The Tale *of the* Himalayan Yogis

The Nirvana Chronicles

STEVE BRIGGS

BALBOA PRESS
A DIVISION OF HAY HOUSE

Copyright © 2018 Steve Briggs.

All rights reserved. No part of this book may be used or reproduced by any means, graphic, electronic, or mechanical, including photocopying, recording, taping or by any information storage retrieval system without the written permission of the author except in the case of brief quotations embodied in critical articles and reviews.

The image of Babaji is from "Babaji and the 18 Kriya Yoga Tradition," with permission from the author, Marshall Govindan

Balboa Press books may be ordered through booksellers or by contacting:

Balboa Press
A Division of Hay House
1663 Liberty Drive
Bloomington, IN 47403
www.balboapress.com
1 (877) 407-4847

Because of the dynamic nature of the Internet, any web addresses or links contained in this book may have changed since publication and may no longer be valid. The views expressed in this work are solely those of the author and do not necessarily reflect the views of the publisher, and the publisher hereby disclaims any responsibility for them.

The author of this book does not dispense medical advice or prescribe the use of any technique as a form of treatment for physical, emotional, or medical problems without the advice of a physician, either directly or indirectly. The intent of the author is only to offer information of a general nature to help you in your quest for emotional and spiritual well-being. In the event you use any of the information in this book for yourself, which is your constitutional right, the author and the publisher assume no responsibility for your actions.

Any people depicted in stock imagery provided by Thinkstock are models, and such images are being used for illustrative purposes only. Certain stock imagery © Thinkstock.

Print information available on the last page.

ISBN: 978-1-5043-9227-3 (sc)
ISBN: 978-1-5043-9228-0 (e)

Library of Congress Control Number: 2018900185

Balboa Press rev. date: 02/05/2018

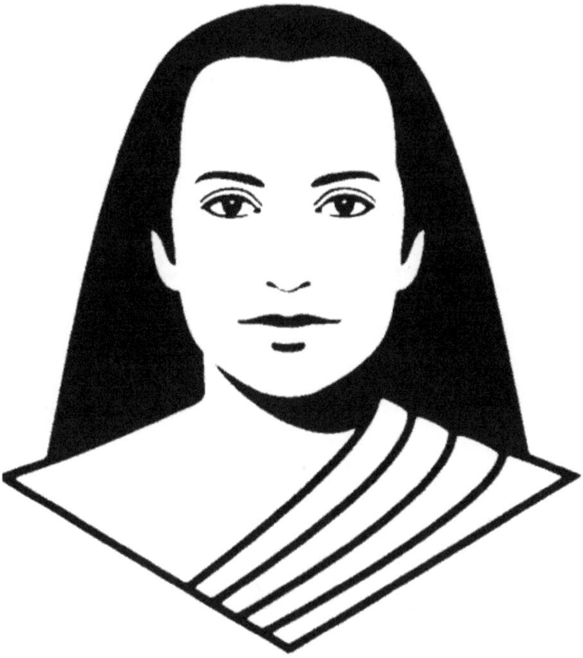

Acknowledgements

I am indebted to my friend, Babaji, who suggested, "Now try your hand at fiction." With timeless wisdom and ample irreverent wit, the Ageless Yogi answered my questions whenever I called on him.

    I would also like to thank Bhumi and Devala for their immense support. Devala's creative contributions were brilliant. Heartfelt thanks to David Renn, Judi Roberts, and Ned Roberts for their suggestions to the story, and to Tony Ellis, whose poems fit seamlessly into the Sufi sections of the story.

Author's Note

India's people possess a gentle disposition. *Ahimsa*, or non-violence, is a cornerstone of the Hindu faith, and foreign aggressors took full advantage of this docile temperament as they bullied the Indian populace. However, not every native son submitted passively to foreign rule.

No group resisted imperialist forces with greater resolve than the Rajputs, a warrior caste possessing a fiercely independent spirit; a spirit epitomized by our protagonist, Prince Govinda. The Rajputs were outstanding horsemen, highly skilled in the art of war.

The Mogul period provides a complex and dramatic backdrop for our story. For six hundred years, the Indian subcontinent was repeatedly invaded, its people and culture compromised. Muslim invaders of Turkic origin arrived in 1206, ruling India for three centuries under the Delhi Sultanate. With the fall of the Delhi Sultanate in 1526, the Mogul Empire emerged, ruling the majority of the subcontinent until they were ousted by the British in 1858.

Muslim rulers ranged from liberal-minded to abusively authoritarian. Emperor Akbar, widely regarded as the Mogul Empire's greatest ruler, developed trade, patronized the arts, encouraged scholarship, and built libraries; however, Akbar's most significant contribution may have been granting India's people their religious freedom.

As cooperative and inclusive as Akbar was, tyrannical Islamic rulers like Tughluq, Babur, and Aurangzeb were responsible for the widespread genocide believed to have claimed 80,000,000 lives.

Addressing the subcontinent's ethnic cleansing, Pulitzer prize winning historian, Will Durant, wrote, "The Islamic conquest of India is probably the bloodiest in history."

Although the yogis in our story are fictitious, I've tried to portray their unique way of living authentically. During my seven years in India, I encountered many sadhus leading solitary lives in remote regions of the Himalaya. Although their practices were wide-ranging, they shared a common goal — all were intent on freeing themselves from the cycle of birth and death. Getting to know these yogis opened a window to an unorthodox lifestyle, a path less traveled.

While supernormal powers are popular in today's fantasy fiction, yogic powers are authentic and well documented in ancient Vedic literature. *The Yoga Sutras of Patanjali,* a renowned treatise on yoga, prescribes precise methods for developing levitation, invisibility, bi-location, communication with animals, reversing the aging process, and restoring life to the dead. According to Maharishi Patanjali, the use of mantras, gems, and herbs aid the development of supernormal powers, or *siddhis*. Those mastering these practices are called *Siddhas*, Perfected Ones.

Accounts of yogis performing feats that stagger the imagination are commonplace throughout Indian history. During the latter years of the British Raj, a yogi named Trailanga Swami was frequently seen floating on the Ganges near Varanasi. The spectacle annoyed British officers, and so they locked Trailanga Swami in the local jail overnight. When the officers arrived the next morning they found the yogi sitting on the jailhouse roof, a broad smile on his face. The account is well documented in the police records of the district.

Sufism, a mystical branch of Islam, has flourished in India for over a thousand years. Sufi fakirs readily embraced traditional yogic practices and even popularized them within their communities. The Hindu *bhakti* movement shared much in common with Sufi sects. Both groups sought exalted states of awareness through meditation, devotional music, and sublime poetry. While orthodox Muslims and conservative Hindus never saw eye to eye on religious matters, Sufi fakirs and Hindu yogis borrowed liberally from one another.

The practice of *johar* (ritual self-immolation) among Rajput clans is well documented. Johar was an extreme measure adopted by Rajput fortress-states to avert the inhumane treatment of their women, children, and elderly. Upon defeating a Rajput army, one Mogul commander agreed to treat the captives humanely, however after the women and children were taken prisoner, they were cruelly ravaged, tortured, and killed. As a result, during the siege of Chittorgarh in 1567, 13,000 Rajputs committed johar rather than allow themselves to be captured.

Gold, silver, and precious gems were offered by royal families to their temple deities over the millennia. In 2011, the Indian Supreme Court ordered the opening of six chambers beneath a Hindu temple in the southern state of Kerala. The estimated value of the temple treasure is in excess of $22,000,000,000.

The Vedas describe seven *lokas*, or heavenly realms, inhabited by human souls. Indian scriptures also offer detailed descriptions of *narakas*, or hellish realms, where the wicked are said to dwell. One such naraka is *kakola*, or black poison. The Agni Purana describes *Kakola* as a dark, bottomless pit inhabited by those who have committed heinous acts. Vedic texts state that a soul does not remain in either heavenly or hellish lokas indefinitely, but embodies repeatedly according to its karma.

Moksha (enlightenment), bhakti (devotion), siddhis (supernormal powers), devas and asuras (divine and demonic beings), Hindu, Tibetan, and Sufi beliefs and spiritual practices, physical immortality, transmigration of the soul, karma, and tantric sorcery are some of the themes explored in our story.

If *The Tale of the Himalayan Yogis* opens a door to a reality beyond the illusions that keep us bound to the wheel of birth and death, the story will have been a success.

Jai Sri Ram
Steve Briggs

Contents

Acknowledgements vii
Author's Note ix
The Sacred Fire 1
The Escape 38
The Return of the Prince 83
The Coronation 91
Varanasi, City of Light 116
Krishna's Leela 136
The Emperor's Harem 177
Among the Lamas 207
The Yogi's Curse 223
Guru and Chela 250
The Vulture and the Lamb 290
Bhumi Mata 303
The Sorcerer's Ploy 337
Conflicting Faiths 380
Revelations and Confrontations 397
Immortal Yogis 435
Exile's End 472
Kashmir 483
The Wedding 500
Abduction 523
Battle 546
The Exchange 558

The Execution	573
The Empress' Doom	602
The Demoness' Curse	615
From the Ashes	649
Epilogue	663
Glossary	667
About the Author	679

The Sacred Fire

Govinda stood among the hushed throng gathered inside the towering gates of the hilltop fortress. His mother stood behind him, holding him close. The civilian inhabitants of the stronghold had come to see their warriors off, and Govinda's father, Raja Chandra, led Krishnagarh's saffron-clad cavalry toward the spike-studded gates of the centuries-old citadel. Fathers and sons rode past their families, their faces streaked with turmeric, the clan's symbol of martyrdom.

Seeing his father's scimitar sheathed in scarlet, its ruby-studded hilt shimmering in the morning light, Govinda wanted more than anything to be riding alongside his father — he was old enough and trained in warfare.

As his father approached, Govinda slipped out of his mother's arms and stepped in front of his horse. Seeing his son, Raja Chandra signaled for the cavalry to stop.

"*Pitaji*, I want to ride with you," petitioned the prince.

"But you're needed here, *Beta*," replied the king.

"If we defeat the Moguls, *johar* won't be necessary."

"Should I not return; your word will be law."

"But you will return, Pitaji… you must return."

Surveying the Rajput clan that he had ruled for nearly two decades, the king replied, "The fate of these good people is in your hands, my son."

Locking eyes with his father, Govinda said, "Then I shall protect our people."

Raja Chandra placed his hand on his son's head, and in the touch of his father's hand, Govinda felt as if a great mantle of power had descended on his shoulders. Stepping back, the crown prince watched the silk ribbons of his father's turban flutter against the king's bronzed neck as he passed through the gates.

A bearded poet rode alongside the cavalry, eulogizing Krishnagarh's ancestors. Drummers marked the balladeer's lyrics with thunderous exclamations; a pair of horns sounded to the rear of the horses. Govinda was certain that Kalki would carry his father to victory and that he would hoist the clan's sapphire-and-gold flag upon his return.

Young and old revered their king, but on this cloudless morning, disconsolate women pulled veils over their faces to conceal their tears. The wives and mothers of Krishnagarh stood in numbed resignation, their hearts shattered by the fate of their men. The riders stole fleeting glimpses of their families as they passed, knowing they would be their last.

Returning to his mother's side, Rukmini pulled her son against her shoulder.

"Pitaji will return, I'm sure of it," Govinda assured his mother.

"I'm praying to Krishna, Beta."

"Pitaji means everything to me."

"He means everything to all of us," replied Rukmini, fighting back the tears. "Now go and find Ravi."

As the last rider passed through the gates, Govinda slipped through the crowd in search of his cousin.

"Davan's tower?" he pointed, slapping Ravi on the shoulder before running ahead. Scrambling up the sandstone steps leading to the turret atop the west wall, Govinda waited for the younger boy, who struggled to keep up.

Standing on the rampart, Govinda followed his father's cavalry as it wound its way down the hill and across grassy plains dotted with scattered hillocks. The warm, amber glow spreading across the sandy grasslands below seemed like that of any other day.

Encamped on the banks of the Banas River, the imperial army was

The Tale of the Himalayan Yogis

poised to snuff out Krishnagarh's cavalry. No enemy had laid siege to the Rajput fortress since before Govinda was born, but the threat of extinction now loomed on the horizon.

"Why are their faces painted yellow?" Ravi asked his cousin.

"In case they don't come back."

"Where are they going?"

"To fight the Moguls," Govinda explained.

"The cooks say they're going to the land of our ancestors."

"Only if they are defeated," replied Govinda. "Let's find Davan."

From the watchtower above the fort's main gates, Davan maintained an unbroken vigil over the terrain beyond the fortress' towering sandstone walls. For decades, the sentry had scanned the countryside from his turret, searching for signs of invaders. Govinda and Ravi knew every sentry on the wall, and Davan was their favorite. The tall, sinewy guard had taught the boys to read the land, sky, and wind.

Impregnable battlements formed a sprawling crown atop the hill, separating friend from foe, and home from the hostile surroundings that extended as far as the eye could see. To the east, the Aravali Hills appeared like emerald illusions rising above the plains. The oval hill crowned by Krishnagarh was an anomaly, a single hump belonging to the chain of camelbacks to the east.

Secure within the fabled fort's walls stood the royal palace, marble temples, military barracks, stables for horse and elephant, water tanks, flowering gardens, mango and citrus orchards, and a bustling bazaar. Govinda often dropped in to see the brightly painted puppets dangling from the ceiling of Vaish's shop, and he eagerly awaited the puppet master's next performance in the palace courtyard.

"Davanji, are you watching?" asked Govinda as he and Ravi reached the side of the greying sentry.

"I'm watching," replied Davan, whose profile he had inherited from descendants of Alexander the Great, some of whom had remained behind after the invasion of India. Stretching beyond his shaven cheeks, the sentry's mustache and crooked nose looked peculiarly like a crossbow. Decades of scanning the landscape had etched deep furrows between Davan's brows, narrowing his unblinking eyes. It was no secret that the sentry's withered arm, the result of an ax blow that had nearly severed the limb, prevented him from riding with the cavalry.

"Is that where our ancestors live?" asked Ravi, pointing to the western horizon.

"The enemy camp is there," Davan replied.

Govinda detected something amiss in the sentry's voice. The old sentry sounded distracted, even haunted. Govinda was skilled at reading men's hearts; he knew Davan was as troubled as his mother.

"But the cook says the soldiers are going to our ancestors," Ravi insisted, struggling to comprehend why the day had begun differently than others.

"The soldiers are going to the land of our *pitris*," Davan agreed, his voice tinged with melancholy. "Tomorrow we will join them."

Ignoring the comment, Govinda peered at Davan, but the sentry avoided his gaze. Turning around, Govinda scanned the courtyard buried beneath great mounds of mango wood. Like a column of ants, laborers hauled wood into the enclosure.

"Don't look at it," cautioned Davan.

"There won't be any need for the wood," declared Govinda. "Father will defeat the Moguls. His cavalry is the best in all of Rajputana."

"But what chance do they have?" countered the sentry. "For every one of our men, there are ten Moguls."

Still haunted by the memory of the battle that had cost him the use of his arm, Davan had frequently recounted the final siege of Krishnagarh. Tales of Rajput fortresses razed to the ground and their inhabitants butchered were little more than murky myths to Govinda's youthful mind — far less real than the clan's legendary cavalry.

Govinda's gaze shifted from the growing stacks of timber to his mother and aunt, who walked arm-in-arm across the courtyard. Ravi's sister Kamala clutched her mother's free hand as they passed between a pair of granite horses and disappeared into the palace.

"Father will return," Govinda insisted. "You'll see."

"The *shakuns* bode ill," warned Davan.

"What omens?"

"As the cavalry appeared outside the gates, a kite downed a young sand grouse. The fledgling had no chance. I fear for our men, and if the army is defeated, the Moguls will overrun the fort."

"I don't believe in omens," decided Govinda. "Fear has no place in a warrior's heart. Father says superstition only casts its shadow on the weak-hearted."

"I fear not for myself. I am old, but you and Ravi are young. I do not wish for you to enter the johar fire."

At the word fire, Ravi grabbed Govinda's arm as he stared at the growing stacks of wood in the courtyard. Instinctively, Govinda rubbed Ravi's neck, causing his cousin to loosen his grip.

Traveling storytellers narrated tales by the night fire, passing along the wisdom of the elders to the next generation. The Land of the Pitris and the tradition of johar were known to every Rajput child.

"But why is johar necessary?" asked Govinda edgily.

"It is the way of our people," replied Davan distantly. "Our ancestors chose johar, and we shall do the same. One does not question such things."

"Even if there is a better way?"

"We Rajputs are proud... maybe too proud. We will not allow our people to become slaves..."

Spotting the tear on Ravi's cheek, the sentry fell silent, fixing his gaze on the expanse below.

"Surrender is not an option, but johar may not be necessary," decided Govinda.

"You are young and hopeful," replied Davan, "but I shall follow the path of my ancestors."

"Should Father die, I would become king."

Davan nodded.

"And if I am king, my people must obey me."

Anticipating Govinda's conclusion, Davan interrupted him. "Raja Chandra met with the Council of Elders. The Council decided that if word comes that the king is dead, johar is..."

Govinda didn't wait for Davan to finish. Grabbing Ravi's arm, he led his cousin down the turret steps.

"Are we all going to burn up?" sobbed Ravi as he struggled down the steps leading to the courtyard.

Govinda couldn't answer truthfully; he didn't want to think about truth.

"If the Moguls come, you and I will ride into the hills," he invented. "They'll never find us there."

Govinda was uneasy about making up the story, but he needed to comfort his cousin. Halfway down the steps, Ravi stopped, his jaw set in a way Govinda had not seen before.

Staring beyond the wall of the fortress, he said, "Cousin, are we all going to die?"

Not waiting for an answer, Ravi reached the courtyard ahead of Govinda. Dust shrouded Ravi's ankles as he raced along the path he and Govinda took whenever they returned from Davan's tower.

Govinda was about to overtake his cousin when Ravi stopped so abruptly that they almost collided. A menacing stack of firewood obstructed the boys' path to the palace. Seeing the blocks of wood, Ravi became as rigid as the granite horses flanking the palace entrance.

Govinda stepped in front of his cousin, blocking the boy's view of the ominous pyre. Peering into Ravi's swollen eyes, Govinda clutched his cousin's shoulders, speaking to him with an authority that surprised them both.

"I promise; no one is going to die." This time his words rang like a great sword of truth clashing against the enemy's armor.

"But Maa said the cavalry is going where Grandpa went when he died."

"Auntie Mira said that?"

Ravi's face contorted with fear. Trembling, he struggled to free himself.

"Ravi, listen to me. You and I are Rajputs… and Rajputs are brave."

"But if the fire doesn't burn us up, they'll torture us!"

"Where did you hear that?"

Ravi's chest convulsed wildly.

"I heard the cooks talking."

Govinda was about to scold his cousin when an unshakeable calm overcame him. The sensation sprang from his heart and spread throughout his body. His arms and legs felt weightless, as though he were floating on the lake in the Aravali Hills. The sensation felt as if some unseen creature were tickling his skin everywhere at once. If not for Ravi's distress, Govinda would have shrieked with joy.

Affection welling up within him, Govinda's eyes met his cousin's as a measured calm gathered behind his forehead. Govinda's hands felt as if he were holding them over a winter fire. The warmth passed into Ravi.

Inexplicably, Ravi stopped shaking. A serene expression came over his face. Govinda knew that no words were needed and he wrapped Ravi in a comforting embrace. Resting his head on his cousin's shoulder, Ravi relaxed so thoroughly that he would have collapsed to the ground had Govinda not held him.

The boy's fright purged, Govinda pressed his finger to Ravi's nose, a gesture that brought a smile to the boy's face. Together, they made a full arc around the wood, racing to the palace where their mothers had entered moments earlier.

Inside the palace, Aunt Mira clung to her sister-in-law as if a desert wind were about to sweep her away.

"Didi, how do we explain johar to the children?" she asked. "Govinda understands, but Ravi and Kamala are too young."

"Our children are young, but they are wise," replied Rukmini. "They will be strong if we are." Her words held more conviction than her heart, which sickened at the thought of the children's fate.

An attendant entered the room bearing a platter laden with fruit. Accepting the sliced mango, Rukmini rested against a satin bolster.

"Where is the fruit coming from?" she asked. "The provisions officer informed Raja Chandra that there was only rice and gram in the granary for two days."

"*Raniji*, fresh produce, dried fruit, and dairy have been set aside for the royal family," the servant reported. "Was it not the right thing to do?"

"Distribute the fruit to those burdened with the task of carrying wood, but set aside a container of cream for Krishna. Give the remainder to families with young children. It is kind of you to think of our family but instruct the kitchen to prepare dal and roti for our meals. Ask Manju to warm a cup of saffron milk for Kamala. It will soothe her."

"I will go and find Ravi," said Mira, leaving Rukmini to her thoughts. As Mira left the queen's apartment in search of her son, she was nearly run over by the boys, who skidded around a row of marble pillars.

"Ravi and I have been to the tower," Govinda informed his mother.

"We saw you," Rukmini replied.

"Davan wasn't himself today."

"Come," said Rukmini, holding out her arms as Govinda dropped onto a stack of satin pillows and leaned against his mother's shoulder. Sensing that the queen wanted to be alone with her son, Mira took Ravi by the hand and departed.

Govinda called after them. "Ravi, when Kamala comes, we'll have a puppet show. Want to come?"

Ravi nodded excitedly.

"I'll send him back shortly," said Mira before leading her son away.

Turning to his mother, Govinda described what had happened in the courtyard. "Ravi was panic-stricken when he saw the wood."

"What has he heard?" asked Rukmini, a look of concern wrinkling her olive skin.

"There's talk of Moguls torturing Rajput children."

"Ravi's too young for such talk."

"When he saw the wood, he started shaking. It was all I could do to calm him down."

"How did you calm him? I've seen Mira spend hours comforting him when he gets that way."

"I can't say, but I stood in front of him so that he couldn't see the woodpiles. I was about to scold him when a strange feeling came over me. It felt like compassion; only it was stronger than anything I've felt before. I was looking into Ravi's eyes when my hands got warm, and my eyes stopped blinking. The calmness inside me flowed right into Ravi. He stopped struggling, and he stopped shaking too."

Rukmini listened but did not speak.

"It sounds odd, doesn't it," said Govinda, unable to better explain the peculiar sensation.

"It was good of you to calm him."

"I did my best. But Maa, it's not just Ravi. Davan's in a dark mood. He went on and on about johar. It seems a cloud has gathered over Krishnagarh."

"Since the men rode out this morning, johar has been on everyone's mind," conceded Rukmini.

"Couldn't they have stayed inside the fort and forced the Moguls to attack? The odds would be better that way. No one has ever conquered Krishnagarh."

"Your father waited as long as he could, but the provisions are nearly gone. It has been four moons since supplies have reached us. Our enemies would have had an easy time once our men were weak from hunger. Surrender is not an option for a Rajput. You know that."

"I do… it just seems there must be a better way than johar."

Etched in Rukmini's mind like an epitaph on a marble crypt, Rana Chandra's instructions now haunted her. *If word comes that I am dead, the priests are to light the fires without delay. The Moguls must not reach the fortress until after johar. You and Govinda will lead the procession; many will be afraid.*

The king's command stabbed at Rukmini's heart, tormenting her brooding mind. The queen searched her husband's words for hope, but found none; it seemed johar was inevitable.

Rukmini stroked her son's head as she considered what lay ahead. Time was running out. Johar could commence at any moment.

Kamala and Ravi rounded the pillars; Kamala was sipping milk as Ravi approached Govinda, his favorite puppet in tow.

"Make Tuglu dance," Ravi pleaded, handing the brightly painted peasant to his cousin.

"All right."

Govinda had been operating puppets since he was his cousin's age. Jumping to his feet, he tugged at the puppet's strings, and the loose-jointed fellow sprang to life, his pointed slippers tapping rhythmically against the marble floor as he sang.

> Those Mogul warts won't live long,
> Our Rajput warriors are too strong.

Long live the Rajput clan,
And foil the Evil Emperor's plan.

Tuglu marched about the room like a soldier and then frolicked like a gypsy. The sprightly marionette leaped off a crimson rug and soared through the air. Kamala shrieked as Tuglu landed on Ravi's head, dancing as he giggled.

"Here I come, little princess!" Tuglu squealed. "Hold out your hands!"

With a tug of his strings, the puppet was flying again. Soaring over the children's heads, Tuglu landed on Kamala's palms. For an instant, it looked as if the stringed doll would topple over, but he righted himself, performing a folk dance for his giggling audience. Wide-eyed, Kamala held her upturned palms perfectly still for Tuglu, who pranced about as he sang.

When the merry puppet finished his dance, he bowed to the children.

"Dakshina," squeaked Tuglu.

"But I don't have anything to give you," moaned Kamala.

"Oh yes you do," the puppet declared as a servant entered the room carrying a platter. "Here come the sweets."

Little Kamala ran to the servant.

"Tuglu, these are for you," Kamala offered, holding out two squares.

"Put one in here," Tuglu instructed, pointing to his open mouth. "And give one to him," the puppet added, pointing at Govinda. Giggling, Kamala stuffed a piece into the puppet's mouth. As Kamala removed her fingers, Tuglu's mouth snapped shut, causing her to shriek.

"Sorry," apologized the puppet. "I haven't eaten all day."

Govinda dropped down beside his mother. Kamala handed him a sweet, following it with a hug. Govinda swallowed the morsel and then held Tuglu behind Kamala's back while he extracted the bite from the puppet's mouth, offering it to his mother.

Rani Rukmini pressed a gentle hand to her son's cheek.

"Thank you, Beta. Now the children are happy."

Inside a spacious Persian tent at the heart of the enemy camp, the Emperor of Delhi and his sons reclined against embroidered cushions spread over plush Kashmiri carpets. Junaid Shah relished a second gilded plate of curried mutton. Between bites, the robust ruler lectured his twins in the art of war.

A servant placed a finger bowl in front of the Emperor, but Junaid Shah waved it away, licking his fingers lustily. The feast had satisfied his appetite, if only temporarily.

Having finished his meal, a Persian cat slipped into the Emperor's lap. The Emperor ran his thick fingers across his favorite pet's back. Ghazi listened attentively to his father, but Hashim's gaze fell on the cat.

"Tomorrow, we feast," the Emperor boasted to his sons, who sat on either side of him. "In the forenoon, you'll have your first taste of blood, and then you will enjoy the sweet touch of a *nautch* girl."

The Emperor's eyes swam in sensuous pools of delight. Ghazi nodded eagerly, but his twin appeared apprehensive.

"Nautch girl?" asked Hashim tentatively.

"Temple dancers," replied the Emperor.

The Emperor wiped his chin with the sleeve of his tunic before speaking to an aide.

"Summon the generals."

Having already been apprised of the enemy, the Emperor wanted to discuss strategy. After spreading cushions, a slippered attendant placed a hookah at the center of the semi-circle. Moments later, a stream of vested generals entered the Emperor's silk-canopied quarters. The mustached officers wore matching turbans and icy expressions.

"Sit," ordered the Emperor, waving at the cushions. "Zaim, what news?"

Commander Amin Zaim had risen quickly through the ranks. He was every bit as shrewd as the Emperor. In lopsided battles, the Emperor devised his plans, but when facing formidable foes, Zaim indeed commanded. His guile was responsible for the imperial army never suffering defeat.

On occasion, Zaim was a fighter as well as a commander; his brow bore the scar of a scimitar's stroke. Backed by Asia's largest army, few dared resist the Emperor's authority; Commander Zaim dealt with those who did.

"The Rajputs are little more than a few mosquitoes buzzing around the head of a bull elephant," scoffed Zaim. "Their numbers are but a fraction of ours."

"Then the outcome is assured," grinned the Emperor, his thick mustache arching beyond the corners of his mouth. "The fun will be in removing the heads of India's finest warriors. What is their count?"

"Three thousand."

"And horses?"

"All have exceptional mounts," reported Zaim.

The Emperor raised his brows. "Fine horses are scarcer than gold. Here is the plan. We will await their attack. General Sadan, position the cavalry behind the Rajputs but do not attack. Should they retreat, your cavalry must contain them. Once the battle starts, Generals Jari and Murad will send line after line of fresh riders. Position a row of archers on either side of me. The Rajputs that survive will wish they hadn't. Their numbers reduced, my sons will savor their first taste of battle."

The Emperor nodded to each of his sons. Ghazi appeared to be savoring the battle in his imagination, but Hashim's face bore no hint of a smile. He was as uneasy about bloodshed as his brother was eager to taste it.

"After we deal with the Rajputs," the Emperor continued, "I will lead the cavalry to Krishnagarh for the victory celebration. I intend to sack the fort before johar commences. This fire sacrifice intrigues me. Women and children entering infernos will make a superb spectacle, but I want to select the loveliest temple dancers before the fires consume them. They tell me johar will not begin until word comes that their king is dead. General Sadan, I'm counting on you to prevent any messengers from reaching the fort. Do you understand?"

"Understood," replied Sadan confidently.

The Tale of the Himalayan Yogis

"We will make short work of the Rajputs," Zaim assured the Emperor. "There won't be anyone alive to warn the fort."

"Agreed, but I want to spar a bit first." The Emperor snapped his fingers. "Basim, a sweetmeat for Muti."

At the mention of its name, the ball of fur purring in Emperor Shah's lap bounded onto the rug, ignoring the assembly of generals. Basim released a mouse onto the carpet, and Muti gave chase to the terrified rodent, zigzagging behind its prey as if the Persian's nose were attached to the rodent's tail. The guards sealed the tent's entrance to prevent the mouse from escaping.

"Watch how he does it," exclaimed the Emperor, clapping excitedly. "Muti has his fun… then he gets down to business. Empress Zahira introduced me to the sport; Muti was a gift from her."

After chasing his prey about the tent, Muti cornered the hapless mouse. Batting the trembling rodent from paw to paw, Muti amused himself until he grew bored. Then, with a terrible swiftness, Muti's dagger-like claw pierced the rodent's heart, and he sipped the warm, vivid liquid, purring contentedly.

"The heat has made Muti thirsty," explained the Emperor, drawing the cat into his lap. "When he's hungry, he removes the head. Tomorrow we shall satisfy our appetite. Like my Muti, I too enjoy the diversion before the execution. Commander, bring the Rajput king's corpse to Krishnagarh. His subjects should view their king before they enter the fire."

"With pleasure, Emperor," Zaim replied.

"Have the old man prepare the hookah," the Emperor ordered a servant who handed him a jeweled cup of Kabul's choicest wine. "A worthy adversary is cause for celebration."

The men's relaxed reverie was interrupted by laughter penetrating the silk walls of the Emperor's tent. Muti's ears stiffened, forming erect little triangles. Sensing a predator in his midst, Muti bared his claws and leaped from the Emperor's lap, clawing his master's arm as he sought refuge under a table.

"Hyenas," muttered Zaim, exhaling a cloud of smoke.

"Filthy scavengers," grumbled the Emperor, examining the scarlet lines etched into his forearm. "Send some men to the edge of camp for a little target practice... and bring the pelts."

After the generals had gone, the Emperor revealed the remainder of his plan to his sons. "Three prizes await us, the least of which are the Rajputs' horses. I have heard their king possesses two priceless gems. The first is his queen, whose beauty is rumored to exceed anything in the harems of Persia."

Junaid Shah's passion was perhaps more legendary than his tyrannical ways. Fifty lovely women from the Emperor's zenana were asleep in the tents surrounding his tent.

"Father, what is the third prize of which you speak?" inquired Ghazi, his youthful blood warming to both battle and banquet.

"My spies tell me there exists a blue diamond in the queen's temple; Babur wore the sister gem on his turban when he conquered Asia. The Idol's Eye is said to be as plump as a Turkish fig. No one outside the fort has seen the gem in living memory, but my spies tell me it adorns the queen's idol.

"Legend says an eagle carried the gem from the Vijayanagar mines after pecking out the eyes of a serpent king, and that the gem possesses divine powers. I plan to see for myself if the tales are true. After claiming the prize, I'll crush the idol and pave the entrance to my mosque with the gravel."

"Father, where is the sister gem that belonged to Babur."

"In good hands," replied the Emperor vaguely. "The diamonds are destined to be together. After claiming the Idol's Eye, I'll reunite them."

"Will Ghazi and I go with you to Krishnagarh?" asked the soft-spoken Hashim.

"As you like," the Emperor replied, casting a withering glance at the meeker of his sons. "A pair of doe-eyed nautch girls awaits each of you. It is time you got to know the people you will one day rule."

Dawn's muted light filtered over the land. In the privacy of their tented quarters, the leaders of the opposing armies prayed. Raja Chandra invoked Krishna while Emperor Shah knelt on his prayer

The Tale of the Himalayan Yogis

rug, facing Mecca the way he had done in his childhood home outside Ahmedabad. The soldiers of both armies performed similar rituals. Both sides prayed for victory, but in truth, superior numbers, and not divine intervention, would determine the outcome.

The brilliance of the ochre orb rising to the east was blunted by the plumes of dust rising behind the Rajput cavalry as it rode headlong into the heart of the imperial army. So as not to harm the horses, the Emperor withheld his missiles, enticing the Rajputs to play his game of cat and mouse.

The Rajputs faced a wall of Mogul pikes, the spears' tips held above the heads of the enemy's horses to prevent their injury. The Rajputs batted the spears aside before clashing with the Mogul ranks. As the clamor of steel escalated, men were flattened and trampled and impaled. Spears stuck into limbs and were left there as swords flashed out to replace them, arcing down and spilling gouts of blood. Spiked maces struck skulls, cracking them like eggs. Ruined bodies lay strewn across the landscape. The parched dust soaked up blood, but there was always more, turning the terrain into a reddish-brown mire.

At the Emperor's signal, his archers fired, and a dozen arrows struck Raja Chandra. Enemy soldiers swarmed like hungry jackals around the fallen Rajput. Seeing their slain king, the remaining Rajputs formed a circle around the rider assigned to inform Krishnagarh that their leader was dead. The rider's escorts broke through the Mogul defenses, sacrificing themselves to secure a narrow opening. The messenger pushed through the opening, eluding flailing swords and whirling maces. An arrow bit deep into the Rajput's shoulder, and another struck his leg. Undeterred, the messenger raced across the plains, a hundred Moguls in pursuit.

The battle raged on, but by sunset the massacre was complete. The Rajputs had been snuffed out, but not before a third of the imperial army had fallen. The Emperor had played his game of cat and mouse, but it had cost him dearly. His left arm hung limply, the result of a battle-ax wielded by a dying Rajput. His bandages soaked red; the Emperor gathered his generals.

"Zaim, what is the report from the cavalry?"

Zaim turned to his general. "Sadan, you stopped the messenger, did you not?"

Sadan nodded crisply. "My men killed the rider's escorts and apprehended the messenger."

"Bring him to me."

"Sir, they have not yet returned," said Sadan.

"Then it is uncertain whether the Rajput has been stopped or not?" bristled the Emperor. "If he reaches Krishnagarh, my plans will be ruined."

"I assure you, he has not eluded my men. I saw my men overtake him," lied Sadan, a cold wave of terror passing through his body.

"Zaim, have the Rajput brought to me. I'll be in my tent."

General Sadan was the only officer who knew that the Rajput had eluded his cavalry. To admit that the rider had escaped would mean his execution, and so, after the army returned to camp, Sadan lingered on the battlefield where his men had been assigned to round up the Rajput horses that were grazing on the sparse patches of grass between the bodies.

Tormented by the prospect that the Emperor would discover the deception, Sadan paced agitatedly among the dead, anxiously waiting for his men to return with the captured rider. As he climbed onto his mount, his men rode up.

"You stopped the Rajput?" questioned Sadan anxiously.

"Sir, the Rajput escaped," a soldier reported, staring at the ground. "His horse was too swift."

"Bungling fools! I dispatch a hundred men, and yet you failed to capture him."

"Sir, the rider's horse was faster than any we have ever seen. We pursued him, but it was hopeless."

"When the Emperor finds out, we will all be better off dead."

Sadan kicked his horse angrily but then brought his mount to a halt.

"I have an idea, but Zaim must not hear of it."

"Sir, we have seen Zaim punish men," replied another soldier.

Sadan pointed at a Rajput lying facedown with an arrow in his back. "Toss that body onto a horse and bring it back to camp. The Emperor shall have his messenger."

Sadan's men rode into camp and presented the Emperor with the evidence the obdurate ruler had demanded. Satisfied that the messenger had not reached Krishnagarh, Junaid Shah turned his attention to his sons, ignoring the seething pain knifing through his body as his physicians cleaned his wound.

"You are both incompetent in battle!" barked the Emperor, drawing on his hookah. "Ghazi, your recklessness would have cost your life had I not been hovering over you like a mother hen. And Hashim, poor wretch, I cannot even look at you. See how your Sufi mystics profit you now. Sadly, you have your mother's blood in you. So long as I am Emperor, you will never be called to battle again."

Hashim stared vacantly at the lion's head woven into the rug beneath his feet. Faced with joining the battle, Hashim suffered an attack of breathlessness, and his father removed him from the contest. Hashim was no stranger to such attacks; they had afflicted him since childhood.

Despite Junaid Shah's disdain for his sons' performance, the Emperor could not deny that he too had been ill-prepared. During his decades-old regime, the Emperor had never faced a foe with greater resolve. True to their reputation, the Rajputs had proven themselves to be the fiercest warriors on the subcontinent.

His wounds stitched and bandaged, Junaid Shah swallowed the opium pods his attendant provided, muting the screaming pain in his arm and soothing his aching body. The Emperor drifted into a dream, conjuring up images of the delights that awaited him, not knowing that a lone rider had escaped into the night.

From Davan's tower, Govinda scanned the countryside for signs of a rider bearing news of the battle. The late afternoon sun glared relentlessly, heating the stone walls of the fortress. Despite the sun's brilliance, Govinda never averted his gaze. By the time he retreated to the queen's apartment, the sun had set.

"Maa, there is hope. The messenger has not come," offered Govinda, seeing the dejection in his mother's eyes.

"I do not feel hopeful," sighed Rukmini.

Govinda's gentle, brown eyes probed his mother's careworn face.

"Maa, why are you so sad?"

"Not knowing gnaws at my heart."

"But Pitaji's army may have already defeated the Moguls."

Rukmini gazed into her son's thoughtful eyes.

"You're as noble as your father."

Govinda barely heard the words for he was probing his mother's heart, searching for a way to lighten her spirit.

"Had the army been defeated, the messenger would have arrived by now."

Pressing his chest against his mother's shoulder, Govinda had always been able to feel his mother's affection, but gloom now shadowed her heart.

"Come, let us go to the temple," suggested the queen, rising from her couch and collecting a tray of sweets.

Outside the palace, Govinda paused before the mountain of logs, trying to imagine how it would feel to be consumed by the menacing flames. Silently, Rukmini led her son away from the pyre.

Offerings of coconut, fruit, a *katora* of honey, incense, camphor, rose petals lay on the temple's stone floor in front of Krishna. Rukmini placed the sweets beside the other offerings.

The sight of Krishna, framed by a pair of brass lamps, calmed the queen. Yellow silk draped across Krishna's shoulders, and a dazzling crown set with emeralds, sapphires, and pearls sat atop his long, black hair. At the center of Krishna's forehead, a magnificent blue diamond glistened, a family heirloom passed down countless generations. A necklace of *tulsi* seeds adorned Krishna's neck. Fingering his wood flute, the youthful deity gazed benevolently at his devotees. The five-thousand-year-old idol had been the pride of Govinda's ancestors, some of whom had also faced the specter of johar.

Rukmini trained her eyes on the form in front of her.

After impaling a coconut on a tall iron spike near the base of the altar, Pundit Ananta chanted mantras while Rukmini placed offerings

The Tale of the Himalayan Yogis

at the feet of the idol. The ceremony completed, Ananta circled a camphor flame in front of Krishna before holding it for Govinda and Rukmini, who swept their hands through the fire, spreading its warmth to their head and heart.

A second priest appeared at the entrance to the shrine. "It is time to prepare for johar," said the newcomer.

Ananta looked at the innocent faces in front of Krishna. "Bhaiya, I have lived a full life, but they are such tender flowers," he whispered, gesturing toward the queen and her son.

"We must not break tradition," admonished the second priest.

Rukmini and Govinda remained inside the temple, softly singing until sleep overtook them. Although temple rules forbade lying down inside the sanctum, tonight would be an exception. The queen would need her strength to lead johar.

As mother and son lay side by side, Govinda whispered. "Maa, is your heart better now?"

"Yes, Beta."

"Death is nothing to fear," assured Govinda, caressing his mother's forehead.

"I remember when you were sick. You told everyone that you were not afraid to die. But how will we comfort those who are not as strong as you?"

"Have you forgotten what Krishna said to Arjuna before they entered the battle? 'This body is known to have an end, but the dweller in the body will never perish.'"

"You are wise for one so young."

"But it's true. Death is little more than a magician's trick, a mere sleight of hand."

"Still, my heart is troubled; almost everyone's is, I think," said Rukmini.

"Maa, I never told you, but I died once."

"What are you saying, my child?"

"When I was sick…"

"I've not forgotten that day. The physician said there was no hope."

"I died that night," repeated Govinda.

"I don't understand."

"Do you recall the physician saying that my pulse was failing?"

She nodded. "The words still haunt my dreams."

"I found myself looking down at my body from above the bed. You and Father and Ananta were there. I heard the physician say there was no hope, but when Ananta put the Idol's Eye in my hand, my body stopped burning. When I woke up, you were holding me in your arms."

"You never told me."

"Now it seems right to speak of it. Maa, death is no more real than a nightmare; and far less frightening."

Rukmini laid her head on the pillow next to Govinda.

Who is this sage in my son's body?

With her arm draped across her son's chest, Rukmini slept, but her rest soon turned fitful, and a dream vision appeared in which she witnessed a fierce battle. The queen watched as her husband's army was overwhelmed by a horde of faceless soldiers. The silhouettes of struggling men faded in and out of the scene, scimitars bit into riders, and crescent daggers gouged deep gashes in torsos and limbs. Slain soldiers littered parched plains.

At the sight of her husband's body riddled with arrows, Rukmini awakened, relieved to find that the scene had been a dream.

"Maa, are you awake?"

"Yes, Beta," Rukmini replied, drawing her son close.

"Maa, what was in your dream?"

Pulling Govinda close, Rukmini related what she had seen.

"I am ready to lead our people into the sacred fires," whispered Rukmini.

Govinda shook his head.

"These are the people we love. I won't let them enter the fires."

"But Beta, a wife does not make a promise to her husband only to change her mind."

"I'm sure Father would approve of my plan. Before riding through the gates, he said, 'Should I not return, your word will be law.' Davan will lead the women and children into the hills where they will be safe. From there they will journey to Bundi."

The Tale of the Himalayan Yogis

"The elders will not approve," protested Rukmini.

"The elders will support me if you do."

Rukmini's gaze fell on Krishna's feet. According to Rajput tradition, a woman was obligated to obey her eldest son in the event of her husband's death. Seeing a resolve in her son's eyes that she lacked the strength to challenge, Rukmini nodded reluctantly.

Govinda lifted an oil lamp and led his mother out of the temple. The courtyard was bathed in moonlight, rendering the lantern unnecessary. Seeing the queen, Pundit Ananta approached.

"Rani Rukmini, we are ready to light the fires."

The queen looked questioningly at the head priest.

"Then you don't know?"

"Tell us," said Govinda.

"The messenger has arrived with news from the battle."

Before the priest could continue, Davan approached, leading a horse with what appeared to be the messenger in the saddle, his turmeric-painted face caked with dust, his uniform reduced to rags. The rider was dazed and wounded, the neck of his horse streaked with blood, both its own and its rider's. The shaft of an arrow dangled from the rider's thigh.

Tumbling off his mount, the man steadied himself with Davan's help as he tried to speak.

"Rani Rukmini... Prince Govinda. I bring news of our army's defeat."

"The king is dead," Rukmini broke in before the soldier could find the courage to say it.

"Yes, the king... is dead," croaked the messenger.

"Are they coming?" asked Govinda.

"They will come," replied the messenger, "but those who pursued me gave up when they saw the swiftness of my horse."

"Then we must act quickly," decided Govinda.

"Johar will commence at sunrise," said the second priest, anticipating the next move.

"Prepare the pyre," instructed Govinda, "but I want to meet

with the people before johar commences. The sentries should gather everyone in the courtyard without delay."

By the time the community had assembled at the center of the fort, sections of the wood were already ablaze, providing an ominous backdrop. Mothers, laborers, sentries, servants, a few of the older children, and the elderly faced the pyres.

Rukmini spoke first. "Elders, brothers, and sisters… our king is dead; the army defeated. This is the news brought by the messenger. The imperial army is advancing toward Krishnagarh. Prince Govinda wishes to speak."

Govinda, who had been standing alongside his mother, stepped forward.

"Respected elders, as Rani Rukmini has said, our army has been defeated, and our king is dead. The destiny of our people has reached a crossroads. Behind me, the johar fires blaze. Johar has been the tradition of our ancestors. We are all prepared to make the same sacrifice our men made in battle. I honor their resolve… courage is the very life breath of our clan. We can enter the sacred fires if that be our wish, but I have a plan that has the queen's blessings."

"Those who wish to do so will leave Krishnagarh through the eastern tunnel accompanied by Davan and the sentries. Shielded by the Aravali Hills, we can reach Bundi where we are welcome at my grandfather's fort. There will be carts and horses for the young and infirm. It will be a difficult journey, but our options are few. Imperial troops are watching the fort, but by using the tunnel, we can reach the hills unseen. Those who are able must walk. I ask our respected elders for their blessings."

"But this goes against tradition!" objected a man from the middle of the crowd.

"Are we to abandon our religion in favor of a boy's fanciful plan?" questioned another man.

"Govinda is not a boy. He is our future king," countered a white-haired man as he stepped to the front of the crowd. Everyone

The Tale of the Himalayan Yogis

recognized General Pratap Singh, Raja Chandra's paternal uncle and a respected voice in the community.

"The news of our king's death saddens us, but there is little time to mourn his passing. Raja Chandra would approve of Govinda's plan; it shows mature judgment and has every chance of success. The Moguls are unaware of our tunnel into the hills. In fact, there is a reason to believe the Moguls have abandoned their positions to the east, knowing that our soldiers have gone west.

"Although I find no flaw in Govinda's plan, johar is the honorable response to the death of our fathers and husbands. Thirteen thousand of our ancestors entered the sacred fire when faced with the dilemma that confronts us now. I want to continue that tradition rather than abandon home and conviction. However, I do not wish for innocent children to join me.

"Govinda, you are young, but I am old. Therein lies the difference in our thinking. I agree that the children and their mothers should go to Bundi, but I ask that you allow the elderly and the widowed who are childless the choice to depart this world with dignity, should that be their desire. According to our ancestors, that dignity is johar. As a military officer, I pray that no one will remain behind."

General Singh's speech stirred the crowd, and many huddled together to discuss the proposals. Govinda turned to his mother.

"What do you think of uncle's idea?"

"I agree with him. We should not deny johar to those who wish to depart," whispered Rukmini. "Govinda, I too wish to enter the fire."

Govinda fixed his gaze on his mother. Tears gathered at the edges of her chestnut eyes. Govinda was about to address the crowd again when a member of the Council of Elders stepped forward.

"I cannot allow this plan. The Council of Elders made a solemn promise to our king. For us to break our word, knowing that Raja Chandra and his men are dead, is unthinkable. Johar should commence immediately."

"I respect your desire to honor my father's decree," replied Govinda, "but there is a higher authority than that of a king, or his son, for that matter."

"Of what authority do you speak?" demanded the elder, annoyed that a boy differed with him.

"I speak of the authority that resides within each of our hearts."

"Are you suggesting that some divine authority has moved you to speak against the wishes of your father?" complained the man.

"My father is divinity to me," replied Govinda.

"Then you must abide by his wish."

"As your queen, I ask that you listen to Govinda, who will soon be your king," interjected Rukmini.

"I see we have no choice but are destined to disgrace," grumbled the elder. "Either we dishonor our ancestors, or we dishonor our future king."

Govinda grew impatient.

"Time is running out if we plan to succeed, but let us consider our elder's words for a moment. Those who wish may enter the johar fire, but not because of my father's instructions. Raja Chandra would not want that; I am sure of it! Therefore, each of you must examine your heart, and decide. Those who wish to go to Bundi should gather at the tunnel entrance before sunrise. Those who wish to perform johar should remain in the courtyard. Let us lose no more time."

The disgruntled elder was about to respond when a voice from the rear of the crowd rang out, "Jaya Raja Chandra! Victory to King Chandra!" The crowd joined in the refrain, raising their arms triumphantly. Then came the words, "Jaya Raj Kumar Govinda! Victory to Prince Govinda!" and the crowd voiced its support.

With Govinda's plan adopted, shuttered shops and abandoned lookout posts appeared deserted. The main gates went unguarded. General Pratap Singh and the elderly gathered in the courtyard, waiting for johar to commence. The others would be well on their way to Bundi by now.

It is time to light the fires, thought Govinda, who hastened to the queen's temple. Removing his sandals, he slipped into the sanctum. Krishna's oiled limbs glistened in the light. Rukmini stood before the statue, staring intently into the deity's benevolent eyes.

"Maa, johar will begin soon."

"I will lead the elders."

Govinda looked at his mother questioningly.

"The queens of our clan have always been the first to enter the fire. I am thankful that so few have chosen johar, but I must uphold tradition," whispered Rukmini, her large brown eyes shrouded in doubt. Taking his mother's hand, Govinda led her outside where Pundit Ananta was sprinkling the elders with sanctified water.

"Dear ones, remember Krishna's words," said the pundit. "'There never was a time when I was not, or you. Nor will there ever be a time when we shall cease to be.'"

Lighting a tuft of *kusa* grass, the pundit led the procession to the johar pyre. Ananta signaled to the attendants, who doused the wood with ghee. Chanting softly, he touched the burning grass to the firewood. Flames quickly engulfed the oil-soaked logs, crackling and fussing as the fire spread. As the inferno grew, Ananta turned to face the assembled elders. The priest was about to usher Rukmini into the blaze when Govinda took his mother's arm.

"Mataji, please don't enter the fire."

"But I must."

"Come, stand beside me so that our elders will have courage."

Govinda gently tugged at his mother's arm, and she offered no resistance. Torn between her duty to lead the procession and her obligation to obey her son, Rukmini stood beside Govinda.

One by one, Govinda gazed into the eyes of the elders. Affectionately referred to as 'aunt' or 'uncle,' these were Govinda's people, now more than ever.

Husbands and wives moved as one, pausing to touch the feet of the royal family. With eyes downcast, the elders took dignified steps as they approached the inferno. Hand in hand, husbands and wives entered the flames. Silver plumes rose above the fortress walls as Krishnagarh's elders departed the world. Lost in contemplation, Govinda felt no sadness as he watched the elders merge with the fire. One day, he too would make the journey to his ancestors, but not this way, he thought.

Govinda led Rani Rukmini back to the queen's temple where Ananta had prepared a blanket at the feet of Krishna.

"Maa, you did the right thing," Govinda reassured his mother.

"I no longer know what is right."

Placing a blanket over her, Govinda stroked his mother's forehead. Satisfied that the queen was resting comfortably, Govinda left the temple and climbed Davan's tower. Gazing down at the fires, which now burned low, he lowered his head a final time before shifting his attention to the galloping horde that approached like a gathering storm.

The tempest of dust and intimidation spanned the horizon, blotting out the sun that would soon set on the first, and likely final day, of Govinda's reign. His people had hailed him moments before disappearing into the tunnel. He now faced a more daunting challenge; the imperial army of the Mogul empire.

It had already been the most trying day of his young life, but the siege that was about to reduce his kingdom to rubble didn't trouble him. The mighty fortress, witness to a thousand years of glory, had been evacuated. Despite the onrush of soldiers about to overrun his home, Govinda considered throwing open the gates so that the invaders could enter unobstructed, saving their elephants the effort of breaking down the barrier.

Like a slithering serpent, the imperial army wound its way up the path to the main gate, led by a pair of helmeted behemoths poised to crush anything in their path. With a prod from their mahouts, the elephants charged the barrier. The collision of skull and barricade shook the walls of the magnificent fort, causing the beasts to trumpet furiously. Again and again, the snorting battering rams slammed into the unyielding barrier, the deafening concussions resounding like great claps of thunder. Splintered wood rained on the ground, but the main gate was not defenseless. The barricade's iron studs dented the elephants' helmets and bruised their heads, infuriating the beasts.

Govinda watched the contest from Davan's turret while keeping an eye on the rope ladders flung over the walls by foot soldiers. Scaling the fortress walls, Moguls scrambled over the ramparts like ants in

The Tale of the Himalayan Yogis

pursuit of sweets. The invaders swarmed the courtyard, darting about like crazed creatures in search of anything of value.

It was time to retreat. Govinda bounded down the steps, relieved that Ravi was not here to witness either the courtyard inferno or the enemy overrunning his home.

Slipping into the queen's temple, Govinda found his mother sitting in front of Krishna.

"Maa, we must hide."

"The chamber is ready," said Ananta, ushering the queen inside the closet behind Krishna's altar.

Sealing the door behind them, Ananta sighed. The pundit's day had perhaps been the most taxing of all, for he had guided eighty-six elders into the conflagration. Bewildered, the priest starred blankly at the solitary flame lighting the hiding place. Having witnessed what few ever would, Ananta was powerless to describe it.

"Will they find us?" asked Rukmini.

"If they search long enough, maybe," replied Govinda.

"My wish was that our elders not suffer," said Ananta, his mind fixed on the johar fires.

"They did not suffer because they were not afraid," Govinda assured him, leaning against the wall beside the priest.

"Govinda is right," said Rukmini. "The elders did not choose johar out of fear."

"In their meditations, the elders journeyed beyond this world many times," said Govinda.

Although there was scarcely space for three, a small opening in the ceiling ventilated the chamber. From time to time, Govinda pressed his cheek to the wall and peered through a tiny hole behind the altar, which afforded a partial view of the sanctum. The oil lamps behind Krishna lit the inner sanctum beyond which a pair of mahogany doors stood ajar at the far end of the temple.

Outside, the Mogul army made fast and strident work of the pillaging. Looters ransacked the queen's palace; soldiers plundered shops, apartments, stables, and military barracks. Whatever would burn was set ablaze. But the wanton destruction was not what

Junaid Shah had in mind for his victory celebration. Finding the fort abandoned and the fires smoldering, the Emperor was furious.

"Where are the temple dancers?" demanded the irate Emperor, striding from fire to fire.

The fires spat sparks at the Emperor as if to say, 'the people of Krishnagarh are victorious.'

"We're too late," observed General Jari, Zaim's second-in-command, pointing to a charred skull.

"But how did they know their king was dead?" wondered the Emperor. "I have brought their king, but his subjects are not here to greet him."

The Emperor's face contorted as he scanned the fort, searching for a means to vent his frustration. A jolt of pain shot through his arm as he mounted his horse. An injured limb hung at his side as he clutched the reins in his right hand. Having enjoyed the spoils of victory countless times, the Emperor had planned to share the plunder with his sons. The angry ruler was determined to find a prize worth celebrating.

Spotting his commander, the Emperor rode over to him.

"How did they know?"

"I'm wondering the same thing," replied Zaim.

"Sadan brought me the messenger's body…" began the Emperor. "… bring me the sentinel posted to the west of the fort."

A burly soldier presented himself before the mounted Emperor.

"Soldier, you were assigned to watch the main entrance to the fort."

"That is correct, Emperor," answered the sentry, his eyes fixed on the ground.

"Did a rider enter the fort last night?"

"Yes, a Rajput came from the battlefield."

"Are you certain?"

"The rider bore wounds… his face was streaked with turmeric."

"Bring me General Sadan!" ordered the Emperor, his eyes flaring. Commander Zaim sent a pair of guards in search of Sadan, who had been assigned to round up any horses found in the stables.

The reason for General Sadan's summons was apparent. The

The Tale of the Himalayan Yogis

evidence was everywhere. The fires burned low, the fort had been abandoned.

"Sadan!" raged the Emperor, reining in his steed. "This will not do!"

Kalki, the white stallion the Emperor had claimed after its master's death, reared defiantly at its rider's beastly growl, but the Emperor brought the horse under control. The Emperor sat atop his mount, his bearded chin protruding like the blade of a battle-ax, his heavy brows arching over angry eyes.

Commander Zaim addressed his officer, his voice singed by the explosive fury within him.

"General Sadan, the sentinel assigned to watch the main gate informed the Emperor that a rider entered the fort last night. Explain yourself."

"They must have dispatched a second rider," Sadan recited, as he had planned since he perpetrated his ruse. "My cavalry caught the first man. You saw the body."

"There are three thousand dead Rajputs out there!" countered Zaim. "Anyone could have been tossed onto a horse."

"But why would I have done that?"

"Because you failed to stop the rider!" boomed the Emperor from atop his horse. "Sadan, you know how much I loathe officers who cover up their mistakes."

Raising his mace, the Emperor dug his boots into his horse and charged at the officer. Junaid Shah whirled the weapon over his head, swinging it violently at Sadan's head as he rode past the officer. Sadan dove to the ground, narrowly avoiding the deathblow.

"You have deceived the Emperor!" shouted Zaim. "Now pay the price of your insolence."

Turning his horse, the Emperor glared down at Sadan, a fiendish expression on his face. But this time, rather than charge, the Emperor let his mace fall to the ground in favor of the battle-ax he pulled from its holster. Swinging the weapon in a full arc, the Emperor flung the weapon end over end through the air. Sadan was not expecting the attack and had little time to react. The ax blade struck a glancing blow to Sadan's thigh, knocking the officer off his feet. Seeing the wounded officer struggling to stand, Junaid Shah jumped down from his horse and unsheathed his dagger. Raising it over his head, he was about to plunge the blade into the officer's chest when he pulled back.

"Too easy to die this way," frothed the Emperor. Turning to Zaim, he snapped, "Stake him in the fort's rubbish pit. The hyenas will take pleasure in picking his bones if they get there before the vultures."

The Emperor retrieved his mace and climbed back onto his horse.

"Bind his thighs," Zaim instructed the men who had already hurried forward. "Without circulation, his legs will wither. I want him alive when the feeding starts."

With a wave of the commander's hand, a pair of guards shackled General Sadan and dragged him from the courtyard.

Wielding the mace had strained the Emperor, and his shoulder bled through its bandages. Ignoring the pain, Junaid Shah galloped about the fort in search of a means to douse his fury. As if the ghosts of Krishnagarh were tormenting the tyrant for his senseless destruction of the fort, the Emperor's tirade caused his men to stop and stare at the bizarre spectacle. Swinging his mace at phantoms in the air as he raced from one end of the fort to the other, the irate Emperor ignored the gash in his shoulder, which stained the silky mane of his white steed. When the tempest finally passed, the Emperor trotted over to Commander Zaim.

"Point me to the Krishna temple. At least one prize still awaits me."

"There," said the commander, pointing to the finely sculpted shrine near the queen's palace. "Go and claim your prize."

Zaim had witnessed the Emperor's epic tantrums in the past and knew to keep his distance until the rage had run its course. The commander watched as rider and stallion disappeared through the temple doors. If the Emperor returned with the diamond, his mood would be as amicable as the Emperor's cat after a successful hunt.

Expecting looters, Govinda peered through the pinhole, willing the Moguls away. Recognizing Kalki, he grimaced as the lone rider entered the sanctum. The sight of a Mogul atop his father's horse angered Govinda, who noticed the rider's injured arm and the stallion's discolored mane. The Mogul handled the horse with his right hand only.

The Tale of the Himalayan Yogis

Govinda watched as the intruder inspected the altar, the Mogul's eyes riveted on Krishna. A slow smile formed on his face, but the half-crazed grin was all that Govinda could see since the rider had come near the altar. Although a wall separated them, Govinda was close enough to touch Kalki's nose, which gently nuzzled Krishna's hand. The rider's eyes widened as he ogled the magnificent blue diamond adorning Krishna's forehead.

Resting the mace across his thighs, the Emperor reached for the diadem on Krishna's head. Holding the crown in his right hand, the sight of the gem-studded ornament sweetened the Emperor's mood. Removing his turban, he placed the diadem on his sweat-streaked head. Perched atop the Mogul's massive head, the delicate filigree crown made the man look ridiculous. Searching for a reflective surface in which to admire himself, the Emperor found none.

Turning his attention to the Idol's Eye adorning Krishna's forehead, Govinda's heart sank as the Mogul plucked the gem from the statue. The rider turned the plum-sized diamond round and round in his fingers. In countless conquests, Junaid Shah had never come across a prize such as this. The Idol's Eye was breathtaking, worth as much as the many chests of gems he already possessed.

"Things are turning out well," he muttered. "I've slain the Rajput king and claimed the Idol's Eye. Surely the queen did not waste her beauty on johar!"

Giddy from his find, the Emperor turned to Krishna, who stood serenely on the altar, his ankles crossed as he fingered his golden flute.

"You failed to protect your beloved Rajputs. This will be the last tune you'll play, idol of dead heathens," sniggered the Emperor.

Gingerly, the arrogant ruler raised the mace above his head, his left arm dangling at his side. He was about to deliver a crushing blow when Govinda emerged from behind the altar.

"Stop!"

The startled rider stared at the boy in disbelief, his mace hovering in the air.

"Who are you?" demanded the flabbergasted Mogul. Their languages were different but related, and similar enough for them to understand one another.

"I am Govinda, son of Raja Chandra Prakash Singh."

The Emperor smiled at his good fortune. Maybe the final prize awaited him, after all?

"Then you are now king of this forsaken place. Where is your mother the queen?"

"Here," replied Rukmini, stepping out from behind the altar.

The Emperor's mind reeled with excitement. Like the flawless diamond he held, the queen was far more beautiful than he had imagined.

"This is turning out better than I had planned," snickered the Mogul.

"Whoever you are, I won't allow you to strike Krishna!"

An indomitable force surged through Rukmini as she spoke. The Emperor shrugged at the queen's reply.

"The rumors are untrue. You are far more beautiful than my spies report."

Ignoring the comment, Rukmini shot back, "I will not allow you to defile this temple."

"Is that so?" replied the Emperor, ever keen for a game of cat and mouse. No one had ever spoken to him in that way, especially not a woman. "Do you know who I am?"

"Commander of the imperial army, I imagine," replied Rukmini indifferently.

"Not merely that!" bellowed the Emperor, rage and passion combusting like wildfire in his veins. "I am the one you Hindus call the Evil Emperor."

Rukmini's heart beat wildly. They were, perhaps, not in greater danger than if it were any enemy officer, but such an infamous tyrant filled them with dread.

"First, I'll crush your idol and then you'll have the privilege of joining my harem," taunted the Emperor.

"Strike a blow to Krishna, and you'll die," warned Govinda, stepping in front of his mother.

"Impudent boy! Your mother will watch a pack of dogs tear your flesh apart. But first I'll destroy this pathetic idol of yours!"

As the Emperor swung his spiked mace at Krishna's head, Govinda grabbed a brass lamp from the altar, parrying the Mogul's blow. The iron mace slammed into the lamp, snuffing out its flame and spilling hot oil on the stone altar. The force of the impact sent Govinda sprawling to the floor, but it had saved Krishna. Rukmini dropped to her knees to see if her son was hurt.

Incensed, the Emperor raised his weapon again; this time no one would prevent him from landing a crushing blow to the smiling Krishna. As the Emperor was about to strike the blow, Govinda, who was too far away to block it, called out,

"Kalki, save Krishna!"

As if the stallion understood, Kalki reared. With the Emperor's injured left arm, clutching the heavy mace in his right hand made it difficult to control the mighty horse, and he lost his balance. As the horse reared, the diadem atop the Emperor's head nearly touched the sanctum's ceiling. Horse and rider suspended in the air for a moment, the diadem slowly slid off the Emperor's head, melodiously ringing as it struck the granite floor. Having lost his balance, the Emperor fell backward off the stallion. Ananta, who had joined Govinda and Rukmini, froze his mouth agape.

With a resounding thump, the Emperor crashed to the floor where he lay motionless at the feet of Krishna. Govinda ran to Kalki, trying to calm the agitated stallion while keeping an eye on the fallen rider, expecting the Mogul, who was a brute of a man, to be on his feet and fighting at any moment. But the Emperor lay motionless below the altar.

Followed by Rukmini and Ananta, Govinda took a tentative step toward the prone body. Picking up the Emperor's mace, Govinda could barely lift it with both hands. Ananta moved cautiously toward the Mogul; Kalki pawed testily at the floor.

Together, Govinda and Ananta bent down to examine the body. Rukmini placed a wary hand on Govinda's shoulder. The Rajputs' eyes fell on a blank and icy stare carved as if from stone. Fearing the Emperor would suddenly wake up, Ananta removed the dagger from the Mogul's sash. The priest pointed to an oval blotch on the Emperor's tunic.

"He's bleeding," determined Govinda, who unbuttoned the tunic, exposing a gruesome wound in the Mogul's massive chest. Rukmini's grip tightened on her son's shoulder. Instinctively, Govinda touched his right hand to his chest, a Hindu gesture of respect. The iron spike used for splitting coconuts had pierced the Emperor's heart.

"Should we move the body?" asked Ananta. Restless from being pent up inside the sanctum, Kalki bolted out of the temple. Govinda grabbed for his reins, but the stallion was too swift.

"When they see Kalki, they'll come," cautioned Ananta.

Ushering her son away from the body, Rukmini stopped to scan the floor in search of the Idol's Eye. As she reached down to pick up the jeweled diadem, voices were heard outside the temple.

"Quickly!" pleaded Ananta. "They're coming!"

Rukmini picked up the diadem and slipped into the hidden chamber behind the others as the silhouette of Commander Zaim appeared at the entrance. Having seen the Emperor's horse outside, Zaim entered the temple cautiously, signaling for his men to follow. Waiting for his eyes to adjust to the dimly lit shrine, Zaim moved warily toward the altar. Spotting the Emperor lying on the floor, the commander discovered the spike that had impaled the Emperor.

"Insallah," he shuddered, running a finger along the scar on his brow.

Zaim scanned the temple, trying to imagine what had happened, but the light was uneven, the shadows playing tricks on his mind. It was apparent that the Emperor had fallen from his horse, but there was no evidence of a fight, save for a twisted oil lamp beside the altar, which proved nothing. The Emperor might have bludgeoned it with his mace.

"Look around," Zaim ordered his men, puzzled by the Emperor's unbuttoned tunic. Zaim had kept a close watch on the entrance; no one had entered or left the temple since the Emperor rode inside.

The soldiers combed the sanctum but found nothing. The weak light caused them to overlook the hairline crack behind the altar. It had been an exhausting day for the soldiers, and they soon gave up their search and returned to the courtyard.

Commander Zaim went in search of the Emperor's sons. He did

The Tale of the Himalayan Yogis

not want anyone suspecting foul play. Investigation of the Emperor's death would exclude no one, not even Junaid Shah's sons.

"Your father has had an accident," the commander informed the twins.

"What kind of accident?" the boys asked at the same time.

"Come!" said Zaim, leading the boys to the temple.

The twins found their father lying on the cold granite.

Hashim reeled at the sight of his dead father while Ghazi stood callous and aloof.

"How did it happen?" asked Ghazi.

"The investigation is yet incomplete," replied Zaim.

Tears clouded Hashim's eyes as he bent down and reached toward his father.

"Touch nothing!" barked Zaim.

"I am only closing his eyes. They hold no clues."

While the sight of his dead father unnerved Hashim, his brother stood unmoved, for Ghazi was determined to be the Emperor's successor, and he lost no time in taking command.

"Is this how you found him?" questioned Ghazi.

"Yes," confirmed Zaim. "It appears the Emperor fell from his horse after riding into the temple to claim the diamond. When I saw his horse outside, I rushed in and found him."

"Have your men search the temple."

"They already have," replied Zaim.

"Search it again!"

It occurred to Hashim that the chasm between him and his brother was about to widen. Already they shared little but their parentage. Hashim was an accomplished poet and student of Sufism, a skilled musician who preferred singing *ghazals* to attending monotonous prayer sessions at the mosque.

Ghazi had inherited his father's temperament. Having rushed headlong into the battle with the Rajputs, he relished the kill. As children, the brothers had gotten along because Hashim willingly acceded to his brother's wishes. But as equal heirs to the Peacock Throne, Prince Ghazi and Commander Zaim were already contemplating who would inherit the empire.

"None of the soldiers entered the temple before the Emperor? No one touched the body?" asked Ghazi suspiciously.

"I'm certain," answered Zaim impatiently. "I made sure no one entered the temple before the Emperor. I was the first among the soldiers to find him."

"But someone got here ahead of you."

"Why do you say that?"

"Explain the unbuttoned tunic." The commander hadn't expected the cross-examination, but he should have. After all, Ghazi was the son of Junaid Shah, the shrewdest man Zaim had ever met.

"Seeing the stallion bolt out of the temple, I entered immediately. The horse must have thrown the Emperor."

"But our father was a superb horseman," said Hashim, who was on his knees beside the body.

"No horse could have thrown him," agreed Ghazi.

"Except that his arm was injured," countered Zaim.

"True," conceded Ghazi. "The stallion is formidable. He would be too much to control with one arm. But how do you explain the open tunic?"

"There must be many hidden chambers and tunnels in the fort. Someone was in the sanctum when the Emperor fell, and that person must still be here. There is only one entrance, and I've watched it closely for the past hour. No one could have escaped. But it's late. My men will search the fort in the morning."

"I want to stay with father," requested Hashim.

"Commander, assign some men to stay with my brother," ordered Ghazi. "Return in the morning with as many men as you need to conduct a thorough search of the fort."

"We'll return at dawn. I'll assign soldiers to watch the fort. If someone is hiding here, we'll find him."

"Keep the gates guarded at all times… and post soldiers outside the temple."

"Good," replied the commander. "Tomorrow I shall make my headquarters in the Rajput's palace."

After Zaim had arranged his men's posts for the night, he returned to the encampment by the river. The commander's thoughts turned again and again to the impaled Emperor as he rode toward the camp.

Emperor Shah's obsession killed him. He injured his shoulder in that dull-witted game of cat and mouse. How unprofessional! He should have left war to me! Rather than finish the Rajput off when he had him on the ground, the Emperor let the man up. Foolish game! The lapse in judgment cost him not only his arm, but his life. But all this may work to my advantage. The twins are but boys. That Hashim is pathetic; Ghazi alone stands between me and the throne.

The Escape

Outside the temple, a curtain of darkness descended on Krishnagarh's most tormented day. The acrid odor of smoldering buildings and charred wood filled the air, penetrating even the closet shared by the Rajputs.

"Ananta, I'm famished," whispered Govinda, who hadn't eaten all day. "Is there prasad on the altar?"

"Fruit and rice pudding… also water. But shouldn't we wait until we're certain the troops are gone?"

"I only want to assure the lion in my stomach that food is coming soon. Can we rest in here?"

"Yes, of course," said Ananta. "The queen must be exhausted."

"Mataji has had the most difficult day of all."

"We all have, Beta!" replied Rukmini.

"We'll need to hide Krishna," decided Govinda. "When the Moguls return they'll destroy the temple."

"Won't they be suspicious when they find him missing?" questioned Ananta.

"I won't let them harm Krishna. We'll move him tonight. And then we'll move. I know the perfect spot."

Govinda peered through the pinhole, but he couldn't see anyone from his vantage point.

"Maa, do you think our people made it to Bundi?"

"I feel certain they are safe," she reassured him.

"Our clan will speak of this day for many reasons, the least of which is the death of a tyrant," declared Ananta. "You have saved our people."

"But I did nothing," Govinda protested.

There was just enough space for Rukmini to lie along the length of the wall. Loosing her plaited hair and removing a gold bangle from her wrist, the queen fell asleep on the mat that Govinda had spread for her.

"I never knew this chamber existed until today," said Govinda.

"When Krishna was brought here from Vrindavan, the Idol's Eye was brought along with him," explained Ananta. "Those who knew of the diamond coveted it, including a temple priest from where the idol came. According to legend, after the priest attempted to steal the Idol's Eye, your ancestor built this chamber."

"With the Moguls nearby, and the rival Rajput clans warring incessantly, my ancestors would have had no peace if others had discovered the diamond," agreed Govinda.

"That is why we keep Krishna and the Idol's Eye in the queen's private temple. The secret isn't shared even with our people. Your ancestor feared that one day the Idol's Eye would be discovered and so he built this secret chamber. He also commissioned a gem cutter to fashion a zircon identical to the Idol's Eye."

"Are you saying the gem adorning Krishna isn't real?"

"It's a forgery. The Idol's Eye is here with me."

"May I see it?"

"Of course!"

From within a fold in his dhoti, Ananta produced a silk pouch which he handed to Govinda. Reaching inside, Govinda felt the hard, faceted surface of a gem which he withdrew.

"It's magnificent," said Govinda, holding the diamond up to the candlelight. In truth, it wasn't noticeably more beautiful than the duplicate that he had already seen — so skilled was the forgery — but knowing the stone's identity made it a privilege to hold.

"Behind that," said Ananta, pointing to a stone like every other in the wall adjoining the sanctum, "is a vault where the real Idol's Eye has been kept since the temple was built. The Idol's Eye touches the idol's foot from beneath him.

"The real diamond adorns Krishna during festivals; the remainder of the year the zircon is displayed. As you know, the Idol's Eye is a centuries-old legacy of our clan. We guard it with great vigilance. Only the Raja of Krishnagarh and the chief priest know about the vault. And since you are now king, I am telling you."

"Until the coronation, Krishnagarh has no king."

"Just the same, I feel it is crucial for you to know," continued Ananta. "The vault also contains a Sanskrit parchment the head priest must read before being entrusted with the Idol's Eye."

"What does it say?"

"The parchment explains the legacy of the diamond. It says that Krishna wore the Idol's Eye while he was king of Dwarka. Our priests knew this, but what is not known is that the Idol's Eye possesses rare powers believed to emanate from the sun. And whoever possesses the Idol's Eye, possesses the powers."

"What kind of powers?"

"The parchment indicates that Krishna will appear to anyone holding the gem in meditation and that whoever possesses the diamond will understand the language of the animal kingdom. Just today, you communicated with Kalki."

"Are you saying that Kalki threw the Emperor because of me?"

"Is there any doubt?"

"It was my sudden shout, not my words. Kalki was upset because the Emperor knocked me off my feet."

"When you were sick with cholera, your father instructed me to place the Idol's Eye in your hand and chant the Krishna mantra. I had not been chanting for long when the room suddenly filled with brilliant blue light. For an instant, I gazed upon Sri Krishna. He was more magnificent than I had ever imagined – than I ever could have imagined. He was speaking to you. Do you remember?"

"One does not forget such a thing, but still I find it hard to believe that a gem can grant such powers."

"According to our scriptures, one gains yogic powers through the use of mantras and gemstones. The parchment also speaks of it."

"May I read it?"

"Of course, but there is more. Aside from the parchment of which

The Tale of the Himalayan Yogis

I speak, there is a letter bearing the royal seal. After a newly crowned king reads the letter, he seals it. I have no idea what the letter says. No living being has read it; your father was the last, and will be until you read it."

"The letter is also in Sanskrit?" asked Govinda.

Ananta nodded.

"According to the parchment, not even the queen knows about the secret vault, or the manuscript describing the diamond."

"The value of the Idol's Eye must be incredible."

"Its physical value is nothing compared to its spiritual worth. The manuscript advises that the king hold the gem while meditating on a secret mantra. After his coronation, I taught your father to do this. The instructions also say the priest should hold the Idol's Eye when performing the last rites. I had it with me during johar."

"Shouldn't we put the diamond into the vault where it will be safe?" suggested Govinda.

"That is for you to decide. The king determines the use of the diamond. Until the Moguls leave, I suggest you keep it with you since the diamond protects whoever has it in his possession."

"And if the Emperor had stolen it?"

"The manuscript warns that the diamond must not fall into the hands of the evil-minded. However, if that were to happen, without the parchment one would not know how to activate the gem's power," explained Ananta.

"Will you teach me the mantra?"

"I will, but you must agree never to speak of it."

"I will keep the secret," agreed Govinda.

Ananta closed his eyes and whispered the mantra into Govinda's ear.

"Now you know how to activate the Idol's Eye. In addition to what I've already told you, the diamond has healing powers. It will surely help the queen. Place the diamond in her hand."

Govinda did so gently so as not to wake his mother. Her hand closed around the gem, but she continued sleeping.

"I feel its power already."

"When word of the king's death came, I feared the Moguls would come for the gem," said Ananta. "If somehow they captured or killed me, the legacy of the Idol's Eye would have been lost forever. I'm relieved to have shared it with you."

"I knew there was a reason why we needed to stay behind."

"Let us hope the Moguls find the forgery. Then surely they'll leave."

"But how did they find out about the Idol's Eye in the first place?"

"I've been wondering the same thing," mused Ananta.

Govinda paused for a moment. "What exactly is the prophecy of the Idol's Eye?"

"I would rather you find out for yourself." Seeing the weariness in Govinda's eyes, Ananta said, "I will open the vault in the morning so that you can read the parchment."

Govinda lay down beside his mother, but before falling asleep, he saw that the queen's fingers had opened from around the Idol's Eye. Covering the gem with his palm, he repeated the mantra Ananta had taught him.

After the troops left, Hashim returned to the temple. Only a handful of soldiers remained behind. As he entered, Hashim closed the temple doors so that he would not be disturbed. Spreading a green cloth over his father, the prince prayed into the night.

Having had no dinner, Govinda roused Ananta. Peering through the tiny hole, he scanned the temple sanctum. Seeing no one inside the sanctum, he and Ananta pushed open the heavy stone door to the closet and stepped out from behind the altar. As Ananta approached the altar, his foot struck the crushed oil lamp. The brass lamp clanged as it rolled across the floor.

"Who's there?" shouted Hashim, having fallen asleep beside his father's body beneath the view from the hole in the closet wall.

"Who are you?" asked Govinda, who was equally startled.

Springing to his feet, Hashim unsheathed his dagger. "I am the son of the Emperor of Delhi. Who are you?"

"I am the temple priest's son, and this is my father," Govinda invented. The broad bands of sandalwood paste on the foreheads

The Tale of the Himalayan Yogis

of Ananta and Govinda supported their story. "Your dagger is not necessary."

"Where is your hiding place?"

"Behind the altar," replied Govinda, who saw no chance of concealing the chamber.

"Stand near the light so that I can see you better." The two stepped close to the altar where one of the lamps still burned.

"Did you kill my father?" questioned Hashim.

"No," replied Govinda calmly, "but we saw what happened."

"Tell me," said Hashim, lowering his dagger but not sheathing it.

"Your father rode into the temple on my fath… on our king's horse. His arm was bleeding."

"He suffered an injury in the battle."

"I imagine your father was a brave warrior," said Govinda, hoping to appeal to the Mogul prince's heart.

Hashim nodded. "Continue."

"Your father rode up to the altar intending to strike Krishna, but his horse reared. He lost control, fell from the horse, and the spike impaled him. I'm sorry, my friend, but that is the truth."

"Then it was you who opened the tunic?"

"I opened the tunic when we saw the wound. Your father died instantly."

"Where is the diamond?"

Govinda hesitated. "May I ask your good name?"

"I am Hashim Shah. What is your name?"

"I am Govinda, and this is my father, Pundit Ananta. We came out to find something to eat. Can we share our food with you?"

"I will not eat, but you may."

Ananta went for the fruit and pudding, and also returned with a pot of water.

"Would you like some water?" asked Ananta.

"I would… to wipe my father's brow."

"For such purpose, use this water." Ananta handed him the bowl at Krishna's feet. Hashim hesitated, then sheathed his dagger and accepted the bowl.

"It grieves us that this tragedy took place in our holy shrine," offered Ananta.

"The sweat of conflict is still on his brow. My father was not a peace-loving man," said Hashim, wiping his father's forehead with the sleeve of his tunic.

"Use this," said Govinda, removing the silk shawl draped across Krishna's shoulders. The gesture surprised both Ananta and the Mogul.

"I am not like my father," confessed Hashim. "Yesterday, I tasted war for the first time. I never want to witness such madness again."

"Not everyone is meant to fight," replied Govinda.

Hashim's eyes flashed uncertainly between his father's body and the Rajputs. His mind cautioned him not to keep such company, but his heart recognized no enemies here; indeed, these seemed among the best of his friends. No one other than Hashim's grandfather and uncle had spoken kindly to him since his mother's death.

Ananta was peeling bananas when Rukmini emerged from the chamber. Upon waking, the queen had found Govinda and Ananta gone, and assumed it was safe to come out. The stranger in the sanctum startled her.

"Who is this woman?" demanded Hashim.

Rukmini drew her pallu over her face; she had had enough of lustful stares.

"This is my mother," Govinda explained. "Mataji, this is Prince Hashim, the son of the Emperor. Father and I explained about the accident," signaling for her to play along with the concealment of their identities.

"We are sorry for your loss," offered Rukmini, catching on immediately. "We are simple people. We have no place to go, and little food."

"Tomorrow, the soldiers will return. They will search the fort, and if they find you, they'll blame you for the Emperor's death."

"What do you suggest?" asked Govinda.

"Stay here in the temple. The commander noticed the unbuttoned tunic and posted guards outside."

The Tale of the Himalayan Yogis

"There is another way out of the temple," confided Govinda, "but we want to take Krishna with us."

It was dangerous to reveal their chance of escape to a Mogul, but in truth, he doubted there was any such chance of moving Krishna without help.

"The commander has seen the idol," warned Hashim. "If it disappears, it will raise even more suspicion."

"Please help us," pleaded Rukmini. "Otherwise they will destroy our beloved Krishna."

"How many soldiers are in the fort?" asked Govinda.

"Only a handful, but the others will return in the morning."

"Where are the soldiers quartered?"

"In the palace."

The Rajputs winced at the news but remained silent.

"Can you find out where the guards are staying in the palace?" asked Govinda. "The tunnel under the temple leads to the queen's apartment inside the palace."

"I'll go and see."

"It is kind of you to help us," said Govinda.

"Under other circumstances, we might have been friends," replied Hashim.

"We still can be," said Govinda, placing his hand on the prince's arm. He felt Hashim's body stiffen. Both of them briefly glanced at Hashim's dagger.

"I'll go to the palace now," said Hashim. Govinda withdrew his hand, and Hashim backed up, then turned and walked quickly away, glancing over his shoulder before exiting the temple.

While Hashim was away, Govinda devoured the bananas and Rukmini nibbled at the rice pudding. Although the queen had no appetite, she felt better than she had earlier.

"Let's try to lift Krishna," suggested Govinda. "Then we'll know whether Hashim's help is needed." The granite statue was almost life-sized, and they struggled to move it from the altar.

Rukmini grew anxious. "Govinda, we've lost the Idol's Eye."

The queen lit a torch and held it high as she scanned the floor. She had almost given up her search when she spotted something glistening in the fire pit.

"Look, here in the havan pit."

"Leave it, Maa," advised Govinda.

"But Beta, the Idol's Eye is our family's most prized heirloom. It's the reason they came here in the first place."

"That's why we must leave it. The Moguls won't leave until they find the gem."

"I see."

Hashim returned from the palace. Soldiers had ransacked the queen's apartment, but it was empty. Holding up a torch, Ananta opened the hidden door to the tunnel. Having made the journey countless times, Rukmini knew every step of the way to the palace. Ananta handed her the torch, and she led the way as the others carried Krishna. The air in the tunnel was heavy and stale. Halfway to the end of the tunnel, a second passage forked to the left.

"This way," Govinda instructed his mother.

"Are we not taking Krishna to the palace?" asked Rukmini.

"He'll be safest in the lotus pond."

The lotus pond was inside the queen's walled garden. The water was deep enough to submerge the statue.

After shuffling along the tunnel leading to the garden, Ananta pushed on a hatch that opened into a gazebo rimmed with marble pillars. A Shiva moon greeted them as they stepped into the garden. The pond lay a few steps from the gazebo, its surface covered with pink lotus blossoms with broad green leaves.

Sweeping the blossoms aside, they eased Krishna into the water, spreading the leafy plants evenly over the water. With the statue concealed, the group returned to the tunnel and continued to the queen's apartment. On their way, Hashim noticed a third passage branching off to the right, but no one spoke of it.

Rukmini sighed as she entered her private quarters. Her belongings were strewn everywhere, the furniture had been set aflame, and a Mogul sword had slashed the portrait of her father. Her beautiful Kashmiri carpets were gone, and the Gujarati wall hangings had been reduced to ashes. Crestfallen, the queen said nothing, not wanting to reveal her true identity.

After securing the doors, Govinda lit an oil lamp and spread some charred cushions on the floor.

"Hashim, I have something to tell you. My mother is Rani of Krishnagarh and Punditji is our family priest."

"But you are her son," confirmed Hashim.

"Yes."

"Then that makes you the crown prince?"

"That makes Govinda the Raja of Krishnagarh," interjected Ananta.

"And soon you may be the Emperor of Delhi," added Govinda.

Astonished to learn Govinda's true identity, Hashim dismissed the preposterous notion of him being emperor. "My brother will inherit the Peacock Throne."

"Friend, I have yet another favor to ask," said Govinda, coming to the reason why he had revealed their identities.

"What is it?"

"Will you take me to the battlefield so that I can perform the last rites for my father?"

"But your father's body is here in the palace."

"How is it possible?"

"My father had the body brought here," explained Hashim.

Rukmini's chest convulsed at the news. The events in the temple had taken her mind off of her husband's death, but now the unbearable loss was suffocating her again. Govinda put his arm around his mother.

"You see; we too are grieving. Ananta and I will go with you to see the body, but Mataji should rest."

After making his mother as comfortable as he could in the ruined quarters, the others entered an antechamber adjoining the queen's apartment.

"Govinda is a name for Krishna, is it not?" asked Hashim.

"That's right, but how did you know?"

"My Hindi acharya gives me books from time to time. I have read the Ramayana and Srimad Bhagavatam," Hashim said proudly.

"What does Hashim mean?"

"'Generous One.' My mother chose the name. Ghazi is my brother's name; it means 'Conqueror.' Perhaps we have modeled ourselves after our names — certainly, they suit us — or at least my brother's suits him."

"Your name suits you well. If what you are doing now is not generosity, then I misunderstand the word."

Embarrassed, Hashim fell silent. He had rarely received praised in his life.

Govinda broke the awkward silence. "Then your brother will become emperor?"

"Ghazi will make an able ruler." Hashim crossed the antechamber to the opposite door. "The soldiers are quartered in the servants' apartment. Your father's body lies in the main hall."

Govinda led the way through ransacked chambers until they reached the throne room, which the soldiers could not enter from the servants' quarters.

The hall was Govinda's favorite in the palace. Fifty elephants had transported the gold-veined marble used to fashion the walls, floor, and columns. Above the teakwood throne hung the clan's emblem – a scimitar rising from the flames.

Govinda noticed immediately that the king's ruby-studded crown was missing from the cushion to the right of the throne. On the wall behind the throne hung portraits of Krishnagarh's kings, including the king who brought Krishna and the Idol's Eye to the fortress. A looter's sword had slashed the painting, which clung awkwardly to the wall.

In the center of the domed hall, a commoner's cloth covered a body. Govinda paused, allowing Ananta to pull the fabric away. Raja Chandra's eyelids were closed, his garments bloodied and torn, and the splintered shafts of a pair of arrows were still lodged in his chest.

"War is cruel," lamented Govinda.

Hashim placed a consoling hand on his back.

"How did my father die?" asked Govinda, kneeling beside the body.

"You were kind enough to tell me how my father died. I shall do the same for you. Our army severely outnumbered your father's. When

The Tale of the Himalayan Yogis

Father pointed to the Raja of Krishnagarh, Ghazi begged Father to let him fight. Father consented but instructed a line of archers to stand ready. Ghazi was no match for your father, and your father knocked my brother from his horse. Dazed, Ghazi lay on the ground. Your father dismounted and raised his sword to strike the deathblow. For some reason, he hesitated; possibly because my brother was so young. At that moment, my father signaled for the archers to fire. My people are to blame for your father's death."

"For a Rajput to die in battle is a great honor. Is it not the same for a Muslim?"

"Death in battle is said to be the highest honor, but to me, these are empty words. Govinda, despite our ill-timed meeting, is it possible that we could be friends?"

"If friendship results from our father's deaths, then they will not have died for nothing," said Govinda. "Do you have a plan to bury your father? The land is rocky here, but I know a grove where the soil is soft."

"And I will help you prepare the pyre for your father. Strangely, I feel closer to you than to my brother," mused Hashim. "I will instruct my men to bring a bullock cart to the temple at sunrise. I shall drive the cart to the grove myself."

"The grove is not far from the fort."

"And your father?" asked Hashim.

"Instruct your men to bring sandalwood to the palace garden. There is ample wood behind the stables. Tell them its needed for cooking fuel. I will light the pyre in the queen's garden."

"That's risky," warned Ananta.

"Surely the soldiers will see the fire."

"Then take the soldiers with you when you bury your father. The grove is not hard to find. Follow the road south, and you'll see it. While you're away, Ananta and I will perform my father's rites."

The shrouded form of Hashim's father lay on the weathered planks behind him. Hashim had witnessed the senseless loss of human life in the previous days culminating in the death of his father, a man he scarcely knew, a man who had never uttered a kind word to him. And yet, Hashim wept silently as the roughly hewn wagon bounced over the rocky landscape outside Krishnagarh.

I am an orphan now, but in reality, I have been one since Maji's passing, thought Hashim.

The black soil turned easily. Hashim insisted on digging the grave himself. Wildflowers blanketed the plot beneath the slender neem trees; the burial was little more than what would be given a peasant.

"Father, I wrote this for you," whispered Hashim as he placed a handful of mustard blossoms on the freshly turned earth.

> tell them when I die
> that I didn't die
> tell them I'm painting landscapes from the sky
> tell them I found love in a grain of sand
> and followed it there
> tell them I'm hiding in the woven basket on the floor
> tell them my heart stopped beating
> because the chase was over
> tell them my body fell away
> like soiled clothes before a bath
> tell them I'm blue and purple and gold
> tell them I'll never grow old
> tell them I now skip from planets
> and smile in starlight
> tell them the sun is my eye
> tell them not to worry or fear
> that I'm near
> tell them when they die
> that they will not die

Govinda and Ananta moved swiftly to complete their task before the soldiers returned. After dousing the wood with buckets of ghee, the bamboo bier on which the shrouded form of Chandra Prakash Singh lay, was positioned on top of the pyre. Ananta lit a tuft of grass and handed it to Govinda, who set the pyre ablaze. Rukmini stood

The Tale of the Himalayan Yogis

beside her son, her pallu drawn over her head. The queen followed Govinda as he circled the fire three times. As the blaze burned down, the mourners walked away without looking back.

Having no idea how long they would be hiding, Ananta collected a cache of food that didn't require cooking. Govinda, who knew every hideaway within the sprawling fort, selected a storage chamber at the edge of the fort's water supply, a deep pool fed by an underground spring at the southernmost end of the fort. The pool was partially hidden by an overhanging ledge, allowing the fugitives to bathe and draw water without undue risk of being discovered.

Govinda and Hashim would rendezvous after dark. If all went according to plan, the Mogul troops would leave in a day or two. Govinda had every reason to be optimistic as he stretched out on the granite floor alongside his mother. The saddest day of their lives had finally come to an end.

Moments before noon, Commander Zaim passed through the main gates with a hundred soldiers and as many servants in tow. The commander intended to stay for a while. Finding no sentries at either the front gate or the entrance to the temple, he headed for the Krishna temple, his annoyance growing with each step. His junior officers trotted behind him.

"Where is Prince Hashim?" bellowed Zaim. "And where are the sentries I assigned to guard the temple?"

Finding not only the Emperor's body missing but also the Krishna idol was gone, Zaim stormed out of the temple.

"Faizon, find Prince Hashim and bring him to the palace at once," he thundered as he marched into the palace. Finding the Rajput king's body gone and the remains of a fire smoldering in the garden, Zaim wanted answers.

Shortly after the commander disappeared into the palace, Hashim, along with the soldiers that had helped him bury the Emperor, rode into the courtyard.

"The commander wants to speak with you." General Faizon informed Hashim.

"What about?" he asked timidly.

"The Emperor's body is missing, as is the Rajput's, and someone has removed the idol from the temple."

"Where is the commander?"

Faizon pointed to the palace.

"Hashim!" barked the commander as the prince entered the hall, the scar above Zaim's brow pulsing. "Where are the bodies? And where is the idol?"

Commander Zaim's thick chest and shoulders made it challenging to stand face to face with him, despite the fact that the two men were of a similar height.

"Come with me, and I'll explain everything," replied Hashim, thoroughly intimidated.

"What have you done with the Rajput's body?"

"I burned it."

"Leaving it for the vultures would have been sufficient."

"My brother would not be alive if not for the Rajput, and so I burned the body out of respect."

"Respect?" fumed Zaim. "From now on, check with me before doing anything."

The two men reached the temple.

"And the Emperor's body?"

"The soldiers helped me bury Father this morning. I found a grove outside the fort where the soil is good. We've just now returned."

"By taking the sentries away from their posts, they have disobeyed orders. I shall punish them for your insolence."

"It's hot here, Commander. I could not bear to see my father's body decay."

"Enough of corpses… where is the idol?"

"When I came for Father this morning, the idol was gone."

Hashim drew the commander's attention to the closet.

"See, the Rajput's hiding place… and look here, a secret door leading to a tunnel. I found both when I came for Father's body. Whoever opened the Emperor's tunic must have been hiding in this chamber, and then, during the night, removed the statue and escaped through the tunnel. I'll show you where the tunnel leads."

"Do you think there was more than one Rajput?"

The revelation of the tunnel and hiding place made Commander Zaim more reasonable. The cool underground air helped soothe his agitated mind as they navigated the passageway.

"I can't say how many," said Hashim, "but it would not have been possible for one man to carry the idol."

The boy has some of his father's intelligence, after all, mused Zaim.

"This passage goes to the palace," said Hashim, pointing to the left. "And this tunnel goes outside the fort."

The passage opened onto the hill beyond the west wall. Squinting, the men stepped into the sunlight. Zaim's mind churned impatiently as he scanned the area.

"So this is how they escaped, but surely they didn't carry the statue across that wasteland," decided the commander, waving his hand dismissively at the sandy expanse below.

Hashim was relieved that the commander was behaving reasonably again.

Returning to the temple via the tunnel, Zaim led Hashim back to the palace.

"Tell me again; what have you done with the Emperor's body?"

"I buried Father this morning. After finding the Rajput's hiding place and the escape route through the tunnel, it seemed pointless to keep the men at their posts, and so the soldiers went with me to pay their final respects. I buried my father in a grove south of the fort."

The boy may not be derelict after all, thought Zaim. *Still, something is wrong here. It will come to me. It always does.*

Approaching his second in command, Zaim issued instructions, "Faizon, gather the men in the palace; including the sentries who abandoned their posts."

When the men had assembled, the commander dispatched search parties and punished those who had disobeyed his orders.

Rukmini awoke with a start. "Ananta, we've left Krishna's crown in the closet."

Inside the palace, a soldier handed Krishna's diadem to Commander Zaim.

"Commander, we found this in a chamber behind the altar," reported the soldier.

As the soldiers turned to go, Zaim gave instructions to his junior officer. "Search the soldiers who have been inside in the temple. You're looking for a diamond the size of a fig. Report back to me when you've completed the search."

Hashim was on his way to the palace when some soldiers hurried past him. Entering the commander's headquarters, he found Zaim waiting for him.

"My men have been looking for you."

"I've been walking."

"This is not a stroll in the palace garden with the queen's handmaids. Tell me, what do you think happened to the diamond?"

"The diamond was the reason for sacking Krishnagarh. Whoever has the idol must also have the gem."

"The soldiers reported that you ordered sandalwood brought to the palace garden this morning. Why sandalwood?"

"My Hindi teacher taught me that sandalwood is sacred to their religion."

"Why have you been learning Hindi?"

"It was my father's idea. He said, 'if you understand the language of the enemy you'll understand the enemy.'"

Zaim stared at Hashim in silence.

"Are we finished?" asked Hashim.

"You may go, but not far."

Commander Zaim's wary eyes followed the prince out of the room.

"Faizon, the boy is up to something. Have one of your men follow him."

Hashim headed for the far end of the fort where Govinda and the others were hiding. Descending the steps to the tank, he moved stealthily along the narrow trail leading to the storage chamber. As agreed, he tapped twice on the door. Hearing the signal, Govinda

The Tale of the Himalayan Yogis

wondered if something had gone awry. Hashim was not supposed to return until night.

Opening the iron-reinforced door, Govinda looked questioningly at Hashim.

"The soldiers are searching everywhere."

"No one will find us."

"Where does that lead?" asked Hashim, pointing to an opening in the floor.

"Our escape route, should I be proven wrong."

"The commander thinks you've fled the fort. He's searching for clues as to whether you left on horseback, or on foot." Hashim added, "Zaim's also watching me."

Wishing he could remain with the Rajputs, Hashim stepped out of the hiding place. Around his people, there was always tension in his heart, but he felt utterly at ease with the Rajputs. Hashim was no longer sure which side he was on.

Hashim had been not expecting his nemesis.

"Who's in there?" barked the commander.

Zaim loomed in front of him, dagger in one hand, a torch in the other. Locking eyes with his tormentor, Hashim blocked the door to the hideout.

Hoping to alert his friends, Hashim shouted, "I've been inside praying."

"You're lying," countered Zaim. "Who let you inside?"

"I told you. There's no one inside. I was praying."

"Without your *namaz* rug?"

"My prayer rug is in Father's tent by the river."

"Stand aside," ordered Zaim.

"There's no one inside, I tell you."

His dagger raised, Zaim stepped forward, but Hashim held his ground; to his left was the water tank and to his right a steep rock wall.

"Out of my way."

"I was planning to swim," Hashim blurted out as the possibility of his imminent death flashed before him.

"Have your swim!" mocked Zaim, shoving the prince into the water before entering the chamber. Passing his torch around the room,

Zaim saw nothing but shadows on the walls. Finding the space vacant, he turned and left.

Hashim pulled himself from the water, his tunic clinging to his trim torso. Zaim stared contemptuously at the prince before heading back to his headquarters.

"Commander, we should not be fighting," said Hashim, catching up with Zaim.

Zaim turned to face Hashim. "Why did you say that your brother will be Emperor? You have an equal claim to the throne."

"It would seem that way," agreed Hashim, wiping his brow with his sleeve, "but years ago my parents decided that it was Ghazi who had inherited Father's disposition. I have no interest in the throne."

Zaim walked away without replying. Hashim did not follow him — any further attempt to improve his standing with the commander would be just as likely to have the reverse effect.

Rather than enter his headquarters, Zaim headed for the queen's temple. Passing the shackled guards, he approached the officer in charge.

"Have you completed the search?"

"We found a half-eaten pot of pudding in a storage closet behind the altar. We also found this."

The officer held out a finely crafted gold bangle.

"You found this in the chamber behind the altar?"

"He found it," said the officer, pointing to a soldier.

"A woman may be involved... a woman of position," Zaim surmised. "It may even be the queen... this is her shrine."

Surveying the scene of the Emperor's death, the commander's gaze fell on the vacant altar before shifting to the iron stake at the center of a circle of stained granite. Imagining how the Emperor fell from his horse, Zaim scanned the temple, fixing his attention on the fire pit in the center of the room. He was about to leave the temple when he noticed something sparkling amidst the grey-white ashes.

Half buried, the Idol's Eye peered up at him. The commander looked to see if anyone was watching before reaching into the pit. As he bent down to retrieve the gem, a pair of soldiers approached from behind. They watched Commander Zaim turn the diamond round and round in his hand before slipping it into his pocket.

"Is that what we've been searching for?" asked one of the soldiers.

"No! It's just a glass trinket someone discarded in the fire pit."

As the commander passed through the temple doors, he stopped to examine the soldiers shackled in the sweltering sun.

"After three days in this oven, you'll learn that a sentry does not abandon his post."

Govinda had worked out a plan.

"Ananta, I want you to take Mataji to Bundi tonight. Tiwari has an oxcart that you can use."

"Will you be safe here alone?"

"I won't be alone. I have the Idol's Eye and Hashim."

"But how will you get to Bundi?" wondered Ananta.

"I'll ride Kalki. I won't leave him for the Moguls. I'll join you in Bundi in a day or two."

"Govinda, this is foolhardy," admonished his mother.

"I'll be fine."

"We should all go to Bundi together," she decided. "Don't you agree, Ananta?"

"Rani Rukmini is right. You don't know what the Moguls are capable of."

"I won't leave Kalki behind. He's a part of me. He's how I shall remember Father."

"But it's too dangerous," Rukmini insisted.

"There's yet another reason. Inside the temple is a vault containing parchments known only to the king and his priest. One of the parchments is to be read by the crown prince before he assumes the throne. As heir to the throne, I can't leave the parchments for the Moguls. According to Ananta, I'm bound by duty."

"But once the Moguls are gone, you can return for them."

"If they destroy the temple, the parchments will be lost forever. Ananta says they contain details crucial to a newly crowned king."

"I've lost your father. I fear I shall lose you as well."

"I'll come with Kalki in a day or two. The journey to Bundi will be taxing. You should depart before moonrise."

"How will we get outside the fort?" asked Ananta.

"That's more than a cellar," said Govinda, pointing to the spot where they had hidden from Zaim. "When I reach Bundi, you and I will take Father's ashes to Varanasi."

Rukmini did not like the idea of leaving Govinda behind but said no more until it was time to depart.

The three descended into the tunnel and walked for what seemed a very long time before Govinda pushed hard against a stone cover. Stars appeared overhead as the night air rushed into the musty passage.

"Do you know Tiwari's farm?" asked Govinda.

Ananta nodded. Tiwari's plot was the only cultivated land in the vicinity of the fort. An underground stream surfaced at the edge of his property, irrigating the old man's homestead.

"When you reach Bundi, keep the queen's identity a secret. No one but Grandfather should know."

Looking up at the fort, Rukmini feared the Moguls would be combing the edifice in search of her son.

"Come with us," she pleaded. "Pitaji wouldn't want you to risk your life for Kalki."

"I'll be all right, Maa. And it's not just for Kalki that I'm staying behind."

"But there are soldiers everywhere."

"I have a plan, but I need to get the parchment first. Now, don't delay. You should go before moonrise; otherwise, a sentry might spot you."

"On the wall of the closet you'll find a pair of tongs," explained Ananta. "You'll need them to open the vault."

Rani Rukmini hugged her son with all her strength. As Govinda was about to climb back into the tunnel, they heard laughter.

Govinda pulled the queen back into the tunnel.

"What was that?" asked Ananta.

"Soldiers celebrating," guessed Govinda. "Stay in the tunnel while I have a look."

Govinda stepped silently in the direction of the sound. Again he heard noises, but this time the commotion sounded like flapping wings. Moving among the rocks, Govinda approached the muffled din until he reached the edge of the fort's refuse pit. Leaning over the edge, he peered into the crater. A flock of vultures lined the far wall of the pit, their puny heads bobbing in the darkness.

But why are they huddled on the wall and not feeding in the pit?

Govinda spotted something at the bottom of the crater, but he couldn't make out what it was, and so he listened and watched. He heard what sounded like groans followed by mocking laughter. Shadowy creatures moved about as he descended into the pit.

Spotting a man lying in the pit surrounded by a pack of hyenas, a tremor of dread swept through Govinda. Repulsed by the unthinkable notion that hyenas were feeding on the man, Govinda descended further into the pit. He had no weapon, no way to run off the hyenas, and so he picked up stones and hurled them at the pack.

A hyena yelped as it retreated, but wasted no time in rejoining the others. Tossing stone after stone, the hyenas backed off, only to rejoin the pack.

Picking up a charred stick, Govinda rushed at the pack, hoping to scare them off. The peculiar beasts retreated up the far side of the pit, then turned, staring hauntingly at the intruder that had interrupted their meal, their narrow yellow eyes trained on Govinda.

Kneeling, Govinda examined the ropes binding the man's arms and legs while keeping a watchful eye on the hungry pack. Scanning the man's legs and feet, he recoiled. The man was an officer, but why had the Moguls done this to one of their own?

"Can you hear me?" he asked. When the man didn't reply, Govinda placed his hand on the man's head, causing him to quake wildly.

"What is your name? Who has done this to you?"

This time the man heard Govinda and opened his eyes. "Sadan… My name is Sadan… punishment."

"But why?"

"I lied to the Emperor. But he found out… of course, he found out."

"The Emperor is dead."

"Dead?"

"I need to find a knife."

"Don't leave…" moaned Sadan.

"I'll move you to a safe place, but I need to get a knife."

"The hyenas will return…"

"But without a knife, I can't cut you free."

The Mogul closed his eyes, resigned to another assault by the pack. Govinda looked up at the chilling silhouettes lining the rim of the pit. The hyenas were oddly proportioned, their hind legs shorter than their forelegs.

A voice called out from above; Ananta was descending into the crater.

"*Hari*, what happened to this man?" flinched Ananta, averting his gaze.

"We need a knife."

"I have one." Ananta wasted no time in cutting the ropes.

"Cut those too," instructed Govinda, pointing to the tightly bound straps on the man's thighs. "We'll have to carry him to the hideout."

"It won't be easy," said Ananta, sawing through the leather straps.

"I won't leave him for them," said Govinda, pointing to the hyenas.

With great effort, they pulled the Mogul up the wall of the refuse pit, into the tunnel, and back to the hiding place. Rukmini followed, horrified by the Mogul's condition. Inside the chamber, Govinda searched for something to sanitize the wounds before settling on a bucket of water from the tank.

"Ananta, you know the way out. Take Mataji and go; it will be too risky once the moon rises."

"But you can't look after him alone," protested Ananta.

"Hashim will be coming soon. I'll send him to the clinic for antiseptics."

"What if the Mogul attacks you?"

"The man cannot even stand," replied Govinda impatiently. "Now go while you can."

"Promise you'll come soon," pleaded Rukmini, hugging her son.

Ananta placed the stone covering over the tunnel exit after helping Rukmini step into the night. Stars dotted the velvet sky, but the moon had not yet risen. Darkness hid the pair as they descended the rocky slope.

The walk to Tiwari's farm was longer than Ananta remembered, but they reached it without incident. Approaching the old man's homestead, Ananta noticed a faint glow where Tiwari's cottage once stood.

"They've burned his farm," sighed the Brahmin. "I haven't been out here in years, but that's Tiwari's land."

Ananta moved cautiously toward the smoldering ruins. The walls and roof of the single-room cottage were gone; only the blackened foundation remained. The pundit stepped inside the stone rectangle in search of clues to the fate of the farmer. Finding nothing, he entered the small lean-to where Tiwari kept his oxcart and plow. The cart was gone, and there was no sign of his spiral-horned ox.

"No sign of Tiwari or his cart," he informed Rukmini.

"Then we must either walk to Bundi or return to the hiding place."

"Bundi is a difficult journey even by oxcart," replied Ananta. "We should return to the hideout."

After carefully fitting the cover over the tunnel entrance, Ananta led the queen back to Govinda's hideout.

"They burned Tiwari's cottage," Ananta reported, pushing his head into the hideout.

"Any sign of Tiwari?" asked Govinda.

"His ox and cart are gone."

"Tiwari knew the siege was coming; he may have eluded them."

"Mataji needs to rest. Are we safe with the Mogul here?"

"He's been asleep since you left."

Rukmini was settling onto her mat when two faint knocks came from the door. Govinda opened the door, and Hashim entered.

"Why hasn't the queen gone to Bundi?" asked Hashim.

"The old man's farm has been burnt to the ground."

"Again, my people make it difficult."

Hashim spotted the body stretched out in the corner of the chamber.

"Who is that?"

"His name is Sadan."

"General Sadan?" asked Hashim, a look of terror on his face. "How did he get in here?"

"I found him in the garbage pit outside the fort. They left him for the scavengers."

"Is he bound?"

"No, but his legs are in bad shape. The hyenas were feeding on him when I found him — his punishment for failing to stop the messenger."

"Commander Zaim's idea, no doubt, though probably on my father's orders. We need to get you out of here. It's only a matter of time before they find you."

"I'm not worried."

"Please, Govinda, do not underestimate Zaim. If he catches you…" Hashim's voice trailed off as he stared at Sadan, making his meaning all too clear.

"Would it be too risky for you to drive an oxcart outside the fort?" asked Govinda.

"I'm willing to try."

"Fill the cart with stones from the quarry. If anyone questions you, say the Emperor's grave is shallow, and you feared coyotes might ravage the body."

"It sounds like a good plan, except that when I return without the cart, they'll ask questions. Zaim has a way of wilting my courage."

"Anyone who would stake his officer for the hyenas is hardly human."

"Make no mistake; Zaim's a devil. I hope you never meet him. What will you do with Sadan?"

"I don't think he can walk. If we don't treat his wounds, he could lose his legs… maybe his life."

"Can I do anything?"

"The clinic is at the end of the row of shops near the barracks. If they haven't ransacked the shelves, you'll find fresh dressing and alcohol there."

"I'll do my best," said Hashim. "Bind Sadan and put him in the tunnel for the night. Otherwise, I fear for your safety."

The Tale of the Himalayan Yogis

"But we just saved him from a torturous death. He's delirious and can't walk. I'm not sure he'll live no matter what we do."

"Then he will be that much more desperate. It doesn't matter what you've done for him. In his mind, you're no better than the hyenas. Sadan didn't become a senior officer out of kindness."

"He'll sleep through the night," decided Govinda.

"It would be a mistake to trust a Mogul."

"But I trust you."

"Then trust me now," pleaded Hashim. "I don't trust these military types, nor do they trust each other; indeed, they trust no one. They have no loyalty to win no matter what you do for them. Tomorrow, I'll try to arrange an oxcart."

"Leave it at the base of the west wall," Govinda instructed. "If Zaim asks where it is, tell him a wheel came off."

"Zaim is uncanny about deception."

After Hashim left the hideout, Govinda lay down on his mat, his mind occupied with Tiwari.

"I think I know where Tiwari is. There's a cave in the hills. Tiwari took me there once. He called the cave his secret fort. He said he needed a place to hide from the enemy."

"Tiwari's old enough to have seen Krishnagarh attacked more than once," mused Ananta.

"Tiwari's cave isn't far. We should go tonight. Even if Tiwari isn't there, the hills will be safer than staying here. The night air is cool. We can make it before sunrise."

The fugitives moved silently through the tunnel. The waning moon overhead scarcely illumined the landscape. Govinda scanned the fort's ramparts but saw no sentries. Angling across the hill, the trio passed the refuse pit. Rounding the corner of the fort, they headed east. Although the Aravali Hills were not visible, Govinda knew precisely how long it took to reach them on horseback. He had, however, never crossed the plains on foot and wondered if their tracks would lead the Moguls to Tiwari's hideout. A high wind would erase their footprints, but the air was as still as death.

Twice they crossed sections of barren rock. Govinda turned north, hoping that anyone tracking them would have difficulty in picking up their trail again. The journey took longer than expected. Rukmini was weary by the time they reached Tiwari's cave, a tiny opening hidden among a hodgepodge of odd-shaped boulders.

Govinda crawled into the cave. Inside, he was able to stand, but there was no sign of Tiwari. Returning to the entrance, he helped the others enter the cave.

"I was sure Tiwari would be here," said a dejected Govinda.

"Maybe the Moguls caught him," Ananta suggested.

"Let's hope not."

"Govinda, we're well on our way to Bundi," observed Rukmini. "We can reach there together tomorrow night."

"But that would mean leaving Kalki and the parchments behind."

The floor of the cave was smooth and spacious, and it was not long before they were asleep.

Govinda woke in the early morning, but finding the cave devoid of light, he rolled over and returned to his sleep. A massive boulder fronted the opening to the cave, which obstructed the morning sun. It wasn't until he crawled outside that he realized how long he had slept. The sun was already well above the Aravali Hills.

Govinda slipped between the rocks, descending the hill to a spring from which he and Tiwari had once drawn water. The mineral spring was pure, and Govinda sipped his fill before splashing his face and arms with the cooling water.

He was about to return to the cave when he spotted what appeared to be the tip of an oxen's horn protruding from a rock a good distance downstream. Dismissing it as a branch attached to one of the scrub trees among the rocks, Govinda was heading back up the hill when he heard the baritone lowing of an ox.

Spinning around, he spotted a gaunt, turbaned figure sitting on a rock. The man was smoking a *bidi* and pulling on his mustache between puffs. An old, grey ox stood beside him.

"Tiwari," called Govinda, bounding out from behind a boulder.

"Govinda?" replied the old man, his sad eyes clouded by cataracts.

"I saw smoke rising above the fort and assumed the fires had claimed everyone."

"I'm sorry about your farm. We were afraid you had died in the blaze."

"If not for my son, I would have."

"What do you mean?"

"I intercepted the messenger on his way to the fort. He told me the Moguls had slaughtered everyone. I waited until nightfall before going to the battlefield."

"But why?"

"My son fought beside your father."

"I see."

"I've witnessed three sieges in my life, but I've never seen anything like it. Bodies so thick I had to leave the cart… wasn't even space for my boot… mostly I just stepped across the bodies. I was determined to find my boy."

"You found him?"

"His ashes are in the pot." Tiwari pointed to a terracotta vessel on the cart. "Bad omen when a father performs the rites for his boy."

"But a soldier who dies in battle goes directly to the higher realms."

"True," nodded Tiwari, pausing to draw on his bidi. "But it bodes ill for the father."

"What will you do with the ashes?"

"I've been thinking about that all morning."

"In peaceful times, a son spreads his father's ashes in the Ganges, but in times of war… I'm taking my father's ashes to Varanasi. You could come along."

"Too old… too weak." The old man's eyes had retreated deep into his skull.

"Have you had food?"

"I've stopped eating."

"We have provisions in the cave," offered Govinda.

"I won't take food. My time is over. One day, when you are a father, you'll understand."

"Then I shall take your son's ashes to Varanasi."

"I would like that. My son died fighting beside Raja Chandra. His ashes should be scattered with his king's."

"Tiwari, I have a request."

"Ask."

"The queen is sleeping in the cave. I need to move her to Bundi where she will be safe."

"Take the cart. I have no use for it. I was wondering what to do with Avani," said the old man, rubbing the gentle oxen's nose. "She's old, but she has the will to serve."

"A good ox is always useful."

"No son… no farm… Avani is my last tie to this world. Now I'm free."

"What will you do?" asked Govinda.

"I will lie in the cave and not get up."

"I'll look after you, and when the time comes, I'll perform the sacred rites as if I were your son."

Tiwari stared into the stream. Slowly, his face brightened.

"Would the crown prince do that for an old man? Would it be right?"

"Of course I would! Of course, it would be right."

"Then there may still be hope for my soul."

"You're a good man, Tiwari. Why wouldn't there be hope for your soul?"

"We are taught that without the rites, one's soul is lost."

"Pundit Ananta and I performed Pitaji's rites yesterday. I know what to do."

"Then I will die knowing that I'll see my son again," said Tiwari, smiling broadly.

"Come with me to the cave, and I'll make sure you're comfortable."

Govinda took hold of the old man's arm, which felt like a stick wrapped in cotton. Old Tiwari stopped halfway up the hill.

"The smoke would bring the Moguls."

"I'm not afraid of them."

"Better leave my body in the cave," advised Tiwari. "Put some rocks in front of the entrance to keep the *pretas* out."

Govinda helped the old man climb the steeper section of the hill.

The Tale of the Himalayan Yogis

When they arrived at the cave's entrance, he sat the aged Rajput on a rock and crawled inside. A small lamp burned on a makeshift altar. Ananta was performing *puja* while Rukmini looked on. When he finished, Govinda revealed his plan.

"I found Tiwari by the stream. We can use his oxcart."

"Then you'll come to Bundi with us?" asked Rukmini hopefully.

"I promised Tiwari I would perform his last rites."

"Tiwari's dying?" asked Ananta.

"He hasn't taken food since his son's death."

"But he might live for days."

"He might, but I promised him," replied Govinda resolutely. "I will come when I can, but only after Tiwari's gone. Tonight, you and Mataji should go to Bundi."

"Thinking his mantra is the best thing for Tiwari's soul," Ananta reminded Govinda.

"What is your plan?" asked Rukmini.

"I will return to the fort through the tunnel our people used."

"But that tunnel goes into the courtyard."

"A second passage connects to the palace."

"That is much too dangerous," complained Rukmini. "You'll end up with the Moguls in the servant's quarters. Sometimes it seems like this is all a game to you."

"It is, Maa."

"Until they catch you."

Hashim drove the rock-laden oxcart into the courtyard, hoping that he would not encounter Zaim. But the commander stepped out of the palace as the creaking cart approached the gates of the fort.

"Stop the cart," ordered Zaim.

The sentries lowered their swords, daring the prince to oppose them.

"Who gave you permission to leave the fort with that cart?"

"I need no man's permission to visit my father's grave," replied Hashim defiantly.

"I told you not to go anywhere without checking with me first."

"You forget, Commander, that I am not one of your soldiers. If you persist in harassing me, I shall inform my brother, and he will deal with you."

"Are you threatening me?"

"Interpret my words as you wish, but I'm sure my brother will understand my desire to spread stones on our father's grave to prevent coyotes from ravaging the body."

"Then you did not dig a proper grave?"

"The land is badly suited for a grave. We found a plot where the soil was soft, but we could not dig deep."

"And so you thought to cover the grave with stones."

Hashim nodded. "I brought the stones from the quarry at the far end of the fort."

"Take some men with you."

Hashim suspected this was Zaim's way of keeping an eye on him.

"The soldiers were with me when I buried Father. I wish to have a moment alone at the grave."

"Grieving?" asked Zaim.

"Did you not also love your father?"

The question caught Zaim by surprise.

"I scarcely knew my father," he replied indifferently. "He died fighting in Afghanistan when I was four."

"Then you've lived with the pain of losing your father for a long time."

"I told you, I hardly knew my father. His death meant nothing to me."

"I'm sorry for you. Now, I wish to visit my father's grave."

Zaim stepped aside, seemingly surprised by Hashim's words.

"See me in the palace when you return."

Hashim tapped the ox's hindquarter with a bamboo stick. The plodding beast moved at an agonizingly slow pace for the prince, who was rapidly wilting under the midday sun and Commander Zaim's glare. Hashim was unsure what to do next, and so he headed in the direction of his father's grave. Arriving at the stand of trees, he placed the stones over the burial plot marked by the wilted flowers he had left the previous day.

The Tale of the Himalayan Yogis

After spreading the stones, Hashim offered a prayer before departing. As he approached the fort, Hashim considered continuing without stopping to see Govinda, but the urge to be with someone who cared about him gnawed at his heart. Hashim was parentless, his brother preoccupied with shoring up his succession, and a cruel commander seemed intent on punishing him for being human.

The hill was too steep for the cart, and so he set out on foot, medical supplies in hand. Seeing no sentries in the turrets overhead, Hashim climbed to a spot where he hoped to find the entrance leading to Govinda's hideout.

Near the fort's foundation, Hashim found the opening he was looking for and slipped through the uncapped entrance leading to the Rajputs' hideout. After shuffling along the musty corridor, he reached the end of the tunnel where the missing slab of stone above his head confirmed that he was beneath Govinda's hideout.

"Govinda!" he called.

When his friends did not answer, he decided they were either asleep or bathing in the tank outside.

Pulling himself up through the opening, Hashim was partway inside the hideout when a crushing blow struck the back of his head, knocking him to the floor of the tunnel. Reeling from the violent assault, Hashim lay half-conscious on the damp floor. Throbbing pain shot through his head; a trickle of warm liquid spread across the back of his neck. Had it not been for his turban, the blow would have crushed his skull.

His vision blurred, Hashim struggled to stand. Steadying himself against the tunnel wall, he slowly regained his balance. Sadan had mistaken him for a Rajput and delivered the blow out of fear. But where, he wondered, was Govinda?

"General Sadan?" called Hashim. "I've come to help."

"Identify yourself," replied a weak voice from above.

"I'm Prince Hashim. Are you alone?"

"Are you alone?" countered Sadan.

"Yes. I'm coming up."

"Don't! You've come to return me to Zaim. He'll stake me in the pit again."

"I won't allow Zaim to harm you."

"Why would you help me? I deceived your father and deprived you of a pleasure slave."

I would have derived no pleasure from a slave, thought Hashim.

"The Emperor is dead, and I must look to my future, not his past. Nor do I hold against you the consequences of your failure. My brother will become the new emperor. He won't allow Zaim to harm you."

"I'm glad your brother will be emperor and not you. If you are as forgiving as you claim, Zaim will feed you to the hyenas before he leaves this place."

"They're searching everywhere. Sooner or later, the soldiers will find you," cautioned Hashim.

"They?" asked Sadan incredulously. "Who are you to call yourself other than they? Unless you are a traitor, they have already found me. But where are the Rajputs who carried me out of the pit?"

"If I am a traitor, then what are you? Let there be no accusations between us. As for the Rajputs, I don't know who you're talking about."

If Govinda had left the hideout, then Hashim saw no reason to admit that he knew him.

"But you must," claimed Sadan. "Otherwise, how did you know that it was I who hit you?"

Hashim was unsure what to say. "The Rajputs are good people. They saved your life."

"They are Rajputs still."

Hashim doubted there was any benefit in attempting to persuade Sadan to befriend the Rajputs.

"I will leave now," he said. "I will not betray you for I would betray myself in doing so. And if Zaim's men catch you, you must also not mention me. Otherwise, I won't be able to prevent Zaim from finishing you off. Do you understand?"

"I understand," replied Sadan.

"Do you have food?"

"The Rajputs left plenty."

"And your wounds?"

Sadan did not answer.

As Hashim turned away from the opening in the ceiling, he stumbled on the medical supplies.

"Sadan, I've brought bandages and antiseptic for your wounds."

"Hand them up."

Hashim extended the supplies into the hideout where Sadan snatched them out of his hand.

"This time I shall go." As Hashim shuffled along the tunnel, he heard groans as Sadan applied antiseptic to his festered wounds.

By the time Hashim reached the fort's entrance, his head throbbed like monsoon thunder. Blood and dust caked on his neck; the sun overhead caused his head to spin. As Hashim drove the cart through the front gates, a pair of guards seized the iron ring in the oxen's nose.

"What are you doing?" asked the bewildered prince.

"Climb down," ordered one of the guards.

"Why?"

"Commander Zaim's orders. He is expecting you."

Beads of sweat lined Hashim's brow as the guards led him into the palace. Seeing the prince, Zaim rose from his cushion.

"Bind his hands and feet."

"What's this all about?" demanded Hashim. "I've done nothing wrong."

"I'll decide that," barked Zaim. "The sentries informed me that they saw you drive the oxcart away from the fort. On your return, the sentries watched you disappear into an opening at the base of the fort."

Hashim's head pounded, he struggled to breathe. "I spread the stones over my father's grave."

"I'm not interested in the grave."

"On my way back to the fort… I stopped." Hashim had no idea what to say next, and so he stumbled on. "… because I thought I saw someone on the hill." Hashim's hands trembled as he spoke. "I climbed to where I saw the man, but he had disappeared into an opening near the wall of the fort. When I stepped into the tunnel, someone struck me over the head." Hashim was now gaining confidence in his story, and he removed his turban to show Zaim the bulbous lump on the back of his head. "When I woke up, I came back to the fort."

Zaim turned to the guards. "Have fifty soldiers with mounts wait for me in the courtyard... and take him to the physician."

"Where are you going?" asked Hashim tentatively.

"First, I'm going to see if the hyenas have finished with Sadan. Then I'm going to have a look inside the tunnel where the attack occurred."

If Zaim discovered the hideout, it would be only a matter of time before he captured Govinda. And what of Sadan? Hashim had promised to protect him, but now Zaim and his men were about to show up in the tunnel.

The physician applied compresses to Hashim's head and neck, easing the stranglehold of tension gripping his body. The physician, a kindly old man, had dressed the Emperor's wounds after the battle with the Rajputs. Stretched out on a mat in the servant's quarters within the palace, Hashim drifted off to sleep. As he left the room, the physician instructed the guards outside the makeshift infirmary not to disturb the prince for any reason.

Govinda ran through the dank tunnel connecting Krishnagarh and the Aravali Hills. The strong smell of dung told him the substance oozing between his toes came from the animals that had carried his people to freedom. Moving through tunnels was second nature for him, and before long he was faced with a decision: should he follow the tunnel leading to the palace, or choose the tunnel that would take him back to his hideout? Without hesitating, he chose the tunnel leading to the palace. As he headed toward enemy headquarters, a thrill of excitement quickened his pace.

Although he knew the tunnel led to the servant's quarters where the Moguls had set up camp, Govinda had never used the passage before. Arriving at tunnel's end, Govinda ran his fingers over the low ceiling, hoping for a clue to the entryway. Locating the false square, he pushed on it, hopeful that he wasn't about to thrust his head into a room full of soldiers.

Govinda created a narrow crack, but the room was utterly dark.

The Tale of the Himalayan Yogis

He opened the slab further. Although he couldn't see anything, the smell of wool told him that a rug covered the opening.

Govinda knew precisely where he was since the servant's quarters had but one rug. Listening for voices, he heard none. It would be risky to push his way into the room blindly, and so he waited for a sign. The sound of slow, rhythmic breathing told him that someone was asleep in the room. Pushing aside the stone cover, he maneuvered the rug out of the way and raised himself into the chamber. A man was lying on a mat at the far end of the room. Govinda was about to open the door when a voice from behind stopped him.

"There are guards on the other side."

Spinning around, Govinda saw that the Mogul was sitting up and watching him.

"Hashim," he whispered, silently moving to his friend's side.

"I am relieved to see you safe if one could call the Mogul headquarters safe. Zaim is on his way to the hideout."

"Is Sadan still there?"

"Yes. I brought bandages, but the sentries spotted me and informed Zaim."

"How did you get out of that one?"

"When I climbed into the hideout, Sadan hit me over the head. The wound convinced Zaim that I was not harboring fugitives."

"Then Sadan is in trouble."

Hashim nodded grimly. "Zaim's riding Kalki to the pit to check on him. When he discovers that Sadan's been cut loose, he'll go straight to the tunnel. I'm afraid there's little hope for him."

"Perhaps... but perhaps not."

"You're not thinking of trying to rescue him?" Hashim shuddered at the thought of saving one Mogul officer from another.

"How badly are you hurt?"

"Just a headache and a sore neck."

"I have a plan."

"Another plan?" asked Hashim, rolling his eyes.

"If the plan works, I'll steal Kalki out from under Zaim, and maybe even save Sadan in the process."

"You talk as if you possess some yogic power."

"I don't, but the Idol's Eye seems to."

"Can I help?" offered Hashim.

"Go and see if anyone's inside the temple."

"You're not going back there again? There are guards everywhere outside the temple."

"There's something I need to get."

"Let me get it for you," offered Hashim.

"Thanks, but I have to get it myself."

"All right, but at least let me keep watch outside the temple."

"Let me know the moment when Zaim returns with Sadan. It is time I met this commander I've heard so much about."

"You want to meet Commander Zaim?" At Govinda's words, an icy chill scaled Hashim's spine, and his breath froze.

"I want to meet all the generals," laughed Govinda.

"That can be easily arranged; they would like to meet you as well. I hope this plan of yours works and that you haven't lost your wits."

When Hashim returned with news that the temple was empty, Govinda vanished into the tunnel connecting the garden pavilion with the temple. Emerging inside the temple, he headed for the closet where he searched for the tongs, but they were gone. Examining the wall, Govinda decided that removing the stone without the tongs was impossible — the stone had been skillfully inserted to prevent theft.

Prying at the stone with a blunt knife that he found in the closet, Govinda wanted the parchment more than anything. If he failed to secure it, there was no guarantee he would ever discover its contents since he fully expected the Moguls to raze the temple to the ground. Frustrated, he leaned against the wall of the chamber, searching his mind for a solution.

So much had happened since his father had led the cavalry out the main gates three days earlier: the army's defeat... the elders entering the johar fires... the Emperor's gruesome death... befriending Hashim... his father's last rites... the parchment... finding Sadan in the pit... his promise to Tiwari. The events now swirled about his mind like fallen leaves swept along the ground by a gust of wind.

"The sentries say troops are approaching the hill," Hashim informed him.

The Tale of the Himalayan Yogis

"Zaim and his men?"

"Not Zaim," replied Hashim. "The troop is much larger."

"Good! They should arrive in time for Zaim's public humiliation."

Hashim looked questioningly at Govinda, who leaned against the temple wall as if he hadn't a care in the world. "Zaim's humiliation? Have you gone mad?"

"Friend," grinned Govinda. "It is the world that's gone mad. You and I are here to rescue it."

"Rescue what… and who? This is not the time for jokes. A thousand soldiers are about to ride through the gates. What chance will you have of escaping then? Have you found what you're looking for?"

"I can't open the vault."

"Then go back to the hills," pleaded Hashim.

"I'm waiting for Kalki."

"You're waiting for the avatar?" frowned Hashim.

"You think I'm waiting for an avatar? Who's mad now?"

"You said you're waiting for Kalki," protested Hashim, a look of confusion on his face.

"Kalki is my father's stallion. I'm not leaving without him."

"Zaim has claimed the stallion. He rode out the gates on a white horse."

"I know. That's part of my plan."

"You keep talking about a plan. Would you mind sharing it with me?"

"You'll see soon enough."

"Govinda, you talk like a madman."

Govinda did not reply. His mind focused on the lamp's flame, his fingers wrapped around the Idol's Eye. Jumping to his feet, he ran to the entrance of the temple and peered into the courtyard.

"I see that your brother is leading the cavalry. I want to meet the future Emperor of Delhi."

"Unless you go quickly, you will meet Ghazi… and his generals."

"All the better. It will be good for the officers to witness what is about to happen."

"You don't seem to understand. These are soldiers, and you're the enemy."

"I do what Krishna wishes for me to do. Here in the temple, his presence is strong. I had a vision just now. I assure you, there is no reason to be afraid."

"I hope you know what you're doing, because if you don't…"

"I plan to confront Zaim but do not try to help me no matter how desperate things become. You can help yourself and me by pretending to be my enemy."

"I'm the one who got hit on the head, but you're the one acting like it," mused Hashim, his voice filled with doubt.

"I'm looking forward to this."

"If you escape, will you ride to Bundi?"

"It would lead them to my people."

"Then what will you do?"

"I'll hide in the hills until they give up their search. Can we meet somewhere in Delhi?"

"So long as it's away from the palace. Inquire about me at Haus Khaz. I study there with a Brahmin named Ramlal. If that fails, my grandfather will direct you to me. His name is Mumtaz Aalim. He lives in an abandoned Shiva temple in a place called Gaziapur. The locals know the place."

"I'll try to come."

"Govinda, I've reached a crossroads. I'm not meant to be an emperor or even the brother of an emperor."

"I too have reached a crossroads," agreed Govinda.

"Maybe we share a common destination."

"I hope so."

Voices could be heard outside the temple.

"There's still time for you to escape," suggested Hashim.

"I won't leave without Kalki."

"The loyal type," Hashim grinned.

"I never forget my friends."

"It's a lethal combination you Rajputs possess: fearless and loyal to the death."

"Some say we're foolhardy too," added Govinda.

"Is this the last time we'll speak?"

"I hope not. I would hate to miss our meeting in Delhi."

The Tale of the Himalayan Yogis

"Be careful."

Govinda nodded.

"Now go and greet your brother, and don't forget to inform me when Zaim returns."

Hashim slipped out of the temple in time to see his brother dismount. Ghazi looked more intimidating than he remembered. Quickening his pace as he crossed the courtyard, Hashim greeted his twin.

"Where is Commander Zaim?" questioned Ghazi.

"Zaim and some of his men are outside the fort."

"I left instructions for him to search the fort. What's he doing outside?"

"A tunneled entrance into the fort was discovered. Zaim suspects Rajput fugitives may be hiding there. He's gone to have a look. You must be thirsty after the long ride. Come, there is fresh coconut water in the palace."

Ignoring his brother, Ghazi instructed two of his men to inform Zaim that he had arrived. But before his men could turn their horses, a sentry called down from the wall, revealing that the commander and his men were approaching.

Ghazi handed his reins to an aide while an officer led the remainder of the cavalry to the far side of the courtyard. Hashim returned to the temple where he signaled to Govinda that Zaim and his men were approaching. As Hashim passed the soldiers chained to the pillars outside the temple, one of them groaned. Hearing the beleaguered man's cry, Govinda disappeared into the rear of the temple, returning with a pot filled with water.

Govinda scooped a handful of rock sugar into his pocket from a bowl near the temple entrance and then glanced at the iron spike that had claimed the Emperor.

Commander Zaim rode through the main gate ahead of his men. He was not expecting to find Ghazi, and the cavalry, waiting for him and his spine straightened at the sight of them. Zaim wanted everyone to know that he, and not Prince Ghazi, was in charge of the army.

Strapped to a horse, his face pressed against the animal's flanks on one side and his ravaged legs dangling over the other, soldiers ushered

General Sadan into the courtyard. Govinda peered past the soldiers shackled to the temple pillars. The soldiers failed to notice the fugitive at their backs.

"Cut him down," Zaim ordered the men flanking General Sadan, choosing to take care of business before greeting Prince Ghazi.

"Congratulations," offered Ghazi. "I see you've rounded up a Rajput."

"Worse than a Rajput... this man's a traitor."

"Traitor? Who is this traitor?"

"General Sadan... Had he done his job, your father would still be alive."

Sadan's body hit the ground like a sack of peasant's rice. He was conscious, but the scarlet lines crisscrossing his torso told Ghazi that they had flogged the officer.

"Stand up," ordered Zaim. "Salute your men like an officer."

The men who had cut Sadan down from the horse lifted him to his feet. Sadan groaned as his swollen feet touched the ground.

"Sadan, I ordered you to salute your men," repeated Zaim. "Help him salute his men."

Commander Zaim took pleasure in making examples out of those who failed to execute orders. A soldier raised Sadan's limp arm.

"What punishment has the general received for his incompetence?" asked Ghazi.

"I had him staked in the garbage pit. The hyenas and buzzards were to be his executioners, but someone cut him loose."

"Who could have done that?" asked Ghazi.

"I cut him loose!" announced Govinda, who had emerged from the temple and was offering water to one of the shackled sentries. It was the first water the man had received all day.

"Who said that?" demanded Zaim, pulling Kalki in a circle and scanning the soldiers. "Step forward so that I can see you."

Govinda examined a second soldier who was similarly bound, but the man was unconscious, and so he tossed the pot to the ground as he strode into the center of the throng of soldiers.

"A cowardly way to punish a man, don't you think?" suggested Govinda.

All eyes were on the Rajput, including those of the sentries who watched from the ramparts overhead.

"What did you say?" snarled Zaim.

"I said it's a cowardly way to punish a man, especially your officer," Govinda repeated.

"Who are you?" asked Ghazi, finding the comment amusing.

"I am Govinda, son of Raja Chandra Prakash Singh. Who are you?"

Govinda now stood but a few steps from Ghazi. Zaim glared at the Rajput from his saddle. Hashim, who was standing at his brother's side, was now convinced that Govinda had lost his mind.

"I am Prince Ghazi, and this is my brother Hashim. We are the sons of the dead Emperor."

"Are you responsible for the Emperor's death?" asked Hashim, remembering Govinda's instructions.

"I was there when he died."

"Then you saw what happened?" questioned Ghazi.

"I saw it all."

"Speak! How did our father die?" demanded Hashim, his forcefulness pleasing Govinda.

Turning to Commander Zaim, Govinda spoke. "Commander, I've been watching your feeble efforts to solve the Emperor's death. You're not clever enough."

Several of the soldiers forming a half circle around the Rajput smirked.

"You dare speak that way to me," thundered the commander, loosening the knot to his battle-ax.

"You've shackled those men to pillars and left your officer to be eaten by hyenas in a refuse pit while you have made no progress at all. Pathetic way to command your troops."

Zaim had heard enough. Raising his battle-ax, he was about to ride Govinda down when Ghazi stopped him.

"Not yet," Ghazi ordered, raising his hand. "First, let us find out how the Emperor died."

Zaim lowered his weapon, his eyes spitting venom.

"Speak," ordered Zaim. "Tell us what you know before I cut your heart out."

"Before I speak, you must agree to one thing."

"I like this Rajput," Ghazi whispered to his brother.

"He's obviously deranged," Hashim whispered back, "but let us hear him out."

"What is that?" barked Zaim.

"Cut those men free," said Govinda, pointing to the sentries shackled in front of the temple.

"What do those men matter to you?" snapped Zaim.

"Every man matters to me. You must also agree not to harm General Sadan."

"Rodent," snarled Zaim. "In what hole have you been hiding? I didn't defeat your father's army and sack this fort to have some lunatic orphan tell me how to run my affairs."

"I'm not asking you to agree to anything, Commander. I'm asking Prince Ghazi. He's to be the next Emperor of Delhi, not you."

"Like my father, I too enjoy a game of cat and mouse," said Ghazi, pleased that the Rajput had proclaimed him to be the future emperor. "I grant the boy his wish."

"Then tell us how the Emperor died!" bristled Zaim, his patience evaporating like spilled water in the desert.

"I'll show you, but it will be safer if you dismount."

"Why is that?" demanded the irate commander.

"Because you appear to be a poor horseman."

At Govinda's remark, Zaim flew into a rage. "Another word and I'll plant this blade in your chest faster than my archers downed your father!"

"Then this is for my father," countered Govinda. "Kalki, are you ready?"

Zaim looked about. "Are you mad? Who is this Kalki?"

"The stallion… FOOL!"

"You mock me!" frothed Zaim. "Now you die!"

Wild with rage at being called a fool in front of his men, Zaim flung his battle-ax at Govinda. End over end it hurtled toward its mark, but Govinda was expecting it and readily dove out of the ax's

The Tale of the Himalayan Yogis

path. The blade dug into the earth beside him, throwing dust into the air. Seeing Govinda on the ground, Kalki grew agitated. Govinda waited, for he knew the commander would climb down to make the kill. He had seen it in the vision.

As the commander's boot slid out of the stirrup, Govinda shouted, "Kalki!"

As if on cue, the stallion rose into the air. With but one boot in the stirrup, Zaim struggled to stay atop the rearing horse. A look of dread froze on Zaim's face as he toppled off the horse, crashing hard to the ground. Leaping to his feet, Govinda grabbed Zaim's battle-ax.

Standing over the fallen commander, Govinda raised the ax into the air. Hashim looked on in awe, fully expecting his friend to decapitate Zaim. Taking perfect aim, Govinda swung the ax, planting the blade in the ground alongside the commander's ear. Cowering in the dust, Zaim watched his foe swing nimbly onto Kalki's back. Twisting around in the saddle to face Prince Ghazi, Govinda called out,

"Now you know how the Emperor died! I expect you to keep your promise."

Turning to Zaim, Govinda mocked the commander a final time.

"You really are a poor horseman."

Kicking Kalki into a gallop, Govinda headed for the gates. Unused to acting without orders, the soldiers hesitated, and their leaders hesitated as well, stunned by the Rajput's brazen actions. Shaken by his brush with death and the fact that he lived only by an enemy's mercy, Zaim issued his command too late.

Govinda rode past the Mogul ranks before they could close, passing through the gates before the archers could fire. The soldiers rushed to the gates to regain their line of sight, but their target was already beyond their range.

Zaim struggled to his feet with the help of an aide, his men looking on like a thousand puppets waiting for someone to pull their strings. None of Commander Zaim's men admired him; some had even found the encounter with the Rajput amusing, knowing that the boy had spoken the truth.

"Go and get the boy," Zaim ordered his cavalry. "Bring him to the palace. I'll deal with the Rajput myself."

"It appears you tried that already," taunted Hashim.

Somehow Hashim knew that even with the entire Mogul cavalry pursuing his friend, they would return empty-handed. After all, Govinda had Krishna on his side, the avatar who had defeated an army without lifting a weapon.

"This beats that dusty camp," said Ghazi with a look of fascinated excitement.

"It certainly does," agreed Hashim.

The Return of the Prince

Like tribal drums, Kalki's hoofs thundered against the earth as he streaked across the plains. It had been too long since Govinda had ridden his father's stallion and the duo delighted in their reunion, riding as they had never ridden before. Warm currents rushed past Govinda's cheeks, the strips of cloth at the back of his turban fluttering like a kite's tail. Hiding in cramped closets and musty tunnels had been a prison of sorts, but now Govinda flew to freedom like a falcon from its jess.

Sensing that Kalki wanted to run, he let the stallion control the pace. The young rider handled his horse the way his father had taught him, allowing Kalki to be an equal partner. As the landscape blurred, Govinda felt the same exhilaration he had as a child clutching the fleet-footed steed's mane as he and Pitaji streaked across the grasslands.

Charting a course past Tiwari's still smoldering farmhouse, he would hide at the southern end of the Aravali Hills, a safe distance from Ananta and his mother. No horse in all of Hindustan possessed Kalki's speed or his stamina. The Moguls would have fared as well pursuing a phantom.

After distancing himself from Tiwari's farm, Govinda stopped to see if the Moguls were pursuing him. Krishnagarh appeared as little more than a fire ant atop its mound. Govinda headed for the last hill in the Aravali range where water and cactus fruit would sustain him. Arriving at a stream, he reached into his pocket and produced a handful of rock sugar. Kalki relished the treat.

Leaving the stallion to drink from the stream, Govinda climbed the hill to see if he had been followed, but the land was tranquil in every direction. A traveler gazing at the sunset from atop the hillock could never have imagined the landscape littered with the corpses of fourteen thousand soldiers.

From his rocky perch, Govinda scanned the cloudless sky. Like a monarch surveying his domain, he entertained a thought that had been vying for his attention since he visited the queen's temple earlier in the day. Ananta would be driving Tiwari's cart to Bundi in the night, and if he could conjure up a rain shower, not only would his tracks be washed away, but those of the wagon as well. Though summer monsoons were scarce, Govinda called upon the Idol's Eye, placing his hands on the gem as he made his wish. Considering the reckless escape the gem had helped engineer, Govinda felt confident the Idol's Eye could summon rain.

Satisfied that Kalki had outrun his foes, Govinda climbed down the hill and removed his tunic. Govinda lay on his back in the stream bed, the shallow creek flowed around him, partially submerging his head and chest. The cooling current revived his tired limbs.

Refreshed, Govinda reclined against a smooth rock at water's edge. Lost in a daydream, he felt something wet against his cheeks and opened his eyes to find Kalki licking him affectionately.

"Kalki, you and I were meant for adventure. I could never leave you for those barbarians."

Govinda had always had a unique way with animals, and they had an uncanny ability to understand him. He liked talking to animals more than to most people; their minds uncluttered by useless thoughts.

As Govinda lay on the rock, he found himself not only talking to Kalki but understanding the horse as well.

"What is it, Kalki?" asked Govinda, sitting up. "Did you say something, or do I imagine it?"

I want to tell you about the battle.

The thought did not come in words; it came all at once, like an

The Tale of the Himalayan Yogis

idea that had occurred to Govinda... but it had not occurred to him; it had been sent to him, like a letter to be read. The message was instant, but it took time to decipher since it was constructed from thought unstructured by language, necessitating a sort of mental translation, the process complicated by the slightly foreign quality of the idea; a horse did not think entirely like a human.

"Kalki, neigh if you're talking to me," said Govinda, wanting to be sure he didn't imagine things, though he didn't know how he could dream up anything like this. No sooner had he spoken than the horse nudged him on the shoulder, neighing softly.

I want to tell you about the battle. It has not left my thoughts since that day.

Govinda understood the message faster this time; he was becoming familiar with Kalki's mind and how to translate his thoughts into words.

"I'd like to know," he said aloud, not knowing how to reply in kind to Kalki, or if he even could. He wondered if Kalki had to perform a similar mental translation, converting Govinda's words into their raw meaning.

Our men mounted us at dawn and Master led us toward the camp by the river. The predators were waiting for us. Their pack spread across the horizon, but we were not afraid. Their horses circled behind us.

Master guided me into the thicket of raging men. They pointed pikes at Master, lifting them over me because they wanted to enslave me, but Master pushed the pikes aside with his lance. The predator-men went wild at the sight of blood. But Master was not afraid. He left his spear in a man's chest and used his sword to slay man after man, fighting two and three at a time. I maneuvered to protect him, but there were so many attackers. We were outnumbered ten to one. Master and the others fought and fought, but whenever a predator-man fell, two more appeared. I grew tired, and so did the other horses.

Then the son of the predator-men's leader rode up to Master. He spoke. It is harder for me to understand humans other than you, and he was the most difficult I have ever heard; he spoke differently than you and Master. Whatever he said, Master didn't like it, and he swung his sword sternly. It was no contest. Master knocked the young predator from his horse and leaped from my back. Master went for the kill. He knocked the young one down and raised his sword. A line of archers fired, hitting Master in the chest, and he fell to the ground.

I stood over Master's body, trying to protect him from the approaching men, but the predator-men's leader forced me away. The leader and his men surrounded Master's body. They laughed at the leader's son as he struggled to stand up. Then a second younger one ran up to help the one on the ground. The two young ones looked the same. Their father pulled the caring twin away by the neck, forcing him to look at Master's body. The boy looked away. He turned and retched. The leader shouted at the boys.

The second boy was not like the others. He did not belong in the battle. I moved nearer to him. I wanted him to climb on me so that I could take him away from the battlefield. With Master gone, I didn't want to be there. I could only look at the boy. The others were like demons in men's bodies.

Then the twins' father, the predator-men's leader, climbed on me. I was furious, but I knew that if I reared, the predator-men might kill me, so I let him have his way. He stayed out of the fight until our men were exhausted, and then he butchered a dozen wounded riders.

An injured man swung his battle-ax at the predator-men's leader, but the leader knocked the man off his mare. The leader climbed down and stood over the man. The leader put the tip of his sword to the man's throat, but let the man get up. As the man rose, the predator-leader thrust at his throat, but the man blocked with his battle-ax. The leader countered, but the wounded Rajput was faster than the leader. The leader pushed the man's battle-ax to the side, but not far enough. The blade bit through the leader's shoulder. The leader screamed, but the wound only angered him. The enraged leader made a clean cut through the man's neck. The leader picked up the head and swaggered over to his sons. The predator-leader tossed the head at the feet of his sons, cursing at them.

After the battle, when the predator-leader rode me into the fort, he forced me to gallop about the fort. Then he rode me into Krishna's abode.

Govinda remembered how Kalki had charged about the fort as a colt, shaking his head violently in an attempt to free himself from his trainer's rope.

"You've always been a spirited horse."

The Tale of the Himalayan Yogis

I wanted that monster off my back. When he hurt you, I reared and kicked with all my might. I wasn't coming down until the devil was off my back. Then he fell off, and I was free. He got what he deserved. That evil man killed Master!

"Kalki, you were magnificent!"

Your father was my hero. No one will ever ride me again, unless, of course, you wish to. I killed the predator-leader, but I feel no remorse.

Govinda whispered tenderly, "Kalki, I can see you are distressed, but you didn't kill the Emperor. He brought about his own destruction. That's always how it is. He swung at Krishna, but how can a mortal strike a blow against immortality? The Emperor was mad."

Master Govinda, I want to leave this place, but where shall I go? I will never go back to the fort.

"I have a task for you. In a few days, you must carry me to Bundi."

I am honored.

Govinda lay on a rock, amused by his uncanny escape from Krishnagarh. He was not at all worried about the Moguls finding him. With Kalki and the Idol's Eye, his defenses were as formidable as any army. Leading Kalki to a concealed place among the rocks, Govinda fell asleep under the starry sky, having forgotten about his wish for rain.

At dawn, as the first drops tickled his cheeks, he rubbed the Idol's Eye to thank Krishna for granting his wish. Soon the shower intensified. Tearing off his tunic, Govinda danced about the rocks like a mad hermit. If Hashim could see him, there would be no doubt in his friend's mind that he had lost his mind. As the torrent cascaded from his shoulders onto the rocks around him, the events of the previous days washed from his mind. Govinda felt purified; ready to face an uncertain future.

Govinda rode through the rain, elated that the monsoon was not receding. Weaving his way between the hills, he headed for Tiwari's cave. There was little chance that the Moguls would discover the grotto.

Leaving Kalki to graze by the stream where he had found Tiwari the previous morning, Govinda climbed to the cave and crawled inside. Tiwari was lying inside the entrance, his chest rising and falling weakly. Govinda softly jostled him.

"Tiwari, are you awake?"

"You try sleeping when you haven't eaten for three days," replied the Rajput.

"Did the others depart last night?"

Tiwari nodded. "And here I am, still waiting. I would have died with my son if I wasn't a coward."

"You're no coward. It is good that you waited; now I can take your son's ashes to the Ganges."

"You're a good boy, Govinda. You'll make a fine king."

"What good is a king without a kingdom?"

"Forts can be mended."

"More easily than hearts, I imagine."

"Walls can be repaired, but the heart is another matter. Did you escape with the stallion?" asked Tiwari.

Govinda nodded. "It was quite an adventure. Do you want to hear about it?"

"Every detail… it could be days before I die."

Nine days had passed since Govinda found Tiwari by the stream, and still, the old man hung on. Tiwari stopped venturing outside the cave, preferring to lie under his blanket. He ate nothing and drank sparingly. From time to time, the old man muttered incoherent tales of *pretas* that were said to roam the hills in search of deer and young jackals. Govinda ignored the delirious rambling, preferring to fill his mind with the serene influence of his mantra.

One morning, Tiwari crawled out of the cave for the first time in days. Govinda followed him down the hill to the stream. The old man stopped, wobbled a bit, and stared vacantly across the water.

"What is it?"

"He's calling me," Tiwari replied absently.

"Who's calling you?"

"Him," said Tiwari, pointing across the stream.

There was no one there.

"I don't see anyone," replied Govinda, assuming the old man was having another bout of delirium.

"He's too tall to come inside the cave, so he called me out. He's a severe one... never smiles. And his dogs... black as a moonless night."

"Dogs?" Suddenly it hit Govinda. "Yama's dogs?"

The Hindu faithful believed that Yama, the god of death, appeared with a pair of dogs when it was time to usher a soul to the other side.

"Friend, are you ready?" asked Govinda, steadying the old man.

"I need to cross the stream so that he can take me."

"Can I help?"

"He's coming."

Tiwari held out a hand as he waded across the stream. On the far side, he rested on a rock. A moment later, Tiwari's body toppled over, and the old man was gone.

Govinda piled the scraps of wood that he had collected next to the stream. Rather than entomb Tiwari's body in the cave, he decided that it would be safe to burn the body. Having observed johar and lit his father's pyre mere days earlier, the ritual was all too familiar. Although the smoke might alert the Moguls, Govinda was confident that their search parties had returned to Krishnagarh.

After the fire died away, Govinda scooped Tiwari's ashes into the pot containing his son's remains. It was time to ride to Bundi. Securing his peculiar freight, Govinda rode north, hidden from view by the Aravali Hills.

Reaching the shores of Kachola Lake, the waters shimmered in the moonlight. Govinda and Kalki drank the refreshing liquid. They traveled no further that night, sleeping on the sandy shore of the lake.

When morning came, Govinda didn't push Kalki, for he was not looking forward to the reception that awaited him at his grandfather's fortress. He knew his arrival would be cause for celebration, but Govinda didn't feel like celebrating. He assumed his coronation was about to take place.

The sentries spotted the lone rider and hastened to inform the king. Only one horse in all of Rajputana carried itself the way Kalki did. When the sentries reported seeing the king's grandson on the horizon, word of the prince's arrival spread to the residents of the fort.

The refugees from Krishnagarh gathered to greet their hero — the same throng that had assembled to watch Raja Chandra lead his men to battle — in addition to the people of Bundi.

Flag bearers hoisted Krishnagarh's colors atop the fortress walls, and officers stood at attention. Trumpets were poised to hail Govinda's arrival, and ceremonial swords shimmered in the sun. Children, dressed in festive attire, looked on expectantly. All eyes were fixed on the gates as Kalki carried Govinda into the courtyard. The Rajput prince was greeted by a welcome worthy of Ram's return to Ayodhya.

"Jai Raja Govinda! Hail Raja Govinda!" the crowd chanted. Drums pounded and horns blared. Kalki sauntered through the throng; his head held high. Govinda sat tall in the saddle as he scanned the crowd. Familiar faces smiled at him from every side as onlookers rushed forward to touch their hero's boots, but it wasn't until Govinda reached the far end of the courtyard that he spotted his family.

Little Kamala and Raja Yogesh stepped forward followed by Ananta and Ravi. Kalki stopped, and Govinda sat for a time, enjoying his moment of triumph. Once more, the crowd shouted, "Jai Raja Govinda! Jai Raja Govinda!" Govinda raised his hand to acknowledge the greeting, replying, "Jai Raja Chandra!"

The Coronation

Hashim was sitting with Ghazi when Junduk, a short, thick-necked, stoop-shouldered servant with unruly eyebrows, entered the Emperor's private audience hall to inform him that Commander Zaim was approaching the palace. Junduk had served the twins' father for two decades. Ghazi appeared edgy at the prospect of meeting Zaim and ran his hand apprehensively over Muti's back.

"Muti has not been the same since Father died."

"Nor have we," agreed Hashim. "We should proceed with the coronation without delay."

"Palace spies inform me that the mullahs favor Zaim. It seems the buzzards are circling, but I shall ensure that Zaim fails in his effort to seize the throne."

Hashim shook his head. "After Zaim's performance at Krishnagarh, I doubt even his generals will support him. We have the Rajput to thank for that."

"The Rajput's caper haunts Zaim. I have devised a plan that will undo the commander."

Zaim entered the hall and seated himself on a cushion.

"Commander, your image has been tarnished," began Ghazi. "You will need to restore it if you intend to lead the army."

"I am in control of my army," replied Zaim testily.

"Since Krishnagarh, the talk on the street has been of two things: the death of the Emperor and your humiliation at the hands of a boy.

Hindus everywhere have taken heart. Thanks to you, they have a hero to rally behind."

"Had I known the stallion was trained to rear at the boy's signal, he would not have tricked me."

"But you did not know, and he did trick you; moreover, he made a fool of you," said Ghazi coldly. Zaim's fist tightened at the word 'fool.'

"If indeed my reputation has been damaged, then allow me to repair it. I will capture the Rajput and put an end to the wave of optimism among his people."

"You have my support. This morning, an imperial spy returned with news that confirms what other palace emissaries report. From Jaisalmer to Chittor, villagers speak of nothing but Prince Govinda's triumph over the Emperor. We must crush the insurrection before it gets out of hand. Bring the Rajput to Delhi to stand trial for the Emperor's murder."

"It would be my pleasure."

"I am told Prince Govinda is staying at Bundi Fort, a place of little consequence. The boy's elderly grandfather rules Bundi, but he has virtually no army and his treasury is empty. There is no need to lay waste to the fort. Go and capture the boy. Do this, and you will restore the Empire's authority throughout Rajputana… and repair your image at the same time."

"I will depart for Bundi in the morning."

"There is another thing. Have you found the missing diadem?"

"The diadem has not been found."

"I expect you to find it, Commander. The soldier who discovered it claims he turned it over to you."

"He lies."

"Commander, your reputation has been damaged. I suggest you mend it."

Zaim's stiffened his jaw.

Ghazi is becoming more like his father with each passing day. He may prove to be more dangerous than I had expected.

"I will go now," said Zaim, standing. Ghazi said nothing; he merely stared at Zaim. Uncertain whether to go, or stay, Zaim hesitated before leaving the room. Hashim recognized the intent of his brother's gesture.

"If I judge Prince Govinda correctly, Zaim will not have an easy time capturing him," said Ghazi. "While Zaim's off chasing the Rajput, we shall proceed with the coronation."

"That's the prudent thing to do," agreed Hashim. "And if he does capture the Rajput?"

"Then Govinda will be executed."

Hashim winced at his brother's words.

"What about the diadem?"

"Zaim has it. While he's away, we'll search his apartments."

"Is it necessary to execute the Rajput?"

"Absolutely!" replied Ghazi.

"But he's just a boy."

"So am I, yet I am to be Emperor of Delhi. My spies tell me troops of puppeteers are traveling about Rajputana. Their dim-witted skits portray Govinda vanquishing the Emperor through the use of yogic powers."

"He does appear to be an exceptional boy."

"Nonsense! Father's injured shoulder caused the fall, and perhaps because the Rajput shouted a signal at which the horse reared. That was what happened to Zaim. If we don't quell this thing, soon you too will be believing in the Rajput's legend."

"I am on my way to visit Grandfather. Will you join me?"

"You go. I have much on my mind just now."

The weight of the Empire was about to fall on Ghazi's shoulders, and he had yet to reach his twentieth year.

"Do you have a message for Grandfather?"

"Invite him to the palace," replied Ghazi.

"But you know he won't come."

After Mumtaz Aalim's daughter died, the twins' grandfather took up residence in an obscure shrine to the south of Delhi, ignoring all requests for him to visit the palace.

Seasoned in the secret practices of Sufism, over the course of his scholarly life, Aalim concluded that the followers of religion were of three types: fundamentalists, mystics, and the submissive masses. He believed the majority of the people fell into the latter group, passively accepting their faith without delving deeply into it. The populous was harmless, but they missed the essence of spiritual life. The fanatics, on the other hand, disturbed him deeply.

Hashim found his grandfather leaning against the trunk of an aged mulberry tree that arched above the decaying shrine. Not far from the old man stood a mule and a rough-hewn cart. Hashim couldn't remember finding his grandfather anywhere but under the tree. It seemed that he was always meditating or composing ghazals in the shade of the tree, which Aalim referred to as his 'guide.'

"Hashim, you've brightened an old man's day. Your eyes are as gentle as your mother's."

"They have witnessed horrors since I saw you last, Grandfather."

"Innocence is short-lived in this age. Your mother was spared the heartbreak of an empire ruled by persecution."

"I think of her often," replied Hashim.

"What brings you to this dusty place?"

"I find no peace in the palace. Intrigue pollutes the very food we eat. Ghazi doesn't touch his dinner until a servant samples every dish. If the servant doesn't fall over dead, we have our meal."

"Power comes at a price. Intrigue is the nature of the palace just as the nature of the snake is to bite."

"But not all snakes are venomous," retorted Hashim.

"You are wise beyond your years. Your mother was that way."

"Maji's wisdom came from her father."

Aalim shook with laughter. "And his came from his father! Is that not the way life is? I've been studying an ancient treatise about the motion of the planets. Surya Siddhanta calculates thousands of years into the past and future in the endless cycle of our earth orbiting the solar deity. India's rishis saw far into the future."

"It seems our mullahs can't see beyond the fringe of their prayer rugs," groused Hashim. "They view Allah as separate from creation, exhorting his people to persecute those who refuse to bow to Mecca."

"Ignore the zealots. One can no more separate God from his creation than one can separate the berries from the limbs overhead.

The tree is in the berry and the berry in the tree. How could it be otherwise?"

"My mind is clouded, Grandfather. I am unable to follow your thoughts."

"Your mind has become ensnared by the world of the palace."

"I feel obligated to help Ghazi."

"You and Ghazi are seeds of the same tree. One seed fell beneath the tree; the other was swept away by the wind."

Hashim nodded. "Though we are twins, I feel we are different."

"Trust what you feel. Your heart is pure; the seeds of truth sprout there."

"Grandfather, I wish to follow your path… not Father's."

"You will know when it is time to leave the palace. Accept your brother's offer to become *vizier*."

"Me? Vizier? But I know nothing of politics. A prime minister should be someone with experience, like Uncle Lufti."

"Ghazi will soon be Emperor. He will need your help."

"I don't want to become consumed by hatred the way Father was after Maji died."

"What happened to your father will not happen to you."

"Why is that?"

"You have shed the skin of self-importance."

"What does self-importance have to do with it?"

"Ego is easily seduced by the opiate of authority. Ghazi will follow your father's path. Power will become his narcotic. You, on the other hand, have your mother's heart."

"How have I rid myself of ego?"

"When its fruits are ripe, the mango tree bends to the ground. Humility is the sign of a soul ripened by the love of God."

Mumtaz Aalim dispensed his wisdom sparingly. Those who asked received it. Unlike Hashim, Ghazi never asked. The old man loved his grandsons, but he knew the tyrannies of fate compelled Ghazi to follow his father while Hashim was destined to walk the path of the mystic.

"Ego has no place in a heart that communes with the divine. If there is one place where ego should not reside, it is religion. Religions are but branches of the same tree. The same soil nourishes all. Divinity is not the sole property of any religion."

"The Persian Khayyam wrote, 'Ego becomes extinct in the will of God.'"

"I would say ego becomes extinct in the love of God," replied Aalim.

"Maji taught me to love when I was small."

"We can nurture love, but cannot necessarily teach it. Otherwise, Ghazi would have learned it too. There is more love than air on this earth, but who breathes it in? Love is the divine on earth. It will not lead you astray. Pursue what you love."

"But at times I am afraid."

"If something frightens you, love it. If something hurts you, surround it with love. If something becomes a burden… probably not enough love. The heart will never lie to you. Pure, innocent love like that of a child. Whichever people you love most; they are your family."

"Grandfather, I want to visit Maji's shrine."

The old man climbed onto his wagon; Hashim sat beside him. Aalim tapped the mule's hip with a stick, and the two-wheel cart lurched in the direction of a slender edifice in the distance.

"Kutubh Minar frees my mind," explained the old mystic, pointing his stick at the pencil-shaped minaret on the horizon.

"Why is that?"

"I point the cart at the mosque, and the mule knows the way. It is the same with meditation. Point the mind in the direction of the divine, and it will find its way. A fakir taught me that when I was young."

"And what does the mind find when it reaches its destination?" asked Hashim.

"It gets lost."

"But if the mind gets lost, how will it arrive at the divine?"

"You misunderstand. The mind gets lost at the goal, not along the way. That is the secret the yogis shared with our mystics."

"Will you share that secret with me?"

"In time you will discover it for yourself, for that is the only way it can be known."

"I long to know the divine more than anything."

"Once the journey has begun, there is no turning back," cautioned Aalim.

"Why would one turn back?"

"The spiritual path is not so simple as pointing a mule at a minaret."

"But you said it was only a matter of starting in the right direction."

"The path involves more than following a mantra back to its source."

"Tell me, Grandfather. I wish to know."

"Spirituality is layered. Religion is like the rind of an orange; its doctrines are devoid of sweetness. The mystic enjoys the sweet juice. Having no use for the rind, he discards it by the road."

"It seems most chew the bitter skin," observed Hashim.

"That is true of every religion. Adolescent souls cling to dogma the way a man clings to driftwood on a stormy sea. He fails to see the ship that follows behind him or the captain who beckons him aboard."

"Why don't our mullahs teach about the sweet nectar?"

"Our mullahs are scholarly, as are the Brahmins. The Sufi seeks ecstasy, not scriptural learning. Where is the sweet juice in a book? The fakir longs for the intoxication of divine union. He has little use for words."

"Is this union you speak of what our poets call *wajad*?"

Mumtaz Aalim smiled.

"In the state of ecstasy, nectar flows from the heart, drowning the seeker in love. Neither our mullahs nor the Hindu clerics can teach this. Wajad is not for the submissive masses."

"During your meditations, I have seen tears streaming down your cheeks. I yearn for that."

"You shall have it as surely as the sons of Islam respond to the muezzin's call," said Aalim, pointing his stick at the crowd flocking to the mosque as his cart came to a halt, its path blocked by a throng of bearded supplicants.

"My Hindi acharya speaks of exalted states achieved by enlightened yogis. He says there are adepts in the Himalaya who live on the air they breathe and never age."

"Sages are nourished by a nectar called *Amrit*. Whether awake or asleep, some yogis live perpetually in God-intoxicated states."

"They're permanently in such a state?" asked Hashim.

Mumtaz Aalim nodded.

"Grandfather, have you achieved such a state?"

"I am content. That is enough. The calming of emotions at the command of the mind is vital if an exalted state is to be sustained."

The tide of worshippers passed, and the cart approached the shrine where the interred remains of Hashim's mother lay. Beyond the tomb, Kutubh Minar stretched skyward like a mullah's finger pointing to heaven. From the slender minaret's balcony, a muezzin summoned his minions. Not far from Kutubh Minar, Hindu women entered a temple bearing offerings of flowers and fruit.

Climbing down from his creaking cart, Mumtaz Aalim led his grandson into the grove of fig trees beside the marble shrine that Emperor Shah had built in memory of his favorite wife. Plucking a handful of fruits, Aalim said,

"I wish your mother were here to see what a fine son she bore, but death calls at its convenience. Your mother had but one wish."

"What was that?"

"She wished that you and Ghazi would not oppose one another. When your mother gave birth to two equal heirs, she worried that you and Ghazi would fight over the Peacock Throne. I advised her to observe your tendencies to see which of you had the disposition of a ruler."

"That would be Ghazi."

"True, but there will come a time when his impassioned spirit will no longer serve the Empire."

"Should I forego my studies to help Ghazi?" asked Hashim.

"Postpone your studies, but continue to grow in wisdom. Learn from your brother, and he will learn from you. Trust him, and he will trust you. Love him, and he will love you. Remain humble no matter how arrogant he becomes."

"Ghazi and I understand each other. There is space enough in this world for the two of us, having shared the womb. I will never hurt Ghazi, and he will not harm me. Of this I am certain."

The Tale of the Himalayan Yogis

"Council your brother not to persecute others the way your father did. It destroyed Junaid Shah. It could destroy Ghazi."

"He'll be crowned soon."

"Better not delay," cautioned Aalim. "The Empire seethes with discontent."

"Grandfather, have you heard of the Rajput, Govinda?"

"I hear very little, and what I hear is of little interest."

"No one in the palace knows this, but Prince Govinda and I are friends."

Mumtaz Aalim closed his eyes.

"Your heart and his are old friends."

"Strange as it may sound I think I've found my family."

"Ghazi is your twin, but Govinda is your spiritual brother."

"But he is Hindu, and I am Muslim."

"Words!" scoffed the old man. "Kabir wrote, 'I am at once the child of Allah and of Ram.' Remember this always. Tell me more about your Rajput friend."

"Govinda was with Father when he died."

"Say no more… I see it all in my mind's eye. The Rajput is one of us."

"Ghazi has ordered Commander Zaim to capture the Rajput. He plans to execute Govinda."

Aalim chuckled. "Do you believe Zaim will catch your friend?"

"No, but I worry. Govinda's just a boy."

"Save your concerns for Zaim. Chasing Govinda, he will bring about his destruction."

"Grandfather, how do you know these things?"

"Invisible beings inform me," he replied, smiling mischievously.

"Is it difficult to hear them?"

"Listen in your heart and you can know anything."

Hashim was silent, listening as his grandfather advised.

"The Sufi's journey begins where religion ends," explained Aalim. "Come, let us enjoy your mother's sweet presence."

His hands laden with figs, Hashim stepped out of his slippers onto the polished marble. The pink lotuses embedded in the pearl-white floor had been his mother's favorites, metaphors for the heart that she employed liberally in her poetry. Empress Kameela's shrine was Hashim's personal Mecca. The graceful pearl dome overhead and circle of marble pillars supporting it housed more than memories. A subtle presence permeated the crypt, wafting about like the scent of flowers in a garden. Hashim felt it whenever he entered his mother's shrine.

After the queen's death, Emperor Shah commissioned Turkish architects to create a monument for his favorite wife. Exquisite symmetry and graceful lines elevated the diminutive mausoleum. Slender minarets topped with onion domes stood at the four corners of the oval tomb. The simple elegance of the inner chamber mirrored the chaste nature of the queen. Hashim marveled at how men who had never known his mother had captured her spirit so perfectly. He did not know that the chief architect had spent many moons studying his mother's letters and poems.

Three verses were inscribed above the slender columns that encircled the vault. Kameela's favorite poet was Attar; a second verse was penned by Rumi. Both were engraved in gold, but Hashim's favorite poem was his mother's, and though he knew it by heart, he paused to read it before placing his offerings on the crypt.

> the sound
> of the sad bell
> tolling
> marks the distance
> between God and me

Hashim touched his forehead to the marble crypt and whispered, "Maji, I feel you in my heart always. I am a stranger among my people. Even Ghazi stands aloof, his passion for the throne consumes him. I have met someone who you would like. His name is Govinda. Like me, he is fatherless. I tell you these things because, aside from Grandfather, there is no one with whom I can share what is dearest to my heart. Now there is no distance between you and God. There has never been between your heart and mine."

Delhi's elite crowded into the imperial stadium to witness the spectacle. The newly crowned emperor's bull elephants were about to enter the arena.

The gate opened, and a mahout ushered a massive beast to the far side of the arena followed by a second bull escorted to the near side. A mud partition separated the behemoths. The titanic battles between Sri Lankan elephants were immensely popular among Delhi's patricians and military leaders. As the mahouts led their beasts onto the field, a chorus of conches sounded followed by the rumble of drums. One of the elephants answered the horns, trumpeting at the sky, his trunk snaking above his head like the spout of a teapot.

The lumbering hulks approached the mud divider, each sensing its adversary on the opposite side. The mahouts scampered off, wanting to be at a safe distance when the brutes squared off.

Tempers were slow to flare, but their fury sufficiently aroused, the bulls would crush anything in their path. The elephant on the far side of the wall lowered his head and smashed through the barrier as effortlessly as a child pushed open a door. As the wall collapsed, Hashim gasped. His childhood friend, Gum Gum, the mildest-tempered elephant in the Moti Mahal, had been selected to fight Airavat, the fiercest bull in the Emperor's stable.

There are thousands of elephants in the imperial stable. Why has Ghazi chosen Gum Gum? Surely he knows Gum Gum is my favorite.

As a boy, Hashim had ridden atop Gum Gum as the female elephants, and their calves marched single file to the Yamuna River for their morning bath. Watching the gentle giants spray one another was among his fondest memories.

Casting a questioning glance at his brother, Hashim was forced to stand to maintain his line of sight when the crowd rose to its feet as the beasts butted heads. The sparring began tentatively, but the contest rapidly intensified.

The collision of skulls shook the arena. The bulls trumpeted as they engaged one another. Known for their modesty, the mammoths were pitted like gladiators one against the other. Propelled by pride and obstinacy, they slammed into one another, mobile mountains tearing at each other's cheeks with lethal tusks. The bigger bull scored first, causing Gum Gum to falter momentarily before summoning his resolve for a counterattack. Charging at his adversary, Gum Gum drove his forehead into the bull's trunk. The stadium quaked as their heads collided.

As the battle escalated, Hashim's stomach knotted like threads on a loom. The suffocating sensation that had visited him during the battle with the Rajputs now wrenched his chest and gut as he watched the superior bull's dagger-like tusks gore his childhood friend. From a gash above Gum Gum's brow, a stream of blood obscured the ceremonial markings on his forehead.

The combatants were poorly matched; Gum Gum's opponent was far stronger and more experienced. Hashim wished his brother would call off the fight. If the face-off continued, he feared Gum Gum would be injured. The battle raged on. Gum Gum stood his ground, enduring a bludgeoning that brought feverish cheers from the crowd and sent saliva spraying about the field.

Wrapping his trunk around Gum Gum's tusk, Airavat yanked hard, causing his foe's head to twist violently to one side. Hashim had heard stories of elephants breaking another's neck, and his fists tightened. His head wrenched until his dilated eyes gazed skyward, Gum Gum struggled to stand. Unable to withstand the pain, Gum Gum rolled onto his side. Airavat hovered over his fallen foe. Raising his trunk to the sky, the king of elephants trumpeted triumphantly.

Seeing the defeated bull lying on his side, a pair of mahouts scrambled onto the field, iron goads in hand. Rushing toward the combatants, the attendants prodded Airavat away from his fallen victim. The bull's rage not yet sated, he pursued one of the mahouts while the other helped Gum Gum to his feet. Exhausted, Gum Gum struggled to stand, falling into the dust twice before righting himself.

The mahout led the defeated combatant off the field as the spectators showered cheers of appreciation on the courageous young bull. Meanwhile, the second mahout fled from the arena, barely

The Tale of the Himalayan Yogis

escaping Airavat's crushing feet. With Gum Gum safely corralled inside the elephant enclosure, Airavat returned to the center of the field. A spray of fireworks signaled the end of the battle.

From his gilded chair beneath the imperial pavilion, Emperor Ghazi Shah savored the titanic battle, sipping wine as he watched. He had worn the crown for less than forty-eight hours, and already he was shaping the future of the Empire. The elephant duel had been his idea, a symbol of his rule. Ghazi now commanded twenty-thousand elephants, all trained in the art of war.

The Emperor acknowledged his adoring minions with a wave of his royal hand. Among the crowd of ten thousand, only one appeared displeased: The Emperor's brother and closest ally.

Ghazi had glanced at his brother from time to time. Puzzled to see Hashim's head buried in his hands throughout much of the contest, the young Emperor knew that violence upset his brother, but the days of indulging Hashim's fragile emotions were over. With a vast empire to govern and new territories to conquer, Ghazi wanted everyone to know that he intended to rule with the authority of a stampeding elephant.

However wretched Hashim felt having witnessed the elephant fight, he was woefully unprepared for what followed. A gate swung open, and a pair of lungi-clad Hindus staggered onto the field. Bare-chested and barefoot, the beleaguered men stumbled about, their bodies tense and frail. The second man to pass through the gate was older and more fragile than the other man. Identifying the easy mark, Airavat charged, narrowly missing the man with his lance-like tusk. The feeble man struggled to his feet, trying his best to avoid the beast, but the man was quick to tire.

Sensing the kill, Airavat charged. The spent man staggered and the rampaging bull wrapped the man in his trunk, squeezing his torso like a boa constrictor. The hapless fellow flailed about crying for help, but the crowd responded with deafening roars of approval. The elephant shook his head violently, hurtling the doomed man high into the air. His body crumpled as it slammed against the ground. The dazed man lay on the dusty field, unable to get up. The enraged elephant trampled the helpless man the way wanton schoolboys crushed insects. Hashim buried his head in his lap as the crowd clamored for more.

An attendant hurried onto the field carrying a pedestal followed by a pair of guards who ushered a shackled man to the center of the arena. The condemned man dropped to his knees, resting his head on the pedestal while the mahouts maneuvered Airavat into position. Trumpeting twice, the bull raised his massive foot above the condemned man's head, pausing until one of the guards gave the signal. As the guard lowered his arm, the brute landed a crushing blow, shattering skull and pedestal.

One man remained. Having delivered death to the others, Airavat shifted his attention to the last of the three convicts. Examining his prey, the bull weighed his options. He could impale the man with one of his tusks, trample him underfoot, or attack with the iron blades attached to his feet.

Keeping his tactic a secret, Airavat charged. Seeing the rampaging bull rushing toward him, the man fell to his knees. A sharpened tusk gored him in the side. Raising his victim above his head, the blood-lusted elephant adorned himself with a morbid trophy. Agitated by the weight of his prize, the elephant shook his head until the impaled corpse was nearly split, and the tusk slid out of its side. As the body fell to the ground, the crowd sang like a chorus of demons.

As the final execution reached its horrific conclusion, Hashim turned to the officer at his side.

"What crimes have these men committed?"

"Two of the men were convicted murderers. The third was given a choice to pay the *jizya* or have his daughter sold into slavery. Rather than lose his daughter, the man bludgeoned an officer with a stone mallet."

Though the infidel's tax was commonplace, Hashim had no idea that the penalty for refusing it meant a child could be taken from her family.

"Is this a new law?"

The officer shook his head.

"Old law. The Emperor uses it as he sees fit."

Elephant executions were frequent in the imperial arena, but

The Tale of the Himalayan Yogis

Hashim had never attended one, and he had not expected such brutality at Ghazi's coronation festivities. Hashim wondered what possessed him to do it. Was his brother testing the limits of his power now that the crown rested on his head? It was Ghazi's hour of triumph and not the time to find fault with his brother. If not for his grandfather's council, he would have fled the stadium.

Delirious spectators clamored for more as soldiers dragged the broken and mangled bodies from the arena. The thunderous ovations pleased the Emperor as well as the generals at his side. Hashim tried in vain to mask his disillusionment.

After acknowledging the crowd with a wave of his imperial hand, Ghazi turned to his brother, who stood numb and expressionless, his chest heaving. Casting his brother a questioning look, Ghazi spared it little thought before turning to his generals.

Slipping out of the royal pavilion, Hashim headed for the *Hati Mahal*. Seeing Gum Gum surrounded by a throng of anxious mahouts, he feared the worst.

"How is he?" asked the prince, kneeling beside Gum's Gum battered forehead.

"He may lose a tusk, but his neck isn't badly injured," the doctor reported. "Had he resisted, Airavat would have broken his neck. He's suffering from exhaustion."

Hashim ran his hand across Gum Gum's forehead and then rubbed his ear the way he had done as a boy. Gum Gum gurgled, acknowledging his friend's gesture. Though sad, the bull's large honey-hued eyes were peaceful.

"Bring fifty buckets of water and sponges," Hashim instructed one of the mahouts. "I want to bathe him."

"Pour warm water over his trunk, but do not touch it," advised the physician.

Seeing Gum Gum's legs chained, Hashim frowned.

"Why the leg irons?"

"Sir, bull dangerous during *musth*," the mahout replied.

Hashim's jaw tensed as he ran his hands over the elephant's swollen temple glands, confirming that the adolescent bull had entered musth.

"Is that why he was chosen to fight?"

"Sir, the Emperor requested it," answered the head mahout.

Hashim pressed his head against Gum Gum's cheek and gently stroked his shoulder.

Late in the night, Hashim passed through the palace like a phantom. Inside his apartment, he stretched out on his bed, a satin sheet spread over him. With the specter of the executions still haunting him, Hashim sought refuge at his writing desk.

Hashim's quill hovered over the blank parchment resting on the buffed mahogany surface. He tried to write, but the pain prevented him, and so he turned to the weaver-poet from Varanasi. Settling onto a divan near his bedroom window, Hashim turned the pages of *The Bijak of Kabir*, reading long after his lamp had yielded to the morning light filtering through the open window. With a clear voice, Kabir challenged the inequities rife within the Empire. Heartened by the poet, Hashim was determined not to be a collaborator in his brother's cruel game.

Kabir's commentaries fomented thoughts of rebellion. Hashim desperately needed to see Grandfather. Forgoing breakfast, he made a detour through the palace, hoping to avert a chance encounter with his brother. His route took him past the harem where the eunuchs were preparing for the day. As he slipped past the entrance to the *zenana*, he heard his name.

"Hashiiiim," slurred the speaker.

Startled, Hashim spun around to find himself standing face to face with a disheveled image of himself. Judging from his glassy stare, Ghazi had smoked opium throughout the night.

"Have you spent the entire night in the harem?" asked Hashim cynically.

"An emperor does not sleep alone, at least not until he has produced sufficient heirs. Say the word, and I'll send a Persian beauty… or a pair of Nepalese dancers, if you prefer."

Hashim was in no mood to confront his brother, but somehow the words escaped his mouth.

"How could you?"

"It is the Emperor's duty to share himself with whomever he wishes," answered the sleepy-eyed ruler.

"I'm not talking about your women," bristled Hashim. "I'm speaking of the executions. You ordered a man killed for saving his child from slavery."

"It was necessary."

"Opium has spoiled your mind," replied Hashim, unable to calm his heaving chest.

"Not all the credit goes to the poppies. The palace wine is second to none."

Disgusted, Hashim turned to go, but Ghazi grabbed his twin by the shoulders and spun him around.

"Brother, what's troubling you? This is a time of celebration. I am Emperor of Delhi and tomorrow you will become Prime Minister."

"I want no part of petty tyranny."

"Hashim, what has come over you?" complained Ghazi.

"You talk like a madman. How can executing an innocent man save lives?"

"The Rajput has given hope to the people."

"And why shouldn't people have hope?"

Ignoring his brother, Ghazi continued: "There is talk of uprising all over Delhi. The elephant executions will not only put an end to the deluded talk but will assure the generals that their emperor is strong. I worry about you, Hashim. An emperor cannot tolerate a weak-willed vizier."

"That's just the point!" protested Hashim. "I *am* weak! You should find a suitable vizier."

"But you're the only person I trust," pleaded Ghazi, his bloodshot eyes shunning the light.

"I spent most of the night with Gum Gum."

"Gum Gum?"

"Have you forgotten your childhood since putting on the crown? Gum Gum was our friend. The physicians say he'll live, but he may lose a tusk."

"I didn't know they chose Gum Gum. I merely asked for a suitable adversary for Airavat."

"The mahouts said you requested a young male in musth."

"What does it matter?" replied Ghazi testily, his mental fog lifting as his patience waned.

"If you intend to rule as Father did, then I cannot help you."

"What was wrong with the way Father ruled?" challenged Ghazi. "Now that I wear the crown, I must think how the masses will be affected by my actions."

"That's what disturbs me. We've just executed a man for protecting his daughter."

"Two of the men were convicted murderers."

"And the third?"

"I told you. It was necessary," replied Ghazi, growing increasingly annoyed. "If you are to be vizier, I will need your unwavering support."

"I shall give you my answer tomorrow."

As Hashim turned to leave the palace, he spotted Itibar Khan, a towering, muscular eunuch, standing among the columns near the harem entrance. Hashim was sure that the eunuch had been listening. He had not planned on confronting his brother outside the zenana.

Alert ears lurked everywhere in the palace; the most trivial scrap of information would benefit the listener, for knowing the Emperor's thoughts gave great sway.

As Hashim crossed the courtyard leading to the drawbridge beyond the palace walls, a hooded figure shuffled past. Despite his distracted thoughts, Hashim took note of the man's attire, suspecting his robes to be those of a *tantric*. The figure's spidery fingers were all that Hashim could make out of the man, for he had not noticed him in time to have a look at his face.

"Who has the sorcerer come to see?" Hashim asked the guard at the front gate.

"Sir, he visits Begum Zahira."

"Then he has been to the palace before?"

"Sir, the man comes daily."

"I see," replied Hashim, looking back in time to see the figure disappear into the palace.

A stream of people entered the palace each day, but this particular visitor troubled Hashim. Why would Begum Zahira, the woman believed to have murdered his mother, invite a Hindu tantric to the Moti Mahal?

The image of the murky figure evaporated as Hashim headed for his uncle's home, a manicured estate overlooking the Yamuna River a short distance from the palace. Mumtaz Aalim had been staying with his eldest son since the coronation.

Attired in a hand-spun coat with cotton pants and pointed slippers, Lufti greeted his nephew. As Hashim entered the sprawling *haveli*, he decided that if executions were to be a part of his brother's rule then, he would move in with his uncle, who lived alone.

"*As-salamu-alaykum*," Hashim greeted his uncle.

"Peace unto you, Hashim. You are about your business early today. I don't recall you being an early riser."

"Uncle, did you attend the festivities?" implored Hashim.

"It was a grand procession; don't you think? Ghazi will make a fine emperor."

"Is Grandfather about?"

"*Baapu* is meditating in the garden. He appears quite lost to the world at the moment."

"Then we shouldn't disturb him," sighed Hashim. "I envy Grandfather."

"You envy an old man whose lamp grows dim when a full life lies ahead of you?"

"Grandfather has attained peace."

Hashim's uncle nodded. "Few find peace before the light extinguishes. Peace found Baapu as a young man."

"That is why I envy him."

"Hashim, what's bothering you?" asked Lufti Aalim. "I can see that you haven't slept."

"Did you attend the elephant executions?" asked Hashim tentatively, eyeing the sandalwood statue of the elephant god Ganesh inside his uncle's palatial home. Seated on a cushion of skulls, the soles of the Hindu god's feet pressed together like those of an infant. It was bold of his uncle to display the icon so prominently, a declaration that would draw the ire of Delhi's elite.

"The executions sadden you," said Lufti apologetically, his eyelids closing unhurriedly as he reviewed the events of the previous day.

"My mind is in turmoil."

"It need not be," replied Lufti, his brows arching over compassionate eyes.

"Were you not appalled?"

"It showed poor taste, but you must have noticed the crowd's reaction; they clamored for more."

"I noticed," said Hashim surveying the mansion where he had spent much of his childhood. Uncle Lufti ornamented his home with treasures from distant lands and diverse cultures. A glimmering Thai Buddha sat in meditative repose in an alabaster alcove. Exquisite Persian rugs formed a mosaic of rectangles leading guests from room to room. Glazed pottery from the Tang Dynasty and lacquered Burmese *Hsun Ok* rested on buffed tables. Tibetan scroll paintings graced marbled walls. Furnishings of burnished teak, mahogany, and sandalwood housed religious artifacts wherever the eye fell. An ivory statue of Ram and his consort Sita stood prominently in Lufti's library, which contained rare manuscripts from Europe and Central Asia.

"We Moguls are easily bored. If not for our women and war, we would find no reason to live."

"No one has the right to crush a man like an insect!" protested Hashim. "The screams of anguish cut like daggers."

"Hashim, you have your mother's sensitivity. When Kameela was small, she rescued every creature in distress. I remember one night when the family had gathered in the courtyard to listen to a learned pundit. When a moth ventured too close to a lamp, my poor sister fled to her room in tears."

"Imagine if Maji had witnessed the elephant executions."

"She would have run onto the field to stop the violence. *Kali Yuga* was far too brutal for your dear mother."

"Why did Grandfather allow the Emperor to marry Maji?"

"A nobleman cannot deny the imperial family their wish. Once Emperor Shah decided that he would marry Kameela, Father had little say in the matter."

"Like Maji, I too am unfit for palace life."

The Tale of the Himalayan Yogis

"The similarity does not escape me," acknowledged Lufti.

"Ghazi plans to have me sworn in as vizier, but how can I offer counsel if he insists on senseless violence? Uncle, you would make a fine prime minister. You have the experience Ghazi, and I lack. Everyone respects you."

Lufti's mind was a finely crafted vessel molded by the Sufi masters of Persia and polished at the feet of his father.

"Hashim, you and Ghazi are young. You have both overreacted; Ghazi in trying to impress his generals and you in your haste to abandon your brother when he needs you most. Ghazi is not as ruthless as he would have everyone believe. Your brother may be insecure, but he is no fiend. If even a few drops of your mother's blood run through him, he cannot be a total stranger to kindness."

Hashim looked around, taking in the magnificence of his uncle's home.

"You are wondering why I live alone. It has been on your mind since you arrived."

"I was wondering why you never married."

"I married not long after you were born. Baapu chose a shy Brahmin girl."

"But Brahmins rarely marry outside their caste. Surely a Hindu family would never consent to their daughter marrying a Muslim."

"Not all are caste-bound."

"No one has ever spoken of your wife," said Hashim apologetically.

Lufti inhaled slowly as if breathing in the fragrance of a flower.

"She was as delicate as the jasmine in her plait of ebony hair. Her chestnut eyes were unremarkable, but when she knelt at her altar, she was as radiant and pure as Laxmi."

"What happened?"

"Our son, Omar, was four." A shadow crossed Lufti's face as he recalled the tragic night. "It was a tradition for our family to take a boat ride on the Yamuna to watch the fireworks marking the end of *Ramadan*. Having fasted excessively, I was too weak to leave the house, and so the family left me behind. Everyone was watching the fireworks when little Omar got too close to the water and fell into the current. Although she couldn't swim, his mother leaped into the water after him. In an instant, they were gone."

"I'm sorry."

"Come, I want to show you something."

Lufti guided his nephew through the library into his bedroom. Removing his slippers, he pulled the curtains open, exposing a waist-high altar lit by a pair of brass lamps. On the altar stood a dozen icons carved from jade, marble, sandalwood, and ebony.

"Shall we make offerings?" suggested Lufti.

Hashim scrutinized the benevolent faces as his uncle offered camphor and rosewater. Both men kneeled on the rug at altar's edge.

"Since my wife's passing, I have opened my heart to the divine mother, and she has taken me in."

"I recognize Kali and the Christian Madonna, but who are the others?"

"The Egyptian goddess Isis," said Lufti, pointing to an alabaster statue of a young woman with an owl perched on her wrist.

"Isis is the power of magic." Lufti picked up a carnelian amulet and placed it in Hashim's hand. "This amulet, and the incantation that belongs to it are said to give the power to travel to the realms the Egyptians call the Underworld."

Hashim pointed to the jade statue of an Oriental goddess. "Who is that?"

"Kwan Yin, the Chinese mother of compassion and protector of animals."

"But Islam opposes idol worship."

"Your grandfather and I kept the idols from you so as not to confuse you, but you are old enough to understand now."

"There are many things I don't understand," admitted Hashim. "Why do other religions honor the goddess, but not ours?"

"I can't say. We hide our women in veils, believing that a bed of virgins awaits us in heaven."

"You don't believe in that heaven?"

"The Sufi masters teach tolerance and love. Though I am a Muslim, would any mullah agree?"

Hashim's grandfather appeared at the threshold of the

camphor-scented shrine. The tiny old man pressed his forehead against the altar and then signaled for his son and grandson to come out.

"I have been expecting you," Aalim whispered. "Do not be disturbed by recent events. They are part of the dream you have agreed to witness."

"But I despise this dream," said Hashim, looking into Mumtaz Aalim's calm, mahogany eyes.

"In a nightmare, a man is paralyzed with fear when the tiger strikes. But when he awakens in the morning, he finds the tiger has not eaten him."

"That may be true of a dream, but the broken bodies were real. They haunt my dreams and my waking."

"Still, it was a dream of sorts, was it not?" asked Aalim.

"For those more enlightened than me… for the victims, it must have been hell."

"Do not underestimate our Hindu brothers. In matters of the soul, we have much to learn from them."

"But it was their bodies that were crushed."

"Hashim, I love you for your compassion, but there are powers greater than an emperor's laws."

"And what of the sons and daughters of the executed men? Are they to understand that their father's death was part of a greater plan? Will that greater plan feed and clothe them?"

Mumtaz Aalim studied his grandson. "The loss of your dear mother remains with you."

"Since Maji died, I have lived with fear."

"In fear of what?" asked Lufti.

"Father… his generals… Islamic Law. Now that Ghazi is emperor, he too frightens me."

"It is time we removed the fear from your heart," determined Aalim.

"I am not afraid of death, but I fear a world where men cheer the death of their brothers." Hashim paused. "Grandfather, I have come for advice."

"About Ghazi?"

"He's become a tyrant."

"Limbs of a tree share the same roots. Serve your brother. That's all I will say. Go and place a rose on Nizam's crypt."

Hashim dodged left and right, threading his way through the throng of pilgrims as he navigated the maze of narrow paths leading to the famed Sufi shrine. Eyeing the nobleman, vendors vied for Hashim's attention, but he ignored the offerings of sweets and chai. Stopping to purchase a flower, Hashim placed a white rose on the crypt before seeking the shade of a nearby tree.

Hazrat Nizam was raised in the capital city two centuries earlier, a saint steeped in love and wisdom. Those who approached the gentle Sufi's crypt inhaled a sweet fragrance said to emanate from the saint's mortal remains.

Hashim was sitting against the tree, trying to make sense of his grandfather's words, when a man with chestnut skin approached. The man's white beard and wrinkled face gave him an aged look, but his calm eyes shone with childlike brilliance. A hemp rope gathered the man's grey robes at the waist. Atop his head sat a peculiar green turban, a yellow sapphire pinned at its front. The turban, Hashim guessed, was of Afghan origin. Hashim pulled a coin from his pocket, but the man waved it away.

Standing before him, the man gazed lovingly at Hashim. Holding a white rose, the fakir touched its petals to the crown of Hashim's head. The unexpected blessing sent a surge of energy coursing through Hashim's body, plunging him into a rapturous state. Hashim's eyes turned to the sky, and his mind receded into his throbbing heart.

How long he remained in the ecstatic state, Hashim had no idea, but a distant voice extracted him from his blissful trance.

"Where have I been?"

"Not necessary to understand," said the fakir.

Hashim noticed that the sun had risen higher in the sky.

"How long have I been here?"

"What does time matter in eternity? Things are happening."

"What things?" asked Hashim.

"Mumtaz Aalim's words... your brother's errant deeds... Govinda's friendship."

"You know about Govinda?"

"Everything is here," explained the old man, placing a finger on Hashim's chest. "past... future... If you look, you too will see."

The man's words floated up through the overhanging limbs, mingling with the pungent scent of frankincense wafting about the shrine.

"Who are you?" asked Hashim.

"Chishti Order," replied the man almost inaudibly.

"Chishti? You mean Sufi mystics?" Hashim was unsure if he had heard correctly.

"Can you recall your vision?"

Hashim vaguely recalled a pillared chamber with fakirs seated in a circle around a whirling dancer.

"Can you see the dervish? Can you feel the energy?" asked the old fakir.

"I was... am... seated in a hall with others like me. At the center, a man is spinning faster than any dancer I've ever seen."

"*Sama* ritual!" whispered the fakir.

"I don't understand."

"Your heart needed healing," explained the fakir.

Miraculously, the fear in Hashim's heart had vanished.

The aged saint gestured toward the mound of flowers atop the crypt before standing up. Hashim bent forward and pressed his forehead against the holy man's feet. Raising his head from the ground, he opened his eyes, but the saint had vanished. Hashim searched the crowd, wondering who the man was. On the spot where the fakir had been standing, a white rose lay on the grey stone in front of him. Its fragrance filled him with hope.

Varanasi, City of Light

Leela sat in the canopied howdah opposite her mother, the Maharani of Jodhpur. Leela's dance teacher, Narayani, sat beside the queen. Escorted by a hundred turbaned cavalrymen, the royal carriage swayed rhythmically toward Osiyan on a sandy, sparsely traveled road linking Jodhpur to the ancient trade center at the heart of the Great Indian Desert. The months leading up to the journey sorely tested Leela's patience.

"I couldn't have waited another day," sighed the young princess.

Since spring, Leela had been preparing for the autumnal festival renowned for its moonlit evenings of music and dance. Other years, Leela had attended the festival in Jodhpur only, but this year she was on her way to Osiyan for the premier dance competition in all of Rajputana.

"Leela dear, you danced beautifully at the palace recital," gushed Narayani, herself an accomplished dancer.

"I felt like I was flying."

"You weren't nervous at all," observed Leela's mother, who had long since grown weary of the swaying conveyance and featureless landscape.

"Why would I be nervous doing what I love most?" replied the queen's precocious daughter.

"You're not tired are you?" asked Narayani. "It was a late night."

"Tired?" frowned Leela. "I'd dance day and night if Maa would allow it."

A wry smile formed on her mother's face. Leela had boundless energy and as much talent. When the young princess wasn't whirling about the palace, she was spending hours mastering the intricate *mudras* peculiar to her South Indian form of dance. From the time when she could walk, the queen's apartments had been Leela's private stage.

"Tomorrow, you'll be dancing in a courtyard under the stars," noted Narayani. "We should rehearse the moment we arrive so that you are familiar with the floor and surroundings."

Leela wondered how grownups conjured up such silly notions. She couldn't imagine why a dancer would require familiarity with her surroundings any more than a bird needed to get familiar with the sky.

"What difference could a floor possibly make?" she protested. "My feet barely touch the ground when I dance."

"All the same, the best dancers prepare before they perform. You'll need to rehearse with your mask on," Narayani reminded her prize pupil.

"I've never worn a disguise."

"It's important," the queen insisted. "Princesses don't normally dance in public."

"It's silly that a girl can't dance in public just because she's the daughter of a king."

Leela had pleaded with her parents for almost a moon before they agreed to let her enter the competition. Although her mother remained opposed to the idea, the queen had consented after her husband came up with the idea of the disguise. Leela would dance the part of the cowherd Krishna. The young princess loved the idea. Even her mother admitted that it was an ingenious plan.

Leela's feet skipped about the floor of the carriage, her heels and toes tapping alternately against the teakwood surface.

The endless expanse of rippled dunes had long since lost its charm. Even the camel caravan in the distance failed to interest the young princess. Preoccupied with her dance routine, Leela formed intricate mudras to match her nimble footwork.

"I wish Pitaji and Satyam were here," she sighed, peering impatiently across the desert in search of Osiyan.

"Satyam is busy with his tutors, and Pitaji has much work to do," the queen reminded her.

"I like dancing for Pitaji best of all."

No matter how busy, Leela's father paused whenever his daughter whirled past. Had it not been for the royal family's upcoming trip to Varanasi, the entire family would have attended the Marwar Festival.

"City of Light… the oldest city in the world," proclaimed Ananta, pointing to the fabled city by the Ganges.

On the far shore, Maharajas' palaces, beehive temples, and ochre ashrams lined the bluff overlooking the cobalt waters swirling past Govinda's feet. Golden shafts of light filtered between the weathered buildings, spreading an aura of piety over the ancient city.

"The river is broad and smooth," observed Govinda, inhaling the sight. On the far shore, at river's edge, silver plumes rose from a dozen fires.

"Varanasi's ghats," noted Ananta. "The fires never go out."

"Let's bathe in the river," decided Govinda.

Dropping Kalki's reigns, he was about to plunge into the river when Ananta placed a firm hand on his shoulder.

"Patience, my friend. Those who bathe on this side of the river are said to be reborn as donkeys."

"I won't have you reborn as a donkey on my account," laughed Govinda.

It felt good to laugh again.

"Did you see them?" asked Ananta, having glimpsed the glistening, grey forms in the current.

"See what?"

"River dolphins."

"What's a dolphin?" asked Govinda, scanning the surface of the river. Kalki also looked, but neither had seen the creature, whatever it was.

"Govinda, you still have much to learn."

"I want to see new things before they put that crown on my head. I'm not ready to sit on a throne all day."

"You're not expected to take the throne yet. Let us enjoy Shiva's city. Come, the ferry collects pilgrims downstream."

Ananta led his charge onto a ferry; Kalki followed reluctantly.

"There must be hundreds of temples," exclaimed Govinda, scanning the far shore.

"On the other side, you'll feel a presence you've never felt before. Some say Shiva himself wanders among the ghats disguised as a mendicant."

The ferry drifted with the current. Govinda stood beside Kalki, captivated by the breadth of the Ganges.

"Kalki, have you ever been on a boat?"

Never.

"Neither have I."

It makes me nervous.

Ananta smiled as he listened to Govinda's side of the conversation. Not so long ago, Govinda did not even believe that a man could talk to animals; now he did so casually and freely.

A sleek, shining, dove-grey creature surfaced for a moment before sliding noiselessly under the water.

"Did you see it?"

Govinda nodded.

"It was as long as Kalki."

Eyeing the water, Kalki shifted uneasily.

"The dolphins migrate from the Bay of Bengal," explained Ananta. "Now the fires are visible. We'll meditate by the burning ghats at sunrise."

"Here in the middle is the best place to spread the ashes," said Ananta. "Release Tiwari's and his son's ashes here."

Govinda removed the urn, which was attached to Kalki's saddle. Reaching over the side of the boat, he poured the ashes into the current while Ananta chanted verses from *Rig Veda*. The current carried the ash away, accepting it the way it had received mortal remains for millennia.

"Why is it auspicious to put the remains into the Ganges?" wondered Govinda.

"The scriptures say the waters purify the subtle bodies so that the soul can move on to higher realms."

"Does the soul stay in a higher realm for a long time?"

"Some souls enjoy celestial *lokas* for a long time… others return quickly."

"If it were up to you, would you return quickly?" asked Govinda.

"I can't say. The celestial realms are said to be enchanting. One might like to stay for a while, but it may not be up to us."

"It seems unnatural to live inside fortress walls rather than by a river or in a forest, but Kali Yuga has so much hatred and conflict that it isn't safe."

"The sages say Kali Yuga is the easiest time to achieve *moksha*."

"But how can that be? Everywhere our people are downtrodden. It's the same for Buddhists. Pitaji and the soldiers died so suddenly."

"The length of life matters little. One can dissolve mountains of karma in a single act," explained Ananta, his eyes focused on the burning ghats.

"Since the siege, I've been buried under a mountain."

"You've been tested."

"But have I passed the tests?" pondered Govinda.

"Karma provides what we need to learn. Again and again, you risked your life for others."

"You would have done the same."

Ananta smiled. "Humility is a sure sign that the journey is nearing its end."

"Should I become an arrogant king, promise that you'll humble me."

"I doubt there will be a need. The throne didn't corrupt your forefathers. Your father was the most modest man in Krishnagarh."

Govinda's mind flashed on his father seated on the throne surrounded by portraits of his ancestors.

"Will the heartache pass?"

The Tale of the Himalayan Yogis

Ananta hesitated. "I placed my father's ashes in the Ganges eleven years ago, but a day doesn't pass when I don't think of him."

"I'm sure I'll think of Father every day for the rest of my life."

The ferry reached the shore. Govinda led Kalki onto the riverbank where steps larger than those leading to Davan's turret connected the river with the temples on the bluff.

"Now we can bathe," advised Ananta.

Govinda slipped out of his tunic and jodhpurs, leaving his clothes on the steps. Wading into the shallow current, Ananta followed close behind. After submerging three times, Ananta retreated, but Govinda lay in the refreshing waters the way he had done at Kachola Lake. His skin glistening as he emerged from the river, Govinda dressed in the warming sun.

"Have you visited Varanasi many times?" asked Govinda.

"I studied here. My uncle is the chief priest at the Shiva temple. Everyone knows Pundit V. K. Mishra."

"If bathing on the other side of the Ganges causes one to be reborn as a donkey, what happens to those who bathe on this side?"

"Our sins are absolved."

"Really?" asked Govinda incredulously.

"According to our scriptures, lifetimes of sin are purified."

Govinda relaxed. "I feel lighter already. My soul needed a good cleaning."

"The Ganges is the best place for scrubbing the soul," smiled Ananta. "Let's find my uncle. He'll be performing *aarti* in the temple, but first, we'll visit Ganesha."

A gathering of pilgrims watched Pundit V. K. Mishra pour water over the rounded Shiva stone and smear ash on its side, forming three horizontal lines symbolizing the holy trinity. Pilgrims placed marigolds and *bilva* leaves on the sacred stone as Ganges water dripped onto the granite lingam from a copper pot hanging from the temple ceiling.

Pundit V. K. Mishra's exposed belly was as round as a harvest moon. His greying beard needed either more time to grow or a visit to one of the barbers that lined the footpaths leading to the river. Pundit Mishra smiled amiably; his winsome eyes twinkled without reason.

Mishraji, as locals referred to the jovial priest, was a central figure in India's oldest religious community.

"*Namaskar, Kakaji,*" beamed Ananta, his hands pressed together.

"*Om Namah Shivaya,*" boomed the affable pundit above the din of street vendors outside the temple. "*Ap Kaisa Hai,* Anantaji?"

"Very well, Uncle… and you?" asked Ananta.

"By Shiva's grace, I am well," replied Mishraji, wagging his head as if his neck were rubber.

"Uncle, this is Raj Kumar Govinda of Krishnagarh. You must remember Raja Chandra."

"*Namaskar.* Govinda, your father is a fine man. How is Rajaji?"

"Uncle, we have come with Raja Chandra's ashes," Ananta explained. "The Moguls sacked Krishnagarh. Our brothers made the great sacrifice."

Mishraji's eyes saddened. "Rajputs are bravest among Hindus! There is talk in the market that the Emperor was slain inside a Krishna temple. Is it true?"

"It is true, but allow me to tell the story later," said Ananta. "We'll be staying in Varanasi for a few days."

"Then you shall be my guests tonight. Tomorrow, I will secure proper accommodations. The Raja of Jodhpur has the finest palace in Varanasi. Govinda will be his honored guest."

"That would be more than we could ask."

"But no more than you will receive," replied Mishraji, his eyes twinkling again. "Ananta, when were you last in Varanasi?"

"I accompanied Raja Chandra five years back."

"In that short span, seven temples have been razed to the ground and mosques built in their places. More and more, we worship underground. The Raja of Jodhpur is helping to rebuild our temples, but imperial forces come here often since we are near to Delhi."

"We've seen the imperial army in action."

Govinda awakened to a commotion in the alley outside the room.

"Mishraji wants you to see an astrologer," said Ananta, noticing that Govinda was awake.

The Tale of the Himalayan Yogis

Sleepy-eyed, Govinda sat up.

"Why is that?"

"Shastri is the most renowned astrologer in all of Varanasi. Let us see if he can shed light on your future."

"Didn't you say once that you wouldn't tell me the prophecy of the Idol's Eye because it was better that I discovered it on my own?" Govinda reminded Ananta. "Should I not discover my future on my own as well?"

"I feel you should see him."

After bathing in the Ganges, Govinda, Ananta, and Mishra stepped around a bull feeding on discarded *chapatis* and entered a small courtyard framed by whitewashed bungalows. A maidservant drew milk from a cow at the far corner of the yard. At the opposite end, a girl lowered a brass bucket into a well. At the center of the courtyard stood a single *tulsi* bush.

Stepping over a brightly colored *rangoli* outside the astrologer's bungalow, Mishra knocked on the door. An elderly woman appeared, held her index finger to her lips, and retreated without uttering a word. Moments later, a man of similar age and stature appeared. The astrologer wore a white dhoti bordered in pale green; his fraying sacred thread ran diagonally from shoulder to hip. A small white hat was poised to topple off at the slightest tilting of the old man's head.

"Namaste Shastriji," said Mishra, bending to touch the astrologer's feet. "I have come with a prince in need of counsel."

The frail man held his hand to his ear and Mishra bellowed the introduction again so that the old astrologer could know the purpose of the visit.

"This is Raj Kumar Govinda," shouted Mishra.

"But the stars indicate a king is to appear at my door today." The astrologer's playful, high-pitched voice was disarming.

"The stars are correct," confirmed Ananta. "Though he is not yet wearing the crown, Govinda will soon be Raja of Krishnagarh."

"Come in," said the astrologer, bowing stiffly. The kindly old man's smile exposed a gold-capped tooth.

"Govinda seeks your advice on important matters," said Mishra.

Placing his ring finger in a bowl of sandal paste, the astrologer put a dot on Govinda's forehead.

"A forehead without the auspicious sign is like a graveyard, my son," said the astrologer, gesturing for his guests to sit on the mats his wife had spread on the floor. "Accept my apologies. My wife is observing silence on her day of fast." With his wife's outstretched hand supporting him, Shastri seated himself on a jute string cot.

"Age?" squeaked the astrologer, who was surrounded by stacks of worn scriptures.

"Fifteen," answered Govinda.

"Place of birth?"

"Rajputana."

As Shastri rattled off a string of questions, he examined Govinda's right hand. Poking his palm, Shastri scrutinized the fingertips and obscure lines that formed a map of his client's life. At one point, the old astrologer pressed Govinda's little finger back until it hurt.

"This is not the first time I have examined this soul," determined Shastri, who had read over twenty-thousand horoscopes.

"Govinda's parents brought him as an infant," replied Ananta.

"I shall read the stars from the palm. From this mound Venus' disposition is known," explained Shastri, pressing the fleshy pad at the base of Govinda's thumb.

"It is not by chance that you have come, for you stand at a crossroads. Just as Varanasi is the junction between this life and that which lies beyond, so is your life in the balance. You are entering a time of adversity called *Kala Chandra,* the Black Moon. The coming years will bring misfortune to your family, even death. During this time, you will live in exile... a king without a kingdom."

"How long will the exile last?" asked Ananta.

"Seven years. Though you will live within the womb of the earth, your soul will shine. During your exile, you will be blessed by a guru. His knowledge, along with your *tapasya,* will awaken you. You know the word 'tapasya'? It means austerity. Our yogis are indifferent to heat and cold and hunger. Like that you will live. But despite hardship, you will be happy."

The Tale of the Himalayan Yogis

"I've heard about sages meditating on mountaintops," acknowledged Govinda.

Shastri continued: "Death has recently visited your family."

"Pitaji died fighting the Moguls."

"You know the story of Krishna's mother?"

"Yashoda?"

"I speak of Krishna's real mother, Devaki, who languished in prison for years."

"King Kansa locked Devaki in a cell," added Govinda, unhappy to hear his mother compared to Devaki.

"Your mother will face trials equal to Devaki, but do not attempt to help her. It would mean certain death for you. She will suffer the grief of separation, but she has strength. Kala Chandra is the dark time. The influence of Saturn is strong these coming seven years. When Saturn transits the natal moon, life turns upside down. Unless you live in seclusion, you will be beset with hardship."

"It sounds terrible," complained Mishra.

"The planets deliver the warranted karma."

"But Govinda is just a boy," replied Mishra.

"Seven years does not make the life. Govinda has an extraordinary Raj Yoga. See this mound." Shastri poked again at the base of Govinda's thumb. "When Black Moon ends, every blessing comes by the grace of Krishna himself. Rare indeed will be your rise."

"But only after seven years," repeated Ananta.

The astrologer nodded.

"Govinda, you know the *Ramayana*. Your Sita will be devoted to you the way Sita was devoted to Ram. And you will be devoted to wife and guru the way Ram was devoted to his Sita and Sage Vasishtha."

"But I don't have a guru."

"Your spiritual father waits for you, but you will not recognize him until he chooses to reveal himself."

"How is it possible that I will not recognize him?"

"You need do nothing. Only follow my instruction. The words I speak are your guru's own words. Is it clear?"

"I understand."

"Your guru will be greater than you may know. He will remain a mystery to you, for he cloaks in detachment. Once in guru's care, you are safe."

"Thank you, Shastri," said Ananta. "This has been helpful."

"One last thing," said the old astrologer raising his index finger for emphasis. "In ten days' time, there will be a lunar eclipse. Before the eclipse, bathe in Ganga, then remain in the temple until dawn. During eclipse, the danger is extreme! Death will follow you as your own shadow. You may even die."

"What can we do?" implored Ananta.

"Mishraji will organize *Mrityunjaya*."

Govinda was about to speak but changed his mind.

"You have questions?" Shastri inquired.

"Mrityunjaya means 'averting death.'"

"Precisely. Mishraji will instruct pundits to begin tomorrow. Twenty-one priests will chant ten *lak* mantras.

"A million repetitions?" shuddered Ananta.

"Do not confront your enemy," cautioned the astrologer. "That is all I will say on the matter."

"But I confronted the Moguls at Krishnagarh, and it worked to my advantage."

"Now it will be different. Others will help you. Do you understand?"

"Yes," replied Govinda.

"Shastriji, this is most discouraging," said Ananta, who looked as if his son was about to die.

"It is fortunate that you have brought Govinda. His kingdom awaits him, but first, he must claim his spiritual treasure. Already his fame is spreading.

"Surely Govinda will succeed," said Mishra.

"Free will is fickle. The mountain Govinda must climb is not without peril. Just see how many yogis have fallen when the summit was within their grasp."

"Govinda will not fall," insisted Ananta. "His mind is like the steel of his sword, his heart pure as the gold on Krishna's crown."

"I know very well Govinda's strength," said Shastri. "Jupiter sits in exaltation with the moon. The guru's grace is unsurpassed in this horoscope. Mishraji will take you to the Kala Bhairav shrine. Make offerings to the planets, then put this on middle finger, right hand." Shastri placed an iron ring in Govinda's hand. "It will win Lord Saturn's favor."

The reading was complete. Mishra helped Shastri to his feet. Govinda pressed his palms together as he backed out the door. Lost in thought, the Rajputs made their way to the river. Of all the predictions, the prospect of his mother's hardship weighed heaviest on Govinda's heart and the fact that there was nothing he could do to help her.

Mishra escorted his guests to Jodhpur Palace.

"Greetings friends. Welcome to our home," said Raja Rao.

"Namaste Rajaji," replied Mishraji. "Thank you for extending such kindness."

"The tragedy at Krishnagarh deeply saddens me," said Raja Rao. "I knew your father well, Govinda. Raja Chandra was a courageous man and a dear friend! Even your clan's adversaries respected him for his integrity."

"Thank you for your kind words," replied Govinda. "Ananta and I have come with Pitaji's ashes."

"We heard the news of the siege and doubled our fortifications. But what can anyone do against the imperial army? Sadly, our Rajput clans refuse to unite against our common enemy. We are no match for the Moguls."

"They are not so fearsome as they would have us believe," Govinda replied coolly.

"We have heard stories of your heroics."

"*Chai wallas* tell a good tale," mused Govinda. "It sells a second cup of tea."

"The rumors are true," Ananta confirmed.

"Govinda, you and Ananta must be our guests," offered Raja Rao.

Trim but sturdy, Raja Rao moved across the room with the prowess of a tiger. Govinda imagined that the raja would make a formidable commander as well as a benevolent ruler.

Ananta's nephew, Nitin, entered the room.

"Nitin, show Ananta to the pundit quarters," instructed Raja Rao. "Govinda will stay in the guest suite."

Nitin led Ananta into an elegant apartment overlooking the river.

"The streets are crowded with men exchanging tales of how Govinda killed the Emperor and eluded the imperial army. Are the stories true?" wondered Nitin.

"What exactly have you heard?" asked Ananta.

"The chai wallahs claim the prince stabbed the Emperor in the heart to stop him from defacing Krishna."

"I shall tell the story at dinner. I'm sure our hosts would like to hear the story as well."

At dinner, everyone was eager to hear a firsthand account of Govinda's heroics.

"Ananta, why don't you tell the story?" Govinda suggested. "Raja Rao might like to know how the Emperor died."

Ananta told the story with the same flair and conviction with which he had shared the tale with Govinda's grandfather, an account which spread to the far corners of Rajputana.

When Ananta finished, Govinda added, "Anantaji, mention the predictions as they relate to the story."

"Govinda is in grave danger. The pundits have already begun recitations in the temple beneath Masjid mosque. When the *yagya* is complete, Govinda will go into exile."

"Would it not be prudent for Govinda to leave Varanasi immediately?" suggested Raja Rao.

"Shastri advises Govinda to remain in Varanasi during the yagya."

"Rajaji, I am concerned for your family's safety," said Govinda. "The Moguls have seen my stallion, which is now in your stable. Is there somewhere safe for Kalki?"

Commander Zaim's spies infiltrated Bundi Fort and confirmed that the boy with the white horse was Raja Chandra's son, the heir to the Krishnagarh throne. His name was Govinda, and he had gone to Varanasi to place his father's ashes in the Ganges. The spies returned to Delhi without news of the boy's mother.

The Tale of the Himalayan Yogis

Zaim was mystified. Rani Rukmini would be in Bundi unless she had joined johar; he was sure of it. Zaim's spies informed him that most of the women and children had fled the fort, and that only the elders had taken johar. The gold bangle convinced Zaim that the queen was alive, and so he led his troops to Bundi. With Rani Rukmini in his possession, he would have the prizes that had cost the Emperor his life. From Bundi, Zaim would ride to Varanasi where he would capture the upstart Govinda, putting an end to the growing insurrection.

"I want to perform Pitaji's rites today," said Govinda.

Ananta nodded. "Raj Ghat is beyond Varanasi. We'll go by boat."

An oarsman pushed the rough-hewn dugout away from shore, and the boat drifted with the current. Govinda trained his eyes on the honey-hued solar deity rising from its dusty bed on the Gangetic plains. In the space between the dugout and the horizon, the Ganges swirled, its liquid contours painted lavender and rose. The murmur of oars was the only sound Govinda heard as he cradled the urn containing his father's ashes.

The boat glided past the ancient city on the bluff, arriving at Raj Ghat where flames engulfed the bodies of India's kings for millennia, a ritual believed to free the soul for its journey to the realm of the ancestors.

Kneeling, Govinda turned the urn over the prow, releasing its contents into the water as Ananta chanted. Through cheerless eyes, Govinda watched the ashes disperse over the water's surface before they vanished altogether.

Pitaji, do you remember how we galloped across the plains together? You told me Kalki could outrun the wind. You had me hold his mane with both hands. Together, we gazed upon mighty Krishnagarh where our ancestors ruled. Now you are with them. Have peace, Pitaji. Om Shanti!

"Maa Ganga will carry the ashes to the Bay of Bengal," whispered Ananta.

A solitary tear dimpled the water below.

Mishra waited for his friends outside the Shiva temple; his forehead streaked with broad bands of vibhuti.

"*Bum Bum Bole,*" Mishra greeted his friends. "Let us go to Kala Bhairav."

A look of contempt wrinkled Mishra's forehead as he passed the Masjid mosque.

"They've built their mosque on the foundation of our oldest temple."

Mishra disappeared through a narrow opening in the rocks below the mosque which sat on the bluff overlooking the river. Govinda and Ananta followed him into the darkness. After twenty paces, the tunnel emptied into a shrine suffused with the scent of incense, camphor, and burning ghee. On a waist-high platform at the center of the room stood nine small, black statues. Govinda had entered the Kala Bhairav temple where pundits would perform his propitiatory ritual.

"Pay homage to the planets," instructed Mishra. "Circle the altar nine times, once for each planet."

Unsure what to make of Shastri's predictions, he scrutinized the stone statues on the altar.

"Saturn," said Ananta, pointing to a statue in the back row.

"Our Vedic rituals must not be interrupted," Mishra explained. "With the Moguls roaming about Varanasi, we have little choice but to perform them underground."

In the dim light, Govinda could make out several rows of priests seated on blankets.

"Sit here," instructed Mishra, pointing to a mat on the floor. "Since Shiva rules the planets, offerings will be made to him. The mantra recitation will counteract Black Moon."

Potent energies filled the chamber as Govinda's mind sank like a stone tossed into the Ganges. Deeper and deeper he plunged until the priests' sonorous chants became a distant whisper before fading away altogether.

The pundits kept a watchful eye on the young prince as they chanted. When the recitation ended many hours later, Govinda opened his eyes, thinking that a brief moment had passed. The rapid-fire performance would be repeated from sunrise to sunset in the coming days.

"Chanting was good?" Mishra asked.

Govinda nodded.

"The pundits will begin again at dawn. Come, let me show you our subterranean world."

Mishra led his friends through an opening into the central chamber in the temple, a cavern much bigger than the one where the pundits chanted. A pair of priests were attending an altar at the far side of the room. Above the altar, a black form held a trident in one hand and a skull in the other.

"Meet Kal Bhairav... the Black Terror. Make friends with him," advised Mishra.

"Is he friendly?" asked Govinda innocently.

"No, but Bhairav will protect you if you befriend him."

"How do I do that?"

"Bring him offerings. And bring some for his friends."

"Who are his friends?" asked Govinda.

Mishra pointed to a pack of dogs asleep on the floor.

"Those are Bhairav's friends?"

Mishra pointed to the largest of the dogs. "Ruru is their leader. They won't hurt you unless disturbed."

"I'm comfortable with animals," replied Govinda confidently.

"Come, there's more."

Mishra led his charge into a smaller cavern; a dozen phantom-like figures filled the space, their bodies smeared with ash from the cremation grounds. In the weak light, the mendicants appeared like apparitions. Tall stacks of matted hair formed beehives atop their heads. A few of the sadhus wore loincloths; others wore lungi cloths. Govinda noticed a pile of weapons in the corner; there were sufficient swords, tridents, and battle-axes to supply a small army.

"*Nagababas*," announced Mishra. "These men are different; their practices are severe."

"Why the weapons?"

"Nagababas are fierce in their beliefs. At our festivals, they lead the processions. Come and see the last shrine."

Through an opening barely wide enough for a man to pass through, the trio stepped cautiously into a small chamber. A cloud of incense choked Govinda's lungs as he entered. The smoke was so dense that he could scarcely see. Mishra held out an arm to prevent Govinda from colliding with the shrine's pujari.

"Kali," whispered Mishra. "Her temple was also destroyed. Our gods are hiding, but Kali is not afraid."

Govinda stepped forward and touched the goddess' feet. Every fort in Rajputana had a Kali shrine where Rajput warriors sought her blessings before riding off into battle. Kali was fierce and black and held weapons in her many hands. The goddess' eyes bulged menacingly; her tongue dripped blood. A string of skulls garlanded her neck.

"I wouldn't want Kali upset with me," whispered Govinda.

"Jai Kali Maa," whispered Ananta, touching his forehead to her feet. "Underneath, she's pure love."

"Look there, but don't go inside," cautioned Mishra, pointing to an opening in the wall opposite Kali's altar. Govinda peered tentatively inside. In the center of the chamber sat a yogi, his matted hair cascading to the floor. The yogi's broad shoulders and taut, lean muscles were those of a man accustomed to physical exertion, and yet the ascetic's smooth forehead suggested a life of unfettered ease. His cheeks were soft, his feet tough like worn leather.

Perfect posture, thought Govinda, admiring the yogi's neatly folded legs supporting his rod-straight spine. *There's something peculiar about this yogi.*

"The yogi wears unusual beads; don't you think?" observed Govinda. The yogi's *malas* were exceptionally large and smooth.

"They're not beads," chuckled Mishra.

In the scant light, it was impossible to see anything.

"Cobras," said Mishra matter-of-factly. A cobra draped itself over each of the yogi's shoulders, and a third snake wrapped around his neck. Seeing more snakes on the floor, Govinda stepped back.

"The cave is full of them."

Mishra signaled that it was time to go. With considerable effort, the rotund priest squeezed through a narrow opening behind Kali's altar. Govinda followed the plump pundit up uneven steps until they reached a hinged covering overhead. Mishra pushed on the covering and a broad shaft of sunlight filtered down the stairs. Govinda and Ananta followed Mishra into an alley behind the mosque. A passel of hogs shuffled by, their pink snouts combing the ground in search of scraps.

"Who is the yogi with the cobras?" asked Govinda.

"Shankar Baba is famous in Varanasi," explained Mishra as he led his guests along a narrow alley near the river. "Some say he's three hundred years old. Others say he was never born — he simply came to be. No one knows. Shankar Baba rarely comes out. Fortunately, his cobras never do."

"Three hundred!" repeated Govinda.

"Shankar Baba hadn't been seen in years until a few days ago when he was seen bathing in the river."

"Hungry?" asked Ananta.

"Very!" replied Govinda.

Mishra led his friends to a stall where they purchased samosas with tamarind chutney.

"It must be dangerous living with cobras," observed Govinda, sipping rosewater lassi. The image of the yogi meditating with deadly snakes remained etched in his mind.

"These traditions are not easily understood," said Mishra, "but I'll try to explain. The cobra is a symbol of kundalini, the serpent energy sleeping at the base of the spine. Through yogic practices, these energies are awakened, bringing immense power and wisdom to the yogi."

The cook brought a plateful of pyramid-shaped samosas, then paused to listen to his customers' conversation.

"I felt kundalini once," said Govinda. "It flashed up my spine. First, it burned, and then it felt cool."

"Kundalini awakens Shiva in the crown chakra," explained Ananta.

"But how can a yogi meditate with a cobra wrapped around his neck? Won't it disrupt his practice?" mused Govinda.

"One would imagine," agreed Mishra, "but *nag yogis* claim cobras have a calming effect."

Govinda burst out laughing.

"The yogi has to be calm, or he'll die."

"That's true, but a snake can be a pet if it's cared for."

"I prefer horses," decided Govinda, dipping his samosa into a *katori* of brown sauce.

"You liked the Bhairav temple?" asked Mishra.

"I couldn't see anything," interjected Ananta. "I almost stepped on one of the dogs."

"That wouldn't be good," said Mishra, rolling his eyes. "Come, let us have a look at Varanasi's sacred mandala."

The affable pundit led his guests into a web of alleyways clogged with pilgrims, beggars, sleeping cows, and scheming monkeys.

"Varanasi is laid out along a series of concentric circles that become progressively smaller. The center point is the Shiva lingam in the Vishwanath temple. In their meditations, the rishis perceived creation as a great cosmic egg containing countless galaxies. The whole universe is mapped out in Varanasi, but now we are forced to hide like thieves."

"One day the treachery will end," vowed Govinda.

Zaim and his men met with no resistance at Bundi Fort. Rani Rukmini was taken prisoner and escorted back to Delhi where she was to await the return of Commander Zaim, a man she feared from the moment he entered her father's palace.

Accompanied by imperial cavalry, Rukmini arrived at Dinpanah Qila, the Refuge of the Faithful. The massive russet fortress rose above the fabled Yamuna River, the river beside which Krishna played as a child. Rukmini's horse carried her past the imperial flag, a moss green standard depicting a lion and the sun, and through the spike-studded gates of a fortification housing the emperor's harem.

The queen's palace was home to a thousand women and as many eunuchs. Delicate Asian women, Persian beauties, and pale Europeans were among those inhabiting the harem. A handful of the Emperor's

The Tale of the Himalayan Yogis

consorts were Hindus. It seemed odd to Rukmini that an emperor couldn't satisfy himself with one wife, or even two. But then, the Emperor of Delhi was no ordinary ruler.

Speaking to a towering eunuch with boulder-like shoulders and the hands of a giant, Zaim's officer issued a series of orders.

"Commander Zaim wants the rani treated respectfully. Provide her with a Brahmin cook and a pair of maidservants. She should have whatever she requires for her puja. Whatever she requests, provide it without delay."

The eunuch wagged his shaven brown head before escorting the new arrival to her apartment in the Moti Mahal.

Krishna's Leela

The guest of honor leaned against a satin bolster, the Raja of Jodhpur on one side, and the Mishras on the other. Forty guests of the royal family had gathered for a banquet at Jodhpur Palace, a sprawling edifice overlooking the Ganges. Govinda felt uneasy being the center of attention. He wished he could escape on one of the fishing boats plying the river. It seemed everyone at the gathering wanted to meet Govinda, and those who lacked the courage fixed their gaze on him from a distance.

The wispy song of a wood flute sweetened the night air. Oil lamps flickered on ledges, framing the rooftop garden in soft, golden light. The night air rose off the river, stirred by a pleasant, autumnal breeze. The Raja of Jodhpur treated his guests to a Rajputana feast that made Govinda long for Krishnagarh.

Leela stared into a mirror in her mother's apartment, rehearsing her dance routine. The queen entered to apply makeup at the corners of her daughter's large, expressive eyes.

"*Jeldi* Maa! *Jeeeldi*!" said Leela excitedly. "I'm ready to dance."

"Hold still, little one, or your makeup will smear. You do want to look like Krishna, don't you?"

Atop Leela's head rested a tiara with a plume of peacock feathers. The young dancer's raven tresses tumbled over her shoulders. Gold ornaments flashed at her elbows, neck, waist, and ankles. Leela's lemon pantaloons, green sash, and rose shawl had transformed the young princess into a little Krishna. Leela was about to perform the dance that had captivated the Osiyan Festival, winning her a grand prize. Only the black eyeliner circling her flashing eyes was needed to complete her costume.

"Finished," sighed the queen. "Now go and enchant our guests."

Leela peered into the body length mirror. Satisfied with her appearance, she was about to run out of the room when her mother winked at her, "He's quite handsome, don't you think?"

"Maa!" admonished Leela, giggling as she disappeared up the stairs to the rooftop garden.

The ceiling of stars rivaled the harvest moon over Osiyan's amphitheater. Surges of energy rushed about Leela's lithe body as she steadied her mind, surveying the space where she would perform. A drummer tapped the goatskin surface of his tabla as the musicians waited for their cue. Leela bowed in front of a sandalwood Krishna. Folding her hands, she whispered,

"Krishnaji. I'm dancing for you tonight. I hope you like it."

As the young dancer glided to the center of the rooftop garden, a flute's melody filled the air.

Govinda blinked and blinked again. Had Krishna himself come to Varanasi?

The nimble dancer mimed the story of the child Krishna stealing butter from his mother's kitchen. Mischief flashed across Krishna's face as he reached to the sky, removed an imaginary pot from its place on a shelf, licked his fingers, and reached for more. With an impish grin, the butter thief shoved his entire hand into the jar. The prank brought a smile to the dancer's beguiling face.

Leela had become Krishna himself. Moving with the grace of a peacock and the poise of nobility, she spun through the night, countless stars lighting her way.

The story soon shifted. Krishna crossed his ankles in serene repose, raising his flute to his lips. The winsome cowherd played intoxicating melodies, luring his adoring gopis from their homes in the night, entrancing his doting milkmaids one by one. Krishna moved about the roof, sporting amorously with his audience.

The dance medley completed, Leela spun to the center of the floor where she stood, her flute pressed to her lips. Little Satyam ran onto the floor and placed a garland over his sister's head. The audience showered flower petals and applause on the dancer.

Raja Rao welcomed his daughter into his arms. Their embrace left a smudge on the king's cheek.

"Isn't our little Krishna lovely?" asked Raja Rao.

"Rajaji, only a true *bhakta* could perform like that," replied Govinda.

"Leela, would you like to perform a folk dance for our guests?" suggested her father.

Leela nodded and then handed Govinda her wood flute before racing off to change costumes. Returning moments later wearing a crimson peasant's skirt and white blouse, the winsome dancer morphed from Hindu deity to peasant girl. The tabla player set the beat with a pair of wooden castanets as the little gypsy stamped her heel to the ground, causing her silver anklets to jingle. Leela spun round and round, covering the rooftop in a flurry of feathery steps. The dancer's boundless energy filled the sky and everything beneath it.

The folk dance was Leela's favorite; the dance she wanted to perform at the Marwar Festival, but couldn't because of her royal blood. Now she was making up for the missed opportunity, and the crowd loved her for it. By the time the folds in her cotton skirt settled after her final flurry, Leela had won the heart of everyone on the rooftop, including Govinda. Pulling herself up from the floor, Leela gazed into Govinda's eyes, and in that moonlit moment, kindred souls recognized one another.

Windows thrown open to the night, Govinda dreamt of folktales told through song and dance in fortress courtyards. Waking at first light, he stepped onto the balcony outside his apartment. Below him, the Ganges glided past. Govinda stepped into his room, returning to the balcony with the *bansari* Leela had given him. Placing the flute to his lips, he played a folk melody that Mataji had taught him years ago. The tune was a simple one, and though he was an accomplished player, the song was his favorite.

The song stirred a longing in his heart. Would he ever see Krishnagarh again? If Shastri's predictions were right, seven years

The Tale of the Himalayan Yogis

without a puppet show or peasant dance lay ahead. Wandering about like a sadhu would be his life.

Leela's dance had created a profound longing within him, and for the first time since leaving Krishnagarh, Govinda felt the ache of sadness in his heart. He wished he could return to the people and place he loved. He knew it was impossible, and yet he longed to be with his family, longed to ride Kalki through Krishnagarh's gates, longed to see Leela perform her peasant dance again. Watching the river's peaceful passage, Govinda wished his life would slow down.

"Such a sad tune."

Govinda pulled the flute from his lips. Looking over the marble railing, he saw Leela standing on a balcony below… she was smiling.

"It's not a sad tune. The player is sad, not the song."

"And why is the player sad?"

"I can't say exactly."

"Come to the roof. Krishna will cheer you up."

"Now?" asked Govinda.

"Right now. Nitin and I do puja every morning."

"Then you love Krishna too?"

"Couldn't you tell?"

"I was sure that Krishna himself was dancing last night."

"It's called Krishna Bhava. Every devotee knows the feeling," said Leela.

"I suppose so," replied Govinda. "I've forgotten."

"How could anyone forget the feeling of being one with Krishna?"

"Too much has happened lately… and too fast."

"Krishna will make you happy again. Meet me on the roof."

A flicker of hope chased the melancholy from Govinda's heart as he bound up the steps, eager to join in the morning ritual.

"Hold these," Leela instructed Govinda, placing a handful of rose petals in his upturned palms.

Nitin circled an oil lamp in front of Krishna, then handed it to Leela, who repeated the rite. Then it was Govinda's turn. After aarti, he and Leela tossed petals at Krishna's feet as Nitin recited Krishna's many names. When the ceremony was complete, the priest dipped his index finger into a bowl of sandal paste and placed a dot between Govinda's brows. He did the same for Leela.

"You *must* be feeling better now," smiled Leela.

"I am, but Ananta says it's inauspicious to perform puja during the period of mourning."

"Such a silly notion. When you're sad, you need Krishna most."

"I hadn't thought of it that way."

"Leela, how many times has your mother scolded you for ignoring our traditions?" Nitin gently rebuked the princess.

"I don't know anything about traditions. I only know that I love Krishna and I doubt he cares much about rules either."

"Krishna certainly didn't listen to his mother when she warned him about stealing butter," laughed Govinda.

"See, Govinda agrees with me."

Smiling wryly, Nitin rose to his feet.

"Bring prasad for Satyam," the priest reminded Leela as he left the garden.

"My parents would be unhappy if they knew their guest was sad," said Leela.

"I'm not sad anymore."

"I'm sorry about your father."

"It's more than that. Shastriji predicted great hardship for Mataji. I know Pitaji is happy where he is, but to think of Mataji suffering is unbearable. I want to be with her, but the astrologer warned against it."

"I don't care much for astrologers. They steal one's freedom like a thief in the market."

"But everyone says Shastriji is the best astrologer in Varanasi. Mishra himself insists that whatever Shastriji predicts is destined to come true," countered Govinda.

"But isn't it a self-fulfilling prophecy? Predictions come true because a person believes they will."

"You could look at it that way. I can see that you don't agree with the old ways."

"Pitaji calls me a rebel," laughed Leela. "Are you a rebel too?"

"I suppose so. When my people were about to perform johar, I persuaded them not to do it."

The Tale of the Himalayan Yogis

"Now that's a rebel!" rejoiced Leela. "Johar is the most sacred sacrament of all."

"At least for Rajputs. It's nice to talk to someone who sees things the way I do."

"Ignore those gloomy predictions. You only need to be happy, and everything else takes care of itself. Have you been to Vrindavan?" asked Leela.

"When I was young."

"We stop there whenever we come to Varanasi. There's a garden there where Krishna and Radha dance in the night, but no one is allowed inside after dark."

"More rules." laughed Govinda.

"That's one rule that makes sense. Even the monkeys stay away at night. There are tombs for those who ventured inside after dark. You see, Krishna and Radha are very romantic; they don't like to be disturbed in the night."

"I felt Krishna's love when you danced last night."

"And he felt yours."

Leela picked up a fistful of rose petals and showered them over Govinda's head. Govinda was about to return the favor when Satyam ran onto the roof.

"Where's my prasad?"

"Don't pout, *Chotu*," teased Leela, handing her brother a sweet.

A moment later, Leela's mother appeared at the entrance to the garden.

"Is anyone hungry? Anil's making *aloo parathas*."

As Govinda stood, the rose petals in his hair floated to the floor.

"The pundits will be starting soon," he said. "I'm not supposed to eat before going to the temple."

Leela shot Govinda a disapproving look. "Now you've got a dilemma. One rule says you shouldn't eat before the yagya and another says you must not disappoint your hosts."

"Leela, don't tease our guest," scolded her mother. "Govinda is right. It's not good to eat before propitiating the gods."

"But we just fed Krishna, and he's the *lord* of food."

"I'd like some parathas," said Govinda as he followed the others down the stairs.

After bathing each morning in the Ganges, Govinda met Leela for aarti before walking to the Bhairav temple where he immersed himself in the melodic chants. Mrityunjaya, the most powerful mantra in the four Vedas, reverberated off the charred walls of the cave temple. Although he felt the raw power of the ritual, Govinda would face death without fear when his time came. Still, Leela's words intrigued him. Did the Black Moon amount to little more than an astrologer's self-fulfilling prophecy?

Sultry days sped past, but Govinda's underground internment spared him the oppressive heat. He befriended Bhairav's attendants, feeding the dogs chapatis from the palace kitchen.

The specter of death lurked in the recesses of his mind — a dagger thrust into his heart or a tortured demise at the hands of Commander Zaim. With caution as his companion, Govinda moved warily along the labyrinthine alleys linking Jodhpur Palace to the underground temples.

One morning a monkey stalked him, swinging from a limb onto a rooftop. The assailant waited for its victim to reach the assigned spot on the path before descending. The thief snatched Govinda's bananas, causing him to lurch out of the way, thinking the enemy had finally caught up with him.

Govinda knew the Moguls were coming. He could feel it in his soul. The old astrologer had predicted it, and the omens confirmed it. He reached for the Idol's Eye, only relaxing after he had it firmly in his grasp. Varanasi did not afford the tactical advantage of Krishnagarh, for the Rajput was a newcomer to the ancient city, and the passages hidden from view at Krishnagarh were plainly visible in Varanasi.

The night the old astrologer warned of had arrived. As the earth passed between sun and moon, the moon disappeared, casting an eerie stillness over the City of Light moments before pundit Mishra reached Jodhpur Palace to collect his friends. They would have their river bath before entering the cave temple where Govinda would be safe.

The Tale of the Himalayan Yogis

Sadhus from as far off as Gaya to the east and Hardwar to the west converged on Varanasi to bathe in the holy waters during the peak of the eclipse. The yogis believed the planetary alignment magnified the power of their meditation a thousandfold. Fakirs and sadhus would spend the night meditating on the riverbank after dipping in the Ganges.

"Tonight you will witness rare sights… maybe even miracles," said Mishra. "Rarely seen yogis will join in tonight. Even the nagas will emerge from their caves."

"Will we see the swami float on the water?" asked Govinda.

"If we're lucky," said Mishra. "Jal Swami is unpredictable."

Govinda and the three Mishras stood knee deep in the river, offering flower petals to the Ganges. Upstream, pilgrims launched banana leaves carrying oil lamps, incense, and marigolds. The tiny green boats drifted about like flaming swans on the water.

The sky blackened; the riverfront pulsed with energy.

Govinda searched the water for the floating yogi, but only flower petals and *divya* leaves bobbed in the current. He stripped away his kurta, carefully setting the pouch containing the Idol's Eye on a step before wading into the river. The river felt soothing, as much a spiritual balm as a cleansing of hair and skin.

The matted locks of a naga bathing near Govinda spread like the tentacles of an octopus over the surface of the water. Emerging from the river, Govinda dried and dressed, and then reached down to the water to free a plantain leaf filled with marigolds.

The Mishras escorted Govinda into the cave temples. The lunar eclipse had begun; the time of peril was nearing its peak.

Since venturing to and from Jodhpur Palace had become increasingly risky, Mishra had arranged for Govinda to sleep in the nagas' chamber. Govinda would not see the sun again until the ritual ended.

Outside, a man clad in a spice-stained *lungi* looked over his shoulder before pointing to the entrance leading to the Bhairav temple. A second man, a Mogul, slipped a pair of mohurs into the cook's hand before disappearing into the night.

At the sound of approaching footsteps, Govinda grew alert. Many pairs of boots passed the nine planets and entered Bhairav's sanctum. No Hindu would enter the temple unless barefoot.

"Come with us!"

Recognizing Commander Zaim's voice, Govinda sprang to his feet. A dozen uniformed men crowded into the chamber behind their leader. The smoke faded before their faces, revealing Commander Zaim and his men.

"What do you want with the boy?" demanded Mishra.

No one despised the intruders more than the corpulent Brahmin.

"The Rajput murdered the Emperor," declared Zaim.

"That's ludicrous," replied Mishra testily. "He's just a boy."

"We're taking him to Delhi to stand trial."

"For execution, you mean."

"Let's go," Zaim ordered Govinda. "You can come on your own. Otherwise, my men will drag you out of here."

"He's not going anywhere!" Mishra shouted defiantly.

Zaim drew his dagger. The soldiers were armed with concealed weapons to ensure that Govinda received no warning of their approach.

"I wouldn't do that if I were you," cautioned Govinda.

Zaim was not about to be fooled a second time. Ignoring the warning, Zaim stepped forward, dagger in hand.

"One more step and you'll wish you'd never come in here."

Heedless of the Rajput's words, Zaim rushed forward, but as the commander grabbed Govinda, a shadowy figure locked its fanged jaws on the commander's arm. Zaim screamed from fright and searing pain as his weapon fell to the floor. Ruru was tearing the Mogul's hand apart. As Zaim's men rushed forward, the other dogs attacked, biting and clawing viciously. The attack happened so unexpectedly, and in such poor light, that the soldiers had no idea how their assailants had materialized.

"Go quickly," whispered Mishra, pointing to the opening leading to the nagas' chamber. "Come to the Shiva temple later tonight."

In an instant, Govinda had vanished. One by one, the soldiers overpowered the dogs, but not before their arms were torn and bleeding. One of the Moguls ran out of the tunnel; perhaps to summon reinforcements.

Govinda sprinted through the nagas' empty chamber. Reaching the Kali shrine, he slipped behind the altar and climbed the stairwell. Desperate, he pushed hard on the covering, but it didn't open. Again and again, he pushed, but it wouldn't budge.

It opened for Mishra. Someone must have latched the outside, thought Govinda. *It couldn't have been the Moguls; how could they have learned of the escape route? But then again, how did they find me?*

Govinda clutched the Idol's Eye for reassurance as he returned to the Kali shrine in search of a hiding place. Pulling the stone from its pouch, he held it up to the goddess and prayed. Then he heard a faint voice.

Is Kali trying to tell me something?

Again, he heard the voice.

"Come in here."

"Where?" asked Govinda.

"Here."

The voice wasn't Kali's at all. It was coming from the chamber with the snakes.

Govinda was about to step into the cave when he remembered the deadly snakes. He peered tentatively into the chamber. The sparsely clad yogi was meditating, a pair of cobras coiled about his neck.

"Come inside," the yogi whispered without opening his eyes. Govinda heard voices from behind him. The soldiers were about to enter the Kali shrine, and so he stepped gingerly into the cave, clutching the Idol's Eye for support.

One misplaced step and I'm dead.

Slipping into a corner, Govinda crouched down. He was alive, but death lurked all around him.

Commander Zaim's voice echoed about the chamber. The Mogul's bloodied face glared at Kali's crimson tongue. Zaim examined his mauled hand. His men searched the shrine, discovering the escape route behind the altar.

"It's locked!" a soldier reported.

So it wasn't the Moguls who locked it, thought Govinda.

"Outside!" ordered Zaim, returning the way he had come. As he turned, Zaim noticed the entrance to the yogi's cave. Looking directly at Govinda, the Mogul didn't appear to see him.

"Has anyone searched in there?" he questioned, pointing a bloody finger at the cave.

Not waiting for his men, Zaim entered the cave.

"*Insallah!*" shouted the Mogul upon seeing the ash-covered yogi wreathed in cobras. Terrified, Zaim slowly retreated. The yogi sat perfectly still, impervious to the commotion. Several soldiers raised their weapons. Inside the cave, hoods flared. Both soldier and snake were poised to strike. Seeing the flaring cobras, Govinda was unsure whether to be relieved or panicked.

"I'll take care of the vipers," boasted a soldier behind Zaim. The Mogul stepped forward, his scimitar drawn.

"Stop, or you'll die," came a deep voice from the darkness. But it was too late. As the soldier stepped into the cave, a soundless wave swept across the floor. Before the soldier could withdraw, the wave struck. A trio of cobras emptied their venom into the helpless Mogul. The soldier collapsed in paralyzed agony.

"Insallah, this is some kind of hell!" shrieked Zaim as a cobra's hood flared above the yogi's shoulder.

"The boy must be in there," barked Zaim. "Get me a lamp."

A soldier removed the lamp from Kali's altar and handed it to his commander. Raising the light, Zaim searched the cave. The horde of snakes coiled on the floor, many poised to strike, drained the blood from the Mogul's face. He was about to withdraw when he spotted the Rajput crouching in the corner.

"There he is," said Zaim in a strangled whisper. "Get him."

"Leave now," the yogi advised. "My cobras grow agitated."

"Did he say that?" asked Zaim, pointing at the yogi.

"Leave," repeated the ghostlike figure.

Zaim stepped back as the snakes slithered in his direction.

"I have your mother," taunted Zaim.

"My mother is dead," replied Govinda.

"Does this look familiar?"

Zaim tossed the gold bangle onto the floor in front of Govinda.

"Come with us, or be your mother's executioner."

The Tale of the Himalayan Yogis

"Mataji is safe," declared the yogi.

"What does this naked sadhu know?" countered Zaim.

"I'm not coming," decided Govinda, drawing courage from the yogi's words.

Seeing the snakes moving toward him, Zaim retreated.

"Let's go," he ordered the others. "The boy will have to come out sooner or later."

"Take the dead one," instructed the yogi. "Weight the body with stones and submerge it in the Ganges. He is more fortunate than you, Commander. The venom purified his hatred."

Zaim stared at the yogi for a time before signaling for his men to remove the body. After the Moguls had gone, the yogi spoke again.

"Now try the escape door."

"Who are you?" asked Govinda.

"A friend," smiled the yogi. "Shastri said there would be a sign. I am that sign. Your journey begins now."

Govinda felt something strangely familiar about the holy man.

"I must save Mataji."

"You cannot."

The finality of the yogi's words cut deeply at Govinda's heart. Careful to avoid arousing the cobras, he reached down to press his head to the yogi's feet, placing the Idol's Eye on the floor beside him. As Govinda reached for the yogi's feet, the yogi pushed the gem away with his hand. When Govinda rose to his knees, the jewel was gone.

"Over there," pointed the yogi. Govinda spotted the diamond resting against one of the cobras.

Now, what do I do?

"Go and get it," instructed the yogi, his eyes still closed.

"All right."

Govinda crawled across the floor, his body soaked in sweat. Measuring his every move, he slowly extended his hand until it was close enough to pick up the gem.

"Put your arm in front of his snout," instructed the yogi.

"Are you sure?" The thought of touching the snake's snout seemed inconceivable.

"No harm will come."

Reluctantly, Govinda followed the yogi's instructions. To his amazement, the cobra slithered onto his arm, coiling itself loosely around it.

"He's cold."

"His name is Shambu. He won't harm you. Now take the diamond."

The snake slowly uncoiled onto the floor. Govinda picked up the gem and retraced his steps to the yogi. A small bag lay near the yogi's feet.

"Take the bag," said the yogi, still not bothering to open his eyes. "Tibetan friends will need it."

Govinda picked up the pouch, stashed it in his clothes and backed out of the cave, his eyes riveted on the snakes. Reaching the opening to the chamber, he thanked the yogi for saving his life.

The yogi nodded, replying, "Remember Shastri's instruction."

"How did you do all of this?" Govinda couldn't help asking.

"I do nothing. I let myself be what I must be."

Frowning at the cryptic reply, Govinda wasted no more time. After bowing to the yogi, he slipped through the narrow opening behind Kali. Mysteriously, the exit at the top of the stairs was no longer locked. In the alley outside, he made a snap judgment where to hide, disappearing through a gate into the courtyard of the mosque.

The mosque will be the last place Zaim will look for me.

The mosque soon filled with people, but there was not a soldier among them. Govinda leaned against a pillar in the back, hoping to avoid drawing attention to himself. When the mosque closed its doors, Govinda went in search of Mishra. As he moved along the narrow lanes, Mogul riders passed him. They did not seem to be searching, but he hid from them anyway.

They must be returning to their camp.

Then he remembered Zaim's words: 'I have your mother!'

A feeling of helplessness overtook him as he watched the last soldier ride past. Govinda had been warned not to try to rescue his mother, but at the same time, Leela's point of view seemed entirely reasonable. Was astrology merely a system of self-fulfilling prophecies? The yogi's words: 'remember Shastri's instruction' flashed across his

The Tale of the Himalayan Yogis

awareness. Govinda's mind reeled this way and that. He knew that attempting to free Mataji would be risky, but it was unbearable to think that Zaim held her captive.

If Shastri's predictions were right, then he would be killed if he tried to rescue her. If Leela was correct, then he was passing up the opportunity to save his mother from untold misery. Once Mataji was taken to Delhi, there would be no hope of rescuing her. It was now, or not at all. Govinda pulled the bangle from his pocket. Was he alone in this decision? Was there a decision to make at all? Govinda slunk along the crumbling walls that lined the alley until he reached the crossroads where he had seen the Mogul riders.

Govinda's mind flashed to Krishnagarh where he had outmaneuvered hundreds more Moguls than were pursuing him now. How easy it would be to slip into their camp while they slept. If he died trying, it would be better than living with the knowledge that Mataji was in the hands of the enemy. There was little time; the Mogul riders were rapidly disappearing.

As he pondered his next move, Govinda heard a shriek, and then another. Racing down the road, he saw riders entering a temple. Keeping out of sight, he made his way to the temple courtyard where an elderly priest stood trembling, his left hand nearly severed from his wrist. Behind the priest lay pieces of what had been a Ganesh statue.

"I raised my arm to stop him from harming Ganesh, and he swung at me," moaned the Brahmin. Govinda tore off the sleeve of his tunic and bandaged the man's arm as tightly as he could.

"How many riders?"

"Four or five."

Shastri's warning echoed in his mind as Govinda searched the courtyard for something to wield in combat.

"Is there something I can use as a weapon?" he asked, ignoring Shastri's words.

Self-fulfilling prophecies... far less real than the enemy.

The old Brahmin pointed to the entrance of the temple.

"Durga's trident."

Govinda entered the temple, touched the feet of the goddess, and removed the *trishul* from her hand. The weapon was heavy but lethal.

As he was about to leave, he paused before the goddess. Seeing her compassionate eyes, he uttered a prayer.

"Durga Ma, it matters little if I die… please protect Mataji."

Hoping his prayer would be answered, Govinda touched the goddess' feet a second time. As he turned to leave the temple, he heard voices; three soldiers had ridden into the temple.

"Stand aside, or I'll cut you down!" ordered the first rider.

Govinda stood his ground, sizing up the intruders. The second rider's hands bled, no doubt the handiwork of Bhairav's dogs. In unison, the soldiers raised their scimitars, glaring murderously at Govinda.

"Stand aside, I say!" repeated the first rider.

"Leave now, while you can," Govinda countered, raising the iron trident. Although it was too heavy for a combative weapon, the trident was usable.

The lead rider was about to strike when a fourth horseman entered the sanctum — Zaim — his hands heavily bandaged.

"I want the Rajput alive," he ordered, freezing the soldier's arm in mid-motion.

The riders climbed down from their mounts, providing Govinda with the opening he needed. He sprinted around them, but Zaim blocked the exit. Govinda rushed headlong at Zaim's horse, Durga's trident poised for the strike. The Mogul's horse reared, but this time Zaim was prepared. Digging his boots into the horse, he forced it down. Zaim's blade arched viciously toward Govinda's neck as he dove out of the weapon's path.

The pouch containing the Idol's Eye fell outside his collar as Zaim's sword slashed through his kurta, severing the pouch's cord without injuring Govinda. Zaim could have killed him, but the Mogul was trying to contain his quarry long enough for the soldiers to subdue him.

The blade made a second pass. This time, Govinda parried the blow with the trident. The collision of weapons sent Govinda sprawling to the ground and the trident sliding across the floor. Scrambling to his feet, Govinda dodged to his right, drawing Zaim after him. He then circled back to his left, sprinting through the opening he had

The Tale of the Himalayan Yogis

created. Bypassing Zaim, he ran out of the temple, his pursuers close on his heels. A platoon of forty riders waited outside.

On the floor of the Durga temple lay the pouch, its whereabouts unknown to everyone.

Govinda ducked into an alley, racing past a bright orange statue of Ganesh, one of dozens like it in the city. The Rajput had entered a Brahmin neighborhood. To his relief, the passage was too narrow for horses to come, allowing him to gain precious distance between himself and his pursuers. Seeing their quarry escaping, the soldiers gave chase on foot. Govinda had no idea where the path led; only the locals could navigate Varanasi's labyrinth of alleys. Govinda needed to find his way back to the river and a secure hiding place.

Dodging fruit vendors and leaping over begging bowls, Govinda ran toward the river, jostling pilgrims and avoiding sleeping cows as he fled. He glanced over his shoulder and saw three Moguls; whether the others had failed to keep up, or whether they were simply out of sight, he did not know.

Sprinting down a cobblestone path, he turned a corner so recklessly that he collided with an old man. After helping the fellow to his feet, he continued along the narrow lane. Directly ahead of him lay a hefty bull, the beast's horns extending to the walls on either side of the path. As Govinda turned to run in the other direction, a pair of Moguls rounded the corner behind him.

Lacking a safer option, Govinda ran toward the bull. Seeing the approaching human, the animal aligned its horns to impale the boy as Govinda soared over them, landing on the bull's hump. Enraged by the boots on his back, the beast stood, but not before Govinda had safely landed on the path beyond the animal. He turned in time to see the irate bull charge the soldiers, not caring who it attacked, so long as it attacked someone. The Moguls reversed their direction, the bull rapidly overtaking them.

"Ganga?" panted Govinda. The fruit vendor wagged his head as a hand holding a plump mango gestured vaguely, confirming his direction.

After countless changes of direction, Govinda stood at the entrance to the Annapurna temple, the sister shrine to the Shiva temple where Mishra served. The river was near; Govinda knew the way from here.

Govinda reached the bluff overlooking the river where he stopped to catch his breath and take in his surroundings. Three priests' flaming lamps circled in unison above the inky waters. Scrambling down to the ghats, Govinda stood on a stone platform where the priests performed a sunset ritual honoring the river goddess. The platform afforded a superb view of the river below and the burning grounds upstream. Behind Govinda, dozens of torches lit the waterfront, a tradition during lunar eclipses.

Seated in the amphitheater above the stone platform, a thousand pilgrims observed the ritual. Govinda scanned the ghats in search of a hiding place, failing to notice a peculiar figure in the water. Floating a stone's throw from shore was Jal Swami. Pilgrims attending the evening ritual cast curious glances at the yogi, who appeared to be floating on the river.

Govinda was about to duck behind a stack of firewood when the enemy arrived. Spreading like noxious vapor, uniformed men appeared on every side. Some brandished swords; others carried guns or bows. Commander Zaim swaggered onto the bluff above him, flanked by a dozen armed soldiers.

"I intended to capture you," Zaim shouted down to Govinda, "but you're elusive like a rat. I won't risk you escaping again."

"To die in Varanasi would be the greatest boon," replied Govinda, reaching for the Idol's Eye.

"*Everything* is a boon to you Hindus," goaded Zaim.

"Death is freedom!" shouted Govinda, frantically trying to locate the diamond that he had counted on since the siege of Krishnagarh.

"Freedom!" sneered Zaim. "Your mother would delight in that, would she not?"

The Mogul's words tore at Govinda's heart; his body tensed.

"Zaim, you're a bully... and a coward! You gloat over tormenting an innocent woman..."

Zaim signaled to his men, who raised their weapons.

"I'd be careful what I say," Zaim's second in command warned. "If the commander gives the signal, you're dead."

The Tale of the Himalayan Yogis

Unable to come up with a better plan, Govinda decided to infuriate his foe.

"Commander, your men loathe you. Sadan himself told me so."

Zaim looked at his men, perhaps to see if they agreed that their commander was a coward and a bully. And maybe he saw that they did, for he signaled his marksmen to hold their fire before starting down the hill.

If Govinda was to die, he wanted Zaim to die with him. That way, at least Mataji would not have to face his cruelty.

Govinda saw his chance. Weaponless, he charged up the hill to confront his foe on the steep terrain. Plunging headlong into the Mogul, Govinda wrestled his opponent to the ground. As they rolled down the slope, Govinda felt the superior size and strength of his adversary. Coming to a stop on the platform below, soldiers surrounded the combatants on every side. Govinda struggled to free himself, but Zaim's crushing grip felt like iron. The Mogul was on top of him, exhaling the stench of his fury. Govinda searched for Zaim's dagger, but the sheath was empty. Zaim held the weapon in his hand, poised to thrust it into Govinda's chest.

Govinda kicked hard, driving his knee into the Mogul's groin. Zaim recoiled, causing the dagger to miss Govinda's heart. Instead, the blade tore through his shoulder. Govinda shrieked, but his kick had loosened Zaim's grip enough for him to wriggle free. The crowd of pilgrims, who had been enjoying the pageant, stood in stunned silence. They had come for evening *aarti*, but the commotion had caused the priests to abort the nightly ritual. Many were willing to intervene on Govinda's behalf, but the platoon of armed Moguls dissuaded them.

Pulling himself to his feet, Govinda grimaced as he touched his hand to his shoulder. Zaim lunged at him, but Govinda's blow had sapped his accuracy and speed.

Summoning his courage, Govinda darted between a pair of flaming lamps held by the priests. Looking over his shoulder, he saw a line of soldiers about to open fire. Sprinting to the edge of the platform, he leaped over the indigo water below.

The descent into the water lasted an eternity. Falling, Govinda felt a freedom he had known only atop Kalki. Down, down, down he plummeted, hurtling toward the inky abyss. From behind, he heard gunfire. Searing flames ripped through his back, the final shot striking him in the spine as he plunged into the water. He felt himself sinking, but there was nothing he could do. He couldn't move his limbs. His body stiffened as the swirling currents engulfed him. Facedown in the water, Govinda gasped for air. Instead, the river poured into him, filling his throat and lungs with liquid fire.

"Bring me the rodent's body," ordered Zaim, sweeping the dust from his uniform.

Descending to river's edge, a pair of soldiers waded into the water to retrieve the body. The water level below the platform was higher than usual, the result of a heavy monsoon. The soldiers struggled after the body which was drifting downstream.

Evening worship in the temples had ended. On the bluff overlooking the river, a crowd gathered to view the colorful ceremony. Among those who had just arrived were Mishra and Ananta. Seeing the soldiers pulling Govinda's bullet-riddled body from the water, Ananta's anguished cry reached the far side of the river.

"*GOVINDA!*"

Every pilgrim on the bluff now knew what had happened. The Moguls had slain their hero. The throng contemplated retaliation, but they were weaponless; many held their sons and daughters by the hand.

"Leave the body in the water," commanded a voice from farther out in the river. Hearing the order, the soldiers paused. The voice belonged to a yogi who appeared to be floating on the water.

"Who are you?" demanded one of the soldiers.

"Leave the boy's body."

Strangely, the soldiers were compelled to do as the yogi instructed. Seeing his men release the body into the water, Zaim flew into a rage.

"What are you doing?"

"The fakir told us to leave the body in the water," answered a soldier.

"I order you to bring me the Rajput's body, and you listen to a naked sadhu?" frothed Zaim.

"But the fakir's floating on the water!"

"These fakirs do all sorts of magic with the help of their *djinns*. Now bring me the body."

"If either of you touches the body, you'll die," said the yogi calmly. The yogi had moved closer to the soldiers. The holy man wore nothing but a loincloth; his girth was exceptional.

"He says we'll die if we touch the body," the soldier relayed to his commander.

"Go and get the body," Zaim ordered the junior officers at his side. "Remind me to whip those men until their bones bleed."

Seeing more Moguls coming for the body, the yogi spoke again.

"All of you should leave now. Otherwise, more than one body will float facedown in the river."

"Shoot him," ordered Zaim, signaling to his gunmen. But before the men could fire, the yogi vanished, leaving only faint ripples on the water.

"He's gone!" gasped a soldier.

"Where did he go?" asked another.

Soldiers and pilgrims alike were stunned by what they were witnessing. The yogi had not only floated on the water, but he had vanished in front of a thousand onlookers.

A moment later, the yogi reappeared cradling Govinda's body in his arms.

"I'm taking the boy with me," said the yogi. Then, to the astonishment of the stunned throng, the yogi disappeared into the river along with the body.

Zaim scanned the water expecting the yogi to surface, but the river flowed peacefully past, the crackling of fires the only sound violating the eerie calm hanging over the river. Zaim's men searched the riverfront, but when they returned empty-handed, he was clueless as to what to do. The yogi was gone, and with him, the prize Zaim needed to restore his reputation.

Ananta rested his head against his uncle's shoulder.

"How could it happen?" he murmured. "Shastriji insisted that he would be safe in the temple."

Pundit Mishra pointed to a sliver of light overhead. The moon had begun moving out of the earth's shadow.

"Come," whispered Mishra. "We will invoke Mahadev's blessings for Govinda's soul."

The distraught Brahmins made their way to the Shiva temple, which was now empty. Inside Varanasi's holiest sanctum, Ananta wept. The lunar eclipse was indeed the darkest night of his life.

"Bring blankets," came a soft voice from behind. Startled, the pundits turned around, unaware that there was anyone else in the temple. Standing behind them was the yogi, Govinda's limp body in his arms.

"Jal Swami?" asked Mishra, rising to his feet.

"Some blankets?" repeated the yogi. Pundit Mishra hurried off, returning with blankets which he spread on the floor. Jal Swami laid the body on a cotton cloth, face down. Ananta grimaced at the sight of the rounds that had penetrated deep into Govinda's back.

"Secure the doors," instructed the yogi. Mishra moved quickly to the entrance and locked it.

"Bring *vibhuti* from the lingam, and collect a pot of offered water."

Ananta removed the paste from the Shiva stone while Mishra collected water from the *yoni*. Ananta placed the paste in the yogi's hand and waited.

Mixing the ash with water, the yogi rubbed the paste on wounds that cut deep into Govinda's back. Like a skilled physician, the yogi tended the injuries. He turned the body over, spreading the mixture over the shoulder and across Govinda's forehead. Ananta lowered his head in prayer.

Jal Swami reached for the pot of water, sprinkling it first on Govinda's head and then over his heart before pouring the remainder on Govinda's feet.

"Swamiji, please bring him back," pleaded Ananta.

"That is for Govinda to decide. I have made it possible for him to return if that be his wish."

"Then he could decide not to return?" asked Mishra.

The Tale of the Himalayan Yogis

"Govinda is a wise soul. If you want him to return, tell him."

Jal Swami opened his hand. In it was the pouch containing the Idol's Eye. Removing the diamond, the yogi placed it on Govinda's chest. He gently blew on the gem while rubbing Govinda's forehead.

"Govinda must be more vigilant," said Jal Swami. "I found the gem lying on the floor of the Durga temple. Otherwise, this could not have happened."

Ananta continued praying.

"Chant the Shiva mantra," instructed Jal Swami. The yogi began the chant, and the pundits followed along. Again and again, they repeated the life-giving mantra. The vigil continued late into the night until a knock came on the temple door.

"It's Nitin."

Mishra looked questioningly at Jal Swami, who nodded. Mishra got up and opened the door.

"The news has reached the palace," Mishra's nephew informed them. "Raja Rao sent me to find out if the rumors are true."

Nitin looked down at Govinda's lifeless body.

"Tell Rajaji that his daughter should pray," replied Jal Swami. "But do not wait until morning. Rajaji should inform his daughter as soon as you reach the palace."

"But Leela's asleep. She doesn't yet know what has happened."

"Jal Swami requests that he tell his daughter without delay. Rajaji will understand."

Nitin departed without another word. Ananta and Mishra resumed their chant until the yogi held up a hand.

"Enough... now we wait."

The hours crawled by until a neighborhood cock broke the silent vigil.

"Take the body to the Ganges," instructed Jal Swami as if he had been waiting for the cock's signal. "Can you secure a bier?"

"There will be one at the widow's quarters," said Mishra.

"Bring a fresh cloth to cover the body."

The pundits retrieved the supplies and returned. Jal Swami placed the Idol's Eye in the pouch and handed it to Ananta, who secured it in his robes. Lifting the body onto the bamboo stand, they covered it with the cloth. The pundits carried the bier to the river's edge where the fires smoldered. A pack of dogs sniffed the ashes in search of food.

"Submerge the body, bier and all," instructed Jal Swami, who waded in ahead of the bier. "No one must see him!"

The pundits pushed the bamboo frame under the water and waited for the next instruction. When none came, they looked up to find that the yogi had vanished.

Expecting Jal Swami to reappear, the Brahmins waited, but there was no sign of the yogi or Govinda's body. Some distance away, Mogul soldiers tied rocks to the ankles of one of their own. They too were submerging a body in the river.

"We should return to the temple," decided Mishra. "The doors will open soon."

After washing their feet, the pundits stepped into the inner sanctum of the temple. Entering first, Ananta froze in mid-stride. Govinda was placing a *bilva* leaf on the lingam.

"Jal Swami did it!" exclaimed Mishra.

The two men ran to Govinda.

"What did Jal Swami do?" asked Govinda sheepishly.

"You mean you don't know?" asked Ananta.

"Know what? I've just been sitting here."

"Then you never saw Jal Swami?"

"I've wanted to see him ever since you mentioned his name."

"Amazing!" said Mishra, shaking his head.

"Do you remember anything?" asked Ananta.

"About the fight with Zaim?"

"Yes, what do you remember about the fight?"

"I remember rolling down the hill with Zaim on top of me. He stabbed me in the shoulder, but I got out from under him. Zaim's men were about to fire, and so I jumped into the river. As I hit the water, I felt excruciating pain in my spine. I couldn't move or breathe... my lungs filled with water. Then everything shifted. I saw myself lying in the water, but I wasn't in the water. I saw soldiers come for the body... my body. Then they appeared and took me away."

"Who took you away?" asked Mishra.

"I can't say for sure, but they took me to a mountaintop where we meditated in the snow. I could see everywhere from the mountain. I saw myself at the center of a vast universe. Stars and planets swirled around me. Somehow, I was the cause of it all. Then I heard voices. I heard Ananta… and others asking me to come back. But I didn't want to return. What was there to return too? I was everything there ever was or ever would be.

"Then one of the beings took me into her lap and showed me many things. She showed me Pitaji and Mataji and you and all the good people from Krishnagarh. Then she asked if I loved these people. I said, 'Yes, of course.' She said that if I chose to return, one day I would be their king. I told her that I wasn't sure I wanted to be a king. That's when I heard Leela. She was sitting on the roof in front of Krishna. Tears were streaming down her cheeks. That's the last thing I remember."

"The temple will open soon," Mishra reminded the others. "The last thing Jal Swami said was, 'No one must see him.'"

"You keep mentioning Jal Swami," said Govinda.

"You owe your life to Jal Swami," explained Mishra. "Well, I suppose it was your choice to return, but Jal Swami repaired your body. The Moguls had damaged it beyond all hope without his intervention."

"I've heard about yogis breathing life into a corpse."

"We chanted all night," said Mishra. "Your body was lying on those blankets." Mishra pointed at the still-damp blankets nearby. "At sunrise, Jal Swami had us submerge the body… your body… into the Ganges. That was the last we saw of him."

"Jal Swami found this in the Durga temple," said Ananta, handing Govinda the pouch containing the Idol's Eye.

"How did the Idol's Eye get there?" wondered Govinda. He examined the pouch and found the severed cord. Then he remembered Zaim's sword and how it had nearly severed his neck.

"Come, the temple is about to open."

Govinda followed Mishra to his quarters. The senior priest washed and put on a fresh dhoti.

"The pundits will continue at Kala Bhairav though they must

not know you're alive," cautioned Mishra. "Varanasi is overrun with Moguls."

"But won't it seem odd for the pundits to perform the ritual for someone who they think is dead?"

"It's done for the deceased all the time," said Mishra.

"I'll stay with Govinda," suggested Ananta. "He'll need a meal and some rest."

"I have a plan that may solve all our problems," smiled Mishra mischievously.

After his meal, Govinda fell into a long, dreamless slumber. It had been days since scenes of brutality hadn't tormented his sleep.

When he awoke, Mishra was hovering over him, examining Govinda's shoulder.

"Amazing!" Mishra exclaimed. "The dagger went in here, but there's barely a scar. Roll over."

Govinda flopped onto his stomach.

"The rounds went in here, here, and here."

"The scars are scarcely noticeable," observed Ananta.

"I guess the scars are proof that I died," chuckled Govinda. "Who would believe such an unlikely tale?"

"It's all arranged," Mishra announced happily.

"What's arranged?" wondered Govinda.

"Your exile, of course."

"My exile?"

"You mean you've already forgotten about Black Moon and your years in exile?"

"I haven't forgotten," said Govinda, rolling onto his side and gazing out a window. "I'm just not sure I believe in these predictions anymore."

"Think about what has happened," Ananta reminded him. "Don't you recall Shastri's warning?"

"Shastri cautioned you not to fight your battle," Mishra pointed out. "He said it would mean certain death."

"His exact words were, 'During a lunar eclipse, danger is greatest. You may even die,'" recalled Govinda.

"Isn't that exactly what happened?" asked Mishra.

"I suppose so."

"You have little choice but to go into exile," insisted Ananta.

"But now that I'm dead, Zaim will return to Delhi."

"Zaim's shrewd," cautioned Ananta. "He knows a yogi intervened. He'll be wondering if the yogi somehow saved you."

"But if Jal Swami is that powerful, why didn't he intervene before the soldiers attacked me?"

"Because you insisted on fighting your battle," Mishra explained. "If you hadn't, maybe he would have helped."

"When Zaim threatened Mataji, I forgot everything and ran up the hill after him."

"Shastriji warned you to stay in the cave temple," said Ananta, recalling the astrologer's words.

"I tried, but the Moguls found me. I didn't fight; I ran away. Fortunately, the snake yogi saved me. I was hiding in his cave when Zaim found me. One of his men attacked the yogi, and the cobras killed him."

"Ouch!" grimaced Mishra. "So that's why the Moguls were submerging one of their men in the river."

"Shankar Baba advised them to do it," explained Govinda.

"When a man dies of a cobra bite, his body is submerged in a river."

"Why is that?"

"We cremate the dead because fire purifies the body, but when a man dies of a cobra bite, the venom itself is said to purify the body. There's no need to burn it."

"I hardly know what to believe anymore," Govinda confessed.

"Since coming to Varanasi, you've changed," observed Ananta.

"I suppose dying will do that to a person," laughed Govinda.

"Even before you died. You've grown up these past few days."

"Mishra, what's the plan?" asked the prince.

"I know some Tibetan lamas. I spoke to *Rinpoche* this afternoon. He's an old friend who has been coming to Varanasi for years. The lamas will be returning to Tibet in a few days. I think you should join them."

Govinda took on a faraway look.

"I'm quite sure I was just in Tibet."

"What do you mean?"

"When I died, those beings took me to Mount Kailash. Isn't that in Tibet?"

"Yes, but who were those beings?" asked Mishra.

"Shiva and his consort."

"Shiva and Parvati?" asked Mishra sheepishly.

"What was Mount Kailash like?" asked Ananta.

"The mountain is buried in snow, but since I didn't have a body, I didn't feel the cold."

Ananta and Mishra pondered the strangeness of Govinda's words.

"It is your body that we're trying to protect," Mishra gently reminded Govinda.

"I could go to Jodhpur and live with Raja Rao's family."

Ananta shook his head. "If Zaim found out, the entire imperial army would descend on Jodhpur Palace."

"I'm like a leper. Wherever I go, people could catch my disease."

"I think you should consider going with the lamas," said Mishra earnestly. "They're good people."

"They're monks aren't they?"

"Rinpoche suggested disguising you as one of them. It would mean shaving your head and wearing robes."

"But we Rajputs never cut our hair!" objected Govinda.

"Exile means giving up some things. In any case, you are safe in this room for a few days, but you can't move around Varanasi. The Moguls are everywhere. This morning I spotted Zaim's men standing guard on the bluff. He'll wreck a few temples before he goes. He finds it amusing."

"I should have killed him when I had the chance."

"That's not the way to talk," reprimanded Ananta.

"Someone needs to rid India of the scourge. Fortunately, Mataji is safe."

"Why do you say that?" asked Ananta.

"I forgot to mention it. Shiva's consort showed me. Maa's not in the Mogul camp after all. She's in the queen's palace in Delhi. Maa has a cook and servants looking after her."

The Tale of the Himalayan Yogis

"Then my prayers have been answered."

For three days, Govinda spent much of his time lying on a mat or meditating in the temple at night after the doors were locked.

"I can't go on hiding here forever," Govinda announced as he stuffed a paratha smothered in mango pickle into his mouth.

Mishra pulled a cup of chai from his lips. "Then you'll join the lamas?"

"I'd like to meet Rinpoche."

"Good, because they're leaving for Sarnath tomorrow."

"I thought they were going to Tibet."

"They're meeting some lamas in Sarnath before heading to Tibet."

"How many lamas are there?"

"I don't know exactly, but a few are your age. Finish your parathas, and I'll take you to meet the head lama."

"I've never met a lama before."

"You'll like them. They never stop laughing."

Donning pilgrims' garb, Mishra and Govinda walked along the same narrow footpaths where Govinda had fled the Moguls. Along the way, they passed a figure of a Laughing Buddha. The sight of the statue somehow made Govinda feel better about joining the lamas.

Finally, they reached their destination, a Buddhist temple at the edge of the city. The pagoda's tiered structure was graceful like the limbs of a conifer. Mishra ushered the young fugitive inside. Varanasi's footpaths seemed even more chaotic when compared with the serene space within the temple.

Govinda knew almost nothing about Tibet or its religion, but he took note of the meticulous care given to the building. He especially liked the golden Buddha at the far end of the shrine room.

"Rinpoche Choden?" Mishra asked the manager.

The man tilted his head to the left, which meant the rinpoche was in the garden where he often meditated. Mishra led Govinda outside where they approached a round-faced Tibetan strolling among the flowering bushes, his hands folded behind him. The lama's head shaved, he wore burgundy robes and a warm smile.

"Namaskar, Rinpoche," greeted Mishra.

"Namaskar," replied the rinpoche. "You bring friend."

"This is Prince Govinda,"

"Mishraji say good thing about Prince Govinda."

"And about you," Govinda replied. "Thank you for offering to take me to Tibet."

"Then you join caravan?"

"If you allow me," replied Govinda. "When do you depart?"

"Sunrise. Lamas walk dawn to dusk then take *tsampa* before sleeping."

"Tsampa?" frowned Govinda.

Rinpoche Choden laughed heartily. "Roasted barley best food for Tibetan."

"How far is Tibet?"

"With good weather, we make Annapurna before winter."

"Annapurna?" asked Govinda.

"Holy Nepal mountain. We spend winter at Yurpa Gompa… then Tibet in spring."

"It sounds like Tibet is far away."

"Tibetan like walking," chuckled the rinpoche.

"I wish I could say the same. We Rajputs prefer horses."

"Horse popular in Tibet, but horse no good on mountain. Only yak and mule good in Himalaya."

"It must be cold in the mountains."

"Very cold," shuddered the lama. "Lama no feel cold."

"I have seen the snow peaks."

"You have seen Himalaya?"

"In a dream," Govinda explained, realizing how ridiculous he sounded.

"Dream vision, good vision," assured the lama, his eyes twinkling magically. "Tibetan believe in dream. All lama make dream travel. Lama use magic body to visit Land of Pure Bliss. Buddha-land beyond this," said the rinpoche waving his hand at the land and sky.

"Do yogis go there?"

"Yogis, lamas… many good souls go to Land of Pure Bliss."

Turning to Mishra, Govinda said, "I want to join the lamas."

"It's the best thing," Mishra agreed. "You'll be safe with the lamas… and happy!"

The Tale of the Himalayan Yogis

"What about costume?" asked the cheerful abbot.

"Costume?" asked Govinda.

"Your disguise," clarified Mishra. "Rinpoche wants to know if his man should shave your head and cut robes for you."

"I suppose it's a good idea."

"Head shave, good idea," grinned Rinpoche Choden. "Make person humble."

"Shave it, then," Govinda agreed.

"My man bring dagger."

"Dagger?"

Rinpoche Choden examined Govinda's scarred shoulder.

"Manager say you fight soldiers. You brave boy!"

"Foolish is the word."

"Govinda already humble. No need to shave head, but we shave anyway."

The head lama disappeared from the garden. When he returned, he was laughing at a joke he seemed to be telling himself. The good-natured fellow reminded Govinda of the Laughing Buddha they had seen along the way. A thickset lama carrying a dagger followed the rinpoche. The newcomer's neck was as wide as his jaw. Govinda, who was of average height, towered over the lama.

"Squat," ordered the newcomer as the head lama watched over his shoulder. Govinda sat on his heels, wincing as the lama's dagger glided across his forehead. Govinda's dark locks tumbled to the ground in orphaned bunches.

"Stand," ordered the Tibetan. Holding a piece of cloth up to Govinda's waist, the lama wrapped it around his torso and laid a second cloth across his shoulder.

"Wait," instructed the taciturn lama, who marched off to the guesthouse.

"He doesn't have much to say," observed Govinda.

"Tingpo speak little," said Rinpoche Choden. "He observe Buddhist vow. No speak mindless words."

"You mean he's always like that?" asked Govinda, shaking his head, which felt almost weightless.

"Three years, Tingpo no speak."

"Why?" asked Mishra, who had trouble keeping quiet for even a few minutes.

"Special vow," replied Rinpoche Choden. Suddenly, the abbot burst into laughter, causing his body to spasm with delight.

"Vow of silence… like yogis make?" asked Mishra.

Govinda ran his hand across the crown of his head and grimaced. "Now I know how sheep feel."

Again, laughter filled the garden, but this time it was Mishra, whose bulbous paunch convulsed. "*Hari*! You look like the Buddha himself."

Rinpoche Choden ran a gentle hand over Govinda's shiny skull. "Govinda make fine lama."

The burly barber-tailor trotted back into the garden, Govinda's disguise in hand.

"Remove cloth," he instructed.

Govinda carefully took out the pouch containing the Idol's Eye before removing his kurta and pants. A moment later, wrapped in burgundy, he was scarcely distinguishable from the lamas in the garden. He stuffed the pouch inside his robes. Rajput or Tibetan, the Idol's Eye was his heart and soul.

"Govinda, one of us," proclaimed Rinpoche Choden, adjusting the cloth over Govinda's shoulder.

"Mishra want robe?" teased the abbot.

Mishra's lips formed a mischievous grin. "I'm considering it." Turning to Govinda, he said, "The caravan leaves in the morning. It is better if you stay with the lamas tonight."

"I have someone I want to see first," replied Govinda.

"It's not safe," cautioned Mishra, his playful mood turning serious. "Even with your robes, they might recognize you."

"I send Dolmo with Govinda," suggested the rinpoche. "Dolmo revered lama."

"After yourself, of course," corrected Mishra.

"Dolmo advanced soul. When Dolmo little boy, I take sandals and walking stick to Dolmo's home to see if he recognize from previous birth. Dolmo choose without hesitation."

The rinpoche summoned Lama Dolmo.

"If one of the lamas accompanies you, no one will suspect anything," agreed Mishra. "Keep your head covered. You don't exactly look Tibetan, you know."

"I'm going to Jodhpur Palace."

"Remind the family to keep the secret. We can't have their servants knowing that you're alive."

The rinpoche returned with the young lama. Govinda liked his companion immediately.

"Dolmo, how long have you been a lama?" Govinda asked as they left the garden.

"I am small when Rinpoche find me."

"He took you from your family?"

"Family happy for me. Rinpoche tell parents many lifetime I am lama."

"But don't you miss your family?"

"I visit family. What about you? Rinpoche say your father is king."

"My father was a king. He died fighting the Moguls."

"Father happy," said Dolmo innocently.

"My father is dead," repeated Govinda, thinking the young lama had misunderstood.

"I understand," said Dolmo, taking Govinda by the hand. "Father happy."

"Why do you say that?" asked Govinda as they navigated the tangle of paths leading to the river.

"Because soul happy in Land of Pure Bliss."

"Do you like India?" asked Govinda. He was not in the mood to talk about his father's soul.

"Gautama Buddha live here. Tibetan like making pilgrimage to India."

"But the Moguls have ruined it."

"Mogul empire little thing. Land of Pure Bliss big thing."

"Never let me forget that," said Govinda.

"You not forget. You lama now." Dolmo's puppy-like eyes gazed innocently at Govinda.

"We're almost to the palace," said Govinda. As they turned onto a broader path, riders forced them to the side. At the head of the cavalry rode Commander Zaim.

"Out of the way… move out of the way," ordered a junior officer, who rode at Zaim's side. The road was packed with pilgrims bargaining with merchants for copper pots used to carry Ganges water back to their villages. Seeing his nemesis, Govinda looked away.

As Zaim passed, Govinda heard the commander grumble, "I detest these Hindu holy men. I shall pay a visit to that yogi with the snakes."

The loathing in Zaim's voice caused Govinda to tighten his grip on Dolmo's hand. The young lama glanced calmly at his new friend.

The Moguls passed, and Govinda and Dolmo soon reached Jodhpur Palace. Raja Rao welcomed the young lamas into the palace, unaware of Govinda's disguise.

"Rajaji," began Govinda, "I have come to see Leela."

A confused look creased Raja Rao handsome face. Why had a lama come to see his daughter? Examining the lama at his door more closely, Raja Rao smiled knowingly.

"Come," he said, leading his guests into the study. The king instructed an attendant to inform his daughter that visitors had come to see her and then closed the door.

"Nitin has explained everything," said Raja Rao. "It's the most extraordinary tale I've ever heard."

"Does Leela know?" asked Govinda shyly.

"I didn't want to tell her, but when Nitin returned with instructions from Jal Swami, I informed her immediately. It was quite a burden for a tender heart, as you might imagine."

"Then she knows the full story? What Jal Swami did and everything?"

"It has taken its toll. Leela hasn't talked much… or danced since she heard the news."

"Mishraji came up with the disguise," said Govinda, plucking at the sleeve of his robe. "I'll be leaving for Tibet in the morning."

"The Moguls destroyed two more temples. They would have destroyed Kashi Vishwanath, but the nagas were inside. The nagas killed a dozen soldiers before the Moguls fled the temple. The shop owners say the Moguls are offering gold to anyone who knows anything about Jal Swami."

"Do you think Zaim suspects that I'm alive?"

"He's worried that Jal Swami has intervened somehow."

"I don't mind Zaim having a few sleepless nights. We just passed him on the road. He muttered something about having his revenge on the snake yogi."

"Foolish man! If Zaim is worried about Jal Swami, then he has no idea what he's in for should he go after Shankar Baba," said Raja Rao. "Leela's in the garden. Dolmo and I will have chai here in the study."

As Govinda reached the door, he turned.

"Rajaji, I have no right to ask this… but promise that you won't arrange Leela's marriage while I'm away."

Smiling, Raja Rao replied, "Leela's mother and I have known since the night Leela danced in the garden."

"Then you aren't opposed to the idea?"

"Not at all! Your father and I were friends. Leela is a princess, and you are a prince. When you return from your exile, you are to be king of not only Krishnagarh but of Bundi as well. Your legend is second to none among Rajputs, and well known to the people of Varanasi too. Why would I oppose the idea of your marriage to Leela?"

"I seem to attract trouble."

"The trouble that you attract is not your doing. I want Leela to be happy, and I doubt she would be happy if I arranged her marriage to anyone but you. Now go and see if she agrees with me; that is an important point that we must not overlook."

Govinda climbed the stairs awkwardly in his new robes. His shaven head covered, he stepped onto the roof where he found Leela gazing at the river below.

"Souls come and go quickly down there," said Govinda, standing behind her.

Leela spun around; her eyes widened in amusement.

"Nitin told Pitaji you might have to wear a disguise."

"What do you think?"

"I'm not sure you're meant to be a monk if that's what you're asking," she giggled.

"I'm quite sure I'm not."

"Nitin told us about your exile. Seven years is a long time!"

"I've been thinking of everything that's happened since the day I met Shastriji."

"Then you'll be leaving," frowned Leela.

"I will, but that's not the prediction on my mind. Shastri said that I would meet a girl as devoted as Sita. I'm pretty sure I've already met her."

"You have?" Leela asked warily.

"Yes, and her father has promised not to marry her until I return."

"Oh, Govinda!" she shrieked. Leaping into his arms, Leela hugged him with all her strength, causing Govinda's robes to slide off his shaven head.

"When Nitin came with the news that you were dead, I was sure I would die too."

"You're the reason I came back," replied Govinda. "I was off on a mountain somewhere when I heard your voice. The next thing I knew; I was sitting in the temple."

"I prayed that you wouldn't die, but they said the Moguls had killed you."

"Can you wait seven years?" he asked.

"It won't be easy."

"Ram and Sita wandered in the forest for fourteen years."

"But that's different," she replied. "They spent their exile together. What if you never come back?"

"Shastriji said the Black Moon lasts seven years. He said that when it ends, I'll inherit a kingdom and live happily for the rest of my life."

"You're just making up the last part," teased Leela.

"I'm not. I'm going to be a famous king with a devoted wife."

"But you're already famous."

"Infamous in some people's minds," he said.

"Forget about those Moguls."

"I'm trying to, but they keep appearing. Just now I saw Zaim on the street. Fortunately, he didn't recognize me."

"You look funny with your head shaved."

Govinda rubbed his head self-consciously.

The Tale of the Himalayan Yogis

"Where will you go?"

"Tibet."

"How will you get there?"

"We'll walk."

"But Rajputs never walk anywhere," she teased.

"We'll be crossing the Himalaya. It's cold, and it snows on those mountains. They rise above the clouds, you know."

"Why not come to Jodhpur? It's not cold there. The sun shines in my window every morning."

"I suggested it, but the others are against it. They say the Moguls would attack your father's fort. It was terrible what they did to Krishnagarh."

"Will you take me to Krishnagarh one day?"

"If you'd like. I plan to rebuild it," said Govinda wistfully.

"After you become a famous king?"

"It's my ancestral home. I owe it to Pitaji to rebuild it."

"What about Mataji?"

"She is safe, but still I worry about her."

"Do you worry about me?"

"No!"

"You don't?" Leela's expression turned to one of disappointment.

"I know you can take care of yourself."

"Maa thinks I'm too independent."

"We're similar in that way," said Govinda.

"As long as you don't become a hermit."

"I've only just put on these robes, and already I'm feeling confined. I wish we could ride Kalki together. I'd like to do that before I go, but Kalki is the only white stallion in Varanasi. If the Moguls spotted him, we'd be starting all over with them."

"Pitaji has a fine stable. We could take one of his horses."

"I have a better idea: After dinner, I'll play the flute for you."

"That's a much better idea," agreed Leela.

"I wish you could come to Tibet with me."

"Maa wouldn't approve. She didn't even want me to go to the Marwar Festival."

"Princesses have rules to follow."

"And princes don't?"

"Tonight is my last night in Varanasi."

"Let's not talk about that," decided Leela. "It will spoil the evening."

"Come, I want you to meet Dolmo. I think Dolmo is a *Bodhisattva*."

"I think *you're* a Bodhisattva."

"Hardly," he laughed. "If you saw me fighting with Zaim the other night, you'd think I was mad."

"Who says a Bodhisattva can't be a little crazy?" she laughed.

"I suppose you're right. The lamas spend most of their time laughing."

"Then you'll fit right in."

"Except for the tsampa!" he replied.

"… and the walking."

"I wish I could take Kalki."

"Why don't you?"

"Rinpoche Choden says only mules and yak can cross the Himalaya."

"If a horse can't make it across those mountains, how will you?"

"Good question."

Although everyone was keen to know the details of Govinda's miraculous recovery, no one dared to ask about it, for Leela's family knew that their guest would be in great danger if word spread that he was alive.

After dinner, Leela slipped out of the room, returning with a kurta, dhoti, and turban in hand. She had changed into a rose *choli* and sapphire skirt that reached the floor. A pair of silver bangles tinkled as she walked.

"Here, put these on," she said, handing Govinda the clothes. "If you're going to play Krishna's flute, you should look like him."

"You don't like my robes?"

"Your robes are fine, but they don't go with Krishna's flute."

Govinda changed into the yellow dhoti and then led Leela to the rooftop balcony overlooking the Ganges. The sultry nights that followed the monsoon had passed, ushered away by breezes sweeping down from the Himalaya.

As the Ganges reached the fabled City of Light, it took an uncharacteristic turn to the north between the Varana and Asi rivers, an anomaly that lent still greater auspiciousness to India's holiest river. Varanasi had flourished for millennia, weathering invasions more destructive than those wrought upon it by the imperial army.

"Ever since Pitaji brought us here when I was little, I've watched the river from this spot. At night, when the fires dance on the water, you can enter a different world."

"Ananta says the ghats burn day and night," Govinda replied, peering at the fires consuming shrouded bodies stretched out atop mounds of sandalwood.

"Nitin says they burn a hundred bodies every day."

"I was almost one of them," replied Govinda, recalling the night of the eclipse.

"Show me where the rounds struck."

Govinda removed the shawl.

"Mishra says there are three scars."

"Here's one," said Leela, touching it with her finger. "Here's another… and here. Do they hurt?"

"Not at all. Jal Swami is a fine physician. And then there's this." Govinda pointed to his shoulder.

"What happened there?"

"Zaim missed with his dagger. He was aiming for my heart."

"His dagger went in there?"

"He has bad eyes," he joked. "And he's a poor horseman."

"What does that have to do with him stabbing you?"

"It's a long story."

"We have all night."

Sparing no details, Govinda recounted his bold escape from Krishnagarh and his encounter with Zaim during the eclipse. When he finished, Leela leaned over the balcony.

"The swirling water inspires me to dance. I watch the river for hours at a time. It's my meditation."

"Krishna played his flute on the banks of the Yamuna."

"Will you play for me?" asked Leela.

"If you like. Here's something Krishna played for his gopis."

Govinda touched the *bansari* to his forehead before placing it to his lips. Caressing the hollowed reed, Govinda coaxed from it a lilting melody. The instrument's simple tune spread, mingling with the breeze on the bluff and river below. The song journeyed into the night.

Like a boat set free, Leela drifted on the enchanting currents flowing from Govinda's soul. Blissful waves cascaded along her spine as she floated onto her toes. Spinning slowly at first, she moved about the balcony, her spirit soaring above the river. Up she rose into the velvet sky as Govinda's fingers moved playfully about the flute.

Ecstatic currents now coursed through Leela's lissome body. Her hands formed *mudras;* her hair was swept about by Govinda's sweet breath. Round and round she spun as if ascending a spiral staircase to the stars. Her *bhava* stole her breath, and she collapsed to the marble, captive to Krishna's hypnotic melody.

The song ended and another filled the night. Govinda played on as Leela spun rapturously about in perfect rhythm with the notes. Govinda's music now possessed her soul as she danced, eyes closed, her vision fixed on heaven.

Moving to the center of the balcony, Govinda played as Leela moved about him the way Krishna's milkmaids circled their lover. Leela touched Govinda's feet. Then, rising to her feet like a windswept wave, the graceful dancer's head fell back as she spun, surrendering to the flute's tender caress. Her outstretched arms reached for heaven; her fingers plucked at her heart. Leela's chest heaved, her feet moved feverishly about the balcony. Intoxicated, she danced on.

The indigo night flowed by with the Ganges. Now tranquil, the young lovers dreamily watched the current glide past the balcony.

"I never danced like that before," whispered Leela.

"I never played like that before."

"You're magnificent."

"It's you who are magnificent," replied Govinda, drying Leela's forehead with his shawl.

"Tonight will sustain us," she whispered.

"For seven years?"

"Forever! My soul knows yours… I can find you anytime."

"Then Shastriji almost had it right," said Govinda, recalling his words.

"What do you mean?"

"He said I'd find my Sita… but I've found my Radha."

"But Radha never married Krishna."

"I've found *my* Radha. I can marry my Radha if I wish to… and if she wishes too, of course."

"Then I've found my Krishna… and of course, I wish to marry you."

Govinda pulled Leela close.

"I have something for you," he whispered, folding Leela's fingers around a peacock fashioned from lapis and jade.

"It's beautiful!"

"It's Krishna's favorite."

"Make a wish," said Leela.

"I wish that when I open my eyes in the morning, the exile will be over," he said wistfully.

"Time means nothing now. But you should sleep. You've never walked from sunrise to sunset before."

"I've never walked anywhere before."

"Do you want to know a secret? When Narayani makes me do those drills for hours at a time, I chant my Krishna mantra. It turns everything into bliss."

"Ananta taught me a Krishna mantra."

"Then chant it while you walk."

"Even with a Krishna mantra, it's going to be a long journey."

"But a bowl of tsampa will be waiting for you at the end of the day," she giggled.

"You'd make a better lama than me. You're the one who's always giggling."

"I think this exile is going to be harder for you than for me," she decided.

"Of course it will, you're not even going into exile."

"When you're cold… or tired… or lonely… know that I'm in there," Leela whispered, pressing her finger against Govinda's heart.

"I know… I hear you giggling."

The Emperor's Harem

Prisms of golden light appeared on the horizon. Dolmo touched Govinda's shoulder, but the Rajput didn't stir. The young lama pressed his friend's shoulder again. The reality that Govinda was about to begin his exile slowly seeped into his awareness as he rose from his slumber.

Without his friend's help, the unwieldy mound of burgundy cloth would never have found its way onto Govinda's body.

"Come," said Dolmo. "First tsampa… then walking."

"Tsampa in the morning too?" asked Govinda, rolling his eyes amiably.

"Tsampa give strength."

"How does it taste?"

"Tsampa best food for lama."

Govinda was not expecting Leela to be awake.

"Have Krishna's blessings before you go," she whispered.

Taking Govinda by the hand, Leela led her guests to the rooftop shrine where she dotted their foreheads with sandal paste from a bowl at Krishna's feet.

"Pitaji asked me to give you this. It's a gift for the lamas. And I have something for you. It will keep you warm when you cross the mountains."

Leela presented Govinda a buttery ring shawl woven from the chin hairs of a goat, her initials embroidered at the corner.

"Perfect," said Govinda. "We must carry everything and the shawl weighs less than the hair I used to have."

"Give good warmth," agreed Dolmo.

"Nitin asked me to give you this," said Leela, handing Govinda a bag of herbs. "He said it's from a yogi."

At the palace gates, Govinda and Leela shared a moment to sustain them until his exile ended.

"Today we reach Sarnath," said Dolmo, quickening his pace.

The Mishras were waiting when they arrived at the pagoda.

"Namaste, Anantaji," greeted Govinda.

"Govinda… is it you?" marveled Ananta. "I recognize your voice, but nothing more."

"Good disguise, don't you think?"

"If Ananta doesn't recognize you, surely the Moguls won't," smiled Mishraji.

"From today, I'm Lama Govinda from Longtong. How is Kalki, by the way?"

"Lonely," replied Ananta.

"Take Kalki to the Aravali Hills and set him free so that he can join the herd when it passes through."

"News of your death will travel fast," said Ananta, seeking Govinda's advice.

"No one in Bundi, other than Grandfather, must know the truth."

"What about Rani Rukmini?"

"Of course, explain everything to Mataji. I have a letter for her, and one for Hashim too."

He handed Ananta two parchments sealed with the stamp of the Raja of Jodhpur.

"Hashim can be found in Delhi at Haus Khaz where he studies with the Brahmin, Ramlal. If you don't find him there, go to an abandoned shrine in a place called Gaziapur to the south of the city. Hashim's grandfather lives there. His name is Mumtaz Aalim. Tell no one other than Hashim."

The Tale of the Himalayan Yogis

Mishra nodded emphatically. "Raja Rao's family and Nitin know, but no one else in Varanasi... except, of course, Jal Swami."

"I owe Jal Swami my life, and I don't even remember him."

"One day you will meet him," Mishra assured him.

"Offer Jal Swami a basket of mangoes for me," said Govinda, placing a coin in Mishra's hand. "Already I miss Rajputana, and my exile hasn't even begun."

"Govinda, your safe return will be my daily *sankalp*," said Ananta.

Ananta reached for Govinda's feet hidden beneath his robes. Govinda pressed his hands together, bidding his friends goodbye before turning to go.

The sunbaked road to Sarnath offered Govinda the chance to distance himself from the tempest that had swirled about him since arriving in Varanasi. Rinpoche Choden and Dolmo walked on either side of him, passing prayer beads through their fingers. Buoyed by the murmur of mantras, the lamas moved as purposefully as the silent stream of pilgrims descending to the Ganges each morning.

It felt good to wear Buddha's cloth and to walk with kindred souls. Govinda's companions tread steadily, gentle souls whose faces shone like beneficent moons.

Buddha is an excellent god, he decided.

Repeating his Krishna mantra, Govinda fingered the Idol's Eye from time to time, his sole link to his Rajput past.

"Brother, Rani Rukmini should be released immediately," insisted Hashim. "Why is Commander Zaim keeping her prisoner in the Moti Mahal?"

"My spies inform me that she was present when the Emperor died," replied Ghazi. "But I agree; she has done nothing to warrant her arrest. It would be a final insult for Zaim to find his prize missing when he returns. I am in favor of ousting the commander as soon as it seems reasonable."

"I favor releasing the Rajput if Zaim captures Prince Govinda."

"That I will not do. The Rajput's mother means nothing, but he is a threat to the Empire. Someone must be held accountable for Father's death. Freeing Govinda would cost me the respect of the generals.

Inside the Moti Mahal, Rukmini spent her days cloistered in her room. One sultry afternoon a knock came on her door. When she did not answer, the door swung slowly open, revealing an immense, muscled, olive-brown eunuch, his head nearly touching the frame above the door.

"Padshah Begum wishes to see you," the giant announced, his gentle speech in sharp contrast to his imposing physique.

"Padshah Begum?"

"Empress Zahira invites you to her apartment," the eunuch clarified.

"But I have nothing to offer."

"I can provide."

Rukmini straightened her sari and pulled the pallu over her head. Reluctantly, she followed the eunuch to Padshah Begum's apartments. The eunuch's size would have been daunting were it not for his exceptional eyes.

"Wait," instructed the eunuch, disappearing into one of the many gardens surrounding the palace. Rukmini stepped onto a veranda overlooking a garden rivaling the size of Krishnagarh's courtyard. Streams cascaded into lotus pools, tempering the oppressive heat. Towering trees shaded teakwood benches flanked by flowering shrubs. Luxuriant swings were attached to the limbs of flowering magnolia trees.

Returning with a handful of jasmine and blue hibiscus, the eunuch offered, "I will present on your behalf."

"It is kind of you," Rukmini replied. "May I ask your good name?"

"I am Bandu," answered the eunuch. "My brother and I look after the harem on behalf of Padshah Begum."

"Padshah Begum was Emperor Shah's wife?"

"One of many, but his favorite after the Emperor's first wife died."

"And his first wife was the mother of Emperor Ghazi?" asked Rukmini.

"That is correct. Emperor Shah also had a son with Empress Zahira. You will meet that son presently."

The Tale of the Himalayan Yogis

"What is his name?"

"His full name is Mohammed Babur Ali Faez Shah Yaman. After Emperor Ghazi, Prince Hashim is next in line for the Peacock Throne, and then Prince Yaman, at least until Emperor Ghazi produces an heir of his own."

The eunuch led Rukmini past indoor fountains and marble ponds stocked with colorful koi. Red and yellow songbirds chirped happily inside gilded cages as Rukmini passed. Parrots and lovebirds with clipped wings perched in the open. Stunningly beautiful women floated past, casting curious glances at the newcomer.

Bandu ushered Rukmini into Padshah Begum's apartments, a pink-veined marble hall furnished with exquisite tapestries, gilded mirrors, Persian carpets, gem-inlaid narcissus pots, and silk-upholstered divans. Eunuchs served sweets and fruit drinks to seemingly bored women leaning against satin pillows.

At the center of the gathering of royal concubines, Empress Zahira reclined on an azure divan, a mountain of pillows propping her up. The Empress' thick ruby lips and masculine chin made her the least attractive woman in the room. A necklace of Hyderabadi pearls softened her features somewhat.

Empress Zahira's hands appeared to be those of another woman; graceful, imaginative, willowy fingers adorned with glittering rubies and diamonds. But the most remarkable aspect of Zahira's appearance was her peach-colored kurta, which was fashioned from Chinese silk and embroidered with jasmine blossoms.

Behind the Empress stood a man who looked like Bandu.

"That is my brother, Itibar Khan," Bandu whispered into Rukmini's ear.

The Empress issued instructions as she examined a stack of documents.

"Tell the Portuguese I expect their cooperation; otherwise their ships will not be allowed into port."

"Yes, Your Majesty," replied Itibar Khan.

Seeing Bandu ushering her guest into the hall, Padshah Begum raised a hand, and Itibar Khan gathered up the documents. The conversations stopped as all eyes focused on the newly arrived guest.

"So you are the legendary Rani Rukmini," said the Empress, inspecting her guest. Inclining her chin slightly, the Empress signaled for a pair of consorts to vacate the divan they shared. The Empress gestured for Rukmini to sit near her.

"It is an honor, Padshah Begum," said Rukmini, taking the consorts' place on the divan.

"You may call me Zahira."

Rukmini nodded to Bandu, who presented the bouquet on her behalf.

"I adore flowers," said Zahira, inhaling the jasmine. "Is your apartment to your liking?"

"It is… thank you for your kindness."

"Bandu will see to your needs. Do not hesitate to advise him in your meal preferences. Our cooks make every conceivable cuisine."

"My needs are few," replied Rukmini.

Noticing that her guest was admiring her garb, the Empress said, "If you stay, one day I will create something for you."

"It is lovely. Do you design your clothes?"

"In fact, most of the gowns that you see are mine." The Empress pointed at several exquisitely attired women. "Safiya, show our guest my most recent creation."

A modest woman rose to her feet, gracefully modeling an aqua *Salwar Kameez* with a narrow Chinese collar. The woman possessed caring, blue-green eyes and pale skin.

"The brocade is superb. Where did you develop such a talent?"

"I have not always lived amidst luxury," revealed Zahira. "My family left Kabul when I was seven. We faced starvation crossing the mountains. When we reached Delhi, I apprenticed as a seamstress to fill my stomach."

"You are a master at your craft."

The Empress smiled briefly and then grew serious.

"Itibar Khan informs me that you witnessed the Emperor's death."

"It is true," nodded Rukmini.

"You need not be apprehensive. It was no secret that Junaid Shah desired you for his harem. I wish to see for myself if my husband died chasing a lie. Remove your scarf so that I may know for myself."

Rukmini let her pallu fall to her shoulders.

"Sadly, I see that my husband was well informed. You are indeed a rare blossom. In time, your bloom will fade, as does every woman. Then you will be forced to rely on cleverness and conversation if you wish to maintain your position."

"I have no position other than at my husband's side."

"But like mine, your husband is dead."

"My wish was to join my husband."

"But you chose not too."

"My son prevented me."

"That would be Govinda, the boy who has outwitted the entire imperial army," laughed the Begum. "Our army is not what it once was."

"They defeated my husband's cavalry."

"Military matters bore me. Tell me, why do Hindu wives carry their loyalty to such extremes?"

"I am not exceptional in any way."

"If we speak of your son, would that not spark a flame in you?" probed Zahira.

"My son has gone to Varanasi with his father's ashes. Your commander aims to capture him."

"Then naturally you are worried for his safety."

"Why must Commander Zaim torment us? My son has done nothing."

"Commander Zaim is no different from any other man. He enjoys his wars and the treasures that accompany them. Without a battle, men grow restless. I cannot help your son. His celebrity has sealed his fate."

"Of what celebrity do you speak?"

"Surely you know that Prince Govinda is a hero among your people... and therefore, a threat to the Empire."

"But Govinda has done nothing."

"It matters little what he has done. What matters is what people believe, and the people believe that your son killed the Emperor."

"But it's not true."

"Then tell me how it happened. I wish to hear how my husband died."

"Even if the telling does not flatter the Emperor?" asked Rukmini hesitantly.

"My husband was a passionate man. These were but a few of the flowers in his garden," said the Empress, waving an indifferent hand at the women in the hall.

"After our army was defeated and our king slain, the Emperor's men laid waste to our fort."

"Your Rajput men rush headlong into battle no matter the odds. Their pride got them killed."

"Their families were without food," countered Rukmini.

"War is a cruel game."

"We do not see it as a game."

"Do you play Pachisi?"

"I played as a child."

"To men like my husband and Commander Zaim, war is no less a game than Pachisi, but we digress. Continue with your story."

"The Emperor entered the queen's temple where we were hiding and removed the diamond from Krishna. He said, 'I have come to claim two prizes, the Idol's Eye and the Queen of Krishnagarh.'"

"You speak as if you were also dead," replied Zahira.

"I died with my husband… only this body goes on breathing, a reminder that my husband died because of it."

"I see… not only are you lovely, but devoted as well. A rare combination… rarer perhaps than the Idol's Eye."

"But you must have the diamond," said Rukmini.

"Why do you say that?" asked Zahira, leaning forward.

"Because Zaim found it."

Empress Zahira's cheeks flushed as she glanced over her shoulder and whispered something to Itibar Khan. The eunuch quickly left the hall.

"You say Zaim has the gem. How do you know that?"

"The Emperor entered the temple on his horse; actually, he was atop my husband's stallion when he fell."

The Tale of the Himalayan Yogis

"Nonsense; the Emperor was a fine horseman," contradicted Zahira.

"I'm sure he was, but his arm was injured. When the horse reared, the Emperor lost his balance and fell."

"… and was impaled on an iron stake. I can see that you are no more capable of deception than I am capable of giving up my position as Padshah Begum."

"I know nothing of deception. I only know the Emperor died instantly and that my son did not kill him."

"But there are stories attributed to your priest that your son caused the horse to rear."

"The Emperor knocked my son to the floor. The horse knew my son and became agitated."

"Then Govinda had a hand in the Emperor's death," decided Zahira. "Zaim will bring him to Delhi where he'll stand trial."

"My son is just fifteen."

Empress Zahira stared at her guest. "How is it that your loveliness sustains itself fifteen years after bearing a child?"

"I was fifteen when my son was born."

"You Hindus marry as mere children."

"I was betrothed at age seven, although I continued to live with my parents for some years. We believe that a girl grows in devotion having known only her husband."

"And what about Rajput men? Are they so devoted?" asked Zahira skeptically.

"I can only speak for my husband. His devotion exceeded my own. He sacrificed his life for me while I have not done as much for him."

"You speak of johar as if it were a sacred act."

"Johar is not easily understood. It is devotion that sanctifies the act."

"I had no choice but to share the Emperor with many women. I cannot say that devotion ever had a chance."

"I am sorry… devotion exceeds everything," replied Rukmini.

"But what about your son? Are you not devoted to him?"

"For him alone I live."

"Then you hope to save your son from Commander Zaim."

"There is little I can do."

"I may be able to help you."

"Please… my son has harmed no one."

"A wound to an officer's pride pains him far more than one to his body. Your son has injured Commander Zaim."

Itibar Khan reentered the room carrying a silver platter on which rested a stunning tiara studded with rubies, emeralds, and diamonds. He whispered into the Empress' ear.

"Krishna's crown," said Rukmini with a sigh. "The Emperor took it from him."

"It was among Zaim's belongings," said Zahira. "But no diamond was found."

Zahira exposed a necklace from within her beautiful silks. Attached to the filigree chain hung a stunning blue diamond.

"Come closer."

Rukmini approached, bending over the Empress' divan.

"It is similar to the Idol's Eye but somewhat smaller in size."

"Krishna's Consort was the Emperor's favorite," explained the Empress.

"I have heard stories that the Idol's Eye had a sister diamond by that name."

"I want you to get the Idol's Eye for me," said Zahira, stroking Krishna's Consort like a pet.

"But I told you, Zaim has it."

"Naïve child. You have watched the world from your palace window. You know nothing of life on the street. If Zaim has the diamond, then you must get it from him."

"To do that I would have to…" replied Rukmini, shaking her head.

"… do what every woman does when she wants something of a man? How do you think I got this?" Zahira caressed Krishna's Consort.

"But I cannot… I will not."

"Even if your son's life depends on it?"

"Please do not bring an innocent child into this. I am unable to think the way you do."

"I do not expect you to think at all, my dear; surely one so beautiful as you possess the instincts to flatter a man."

"I have known only one man, and he desired no flattery."

"Listen to me." The Empress rose from her divan, her dark eyes flashing. "I am trying to save your son's life, but you speak as if you were dull-witted."

"You do not understand what is sacred between husband and wife."

"Tomorrow we shall meet in the garden for a game of Pachisi. For your son's sake, I hope you will have changed your mind."

"My heart will not change, nor would my son want it to."

"Do you not wish to save him?" repeated Zahira.

"May I have permission to take your leave?"

Zahira stared at Rukmini before answering, "Bandu will come for you at the same time tomorrow."

Bandu led his charge back to her apartment, his powerful strides making it difficult for Rukmini to keep up.

"Raniji, do not contradict Padshah Begum. She can strike like a cobra without warning."

Reaching Rukmini's apartment, Bandu said, "I shall send a bearer with a cool drink. A massage might lift your spirits."

"Thank you, Bandu. You are kind."

Rukmini collapsed on her bed, imagining what would be expected of her when Commander Zaim returned.

Having spent the morning contemplating the Empress' offer, Rukmini was expecting the knock. She would do anything to save Govinda.

"The Empress is waiting in the garden," Bandu announced.

Rukmini was still observing her period of mourning and had little desire to spend the afternoon with the Empress, but the possibility that Zahira might intervene on Govinda's behalf offered her a faint ray of hope.

"What interest does the Empress have in me?" she asked the eunuch.

"In the harem, the Empress knows all things. She knows of every quarrel, every unhappiness, every illness among her women. You are new here, a guest of sorts. Empress Zahira finds you intriguing, possibly because the Emperor was fascinated with you."

"But he had never met me."

"These people are different from you. They only know what they want and will dispatch an army to acquire it."

"And Zahira wants the Idol's Eye."

"Apparently, though I cannot say why. You saw the pearls and rubies. Zahira's gems are as plentiful as pebbles by the Yamuna. She dispenses rubies to court nobles like sweets given to well-behaved children."

"The Empress believes the Idol's Eye is special."

"I heard her speak of the diamond with a Hindu sorcerer."

"What did they say about it?" asked Rukmini.

"The sorcerer claimed the Idol's Eye and Krishna's Consort carry extraordinary powers, and that he who possesses both diamonds will rise above all others."

"Legends are unreliable."

"I am an ignorant man, but I listen and learn."

"It seems there are ears everywhere in the Moti Mahal," observed Rukmini.

"Trust no one. There are spies in all places. These people value information more than Hyderabadi pearls."

"Should I not trust you either?" Rukmini knew the answer to her question before she asked it. Bandu's eyes told her that, though he possessed the strength to crush her like a strand of straw, he was guileless.

"Raniji, I am not a Mogul," said the giant. "My brother and I were brought from Tunisia as slaves. We had no choice but to adapt, or be quartered and fed to vultures."

"Then you too know what it feels like to be looked upon as an object to be bartered over."

The Tale of the Himalayan Yogis

"Perhaps that is why I have taken you into my confidence," replied Bandu softly.

"To protect my son, I must submit to the whims of Commander Zaim."

"In the palace, one must adapt. That is the rule. Now we should go; the Empress does not like to be kept waiting."

Bandu escorted Rukmini to the Empress' royal garden where he had picked flowers the previous day.

"I presume the Empress does not like losing at her pastimes?"

"Empress Zahira enjoys her games, and Pachisi is her favorite."

The gardens spread in all directions. Rukmini had not seen the alfresco board built into a flat square of ground. From a path hidden among a profusion of flowering bushes, Safiya approached with a young woman at her side.

"Greetings, Rukmini," said Safiya, extending her hands. "I would like you to meet Nada."

"It is a pleasure," said Rukmini, immediately taken by the beauty of the young woman.

"Come," said Safiya. "The Pachisi game is about to begin."

A towering banyan tree shaded the game board.

"Rani Rukmini has arrived," announced the Empress. "Choose your color. White is not a choice; I would suggest green."

Rukmini sat in the green chair opposite the Empress. She was conscious of her white clothes; the other players dressed according to their game colors.

"Are we playing with teams?" Rukmini asked. Pachisi, she remembered, was typically played with teams.

"Everything has one of two outcomes," said the Empress. "I wish to share neither."

"Are you lucky with the cowries?" Safiya asked Rukmini, gently shaking her shells. Rukmini liked Safiya far more than she did the Empress.

"Not especially," Rukmini replied, fingering her delicate cowries.

"Do you know the rules?" asked Safiya.

"It has been many years. I played Pachisi as a child."

"Then I shall refresh your memory. The strategy is quite simple. In the end, luck determines the outcome."

"I disagree," Empress Zahira broke in. "The game has subtleties that a novice like Safiya does not comprehend."

"You are quite right," agreed Safiya. "Who is our fourth player?"

"Yaman."

Begum Zahira's response drew muffled groans from several of the spectators.

"Yaman is playing today?" asked Safiya, unable to hide her disappointment.

"He needs a diversion; his tutors bore him. Here he comes now. Come, *Bacha*; the pawns have already assembled."

"I'm red!" bellowed the bulbous-skulled youngster clad in fiery red. Pushing his way through the pawns, he plopped onto the red chair at the edge of the game board.

"Let's throw the cowries to see who plays first," suggested the Empress. The players lifted their cowries and tossed them onto their tables.

"I threw *pachis*," Safiya said. "Did anyone else?"

When no one replied, Safiya gathered up her shells and was about to take her turn when Yaman let out an ear-piercing shriek.

"I shall go first!"

"Bacha, Auntie Safiya goes first," the Empress explained. "Then it will be my turn, then yours."

Ignoring his mother, Yaman flung his shells onto his table.

"Nine!" he declared. "Someone advances nine squares!" A red pawn hastily moved down the red column. Yaman leaned forward in his chair, admiring his fast start.

"Go ahead, Rukmini," said the Empress. "It's your turn now."

Rukmini was about to toss her shells when the fidgety prince let out another deafening shriek.

"Wait! I'm taking another turn."

"Bacha, wait your turn!" snapped the boy's mother.

"I'm taking my turn now," the boy decreed, scattering his cowries across his table.

"Yaman, you must play by the rules," scolded the Empress. "Otherwise, it's no fun for the others."

"I'll have as many turns as I like," insisted the pudgy prince, glaring defiantly at his mother.

The game progressed awkwardly with Yaman rolling according to his whim. As a result of his extra turns, the prince's first pawn was about to return to the inner column, ensuring the pawn's safety, when one of Safiya's pawns captured his pawn, sending it back to the starting point.

Seeing his lead pawn shuffling back to its nest, Yaman bellowed, "I don't care if she captured my pawn, it's not going back!"

Thrashing about in his chair, Yaman kicked the ground, throwing up a cloud of dust. Yaman's pawn hesitated, wondering whether the Empress or her son, was more dangerous to disobey.

"Yaman, play by the rules or I'll send for your tutors," threatened the Empress.

"Stupid game," Yaman complained, pushing over his table and scattering his cowries on the ground. "I'm going fishing."

"That will be better. Now calm down. Itibar Khan will bring your spear."

Rukmini wondered what type of fishing the ill-mannered boy intended to do with a spear and looked on apprehensively as the eunuch brought the boy his weapon. Together, the brown-skinned eunuch and his fleshy charge disappeared to a distant corner of the *charbagh*.

Yaman's pawns departed and the Pachisi game resumed with the three women competing. The Empress skillfully maneuvered her pawns past her opponents. Zahira was ushering her last pawn to the finish line when Yaman stormed onto the board, a magnificent blue butterfly koi impaled on his spear. The dying fish wriggled about as Yaman struggled to pull it free.

"I told you not to catch my blue koi," scolded the Empress. Ignoring his mother's admonition, Yaman was ripping the fish from the spear's tip when a band of red-faced monkeys descended onto the game board and made off with the boy's catch. Enraged by the audacious theft of his fish, Yaman charged after the monkeys, waving his spear over his head.

"I wish I could say I sent for those monkeys. Blue butterflies are scarce like blue diamonds," said Zahira, glancing at Rukmini. "Yaman knows they're my favorites."

Empress Zahira's mood brightened as her final pawn arrived safely at the goal.

"Pachisi!" she declared, relishing the muted applause as the game came to a close.

"Good playing!" Rukmini complimented her hostess. Her own pawns had come up just short of winning. "I never knew the game could be played so cleverly."

"Cleverness runs in my family," confessed the Empress. "Bandu, everyone is parched. Summon the *safarchi*. And bring fans; the air in the garden is stifling today."

"As you wish, Padshah," bowed the eunuch.

The Empress' eyes met Rukmini's. "Have you reconsidered?"

"I will do whatever is necessary to protect my son."

"A wise decision… you will not be sorry. Flattering a man, after all, is not so difficult. The Emperor had no intention of presenting me with Krishna's Consort, and so I plied him with opium and wine. I convinced him that the diamond would bring misfortune to an emperor and was only safe in a woman's possession. Men are easily manipulated. Commander Zaim is no different."

"Thank you for the advice, Your Majesty. I see that you are clever at games other than Pachisi. You always seem to win."

"*Always!*" replied Zahira, a wicked grin forming on her lips. Safiya flinched at the Empress' reply.

"The Emperor placed great trust in your judgment," noted Rukmini.

"The Emperor relied on me."

"With good reason."

Itibar Khan, who had been waiting beneath a tamarind tree, stepped forward to discuss a matter of some urgency with the Padshah. The Empress, wanting to impress Rukmini, permitted her guest to listen as she examined a document held by the eunuch.

The Tale of the Himalayan Yogis

A bevy of servants arrived with fruit punch and sweets. The mood in the shaded garden was merry; laughter bubbled from conversations. As servants dispensed chilled goblets of *khus* to the women, Yaman returned from his adventure with the roguish *bandar*.

"Did you catch the rascals that made off with your fish?" inquired his mother.

Yaman did not answer, but attempted to intercept a pair of goblets, spilling one on the Pachisi board.

"Yaman, that's enough!" reprimanded the Empress. "Bandu, summon his tutors."

At the word 'tutors,' Yaman flew into a rage, flinging his half-spilled goblet at his mother's feet. Her gown doused by the punch, Zahira sprang from her chair, a tigress poised for the kill. Seeing his mother on her feet, Yaman raced off in the direction of the monkeys, running as fast as his chubby legs could carry him.

Empress Zahira settled back into her chair.

"Rukmini, you should not feel like a prisoner here in the Moti Mahal," said Zahira. "Many of us spend our entire lives within these walls."

"Bandu looks after my needs. He is most kind."

With Yaman off terrorizing distant parts of the garden, the Empress settled onto a shaded swing, scrutinizing an endless stream of documents; a routine she had become accustomed to when the Emperor was off fighting his wars of expansion.

"Bandu, I'll escort Rani Rukmini to her quarters," suggested Begum Safiya. The gentle eunuch nodded, his giant hands folded behind him.

"May I show you the gardens?"

"More of Zahira's creation?" Rukmini asked, admiring the sprays of lavender, rose, and azure lining the path.

"Zahira has a gift, and she shares it generously, though you would not know it by her personality."

"How long have you lived in the Moti Mahal?" asked Rukmini.

"Fourteen years, but I will be leaving soon."

"Why?"

"I long to return to my beloved Kashmir," confided Safiya.

"How did you end up in the harem in the first place?"

"My ancestors were carpet makers from Persia. My father is known for weaving the finest carpets in Srinagar. One day Father was summoned to the summer palace to present his carpets to the Emperor. He never forgave himself for allowing me to come along, but I was an obstinate child and he a doting father. I was fourteen when Emperor Shah selected me for his harem. My parents were heartbroken, but what could they do? The Emperor's word was law; to disobey him… well… no one considered such a thing."

"You must be miserable in Delhi."

"It is difficult. The women content themselves with mindless entertainment. They watch us continuously."

"So you became one of the Emperor's wives?"

"One of many. For other parents, it was considered a great honor to have their daughter chosen for the harem, but my father has never forgiven himself."

"What was he like?"

"The Emperor had a volatile disposition, but he also had a gentle side. These gardens were his creation. He commissioned merchant vessels to sail to China and Bali to procure songbirds and rare species of flowers."

Peering into a glassy pool, Rukmini sighed.

"The lotuses are lovely… and I've never smelled such fragrant frangipani. May I take some flowers to my room?"

Reaching out, Safiya plucked a handful of delicate blossoms.

"You are all kind," said Rukmini. "I was terrified when the soldiers led me through the palace gates that first day, but now I feel quite safe."

"It pleases me that you are comfortable, but I must warn you that not all are as kind as they would have you believe."

Taking Rukmini by the hand, Safiya led her through the tropical paradise. Torch Ginger, Oleander, and Pagoda Flower flourished beside the walkways. Yawning banyan trees sheltered timid orchids hiding among the trees' buttressed roots. Mango, *amlak*, and orange trees were laden with fruit. The drone of bees and twitter of birds filled the air. The walled paradise was off-limits to men except for

The Tale of the Himalayan Yogis

the Emperor, his brother, and the eunuchs who looked after the concubines.

"I hope you'll stay a while longer," said Rukmini, sensing that she had a friend in Safiya.

"I will not leave immediately, but with the Emperor's death, it is up to me whether I stay or not. Many know no life beyond the Moti Mahal, but Kashmir will always be my home."

"Did you know the twins' mother?"

Safiya sighed deeply. "Kameela was the sister I always wanted. Her kindness made life tolerable when I first came here."

"I'm told she was a fine poet… a woman of grace and wisdom."

"Kameela was the Emperor's favorite. She was both kindhearted and generous. Everyone in the harem loved Kameela, except, of course, Zahira. When Kameela became Padshah Begum, Zahira was tormented by jealousy."

"I should think Zahira would only be happy being the Emperor's favorite."

"Out of jealousy, she poisoned Kameela," whispered Safiya, her eyes darting left and right.

"Zahira did such a thing?"

"And she would do more! I fear for Kameela's sons. Zahira has designs on the Peacock Throne."

"That rascal, Yaman, as Emperor? He could no more rule the Empire than I could spear a fish."

"Yaman is not to blame for his rude behavior. Everyone doted on him when he was little. He had a legion of mothers, but no one looked after him properly. We sought his affection with flattery and sweets. You see the result."

"But Zahira doesn't need Yaman. It seems she rules already."

"Only until Ghazi marries, which will be soon. The Emperor's wife will assume the mantle of Padshah Begum."

"Then Zahira will lose her position?"

"Would… not will. As you have seen, nothing will stop Zahira. She would never be satisfied as a dowager."

"Bandu warned me that Zahira could be ruthless."

"You can trust Bandu to an extent, but he has little choice but to be loyal to Zahira. However, unlike his brother, Bandu has a sense of honor about him. Itibar Khan, on the other hand, is Zahira's henchman. Keep your distance from him! Itibar Khan poisoned Kameela, and there are rumors that he's bloodied his dagger on occasion.

"Bandu and Itibar Khan always reminded me of Ghazi and Hashim… brothers who look almost identical, but whose souls could hardly be more different. It is simply that Bandu and Itibar Khan have less freedom to show their differences since their status is so far below that of Ghazi or Hashim. A person with a great soul could never achieve great status in the Empire, save for rare exceptions, such as Hashim."

"And you," submitted Rukmini.

"If you are suggesting that mine is a great soul, then I must thank you and disagree. And if you are suggesting that mine is a high status, then I must also disagree," replied Safiya.

"There may be those of higher status, but you are a begum."

"There are countless begums. It means that the Emperor desired me, nothing more. Only Padshah Begum holds any real status among the Emperor's wives."

"With so many wives, all chosen out of the Emperor's passion, why are there so few children in the Moti Mahal?"

Safiya waited while a pair of nubile concubines passed them on the path.

"We must be cautious. Zahira does not tolerate this sort of conversation," whispered Safiya. "She sends the children away. She takes no chances that an heir other than Yaman might assume the Peacock Throne."

"Where do they go?"

"There are stories of an abandoned fortress converted into a prison where discarded royals are locked away. The rumors of what takes place there are too horrible to speak of."

"Why did the Emperor allow it? After all, they were his children."

"In the beginning, he didn't, but over time Zahira dominated his thinking more and more. Finally, he pretended not to know what she did. Like a tree choked by a creeper, Junaid Shah sought to escape."

"In what way?"

"He led conquests of distant lands for no reason other than to escape Zahira, who he feared and hated and thought he loved as she had caused him to feel. And when he was at the palace, he fell under the influence of opium so that he could enjoy Zahira as he would any other begum, and forget that she was Zahira.

It was Zahira, not Junaid Shah, who learned of the Idol's Eye from a shaman. It was Zahira who told him of the diamond, and that any man who possessed the gem would rule at Allah's side – any *man*, she said, so it would not occur to him that Zahira could claim the Idol's Eye as she had already claimed Krishna's Consort.

"Zahira was destroying Junaid Shah from within, even as she played him like a puppet. He was beginning to realize that. His fear and hatred of her were beginning to gain the upper hand, and she knew it. She decided that he should not return from Krishnagarh. It was Zahira who taught the Emperor to think of war as a game. And before his conquest of Krishnagarh, she taught him a new game. Without him realizing it, she untrained him in war; she made him inefficient and foolhardy. And her plan succeeded. Commander Zaim may be in Varanasi hunting your son, but if he sought the Emperor's true killer, he need not have left this palace. And there are deeper secrets here, as well, and darker… but I shall not speak to you of that."

"But now Ghazi is Emperor. He could rule for decades."

"Those with ears say that Zahira is scheming again. She has already proven that she possesses ways of destroying a man if she chooses."

"Then the twins must be warned."

"You are innocent, Rukmini. Remain so, and Zahira will not harm you. But if she suspects meddling, then you will find Bandu's words to be true."

"Then I should not interfere?"

"Zahira does not tolerate opposition. She would turn you over to Zaim, or worse."

"I understand something of palace politics, although Krishnagarh was little more than a walled village compared to this."

"With the passing of the Emperor, we have fallen on perilous times; not only the Emperor's sons but also the women in the Moti Mahal. Our futures are uncertain."

"Why don't the women leave if they are unhappy?" asked Rukmini.

"The harem is their home. Zahira provides generously for them."

"You will be happier in Kashmir."

"Yes, I will be happy in my parent's home."

"Did you bear the Emperor a child?"

"The Emperor wanted it, but I couldn't live with the thought that my child might be imprisoned, or worse. When I told him so, I first saw his true feelings for Zahira. My reminding him of those feelings disturbed him so that he was never alone with me again, for fear of what I might say to him, and awaken in his mind."

"I understand. The specter of Govinda's execution haunts me day and night."

"Should Govinda be captured, Zahira is the one person who can help. She can be one's best ally or bitterest enemy. Better not the latter."

"Was Zahira's account of her childhood true?" wondered Rukmini.

"I am almost certain it was."

"How could someone with a common beginning, and such an eye for beauty, do what Zahira has done, and plans to do?"

Safiya contemplated for a time before answering. "I said earlier that almost all of those with the highest status in the Empire have lesser souls than many of those with barely any status, save for rare exceptions. Zahira is not a unique exception. When Junaid Shah took her, she was a common soul like many others, and like many others, her fear overwhelmed her. Her only rarity was her ability to quickly, and masterfully, learn things. You saw her skill as a seamstress and as a Pachisi player, and I hope, for your sake, that you begin to see her ability as Padshah Begum.

"She became a seamstress to avoid hunger. She learned to be a Padshah Begum out of necessity as well to avoid the treachery of jealous wives. Junaid Shah taught her the rules of this game, and he came to regret it, for she mastered the game far better than he had. He created Begum Zahira, and she destroyed him in return, and now seeks to replace him. Only the twins stand in her way."

The Tale of the Himalayan Yogis

"Were the boys raised here in the Moti Mahal?"

"For a time, but when their mother died, their grandfather intervened. Ghazi stayed with his father while Grandfather raised Hashim."

"How sad to separate the twins."

"It was the best thing. Kameela feared that the boys would vie with one another for the Peacock Throne. Ghazi, who was raised by his father, was chosen as the heir."

"That explains their difference in personality. I was fortunate that my husband never demanded many wives."

"That is fortunate indeed."

"But what I fail to understand is why the Emperor insisted on keeping so many wives, if, after they bore him heirs, their lives were in jeopardy."

"Ours is a peculiar system," continued Safiya. "The principal purpose of the *zenana* is to produce heirs to the Peacock Throne… the more, the better, except in Zahira's mind. Some of the Emperor's marriages were also political. Several of his wives were Rajput royals or daughters of Mongolian khans."

"But only one can rule, and it must be a male; is it not so?"

"It is so, but it is not only rival wives who threaten the Emperor's sons; the siblings themselves go about plotting to take each other's lives."

"Such a horrible way to live."

"Many princes do not turn out well. They choose opium and wine."

"Wine, women, and war are said to be the burden of kings," mused Rukmini.

"So you see why I wish to return to Kashmir where the air is sweet and pure. After my dear Kameela died, I was forbidden to leave the Moti Mahal. Kameela and I were like sisters, and those who despised her despised me. For fourteen years, I have been a prisoner in the harem, seeing the sun in a garden patrolled by eunuchs."

"How have you survived?" asked Rukmini, unable to imagine such a life.

"I befriended the enemy. But now that the Emperor is dead, I have asked for my freedom."

"Zahira has agreed to release you?"

"Grudgingly," replied Safiya. "Once she realized that I was not a threat, she grew to like me."

"I have enjoyed today," said Rukmini, pressing Safiya's hand.

"There will be more Pachisi games… perhaps without Yaman's interference."

"What I mean is, I have enjoyed our time together."

"I too have enjoyed our time together. Shall we walk again?"

"I would like that."

"Mornings are especially fragrant… and Zahira is occupied with the affairs of the Empire."

Hashim accepted the position of vizier in exchange for Ghazi's promise to free Rukmini.

"Zaim's obsession with the Rajput queen may work to our advantage," said Ghazi. "My harem spies inform me that Zaim has the Idol's Eye in his possession."

"How did they find that out?"

"Rani Rukmini mentioned it to the Padshah. Do you know anything about it? You were at Krishnagarh when Zaim searched the temple."

"I remember Zaim's men finding a jeweled crown, but I was not interested in such trivial matters. I was thinking only of Father."

"The Idol's Eye is no trivial matter. The Emperor waged war over it. The diamond is the property of the Emperor. By stealing it, Commander Zaim has committed a traitorous act against the throne. I shall discredit him for his duplicity."

Hashim suspected that Commander Zaim had committed countless traitorous acts against the throne over the years, some probably known to Junaid Shah. Hashim had learned at least one thing as vizier: The Emperor did not punish the guilty; he punished his enemies, whether guilty or not. The Emperor's allies could do what they liked so long as they remained allies.

"Then let us call him back without delay," Hashim suggested.

"And let the Rajput go free?" Ghazi shook his head. "I won't do it.

The Tale of the Himalayan Yogis

The hope of every Hindu rests with Govinda. Let Zaim capture their hero; then we'll deal with him."

Hashim relished any opportunity to be with his teachers. However, since being appointed vizier, he had little time to himself. Stealing away from the palace one morning, he headed for Haus Khaz for a meeting with Ramlal. Teacher and student were sitting in a grassy alcove within the red sandstone complex when a stranger approached; his upper cloth draped over his head to protect against the midday sun. Ramlal could see by the thread angling across the man's chest that he was a Brahmin and rose to greet him.

"Namaste!" nodded the man respectfully.

Turning to address Hashim, the Brahmin spoke in a hushed tone.

"It is I, Pundit Ananta. I have news from Varanasi."

Hashim jumped to his feet to greet Govinda's friend.

"News of Govinda?"

"Is it safe to speak?" asked Ananta.

"Speak freely. Pundit Ramlal is my *acharya*."

"Although you may have heard otherwise, Govinda is safe. He asked me to give you this."

Ananta handed Hashim a letter, which read:

Dear Hashim,

My exile has begun. Ananta will explain all. I dare not put too much on this parchment. While in Varanasi, I opened a volume of Kabir. This verse made the prospect of my exile bearable.

Dying, dying, the world
Is dying only.
But lo! None knows how to die
In such a way
That he dies never again.

With devotion to our friendship,
Govinda

"What have you heard since Govinda's escape from Krishnagarh?" Ananta inquired.

"Commander Zaim's spies report that Govinda is in Varanasi and that Zaim intends to capture him."

"Then Commander Zaim and his men have not yet returned?" asked Ananta.

Hashim shook his head.

"Is Rani Rukmini here? I have a letter for her also."

"She is a guest at the Moti Mahal, a prisoner in all but name. Zaim has claimed her. I accepted the position of vizier in exchange for Emperor Ghazi's promise to release her. He has yet to honor his word, but I don't doubt him. I shall deliver the letter to Raniji, but kindly tell me the story so that I may share the news with her. Ramlal will tell no one."

Ananta handed Hashim the second letter.

"What befell Govinda in Varanasi will add yet another chapter to his legend," said Hashim.

Being an exceptional storyteller, Ananta spared no details in the telling.

Hashim paced anxiously about his apartment, waiting for Bandu to arrive. He had no idea where Rukmini's quarters were, and he trusted no one other than Bandu to show him to them.

The heavy knock at his door told him the African was outside.

"Sir, you called for me?"

"I wish to visit Rani Rukmini. Will you show me to her quarters?"

Bandu led Hashim into the *zenana* where the women were returning from their midday meal. Many curious eyes followed the vizier; all were keen to know his purpose.

Upon reaching Rukmini's apartment, Bandu tapped lightly on the door, which opened slowly. Seeing Hashim at the entrance, Rukmini's eyes widened, but she did not speak.

"May I come in?"

Rukmini gestured for her visitor to enter. She led Hashim to her parlor, which had a balcony overlooking the courtyard. Bandu closed the door behind them.

"I am happy to see the face of Govinda's friend," said Rukmini, offering her guest a seat.

Rukmini sent Bandu for chai, and then returned to the parlor.

"I have news," said Hashim.

"About Govinda?"

"He is safe."

"You can't know how those words ease my heart. I have imagined Govinda's death, and, although I didn't believe it, still the possibility tormented me."

"I've brought a letter from him."

Hashim handed the parchment to Rukmini, who examined the seal before breaking it.

"But the letter bears the seal of the Raja of Jodhpur."

"Perhaps the letter explains," said Hashim.

The letter read:

Namaste Mataji,

I am well, but the thought of the journey ahead leaves me homesick. The rumors of my death are true, but I am alive and well again. I owe my life to two yogis who protected me from the Moguls and healed my body.

Tell no one other than Grandfather that I am on my way to Tibet. My exile has begun. It will ensure your safety and mine.

Though peaks of unimaginable size shall stand between us, we shall remain forever one in spirit. I draw strength from your loving presence, which is always in my heart.

May Sri Krishna bless and protect you,

Govinda

Rukmini read the letter silently and then held the parchment close to her heart.

"Exile?" she murmured. "What does it mean?"

"Pundit Ananta told me everything."

"Spare not a word."

Over several cups of chai, Hashim related the story of Govinda's escape. When it was time for Hashim to leave, Rukmini did something Hindu women were taught never to do: She hugged her guest with all the affection she held for her son.

"Thank you, Hashim. Your words will make Govinda's exile bearable."

"Shall I dispose of the letter?"

Rukmini shook her head.

"I wish to keep it."

"Keep it safe," Hashim advised. "There are many spies in the zenana."

As Hashim stepped out of Rukmini's apartment, Itibar Khan's stared contemptuously at him.

"Come," the eunuch ordered. "Padshah Begum wishes to see you."

"But I do not wish to see her," Hashim answered, his gentle mood disturbed by the menacing eunuch.

"It is expected that a visitor seeks Begum Zahira's permission before entering the Moti Mahal. Bandu knows this; I shall deal with his indiscretion directly."

"But I am vizier. I do not need Padshah's approval," complained Hashim.

"You can tell her that yourself."

Hashim's chest tightened, reminding him of what it felt like to be summoned by Commander Zaim.

The eunuch led Hashim into a cheerless room appointed with heavy mahogany furnishings and an assortment of accouterments taken from conquered forts. Begum Zahira leaned against a stack of grey satin pillows, her divan stretching beyond her feet. A servant massaged her neck while another pressed the fleshy bottoms of her feet. A handmaid held a platter of *pan* at her side. Ignoring her guest, Zahira examined the fresh leaves stuffed with shaved betel nut, date paste, coconut, cardamom, and lime zest. After making her selection, the servant removed the leaf's staple before slipping the mild narcotic into her master's mouth.

"Care for one?" Zahira asked Hashim, her words smothered by the contents in her mouth.

"No," Hashim replied. "I've just had chai."

"Many cups, I'm told."

"Your spies speak the truth." The admission relieved the constriction in Hashim's chest.

"You have compromised Bandu," reprimanded Zahira, her fierce eyes probing. "He has forgotten to whom he is answerable. I shall need to find a way to remind him."

"Do not be hard on Bandu. It was I who insisted that he take me to see the Rajput."

"You seem to have forgotten who runs the Moti Mahal. Out of courtesy, you should have sought my permission."

"I saw no need to bother you over such a trivial matter."

"Nothing in the Moti Mahal is too trivial for my ears," replied the Empress, her tongue reddened with *pan* juice. "What was the purpose of your visit?"

"The Emperor also has his spies, and they have informed him that Rani Rukmini has information about our father's death."

"Is that so? I have not heard anything of the sort."

"According to our spies, that is not true. You were overheard discussing his death as well as other topics that concern the Emperor."

"Such as?" The Empress's toes stiffened as her masseuse's thumbs dug into her feet.

"There is a matter of a misplaced tiara, and a diamond, which you discussed with Rukmini."

"You lack discretion, Hashim. When I find out who the Emperor's spies are, I shall have their eyes and ears removed."

"Then you will be surrounded by the deaf and dumb."

"Do not think that you can enter the Moti Mahal at your whim. In the future, come to me first, or face my censure."

"Are you threatening me?"

Zahira leaned to her left, releasing a stream of scarlet into a silver spittoon. Waving away the servant at her feet, Zahira cast a withering glance at the vizier.

"I have some advice for you. Do not meddle in the affairs of the Moti Mahal. Your mother is dead for a reason. I would not want you… or your brother… to suffer a similar fate."

"We do not fear you."

"You should," hissed Zahira, betel juice staining the corners of her mouth. "You have many enemies, and should I give the word, they will remove you and your twin."

"Are you threatening the Emperor? Such is a serious matter."

"Run and tell your brother before his spies do. Now remove yourself from the Moti Mahal before I lose patience with your foolish prattle."

"What do you intend to do with Bandu?"

"I have not decided. The eunuch has been useful to me in the past, but everyone is expendable, including the vizier."

"We shall see who is, and is not, expendable."

As Hashim turned to go, Itibar Khan appeared out of nowhere and led him out of the harem.

"I shall remember this," muttered the eunuch. "You have caused my brother much pain.

AMONG THE LAMAS

The sun-drenched trail to Sarnath was well traveled, and a stream of pilgrims passed the lamas along the way. The Tibetans had not been on the path for long when the ground began rumbling beneath their feet. Lama Choden was familiar with the sound from Tibetan bandits who frequently raided caravans. Sensing that soldiers were approaching, he worried that Govinda's disguise might not be adequate.

"Govinda, pull cloth over head," he instructed. "Tashi, Jinpa, do same. Govinda must not be the only lama with head covered."

As the riders approached, the thunder of hooves stirred choking clouds, forcing the lamas to cover their mouths with the ends of their robes. The officer in charge stopped alongside the Tibetans. Govinda recognized the man; he had helped Zaim search the queen's temple in Krishnagarh.

"Where are you going?" demanded the officer.

"Sarnath," replied Lama Choden.

"And then?"

"Tibet."

"Your feet will blister if you don't freeze to death," snickered the officer.

Signaling for his men to follow, the Mogul kicked his horse into a gallop.

The walk from Varanasi to Sarnath tested Govinda. The group of seven arrived in time for *solja*, a salty drink that Govinda liked even less than tsampa.

The stupa dominating the landscape intrigued Govinda. Scores of monks attired in wine-red robes circled the shrine where Buddha gave his first lecture, many prostrating with each step. As the day faded, a sea of butter lamps lit the grounds surrounding the shrine.

The common cloth worn by the monks made Govinda feel secure; an average ant in the colony. Lama Choden took Govinda inside the gompas and shrines where they viewed Buddhas of every size and disposition. Many of the statues had extended fingers and toes, aquiline noses, elongated earlobes, protuberances on the tops of their heads, and broad shoulders. A few of the Buddhas were emaciated.

"Buddha's poses have special meaning," Lama Choden explained, stopping before a standing Buddha.

"Why are some Buddhas emaciated?"

"Big Soul Buddha born a prince. Later he practice starvation."

"Will we practice starvation?" asked Govinda, half seriously.

"Hope not," laughed Lama Choden.

"Why do they have points on the tops of their heads and long earlobes?"

"Mind grow BIG! Barely fit inside head!" Lama Choden's hands spread apart, mimicking an expanded mind. "Long ears mean Buddha have divine hearing."

"I want to know more about Buddha's teachings."

"Long journey… much time to learn."

The lama caravan grew to thirty by the time it departed for Nepal. From the lamas' relaxed gait, Govinda could see that he was the only one in the group with anything on his mind. The others ambled along without a care in the world, murmuring mantras as they walked.

Late one afternoon, his legs heavy from fatigue, Govinda imagined himself riding Kalki. Atop a horse, he could reach Tibet before the snows closed the passes. By the third day, Govinda had fallen into the rhythm of the journey, buoyed by the Krishna mantra Leela had suggested he repeat.

In the midday heat, the group sought shade beneath a grove of sal trees.

The Tale of the Himalayan Yogis

"Rinpoche, the lamas hardly speak," observed Govinda.

"Lamas practice *shunyata*... empty head meditation. Less talk make less thought. Empty mind best mind."

"But you said Buddha had big mind."

"Emptiness can get very big!" laughed Lama Choden.

"Will you teach me empty head meditation?" asked Govinda, wanting to purge the memories of the previous moons.

"Govinda make fine shunyata lama. Get twig from tree."

Govinda picked up a slender stick slightly longer than his hand. The twig had a slight bend in it.

"Spin stick." The lama spun the stick between his thumb and index finger. "Fix mind on stick. First practice spinning, then add mantra. This shunyata meditation."

"Should I use my Krishna mantra?"

"Krishna make good mantra."

Crescent blades and sunburnt backs harvested the wheat and sugarcane cultivated on the Gangetic plains. By the time the lamas reached Nepal, the jetsam of Govinda's unwanted thought was purged; his mind was free and optimistic.

"Lama not repeat same thought twice," explained Lama Choden.

"Is that why the lamas have so little to say?" asked Govinda.

"Lama empty mind... like pouring water from pitcher."

"But when the pitcher is empty, one fills it again."

"Villager fill pitcher again... lama no fill pitcher."

"I never thought of having an empty mind."

"Empty mind not empty. Empty mind fill with Big Soul Buddha."

The independent spirit Govinda had inherited from his Rajput ancestors was falling under the spell of the humble lamas who surrendered personal ambition for the greater good of the group. Govinda had been raised with servants looking after his needs, but the lamas, including Rinpoche Choden, served one another. Govinda was not expected to help with meal preparations, but he willingly joined Dolmo in gathering kindling and chopping cabbage. Though Tibetan culture was thoroughly foreign to him, Govinda found wisdom in it.

Had the Rajput clans looked after one another the way the humble lamas did, they would not have been so vulnerable.

The daily bowl of tsampa always tasted the same, but Govinda didn't expect life as a wandering mendicant to be comfortable.

Near the border of Nepal, the lamas purchased provisions in the city of Gorakhpur, a luxury made possible by Raja Rao's gift. From the feudal capital, they slogged through low-lying jungles and swamps. The narrow paths cut by villagers through stands of elephant grass reduced visibility, leaving the lamas vulnerable to stalking tigers and rampaging rhinoceros.

Govinda was relieved to be leaving the swampy lowland; swarming mosquitoes had kept him awake for much of the night. By the time the caravan reached the hills beyond the Terai, three lamas had fallen ill, their robes soaked by fever-induced sweat. Lama Choden masked his concern, but his stoic smile didn't fool Govinda. The delirious lamas shivered uncontrollably one moment while sweating profusely the next. Unable to eat or drink, Norbu, the oldest of the stricken lamas, was caught in the throes of death.

"Malaria… we have no medicine," lamented Lama Choden. "Lama Norbu may not live through night."

"What can we do?" asked Dolmo.

"Pray to Tara!" replied the rinpoche.

Govinda remembered the pouch that Shankar Baba had given him and the instructions that had gone with it.

"In Varanasi, a yogi gave me this."

Govinda applied the powder to the foreheads of the men. The night passed slowly. Govinda fell asleep a few hours before dawn. Lama Choden sat with the sick lamas until dawn. When Govinda awoke, he found Lama Choden sitting next to him.

"How is he?" asked Govinda, rubbing the sleep from his eyes.

"Weak!" replied the head lama, pouring Govinda a cup of solja. "Drink."

Govinda put the cup to his lips but rejected the salty liquid.

"Solja not for me."

"Acquired taste," grinned Lama Choden.

"I think you need to be Tibetan."

The Tale of the Himalayan Yogis

A lama joined Lama Choden and Govinda by the fire. The newcomer announced that Norbu was speaking.

"Yogi powder, good powder," said Lama Choden.

The rinpoche had never seen a man in Norbu's condition survive malaria, but within a few days, the elderly lama was on his feet. Traveling was out of the question until the lamas regained their strength. Govinda welcomed the rest. However, the delay worried Lama Choden. The snows were coming, and the group needed to arrive at the monastery before the trails became impassable.

After ten arduous days, the caravan reached the foothills of the Himalaya, having forded streams and skirted emerald paddies along the way. Terraced hillsides rose above verdant valleys. Rice, barley, and potatoes harvested from the small, rectangular fields sustained the villagers, whose round faces burned from long hours in the sun.

The nights brought a chill, and the lamas sought refuge inside slate-roofed shelters, sharing the sheds with heavy-eyed yak and fidgeting goats. As the hot, humid air of the Terai collided with the colder currents of the high Himalaya, storms buffeted the lamas. Rain fell for three days; precipitation that fell as snow higher in the mountains.

At the edge of the high Himalaya, the trail ended abruptly at a deep gorge carved by a raging river. The caravan had no option but to navigate the feeble rope bridge spanning the river. One by one the lamas inched their way over the turbulent water like daring performers in a circus. A misplaced step would be their last. As Govinda took his turn dangling above death, he wondered if he would live to see Rajputana again. Hovering over the roiling rapids, Govinda crept across the gorge. Upon reaching the far side, he watched the others take their turn.

Beyond the chasm, the lamas ascended single-file through a region so enchantingly beautiful that Govinda found it challenging to keep his eyes on the rough-cut trail. Deprived of his favorite curries, Govinda feasted on visual delights unlike anything in his native Rajputana. The scent of wildflowers and cedar trees buoyed his spirit.

A wall of white loomed ahead; a fortress no army could plunder. A peculiar forest flanked the trail leading to the peaks.

"What is it?" asked Govinda, pointing to the needle straight stalks, which looked like hairs on the head of a jade giant.

"Bamboo," replied Dolmo. "We use for many things."

"We make our flutes from bamboo, but I never saw a tree."

"Bamboo grass, not tree. Make fine house."

The stunning landscape and exotic flora were a novelty. Except for the Aravali Hills, Govinda's world was monotonously flat. As they climbed, he experienced gnawing cold for the first time. Wrapping himself in the shawl which Leela had given him, his hands stiffened from the biting winds and frigid nights. Upon reaching a hot spring, Govinda plunged in ahead of the others. The steaming water soothed his weary body, relaxing it fully for the first time in many days.

Further up the trail, a primitive staircase disappeared into a ceiling of clouds. The weathered slabs reminded Govinda of the steps descending to Varanasi's burning ghats.

"Do they lead to Tibet?" wondered Govinda, who longed for the comfort of a soft bed. The thinning air burned his lungs and made his head spin.

"Steps lead to pass, but we not reach Tibet until spring," said Lama Choden, placing a sprig of tulsi in Govinda's hand. "Breathe this…"

"Breathing isn't easy up here in the clouds," Govinda replied as he stopped to inhale the herb.

Another set of grey slabs disappeared into the fog, forcing the group to climb blindly. Groping for invisible steps, Govinda wondered which was more dangerous, walking to Tibet or confronting the imperial army. Emerging from the clouds, a blinding sapphire sky greeted the lamas.

The caravan had scarcely overcome the steep ascent when yet another staircase appeared, a cruel trick played by the mountain gods. Govinda trudged up the path, his chest heaving. The stones were icy, and the lamas stepped cautiously to avoid a mishap.

Frigid winds numbed Govinda's face. His fingers and toes stiffened, his mind grew uneasy. He had no idea that air could be so cold; his body was at a loss as to how to deal with it. Shuffling stiffly

The Tale of the Himalayan Yogis

along, Govinda moved like one of his puppets, his frozen fingers unwilling to spin the shunyata twig.

As the caravan crossed the face of a scree-covered peak, thunder rumbled in the distance. From Dolmo's expression, Govinda knew the sound was not a good omen.

"Storm?" coughed Govinda.

Dolmo shook his head.

"Avalanche."

"Avalanche?" Govinda mouthed to himself. He had only the vaguest idea what the word meant.

"Watch," Lama Choden cautioned the lamas, pointing up the mountain. Avalanches were as prevalent in the Himalaya as malaria was in the Terai, and far more deadly.

Govinda gulped air; the altitude choked his heaving lungs. Falling behind, he was unable to keep pace with the Tibetans. If the journey had been on horseback on the Rajputana plains, he would be leading the way.

Lama Choden's eyes trained themselves on the wall of white looming overhead like an executioner. As a young man, he had been buried by an avalanche, and he wanted to make sure that none of his companions experienced the horror of an icy grave.

More rumbling shook the valley, echoing ominously from peak to peak. The muted rumble intensified. The mountain trembled; the din grew louder and closer. Pointing at the rapidly advancing wall of snow, Lama Choden shouted warnings, but it was too late. The avalanche sprayed powder into the sky as it aimed at the lamas at the head of the caravan. The lead lama turned back, but there was little time. Govinda watched as a white wave buried three figures in the distance, snapping the scrub conifers in its path as it thundered down the mountain.

The lamas waited to see if more snow would follow, but the mountain fell silent, having shed its blanket. The ensuing stillness was as eerie as the deafening roar had been moments earlier. The lamas stood motionless, not knowing whether to retreat or proceed ahead, or whether moving forward was even possible.

Hopeful that the slide was over, the lamas rushed to the aid of their buried comrades. They found the first man under a shallow blanket of snow, badly shaken, but uninjured. The second man was not so lucky as the other lama. He suffered a broken neck, dying instantly. Jinpa, who had been farthest up the trail, had vanished. Where was the young lama buried? Had the avalanche swept him further down the mountain?

The searchers dug feverishly, ignoring exhaustion and frostbite. Jinpa could be anywhere beneath the white shroud. Govinda dug alongside Dolmo. The boys drew labored breaths as they worked against time and the mountain to save their companion. Govinda's hands were raw, his body sweating despite the cold. How futile it was to be digging when Jinpa could be buried anywhere on the mountain.

As exhaustion set in, a voice inside Govinda's head spoke to him.

Farther down the mountain.

Being no stranger to the inner voice, he stopped to ponder the words. Scanning the slope below the trail, he sensed the spot. No one was digging lower down the mountain because the terrain was steep and treacherous.

"We're digging in the wrong spot," decided Govinda. "We need to go lower."

"Then not much we can do," Dolmo replied. "Too risky."

"We need a rope. I'm going down there," said Govinda, who was lighter than the others.

Dolmo returned with a frayed rope and a second lama who helped lower Govinda down the mountain. His frozen fingers clutching the cable as best they could, he descended to the spot he had identified as Jinpa's icy grave. Govinda dug with his hands, not knowing whether he was in the right place. Deeper and deeper he tunneled, but he found nothing. Discouraged by fatigue and frozen hands, he was about to give up when three icy fingers pushed through the snow.

"He's here!" shouted Govinda. The lamas rushed to the spot where Dolmo held the rope that prevented Govinda from tumbling into oblivion. The slope was far too steep to descend without support, and so the lamas stood and watched as Govinda dug feverishly, uncovering Jinpa's arms, chest, and head. The lama breathed faintly. He was near death.

"He's alive!"

The Tale of the Himalayan Yogis

Govinda secured the rope around Jinpa's waist and then signaled. Four lamas pulled with all their strength to save their brother. Slowly, the body slid up the slope. As Dolmo reached for Jinpa, the rope snapped, sending the lama tumbling headlong down the mountain. Seeing the body hurtling toward the precipice beyond him, Govinda grabbed the rope fastened around the lama's torso. Govinda's effort slowed Jinpa's momentum but didn't stop it. Govinda was pulled head first after Jinpa. As the two slid down the escarpment, connected to one another by a fraying rope, Govinda believed that he was about to die.

Jinpa's body reached the precipice first, and as it did, Govinda heard a ripping sound followed by a loud thump. As Jinpa's body lurched to a halt, Govinda catapulted head first over the cliff.

Just as it had when he plunged headlong into the Ganges, time slowed as Govinda hurtled through the air. Flying through the air, he felt the same sensation in his solar plexus that he had felt while hovering over his dead body as it floated in the Ganges.

As suddenly as he had become airborne, his body snapped to an abrupt stop, his descent into the abyss aborted. His hands screamed in agony. Govinda was desperate to release the rope, which felt like red-hot coals. Though the jute rope burned unbearably, instinct forced him to clench his fists as tightly as he could.

Dangling at the end of the worn rope, Govinda groped for a foothold to support his body. A white chasm loomed beneath him, poised to devour him. The wood flute Leela had given him slipped from his pocket, plummeting into oblivion.

A profusion of messages vied for Govinda's attention. His hands begged him to let go… the pain was too much. His mind ordered him to hold on, but his heart asked, 'why?' It would be so easy to float into infinity. He had already done it in Varanasi. Precious seconds passed. If he were to have any chance of saving himself, he must act.

Summoning an inner resolve that he didn't know he possessed, Govinda extended a raw hand up the rope and squeezed. Despite the excruciating pain, he placed a second hand above the first, pulling himself toward the cliff's edge. By the time he reached the cliff, his hands were beyond recognition. Spent from exertion, Govinda

Steve Briggs

slumped to his knees alongside Jinpa. The snow and ice on his raw hands numbed the pain and stopped the flow of blood.

Drawing ragged breaths, Govinda peered up the mountain to see how far they had fallen. In the gloaming, he could barely make out the lamas. Jinpa's robes had snagged on the splintered trunk of a craggy cypress. Still reeling from his narrow escape, he examined Jinpa to see if the lama had survived the fall. Red blotches dotted the snow near Jinpa's body. Placing a hand on the lama's shoulder, Govinda rolled the body over. Grimacing, he now knew why Jinpa's body had stopped so suddenly. As the lama had been about to plunge over the precipice, his torso snagged on the splintered tree trunk, tearing his robe and ripping open his side. Probing Jinpa's chest in search of a heartbeat, Govinda found one, though it was frantically fast and weak.

Peering up the escarpment, Govinda waved feebly to the lamas watching from the trail. A second rope sailed through the air, landing near the spot where Govinda had uncovered Jinpa.

Govinda watched Dolmo inching down the slope. Reaching the end of the rope, Dolmo was still a fair distance away.

"Are you all right?" asked Dolmo.

"I'm okay. Jinpa's hurt, but he's alive."

Govinda wondered if the frayed rope that had saved him was long enough to reach Dolmo. He untied the knot at Jinpa's waist and tossed the rope in Dolmo's direction. After falling short three times, an additional length of line was extended by the lamas above. This time, Dolmo caught Govinda's rope. After securing it to his rope, he descended to where Govinda was kneeling beside Jinpa.

"Hands!" cringed Dolmo, examining Govinda's wounds.

After inspecting the splinters protruding from Jinpa's stomach, Dolmo packed snow around the wound.

"First snow freeze wound," he explained. "Then take out tree."

While they waited, Dolmo tore a section of cloth from his robe and wrapped Govinda's hands.

"Better?" asked Dolmo.

"I can't feel anything."

"Lamas pull you up."

The Tale of the Himalayan Yogis

Govinda offered no resistance as Dolmo fastened the rope around his waist.

"Is the rope strong enough?" he wondered.

"You lighter than lama."

Govinda was lighter than the lamas, and climbing the slope would reduce the strain on the rope.

"But how will you get up with Jinpa?" Govinda asked.

"You first, then Jinpa."

Govinda was too exhausted to object. Slowly the lamas pulled him to the trail. After tying a rock to the end of the rope, the lamas flung it to Dolmo, who kneeled beside Jinpa.

Daylight was nearly gone, but Dolmo made no effort to secure the injured lama to the rope. Instead, he knelt beside his friend at the edge of the precipice. With the lamas looking on, Dolmo placed his hand on Jinpa's chest and slowly raised his body against his shoulders. After hugging Jinpa, Dolmo released his friend over the cliff's edge. Dolmo bowed as Jinpa disappeared into the silent, white expanse.

"What are you doing?" screamed Govinda, not believing what he had seen. Lama Choden placed a hand on Govinda's shoulder. Without looking up, Dolmo secured himself to the rope. Not waiting for the lamas to pull him up, he began the slow ascent.

After securing the other body to one of the yaks, the lamas trudged single-file into the descending darkness. The caravan still had a long way to go before reaching Yurpa Gompa. The group had not yet passed the avalanche region when more rumbling echoed in the distance. The faint thunder grew louder and louder until it was deafening. Though the fading light made it impossible to see the avalanche, Govinda judged the wall of snow to be behind them.

"Go fast!" shouted Lama Choden, striking the yak ahead of him with his walking stick.

The fate of the lamas was in the hands of the mountain, for there was nothing they could but plod blindly ahead. The lamas shuffled along blindly, expecting death at any moment. The lama to the rear of the group was but a few paces out of reach when the avalanche buried the trail behind him.

The moon emerged timidly from behind a cloud, the snowfields sparkling beneath its brilliance. The lamas trudged on, knowing that it would not be possible to rest until they reached the monastery. Though beyond exhaustion, Govinda did not complain.

"You ride yak," urged Lama Choden.

"I'm okay," Govinda muttered, frosty vapor escaping his mouth.

The lamas followed as the yaks trampled a path through the snow. They were passing through the remnants of an avalanche, although most of the snow had rumbled down the mountain rather than accumulating on the trail.

Numbed fingers prevented Govinda from adjusting his shawl, which Lama Choden willingly did for him. Govinda had entered a cold, colorless dream from which he desperately wished he could awaken. On he plodded, trying to make sense of Dolmo's actions, perplexed by the seeming indifference of the lamas. He had risked his life for Jinpa only to watch the young lama discarded like a worn-out robe. Was this the Tibetan way? And, if so, did he want to be a part of it? If he were injured, would he too be discarded?

Govinda's thoughts pained him even more than his body, and so he mumbled his mantra, hoping to numb his tormented mind. Sensing the boy's distress, Lama Choden walked alongside him.

"How you know where to look for Jinpa?" he asked.

"What difference does it make… Jinpa's dead."

"Govinda brave lama."

"I'm not a lama. I could never push someone off a cliff."

"You no understand," replied the head lama.

"I don't understand any of it. I tried to save Jinpa, but Dolmo pushed him over the cliff."

"I think you understand," said Lama Choden softly.

"I don't understand… someone ought to explain."

"Dolmo speak to Jinpa. Jinpa want to go to Buddha-land. Dolmo help him."

"I don't know anything about this Buddha-land you speak of."

Though the tragedy deeply disturbed Govinda, was Dolmo's decision so different from his ancestors' johar rite? Then again, he had been opposed to that too.

The Tale of the Himalayan Yogis

"Tibetan not think life or death," explained the rinpoche. "No death… only life. Life also in Buddha-land."

"But still, Jinpa could have been saved."

"Maybe. But Jinpa no want to be saved. Dolmo obey friend's wish."

"Are you sure Jinpa wanted to die?" asked Govinda incredulously.

"Dolmo no make mistake. He wise like you. Dolmo no ordinary lama."

Govinda's frozen heart was thawing, and with it, the pain in his limbs eased.

"Yurpa Gompa beyond next mountain," said the rinpoche. "Govinda, how you know where to dig?"

"A voice inside my heart."

"Only pure heart hear voice."

"But the voice almost got me killed."

"Always listen in heart."

"I try to, but I don't always understand," replied Govinda.

"Many years ago I am buried under snow. I not believe Jinpa far down mountain."

"Knowing nothing helps sometimes. If I was meant to find Jinpa, weren't we meant to save him?"

"You desire to help lama. Voice help you. Jinpa desire to leave body. Dolmo help him."

"Your world is simpler than mine," replied Govinda.

"I not agree. Govinda have compassion like Buddha."

"But why does Dolmo have no compassion?"

"Dolmo have compassion!" Lama Choden spoke passionately, something Govinda had not seen before. "Walk with Dolmo. Then you see."

Govinda was too exhausted to catch up with the young lama. He only hoped they would arrive at Yurpa Gompa soon, for every step was more agonizing than the previous. The lamas labored up the slope. Although the trail was shrouded in darkness, the first rays of light glinted against the peaks overhead.

"Yurpa," sighed Lama Choden, pointing to a tiny orange cube in the distance.

Govinda had been plodding along with his head down. Looking up, he nearly fell off the mountain.

The old monastery floated in a sea of white. An icy citadel surrounded the monastery perched at the edge of a precipice. Govinda imagined that an avalanche would bury the gompa at any moment.

Eager to be out of the chilling wind, Govinda kept pace with the others, though his legs begged him to stop. Able to take in the landscape for the first time since night had fallen, Govinda found the frozen stillness utterly foreign to him.

As the caravan ascended the ridge, the building grew in size. The carrot-colored, three-tiered monastery stood on a crag more precipitous than the one from which Govinda had nearly fallen. Glistening massifs loomed overhead like silent sentries; the remote amphitheater of ice and granite was like no fortress Govinda had ever seen.

The trail to Yurpa Gompa snaked up the mountain, leaving Govinda breathless by the time he reached the front gate. Before entering their wintry abode, the lamas spun brass prayer wheels flanking the entrance. The weathered, wooden door to the monastery groaned as it opened, sending icy blasts whistling through the stone corridor.

Inside the main hall, Lama Choden issued instructions.

"Govinda and Dolmo sleep in upper closet."

A resident lama led the boys up uneven stairs and then pointed to a rough-cut ladder. Arriving at their loft, they stretched out under shaggy yak rugs, falling asleep beside a cast iron urn filled with softly glowing embers.

When morning came, Dolmo led Govinda onto the roof where a wooly yak greeted them. Dolmo coaxed the sluggish beast out of their way before they stepped onto the roof, leaving footprints in the freshly fallen snow. The fresh Himalayan air invigorated Govinda, lifting his still flagging spirit.

The boys surveyed the precipices that surrounded them. On every side, above and below, hushed whiteness blanketed the craggy terrain. Overhead, crystalline peaks framed a patch of the bluest sky that Govinda had ever seen.

The Tale of the Himalayan Yogis

"We've reached the end of the world," he whispered, dizzied by the enormity of the vertical landscape.

"Tibet end of the world," laughed Dolmo, pointing beyond the peaks.

Stepping to the far side of the roof, Govinda glimpsed the thread of trail the caravan had ascended in the night. Looking down, Govinda peered into a chasm that disappeared into the shadows. His mind flashed to the frayed rope that had prevented him from plummeting into a similar abyss.

"Why Govinda not happy?" asked Dolmo, taking his friend's hand.

"Why did you let Jinpa die?"

"Better Jinpa die then all lama die."

"I don't understand."

"Two avalanche coming. One bury three lama. Other bury no lama."

"But what does that have to do with Jinpa?"

"I see second avalanche coming. No chance to save Jinpa. I decide to save other lamas. Jinpa agree."

Dolmo's actions were finally beginning to make sense. Had they rescued Jinpa, the entire caravan would have been buried by the second slide.

"Lama Choden is right," decided Govinda.

"What Rinpoche say?"

"He say, 'Dolmo have much compassion.'"

"Like you, my friend."

"I'm hungry," declared Govinda, the tension of the previous day draining from his body. "Do you think we can find something besides tsampa in the kitchen?"

"For you, Norbu make momo."

"Momo?" frowned Govinda.

"You like!" Dolmo reassured his friend.

Gathered around a cast iron stove occupying half the space in the kitchen, the lamas sipped chia, cradling their mugs with both hands. At the sight of Govinda, their round faces brightened. The smiling lamas were as warm as the stove they huddled around.

Steaming milk tea flowed from an enamel pitcher decorated with gold dragons. Dolmo handed a cup to Govinda.

"No tsampa today," grinned Dolmo.

As if rebelling against their tasteless staple, in unison, the lamas repeated, "No tsampa today."

"I make feast for Lama Govinda," said Norbu.

Seated on a threadbare carpet near the stove, Govinda welcomed the warmth. He clutched his cup in his palms, his fingers badly swollen from the cold and chafing of the rope.

Although the lamas said little, they admired Govinda's courage. Everyone had heard the accounts of his heroics, and after witnessing his daring attempt to save Jinpa, no one doubted their accuracy.

The lamas had adopted their Rajput friend as one of their own. The gentle spirit of the Tibetans seeped into Govinda's heart, quelling the memory of Moguls whenever it tested his equanimity. The long Himalayan winter passed like a peaceful meditation at the feet of the Buddha.

The Yogi's Curse

Commander Zaim seethed with frustration. He and his beleaguered men rode out of Varanasi without evidence of their success, seventeen soldiers fewer than when they had arrived. The memory of his final day in Varanasi repeatedly played out in his head as he and his men headed for Delhi.

Zaim had returned to the caves to settle his scores with Bhairav's dogs and the snake yogi. Upon spotting the soldiers, the dogs attacked. However, this time the Moguls were ready, and Bhairav's dogs were maimed and left to die on the floor of the temple. Having taken his revenge on the dogs, Zaim headed for the yogi's cave, an odd mix of fury and fear propelling him through the dark corridors leading to the cobra den.

On their way, the Moguls passed through the nagas' chamber, which had been vacant on their previous visit. Alerted by the howling dogs, the nagas armed themselves with battle-axes and tridents. They spared no one. As the unsuspecting soldiers marched into the nagas' abode, they were cut down like goats sacrificed at a tantric rite. Zaim managed to escape, but the nagas slaughtered twelve of his men.

Undeterred, the commander led his troops to the mosque for morning prayer, convinced that Allah would provide whatever was needed to conquer the yogi. First, Zaim would crush the Kali statue outside the yogi's cave, and then he would have the yogi's head.

In the mosque's courtyard, the commander mapped out his

strategy. Half his men would enter the caves through the riverside entrance while he led the remainder down the stairs behind the Kali shrine.

Inside the Kali shrine, Zaim grinned wickedly as he raised his torch before the goddess' face.

"Faizon, your mace," Zaim ordered his second in command, who stood behind him. Summoning the rage that had led him to victory in countless battles, Zaim swung the weapon at Kali's head, but that was the last that he remembered of the night.

It was morning when Zaim awoke in his camp outside Varanasi. General Faizon sat nearby, facing the fire.

"Faizon!" Zaim called meekly. "How long have I slept?"

Looking haunted, the officer turned toward him.

"From the time you lost consciousness in the night."

"Lost consciousness? What do you mean?"

"You don't remember?" asked Faizon, his eyes full of fear.

"Remember what?"

"What's the last thing you remember?" Faizon asked his superior.

"I was about to crush that disgusting Kali."

"You remember nothing after that?"

"Nothing. Is that when I lost consciousness?" questioned Zaim.

"You lost consciousness sometime after that. You truly remember nothing?"

"I have told you." Zaim meant to sound threatening, but he could not find it in himself; instead, his heart filled with raw fear.

"After you took the mace, the yogi spoke from within his cave. 'Again you enter my abode,' he said. As you raised the weapon, the yogi issued a warning, 'Do not strike her!' As you swung the mace at the idol, you suddenly dropped it as if it were a burning log.

"The yogi said, 'Neither you nor your men will harm her.' You said, 'Devil, you are possessed by a *djinn*. I shall spare the idol, but I will not spare you.' The yogi sat with his eyes closed the way we found him during the previous encounter. He said, 'Leave while you are able.'

"You ordered the soldiers to shoot the yogi. The yogi said, 'This is

The Tale of the Himalayan Yogis

my last warning. Leave now before a curse falls upon you.' You said, 'I fear no man's curse. Allah protects me.' The yogi said, 'Commander, you act on your behalf. Allah serves my will, not yours.'

"You ordered the archers to fire, but the cobras struck first. You stepped back, but the soldiers were bitten and collapsed to the ground. The yogi said, 'Take your men and leave!' You grabbed a scimitar from the soldier nearest you and entered the cobra den.

"As you stepped into the cave, the yogi raised his open palm, and said, 'I have given you ample opportunity to save yourself. You shall live the remainder of your days under a curse.' You faltered and collapsed to the ground.

"The yogi told me, 'Take your commander away! Only a madman would attempt what he did. When he awakens, tell him that his diseased body is the result of his hatred, and not a yogi's curse.'

"We carried you out of the cave and returned here. You have been sleeping until you awoke just now."

Zaim himself remembered almost nothing of the episode with the yogi even after the telling. Though he scoffed at the powers of the yogi, the idea of a curse troubled the Mogul commander as he rode toward Delhi.

Though his days in Varanasi had been nightmarish, by the time Zaim reached the outskirts of Delhi, his mood brightened at the thought of the prizes awaiting him. He would find pleasure in Rani Rukmini and the Idol's Eye. With the diamond safely hidden, he was one of the wealthiest men in Delhi, and with the Rajput queen in his possession, he was one of the most fortunate.

As Zaim and his troops approached the city's eastern gates, a lungi-clad beggar darted in front of his horse. The emaciated outcaste shrieked,

"Curse you, Commander! Curse your evil ways!"

"Flay him," ordered Zaim. But before his men could capture the beggar, the man rushed at Zaim, grabbing the hand that had been ravaged by the dogs. Drawing his scimitar, Zaim was about to lop off the man's head when he noticed the rotting fingers which had touched Zaim's wounds.

"Kill the leper!" snapped Zaim. He had scarcely given the order when one of his men fired at the beggar, who threw himself to the side. The round struck the beggar's hand, which disintegrated like pottery clay. An arrow pierced the leper's chest, and he collapsed in the dust.

"Burn the body where it lies!" ordered the commander as he galloped away. Most of the men followed their leader, but a few stayed behind to carry out his orders. As he approached the army's fortress, Zaim looked back to see smoke rising in the distance. At that moment, a gust of wind blew the smoke in Zaim's direction. Shutting himself inside his quarters, he feared the smoke was entering into his room, and that it carried the yogi's curse.

In the weeks following Commander Zaim's return to the capital, every day proved to be the worst day of his life thus far. The wounds inflicted by the dogs turned to ugly scars, his hand wouldn't heal, and his vision became increasingly blurred. Lesions formed on his face and arms. His fingers refused to function properly. His blood ran hot by day, and by night he tossed about his bed, haunted by the yogi's curse and the specter of the leper.

Impatient for his wounds to heal, the commander turned reclusive. However obsessed he was with Rani Rukmini, his vanity kept him away. As the lesions on Zaim's face worsened, his confidence slumped. The commander bore the symptoms of leprosy. Typically, the disease took years to deform a man, but it seemed that was not the case with Zaim; the yogi's curse appeared to have accelerated his decline.

Emperor Ghazi called a meeting of the generals to review Commander Zaim's failed mission and assess his physical condition. Upon seeing the pitiable commander enter Durbar Hall, Ghazi seized his opportunity.

"Commander, you don't look well."

"I'm fine," insisted Zaim. "I had little choice but to drink from that putrid river. The Ganges is full of bloated corpses."

"But your soldiers returned healthily," countered Ghazi.

"I'm fine, I tell you."

"I'm told a yogi cursed you."

"These yogis possess no powers."

"According to your men, they – and you – witnessed a yogi floating on the Ganges, and another living with cobras that did his bidding."

The Tale of the Himalayan Yogis

"There was nothing extraordinary about these men."

"Yet one put a curse on you, and the other made off with the Rajput's body."

"I know nothing of a curse."

"It seems a yogi cursed you with leprosy."

"Lies!" barked Zaim. "I was poisoned by that foul river. I'll be fine by the next moon."

"Until you recover, the generals and I feel you should take leave of your command."

"Nonsense. I'm as fit for command as ever."

"The court physicians shall decide that. Now, tell us, Commander, why have you failed to return with the Rajput's body?" asked Ghazi, enjoying the upper hand.

"What does it matter? The boy is dead."

"If, as you claim, those yogis possess no powers, then surely you could have retrieved the body."

"The body sank to the bottom of the river."

"I think you know better than to lie to the Emperor. Despite having a hundred armed soldiers at your side, a weaponless holy man made off with the body," accused Ghazi.

"The point is the Rajput is dead. My soldiers put three rounds in him."

"For your sake, Commander, I hope you're right."

"Are you threatening me?"

Zaim looked to his generals for support but found none.

"Enough about the Rajput," said Ghazi. "Where is the Idol's Eye?"

The question caught the commander off guard.

"The what?"

"The diamond the Emperor sacked Krishnagarh to claim."

"I know nothing about a diamond," replied Zaim, concealing the truth as best he could.

"You're sure?"

"Are you suggesting...?"

"Two of your men informed the council that you found the Idol's Eye in the Rajput temple."

"They're lying. I'll have the soldiers beaten."

"Maybe this will help your memory." Ghazi waved to an attendant, who promptly produced a glittering diadem on a silver platter. "According to Begum Zahira's eunuch, this diadem was found among your belongings. It's from the Rajput temple."

"What of it?" seethed Zaim. "We plunder temples all the time."

"It is from the temple that contained the Idol's Eye."

"I know nothing about the diamond."

"Then take leave from your command until your health is better… and possibly until your memory improves as well."

"I have rid the Empire of its greatest threat, and yet you interrogate me as if I were a traitor."

"You returned from Varanasi with little more than a yogi's curse," said Ghazi, continuing on the offensive.

"A hundred of my men witnessed the Rajput's death. Is that not sufficient?"

"Commander, as you know, it is customary to present the Emperor with the head of an adversary," interjected General Jari.

"What does it matter? The mission was a success."

"Commander, the evidence suggests that you put personal ambition above duty," declared Ghazi.

"*Jhootha*," muttered Zaim under his breath. Then, more loudly, he scowled, "You wear the crown a fortnight, and already you plot my ruin."

"To the contrary, I am only concerned for your health."

"It is your health that should concern you," warned Zaim.

"Are you threatening the Emperor?" questioned General Jari.

"You heard me. I will not allow an upstart to accuse me of treason."

"You may go," declared Ghazi. "The generals and I wish to discuss your situation in private."

Zaim scanned the generals, all of whom he had commanded for a decade. Had they all turned against him? Like a cornered animal in search of an escape route, the commander fled Durbar Hall.

Zaim's scarred skin, unsightly though it was, paled in comparison to his battered confidence. The Emperor seized the opportunity to discuss a replacement for the ailing commander.

"Fifteen soldiers and two officers dead chasing a mere boy,"

The Tale of the Himalayan Yogis

recounted Ghazi. "And to make matters worse, Zaim returns without the Rajput's body. Though he insists the boy is dead, it appears that a yogi made off with the body. We need to stake the Rajput's head outside the palace for all to see. Without evidence, victory cannot be claimed. Commander Zaim's mission has nothing to do with truth, but what the people believe. Did the Rajput single-handedly kill my father? No, however, the people believe that he did, and so he is as dangerous as if the tale were true. Did Commander Zaim and his men kill the Rajput? It seems so. But the people may believe otherwise, given the evidence, and so Commander Zaim has failed his mission."

"Emperor, we have interviewed the soldiers who accompanied Commander Zaim, and your conclusions are valid," declared General Jari. "The commander underestimated the Rajput and exercised poor judgment in seeking revenge on a yogi. The story was so unlikely that we questioned every soldier present, but the account of the cobra attacks appears to be true."

"How is it that we lost so many men?"

"Apparently, three of the men died of cobra bites, and the rest were slain in a battle with naked sadhus."

"Poor execution! Look at Commander Zaim now. He slinks about like a beaten dog. I suggest he take a leave of absence. In two moons' time, we'll evaluate his condition."

General Murad spoke. "Emperor, it is a suitable time for Commander Zaim to recuperate as no invasions are planned. May I recommend that you put General Jari in charge during Commander Zaim's absence?"

"Agreed," said the Emperor. "If Commander Zaim's health is not fully restored within two moons, then we shall consider a permanent replacement."

The meeting was adjourned, the Emperor's proposal having met with the council's approval. Ghazi had not expected Zaim's removal to be so easy. Nonetheless, he assigned spies to watch the commander day and night.

After dismissing the council, Ghazi headed for his brother's apartment. He wanted to share his triumph with Hashim, who greeted his twin at the door.

"I have dealt with Zaim."

"With what result?"

"Zaim has been reduced to little more than another corpse floating on the Ganges River."

"Then the council has backed you?"

"Completely!" said Ghazi triumphantly.

"Well done. That leaves only Zahira and her mullahs."

"With Zaim out of the way, I can deal with Zahira."

"Why not free the Rajput queen as you agreed?"

"It's a good idea. With her son out of the way, there is no reason to detain her."

Wasting no time, Hashim went to the Moti Mahal where he was told by the guards to wait. Moments later, Itibar Khan appeared at the gate.

"Begum Zahira has instructed me to tell you that she will send word to the palace when Rani Rukmini is to be released."

"The decision is not Zahira's. The queen is to be released immediately."

"I will inform Begum Zahira." The eunuch glared at Hashim before departing.

Itibar Khan returned to Zahira, who soaked in a sunken tub, attended by a half dozen slave girls. Zahira disliked having her bath interrupted, but the eunuch had little choice but to relay Hashim's words.

"Bring me Rani Rukmini."

Itibar Khan bowed as he backed out of the clammy chamber.

A knock came on the Rajput queen's door. Rukmini opened the door, and, judging by her attitude of familiarity, mistook Itibar Khan for his brother, as was intended. Although Itibar Khan was slightly shorter and broader than Bandu, both eunuchs towered over her. It was unlikely that she would notice the difference. Hindu custom prohibited Rukmini from looking in Bandu's eyes when he escorted her to the daily games of Pachisi, nor did she meet Itibar Khan's eyes today.

"Your Highness, Begum Zahira requests your presence," said the eunuch, imitating Bandu's voice.

The Tale of the Himalayan Yogis

Rukmini followed the eunuch to the Empress' quarters.

"Why does Begum Zahira wish to see me?" she asked, passing a stream of female servants bearing platters of fruit.

"The Emperor has ordered your release."

"Then I am not to be detained any longer?"

"The Emperor wishes to extend his kindness to the mother of the dead Rajput."

Itibar Khan glanced down to see Rukmini's reaction, for he was sure that no one within the harem had informed her of her son's death.

"I see," she said, showing no outward sign of anguish.

"You are not disturbed by the news of your son's death?"

"Better he died suddenly than be tortured."

"It is true. Zaim is known for his cruel methods," replied Itibar Khan, playing along.

"As is Begum Zahira, I'm told."

"Told by whom?"

Rukmini glanced up at Itibar Khan, who had abandoned his impersonation and was staring mercilessly at her.

"I... I heard it in the garden the other day," she stammered. "Two of the concubines were talking."

"Point the women out to me," the eunuch ordered, his voice callous. "Begum Zahira does not tolerate such talk."

Rukmini followed the eunuch down the stairs to the Empress' private bath. At the entrance to the chamber, he instructed her to wait. Circling the sunken bath, Itibar Khan passed the Roman-style pillars framing the basin. The servants pouring steaming water over the Empress' shoulders stepped away to allow her to converse privately with the eunuch. Kneeling, he spoke to the Empress. Rukmini trembled as she watched.

Having spoken to Begum Zahira, Itibar Khan led Rukmini to a bench near the Empress. Before seating herself, she bowed.

"The Emperor has ordered your release," Zahira informed Rukmini, dispensing with her customary greeting.

"It is kind of him," she replied guardedly.

"I had hoped you would find the Moti Mahal to your liking, and that you would decide to stay with us."

"The Moti Mahal has been comfortable in every way. I am grateful for your generosity, Your Majesty."

"But not grateful enough to accept my friendship." The sharpness in Zahira's voice cut through the dense air like a scimitar.

"As Empress, you must know that a queen is cautious in forming alliances. We are bred to be wary," replied Rukmini diplomatically.

"I understand. That is the very reason why I have enjoyed your company. You and I stand apart from the others; equals, as it were."

"I am hardly your equal."

"I disagree. We are alike in many ways. Our husbands have recently died… we have both sired heirs to the throne."

"But your son lives while mine is dead," replied Rukmini.

"And yet, if anything, you've seemed happier of late."

"It is a relief to know that Govinda died suddenly, for now, there will be no trial, no prolonged agony, no public execution."

"You think us… *cruel*…" Zahira paused, letting the word fill the air like noxious vapor.

"I have not found you to be cruel," Rukmini replied softly.

"But others with whom you have spoken find me to be."

"I speak with almost no one."

"No one but Safiya," retorted Zahira.

"We enjoy our walks in the garden."

"More than you enjoy the time *we* spend together?" probed the Empress, her words tinged with jealousy.

"No, I would not say that."

Zahira signaled for her servants to resume their work.

"You have been fortunate enough to know love," said Zahira. "I was not so fortunate. My husband found love, but it was not for me, and when she died, his heart grew hard like the steel of his sword."

"It must be terrible having another woman competing for your husband's affection."

"Wives, concubines, servant girls no older than my son… all were rivals. But then your husband also ruled. With a wave of his hand, he could have summoned any number of *nautch* girls to his bedchamber."

"My husband was not like that."

"You were fortunate. But what does it matter? Our men are dead."

"My love lives on."

"I can see that," conceded Zahira. "But why the indifference to your son's death?"

Rukmini hesitated before speaking. "We Rajputs accept death as part of life. Is death not the fate of every man? May I ask why the Emperor has decided to free me?"

"To satisfy his brother. It seems Prince Hashim has agreed to be vizier in exchange for your freedom."

"Why is that?"

"You tell me," probed Zahira. "My spies inform me that Prince Hashim and your son knew one another."

"But that's impossible," replied Rukmini, burying her shaking hands in her silks.

Zahira summoned her servants. Rising from her bath, the Empress was wrapped in towels as she emerged from the water.

"As I said, it puzzles me that you were not distraught at the news of your son's death," the Empress repeated.

"I choose not to share my emotions."

"According to witnesses, a Hindu holy man made off with the body."

"I find solace knowing that Govinda died in the arms of a yogi."

"If, in fact, he died at all," replied Zahira doubtfully.

"Are you saying Govinda isn't dead after all?"

"I'm saying Zaim has never failed in the past. He didn't return with the body; a first since I've been Empress." Zahira stared at Rukmini for some time before asking, "Where will you go?"

"I shall find a Krishna temple and live near it."

"Without servants to look after you?"

"Krishna looks after his devotees."

"Surely you won't go begging for your meals."

"The temple will provide. I shall be content."

"Life is simple for you."

Zahira examined a stack of brightly colored *salwar kameez* that had been brought by her maidservants. Waving away a dozen stunning outfits, the Empress settled on a violet ensemble.

"Life is simple, but not always easy," agreed Rukmini. "Since Raja Chandra's death, I find myself numb most of the time."

"Why not marry again… or take a lover?"

Rukmini did not answer.

With the help of an attendant, Zahira slipped a chiffon kameez over her head.

"I used to lie in bed wondering who the Emperor was with," Zahira confessed.

"You are more courageous than me. I could never have shared my husband with another."

"If not uprooted, weeds overtake a garden. I do my best to weed my garden."

"Your garden is lovely. I have never seen such a profusion of exquisite blossoms."

"The garden is yours if you stay," offered Zahira.

"You are kind to offer. We two share a peculiar bond. Though our husbands were enemies, we understand one another."

"Then why not stay?" A glimmer of hope lit Zahira's ebony eyes.

"My place is at my husband's side," replied Rukmini, "and he is with Krishna."

"Then go if you must," said Zahira unhappily, "but if you are ever inclined, return."

"I shall remember your kind offer, and I shall remember our games of Pachisi."

Rukmini bowed, performing the *taslim* correctly, having practiced in front of the mirror in her apartment. As she turned to go, the Empress called to her.

"Rukmini, I have a gift for you. I am aware that you wish to wear only white," said the Empress, "and so I made this for you."

The Empress held up a lovely pearl-colored salwar kameez.

"I shall not forget your kindness," said Rukmini, accepting the gift and kissing the Empress on the cheek.

A tear formed at the corner of Zahira's eye. In a voice more vulnerable than her servants had ever heard, the Empress whispered, "Now, go."

The Tale of the Himalayan Yogis

Bandu stepped through the misty air and escorted Rukmini out of the room.

"Vizier Hashim is waiting for you," Bandu informed her. Itibar Khan had not left Rukmini's sight while they were in the bathhouse; this time, she was sure of with whom she spoke.

"I mistook Itibar Khan for you earlier."

"It nearly cost you your freedom. However, you recovered satisfactorily. Begum Zahira is very fond of you."

"She seemed sad."

Bandu nodded. "She was counting on you for a friend."

"Fate alone decides these matters."

As Rukmini followed Bandu through the pillared corridors of the zenana, they passed a veranda leading to the garden.

"May I pick some flowers for Safiya?"

Bandu nodded. "I'll help you." Together, they stepped into the sunlight, which burned Rukmini's fair skin.

Rukmini had collected a colorful bouquet when she spotted Safiya entering the garden.

"Rukmini, I have heard the news."

"The Emperor has granted my freedom," confirmed Rukmini.

"I too will be leaving soon," confided Safiya.

"Then you've spoken to Zahira?"

Safiya nodded.

"I am happy for you," replied Rukmini, taking Safiya's hands.

"Won't you come to Kashmir with me? Srinagar is like no other place on earth. You'll feel like you're living in heaven."

"Maybe one day I shall come, but until the period of mourning is complete, my place is near Krishna."

"I understand, but where will you go? I worry for your safety."

"Vrindavan."

"Vrindavan is a lovely place."

"You've been there?" asked Rukmini.

"The Emperor took the entire harem down the Yamuna on barges. We docked at Vrindavan. You will be safe there."

"These flowers are for you." Rukmini handed the bouquet to Safiya.

"I shall miss you. You have become like a sister to me."

The two women clasped each other's hands. With their foreheads nearly touching, they whispered, "Namaste."

Hashim, who had been waiting nearby, stepped forward. "Raniji, palace bearers will take you to south Delhi."

"South Delhi?"

"Pundit Ananta is waiting there for you," explained Hashim, guiding her across the palace courtyard. "It is a great relief to know that you are finally free."

"Can there be freedom with Govinda exiled to Tibet?" questioned Rukmini, sensing the loneliness that awaited her outside the palace gates.

"Govinda will return... I promise you."

"We must keep his secret."

"I shall," replied Hashim.

As Rukmini settled herself on the gilded palanquin, Hashim bowed to her before closing the ruby curtains, shutting out the people who had taken everything from her.

When Zaim's spy arrived with word that Hashim had escorted Rani Rukmini out of the Moti Mahal and arranged her transport to a Brahmin neighborhood to the south of Delhi, he cursed the pale sky overhead. What Zaim had suspected from the outset had been confirmed. Hashim had been lying all along. Prince Hashim had indeed helped the Rajputs escape.

But why? Zaim wondered. *Why would he help the people who murdered his father?*

Zaim was determined to find out even if it brought an end to his wretched existence. Had it not been for Hashim, Zaim would not have been forced to hunt down Govinda. Had it not been for Hashim, he would never have been cursed by the yogi or attacked by a pack of dogs. Had it not been for Hashim, he would still be commander of the mightiest army in Asia.

Zaim awaited his transfer to the Moradabad leper colony. The door to his windowless cell moaned as it swung open. A voice commanded the inmate to emerge from the darkness. Zaim stepped out of the cell

The Tale of the Himalayan Yogis

and shuffled across the courtyard, accompanied by a pair of guards who kept their distance from the diseased figure.

Soldiers passed without recognizing their former commander. Gnarled lumps marred Zaim's cheeks and neck, and hideous lesions appeared everywhere on his body. His hands and feet were bandaged to conceal flesh that wouldn't heal. Faltering toward the gate, the once proud officer struggled to walk. Sunlight tortured his eyes, forcing the wraithlike figure to shield his face with a scarred forearm.

The newly appointed Commander Jari and his generals approached the prisoner. Wincing at the sight of his former superior, Jari scarcely recognized the man alongside whom he had fought for over a decade.

Jari addressed his former commander.

"Due to your illness, the Emperor has ordered me to deliver you to the Moradabad leper colony. A small bungalow awaits you. Provisions will be delivered once a fortnight. You have been permanently relieved of title, pension, and position."

Winter swept through the barren halls of Yurpa monastery like a lonely ghost in search of companions. Opaque cloud banks, frosted glass, and fluttering snow obscured the crystalline peaks for days at a time. Still, Govinda's spirit, along with his appetite, grew with each passing moon.

The lamas spoke little. Govinda grew accustomed to nuances of silence that both amused and amazed him. Winter was the season when the lamas turned inward, attuning their souls to the cosmos with practices that continued unbroken for weeks at a time. The daily trumpet of horns, thumping of drums, and ice crashing to the ground scarcely violated the gompa's hushed mood.

None of the lamas spoke much Hindi except for Rinpoche Choden and old Norbu, both of whom had spent a few years in India. Some of the lamas didn't speak at all as they moved like cheerful phantoms along the long, lonely corridors of the monastery.

One day, after instructing Govinda to sit with Lama Norbu while the old lama read from *Bardo Thodol*, Rinpoche Choden disappeared. The head lama had retreated to a cell beneath the monastery, taking his daily bowl of tsampa through an opening in the door. After five moons, Govinda wondered whether he would ever see the senior lama again.

Though the monastic atmosphere was decidedly austere, an inner fire fueled the lamas, and they went about their routines with smiles fixed to their polished faces. Their half-closed eyes told Govinda that, even while cooking and cleaning, these monks dwelled in other worlds.

Lama Norbu sat on a fire-breathing dragon woven into the rug beneath him. Leaning over a low table, the lama read from *The Tibetan Book of the Dead*, painstakingly translating each verse to ensure that Govinda understood. Seated beside the lama, Govinda watched the smoke from a braid of rope incense waft about the room like a scented ghost. He liked the resinous juniper better than most. Old Norbu read on, occasionally stopped to ring the *vajra* bell or point to one of the colorful murals decorating the walls of the shrine.

"Lama Govinda, your eyes good, but my mind see clearly. I describe. Okay?"

"If you make a mistake, I will correct you," replied Govinda, peering at the mural through the haze.

"My mind see Buddha-land," began Norbu. "Many Buddhas and Bodhisattvas living peacefully, waiting to return to earth to help others attain Buddha-land. Big Soul Buddhas happy in Buddha-land."

The scene was indeed idyllic. Some of the Buddhas immersed themselves in samadhi meditation. Others taught the Threefold Truth beneath shade trees. Buddhas embraced their consorts, uninhibited, free, and joyous. Deer lay in the grass and monkeys played about the trees.

Paradise thought Govinda.

Another mural depicted scenes of intense suffering, which Lama Norbu ignored.

"What about those who know nothing of Buddha-Land?" asked Govinda, his gaze fixed on a group of tormented souls battling one another.

"Every man must make effort. Otherwise, he continues to be bound by the chains of his forging. Without spiritual training, one may indulge in destructive acts. Hostile thoughts and feelings are diseases far worse than malaria, for they infect the soul lifetime after lifetime. Fortunate are those who practice the eternal truth — whatever you meditate upon, you become."

"Those who will not accept the freedom that exists in Buddha-Land remain on the wheel of birth and rebirth until one day they awaken."

Day after day, Lama Norbu read from the holy book. Memorizing, and then rehearsing various scenes, the old lama imagined the realm of the Buddhas, where, upon his death, he would go. If a lama's passing was traumatic, or he required assistance in arriving at his otherworldly abode, his mentors and fellow lamas were there to help.

Govinda lay beneath the yak fur he shared with Dolmo in the chill attic, his mind full of questions.

"Dolmo, are you awake?"

"Awake."

"Why is it important to prepare for death?"

"When death come, soul can go high. Lama want to go to Land of Pure Bliss. Lama Norbu prepare for liberation."

"Lama Norbu says it is possible to gain Nirvana instantly; that the soul can bypass countless incarnations if one prepares properly. You achieved Nirvana and reached Buddha-land, and yet you came back. It seems so perfect there. Why did you return?"

"Buddha teach... those who achieve Nirvana help others."

"What is Buddha-land like?"

"Buddha-land radiate clear light to world. Buddha-land place of pure bliss. I like it very much."

"Returning to the world of men must be a sacrifice," decided Govinda.

"All is Buddha-land for me."

"But if preparation for dying is important, then what about Lama Jinpa? He died suddenly."

"That is why Tibetan learn about death while living. Who can say what breath will be last breath?"

"Will Lama Jinpa's soul be all right?"

"Rinpoche helping Jinpa. That is why he stay in cell. He take Jinpa to Buddha-land."

"But Rinpoche has been in his cell for nearly five moons. Does it take a long time to reach Buddha-land?"

"Maybe take five days. Lama Choden enjoy Buddha-land. That maybe take five moons." Dolmo giggled.

"Can we visit Buddha-land?"

"If you like."

"I would like to," replied Govinda.

"We go tonight, but we must be fearless."

"I am not afraid."

"I know Govinda not afraid. To go to Buddha-land, we make clear dreaming."

"Clear dreaming?"

"Tonight, we go to Buddha-land in dream body," clarified Dolmo.

Under the yak cover, Govinda's dreams were unlike any he had ever dreamt before. When the friends awakened, they smiled knowingly at one another.

"Buddha-land good?" asked Dolmo.

"Buddha-land very good!" replied Govinda, lying under the yak fur and savoring the experience. The Land of Pure Bliss had lived up to its name, surpassing anything Govinda had imagined.

The following day, after spending the morning with Lama Norbu, Govinda sought out Dolmo. It seemed that every wall in the old monastery depicted the life of Buddha and the hall where Govinda found Dolmo was no exception. Slipping in silently, Govinda seated himself on a small rug outside a ring of robed musicians. The lamas held odd shaped instruments; some had a second one at their side.

Dolmo sat cross-legged on his rug, a row of metal bowls spread before him. The others waited for him to intone a note before joining in. Using a rounded wooden instrument, he struck the side of the largest bowl and then listened. The other lamas listened with equal concentration as Dolmo struck a somewhat smaller bowl, creating a harmonic between larger and smaller bowl. Then he struck a third bowl. As the notes reverberated, a second lama struck a drum while

The Tale of the Himalayan Yogis

a third sounded a prehistoric looking horn that, considering its size, produced a subdued sound.

The tones faded into the walls. Once again, Dolmo struck one of the bowls, a smaller bowl this time. As the sound faded, the other lamas joined in with drums, horns, and cymbals. The melodic ritual repeated itself over and over.

When the session was over, Dolmo sat next to Govinda.

"You like?" asked Dolmo, still holding the wooden stick in his hand.

"The music was like a deep meditation."

"This special music. This music awaken mandala."

"I don't understand."

"Come." Dolmo led his friend over to the brightly painted circle on the wall. "This sacred mandala."

"Lama Norbu taught me about mandalas."

"I strike *panchdhatu* bowl. Vibration make mandala spin," explained Dolmo, circling the wooden instrument in the air. "Vibration spread beyond gompa. Mandala make harmony everywhere."

"Like tossing a stone into a pond?"

Domo nodded. "Ripples going everywhere."

Spring arrived but was chased off by a blizzard. Rinpoche Choden had not emerged from his cellar dwelling. Although some of the lamas were concerned, no one spoke of it.

Dolmo and Govinda were huddled near the hearth, sharing a plate of momos, when Lama Choden ambled into the kitchen. The lamas were delighted to see their leader, and a spontaneous celebration took place. Spiral horns sounded, brass bells chimed, goatskin drums thumped, and lamas chanted. The monks escorted their leader into the central hall, seating him on a velvet chair reserved for the presiding abbot.

Lama Choden, though frail from his extended austerity, smiled benevolently at his friends before addressing the group.

"Humbly, and most honored am I to sit with you, my brothers. I return from worlds I cannot describe. Happy I am that our brother,

Lama Jinpa, arrive safely, though his departure was sudden. Jinpa send greeting to all, with special good wish to Govinda for his selfless act."

No sooner had the snows melted than the lamas departed for Tibet. Not long after leaving Yurpa Gompa, the lamas descended through a forest of flowering rhododendron. A profusion of crimson blossoms blanketed the forest like exquisite Kashmiri rugs. Further down the trail, Govinda inhaled the scent of wild rose and cherry blossoms.

It wasn't long before the trail reached the twisting Kali Gandaki River. Swollen by spring melt, fierce rapids raged at the feet of the tallest peaks on earth. The brutal force of the churning waters cut deep chasms as the river rushed to the paddy fields in the south. Tumultuous torrents roared through narrow gorges. The lamas stepped gingerly across rope bridges, their lives depending on nimbleness, aging ropes, and the grace of Buddha.

As the lamas headed north, the trail shadowed the river. Villages dotted hillsides, and modest shrines appeared at trail's edge. Further up the valley, the river basin broadened, and rivulets cascaded down the mountains, forcing the lamas to traverse a slender path above the valley floor. The caravan marched past stone and wood settlements, some with ochre gompas perched on hilltops. Walking single file through fruit orchards and barley fields, the lamas murmured salutations to the Buddha. Like their monastic brothers, the villagers were of resolute stock, an inner calm guiding their hands as they toiled in the fields.

Tibetan families plodded along the trail. Their goatskin gowns, hairy yak boots, and leathery skin appeared odd to a Rajput, though the peasants' toothy smiles were warm and sincere.

Vegetation grew sparingly. Thorny bushes battled howling winds for survival in this far-flung place; Kalki would have found little to graze on. The landscape of the high-altitude desert donned muted shades of olive, slate, and khaki. If not for the winsome smiles of the locals, Govinda would not have felt welcome.

After following the river for five days, the monks arrived in Lo, an ancient kingdom traveled by salt caravans as they journeyed to

The Tale of the Himalayan Yogis

and from the Indian plains. The lamas rested in Lo Manthang before heading over Mustang Pass, which descended into Tibet.

Old Norbu struggled to keep up. Since his bout with malaria, his stamina had not returned. Everyone noticed, but no one spoke of it. Rinpoche Choden walked with Lama Norbu, but by the end of each day, the senior monks had fallen far behind the others. Rinpoche suggested that Norbu sit atop a yak, but the old lama insisted that he cherished every step he took toward Kailash Lo. Although the group had yet to reach the higher altitudes of the Tibetan plateau, Lama Norbu was breathless much of the time. Govinda fared only slightly better.

At Lo Manthang, Dolmo and Govinda purchased supplies. In the windswept bazaar, they heard talk of a band of horsemen that robbed and even murdered. Dolmo questioned the traders about the bandits. According to a caravan leader, riders had appeared out of nowhere, making off with several mules laden with supplies. Two Mongolians were injured in the attack.

Everyone welcomed the stopover at Lo Manthang, but Lama Norbu's condition steadily declined. The lamas took turns kneading the senior lama's back while he fingered prayer beads for hours at a time.

"Why doesn't Norbu stay here in Lo Manthang?" Govinda asked Dolmo. "The long days on the trail are too much for him."

"Lama Norbu prepare since we arrive at Yurpa," Dolmo replied. "He know death coming."

"Climbing mountains isn't helping."

"Lama Norbu happy. He reach Kailash Lo, then depart this world."

"Do all Tibetans prepare for death?" asked Govinda, recalling old Tiwari's final days in the cave.

"Lama make special meditation. When end near, lama visit higher realms where soul destined to go. Lama own nothing… no house… no yak. When lama die, he free. Lama collect wisdom, not wealth. Wisdom useful for soul journey. Life experience only thing he take with him. Soul have no use for house, no use for land. Final hour chance for big leap if lama have courage."

"I'm beginning to understand."

"Seven gates," explained Dolmo. "Lama practice entire life what gate his soul pass through."

"Which gate should one go through?"

"Thoughts at time of death determine gate. Lama want to exit here," said Dolmo, placing his finger on the crown of Govinda's head. "Higher gate take soul to higher realm… Land of Bodhisattvas. Lower gate take soul to lower realm… no peace in lower realm."

"Why doesn't Norbu ride a mule? It would make it easier for him."

"Tibetan born walking. Buddha's last word was, 'Walk on.'"

"I'm exhausted, but the lamas never grow tired."

"Laughing and walking Tibetan pastime."

Upon reaching the Tibetan border, the lamas had another twenty days journey to Manasarovar, the sacred lake where Gautama Buddha's mother prayed for a divine child. Govinda's muscles burned, and his head throbbed as he reached the summit of Mustang. Aside from old Norbu, who stopped often, the others might have been strolling through a meadow of wildflowers. Their stamina was uncanny; the drone of their mantras rolled on. Some of the lamas spun *damaru*; others fingered prayer beads.

After reaching the pass, the group descended to the Tibetan plateau. Ahead lay barren landscape for as far as the eye could see. Behind the caravan stood a wall of towering pyramids separating the lamas from Yurpa Gompa. Everyone but Govinda felt happy to be in Tibet. For the young Rajput, the bleak terrain and testy winds whipping across the trail were even more desolate than the snowfields surrounding Yurpa. Govinda began to wonder whether he would ever feel the warmth of the Rajputana sun again.

From a ridge, Dolmo pointed to a distant peak.

"Chomolungma," whispered the young lama reverently. "Mother Goddess of the world… highest peak in Himalaya."

Night descended, and with it the cruel cold. Fuel was scarce on the high plateau, and feeble fires failed to ward off the bone-chilling temperatures.

"How will we defend ourselves if bandits attack?" asked Govinda, finishing a bowl of salty tsampa flavored with a drop of yak butter. It was the middle of summer, and still, he shivered by the fire. Govinda couldn't imagine what winter would bring in this austere land.

"Lamas protected," replied Rinpoche Choden matter-of-factly. "We no carry weapon."

Remembering how the yogis in Varanasi had protected themselves against the imperial army, Govinda was satisfied with the lama's answer.

"Weapons invite use," Choden explained. "Lama cloak himself in peace."

"We Rajputs invite conflict," admitted Govinda. "My ancestors took pleasure in battle."

"Lama no desire fighting... bandit no attack. That is way of karma... that is way of universe."

"Before I joined you, I attracted Moguls wherever I went."

"Now you lama like Dolmo. You have peace in heart?"

"Yes, but lamas are warriors too," decided Govinda. "Dolmo is a peaceful warrior."

"Dolmo *tulku*," replied Lama Choden respectfully. "Dolmo Bodhisattva."

"Dolmo is a fine Bodhisattva."

Govinda had no idea where he was ultimately going, but he was slowly becoming accustomed to his wandering way of life. Vast stretches of black sands stretched before him. As the group reached the crown of a hill, Dolmo pointed to a shimmering, blue-grey expanse on the horizon.

"Manasarovar... sacred waters of my people."

At the sight of the lake, Dolmo's pace quickened, but it would be two days time before the lamas bathed in the frigid waters.

The weathered gompa near the pebbled shore of Lake Manasarovar was a welcome sight. Embedded in the side of a rocky crag, Seralung Gompa faced the holy waters. Though cramped, cold, and overrun with rodents, the gompa felt like a king's palace after the long journey.

The legends surrounding Manasarovar were ancient and varied. Wish-fulfilling trees were said to stand on the shores of the lake, and yet Govinda saw no vegetation. Yogis and Bodhisattvas were rumored to meditate by the pristine waters. Although Govinda felt their presence, only pebbles smoothed by wind and water populated the shores. A pair of swans glided across the placid water. Perhaps the graceful waterfowl were yogis having their morning bath.

Lama Norbu lay beneath his yak fleece, exhausted from three moons on the trail. The old man had reached Mustang Pass on determination alone. The lamas knew he would not give up until he saw Kailash Lo, the most sacred mountain on earth.

The clouds lifted the morning after the lamas arrived, offering a glimpse of the domed peak, the center of their universe. Shiva's abode shimmered in the sunlight.

A family of Tibetans had taken up residence in the crumbling gompa where a toothless lama served as caretaker. The lonely lama dutifully filled the oil lamps each morning and swigged home-brewed *chaang* before retiring to his mat near the Buddha.

The peasant family would circumambulate the holy mountain a hundred and eight times before returning to their village, a moon's journey away. Halfway to their goal, they would need favorable weather if they were to complete their pilgrimage in time to return home before winter arrived. Hearing of the peasants' ambitious scheme, Govinda shrugged. Dolmo had not exaggerated when he said Tibetans loved walking more than anything. What amounted to torment for Govinda had been a lifetime ambition for the village family.

On the lamas' third day at Manasarovar, the domed crown of Mount Kailash came into view again. Fording shallow streams that flowed from Lake Manasarovar, they approached the sacred mountain. Govinda had crossed the Himalaya, the fabled House of Snow, but he had never set eyes on anything quite like Mount Kailash. The site of the peak's pearl-shaped dome caused powerful energies to surge within him. Certainly, the mountain was majestic to gaze upon, but the peak resonated deeply with his soul, as well as those of the lamas. The solitary dome dwarfed the surrounding peaks, its aura enveloping everything in its vicinity. For Hindus, Mount Kailash was Shiva's place of eternal transcendence. For Buddhists, the mountain was Kang Rinpoche, 'Mountain of Precious Snow' and altar of their gods.

As Govinda stood with the lamas, humbled by the site of the mountain, a lonely figure passed them on the trail. The broad-shouldered

The Tale of the Himalayan Yogis

yogi wore renunciate robes; a swath of faded cloth covered his head. The yogi walked purposefully up the footpath, his powerful strides distancing him from the lamas. Something about the yogi compelled Govinda to watch him until he disappeared among the rocks.

"Long ago, Milarepa live here," Dolmo explained as they moved toward the peak. "Milarepa born to wealthy family. Father die. Uncle and aunt steal family wealth. Milarepa's mother tell him to study sorcery to make revenge. Aunt and uncle celebrating son's marriage. Many guests at their house. Milarepa summon giant scorpion. Scorpion demolish house, kill son and bride, and thirty-three guests. Uncle and aunt survive. Villagers search for Milarepa, but mother warn him. He summon hailstorm to destroy crops. Disaster for villagers.

"Milarepa feel remorse. He turn to spiritual path. He challenge Naro Bonchung, leader of Bon Po religion. Milarepa say, 'Whoever reach Kailash summit first, his religion become Tibetan religion.' Naro start at dawn. Milarepa meditate. Naro almost reach top. Milarepa make magic and fly to summit. Milarepa defeat Naro Bonchung. Buddhism become religion of Tibet."

Peering up at the peak, Govinda laughed, "I could use some of Milarepa's magic."

The circumambulation of Kailash Lo was about to begin. The lamas crossed a field of scree, gazing up at the south face of Kailash which shimmered against the azure sky. Lama Norbu fixed his eyes on the magnificent pearl dome as he plodded along, falling further and further behind the others. Govinda kept an eye on Norbu, wary of a pack of mastiffs that appeared to be following him. The lamas had encountered several packs of *bhutia* dogs on their journey. The fierce dogs were unnerving at their best and deadly at their worst. Touching Dolmo's shoulder, Govinda pointed to the hungry pack shadowing Lama Norbu. Govinda and Dolmo dropped behind the others when Lama Norbu paused to rest on a rock.

"Bhutia hungry," said Dolmo.

"I understand. I'm hungry too."

The dogs closed in on Lama Norbu, who was oblivious to any danger.

Dolmo picked up a handful of stones. The boys reached Norbu

a step ahead of the dogs, positioning themselves between the hungry canines and their quarry. The lead dog bore knife-like fangs, growling testily. The other dogs mimicked their leader, their fierce barks echoing off the mountain.

Poised to hurl a rock, Govinda warned the dogs. Ignoring him, they moved in. Dolmo threw the first stone, striking the lead dog on the shoulder. Undeterred, the dogs came on the attack. Govinda and Dolmo tried to drive them off, but the ravenous pack refused to retreat. As rock after rock pelted them, the dogs grew increasingly hostile. The lead dog sprang first, but Govinda lurched in front of the beast, kicking it soundly in the chest.

The dog leaped again, but as it sprang into the air, a stick came crashing down on the animal's skull causing the mastiff to recoil in pain.

Before the dog could recover, a second crushing blow descended on the mastiff's shoulders, followed by another that put the yelping animal on the defensive. Another blow struck the beast squarely on the nose, causing it to run off. When the lead dog retreated, the others followed.

"Mastiff have no food," said the peasant, waving the stick above his head. "I see dogs attack other pilgrims. Now I carry stick. Not allow wife to fall behind."

"We'll be more careful," said Govinda, still clutching a handful of rocks as the dogs kept their distance.

Lama Norbu, it seemed, had taken no notice of the fray. Govinda assumed that he had fallen under the spell of the mountain.

By now, the others had backtracked to the scene of the assault. Govinda peered questioningly at Lama Choden, who was muttering prayers. The other lamas joined in. Govinda turned to Lama Norbu, realizing what the others already knew. His friend and teacher had departed, the kindly lama's gaze fixed on the sacred mountain. Old Norbu's lips formed a faint smile; his eyes blazed with the fire of realization. His journey to the Great Between had begun.

Huddling near the faintly glowing embers, Govinda felt the chill air more than other nights. The fire struggled against the thin air and frigid winds sweeping down from the snowfields.

"Lama Norbu choose well," said Rinpoche Choden solemnly. "Tonight auspicious moon."

Govinda shivered; his stomach begged for a bowl of tsampa. The lamas would fast until morning and he with them.

"Lama Norbu reach sacred mountain," said Dolmo.

"Norbu request sky burial," said Rinpoche Choden. "I send word to Darchen. Men carry body from mountain."

Foregoing their tsampa, the lamas slipped under yak furs and fell fast asleep. Govinda moved closer to the fire, but no matter how close he got, the cold tormented him. The gnawing of an empty stomach didn't help.

"Dolmo, are you awake?" Govinda whispered.

"Awake," came the familiar reply.

"Rinpoche says you're a tulku."

"Rinpoche say that?"

"Yes, but he didn't explain."

"Tulku is lama who come back to help others."

"Are you a tulku?" asked Govinda.

"I can't say. Everyone come back. My reason no better than another man."

"But a tulku has attained Nirvana. Rinpoche Choden says that a tulku has a choice whether he comes back, or not."

"Rinpoche wise man."

"Dolmo, I'm glad you came back."

"I glad Govinda here too. Bhutia dangerous, but you not afraid. Avalanche big danger, but you not afraid. Lamas happy Govinda here."

"But I feel sad tonight."

"No feel sad. Lama Norbu happy."

"I'm not sad for Lama Norbu, but I feel my journey with the lamas is almost over... that our paths will part soon."

"I too see new path for you."

"But the lamas are my family now. I want to go with you to Shey Gompa."

"If Shey Gompa right path, you come. If not, you not come."

Guru and Chela

Govinda lay awake, the pulsing energy of the mountain preventing him from sleeping. Cold and hungry, he slipped out from under his yak fleece and walked to the edge of the camp. A trance-inducing moon bathed the mountain. Govinda felt sure that he was in the presence of a god. The mountain drew him toward it like a mighty magnet. Though other pilgrims camped nearby, the night was perfectly still. As Govinda stumbled toward the resplendent dome, he heard someone faintly calling his name. He scanned the camps to see who had spoken, but everyone was asleep; only the occasional crackle of a fire disturbed the silence.

Again he heard the voice.

"Govinda."

He walked further, wondering if altitude, exhaustion, and hunger were playing tricks on his mind.

"Govinda, come."

There it was again. Govinda felt compelled to follow the voice which led him to a small shrine used by Hindu priests. Sitting in the moonlight, he spotted a robed figure facing the mountain. It was the yogi who had passed the lamas on the trail at Manasarovar.

"Sit," the hooded phantom instructed. Govinda sat next to the mysterious figure who was concealed by his robes.

"Who are you?"

"Shiva is our guru," replied the sadhu, ignoring Govinda's question. "We honor Mahadev tonight. Guru Purnima moon is blessing us."

The sadhu's voice sounded familiar, but where had he heard it?

"Guru Purnima moon?" asked Govinda, who had lost track of time on the long journey. Guru Purnima was the most auspicious full moon of the year, celebrated by Hindus and Buddhists everywhere, but here in this remote place, the ancestral traditions seemed part of a former life.

"Make offerings," instructed the yogi, handing Govinda a small pot of milk. In front of the yogi was a small oval stone, the symbol of Lord Shiva.

"Pour milk over the lingam the way the priests do in Varanasi," instructed the yogi.

The word 'Varanasi' awakened a faded memory, and Govinda realized that he was sitting beside the yogi who had saved him from the Moguls.

"Shankar Baba?"

"You remember," said the yogi, turning to face Govinda, whose eyes met Shankar Baba's for the first time. Deep, ageless, and perceptive eyes, like those of a poet or a philosopher; great pools of understanding whose inky pupils flashed gold. Seeing the yogi's face, Govinda fell to the ground, pressing his head against the holy man's feet as he had done in the cave.

"But how did you know I was here?"

"A yogi knows what he wishes to know," replied Shankar Baba. "Do you remember the diamond in the cave?"

"The Idol's Eye?"

"Did it not surprise you to find it missing?"

"I panicked."

"Did you not wonder how it came to be near Shambu? Had fear overtaken you, I would not be here tonight."

"You came all the way from Varanasi to be with me?" asked Govinda incredulously.

"Travel is easier for a yogi than for others."

Govinda suspected that Shankar Baba had not walked from Varanasi the way he and the lamas had.

"When you allowed Shambu to coil around your arm, I knew you had mastered your fear," the yogi continued.

"I'm not comfortable with snakes, you know."

"Nonetheless, you passed Shambu's test."

"But why were you testing me?"

"In time you will understand. Tonight we honor our guru. Make offerings to Shiva."

Govinda took the pot and poured milk over the Shiva stone. The yogi chanted softly as the liquid cascaded down the sides of the small lingam.

"See the snow on Kailash," said Shankar Baba, pointing at the moonlit mountain.

"The snow is like the milk offered to Shiva," observed Govinda.

"Shiva is silent like falling snow. Not a sound is heard in his vicinity. Shiva needs nothing from us."

"If Shiva needs nothing, then why make offerings?" asked Govinda.

"What divine being could ever need anything? But still, milk happens to be Shiva's favorite food. Milk increases Shiva's shakti. When a devotee offers him milk, Shiva's power increases. He shines with *ojas*. Milk is a slippery substance. It gets into the brain and connects us to Shiva's silence. Feel the liquid on the stone."

Govinda placed his hand on the stone.

"Offer the remainder of the milk," Shankar Baba instructed.

Govinda emptied the copper pot onto the lingam and set the vessel down.

"Govinda, you are ready. Pay obeisance to your guru, who sits beside you."

"My guru?" repeated Govinda, his body tingling with excitement. Pressing his forehead against Shankar Baba's feet, Govinda felt a pleasant liquid flowing over his head, cascading down his neck and back until it covered his entire body.

"Can you feel it?" asked Shankar Baba. "Shiva is returning your offering."

"It feels as if liquid is flowing over me."

"The nectar of the gods is being showered on you."

Govinda no longer felt hungry, or cold, or unsure of his future.

"You know much about me, don't you?"

"You are ever in my awareness," said Shankar Baba, gazing into Govinda's eyes. "Who do you imagine sent the man that saved you from the dogs earlier today? Your fearlessness is admirable, but your recklessness exposes you to danger."

"The man appeared out of nowhere."

"I waited for the lamas to bring you to Kailash before I claimed you. Now receive the blessing you richly deserve."

Govinda fell again at Shankar Baba's feet, clutching his master's ankles like a drowning man clinging to a life raft. The yogi placed his hands on Govinda's head. What happened next he couldn't explain. Govinda plunged into a sea of silence deeper than what he had ever experienced. In a flash of brilliant light, Govinda's thoughts, memories, attachments, and desires; all the things that occupied his mind, evaporated like water spilled over hot coals. His mind fell away like dust shaken from his robes. Nothing remained but stillness, and in that tranquility, Govinda knew that he and his guru were one.

Shankar Baba whispered a mantra into Govinda's ear and instructed him how to use it. Govinda bowed to the pearl-white peak that was aglow in the moonlit sky, and then closed his eyes. Into the vastness of space, he soared, a void so great that his body seemed less significant than a grain of sand. Then even that grain of sand dissolved and Govinda merged with infinity itself. Hand in hand, master and disciple meditated on the awesome presence of Lord Shiva.

"Govinda," whispered a voice as if spoken through a long, narrow tunnel. "Complete your pilgrimage with the lamas. When the lamas turn north, go to Rakshas Tal."

Before Govinda could extricate himself from his state of inner absorption, Shankar Baba had vanished. Govinda peered left and right in search of the yogi, but he was gone; there was no sign of him anywhere. Above Govinda, dawn's first light illumined Kailash. He stared at the imposing sight, immersed in the solitude and peace the mountain had filled him with during the night. He knew that he would never be the same.

As the sun sparkled against the ice-flecked dome, Govinda

surveyed the sky-touching pass with detachment. He now understood the spellbound look on old Norbu's face. If it all ended, Govinda would be content, satisfied that life had given him the very best it had to offer.

The lamas trudged silently up the trail as a dozen Tibetans donning black *chubas* descended from the opposite direction. The dusty forms circled the mountain counterclockwise, a tradition of ancient Bon Po, the religion that nearly vanished after Milarepa scaled the summit ahead of Naro Bonchung. Shielded by sheepskin aprons and padded wraps covering their hands and knees, the pilgrims fell to their knees every fourth step, a penance that perplexed Govinda, who glided up the mountain as if he were weightless. Why he felt such elation, he couldn't say, but as he climbed his body felt light and buoyant. The lamas resorted to a unique meditation that slowed their heartbeat and conserved what little breath they could gather.

The meager rations carried by pilgrims were shared freely between Hindus and Buddhists. Govinda watched an elderly couple carried by wooly yaks overtake him, but he walked on, feeling lighter with each step. Climbing as if to heaven itself, he ascended past ice falls and snow melt cascading off the holy peak. Tattered prayer flags fluttered in the wind. Cairns carved with mantras marked the timeless trail.

On the second morning, the lamas reached Drolma La. The summit looked out over a broad and barren expanse to the north.

"Shey Gompa," said Dolmo, pointing to a distant mountain.

"I will not be going with you," replied Govinda.

"Your guru calls."

Pilgrims paused at the summit to take in the vista. Between labored breaths, they whispered mantras that had lived in the background of their minds since childhood. Govinda sat on a rock with the lamas as they offered a prayer for Lama Norbu's soul.

The lamas descended quickly, passing a glacial pool near the trail. The climb down, while easier on the lungs, tested their legs which were heavy from the climb. Attaining the summit had taken a full day; the descent required an afternoon. As the lamas reached the base of the mountain, vultures circled ominously overhead. Passing a cluster of boulders at the bottom of the mountain, Govinda heard sharp-sounding blows and the splintering of wood.

But there are no trees here, he thought, scanning the rocky terrain.

As the lamas rounded the boulders, a bizarre ritual accounted for the vultures' presence. Two men were preparing a corpse for sky burial, their blades hacking at its limbs. No one spoke, but the lamas knew the body belonged to their friend. The mastiffs kept their distance, respectful of the blades and their wielders. Instinctively, Govinda picked up a rock to fling at the dogs, but let it fall to the ground. Viewing a sky burial was considered inauspicious, and seeing the lamas looking away as they passed, Govinda kept his eyes to the ground.

The splintering of bones and cawing of crows awakened childhood memories for the lamas, who were accustomed to sky burials on the hilltops outside their villages. Tibetans didn't dispose of all bodies in this manner; the scarcity of wood and rocky terrain often made it the best available option.

Govinda was relieved to be distancing himself from the uncouth burial.

"Dolmo, an astrologer once told me I would witness much death in my life," he said. "I have lost my father… and Jinpa… and now old Norbu has gone. I died, and a yogi brought me back. Death follows me like a shadow."

"Kailash is abode of immortality," said Dolmo. "Here no death."

"I never thought of it that way. The priests in Varanasi made offerings to the god of death to keep me alive."

"Buddha-saint Asanga say, 'Do not feed your body to the first tiger that comes along.'"

"Why would you feed your body to any tiger?" wondered Govinda.

"Buddha teach compassion. Seeing hungry animal, lama may give up his life to feed tiger."

"But the tiger will soon be hungry again."

Dolmo smiled.

"Soul occupy body only little while. Sickness or old age slay body, but nothing slay soul. When Tibetan hear chopping, he think woodcutting. Is it so different?"

The following evening, the lamas reached Seralung Gompa.

"Rinpoche, may I speak with you?" asked Govinda after finishing his tsampa.

"Sit." Rinpoche Choden motioned to a worn mat near him.

"I had decided to stay with the lamas, but now a new path has been revealed. I am not confused… only I am drawn to both paths."

"No confusion, spirit of lama in you now."

"When the lamas head north I will take a different path."

"I know well what you must do. Your guru has claimed you."

"I am grateful to my lama friends."

"Go and be with Dolmo. He sad that you are leaving, but he understand."

Govinda touched Rinpoche Choden's feet before approaching Dolmo.

"Come, moon is over Manasarovar," said Dolmo.

Dolmo took Govinda's hand as they gazed at the moon and its equally brilliant reflection on the placid water. In the distance loomed Kailash Lo where Lama Norbu departed, and Govinda met his guru.

"Tell me about Shey Gompa," said Govinda, as they walked along the shore. "I want to see it in my mind the way you imagine my world."

"No time to think about Shey Gompa. Your master has claimed you."

"But Shey Gompa is where my friends will be."

"Now you find other friends… true friends."

"If you are not a true friend, then who is?"

"The gods are our true friends. Krishna is friend. Buddha is friend. Guru is friend."

"Lama also friend."

"Yes, lama also friend." Dolmo nodded. "Out of love, your guru will test you."

"He already has."

"Guru test to see if soul stronger than ego. Make guru's wish your life."

"I'll try," said Govinda.

"We walked together many moons. Tomorrow you take new path… guru's path. I will be sad when you are not at my side."

"So will I."

Govinda felt the cold on his back and rolled over. He had grown accustomed to being greeted each morning by the frozen earth beneath him. The lamas had risen silently, performed their morning oblations, and were sipping yak butter tea sprinkled with barley grounds. After a cup of steaming tea, Govinda bowed to his adopted brothers, whose faces shone like butter lamps at the feet of the Buddha. Although their journey across the vast Himalaya had linked them for life, Govinda doubted that he would see his friends again.

One by one the lamas bowed to Govinda before departing, their burgundy robes fluttering in their wakes. Unable to ward off the gloom invading his heart, Govinda watched the lamas disappear one by one over a ridge.

Govinda followed the trail to Rakshas Tal where he hoped Shankar Baba would be waiting for him. The full moon night with the mysterious yogi seemed more a dream than a reality now. A faint shadow entered Govinda's mind. Would Shankar Baba appear as he had promised, or would he be alone in this inscrutable land, wandering about a barren plateau beneath a sky that stretched forever?

Govinda was without food or water in a place seemingly as remote as the moon, following a trail to a lake the scriptures claimed to be the abode of fierce demons. Even Shiva himself was silent in this vast and inhospitable place.

His eyes fixed on the trail, Govinda continued to Rakshas Tal, the lake where bloodthirsty creatures had come to vanquish the gods. Arriving at the lakeshore as the shadows stretched, Govinda scanned the shore in search of Shankar Baba, but there was no sign of life anywhere; nothing but the haunting legend of Ravan, the demon Ram had defeated in an epic battle. Discouraged, Govinda leaned against a boulder. He hadn't slept much on the mountain, having repeatedly been awakened by bouts of breathlessness. Sitting at water's edge, Govinda fell asleep.

Startled by the ten-headed demon before him, Govinda asked, "Who are you?" In each of his hands, the *asura* held a weapon.

"I am Ravan, king of Lanka," boasted the demon. "You sleep having not paid obeisance to me."

"And why should I pay obeisance to a defeated demon?"

"Because I rule this place."

"Lord Ram vanquished you in Lanka."

"Never! I cannot be killed. Take this sword and try," taunted Ravan, tossing a sword to the ground. "See if you can slay me; Ram couldn't."

Govinda picked up the sword and whipped the blade in a blurred arc, severing all ten of the demon's heads in a single stroke.

"Ha, ha, ha!" roared the severed heads from the ground as ten new heads appeared. "Try again!" jeered the chorus of twenty identical demonic voices.

Govinda swung again. Ten more heads fell to the ground and ten more appeared. To his disbelief, the new faces were more horrific than the previous ones; each was the face of Commander Zaim. As Govinda watched, leprous lesions grew on the faces, covering their skin and peeling it away like rotting masks.

"Now I will devour you, for I am Ravan, the most powerful being in creation. Even Ram fears me," the rotting faces whispered in a chorus.

"Lord Ram fears no one," Govinda declared defiantly. "He conquered you, just as I will if you dare to face me."

"Is that so?" snickered Ravan. "Then you're not afraid."

"Never!"

At his words, the demon vanished, and the scene shifted. Govinda sat in a cave, a low fire before him. Terrifying shrieks echoed off cavern walls, and blinding flashes of lightning filled the hollow chamber. Shadows darted about; the wind howled like tortured devils. Phantoms swirled overhead.

"Time to die," echoed a voice from every side. "I am everywhere, but you cannot see me."

Govinda's sword had vanished, and so he took a stick from the fire and drew a circle on the floor of the cave before sitting at its center.

"Ravan, you haven't the power to enter this circle," he declared.

"Fear is the only way by which you can enter, and I have none. Try to enter this circle, coward who hides like a frightened deer."

The flame near Govinda flared to the ceiling of the cave. A chorus of demonic voices shrieked, "Prepare to die!"

Govinda felt burning wind, or perhaps breath, on his neck and back. An immense power was sucking him from his seat. At any moment, Ravan would pull him out of the circle.

"You cannot move me, weak-willed one," Govinda stated resolutely.

"Silence!" roared the voices, shaking the cave.

"You're the fearful one," Govinda countered; "otherwise you would not hide."

Govinda was growing tired of the game when Ravan appeared on the far side of the fire.

"Fear me now!" raged Ravan, filling the cave with an infernal presence.

"I cannot fear you because you don't exist, deluded one," said Govinda. "Ego is not welcome here; otherwise you would have slain me already. Now go. Your pranks bore me. Find a victim elsewhere."

At Govinda's words, the demon disappeared, and he woke to find Shankar Baba standing beside him at lake's edge.

"Having a pleasant dream?" inquired the yogi, a mischievous grin on his face.

Govinda had never been so happy to see anyone in his life. At the sight of his guru, the heaviness left his heart.

"Pleasant is not the word," smiled Govinda, "but yes, I had a dream."

"Your mind is strong, young one," observed Shankar Baba. "Your training has begun. I have been waiting for this day for longer than you know. Have prasad from your initiation last night."

The yogi handed Govinda the copper pot filled with the milk he had poured over Shiva's stone.

"Are you ready to climb mountains with me?" asked Shankar Baba as Govinda drank from the small pot.

"It seems I've done nothing *but* climb mountains since leaving Varanasi," laughed Govinda, emptying the pot in a single gulp.

"It will not be so difficult now that I am here."

"Crossing the Himalaya may be easy for Tibetans, but we Rajputs prefer horses."

"The peaks we will climb are different. Last night you had a taste. Did you like it?"

"There is no place like Shiva's mountain. My mind is unable to conjure up the memory of it."

"The memory of Shiva is not Shiva."

"And a dream of Ravan is not Ravan?"

"Ravan was more real than you think," replied Shankar Baba. "Whether waking or sleeping, awareness is a yogi's greatest ally. Dreams are not mere dreams in the higher realms. But you already know that from your soul journeys."

Does Shankar Baba know everything, wondered Govinda?

"Not everything," smiled the yogi.

"But you just answered my thought."

"I know what I care to know, but I don't interfere. Your dialogue with Ravan was of interest to me, and so I listened from within the fire. Wind, water, fire… the elements are all within our bodies. By focusing on the fire within me, I became the fire that warmed you. In time, you'll know how to do this, and more."

"You found that boorish demon interesting?"

"I wished to see how you handled yourself. You did well, but never forget that ego wears a thousand masks. Ego manipulates the mind. It grows a new head whenever one is cut off. Never assume the ego is dead! If you learn that lesson, you will not fall the way Vishwamitra fell."

"How *did* he fall?"

"The sage performed severe penance, but as he reached the summit, anger pulled him down, and he had to begin the climb again."

"If a great yogi like Vishwamitra could fall, what hope is there for me?"

"We shall find out. Come; there's a small lamasery beyond the Mandhaka hills. I know the lama there. He'll prepare you a tasty meal."

"Tsampa, no doubt," replied Govinda unenthusiastically.

"Lost your taste for roasted barley?"

"Only after having it twice a day since leaving Varanasi. It's no Rajput banquet…"

"I'll have the lama make something special. How does cabbage sound?"

Govinda laughed out loud. He was enjoying his new friend, who he shared more in common with than the implacable lamas.

"Cabbage and Tibetan flatbread, that would be a feast," agreed Govinda. "Will he make momos?"

"You talk like a Tibetan… but I can see you're missing Rajputana."

"Not while circling the mountain. Nothing mattered at Kailash. But this morning I missed the lamas, and I miss Krishnagarh too."

"Kailash is beyond even the highest realms of human experience. Time itself is different there."

"Time didn't seem to exist at all. I meditated for the entire night, and when the sun came up, it seemed as if I'd been sitting for a few moments."

"Do not think of the years ahead as an exile. It will be the most exciting time of your life, and it will pass like a night on Shiva's mountain."

"Shastriji's predictions discouraged me," said Govinda. "He made it sound like Saturn intends to kill me."

"Don't limit yourself by thinking a planet will somehow hurt you. There is always a shadow ready to take advantage of one's fear. If given a chance, the shadow may try to harm you. Planetary cycles should in no way slow you down. *Mangal* is the warrior, and yet Mars helps a person battle the stronghold of ignorance inside, and it will also help you battle the ignorance of humanity. The same is true of Saturn."

"But Black Moon sounds ominous."

"The true value of Jyotish has been almost entirely forgotten. Every planetary situation is positive. There's no such thing as a negative period in Jyotish. A shift in the planets just means there is a different way for a person to think and act. Perfection in your action always exists, and that's possible no matter what your Jyotish cycle. There is never an inherently bad time."

"Coming from you, I almost believe it," said Govinda.

"Why shouldn't you believe it?"

"The things you say sound too fantastic."

"You will get used to my words. It will be my actions that will be difficult to comprehend."

Guru and chela walked in silence before reaching Rizong Gompa. After the vastness of the Tibetan sky, the small monastery seemed confining.

Shankar Baba had the manner of one who followed no rules but broke none. Monastic life, on the other hand, adhered to disciplines established centuries ago. Govinda was confident that he had chosen well when he decided not to accompany the lamas to Shey Gompa.

Tender momos and golden flatbread appeared before Govinda; tsampa was not a part of his meal for the first time since departing Yurpa Gompa.

"Now I *know* you can perform magic," he laughed.

"Did you ever doubt it?" asked the yogi, a twinkle lighting his eyes.

"After seeing you deal with Commander Zaim and his henchmen, I wonder if there's anything you can't do. You never even opened your eyes when they attacked."

"A yogi is careful to keep the ego underfoot, but yes, Commander Zaim's is an interesting soul. The man held much fear and hatred in his heart. When the floodgates opened, he went mad."

"But how did you put that curse on him?" wondered Govinda. "How does a curse work?"

Shankar Baba smiled like a naughty child.

"Whether good or bad, one's actions find their way back home. I simply accelerated the process. In reality, Commander Zaim cursed himself. I just helped a bit by returning his hostility to him. You wouldn't recognize him now. The emperor banished Zaim to a leper colony. The disease will worsen until he frees himself from his loathing."

"And if he does?"

"Then there would be a chance that he could be healed. But he may not free himself in this life. If one is foolish enough to injure another of God's children, then the penalty must be paid in full, whether it be disease or dejection in life." Shankar Baba paused to reflect on Zaim's fate.

"Freeing oneself from the wheel of karma is never easy. The sense appetites of previous lives become the driving forces for the next life. Like a slave, one is bound to the chariot wheels of misery until kindness overcomes selfishness. There is only one way to free oneself from the wheel of cause and effect, and that is holding firm to the inner Self regardless of the outer condition. Until one discovers divine love, one whirls about from life to life."

"It's never good to be the deliverer of karma because being the deliverer keeps you on the wheel. Masters often set up circumstances to deliver karma, but they are not immune. Masters age because they willfully take on their disciple's karma. An arrow wounded even Krishna. Mahatmas do not suffer the way normal people do, but they feel it, and it can slow them down."

"Mishra says you're famous around Varanasi. Everyone is in awe of your snakes."

"What is fame among misfits?" the yogi chuckled. "Cobras are sensitive creatures. Have you not seen Shiva with cobras draped about his neck?"

"Yes, but how did the cobras know to attack the soldiers?"

"They sensed danger and reacted. There was little magic involved."

"Will I meditate with snakes?" asked Govinda.

"Only if you want to."

"Guruji, where are you taking me?"

"To your cave."

"Shastri predicted that I would live within the earth."

"You have not seen this cave in this lifetime."

Govinda noticed that Shankar Baba wasn't eating.

"I stopped taking food long ago," he said, answering his chela's thoughts. "I take Ganges water and a cup of cow's milk from time to time. Eating is inconvenient, don't you think?"

"Living on roasted barley certainly is," replied Govinda, rolling his eyes.

"Have you observed how food shapes the personality? Your lama friends have eaten tsampa their entire lives, and they are unflappable characters. You, on the other hand, have been raised on spicy curry. See the passion in your personality!"

"I never thought of it that way."

"I live on air and water. Less *dosha* that way."

"Dosha?"

"Impurity."

"Why did the Tibetans chop up Lama Norbu's body?" asked Govinda.

"Sky burial benefits the soul."

"I don't understand."

"The soul often lingers to see what the fate of the body will be. Sky burial encourages the soul to move on. The ritual prevents the soul from becoming bound to its former abode. Still, cremation is the better way. If the body is not disposed of properly, a soul may languish in an earthbound state. This can happen when the body is buried in the ground.

"Discarnate beings linger near the home or village where they once lived. Their physical appetites often bind them there in the hope of further gratification. Without cremation, base desires are not burned away at the time of death.

"Due to the lethargy of their minds, discarnate beings may behave like a tiger in a cage. When there is a disturbance, they roar. They may even take revenge on those they dislike or behave cruelly toward people in general."

"Now I understand the burning ghats in Varanasi."

"Come, take some rest. We have a long way to go before we reach Kumaon."

While Govinda slept, Shankar Baba meditated. The yogi had little more use for sleep than he did for flatbread.

The resident lama at Rizong Gompa offered Govinda dried apricots and walnuts before yogi and chela went on their way. Master and disciple were crossing the bronzed grasslands of southern Tibet when a herd of mustangs came into view, reveling in their freedom. Govinda eyed the grey stallion at the head of the group.

"Pitaji rode a stallion more powerful than the grey."

"You miss him, don't you."

The Tale of the Himalayan Yogis

Govinda nodded.

"You need not, for the guru is both father and friend. If you like, you may call me, Baba," said the yogi, "for truly I am your spiritual father."

"I would like that," replied Govinda.

"The guru finds his chela lifetime after lifetime. His work is unfinished until the disciple reaches the goal."

"It must be a great sacrifice."

"To help another attain the goal is service... not sacrifice. When all is of the Self, there can be no sacrifice."

The undulating terrain rolled past grassy dunes where antelope and mustangs grazed. Shankar Baba instructed Govinda to keep his mantra going the way the lamas did, except that he was to do it silently. Govinda followed the footsteps of his guru, happy to be in the presence of a yogi.

The summer sun warmed the high plateau, but by late afternoon the chill that Govinda had never grown accustomed to, returned. Shankar Baba suggested they rest at the edge of a shallow stream.

"Do you hear it?"

Govinda heard only the gurgling of water.

"Hear what?"

"Listen with your heart. What do you hear?"

Govinda heard a faint rumbling in the distance.

"I hear the sound that came before the avalanche buried the lamas... only fainter."

"Riders. Can you feel their intention?"

"I don't feel anything."

"These men have bad intentions. Try again. Their thoughts will speak to you."

Govinda listened.

"I'm not sure."

"In time, you'll learn. Shall we go and greet them?"

"Shouldn't we hide here among the rocks?" suggested Govinda.

"We'll do whatever you decide."

"Then let's greet them." Govinda felt confident with Shankar Baba at his side.

The bandits rode over a hill, kicking up a dusty wake. Though Hindu sadhus rarely had anything of value, the gang had every intention of robbing Govinda and Shankar Baba.

The bearded headman rode up to the mendicants, his coarse garments stained and tattered. His leathery skin was an odd russet color. The man smelled foul.

"Remove your cloth," the headman ordered, his voice like gravel.

Govinda replied in Tibetan, "We have nothing of value, good man."

"You speak Tibetan?" replied the surprised bandit.

"Lamas teach me. Tibet good place." Govinda hoped the bandits would accept his words as a peace offering. If his strategy failed, he knew that Shankar Baba had more weapons in his mind than the bandits held in their hands.

"Tibet not good place," huffed the ill-tempered leader. "People poor. No crop."

"We have a little water." Govinda held out a container.

"Give me," demanded the headman, pointing to the pouch around Govinda's neck.

Govinda had forgotten about the gem and glanced at Shankar Baba questioningly.

"Better give it to him."

Govinda removed the pouch and handed it to the bandit, who opened the silk bag and held the priceless diamond up for the others to see.

"This what we want," proclaimed the bandit lustily. "Where you get it?"

"It belonged to my father."

"You may have the gem's blessings, but the diamond belongs to my *chela*," Shankar Baba said sternly.

"Gem mine," replied the bandit. "This my territory. You pay if you wish to pass."

"Return it to its owner," ordered Shankar Baba.

Shankar Baba stepped toward the bandit leader, who glared defiantly at the yogi from atop his horse.

"And if I don't?" challenged the bandit, raising his bushy brows.

The Tale of the Himalayan Yogis

"Then the gem will burn you."

The Tibetan unsheathed his knife.

"Drop the gem," ordered Shankar Baba. The bandit laughed at the yogi's command as he continued to admire the gem. Then, as if bitten by a snake, the bandit shrieked as he dropped the jewel, which fell to the ground among the horses. Govinda quickly retrieved the Idol's Eye and returned to Shankar Baba's side.

"Give it to me," ordered the head bandit, rubbing his hand.

"I told you it would burn you if you tried to keep it," said Shankar Baba calmly.

"Nonsense!" bellowed the Tibetan, his face red with anger. "Put in pouch and give to me!"

Govinda slipped the diamond into the pouch and handed it to the bandit. Again the Tibetan shrieked as he dropped the bag.

"Get it," the bandit ordered one of his men. Dismounting, the man reached for the pouch, but as he did, it burst into flames. The startled man jumped back.

"Go on your way," ordered Shankar Baba. "You cannot have this gem."

"The gem's cursed," hissed the chief. "Remove curse, yogi, or my men kill you."

"You can kill us, but the curse will remain. Now be gone!"

"Kill the boy," ordered the chief, signaling to the riders at his left. Three weathered brigands dismounted and approached Govinda, daggers drawn. But before they reached him, Shankar Baba reached inside the burning pouch, withdrew the Idol's Eye, and tossed it at the feet of the attackers. When the diamond hit the ground, it burst into an inferno, causing the attackers to retreat.

"Now go," ordered Shankar Baba. "If you harm my chela you will all die."

Shankar Baba's threat infuriated the bandit chief.

"Wrap gem in this," the chief ordered a subordinate, tossing a shabby yak skin to the ground.

"It won't help," said Shankar Baba. "Now go while you are able."

The gang's leader climbed down from his horse. Dagger in hand, he approached Shankar Baba.

"Leave before your rage consumes you," said Shankar Baba coolly. Too incensed to listen, the bandit leader charged, his crescent dagger raised. Before he reached the yogi, Shankar Baba waved his index finger at the attacker, and flames engulfed the Tibetan. Screaming, the bandit ran about like a madman, his beard and shirt in flames. His companions wrapped him in the yak skin, snuffing out the fire, but not before their leader's hands were blistered, and his eyebrows and beard singed.

"Your greed is a curse on your life," declared Shankar Baba. "Now go!"

The men helped their injured leader to his horse. Without another word, the gang rode off as Govinda gathered up the Idol's Eye. Surprisingly, the diamond felt cool in his hand.

"It's not hot at all. How did it burn?"

"The diamond did not wish to be in the hands of thieves," said Shankar Baba matter-of-factly.

"How do you know that?"

"It told me."

Govinda rotated the gem in his hand, wondering how the stone had spoken to the yogi.

"In time you will learn the secrets of nature," said Shankar Baba.

"How did you create fire?"

"A yogi's mind is in tune with the will of nature. He uses the elements as he wishes, so long as his purpose is pure. I told you how I listened from within the fire at Rakshas Tal. To create the flame, I simply invoked the fire element; the Idol's Eye did the rest."

"You make it sound like the Idol's Eye is alive."

"Everything is alive. It's a matter of understanding nature's language and seeing deeply into things. But one must not abuse these powers."

"How could one do so?"

"If the bandits possessed these powers, they would use them selfishly."

"I can't imagine what would happen if Zaim had possession of the Idol's Eye.

The Tale of the Himalayan Yogis

"There are others more dangerous than Zaim," revealed Shankar Baba. "Have something to eat. I can see that you are hungry."

Govinda ate the last of the apricots and walnuts while Shankar Baba watched a flock of cranes overhead.

"We have not seen the last of those *dacoits*," cautioned Shankar Baba. "The Idol's Eye is a rare prize. They will not let it slip through their hands so easily. No doubt, they will return in the night. Many will want to have it. You are the gem's custodian. I am thinking of a way to disguise it so that in the future you will not be in danger."

After sipping from the stream, Govinda and Shankar Baba continued on their way. The trail was undemanding, and by dusk, the travelers arrived at a small stupa. A friendly lama welcomed them inside. The single room shrine housed a dazzling golden Buddha whose head nearly touched the low ceiling. An oil lamp flickered at his feet.

"Swamiji, you and your chela are most welcome," said the lama, inviting them inside. "I am Lama Nima."

"Earlier we encountered thieves on the trail," said Shankar Baba. "They will come again in the night."

"Pasang and his men have been robbing pilgrims since before I came here. Should they come, I will speak with him."

"Their leader is foul-tempered."

"Pasang drinks too much, but he will not harm you. What is it that Pasang wants?"

"My chela has a gem. A gift from his father."

After his meal, Govinda stretched out on a plank of wood and was soon fast asleep. Shankar Baba meditated at the feet of Buddha while the lama transcribed an old text by the lamplight.

Late in the night, Govinda woke with a start, sitting stiffly on his austere bed. By the lamp in front of Buddha, he observed Shankar Baba. The yogi sat as still as the Buddha himself. Like mirror images, Shankar Baba and the golden Buddha faced one another, smiling at their shared secret. Govinda scanned the room, but the lama was not inside.

Outside, men were arguing, but the stupa walls muted their voices. The stupa's weathered door flew open, and a horde of foul smelling men stormed inside. Govinda recognized the bandits from the previous day.

"I want diamond," demanded the first man into the room. The bandit chief reeked of chaang; his hands bound by grimy rags.

"Pasang, the yogi and his chela are my guests," pleaded the kindly lama, who followed the bandit toward the altar. Pasang recklessly overturned a brass bell as he approached Shankar Baba.

"That sadhu burn my hands," accused the drunken Tibetan.

"It is wrong to steal, especially from a holy man," said Lama Nima, trying to calm the intruders.

Shankar Baba paid no attention to the commotion but continued his silent communion with the Buddha.

"Where is boy?" demanded Pasang. "I want diamond."

Govinda clutched the pouch which hung from his neck. He searched for a place to hide the Idol's Eye, but the stupa had only one room.

Lunging violently, Pasang ripped the pouch from Govinda's neck, tentatively pouring its contents into his bandaged hand. Confused by the object in his hand, the Tibetan stepped nearer to the lamp.

"Where is it?" he demanded, holding a lump of coal up to the light. "I want diamond."

"Have your hands not suffered enough?" asked Shankar Baba, not bothering to open his eyes.

Remembering his pain, Pasang grabbed a talwar from the man at his side.

"Pasang, no!" pleaded Lama Nima, stepping between bandit and yogi. But the drunken Tibetan had already committed his strike, and the blade fell on the old lama's arm. Lama Nima slumped beside Shankar Baba, who jumped to his feet, knocked Pasang's weapon aside, grabbed his bandaged hands and twisted them, causing the bandit to wail in agony. Snatching the weapon away, he pressed its tip against the Tibetan's bearded chin.

"You have harmed a pious man. Choose your fate. Leave now, or die by this sword."

Letting the lump of coal fall to the floor, the Tibetan turned and fled, his gang of misfits close on his heels. As suddenly as they had

The Tale of the Himalayan Yogis

appeared, the bandits were gone, leaving Govinda to ponder whether the midnight attack had occurred in a dream. But the sight of Lama Nima's bloodied robes confirmed that it had not.

"Govinda, do you have the powder from Varanasi?"

"A small amount."

Govinda had but a few possessions; the ring shawl Leela had given him, a metal bowl from which he ate tsampa, and a small bag with the powder. He handed the bag to Shankar Baba.

"Bring water to mix with the ash."

Shankar Baba applied the mixture to the wound, then bandaged it with a silk cloth draped over the Buddha.

"Rest," said Shankar Baba tenderly. "In three days time, your wound will be healed."

"Guruji, how did you turn the Idol's Eye into coal?" Govinda asked as he followed Shankar Baba along the trail, the bizarre events of the previous night replaying in his mind.

"Krishna mantra," replied the yogi.

Shankar Baba stopped on the trail.

"Hold the gem and intend for it to turn into coal, then repeat the mantra your family priest taught you."

Govinda removed the Idol's Eye from the pouch and closed his eyes. He repeated the mantra three times before opening his palm.

"Magic! I performed magic!" exclaimed Govinda, proudly turning the piece of coal in his hand.

Shankar Baba glanced disapprovingly at his young charge.

"That way of thinking will prevent you from ever attaining yogic powers."

Govinda looked at the yogi questioningly.

"The thought of 'I' must never be associated with yogic powers. It would mean your ruin, which I will not allow."

Govinda's euphoria was short-lived.

"However great the temptation, yogic powers are not to be used for personal gain. The higher the yogi climbs, the further he could fall."

"The way Vishwamitra fell because he couldn't control his anger?" asked Govinda.

"And others, some of whom you will soon meet. To gain yogic powers, one must meet three requirements. The yogi must acknowledge the divinity within, he must maintain perfect calmness under all circumstances, and he must be beyond temptation of misusing the power."

Crestfallen, Govinda replied, "then I shall never have yogic powers."

"In time you shall," replied Shankar Baba, placing a hand on Govinda's shoulder.

A wall of snow-laden peaks loomed on the horizon. By the third morning after departing Lama Nima's stupa, yogi and chela reached an icy pass, signaling their arrival in the Indian Himalaya.

"My *gufa* is there," said Shankar Baba, gesturing toward a mountain buried under a white blanket.

Another freezing winter, thought Govinda, remembering the bitter nights at Yurpa Gompa.

Shankar Baba wagged his finger playfully. "The cave is warm. You will like it."

"Do you know all my thoughts?"

"Your thoughts are as plain as the nose on your face," smiled Shankar Baba.

"But how do you do it?"

"I have good hearing."

"You can hear my thoughts?" asked Govinda.

"Everything in creation is based on sound," explained the yogi. "You try."

"But how?"

"Breathe in. Fill your heart with *prana*. When your mind becomes calm, listen for the thought that comes. It will be mine."

Govinda inhaled slowly, quieting his mind, which had few thoughts at the moment. Then he waited.

"Tell me my thought," instructed Shankar Baba.

"But I didn't hear it."

"Are you sure? What came to your mind?"

"I was thinking how lucky it was that the lamas taught me Tibetan."

The Tale of the Himalayan Yogis

"You got it," smiled the yogi. "I was thinking how surprised the bandits were when you spoke their language. Easy, isn't it."

"For you."

Govinda wasn't sure he wanted his guru to know his every thought.

"A yogi trusts his mind," explained Shankar Baba. "It is an illusion to think that your mind, and mine, are separate."

"But aren't they?"

Shankar Baba shook his head. "We are all part of the One, but the perfected yogi is conscious of the life stream underlying everything, while others are not. That is what you have come to the Himalaya to discover."

"I thought I was here to escape my execution."

"That was just an excuse to bring you to me," smiled Shankar Baba mischievously.

As the duo moved along the trails, climbing and descending ridge after ridge, Shankar Baba pointed to another flock of cranes. Members of the flock called continuously to one another as they soared across the sky, gaining altitude to avoid threatening weather.

"We have arrived none too soon."

Another Himalayan winter was near, and the prospect of cold and snow discouraged Govinda. Shankar Baba led his chela past a cluster of slate-roofed houses near a stream that descended from higher up the mountain. Cows grazed near the water, and tethered goats bleated outside the simple dwellings. Perched on a slope above the Gomti River, the tiny village enjoyed an unhindered view of an emerald valley bordering Nepal.

"Champa. The village got its name from an ancestor of that tree," said Shankar Baba, pointing to a yawning magnolia ornamented with peach-colored blossoms.

Harvesting wheat, millet, pumpkin, and potatoes from terraced plots, brightly clad women paused to watch the yogi and his chela pass by on the trail below. The villagers were happy to see Shankar Baba, and they pressed their calloused palms together to welcome him. Shankar Baba, in turn, touched his heart as he climbed a steep trail above the village.

"Heaven is up there," gestured the yogi to a ridge above the terraced plots.

With the agility of a snow leopard, Shankar Baba's pace quickened as he climbed the slope. Govinda's chest heaved by the time the travelers reached the yogi's abode above the tree line. It had not been easy keeping up with Shankar Baba whose strides were like those of a giant.

"Come inside."

Govinda slipped off his *chappals*. Together, they stepped into the yogi's cave, its entrance shaped like the mouth of a cow. Govinda recognized the chamber immediately. He was sure that the cavernous hollow, with its fire pit in the middle, had been the scene of his encounter with Ravan.

"This is the cave from my dream!"

"Only now Ravan can't enter. Tonight we rest. Tomorrow I will show you more."

Govinda slept while Shankar Baba meditated through the night. Dawn's first rays filtered through the cave's entrance, waking Govinda. He slipped outside without disturbing his guru, who sat perfectly erect, his legs neatly folded in a yogic posture. From the granite balcony outside, Govinda scanned the horizon. A cloudless sky framed some of the tallest peaks on the planet. Five serrated, snow-capped giants formed an impregnable fortress defining the eastern horizon. The massifs cast a quiet spell over the valleys that lay in their shadows.

"Panch Chuli," said Shankar Baba, who was now standing behind Govinda.

Beneath the massifs, a silver thread twisted through the valley. Smaller springs formed by waterfalls fed by glacial melt higher up joined the river. Countless terraced plots stood between the falls and the valley floor. Forests of cedar, pine, and spruce stood to the north of the river, and terraced wheat fields stepped down the mountainside to the south.

"Like the view?" asked Shankar Baba. "The villagers call it Bam-I-Duniah, the rooftop of the world."

Govinda stood spellbound.

"Trishul," said Shankar Baba, pointing to a trident-shaped peak at the heart of Panch Chuli.

"The Moguls won't get past that fortress," joked Govinda.

"Not even Zaim will find you here."

"I wonder what has become of him."

"For those who deny the soul, suffering serves as their guru. Zaim's disease has brought him to the precipice. His life lesson is at hand. Men can take whatever perverse pleasure they wish, but when it is time to pay the debt, it may be paid with tears. Fruit ripens slowly but falls suddenly. Zaim's karma is ripe."

"With a little help from a yogi," laughed Govinda.

It pleased Shankar Baba to see that Govinda was utterly at ease with him.

In a desolate canyon outside Delhi, a stooped figure prepared a tasteless meal. Zaim's day was unfolding as every other day had since his internment in the leper colony.

A team of soldiers arrived with a wagonload of his personal belongings, tossing the trunks a fair distance from Zaim's hut. Ignoring their former commander, the soldiers rode off, fearful of the scourge. Zaim set aside his plate of watery lentils and shuffled over to collect his possessions. The prize he was counting on to ease his torment had arrived. He wasted no time in dragging one particular trunk into his shabby abode. Clutching the key that had hung from his neck since leaving Delhi, he carefully turned the lock. Inside, Zaim had painstakingly hidden the Idol's Eye.

Slicing open the trunk's cloth lining, Zaim found the gem where he had hidden it. Gripping the diamond in his mottled hand, he breathed a ragged sigh of relief. His tactic had worked. Rather than risk carrying the gem with him, he had opted to hide it. Either way, the Emperor's men could have found it, but he had judged it safer with his belongings than with him, and now it was safely in his hands. The gem was his ticket out of the leper's hell. A wry smile formed on Zaim's face, but it quickly morphed into a pained grimace, for the flesh at the corners of his mouth was raw.

Zaim was now one of the wealthiest men in the Empire. Despite having his assets seized – booty from a dozen campaigns and countless sacked temples – with the Idol's Eye, Zaim had all the wealth he would ever need. He had imagined the *haveli* he would build, filling it with a harem to cool the fires that burned him night after night. What others said was true; there was no blight worse than that of a leper. The sale of the Idol's Eye would provide him servants, opium, women, fine food… Life would be tolerable if only he could rid himself of the curse. The diadem was gone, but it mattered little; the diamond was worth more than the fortunes of all the noblemen in Delhi.

Zaim would take the gem to Chandni Chowk where he knew a merchant who would find a suitable buyer. In the past, Amal had fetched favorable prices for the jewels Zaim brought him.

Zaim would be free of the leper colony with its wretches groveling about hounding him for potato scraps. The stench in the canyon was foul enough; the fingerless hands and stumped feet were constant reminders of his disease. Diamond in hand, Zaim would not spend another night in Moradabad. Hitching the colony's oxcart, he made the journey to the city in the searing midday heat, having rewarded the guards for his freedom.

Though it was hot, Zaim wrapped himself in a blanket as he made his way to Delhi's oldest bazaar, his head covered to avoid the scorn shop owners heaped on beggars.

Amal didn't recognize Zaim as he shuffled into his shop. The plump shopkeeper's servant was about to run the leper off when the wraithlike figure raised a bandaged hand.

"I am not here for a social visit," he muttered, placing the blue diamond on a burgundy velvet tray in front of the merchant. "I'm here to sell this."

Recognizing Zaim's voice, Amal recoiled twice; first at the sight of the disfigured commander, and again upon viewing the gem before him.

"It must be three hundred *ratna*!" exclaimed the Hindu shopkeeper.

"And flawless," added Zaim, barely moving his lips. "How much can you get for the diamond?"

Amal turned the gem slowly in his hand.

"There's not another like it in the world," Zaim insisted.

"The cut is impeccable. Where did you get it?" Amal asked cautiously.

"What difference does it make?"

Beads of perspiration formed on Amal's forehead. "I'm having doubt."

"Doubt?" Zaim placed his hand on his dagger. "Cheat me, and I'll cut your throat."

"You know me better than that."

Amal turned the gem in his hand. After examining the stone from every angle, a look of vexation came over the shopkeeper.

"The gem is superb… but it's not a diamond… the gem is zircon."

"You're wrong!" Zaim's bony frame shook uncontrollably. "I took the diamond from a temple myself. It's worth all the gems in the Emperor's harem."

"Had it been real, the diamond would be worth much more than that, but you've been tricked. The stone is common zircon."

"You're lying," growled Zaim, rising to his feet.

"Calm down. It's not as if the gem isn't valuable. I can get you three, maybe four cows for the stone."

"Cows?" Zaim pulled his dagger from its scabbard.

"There is a way to prove whether the gem is authentic, or not. If it is a diamond, it won't be damaged when I strike it," said the merchant, picking up a wooden mallet. "But if the stone's a zircon, it will be ruined."

"I'll strike it myself." Zaim snatched the mallet from the shopkeeper's hand. "You'll see… the diamond is authentic."

Raising the mallet, Zaim struck a violent blow that shattered the gem, scattering ice-blue shards about the room. Zaim looked on in disbelief as the mallet slipped from his misshapen fingers, his future crushed into a thousand useless pieces.

"I'm sorry," said Amal, rising to his feet. "Had it been a diamond, you would have been one of the richest men in Delhi."

Zaim stared vacantly at the shattered remains of his false dream.

Without uttering a word, he slunk out the door, disappearing down a dusty alley, foul tears leaking from his sunken eyes.

Emperor Ghazi met with his generals to discuss plans to form a military alliance aimed at conquering South India's most prosperous kingdom, a scheme Hashim vehemently opposed.

The prize was Vijayanagar, a southern capital where the women were said to be so heavily laden with jewels that they required the support of servants as they walked. Persian ambassadors and Portuguese adventurers departed Vijayanagar dumbstruck; the opulence and attendant decadence of the capital, known as the City of Victory, surpassed anything they had seen in their travels.

Ghazi viewed the conquest of Vijayanagar as an opportunity to make his mark, to prove to the generals that he possessed his father's mettle. However, he needed to convince his officers that the journey was worth the effort. An envoy was dispatched to confirm the kingdom's rumored wealth.

"I have seen the Imperial treasury," said Hashim. "No Emperor in Asia can boast of such riches."

"It's not for the riches that I must do this," Ghazi explained to his brother. "I must prove my ability to the generals to win their loyalty; otherwise they might betray me at any time."

"With Zaim out of the way, that will never happen."

"I am counting on you to look after things while I'm away. I'll make it worth your while. Vijayanagar's palaces are said to be gilded in gold."

"Gold means nothing to me," protested Hashim.

"Whatever it is you value, you shall have it. All I ask is that you keep an eye on Begum Zahira in my absence."

"Father died chasing riches for which he had little use. I don't want you to suffer a similar fate."

"Every Mogul emperor has proven himself in battle. Babur conquered his first empire at age twelve."

"The Empire will not survive if war supersedes worship."

"You talk like a hopeless romantic," said Ghazi dismissively.

"I shall open schools while you are away."

"What kind of schools?"

"I want to encourage art, music, and poetry among the people. Not just among Muslims, but all the faiths," said Hashim.

"We don't need the mullahs rising against us."

"I shall encourage religious debate. The number of Christians is growing. We can no longer ignore their efforts to convert Hindu and Muslim alike."

"Do what you will, but do not neglect that which sustains the Empire," cautioned Ghazi. "Should the reports from Vijayanagar prove accurate, we will depart within the moon's cycle."

Winter arrived, blanketing terraced field, roof, and humble conifer. Shoulder high drifts buried the trail from Shankar Baba's cave to the river. In the aftermath of a storm, the village men cleared the trail so that the yogi could reach the river for his morning bath. Whether the path was open, or not, mattered little to Govinda. His bath consisted of snow melted over the fire.

Wrapped in blankets woven by Champa's women, yogi and chela moved about the mountain, their feet exposed to ice and snow. Govinda had grown accustomed to the cold, and although he didn't like it much, he found his second winter in the Himalaya more tolerable than the first. His cave was always warm, and the village woodcutter provided ample oak and pine logs.

Fresh milk, boiled rice, roasted pine nuts, and dried berries appeared outside Shankar Baba's cave each morning. Govinda caught occasional glimpses of the boy who brought the provisions; the shy fellow moved noiselessly up and down the mountain followed by his dog.

Govinda's routine depended wholly on his guru. After a night's sleep by the fire, meditation began hours before sunrise and ended with a walk to the river for Shankar Baba's bath. After removing his woolen blanket, the yogi stepped into the freezing water, breaking through whatever ice clung to the river's edge. Reaching the deepest section of the river, the yogi plunged headlong into the waters. Following the bathing ritual, the yogi made offerings to the sun. Filling his cupped hands with water, Shankar Baba poured the shimmering liquid over his fingertips as the sun rose above the Five Chimneys.

"Guruji, why do you offer water to the sun?"

"I wish to pay homage to the place of my soul's birth. You and I come from the great sun and will one day return there."

After the yogi's bath, the pair retreated to the cave where Govinda warmed a bucket of snow for his bath while Shankar Baba knotted his matted locks on the crown of his head. Breakfast followed Govinda's bath; a cup of milk flavored with wild honey and cardamom. Rice, nuts, and dried fruit formed a spartan lunch, a meal Govinda found only slightly more satisfying than tsampa.

Shankar Baba's only rule was never to complain, and Govinda was determined not to break it. Though his exile meant meager rations, Govinda had long since stopped yearning for the sumptuous banquets served at his family's table. He was fit, and not a pound of excess was found anywhere on his athletic frame.

After breakfast, Govinda removed the ash from the fire pit, brought fresh logs, cleaned bowls, and tidied the cave. Neither of the cave's inhabitants owned more than the cloth that covered them and a blanket. Govinda assembled the items required for Shankar Baba's daily puja; a copper cup filled with milk, a dab of honey, some sandal paste, a dried fig, and three bilva leaves.

Puja completed, master and disciple headed for the forest where they walked among the conifers repeating their mantras. The daily sojourn was Govinda's favorite. The deep calm in the woods was interrupted only by the calls of a cuckoo and its mate. The scent of fires and the woodsman's tracks were scant signs that humans lived nearby.

Deer roamed among the majestic conifers, but the langurs had retreated to forests further down the valley. A black bear hibernated under an outcropping beyond the river, and a rarely seen leopardess stalked the region.

Unless Shankar Baba had a lesson to impart, the pair moved in silence, the taller figure shadowed by his young pupil. The fresh snowfall weighting down the conifers caught the yogi's attention, and he stopped to examine the frosted limbs.

"The trees teach us never to complain. They flourish despite deprivation and difficulty," explained Shankar Baba. "One winter the mountains were beset with storms. Ice weighed heavily on the limbs, then the snows came, adding to their burden. Night after night the snow fell until the cave was walled shut. The villagers removed the snow, but the trees continued to suffer, though they never complained. Patiently they endured the hardship, although their limbs were damaged and some trees died."

"You speak of the trees as if they were people."

Shankar Baba smiled. "The trees tolerate our ignorance, but thankfully, the woodcutter follows my instruction to cut only the dead, though it means hauling logs a greater distance."

"You think of the trees as friends, don't you?"

"As should you. Without trees, man cannot live."

"But we have few trees in Rajputana."

"Nonetheless, without trees somewhere, humans would be nowhere. Soon you shall recognize the wise souls that inhabit these trees. Here in the forest, there is no need for a shrine; the trees themselves are equal to gods." Shankar Baba pointed to the top of a towering cedar. "From high above they silently observe us, ever tolerant of man's folly."

"But aren't they bored standing here year after year? The woodcutter claims the trees in this forest are hundreds of years old."

"Even older," claimed the yogi. "Most of the trees in this forest have grown up since I first came here, but a few were here before me."

"But how can that be?"

Govinda tried to calculate his guru's age and came up with an impossible number. He had never properly learned mathematics and gave up.

"In time, everything will be known to you."

"But I feel impatient to know things," Govinda protested.

"That is why I bring you to the forest. As I said, there is much to be learned from the trees. See how straight and tall they grow; they

Steve Briggs

want to rise to heaven itself, to reach for the sun and moon, which they worship, as men should."

"Is that why you offer water to the sun?"

Shankar Baba nodded. "Man's mind and body absorb God's limitless light and energy the way the plant kingdom absorbs the sun's rays. Come, stand here."

Shankar Baba led Govinda off the dappled trail to an opening among the trees where he felt the sun on his face.

"Divine beings live in the realm of the sun… and the moon too," explained the yogi, gazing at the brilliant sphere in the sky. "Beings that guide and teach us. At night, the moon casts her benevolent rays on the earth, which nourishes the trees. The entire plant kingdom is happy when the moon shines on it. Not only the plant kingdom; the moon also nourishes the mineral and animal kingdoms."

"Is that why we meditate under the full moon?"

"When the moon is full, it showers *soma* on the earth."

"Ananta said the gods once fought an army of demons over soma."

"Soma is the nectar that brings immortality… gods and demons alike wish to be immortal."

"Men too, it seems."

"After performing severe austerities, three yogis reached the abode of the gods where they received the elixir of immortality. When they drank the nectar, the amount decreased, which never happened when the gods drank from the pot. The yogis were sent back to earth until they become purer," explained Shankar Baba. "From today, you should make offerings to the sun."

"Shall I offer water as you do?"

"Offering water is a good thing, but offering gratitude from the heart is better. The great cosmic sun that illumines our world hardly needs a handful of water. Surya appreciates devotion most."

"Then the sun receives my offering?"

"Of course," replied the yogi.

Govinda scanned the forest around him. "What else do the trees teach us?"

"Trees are givers. The forest never asks anything of anyone."

"The forest needs the monsoon," noted Govinda.

The Tale of the Himalayan Yogis

"Have you not noticed the clouds forming above forests, showering the mountains with rain? The trees create the rain they need."

"Is that why monsoons in Rajputana are rare? Because there are no forests?"

Shankar Baba nodded. "Come; I want you to meet a friend."

The yogi strode through the snow as if it weren't there. Govinda tried to step in his tracks, but the yogi's stride was too long. Soon, Shankar Baba was out of sight. Deep in the forest, Govinda caught up with his guru. Had it not been for the footprints, he would have lost his way.

In front of them loomed a towering *deodar*. The girth of the cedar was many times that of the other trees in its vicinity.

"How old is it?" asked Govinda, craning his neck to glimpse the top of the massive conifer.

"Why don't you ask her?"

"Her? You mean the tree is female?"

"Neither male nor female, she says. During the waning half of the moon's cycle, the tree feels more feminine."

"Should I offer something?" asked Govinda.

"If you like."

"But I have nothing with me."

"You have your heart. Offer the tree something from that."

Govinda pressed his hands together, thanking the tree for teaching him patience and wishing it a long and healthy life.

"The Elder of the Forest thanks you for your wish," relayed Shankar Baba, "but she says she is already more than a thousand years old."

"The tree spoke to you?" marveled Govinda.

"In a way."

"Tell her that I want to be her friend."

"She says you already are her friend."

"Then I shall visit her often," decided Govinda.

"She would like that. Place your hands on her, and she will bless you."

Govinda reached out and touched the tree's trunk.

"You feel it, do you not?" asked Shankar Baba. "That is how she shares her love."

"I'm happy to have a friend."

"I am thinking of how you can have more friends. A boy should not spend the whole day meditating. Now come; there are other things in the forest that I want to show you."

It was late when the adventurers returned to their cave. Govinda was famished, and he ate everything on the shelf while Shankar Baba smiled at his gluttony.

"Baba, you eat nothing while I devour anything I can find."

"I eat plenty," protested Shankar Baba.

"But you stopped taking milk so that I could have yours."

"The trees in the forest eat, but who sees them eating?"

"I forgot. Sunlight is sufficient food for you."

"Sunlight and *prana* sustain me nicely, don't you think?"

There was no denying that the yogi's limbs were hard like granite.

"If a tree survives on light and air, is it not possible for a yogi to do the same?"

"I suppose so," agreed Govinda, "but trees draw from the soil too."

"The minerals in the earth are also enriched by the sun. The sun and moon have a hand in everything. Life itself sustains itself by their presence, yet few honor them. One day, I will teach you to draw the energy you need directly from the sun."

"Why not today?"

"Because you've already stuffed yourself. What good would it do to eat more after the meal you've just devoured?"

"I have eaten quite a lot, haven't I?" Govinda laughed.

"Bring a fresh log for the fire."

Govinda stepped outside the cave, returning with a pair of pine logs, which he carefully placed on the fire.

"Fire is a yogi's friend. Do you know why?"

"It cooks our food and keeps us warm."

"It has a higher purpose yet. A yogi's fire is not like the kitchen hearth. A yogi never prepares food over his fire. His fire increases the power of his meditation, which is why we call his fire, *dhuni*. Sitting near his dhuni, the yogi repeats his mantra, offering it to the spirit within the fire, who in turn conveys the offering to the yogi's *Ishta-Deva* – in your case, Krishna."

"What about you, Baba? Who is your Ishta-Deva?"

"Shiva," replied Shankar Baba. "The dhuni is a yogi's message-bearer to the gods. Toss some grains into the fire."

Govinda sprinkled black sesame into the flames. The grains hissed and sputtered, bursting in brilliant flashes.

"Notice how the kernels combust," said Shankar Baba. "Fire roasts the seeds the way meditation roasts a yogi's *sanskaras*."

"Sanskaras?"

"Sanskara is the residue from one's past that has collected in the mind."

"Like memories?"

"Sanskaras are more than memories; deeper impressions that color the mind and distort our judgment. Sanskaras compel us to act in ways we often regret."

"Are they the reason men like Pasang are angry?"

"Pasang's mind is polluted with sanskaras. His taste for alcohol compounds his rage."

"Is greed also a sanskara?"

"Whatever exists in a man's mind that distorts his ability to discern truth could be called a sanskara."

"Junaid Shah was obsessed with the Idol's Eye."

"The Emperor craved wealth. No amount of gold and gems satisfied him. No matter how great his treasury, he wanted more."

"His insatiable appetite led to his death."

"Indeed," said Shankar Baba. "Wherever a tiger roams, he leaves a scent that alerts the other animals. Though the tiger may be off hunting on a distant mountain, the monkeys and deer are afraid due to the lingering scent of the tiger. Sanskaras are like the scent that lingers after the tiger is gone. Fear, anger, lust, hatred; all are impressions that linger in a man's mind. They prevent us from knowing truth."

"Ananta said *Maya* keeps us from knowing truth."

"There exists a veil that blinds men. The sages called that veil, Maya. The threads of our sanskaras weave the veil of a man's Maya."

"I'm still confused about sanskara."

"Think of the Moguls. Though you are safe here with me, from time to time, you worry about Zaim and his men."

"I still dream about them," admitted Govinda.

"Dreams are the result of impressions from your past; in the case of the Moguls, your recent past. In time, it will become clear. You have experienced countless incarnations, human and otherwise. In each incarnation, the soul carries with it impressions that lie dormant in the mind like seeds waiting to sprout. The yogi roasts those seeds before they sprout. That is how he frees himself from the binding influence of sanskara."

"Like the seeds I tossed into the fire."

"The yogi roasts his sanskaras in the fire of his meditation to free himself from the veil of ignorance. Roasted, the seed will never sprout again. You are about to undergo a purification that will free your mind from the wheel of bondage for all time."

"I want *moksha* more than anything."

"Had I not arranged things, you would be sitting on a throne with little time for thoughts of moksha. The desire for liberation, though stronger in some, lies within every man, yet only the fortunate can free themselves. To attain liberation, the yogi's spiritual fire must burn strong. Your good fortune has brought you to me. I will see that you reach the goal."

Govinda's second winter in exile passed. The forest shed its white gown, wildflowers bloomed, the black bear lumbered about, and the langurs returned along with the songbirds.

With the melting of the snows, Govinda joined his guru for his morning bath. Though the freezing waters turned Govinda's skin blue, it did not deter him; he was resolved to achieve liberation even if it meant plunging into glacial melt before breakfast. Shankar Baba insisted on the icy bath, explaining that it directed subtle energies in the body upward, which was of benefit to a yogi.

Reaching into the fire one night, Shankar Baba pulled a charred stick from the embers, its tip glowing brightly.

"Take this and follow me," he instructed.

The Tale of the Himalayan Yogis

Govinda followed Shankar Baba out of his cave. Treading the moonlit path, he wondered where Baba was taking him in the night. The upper half of the mountain had been unreachable in winter, but now a sliver of a trail snaked past dislodged boulders and over rock ledges.

Shankar Baba stopped.

"This will be your home now."

"Here on the side of the mountain?" asked Govinda, standing beside Shankar Baba.

"Go inside and light your dhuni," instructed Shankar Baba, pointing to a small opening in the rocks.

Govinda had forgotten about the stick he carried; miraculously, its tip still glowed orange.

Ducking through an opening in the rocks, Govinda entered blackness. Waiting until his eyes adjusted, he spotted some firewood in the middle of the cave and placed the burning stick beneath it.

"For however long you stay here, your fire should burn," explained Shankar Baba, "At Triyugi Narayan, where Shiva married Parvati, the sacred fire has burned for yugas. Like that, your dhuni should burn continuously."

As the logs caught fire, Govinda took in his surroundings. The cave was a smaller version of Shankar Baba's. Scanning the chamber, Govinda spotted a stack of items in the corner of the cave.

"I have left some of your belongings for you," said Shankar Baba.

Govinda examined the objects by the firelight: rudraksha beads, a goat's hair shawl, a pot fashioned from various metals, and a grass mat. The articles felt vaguely familiar.

"These were mine?" he asked, holding up the rudraksha *mala*.

"From your past. The beads will benefit your spiritual practice just as this cave will."

"I lived here?" asked Govinda, perplexed by the notion that he had lived in a cave.

"In a former time. Place the rudraksha outside. The moon will restore their power. Now I will leave you to become reacquainted with your past."

Shankar Baba slipped out of the cave, leaving Govinda to sift through a past his conscious mind had long since forgotten.

Since their meeting in Tibet, Govinda had rarely left his guru's side. Stepping outside the cave, he expected to find Shankar Baba, but the yogi had vanished. After carefully placing his beads on a rock, Govinda spread the grass mat on the floor of the cave and wrapped himself in the buttery shawl. With his dhuni softly crackling, he fell into a faint rhythm with his mantra.

Govinda was asleep by the fire when someone slipped into the cave.

"Come," whispered Shankar Baba. Together they stepped onto the ledge outside.

"So many stars!" exclaimed Govinda, admiring the sea of sparkling gems overhead.

"Tonight the moon is full."

"Baba, have you been awake all night?"

"Soon you will master yogic sleep," said Shankar Baba. "It is different from the villager's sleep. A yogi never loses awareness. He dreams if he likes, but he controls the dream. When he sleeps, he views his body the way a man views his reflection on the water. Yogic sleep is an intensely blissful form of samadhi."

"If the yogi is awake, what does he do during the night?"

"He visits far-off places," explained Shankar Baba, waving his hand at the stars overhead. "There are countless places to explore. The realms where such journeys take place are vast; the stars far outnumber the pebbles around Manasarovar. They pass through one's body like liquid music."

"Do you go there?" wondered Govinda, pointing to the stars overhead.

"And further. Soon you will join me."

"I'd like that."

"The gateway to the heavens is here," explained the yogi, placing his hand on the crown of Govinda's head. "To help you attain the divine realms, I shall explain something about the mantra and its use. If you are fortunate enough to understand the connection between your mantra and your Ishta-Deva, that is because your god has granted you that knowledge. If you don't know, then it is because the god has kept it a secret. A person will discover the real nature of his mantra when his god wills it. It is not necessary to be told. It is self-revealing. The mantra and its associated deity are identical. If your mantra's form is Krishna than he'll reveal himself in due time, and then he will grant you knowledge.

"From that moment on the person will love his god, privately, in the heart of the god and devotee. The value of a mantra is just that. When you finally experience who you've been calling, and enter into a personal relationship with your Ishta-Deva, you are close to the goal. On the other hand, there can be hide and seek... part of the Lila. It is the grace of the god that matters. Not even a matter of deserving... more a matter of grace."

"Nothing can hurt you when you are repeating your mantra. Your mantra is a magic charm of protection.

"When you close your eyes to meditate, be with your personal god. The nature of the name is such that it calls forth the bearer of the name. Whoever you beckon by name, appears before you. Therefore, repeat his name. Then you will feel a joy emanating from your Ishta-Deva, which you never experienced before."

"Let the mantra flow like a current within you. Remembering one's Ishta-Deva is man's sole duty in life. God is deep within us. He dwells there as pure and innocent love. Meditate on him in your heart."

"Now, continue with your meditation until the sun rises over the Five Chimneys. *Brahma Mahurta* is the time when yogis meditate for the benefit of the world."

The sun was well above the horizon when Govinda stepped onto the ledge outside his cave. Outside the entrance, he found a fresh pot of milk and a wooden bowl filled with pine nuts and dried mulberries.

The Vulture and the Lamb

From the balcony outside his cave, the peaks to the north pierced the cloudless blue overhead. Govinda was chewing on a dried apricot when a herd of blue *bharal* wandered down the mountain, grazing the grassy slope as they descended. Govinda watched the animals, noticing that among them was a lamb so small that it struggled on the steep terrain. Venturing into the area where the herd grazed, the sheep, alerted by the human in their midst, sniffed the light, summer breeze. Satisfied that the young mendicant meant no harm, they continued grazing. Taking a pot of milk, Govinda placed it on the hill near the lamb and retreated.

The infant was hungry, but its mother was nowhere in sight. Discovering the milk, the tiny one drank eagerly, licking every drop from the pot's bottom. The following day the herd returned. Having encountered yogi's in the past, the bharal knew instinctively that the humans posed no threat and ignored the intruder while they ate. This time, Govinda decided to feed the lamb himself. He inched his way toward it, milk in hand. The timid creature flinched, but being without its mother, the hungry infant accepted the food offering, drinking from the pot, which Govinda held while the rest of the herd moved further down the mountain.

The feeding ritual continued day after day despite the fact that the

The Tale of the Himalayan Yogis

herd now grazed a lower portion of the mountain. Govinda decided that a leopard, or possibly wolves, had killed the lamb's mother, and so he adopted it, giving it the name, Neelam.

Neelam made amusing noises when she was hungry, which was always the case. Govinda brought extra milk, often feeding the little animal while rubbing its ears. The lamb responded warmly, and a friendship developed between Govinda and the affectionate blue yeanling. Neelam had moist lips, and the fur above her eyes curled away from her forehead. Despite the fact that Shankar Baba towered over the tiny animal, Neelam didn't run away when the yogi approached, for it trusted its human providers.

Curious to know more about the boy who brought him milk and nuts, Govinda called to him one morning as the boy retreated down the mountain.

"Bhaiya… have you seen Baba?"

"Baba is at the stream," replied the boy before disappearing among the rocks.

Approaching the river, he found Shankar Baba bathing in the stream. The yogi's matted locks drifted downstream as he submerged his head in the water.

"Baba, who is the boy that brings milk?"

"His name is Devraj. Devraj's father is the village headman."

"After your bath, go and help Devraj with the cows."

Govinda liked the idea of tending cows and headed down the trail in search of Devraj. He found the boy gathering eggs outside the family barn.

"Can I help," asked the young mendicant.

"I can use some help," replied Devraj.

"Devraj, I am Govinda."

"Everyone knows your name, but how do you know mine?"

"Baba told me."

"Baba knows my name?" beamed Devraj.

"Baba instructed me to help with the cows, but you'll have to teach me."

"It's not so easy at first," said Devraj apologetically.

"Thank you for bringing food to my cave. Without it, I would go hungry."

"We would not let you go without," said Devraj, who was happy to meet the chela of Shankar Baba. "My village owes everything to Shankar Baba."

"Why do you say that?"

"One winter, many children fell sick. Papa went to Shankar Baba for help. Baba gave him ash to rub on the foreheads of the sick. No one expected me to live, but the ash cured me. My father would do anything for your Baba."

Devraj, who was undersized for his age, looked away as he talked.

"Himalayan cows are smaller than those on the plains," observed Govinda. "What are their names?"

"That's Tulsi with the white markings. Poonam and Pushpa are her calves. The others are up above." Tulsi was the prize of the village, adored by everyone for her gentleness.

"How long has Baba lived in the cave above the village?"

"Papa says Shankar Baba has lived there since my great-grandfather was a boy, but he disappeared for a few years."

"Maybe he went on a pilgrimage."

"After Baba cured the children, news of the healing spread. People brought their sick relatives from as far away as Kathmandu Valley. Baba never complained, but one day Baba told the elders that he could help our village more if he were left alone, and so our people stopped going to him, but others kept coming. One day a Sherpa family was climbing to Baba's cave when they saw a leopard on the trail. The family ran away. Then a few weeks later it happened again when some villagers brought a sick elder. That's when Baba disappeared."

"Do you remember when he came back?"

"A few weeks before you arrived, but then he disappeared again."

"What else can you tell me about Baba?" asked Govinda.

"I have taken milk to his cave every morning since I was old enough to climb the mountain. Papa says it's my way of repaying Shankar Baba for saving my life. One day, after leaving the pot of milk outside his cave, I looked inside since I didn't see Baba sitting on his tiger skin. I thought Baba might have gone to the forest. When I looked in, I got scared and ran down the mountain."

"What frightened you?"

"Baba was inside the cave, but I didn't see him at first because he wasn't sitting on his skin."

"Where was he?"

"Floating in the air." Devraj's eyes widened as he told the story.

"You saw Baba levitate?"

"I understand if you don't believe me. The other boys don't."

"I believe you," Govinda reassured his friend.

"Baba was sitting like he always does; only he was up in the air. When I told Papa what I had seen, he told me never to look inside again. He said that if I disturbed Baba, he might put a curse on me."

"Baba would never curse you," laughed Govinda. "Why don't the village boys believe you?"

"Because of Subahu."

"You mean that shaman who pretends to be a priest?"

"No one likes Subahu much."

"What does Subahu say about Baba?" questioned Govinda.

"Bad things, but everyone knows Subahu is jealous."

"Why is that?"

"When the plague came, Subahu mixed herbs, but it didn't help. It was Baba who saved us. That's why he's angry with Baba."

Govinda continued sharing his milk with Neelam, who had grown little over the summer. He spent carefree afternoons with Neelam until one day Shankar Baba cautioned him.

"The lamb will be better off with the flock."

"But Neelam has no one to look after her."

"It won't be good to grow too fond of her," admonished Shankar Baba.

"But winter is coming. The little one will find it difficult to survive."

Although he was not happy with his master's words, Govinda did not complain. He had no intention of breaking the one rule Shankar Baba had set out for him. The infant bharal continued her daily visits, but one sunny afternoon Shankar Baba kept Govinda occupied in his cave longer than usual. The devoted *chela* performed his chores quickly, hoping he would reach the lamb before it wandered off in search of food.

When Shankar Baba finally allowed him to go, Govinda sprinted up the mountain, splashing milk over the sides of the pot as he ran. Scanning the mountainside in search of the lamb, he spotted the little bharal heading back to the herd and called to it. Hearing the voice, Neelam ambled across the rocky slope, knowing that a meal awaited her.

As the lamb neared Govinda's cave, it paused, nervously chirruping as it sniffed the air. Govinda sensed that the bharal was anxious about something and held the pale high so that she knew there was food. Seeing the pot, Neelam sauntered up the slope. The lamb was approaching the ledge outside Govinda's cave when a shadow passed over the rocks. Looking up to see what had cast the ominous profile, Govinda spotted a bearded vulture, its ten-foot span adjusting to the drafts as it descended.

Seeing the odious creature diving toward Neelam, Govinda set down the pot and ran toward the lamb, but Neelam was still a fair distance away. The vulture dove with alarming speed and precision. Like an arrow of death, the predator shot toward the lamb, its dagger-like talons extended. Govinda shouted at the bird, and then tossed a rock near Neelam, hoping she would run off. The vulture slowed its flight, hovering over Neelam briefly before grabbing its prey by the shoulders.

Neelam shrieked as the bird's talons pierced her tender flesh. Having secured its quarry, the vulture flapped its broad wings violently, struggling as it lifted its prey from the ground. Rising above the slope with Neelam in its claws, the immense bird gained height, its close-set eyes glaring defiantly at Govinda as it flew overhead, a flurry of feathers falling to the ground in its eerie wake.

Govinda hurled a rock at the winged demon, but it was too late. The vulture crowed triumphantly as it disappeared over the ridge above his cave. Sickened by what he had witnessed, Govinda ran down the mountain in search of Shankar Baba. Rushing into the yogi's cave, Govinda breathlessly described what had happened.

"Baba, you must save Neelam."

Viewing the attack in his mind, Shankar Baba replied calmly, "But we don't know where the vulture nests, or whether the lamb is even alive."

"You healed the injured lama. Surely you can save Neelam even if the vulture has harmed her."

"This is different," replied the yogi patiently.

"How is it different?"

"We were the cause of the lama's injury. In this case, nature knows what is best. Sit with me," said Shankar Baba calmly, his eyes full of compassion.

"But I must save Neelam."

"What has happened is according to destiny. We cannot interfere every time a bird seeks food for its chicks."

"But Neelam is my friend."

"I cautioned you not to become too attached, but you did not take me seriously."

Govinda, who had been standing beside the fire opposite the yogi, ran out of the cave, determined to save his friend. As he sprinted up the mountain, his mind flashed to the refuse pit where Zaim had staked one of his officers. The hungry eyes of the vultures lining the cavity haunted Govinda as he stumbled over rocks, scrambling at times on four limbs, desperate to find little Neelam. Higher up, countless crags and ledges provided suitable shelter for a vulture's lair. Govinda searched and searched, but his efforts proved futile. It was dark by the time he returned to his cave. Distraught, he slipped inside where he found Shankar Baba, his prayer beads turning slowly in the firelight.

"I was about to come for you. It's not safe up there in the night. I saw a leopard prowling about not long ago."

"I searched everywhere," said Govinda disconsolately.

"I have let you down," replied Shankar Baba plainly.

"It is I who have let you down, Baba. I should not have made a pet of Neelam. If she had stayed with the herd, she would have been safe."

"Do not blame yourself. There are two paths to the divine, that of a renunciate and that of a bhakta. The latter is the nobler path.

The yogi remains indifferent to the world, while the bhakta shares the pain of every being."

"But you're also a bhakta, Baba."

"I am not troubled by the coming and going of souls. Whether that is my good fortune, I cannot say, but the divine play is destined to unfold. One day I will take you to Bhumi Mata. You and she share much in common. She suffers from the distress of the lowliest creature."

"Then it was Neelam's destiny to die?"

Shankar Baba nodded.

"You tried to tell me. I have disobeyed my guru."

"Govinda, the only obedience I ask of you is that you obey your own heart."

"But Baba, you knew Neelam's fate from the beginning."

"I knew Neelam would not live long. How she would die, I did not care to know. The destiny of every being is written in its soul, which the yogi reads as easily as a learned man turns the pages of a book. Go and bathe in the river. It will help wash the pain away. Then we shall meditate together."

"I cannot meditate," protested Govinda. "My mind is troubled."

"It is your heart that aches. Give me your pouch."

Govinda placed the pouch in Shankar Baba's hand. Removing the Idol's Eye, the yogi pressed the stone against his chela's chest. Instantly, the pain in his heart eased.

"Now go for your bath."

Govinda's legs ached as he trudged past the village. He had scoured every outcropping on the mountain, but the vulture's lair was well hidden.

Evening worship was in progress inside the temple, but Govinda was in no mood to go inside. Instead, he slipped into the current, silent tears mingling with the rushing water. The brisk current cooled his heated mind, but his heart would need time to heal.

Entering his cave, Govinda took his place beside his guru, who had spread a mat on the floor by the fire.

"I see the river has not washed your questions away."

"May I ask?"

The Tale of the Himalayan Yogis

"What the son doesn't know, he asks his father." Govinda was happy to hear the words of affection from his guru.

"Devraj told me about the plague that struck the village. He said you cured the children, but then you went away."

"A yogi grows restless when he loses his freedom; attachment brings bondage."

"Like the attachment I felt for Neelam?"

"Like that."

"But you are not attached to anything."

"No, I am not attached. The villagers came from great distances, hoping I would heal their dying elders even though their bodies were old and worn out. Many were ready to die, but their sons and daughters were afraid."

"What were they afraid of?"

"What does every man fear? I left this place so the elders could depart peacefully."

"But is it wrong to help the villagers? When Pitaji died, I wanted him to come back. And now I wish Neelam could come back? Is it wrong to want that?"

"It is only natural for a son to miss his father, but who can tell death to go when he stands at the door? No man owns the house he inhabits. When the owner tells us to go, we must leave at once. To ask a Mahatma to appeal to the landlord is unfair."

"Devraj says the villagers depend on you to protect their crops and animals. It seems they even expect you to prevent them from dying."

"A body does not last forever. When it is time to vacate the house, the man falls asleep in his bed and awakens in another world, where again his stay is transitory. Like the wheels of an oxcart, the soul revolves from life to life, from earth to heaven, and back.

"If Bhagawan wanted most humans to be immortal, he would have made it that way, but there is value in changing forms. For most souls, to have one body forever would be like reading one book, and assuming you understand all of literature. Most souls learn faster by taking various bodies with which to evolve.

"When I was younger, I saw beyond the veil of death," said

Govinda. "I am not afraid of death for my sake, but it hurts to see an innocent creature die."

"Compassion is the natural response."

"The villagers fear death. They believe their jadoo magic protects them from the spirits that come for the dead."

"It is that way with most men," agreed Shankar Baba. "The yogi has seen his death countless times. He knows there is nothing to fear. Out of ignorance, the villager does what he can to delay that which he cannot avoid. Men live in fear until they learn that the soul lives on. Neelam's soul lives on."

"And yet death is not welcome at the door."

"Death terrifies all but the knower of reality. The yogi knows the body is but a shell. When it breaks, he discards the body the way a chick leaves an egg behind."

"But what if a man dies before he's ready?"

"Who knows when death will call? There is no thought of appealing. For Neelam, the time came sooner than for most. When it is time for the harvest, the scythe cuts cleanly. God is supremely compassionate. Our karma decides when we must go."

"Even when an infant dies?"

"In that case, the child has done what it came to do."

"But will its mother understand?"

"The world is an ashram, my son. We learn from experience. A passing cloud eclipses the light of the sun, but it doesn't diminish the sun's warmth. A man lives until his karma is exhausted… not a day longer. That may be a hundred years or a few days."

"The lamas prepare for death from the time they are children."

"Whether due to accident, disease, or old age, the soul departs until it is time to enter a body again; hopefully a better body, but that is not always the case. Back and forth the soul migrates until one attains liberation.

"According to our actions, one may be born an insect, bird, monkey, or tiger. In time, one gains higher births; eventually, the soul gains a human body. But if a man chooses to live like an animal, he may again be born with four legs. The previous birth determines the next. Countless souls wait for the chance to get a human body. After many births, the soul begins the search for liberation."

"How does the soul gain liberation?"

"You hold the key."

"What is that?" asked Govinda.

"The guru's love."

"I was fortunate to find you."

"It's not like that. The guru finds the disciple; not the other way. I have been waiting for you for a long time. I instructed Mishraji to disguise you as a lama and waited for you to reach Kailash. When the veil grows thin, the guru appears, not before. When the guru appears, the journey is almost complete."

"Pundit Ananta read from the scriptures, but I was young and didn't understand much."

"Scriptures may describe the way, but to reach the goal, one must make the journey. Without a proper guide, one can lose the way."

"The scriptures speak of a pathless path."

"The path is straight when the guru shows the way. A yogi's path is narrow like the blade of a dagger. It cuts swift and deep.

"Like a bee sipping from an orange blossom, the nectar is sweet beyond words. When the mind swims in ecstasy, it ceases to exist just as a wave ceases to exist when it merges with the ocean. A wave is only water. It rises and falls, but the ocean never changes. Like that, the Self is ever the same."

"How does one find the Self?"

"A wave draws upon the vastness of the sea. Realizing that the wave is the sea itself, it dares to rise like a tidal wave. To know one's source is to be powerful. A yogi can make the universe tremble. But truthfully, there are no such things as miracles. Soon you will awaken from your dream. I shall ring the bell to rouse you from your slumber."

"What is it that a Mahatma knows that others don't know?"

"A Mahatma is ever awake. When you can see beyond death, you will know that nothing is born, and nothing dies; then you will know what the Mahatma knows."

"What exactly is it the Mahatma sees?"

"The Mahatma beholds the ineffable light of his God-Self, which contains the sun and moon and countless worlds beyond our own. The yogi sees the divine in all things. He sees heavens and hells and their inhabitants all within himself. Predator and prey alike are his very Self."

"Then vulture and lamb are one in the eyes of a Mahatma?"

"I see the difference, but am not bothered by it. Lift the veil, and you will gaze on worlds more magnificent than you can imagine. I travel the cosmos, but there are infinite destinations to explore. The journey goes on without limit. From the valley, the villager cannot see far, but higher up the mountain; the sky is full of stars. Only the courageous venture up the mountain."

"Guruji, how does one awaken?"

"When the guru turns lead into gold, it becomes gold for all time. The secrets of alchemy are shared only with the virtuous."

"Am I worthy of such secrets?"

"You would not be here otherwise. Lose yourself in love. Krishna is the ocean of love. Drown yourself in him."

"But how?"

"To find water, a well must be dug. Divine love dwells deep in your heart. Search there, and you will find the well-spring of love."

"It seems difficult."

"It isn't so difficult; there is more love than oxygen on this earth. It is available to everyone."

"How does one find Krishna?"

"Devotion is the key that unlocks his inner sanctum."

"But when I needed him most, I couldn't find him because my heart was troubled."

Shankar Baba looked up at the moon. "When the lake is turbulent, there is no reflection, but when it is calm, the moon is reflected perfectly. To know the Self, one needs a tranquil mind. For this reason, we meditate. The mantra is like a ship's anchor. Throw it overboard, and it will sink. In the depths, one discovers the treasure chest your Tibetan friends call Nirvana."

"I am tired of pain, Guruji. It hurt when the vulture carried Neelam away."

"Now you know that death is not the end."

"I knew that already."

"But you forgot."

"Yes, I forgot. Will you help me remember?"

"That is why I am here. Now sleep; when you awaken your mind will be peaceful again."

One evening, the woodsman returned from the forest, waving his ax at the sky like a madman. The woodsman rambled on about seeing *bhutas* near the stream that irrigated the wheat fields. Fearing the evil spirits would pollute the villagers' water, Devraj's father dispatched Subahu to chase them off. The village shaman disappeared into the forest, returning the following evening claiming to have driven off the menace. For his bravery, the villager awarded Subahu a generous store of wheat.

Suspicious of the tale, Govinda wanted to know the truth of the matter. Although Shankar Baba did not deny that spirits roamed the forests, he scoffed at the notion that spirits had sullied the village water supply.

"Subahu and the woodsman will share the reward. Go and find Devraj. He longs to see you."

As Govinda and Devraj prepared to swim, Govinda carefully placed his pouch on a rock.

"What's in your pouch?" Devraj asked. He had observed Govinda placing it on a rock many times but had lacked the courage to inquire about it.

"Diamond," said Govinda, removing the Idol's Eye from the pouch.

"I've never seen one."

The hill people were poor; the Idol's Eye was undoubtedly the only diamond in the valley, and probably the only one in many, if not all of the surrounding valleys.

"Have a look," said Govinda, holding the gem up to the sunlight.

Devraj's eyes grew at the sight of the gem.

"It's bigger than a hawk's egg."

"It belongs to Krishna," Govinda told his friend. "My ancestors kept it for him for two hundred years."

"Only a king could have a diamond like that."

"You're probably right. There's not another like it in all of India – probably even in the entire world. The Emperor tried to steal it. It's called the Idol's Eye. Do you want to hold it?"

Devraj hesitated.

"It has yogic powers," said Govinda, placing the gem in his friend's palm.

"Like Baba?" asked Devraj nervously, trying to hand the gem back to Govinda.

"Something like that," Govinda replied.

"If I hold it will I turn into a tiger?"

"I don't think so, but when thieves tried to steal it, it burned their hands."

"You better take it."

"It won't harm you," Govinda assured his friend. "I wear it for protection."

"Nothing could hurt you with the Idol's Eye around your neck."

"It seems that way," agreed Govinda.

"Why is it called the Idol's Eye?"

"Because Krishna wore it on his forehead."

"It is blue like Krishna was."

"Like Krishna *is*," Govinda corrected his friend. "Krishna lives always."

"I know, I forgot."

Devraj handed the gem back to Govinda.

"You must never speak of the gem," cautioned Govinda. "I promised Baba I would keep it a secret. The secrets we share must remain secrets. Agreed?"

Devraj nodded.

Other than Kalki, Govinda had never had a closer friend.

"What do you miss most about your life before coming here?" Devraj asked.

"My flute. I lost it on my way to Tibet."

Govinda had never considered the question before and was surprised by his answer. He doubted the truth of his words… he missed his parents most.

Bhumi Mata

Another winter arrived. Though navigating the icy path between his cave and Champa was treacherous, Govinda helped Devraj tend the cows each morning unless a blizzard rendered the path impassable. The boys had become inseparable, which pleased Shankar Baba, who knew that Govinda needed a friend as well as some tasks to strengthen his body. Shankar Baba himself had few needs. The yogi sent Govinda to fill the pot at the river, but he never treated his disciple like a servant whose duty it was to look after him. Govinda was indeed like a son to the yogi.

Two village girls were washing cloth in the river when Shankar Baba and Govinda approached. The yogi waded into the icy current until he stood waist deep in the water. Extending his arms into the stream, Shankar Baba pulled a large, glistening object from the stream-bed and carried it ashore. The object appeared far too heavy to be moved, but Shankar Baba had no difficulty lifting it. The village girls, who had been watching from a distance, timidly approached to have a look at the unusual object, which Govinda realized was a handsome statue of Lord Krishna. Dumbfounded, the girls ran back to their homes to inform their families.

"It is time the owner returned home," announced Shankar Baba, hoisting the *murti* over his shoulder as if it were weightless.

"Baba, how did you know Krishna was in the river?"

"The sound of his flute led me to him."

"But how did Krishna get in the river in the first place?" wondered Govinda.

"Long ago Buddhism came to these hills. Rather than destroy our idols the way the Moguls do, the Buddhists submerged them in rivers and lakes. Come, let's return Krishna to his temple."

By the time they reached the temple, the entire village had gathered to see what Shankar Baba had found. Subahu eyed his nemesis suspiciously.

"Krishna is returning home today," the yogi announced.

"But this is Kali's temple," declared the recalcitrant priest, blocking the entrance to the temple.

"Stand aside," Shankar Baba commanded the shaman.

"The goddess will be angry. Krishna is not welcome in her temple."

"This is his temple as much as hers. Kali will be happy to have her son by her side again."

"We shall see," grumbled the shaman, stepping aside as the yogi strode into the temple. Govinda followed Shankar Baba into the sanctum. The yogi had never brought his chela inside the temple; Shankar Baba had little interest in temple worship.

"We can make an altar for Krishna opposite Kali," suggested Devraj.

"The village ancestors worshipped Krishna," explained Shankar Baba. "The elders must know the stories."

"Baba is right," confirmed a white-haired man. "Krishna is on the altars in our homes."

"If we anger Kali, calamity is sure to follow," warned Subahu.

As the taciturn shaman stormed off, worried looks appeared on the faces of the villagers.

"Pay no attention to him," shrugged the yogi. "Subahu knows little about the art at which he dabbles. His misguided practices should stop now that Krishna has returned."

"But everyone fears Subahu," said a slight man in a rust-colored kurta.

The villagers lived in the shadow of jadoo, a form of black magic passed down from their ancestors. They feared the night and believed

The Tale of the Himalayan Yogis

that evil spirits snatched the soul from the womb when a woman miscarried.

"Leave Subahu to me," Shankar Baba replied. "Install Krishna when the moon enters the star, *Rohini*."

Shankar Baba turned and left the temple. Govinda followed his guru through the courtyard and up the trail.

"Baba, why are the villagers superstitious?"

"These hills are full of ignorant beliefs. Men like Subahu prey on the villagers' ignorance."

"The villagers, including Devraj, have a lot of fear."

"Fear holds them back. Without trust, they cannot move forward. Help your friend understand these things. When real danger exists, he should call on his god to protect him. Liberation means freedom from fear forever. Fear is a little boundary. Freedom is expansion!

"No other negative emotion exists other than fear. Every time the villagers indulge in worry, anger, or grief, they fall under its influence. All negative emotion is illusory, and can be instantly eliminated if one decides to be happy, and chooses to do whatever it is that makes them happy."

They reached the entrance to Shankar Baba's cave.

"I have something for you," Shankar Baba told his chela, handing Govinda a spotted deerskin. "Sit on this."

"Deerskin?"

Shankar Baba nodded. "A villager offered it. I accepted it when he assured me the deer died a natural death."

"Why?"

"Subtle currents pass between the earth and the yogi's body. Your body's rhythms are becoming attuned to those of the earth. The deerskin will benefit your meditation and protect you as well."

"Guruji, in my meditation, energy rises up my back, filling my head with light. Is that the current you speak of?"

Shankar Baba nodded. "Divinity dwells in your spine. Her energy may be hot, and at other times, cool. Shakti ebbs and flows like an ocean tide. She has many blessings for you, among the greatest of which is wisdom. In time, she will reveal her secrets."

In the Himalaya, winter was the time when yogis retreated to their caves; their minds turned inward for days at a time. In their third winter together, Shankar Baba was rarely seen.

One morning Govinda and Devraj were collecting fodder for Tulsi when they heard rumbling in the distance. It was the same thunderous din that Govinda had heard moments before the snow buried the lamas. Devraj pointed to the rampaging snow sliding down the mountain.

"One winter a village was buried," said Devraj.

"The whole village?"

Devraj nodded. "It happened while Baba was away. In the spring, we found the bodies."

"Did anyone survive?"

"Only a mother and her daughter who were visiting relatives in another village."

Though Govinda marveled at the many perils the villagers faced, the threat of Moguls was not among them.

When Govinda returned to Shankar Baba's cave, his guru was waiting for him.

"It is time you increased your *sadhana*," Shankar Baba informed his chela. "Spend your days and nights in meditation."

The instruction excited Govinda as he retreated to the solitude of his cave. Seated on his deerskin, Govinda's dhuni warmed his feet. Passing the rudraksha beads from finger to finger, he repeated his mantra for hours at a time, increasing the count until the days passed without his notice.

One night, the smell of wild rose filled his cave. Govinda inhaled deeply, wondering where the sublime scent originated.

As the moon waxed and waned, Govinda's body grew lean. A fire raged within him. Seeing the intensity in his eyes, Shankar Baba applied sandal paste to Govinda's forehead, throat, and arms to cool his body. Govinda was becoming a yogi.

Spring arrived in the valley to the west of the Five Chimneys.

"We will go now," said Shankar Baba, surveying the terraced plots from the ledge outside Govinda's cave. "The seeds have been sewn. The villagers will not mind if we disappear for a while."

"Disappear?" Govinda had grown accustomed to his solitary life on the mountain and had no desire to leave. "Will we return soon?"

"We shall see," replied the yogi vaguely.

"Where are we going?"

"We yogis wander from time to time. Otherwise, we grow soft."

With those words, Shankar Baba started down the trail, leaving Govinda to scoop up his meager possessions and follow. The mendicants followed a stream originating in the glacial fields at the base of the Five Chimneys. Having walked since dawn, they conquered ridge after ridge until Govinda slumped against a rock, unable to go farther. Fatigue furrowed his forehead.

During the years that he had been with the inscrutable yogi, Govinda had grown long and lean, but still, he could not keep up with Shankar Baba. When climbing, Shankar Baba drew long, easy breaths while Govinda gulped air unevenly.

"Exhaustion," he panted.

"We have further to go," said Shankar Baba. "When you climb, move like a leopard rather than lumbering like an elephant."

"If Kalki were with me, I could conquer any peak."

"A surefooted mule would serve you better."

The path ahead ascended yet another daunting ridge.

"Baba, I can't make it over that one," Govinda protested.

"This is no place to spend the night," said Shankar Baba. "Shamans have spread their web of magic everywhere in these hills. Can you hear it?"

Govinda listened. Above the sound of his labored breath, he heard drumbeats echoing through the valley.

"They invoke spirits," explained Shankar Baba.

Govinda shrugged.

"Fertility rite. The shamans perform it for the village women." A mischievous smile dimpled the yogi's cheeks. "I know a way over the ridge that isn't so exhausting."

"Anything is better than climbing."

Shankar Baba led Govinda in the direction of the drumming. They reached a village where the women and girls gathered outside a small slate-roofed temple. Unable to bypass the settlement, the mendicants marched through the heart of a cluster of stone and wood dwellings.

The entire village had turned out for the ritual, but only the women were on their feet. The men sat to the side, drawing on their bidis as their wives and daughters drifted about like sleepwalkers in the sunlight. The women moved to the beat of goatskin drums, gliding aimlessly about, vacant expressions on their bronzed faces. A red-robed shaman uttered incantations, tossing grains into a low fire from time to time.

"Why do they walk that way?"

"Trance," Shankar Baba replied. "The priest invokes spirits. Keep moving… we should not disturb their jadoo."

Govinda kept a wary eye on the strange scene as he navigated the trail past the temple.

"What spirits possess these women?" Govinda asked, watching the mindless walkers.

"Nature spirits," said the iron-willed yogi, waving his hand dismissively.

"Why?"

Govinda caught the eye of the shaman at the edge of the yard. The tantric's eyes were wild from contact with invisible beings, his mind the link between the villagers and another world.

"The villagers believe the ritual summons souls into the wombs, but they give away much life energy," Shankar Baba explained, his eyes fixed on the trail.

Govinda stopped to observe the odd rite. When he looked ahead, Shankar Baba had disappeared into the forest.

"What is the effect of their ritual?" asked Govinda breathlessly as he reached Shankar Baba's side.

"Mostly, it gives the villagers faith. Every family wants a son. Tonight, they will make offerings to the moon. Then the women will invite the souls of their ancestors into their wombs."

The brief encounter with the villagers was soon forgotten; another daunting ridge blocked the way.

Govinda looked up in dismay. "Baba, can't we stop here?"

"No!" exclaimed Shankar Baba, studying the steep trail ahead.

The Tale of the Himalayan Yogis

"Take hold of my shoulders and close your eyes. Don't let go or open your eyes for any reason."

Govinda followed the instructions and waited. As Shankar Baba inhaled, an unseen force moved within Govinda. Tightening his grip on his guru's broad shoulders, Govinda was swept off his feet by a force that felt like a mighty wind. His mind spun, his body felt like a swirling leaf. Then, as suddenly as it had arisen, the sensation subsided, and he felt the earth beneath his feet again.

"Open your eyes," whispered Shankar Baba.

From high on a ridge, Govinda looked down at the treetops in the valley where he and Shankar Baba had been walking moments earlier.

"How did we get up here?"

"*Vayu gaman sidhi*," replied Shankar Baba nonchalantly.

"Could we go over every mountain that way?"

"We could… but we won't. A yogi uses his legs like everyone else. Now come, we still have further to go."

"I want to know more about flying."

"One day you will know everything there is to know. For now, know that a yogi understands nature in ways that others do not."

"Baba, I want to know what you know."

"To fly, you must perceive what others don't." Pointing at the leafy canopy of a gnarled oak overhead, Shankar Baba continued, "Everyone sees the leaves and limbs, but who sees the roots in the ground? Staggering forces lie hidden from view. The adept command these forces as easily as an emperor commands his army. Nature is obedient to the yogi so long as his mind remains uncorrupted. Being free, the yogi soars through the heavens at his ease."

"I want to fly."

"You will fly, and more. A *sidha* can leave his body at will, or create a second body, or disappear in one place and appear in another. According to his wish, he can become invisible, or possess the strength of an elephant. A sidha knows the future and the past; he can become smaller than a grain of sand or larger than a mountain if it serves the good of all. However, inner calm is crucial for nature to serve you fully."

The yogis had been wandering for days when, one sun-drenched morning, the shrill cry of a *kakad* roused Govinda from his meditation. A fawn was calling for its mother.

Setting out on the trail, Shankar Baba and Govinda had not gone far when a *hoopoe* appeared. The jittery bird flitted about, its black-tipped crest spread above a long, narrow bill. Seeing the humans, it flew a short distance before alighting on the trail. Shankar Baba followed it, and Govinda, in turn, followed Shankar Baba. The hoopoe repeated the ritual, swooping beneath overhanging limbs as it led the new arrivals deeper into the forest.

Landing a safe distance away, the bird chirped twice before taking off again, dodging limbs left and right as it veered off the trail in the direction of a wisp of smoke rising above the forest. Govinda traced the smoke to its source — a stone shelter partially hidden in a cedar grove. Above the sanctuary, a waterfall cascaded down an escarpment.

"Without the bird, we might have missed her," said Shankar Baba.

"Missed who?"

"Bhumi Mata. She was living up there the last time I saw her." Shankar Baba pointed to a glacier overhead.

"Do you know her?"

"Better than my mother. We who have no parents have Maa for our mother. We should not go to her empty-handed."

"Shall I gather some wood?" suggested Govinda, scanning the forest for a fallen tree.

Shankar Baba pointed to a stream of bees crossing the trail behind them.

"We'll follow the bees to their hive."

As he walked, Shankar Baba picked up a thin, but sturdy stick. A high-pitched drone filled the air as they approached a rock overhang. Shankar Baba ducked under the outcropping, and Govinda followed. The space behind the jutting rock teemed with swarming bees. A colony of bees had built a hive in the cavity under the overhang. The bees paid no attention to the trespassers, continuing their flights to and from the nest.

"We'll ask permission to take some honey," said Shankar Baba, examining the nest. "Inform the bees that their honey is a gift for Bhumi Mata."

Govinda had never communicated with the insect kingdom, and so he tried the same method he had used when communing with Kalki. Sending a message into the hive, he waited for a reply.

"Did you hear their response?" asked the yogi.

"I'm not sure."

"The bees invite us to take their honey. They won't harm us. Nonetheless, we should take care not to disrupt their hive."

Reaching up, Shankar Baba carefully punctured the hive with his stick. Undeterred, the bees continued their flight. Govinda rummaged through his bag and extracted a bowl, catching the honey in it. When the bowl was half full, Shankar Baba sealed the opening with his finger. The yogi ducked under the outcropping and headed toward the trail.

Shankar Baba suddenly diverted from the trail and approached the hidden cottage. A small glade fronted the entrance to the dwelling. A tarnished bell hung from moss-covered eaves. A fig tree laden with fruit stood at glade's edge, seemingly out of place in the mountain setting. In front of the weathered abode, wildflowers carpeted the ground. To the side of the cottage, a lean-to sheltered firewood, and behind it stood a grove of deodars. Above the trees loomed Trishul, Shankar Baba's favorite peak.

The smell of wild roses filled the air. It was the same intoxicating smell that had mysteriously filled Govinda's cave one winter night.

As they reached the entrance, Govinda noticed the inscription, 'Durga Mandir,' above the door. The saint's abode had been a forest shrine.

"Some say Bhumi Mata is the goddess Durga herself," offered Shankar Baba.

Shankar Baba tugged on the bell rope and then waited.

Sensing something, Govinda looked over his shoulder. Birds of exquisite color and plumage had congregated in the surrounding trees.

The bell brought no response. Shankar Baba pushed the door open, gesturing for Govinda to enter. Holding the bowl of honey, Govinda stepped into a room faintly illuminated by glowing embers in a fire pit. He listened while his eyes adjusted to the darkness. A profound silence permeated the modest abode. The room was warm and smelled of cedar.

Gradually, the objects in the room came into focus. Directly in front of Govinda stood a waist-high altar. On the ledge stood the diminutive form of a goddess, her face wreathed with dried flowers. Fresh berries clustered at her feet. A tiger skin covered the floor in front of the altar. The coat was not the brilliant orange and black of a Bengali cat, but a rich, creamy hue marked with black semi-circles.

Govinda turned to Shankar Baba, but the yogi had vanished. Although the hospitable shrine beckoned him to stay, Govinda retreated to the garden in search of his guru. Scanning the forest glade, the only signs of life outside were chirping birds whose numbers were rapidly increasing.

Having walked all morning without food, the plump apricots on a tree near the cottage attracted Govinda's attention. Plucking a handful, he stuffed some into his mouth. No sooner had he eaten the fruit than his eyelids grew heavy. Feeling drowsy, Govinda propped himself against a tree and drifted into a deep and satisfying slumber.

Govinda found himself standing at the base of a crystalline peak refracting iridescent shades of blue, violet, and gold. His eyes followed a path to the summit of the icy pyramid from where two robed figures observed him.

The taller being gestured for Govinda to climb the trail. Stepping tentatively, Govinda found that he was weightless. Rising like a leaf swept along by a breeze, he floated to the top of the mountain where he stood before the beings who had summoned him.

At Shankar Baba's side stood a tiny woman whose face was round and lustrous. Shining ebony tresses cascaded the length of her back. Her olive skin glistened. She wore a robe like those of Tibetan lamas, its fabric glowing faintly. Her feet were visible from beneath her gown. The symbol of the sun appeared on one foot, and that of the moon on the other. A necklace of blue lotus seeds hung about her neck. Her fathomless eyes held Govinda in a tender embrace. Somewhere in the recesses of his mind, he recognized the yogini.

Shankar Baba pointed to the ground. Govinda dropped to his knees, taking hold of the yogini's feet, which fit into his hands. As

The Tale of the Himalayan Yogis

he clasped her feet, a hand touched the crown of his head. He felt as if someone were pouring a liquid into him. The flow of nectar, a substance denser than air, yet lighter than water, continued until his thoughts subsided altogether. The sublime sensation overwhelmed him, drowning Govinda in a torrent of bliss so potent that he half expected his life to end. Surrendering to the pulsing energy, he found himself floating in a womb of liquid bliss. Whether an instant, or eons, passed in the happy state, Govinda had no idea, nor did he care.

Upon opening his eyes, Govinda was sitting in the forest glade at the feet of a figure robed in peach cloth.

"My child, I have been expecting you."

The yogini's gaze wreathed Govinda in kindness. Dappled light framed her angelic face.

"Maa is pleased to see you," Shankar Baba said, holding a bowl filled with plum berries and slender leaves.

Govinda reached for the honey bowl and then stood up.

"The bees offer their gift," he said, handing the bowl to the yogini.

"They are dear," replied Bhumi Mata in a gentle voice. "They fly here and there, collecting nectar with great devotion."

"Have a taste," she said, dipping her finger into the bowl and extending it to Govinda's mouth. Like an infant at its mother's breast, Govinda licked the honey from her finger. "My children have come to greet you."

Govinda looked around the sylvan glade. The birds had mysteriously multiplied; brightly painted faces peered down from every limb.

"Kakini," called Bhumi Mata. A spotted fawn emerged from behind a bush, a garland of dried wildflowers hung from its neck.

"She's the shy one," the yogini confided, stroking the fawn's back.

Govinda had heard the fawn's call in the forest, but the deer was much smaller than he had imagined. He thought of little Neelam, wondering how such meek creatures survived with leopards prowling the forest and raptors patrolling the sky.

A bird fluttered onto Bhumi Mata's shoulder, chirping noisily. Several more landed at her feet.

"These are my children. You are my child as well, Govinda. Stand beneath the fig tree and make a wish," Bhumi Mata instructed him. "What fruit do you like best?"

"Mango and Sitapal," he replied without hesitation.

"Good choices," said Shankar Baba.

"So be it," said Bhumi Mata, waving her hand at the tree. Govinda rubbed his eyes in disbelief. Hanging from some of the branches were golden mangoes and pale green custard apples. Govinda scrambled up the tree and plucked the fruit, tossing them one by one to Shankar Baba, who found catching them to be amusing.

"You yogis don't eat enough," Bhumi Mata scolded. "Tonight we shall feast. I'll spice the vegetables exactly the way you like them, my child. Come, sit with me."

Govinda sat under the fruit tree with Kakini and Bhumi Mata. The diminutive yogini removed a seed from a section of creamy sitapal and slipped the pale flesh into Govinda's mouth. She did the same for the fawn. Back and forth she went, feeding her guests until they had had their fill.

"Rest your head in my lap," invited the yogini, pulling him close. "You are a brave one. I see your courage and every act of kindness. Your selfless deeds adorn you like jewels. They have earned you the best of gurus."

"But anyone would have done what I did."

"Not so, noble heart."

Bhumi Mata stroked his raven hair.

Shankar Baba pressed plump berries through hand-spun cloth and ground leaves with a pestle, preparing a concoction of berry juice, herbs, and wild honey. When he finished, he handed the potion to Bhumi Mata. Holding the rim of the bowl in her slender fingers, she closed her eyes.

"Govinda, it is time," said the yogini. "Your destiny demands nothing less than the highest spiritual attainment and the nobility to rule wisely. Drink this juice, which Guruji has prepared for you. It will awaken slumbering powers within your soul."

Bhumi Mata held the bowl to Govinda's lips. The potion was tart from the berries, yet sweet with honey. No sooner had he drunk the potion than a vast ceiling of stars spread across the sky above him.

The Tale of the Himalayan Yogis

One by one, the stars entered his body, each finding its assigned place. Stars poured into his feet, knees, hands, and shoulders. A shining sphere came to rest at the base of his spine, and another at the crown of his head. Glowing orbs slipped behind Govinda's eyes and into his ears. Larger gold stars illumined his forehead, throat, and solar plexus. Finally, a violet-pink orb in the form of a flowering lotus entered his chest, seating itself in his heart.

"The body has seven principle chakras and many others. It is time they awakened," explained Bhumi Mata.

When the parade of stars was complete, a great golden egg appeared before Govinda. The egg was alive, swelling and contracting, pulsing like a human heart. Within the throbbing egg were life forms cosmic and minute. Emerging from the vast Oneness, a progression of spiraling energy formed galaxies, constellations, and planets, which circled one another in a divine dance. Govinda saw himself at the center of the golden egg, the living Self of all beings.

Could this be what the ancient sages saw in their meditations, he wondered?

A gentle voice interrupted Govinda's vision.

"The great dance of creation begins and ends in mystery, my child."

"I saw stars enter my body."

"Each star is a *sidhi* to be called upon at the proper time, but before you can use them, you will face a few more trials," explained Bhumi Mata. "Each star is a gift for you. In due time, these gifts will materialize. Use them wisely, for the One has entrusted them to you."

"Will these stars help me fly?" asked Govinda excitedly.

Bhumi Mata drew Govinda close to her heart.

"Rest now."

Men were hacked and slain, rivers flowed red, and burning fortresses lit the night sky. Govinda was leading his men to battle when a barrage of arrows rained down on him. Roused from his fitful slumber by the crackle of wood, he awakened to find himself lying by the fire; a blanket pulled close under his chin.

"Come, let us bathe," said Shankar Baba.

Govinda had heard the summons on countless mornings, but

after the tormented scenes that had gripped his mind in the night, he welcomed his master's invitation.

"How long have I slept, Baba?"

"Long enough. After your bath, we'll gather berries."

Suspecting that Shankar Baba knew his night had been anything but restful, Govinda replied, "I'm tired of fighting."

"You will live those visions one day."

"Then I am destined to die in battle like my father."

Govinda paid little attention to the path leading to the stream.

"What follows the dream will be of interest to you," said Shankar Baba, "but for now, the glacial melt will wash away all thought of war."

Govinda pushed the dream from his mind, focusing on what was in front of him. He stood at the edge of a cobalt pool fed by plunging falls that struck a granite boulder, sending misty showers into the air.

"Can we stay with Maa?"

"We shall stay for a time," said Shankar Baba. "The lean-to will be our shelter."

"I'd sleep with snakes to be near her."

"That too can be arranged," chuckled Shankar Baba. "It will be good for you to have a mother. Ascetics like me don't know much about raising boys."

"Baba, this forest is like nothing I've ever seen," said Govinda, wading into the icy pool. "Even the water feels alive."

"Maa has raised your perception. Remember, the world will always be as you are."

"I've never felt so alive."

"Maa has sewn the seeds of your awakening, but it is up to you to keep your garden free of weeds."

"How does one do that?"

"Purity of being. You already breathe pure air, drink pure water, eat pure food, and perceive purity through your senses. That is of benefit, but also your thoughts need be pure, and your dreams too. Pure thought comes from a pure heart, and you have that."

"I want to be free more than anything."

"Then it shall be. As you experienced after drinking the potion, the universe lies within you, as does its infinite power. Use that power wisely, and there will be no limit to what you can do."

"It sounds simple."

"For those who are truly fearless, it is. Bhumi Mata will share nature's secrets with you, and I will teach you the secrets of yoga. Ultimately, they are the same. You will need both one day."

"I'd like to know how those mangoes appeared on the fig tree."

"Sidhis are the divine in action. Sage Patanjali taught that one attains yogic powers through the use of gems, herbs, and mantras. Your powers will come from some of each."

"Then a gem like the Idol's Eye can grant yogic powers?"

"Yes, as will the elixir Bhumi Mata gave you," replied Shankar Baba. "Come, let us gather berries. You are hungry, aren't you?"

The yogi walked deeper into the forest.

"Baba, what was in that drink?"

"Berries, honey, herbs..." said Shankar Baba vaguely. "You liked the taste?"

"My vision hasn't been the same since I drank it."

"Then you are beginning to perceive the essence of things?"

"I walk as if through a dream. The plants speak to me, and I see friendly beings everywhere in the forest. Are they real, or is this some illusion?"

"They are real. Remember our talk with the deodar tree?"

Govinda nodded. "I could never cut down a tree now that I'm aware of the soul within it."

"Countless beings live in the forests."

"They're everywhere."

"Maa has opened your spiritual eye. You are beginning to glimpse the hidden world the yogi perceives. Your vision will become clearer with time. What once seemed strange and unusual will become commonplace as your vision becomes accustomed to new ways of seeing. Can you feel the oneness?"

Govinda nodded. "It overwhelms me. Inside and out; there is little difference."

"Shakti is limitless energy. However much it is awake within you, that is your level of spiritual attainment. We yogis call it *kundalini*, the life force born of the divine mother. As kundalini awakens, she travels from the base of the spine to the crown of the head where she unites with Shiva. Kundalini is expanding within you… there is no turning back. Approach her with devotion, and she will not lead you astray, but know that yogis fall when the ego rebels."

"Will I fall?"

"Should you fall, I am here to catch you."

"Then kundalini is not entirely benevolent?"

"The fire that cooks our food can just as easily destroy the house. Kundalini is no ordinary power. She is the unseen force within all things; both creative and destructive. She grants our wishes, including those that would ruin us. So long as your mind is pure, you are safe."

"I will try my best. From the moment Maa awakened this power, my body has hummed like that beehive."

"Kundalini is the crown jewel sought by every yogi. You are safe in Maa's lap."

Shankar Baba led Govinda further into the forest, where they came upon a stand of bushes laden with purple berries. Govinda shoved a handful into his mouth, delighting in the sensation.

"Satisfy yourself without eating too many. The berries are medicinal. Let us collect some for Maa."

The two gathered fruit before returning to the cottage glade, but Bhumi Mata didn't reappear that day.

The following morning, Govinda walked alone in the forest where he heard a strange hum. He wasn't sure whether he heard the sound with his ears, or with his mind. Then he heard the faint drone of a chant. Although he could not hear the words, he felt the pure, radiant essence of its meaning.

In the distance, a light shone through the forest. The light was white, silver, and yellow, and it was moving. As the light approached a narrow clearing, two yogis appeared. Strangely, they were chanting with closed mouths.

Govinda sensed the beings were friendly toward him, but that he was not to approach them. He watched as they walked through the forest, passing out of sight. The light that shone from within them

The Tale of the Himalayan Yogis

remained visible for a time before fading into the woods. The hum of their chant dissolved as well.

Not long after Govinda returned to the cabin, Bhumi Mata approached the cottage followed by a pair of village boys, who were bent low by the weight of the jute sacks strapped to their backs.

"I intend to fatten you up," giggled the yogini. "You yogis stand tall like cedars but are as thin as bamboo. Prepare a fire. Tonight we feast."

Govinda brought wood, and within moments a fire was crackling inside the cottage. A sliver of smoke escaped through an opening in the beamed ceiling.

The boys pulled spices, dal, wheat flour, vegetables, nuts, and clarified butter from their bags. A banquet was in the making. Spices sizzled, and pots bubbled. Govinda rolled flatbreads into thin discs. Even Shankar Baba helped. Bhumi Mata's skilled hands orchestrated the preparations, which continued until sunset, punctuated by short breaks to prepare smaller meals throughout the day.

While dinner simmered, Bhumi Mata stepped outside and rang the bell. As if it had been waiting for the call, a cobra slithered out from behind a conifer. Keeping a wary eye on the snake, a monitor lizard moved higher up the trunk of the fig tree.

"Bring milk," Bhumi Mata instructed Govinda, who disappeared into the cottage.

"You see," said Shankar Baba, "I am not the only one who is fond of cobras."

"Cobras are sacred, my son," Bhumi Mata explained. "Yesterday, I awakened your kundalini, the internal fire that illumines the spiritual world. It is Goddess Kundalini who opens the spiritual eye between the brows." Bhumi Mata touched Govinda's forehead. "Through this eye, you will perceive realms known only to the sages."

"It's as if I've awakened from a dream."

"The masters perceive light in everything."

Bhumi Mata scanned the edge of the glade.

"Some of my children are unsure of my guests," she said. "The leopard and her son have not come. The peacock stays away too."

After feeding the animals, the village boys served steaming

plates of food to Bhumi Mata's guests, who sat in the glade. Govinda surveyed his dinner in disbelief. All his favorite dishes were there, including Mataji's mango chutney.

"Maa, how did you know these are my favorites?"

"I have served them to you since you were a baby," she smiled.

Tearing off a piece of roasted flatbread, Govinda scooped up a dumpling smothered in gravy.

"I never tasted *kardhi* like this before."

"The food is the same as what you had as a child, only now your senses are awake," explained Bhumi Mata.

Savoring the *masala aloo* blanketed in yogurt sauce, Govinda was transported by the velvety sauce back to Krishnagarh where palace *bawarchis* served sumptuous dishes for the royal family and their guests. Govinda missed his home, his family, and his friends. The pungent aromas filling the air were sweet reminders of a past he had been forced to relinquish.

"Is the chutney to your liking?"

Govinda nodded. "Sweet mustard leaves with ginger… but how did you know Mataji prepared it that way?"

"My son, I reside within every mother. What your mother has done for you, I have also done. There is no place where Mother does not dwell. She lives here in the forest, in the villager's hut, and the king's palace. How could I not know how my son likes his chutney?"

Shankar Baba slipped a saffron-flavored *rasgulla* into his mouth, and then set the bowl at his feet. The cobra curled around his ankle sipped the sweetened cream.

Govinda had no sooner finished his plate than another appeared. Even Shankar Baba relished the savory delights. The village boys served the tiny gathering as capably as Krishnagarh's servants had looked after the king's guests.

"The forest celebrates tonight," said Bhumi Mata, stroking Kakini's neck. "Here there are no predators. Little Kakini is not afraid of the leopard, and the mongoose does not quarrel with the cobra. I feed those who would otherwise hunt their food, and I do so without harming anything. Shankar Baba, you must stay for some time so that I can teach Govinda the secrets of the plant and animal kingdoms.

The Tale of the Himalayan Yogis

And while you're here, I will fatten you up. Mother is unhappy seeing her children so thin."

"Maa, you know the way of yogis," smiled Shankar Baba, who had allowed the cobra to wrap itself around his calf. "You must not turn my chela into a pumpkin. We yogis prefer going to sleep a bit hungry. It trains the mind to be indifferent toward sense pleasures."

"A silly notion!" teased Maa. "I shall turn you both into pumpkins."

"Then we shall resume wandering in the morning."

Ignoring his comment, Bhumi Mata placed a second plate on Shankar Baba's lap. "The monsoon will keep you here despite your ascetic ways."

"This is more than I eat between moons," Shankar Baba protested.

"It shows, Baba. I won't have my guests going to sleep hungry."

"But I never sleep."

"You yogis lead peculiar lives," laughed Maa.

"If I eat another plateful I'm sure to sleep like a villager."

"Would that be so bad? A night's rest will do you no harm."

"Sleep is a waste of life," replied the yogi.

"Why so stern?"

"Habits from the solitary life," chuckled Shankar Baba.

"Maa, do you feed the animals every day?" Govinda asked.

"They are my children. Here they live without fear."

"Animals have always been my friends."

"Accept my grace as the creatures of the forest do. Grace wishes to surround you. Depend on her for all you do; otherwise, the task ahead may overwhelm you."

"What task is that, Maa?" Govinda asked, sensing that he knew the yogini from somewhere in his past.

"I restored your body for a reason."

"Restored my body?" Probing his mind, Govinda couldn't penetrate the veil shrouding his memory.

"One day you will understand," said the yogini. "How fortunate you are to have a master like Shankar Baba. At the moment, he is enjoying my hospitality, but he won't stay long. Soon he'll be wandering again. Now take some rest. Come, sleep inside the shrine tonight."

Govinda curled up near the fire while Shankar Baba ventured into the forest in search of a suitable spot to meditate. The faint sound of a bell awakened Govinda in the night. Stepping outside, he observed shadows moving in the moonlight. At the far corner of the glade, Bhumi Mata was feeding someone. Govinda stepped closer, wary of the creatures at Maa's feet. A pair of leopards were drinking from a bowl held by the yogini.

"They were reluctant to join us earlier, but now they have come."

Having finished their meal, Bhumi Mata stroked the cats' heads before they disappeared into the night.

"Come," said Maa, leading her young guest back to the cottage.

"You'd like to make offerings," suggested Bhumi Mata, gesturing to the altar.

Taking a handful of fruit from a basket beside the altar, Govinda placed berries and figs at Durga's feet before seating himself on the tiger skin near the fire.

"The Supreme Mother invites you to her secret abode. You'd like to come with me?"

After meditating for some time, Govinda felt a hand on the crown of his head. The instant Bhumi Mata touched him; a measured current spread throughout his body. Then there was no sensation at all.

Govinda found himself soaring through the air. The scenery below was of indescribable beauty.

"You wish to fly," Bhumi Mata conveyed wordlessly.

Govinda and Bhumi Mata soared hand in hand over an azure lake with gentle, silver-tipped waves. Together, they journeyed to an emerald island at the center of the exquisite body of water. On a hill stood an opalescent temple surrounded by a grove of conifers. The shade of the smooth, pearl-like walls of the temple shifted with the light. Peach, pink, and blue flowed into one another and then separated again. A pair of lions lounged at the entrance, their majestic manes framing regal faces. The beasts were massive, but like the animals in Bhumi Mata's forest, they lay passively as Govinda and Bhumi Mata descended toward them.

As Govinda's feet touched the ground in the courtyard of the

The Tale of the Himalayan Yogis

temple, inexpressible joy filled him. Instinctively he bent down to feel the grass.

What is this place? Is this all a dream?

"Come," whispered Bhumi Mata, leading him to the entrance of the shrine.

Govinda placed a hand on each of the lions' heads. The beasts purred agreeably. Led by Bhumi Mata, he stepped across the threshold into an oval sanctum permeated with the scent of lilies. A soft chant filled the air; the source of the melodious mantra was a mystery. In the center of the sanctum was a shallow pool lined with marble columns. Accompanied by Bhumi Mata, Govinda waded into the crystalline waters, which reached his knees.

"Splash some on your face, my son." Govinda cupped his hands, filling them with the refreshing liquid. A sparkling chalice mysteriously appeared in his hand.

"Sip from the cup," she instructed. The effects of the liquid melted every care in Govinda's heart.

"Come," beckoned Bhumi Mata. Stepping out of the pool, she led Govinda through an arched entrance into the inner sanctum of the shrine. The ceiling was domed, the walls and floor white alabaster. At the far side of the sanctum stood a throne enveloped in light. Three steps ascended to the base of the throne.

The throne's brilliance drew Govinda toward it. As he stepped across the threshold, Govinda's heart throbbed in anticipation – of what he wasn't sure.

Welcome, Beta.

The words floated like butterflies into Govinda's mind. He turned to Bhumi Mata, but she had vanished. Govinda was alone in the sanctum.

As he approached, a form took shape in front of him. A stunning goddess robed in white materialized on the throne. She wore a tiara of blue, amber, and emerald gems. Long black tresses framed the goddess' face. *Kum kum* dotted her smooth forehead; her cheeks were round and soft. The goddess held Govinda in her spellbinding gaze. She appeared to be gazing into eternity, and yet her kind and familiar eyes drew him toward her like a mother cow attracting her calf.

As Govinda fell to his knees, the goddess stroked his head. Govinda gazed into chestnut eyes that bathed him in love. His mind reeled. He had little choice but to let go.

Who is this Devi?

"Beloved, I am the Mother of All," the goddess said aloud. "You have come to my holy abode, but truly, I live in the hearts of all beings. One day you will travel through my inner realms. Countless universes exist there for your enjoyment. On your soul journeys, come first to me. I will ensure that your journeys are fruitful. Now go into the depth of your heart."

Govinda closed his eyes and sank like a pearl dropped into the sea. Beautiful and extraordinary scenes appeared. The world he knew was but a shadow compared to the magnificence of this one. The goddess appeared before him, sitting on the same throne.

"You are enjoying my Maya?" she whispered.

"Supreme Mother, where am I?"

"You have come to the realm of the heart's purest intent. In this world, whatever you wish for, appears instantly."

"Is this world real?"

"Both inner and outer worlds, though transient, are real. Mother's play is eternal. Her Maya dazzles even the wisest sages. My son, what is your wish?"

"I want to see Mataji."

"But you are looking at her!"

"I would like to see my earthly mother."

"So be it."

The stunning goddess faded into a misty oval, re-emerging as Govinda's mother.

"Mataji, can it be you?"

Rukmini caressed his cheek the way she had when he was a child.

"It is I, Govinda."

"But a moment ago a goddess sat before me."

"Beta, it is time you knew that we are all gods in human form."

"But still, I like to see *my* Mataji's smile."

"And so I am here," said Rukmini, kissing her son on the forehead.

The Tale of the Himalayan Yogis

As unexpectedly as the vision had come, it dissolved, and Govinda found himself at the feet of the goddess once again.

"But where has Mataji gone?"

"As your mind sees her, that is how she appears to you," said the goddess. "My son, forms are fluid here. The Mother who you kneel before is the very essence of every earthly mother, for I am the Mother of All. Ask for a boon, my son."

"I wish that Mataji be safe."

"Even your greatest wish concerns the well-being of another."

Pleased, the goddess reached toward Govinda. Her hand passed through his gown and into his chest. The goddess removed her hand, which held a pink lotus, its petals partly open. Lovingly, she fingered the blossom, caressing the petals one by one.

"Son, I hold the essence of your heart in my hands. Each petal is a divine emotion. This petal is kindness and this one compassion, and this is your courage."

As the goddess stroked each petal, Govinda's heart pulsed with joy.

"If men knew the delicacy of the human heart, they would take care not to damage it for themselves, or others," continued the goddess; "especially their children, whose hearts are tender."

As the goddess was about to return the lotus blossom to Govinda's heart, he held up his hand, and said, "Maa, it will be safest with you."

The goddess smiled knowingly before fading into a mist. Govinda found himself back on the temple steps, Bhumi Mata standing beside him.

"What just happened?" asked Govinda searching Bhumi Mata's eyes.

"Only your heart can answer that," she replied, "for within the human heart lies the power of creation itself, and what you create is yours alone."

"If this is the world of intention, as the Supreme Mother said, then I should be able to manifest anything."

"That is how life was intended to be, and how it once was, but when discord came into being, life became a struggle. Come, it is time to return to the forest."

Bhumi Mata took Govinda's hand. Together they rose above the enchanted island, soaring over the aquamarine waters.

"Let us shower blessings over the earth before returning to the forest," suggested Bhumi Mata.

Together they soared over land and sea. Streams of light poured forth from Bhumi Mata's hands, a shower of stars fell to earth like snowflakes. Smiling with satisfaction, Bhumi Mata flew like a mother eagle, her young one in tow.

"This is how the Great Ones dispel darkness. In your meditations, you should circle the earth this way. By mere intention, you can create peace."

Having circled the earth, they reappeared in the forest shrine where they found Shankar Baba peering into the fire.

"I see your journey has been a success," said Shankar Baba with a knowing smile. "Your progress is ahead of schedule. In the morning we will depart for Champa."

Govinda sat near the fire, his head spinning from the surreal flight. Bhumi Mata slipped mango slices into his mouth.

"Baba, can we stay awhile longer?"

"*Sanyasis* don't stay in one place for more than a few days," Shankar Baba reminded his chela.

"But we've lived in caves for years."

"There is nothing in a cave to grow attached to."

"Shankar Baba is fond of his freedom," acknowledged Bhumi Mata. "Guruji knows best, but accept my hospitality for a few days more."

"We sanyasis are creatures of habit," replied Shankar Baba.

Bhumi Mata sat on her tiger skin near the altar.

"Tomorrow Shankar Baba will take you away."

"I don't want to leave," Govinda replied, his finger tracing the tiger skin's concentric circles.

"I have a gift for you."

Reaching up to the altar, Bhumi Mata removed a bowl fashioned from five metals. 'Fullness of Emptiness' was etched in *Devanagari* on the side of the bowl.

The Tale of the Himalayan Yogis

"When Shankar Baba forgets to feed you, you need only whisper 'Annapurna' into the bowl, and you will never go hungry."

"Never?" Govinda asked, running his fingers over the vessel, which had been worn smooth by time and use.

"Devi Annapurna granted a boon to the yogi who kept this bowl. The boon goes to whoever possesses the bowl."

"Maa, you pamper the boy," chided Shankar Baba.

"You forget that Govinda is a prince."

"Then he shall be a yogi-prince."

"The robes of asceticism do not fit a king."

"I don't dress my chela in robes of any sort," bantered the yogi.

"You yogis scarcely dress at all," laughed Bhumi Mata.

"Kings have cast off their crowns in search of worlds known only to the yogi."

"That is true," agreed the yogini. "A king's treasury cannot buy wisdom. Still, one need not roam the forest naked."

"We are hardly naked, Maa," said Govinda, defending Shankar Baba. "When we are cold, we smear ash over our bodies."

"It will not always be that way," assured Bhumi Mata, wrapping Govinda in a handspun shawl and pulling him close. "You will never feel the cold inside this shawl, no matter how high you climb."

Bhumi Mata placed her thumb on Govinda's forehead, whispering words he didn't understand, causing him to slip into a deep state of inner awareness. Under her influence, he saw many things: a veiled bride circling the sacred fire, soldiers' bodies strewn across the battlefield, a demoness receiving blood offerings, lions ravaging a slave. Disparate images flooded his mind, but the image Govinda would never forget was that of an ageless yogi seated at the center of a blazing fire. He was on the verge of recognizing the yogi when Bhumi Mata removed her hand, and the vision ended.

Govinda pressed his head to Bhumi Mata's feet before peering into her fathomless brown eyes. He suspected the yogini was looking into his soul, but he had nothing to hide.

"Give me your hand, my son," she instructed, turning Govinda's palm to the ceiling. Dipping her finger into a bowl of *dolu*, Bhumi

Mata drew an image on his right palm. Then she took his left hand and drew a second figure.

"These symbols represent Mother's healing power, which I am placing in your hands. On your right hand, I have drawn the wings of a swan. On your left hand, I have drawn a triangle, symbol of Mother's strength. You can now heal. Use it wisely like your Shankar Baba."

"I shall miss you as much as I miss my mother."

"I am ever with you," said Bhumi Mata, stroking his forehead. "You need only call me, and I will come."

Govinda awoke to find that he was alone in the lean-to. Scrambling to his feet, he grabbed the gifts Bhumi Mata had given him and went in search of his guru. Finding no one inside the shrine, he started down the trail. He had gone but a few steps when Shankar Baba emerged from the forest.

"We shall go now."

"Shouldn't we say goodbye?" asked Govinda, rubbing the night's sleep from his eyes.

The yogi shook his head and started down the trail.

The morning sun backlit the peaks, its golden rays falling through the conifers. Shankar Baba's long strides carried him deep into the forest; Govinda followed close on his heels.

"But Baba, we left without seeing Maa," Govinda protested.

"Words are like the puppets you were fond of as a child."

"But Maa was kind to us."

"Yogis don't rely on words. Love is the only gift worthy of her."

Govinda wanted to turn back, to spend another day in the warm cottage, but he knew that convincing Shankar Baba was out of the question. He followed his master through the forest, past gnarled oaks and old conifers, up and down steep trails, across ridges where a misplaced step would be his last.

Late in the afternoon, Shankar Baba stopped at a stream descending from a glacial field. A quiet pool reflected the bulbous boulders and stunted junipers at water's edge. Weary from the journey, Govinda waded into the glassy water. The freezing water numbed his legs and stabbed daggers at his lean body. Peering absentmindedly into

The Tale of the Himalayan Yogis

the pool's smooth surface, he surveyed the inverted images of trees and rocks. Splashing water on his face, he refreshed himself.

Wiping the watery canvas with a sweep of his hand, a look of disbelief spread across his face. The pool settled, and again he saw the peculiar sight, confirming the impossible. At the center of the glassy reflection, Bhumi Mata was smiling at him.

Convinced that he had fallen into a trance, Bhumi Mata was sitting on a rock at water's edge. The yogini flashed childlike smiles, her eyes betraying mischief. Her tiny feet wiggled playfully in the air.

"Mother's Maya bewilders all," grinned the yogini.

"We didn't say, 'goodbye,'" complained Govinda.

"Before I finished with you, that impetuous guru of yours ran off with you. He thought he could slip away without a word. I felt your heart's longing, and so I came. There are some things an ascetic doesn't understand; like the devotion shared between a mother and her child."

"Come with us, Maa. Baba won't mind."

Just then, the yogi appeared at the edge of the cobalt pool.

"Govinda's heart called, and so I came to say goodbye."

"So be it," replied Shankar Baba.

"Come, before Shankar Baba takes you from me," said Bhumi Mata tenderly, holding her arms out.

Govinda waded through the shallow water, pressing his chest against the yogini's knees.

"Maa, how did you find us? We've climbed many ridges since leaving your forest."

"I know where to find you. I'm always watching over you."

Taking Govinda's hands in hers, Bhumi Mata traced the symbols she had drawn on his hands the previous day. Govinda had tried to wash off the die, but the color was fast. To his astonishment, with a sweep of her hand across his palms, the images vanished.

"The power of the symbols is within you now. Use it wisely. Now you should go. Shankar Baba grows impatient."

Govinda clasped the yogini's feet before climbing out of the water, leaving Bhumi Mata seated on the rock above the pool.

Like a soldier's boots, Shankar Baba's feet were weathered and tough, but in the forest, there was no need for leathery soles; the soft, fertile soil massaged Govinda's feet. A fragrant breeze caressed his cheeks and chest. The measured cadence of his mantra matched his rhythmic strides.

When evening came, the wandering ascetics stopped by a stream. Staring at the gurgling water, Govinda lost himself in thought.

"What occupies your mind that your mantra isn't present?" asked Shankar Baba.

"Bhumi Mata."

"That is as it should be. Maa has filled you with her love."

"Since the first day when she fed me fruit, my mind has struggled to remember."

"She gave a clue."

"A clue?" puzzled Govinda, trying to remember her words.

"I'm surprised. Usually, you miss nothing."

"Tell me, Baba."

"Surely you remember her words, 'I restored your body for a reason.'"

Govinda pondered the words. Then, a veil lifted, and it came to him.

"I remember now. When I died in Varanasi, it was Bhumi Mata who came for me."

The broad smile on Shankar Baba's face told Govinda everything he needed to know.

"Baba, what do the symbols mean?"

"As Maa explained, they possess the power to heal."

"Is that how you came to have the power to heal?"

"Long before your great-grandfather was king, Yogiraj sent me to Bhumi Mata, who blessed me in the same way she has blessed you. So long as your hands commit no wrong, you will possess the power to heal. Rare is it that a man's body needs healing so much as his mind. Disease is rooted in sanskara, if not from this life, then another."

Several days journey from Bhumi Mata's shrine, Govinda and Shankar Baba entered a forested valley to the east of Champa.

"Tonight you will stay in the forest," Shankar Baba informed his disciple. "Make your fire under the deodar. Fill your bowl with fresh milk, but do not drink it. Keep your fire burning through the night."

Govinda had invoked Annapurna each day since leaving Bhumi Mata's cottage. The bowl had filled with food, just as she said it would. Govinda had little doubt that the vessel would fill itself with milk according to his wish.

"What am I to do in the forest, Baba?"

"Spend the night with your eyes fixed on your fire. Do not let the fire go out for any reason."

Shankar Baba's instructions puzzled Govinda, but he did not question his guru. The fire was always a good friend, keeping the cold away as it sputtered through the night.

Govinda had never known fear. When others spoke of it, he listened blankly, for he was unfamiliar with the emotion men dreaded most. Govinda loved the forest and greeted the elder deodar like an old friend. After preparing his fire, he leaned against the tree's gnarled trunk, watching the fire gain strength. Noticing a bronze cluster attached to the bark above his shoulder, he cut away a portion of the fragrant resin and tossed it into the fire. Sizzling lightly, the resin spread a pungent aroma across the forest floor.

Govinda rested his head against the massive tree, listening to the silence while watching the flames envelop a splintered log. The forest was alive with creatures monitoring the night. The hoot of an owl alerted rodents not to venture far from their dens. A breeze whistled through the trees. Rooted to the earth like the trees he sat beneath, Govinda passed the night in silent reverie.

Meditation was different in the forest than in Bhumi Mata's cottage, or his cave, for that matter. The hours slipped by under Govinda's vigil, and only the need to add a fresh log to the fire brought the young sentry out of his meditation.

A fresh vitality spread through the forest. The hour of Brahma had arrived, a yogi's favorite time for meditation. While humanity slept, yogis surcharged their souls in ways known only to them.

Govinda felt it, though he never heard it. There was no mistaking; something, or someone, lurked beyond the ring of firelight. He scanned the blackness but saw nothing, and so he returned to his mantra. Still, he sensed something… a heartbeat… a breath… a paw carefully placed on the ground. A stalker lurked… he was sure of it.

Again he scanned the forest but saw only faint outlines beyond the soft radiance of the fire. He gazed into the fire, which was little more than an amber glow. Looking up, he spotted the intruder. Between two conifers, a pair of pale yellow eyes studied their owner's prey. A leopard, Govinda decided, for only a cat could steal so close without disturbing the forest, though not even a leopard could silence its heartbeat or conceal its presence altogether. Calmly, he observed the one that observed him.

The stalker knew just how close it could venture without being exposed by the fire. Govinda did not panic, nor had he reason to, for the wary cat knew that it too was being watched. The feline stalked its quarry with the deftness of a Hatha yogi. Govinda followed its movement, his vision growing sharper by the moment, his pulse steady. The slinky cat circled behind him, forcing Govinda to look over his shoulder.

Govinda wondered if this was the same leopard that had frightened the villagers away from Shankar Baba's cave. Or was it one of Baba's tantric tricks? After all, it was Shankar Baba who had instructed him to spend the night in the forest, and it was Shankar Baba who had advised him to fill the bowl with milk.

Govinda decided that he and the leopard had observed one another long enough. He would speak to his stalker to find out who it was, and why it had come.

"Are you my guru's illusion, or have you come to eat me?"

I have come to eat you, answered the leopard, its intent reaching Govinda's mind instantly.

"I appreciate your candor, but if it's food you want, I have milk for you. Come closer, and I shall feed you."

Milk I would like, but humans I do not trust. They have tried to harm me many times. An image of villagers hunting a spotted cat poured into Govinda's mind.

"The villagers are only trying to protect their animals. You should not kill their pets. If you would like milk, come."

I do not feel hate in you like other humans, conveyed the leopard soundlessly as it inched closer, exposing itself to the firelight.

"You are magnificent, my friend," said Govinda, admiring the cat's silky, spotted coat. "What is the need to hide in shadows?"

The cat's savage intent softened as it moved closer. The animal rubbed its head against Govinda's leg.

Won't you allow me to touch your beautiful coat?

The leopardess paused to consider the request. Having decided that it was safe with the young mendicant, she lowered her head.

"I am Govinda," he said, gently stroking the head of the cat. The leopard's fur was thick and soft and beautiful.

I am Shakti, said the leopard, lying down and rolling about like a kitten.

"I have milk for you."

Govinda set the bowl in front of the leopard. Shakti rolled onto her feet and slipped her tongue into the rich liquid, lapping up a mouthful.

This is good. I will not eat you so long as you feed me.

"Milk like this comes from the villagers' animals. If you kill their pets, there will be no milk for their children."

But I am hungry.

"Do you know my guru, Shankar Baba?"

The leopardess glanced at the fire again.

Shankar Baba is my friend, but he went away. He named me Shakti. He communicated with me better than you do. When I was younger, he asked me to protect his cave from the humans. I was to stand on the trail but harm no one. I did not understand why I was not to hurt the humans, but I obeyed. Shankar Baba understands the creatures in the forest. You also understand, though not as well as Shankar Baba. If Shankar Baba is your friend, then you are my friend, and I will never eat you.

A feeling of friendship flashed between the night watchers.

"Shall I try to communicate with you without the use of sound?" asked Govinda.

Your sounds are simpler to understand than those of other humans, but still, I find it difficult.

Do you understand this? Govinda thought the same way that he thought his mantra, projecting the thought to Shakti.

Better, but it would be best not to think the sounds; just think the meaning, as I do. That way is best. Shankar Baba communicates that way with me.

Govinda tried, but he could not suppress the lifelong training of his mind to structure meaning with words. Perhaps he could express a vague concept without language, but if he tried to specify an idea, his mind instinctively put it in words.

Never mind, Shakti thought to him. *Though you are much better than other humans, you are still a human; I will not expect you to be as good as a leopard.*

There was no ego in Shakti's thought; merely honesty.

Is Shankar Baba as good as a leopard? Govinda thought to Shakti, still in words, but not spoken aloud.

He might be better, the leopardess thought back, staring into the fire, *though I do not understand how.*

Shakti did not dwell on the thought; the concept left her mind almost immediately as she returned to the bowl of milk. Although she drank and drank, the container remained full.

How is the milk replenished, questioned Shakti, sniffing the bowl? *This is no animal that produces milk, nor is it a spring; there are no milk springs.*

The bowl was a gift from a yogini.

Having satisfied her hunger, the leopardess was about to retreat into the forest when Govinda extended his hand and laid it on her head.

My closest friends have always been animals, Govinda reassured the cat.

I feel your friendliness. Unlike other humans, your hand has the power to heal.

"Does it?" he asked, using his voice again.

Shakti purred softly in response…

Then Bhumi Mata's blessing is real, thought Govinda.

I was taken to Bhumi Mata when I was small. All the animals in the forest go to her.

The milk you drank was a blessing from Bhumi Mata.

I have never tasted milk like that. A surprisingly powerful understanding and gratitude emanated from the leopardess, directed toward both Bhumi Mata and Govinda. *You bear her blessing. Now I understand why you are different than other humans.*

If you come to my cave above the village, I shall share my milk with you.

I cannot go there. The villagers try to hurt me. I have little Durga to feed and protect.

All the more reason you should come for milk. Durga will grow strong if he drinks from Bhumi Mata's bowl.

Too dangerous. Already a hunter from the village has tried to harm Durga. The leopardess unhurriedly raised her head from Govinda's lap and sniffed the morning air. The first rays of light now filtered through the trees overhead.

Will you see Shankar Baba?

I hope so, replied Govinda.

Shakti gave the fire a final look.

Give him my gratitude, thought the leopardess.

If ever you are hungry, come to my cave. The villagers sleep in the night. No one will spot you.

There are some who do not sleep in the night. I shall go now.

The leopardess retreated noiselessly into the forest.

Soft light dappled the forest floor, and hungry creatures combed the forest in search of food. Before returning to his cave, Govinda bathed in a blue pool that was not so cold as the stream flowing past Champa.

Overhead, a family of Hanuman langurs watched the human splashing around. The primates' silver coats shone against the green of the forest, their black masks disguising clever minds. After his bath, Govinda gathered a handful of pine nuts to share with the highflying primates.

After snacking from his bowl, Govinda climbed to his cave. Though he missed Bhumi Mata, it felt good to be home.

Seeing Shankar Baba's feet pointed skyward, Govinda climbed faster. He loved watching his guru's nimble limbs arrange themselves in ways few human bodies could. Whenever Govinda attempted one of Shankar Baba's yoga asanas, he soon gave up in frustration.

"How was your night in the forest?" asked Shankar Baba, who was now lying on his mat like a corpse.

"The forest was alive," replied Govinda vaguely.

"What did you learn from your fire?"

"I can't say for sure."

"Nature has much to offer," said Shankar Baba, who had drawn his abdomen under his ribs. "Attune your ear to the elements… rain… wind… the call of an owl; all are voices of wisdom and friendship."

"I made a friend. Her name is Shakti."

"You met Shakti?" Shankar Baba replied, playing along.

"Yes, but somehow I think you had a part in it."

"Why is that?" smiled the yogi, his arms extended above his head, palms pressed together.

"Because she knows you."

"But I haven't seen her in years," replied Shankar Baba as he bent forward and touched the ground with his forehead.

"Shakti planned to eat me, but I gave her milk, and we became friends."

"You need more friends. Bhumi Mata scolded me daily. She's right; you're not a hermit like me."

"Then you planned this adventure?"

"I had a hand in it," admitted the yogi. "There are hidden purposes behind my instructions. *Ahimsa* is something every yogi must master. You did well. I was keeping an eye on you."

"From within the fire?"

Shankar Baba nodded.

"Like the night I dreamed of Ravan?"

"Like that. Fire is my friend the way the animals are your friends."

"Can a fire talk?"

"Better than most villagers," grinned Shankar Baba.

The Sorcerer's Ploy

The monsoon arrived with the force of an invading army. Battling the peaks for supremacy, the daily clashes between sky and mountain thundered overhead like canons on a battlefield. Sudden flashes streaked across the heavens, exposing heaving clouds as they marched across the sky, bombarding village and valley with torrential rains. Streams spilled beyond their banks; waterfalls plummeted from granite cliffs. Watery assaults filtered through pine and spruce, soaking the forest floor.

The fury shook the earth beneath Champa. Jagged flashes splintered trees and earsplitting booms sent children scrambling to their mothers' arms. Animals grazing on high meadows herded themselves into chaans, cowering from fright. Indigo shrouds obscured the landscape outside Govinda's cave. Indra, the lord of tempests, delighted in his sport, wantonly thrusting thunderbolts at the peaks.

The torrents loosed a section of mountain that buried a forest, but still, the villagers welcomed the rains. Weary of the soggy skies that imprisoned him, Govinda longed for the storms to pass. The fog enveloping the mountain prevented him from seeing the back of his hand.

How Devraj reached his cave each morning baffled Govinda, and he pulled his friend inside one morning as the winds buffeted the mountain, threatening to uproot the stunted junipers. Chill rainwater soaking his skin, Devraj sat with Govinda, sipping muddy chai made from the milk he had delivered.

"Baba doesn't like me to make chai over the fire," confessed Govinda, "but you'll catch a fever if you don't warm up." He hoped Shankar Baba wasn't observing them through the fire.

"I'll be fine," Devraj insisted, wiping the water from his face with a wet sleeve, making no noticeable difference in the wetness of his skin. Stripping off his *kurta*, Devraj appeared like a sapling, his scrawny body lacking muscle.

The boys shared stories as they sipped chai.

"I met a yogini named Bhumi Mata," began Govinda.

"Is she a sorceress? Does she make potions and cook weasels?"

"Bhumi Mata would never harm an animal, but she did cook the most delicious food I've ever tasted. All the animals in the forest come to her."

"Even weasels?"

"Leopards, peacocks, *monal*, deer, monkeys, cobras… all come to her. She gave me a magic bowl that fills with whatever I ask it to."

"See; I told you she knows jadoo."

"It's not jadoo. The yogini invokes Vedic mantras, just like Shankar Baba."

"Subahu did something terrible while you were away," said Devraj, mustering the courage to speak against the shaman.

"Now there's a sorcerer who uses jadoo. What mischief is Subahu up to?"

"Krishna has disappeared from the temple. Papa asked Subahu about it, but he denies having anything to do with it."

"Baba will deal with Subahu."

"Subahu has been in a dark mood. He asks a lot of questions, and scolds me whenever I enter the temple."

"Why does he scold you?"

"Because I bring you milk. Subahu wants Baba to go away. He's been upset ever since Krishna came to the temple."

"Never mind about Subahu."

"But there's more. A tantric visited Champa while you were away.

The stranger scares me. He speaks to no one but Subahu. He's said to be a powerful sorcerer known to many in Kathmandu Valley."

"I shall inform Baba."

"Remember when you showed me the Idol's Eye?"

"You didn't tell anyone about it, did you?"

"I told Papa."

"He won't tell anyone."

"And I told Subahu." Govinda grimaced at the confession. "He watches us swim in the river. He has seen you leave the pouch on the rock. While you were away, he asked about it."

"But you could have told him anything… that its full of leopard's teeth… or sacred ash… anything."

"He frightens me."

"Baba will know what to do."

"Are you upset?"

"It's Subahu's fault… not yours."

"Everyone is happy now that Baba has returned."

"I hope we stay. Subahu waited until Baba was away before removing Krishna from the temple."

"You're probably right."

"Of course I'm right. Subahu is the worst thing about this valley."

"I better go," said Devraj, who was uncomfortable with the open talk against Subahu.

After finishing his chai, Devraj slipped into his dried shirt. The fog was denser than usual, the rain severer.

"How will you find your way?"

Devraj shrugged.

"The cows are on the mountain. I wasn't expecting a storm. When I left the *bugiyal*, the sky was calm."

Monsoon storms punished any creature without cover. The previous year two water buffalo had died when lightning struck the ground near where they grazed.

"I can't see a thing," said Govinda, peering into the clouds.

"I should go."

"But it will be slippery."

"Somehow, my feet find the trail."

"I'll go with you," decided Govinda.

Though he shuddered at the idea of climbing to the high meadows in a storm, he could not let his friend go alone.

"It's not necessary," Devraj countered. "I know you don't like storms."

"I'm coming," Govinda insisted.

Crouching low, the boys avoided a blast of wind that nearly swept them off the mountain. From Champa, Devraj led the way up the trail, his feet navigating by memory alone. Every step was precarious. The boys lost their footing often, sliding a step down the mountain for every few they took.

The climb to the high meadows beyond Champa was perilous even under calm skies. Numbed by frigid blasts and pounding rain, the ascent was every bit as grueling as Govinda's struggle the day the avalanche buried the lamas.

The smaller Devraj moved nimbly, but Indra spared neither boy. The Lord of Heaven tossed thunderbolts like a boy skipping stones across a pond. Above the ridge, a blinding flash lit the sky, striking the mountain. Moments later, a numbing explosion shook the ground. The sudden burst of light exposed the terror etched on Devraj's face. Great claps of thunder, a thousand drums beating as one, echoed off the concealed peaks.

The trail had become a rivulet of gushing water. Blindly, the boys battled the storm. Whirling winds forced them to their knees. Hot blasts of white light ripped through the sky, exposing the mountain for an instant before darkness obscured it again. The boys' mud-smeared clothes flapped like a ship's sails in a tempest. The stinging rain lashed at their faces. The boys had forgotten why they were climbing.

Scaling the final distance on their hands and knees, they scrambled up a steep incline. Devraj searched for familiar footholds but found none. Protruding rocks pushed through the mud, tearing at their hands and feet. Desperate for refuge, the boys reached the bugiyal. Blinded by the foggy gloom, Devraj called to his friend, unaware that Govinda was standing beside him.

"Let's check the chaan!" shouted Devraj over the din, hopeful that the herdsman had corralled the animals safely inside the shed.

As the boys approached the chaan, Tulsi greeted them. Huddling under an eave that dumped more water on them than the storm, they peered into the mossy shelter, checking the animals whose matted coats were caked with mud. Floppy-eared faces stared innocently at the newcomers. Pressed one against the other, the animals waited patiently for the storm to pass.

Perched on his haunches on a crumbling window frame at the far side of the shed, the herdsman contemplated the smoke issuing from his bidi. Puffing impassively, he exhaled above the animals.

"Are all the animals accounted for?" Devraj asked the herdsman.

"All but my goat," muttered the man, his cataract-glazed eyes staring blankly over the herd. "Lightning got her."

Devraj maneuvered past the herd until he reached Tulsi, who stood near the shepherd. Scooping up an armful of fodder from a bin, he fed his favorite cow. Tulsi mooed twice, gazing affectionately at Devraj while he massaged her rubbery ears.

"Where is the goat?" Govinda asked the herdsman.

"When the storm passes, I'll show you," the herdsman replied. "I planned to sacrifice her at *Dussehra*... but the storm got her first. She was hit near the chains."

"Chains?" questioned Govinda.

"The *pisacha* chains. The lightning struck higher on the hill, but my goat collapsed lower on the mountain."

"She died instantly?" asked Govinda.

"Bleated once, then dropped like a stone."

"You saw her fall?"

"Couldn't see anything... found her in the grass."

It was late afternoon when the fury subsided, and a yellow sun shone through the parting clouds. The drenched terrain was far too treacherous to move the animals down to Champa. They would spend the night in the chaan. After descending to Champa to retrieve a shovel, Govinda and Devraj returned to the *bugiyal* to bury the dead goat.

"What's a pisacha chain?" Govinda asked as they zigzagged up the mountain.

"Subahu uses the chain to drive out demons, but he hasn't used it since the woodsman's wife went mad one summer after her baby died. Subahu chained her on the *bugiyal*, burned grasses, and made incantations. He left here there all night. As head of the village, Papa was allowed to watch.

"Did she recover?"

Devraj shook his head. "She died in her sleep a few days later, but Papa still has dreams about her being chained to the mountain. Subahu claimed the woodsman's wife was mad, which we all knew anyway. He said pisachas tormented her soul."

"Do you believe demons got her?" asked Govinda.

"I suppose so. But only Subahu knows about pisachas."

"And he's convinced the villagers that pisachas were the cause. But why chain someone to a mountain?" wondered Govinda.

"Jadoo ritual… jadoo's been here longer than the hill people."

"Every time you say that word I feel your heart quicken."

"Our ways are strange," admitted Devraj. "Come, the chain is up there."

The two climbed to a spot where the herdsman was sitting on a boulder near a wood pole standing twice the height of a man. The pole was once a conifer whose limbs had been stripped away and upper section cut off. A heavy iron chain had been threaded through a hole bored through the pole. Govinda had seen a man chained to a pole outside the barracks at Krishnagarh once, but to chain a woman in the night seemed cruel, especially with predators on the prowl.

"Over there," said the herdsman, nodding his head.

The goat's carcass lay in the grass a few steps from the chain. Its neck had been severed.

"If lightning struck higher up the hill, then why is its neck sliced open?" Govinda questioned.

"Can't say," muttered the herdsman. "Pisachas are always hungry. I figure it must have been pisachas by the way her entrails are scattered about."

"This pisacha talk makes no sense," said Govinda, standing over the dead animal. Examining the goat's hindquarter, he grimaced.

"Explain that," muttered the herdsman through a cloud of smoke.

"I can't," Govinda admitted. "Let's bury her."

"There's a good place to bury it," said Devraj, pointing toward a patch of thick, knee-high grass a short distance down the slope. "The grass is thickest where the soil goes deepest."

Govinda plunged the shovel's blade into the soft earth. As he dug, he noticed a patch of freshly turned soil nearby. After digging the goat's grave, he examined the other hole while Devraj and the herdsman lowered the mangled carcass into the ground.

The second hole appeared to be another freshly dug grave. Reaching for his pouch, Govinda removed the Idol's Eye. Oddly, he felt attracted to the hole. It was as if the diamond were telling him to dig, and so he turned the soil with the shovel. Expecting to unearth another carcass, Govinda shoveled the earth away until he struck something impenetrably solid. Digging up another section, again he hit a solid surface.

Why would someone dig here when there's rock just beneath the surface?

Crouching to examine the hole, he noticed a black object beneath the soil. Pushing his hand into the moist earth, he discovered a smooth, contoured surface. Scooping away more soil, he exposed a larger section of stone. Excitedly, Govinda dug with both hands, unearthing first a torso, and then two arms. Taking hold of the arms, he pulled gently, then with greater force. Govinda eased Krishna out of his shallow grave, employing his kurta to clean the dirt from Krishna's face and chest.

"I've found Krishna!"

"No one but Subahu goes near the chain," claimed Devraj. "The entire village believes this place is haunted."

"Let's bathe Krishna in the river and take him to Baba," suggested Govinda.

The boys trod down the rain-soaked mountain, Govinda cradling Krishna's head in his hands while Devraj carried his feet, both boys claiming to be holding the more auspicious end of the statue.

Together, the boys plunged into the river along with the statue, submerging its smooth, black surface. When they lifted Krishna out of the water, his chest glistened in the sunlight.

"The woodsman says the gods aren't real," Devraj blurted out as he dried his arms.

Embarrassed by his comment, Devraj ran off without waiting for a reply.

Hoisting the murti over his shoulder and supporting it with both hands, Govinda began the climb to Shankar Baba's cave.

Passing through Champa, Govinda was met by curious glances. Reaching the edge of the village, he spotted Subahu approaching from the temple. The shaman stood in his path, but Govinda was not about to let the shaman intimidate him. After facing Zaim, the shaman was pathetic.

"What is it you carry?" asked Subahu, his voice filled with malice.

"How dare you bury Krishna near the pisacha chain. Even a derelict would not dishonor him so."

"Where are you taking it?"

"Shankar Baba will want a word with you when he finds out what you've done."

"Your yogi doesn't impress me."

"Nor would he care to. You pander fear for a living."

"Hold your tongue, boy."

"Your tongue shall utter no more lies if I have a say in it. Stand aside. If your hand touches Krishna again, I'll cut it off myself."

"You talk boldly, though the yogi is not at your side."

"I don't need Baba's help in dealing with swine."

"I said hold your tongue, or my curse will seek you, and when it finds you asleep, the pisachas will sever your neck like they did the goat."

"Then you admit to having a hand in the animal's death?"

"What if I did? The animal was to be offered anyway."

"I have known a hundred Brahmins, but none so arrogant as you."

"Your tongue shall make my curse more potent. Be gone, but do not sleep tonight, for with the dream comes death."

"Your threats may frighten the villagers, but I find them childish."

"Soldiers turn and run when they encounter a foe of superior skill."

Govinda laughed. "You don't know Rajputs."

The Tale of the Himalayan Yogis

Eyeing the pouch around Govinda's neck, Subahu grabbed it and pulled hard, snapping the string that held it. Bearing the weight of Krishna in both hands, Govinda was helpless to stop the shaman. Turning the pouch upside down, the Idol's Eye dropped into his palm.

"Where did you get this?"

"Return it, or the stone will burn you."

With Krishna in his hands, Govinda could do little; tradition forbade placing the idol on the ground. If not for the statue, he would have pounced on the shaman.

"This stone is the price for turning the villagers against me," declared Subahu.

"Your poverty is your own doing."

Govinda invoked the mantra that Shankar Baba had taught him. Repeating it over and over, he was desperate to make something happen.

The shaman snickered. "Your magic is weak."

A strange power suddenly welled up inside Govinda. The force flowing through him entered the mantra, causing him to utter it with great intensity.

Subahu was about to stuff the gem into his pocket when he suddenly dropped the Idol's Eye, clutching his singed hand. Govinda bent down and scooped up the diamond while balancing Krishna on his shoulder.

"Out of the way before your entire body combusts."

"Keep your gem for now," hissed Subahu, "but should you sleep tonight, you will not awaken in the morning."

"Stand aside… If not for me, then for Krishna. Or have you adopted the ways of a Mohammedan?"

"I shall allow Krishna to pass, but his bearer is duly warned."

The shaman stepped aside, allowing Govinda to continue along the trail. Upon reaching Shankar Baba's cave, he found his guru sitting by the fire.

"Bring Krishna inside."

"Then you know?" asked Govinda.

"I knew enough to find him in the river. Should I not know that Subahu buried Krishna on the mountain while we were away?"

"The fool tried to steal the Idol's Eye."

"You did well. Bhumi Mata's gifts are almost at your fingertips."

"The mantra worked, Baba."

"Of course it did. All that was needed was Maa's blessing. At first, you doubted, but now your conviction runs deeper than your doubt."

"Subahu's hand is burned."

"The first of his karma has returned."

"I would have beaten him had I not been carrying Krishna."

"Do not think of involving yourself in trifling matters. Let your mind fight your battles."

"But he tried to steal the Idol's Eye."

"One would hope that a fallen priest would reform from the touch of a gem like that, but Subahu has fallen too far; that is the risk one takes when one dabbles in dark magic."

"He cursed me."

Shankar Baba burst into laughter. "Subahu may command a few ghouls, but Krishna himself protects you. Even ghouls bow before Krishna."

"The villagers fear Subahu."

"Do not confront him. He is unpredictable, at best. One doesn't know whether he controls his pisachas, or they control him."

"I don't like him… or his superstitions. Devraj said a tantric visited Champa while we were away. Devraj claims many in Nepal know the man, including a Champa elder. The tantric is said to be a powerful sorcerer. He spoke with Subahu. The woodsman saw them meeting in the night."

"That would be Kritavat," said Shankar Baba, his tone more serious than Govinda had heard before. The name sounded vaguely familiar.

"I've been expecting him. I planned our visit to Bhumi Mata so that he would not find you here."

"Then you know him?"

Shankar Baba nodded. "You also knew him once. Kritavat is Subahu's guru. Do not venture outside in the night without me. With Kritavat stalking about, anything could happen."

"But what could he do?"

"Nothing, so long as you follow my instruction."

"Baba, Devraj is confused. The woodsman told him the gods aren't real."

"Whether or not the gods exist will not depend on what a person believes, but ask your friend whether it makes him happier to believe that they exist, or not. Is he happier thinking they do not exist? The woodsman has lost faith in his gods and has placed his trust in jadoo. Whether one believes in this god, or that, it does not affect the god."

"I'm sure Devraj believes in the gods," Govinda answered, defending his friend.

"You can tell what the gods are like by what the people are like. Think about that. What are the Muslims like, really like? What are the Buddhists like? What are Hindus like? It is the same with tribals because their gods bless them with their love and their help.

"How is a soul created?" asked Govinda.

"That's a deep one," smiled the yogi. "Souls are created out of Bhagavan's breath along with the light that accompanies them."

"Devraj says you've lived here since his grandfather was a boy. How old are you?"

Shankar Baba shrugged. "What are a few centuries in the span of eternity? My guru is ageless, but he appears no older than you."

"How is it possible?"

"It's a matter of restoring the body to a pure state. In doing so, the yogi creates balance. Some do it with herbs; others use mantras, but for those desiring a youthful body, light, along with *prana,* is the key to restoring the form to a state in tune with the great life stream. The mind controls the body. When the mind is singularly focused, balanced, and fully wakeful, the body follows wherever the mind leads it. An ageless body results."

"To the ordinary man, it sounds miraculous, but to the yogi, who has opened the gates to infinity, this is life as it was meant to be," said Shankar Baba. "But few yogis are interested in living forever. Some even cast off the body at a young age. Janeshwar was your age when he discarded his."

"Why would he choose to leave his body at such a young age?" asked Govinda.

"The pull to merge with the One is strong. Your grand guru is a rare exception. It's a matter of free will, and agreement. Think of your lama friend who agreed to come back to help others."

"Are you here by agreement too?"

"In a way," replied Shankar Baba. "When your training is complete, I shall return to the Mahatmas. But to join the Mahatmas, control of one's speech is necessary."

"Then I may not be ready," lamented Govinda. "You asked me not to talk about the Idol's Eye, and yet I told Devraj."

"And Devraj told Subahu."

"Devraj blames himself for the shaman's mischief."

"Without self-control, certain things cannot be shared. It would be too dangerous."

"I don't understand," said Govinda.

"Imagine if the Emperor's spies discovered that we yogis knew the secrets of immortality. They would seek us out and, if they found us, they would torture us until we shared our knowledge with them."

"But wouldn't that be like allowing the army of demons to steal the Amrit?"

"Of course we would never allow it."

"I should not have told Devraj about the Idol's Eye."

"Had the Idol's Eye been kept a secret, Krishnagarh would not have been sacked."

"And Pitaji and the others would still be alive."

Weary from the struggle with the storm and carrying Krishna up the mountain, Govinda fell asleep by the fire, having forgotten about Subahu's curse. When inhuman laughter roused him, Govinda opened his eyes, but his fire had gone out.

Surrounded by darkness, the laughter came again; nightmarish and unnatural. The laughter was coming from outside the cave. Whatever was laughing, there was more than one.

Govinda scrambled to his feet, but there was only one way out of the cave. To go that way would be to go toward the laughter. The laughter erupted again, otherworldly and demonic, freezing Govinda in his place. He searched the cave for a weapon, but found none; the cave was empty, apart from his presence. There wasn't even a loose rock on the floor.

The laughter was nearer now. A silhouette came into view from around the corner of the cave's entrance, barely visible against the night sky behind it. The creature reminded Govinda of a hyena, but it was larger and much deadlier. It stopped just outside the cave and then slowly turned toward him, its blood-red eyes probing the blackness. The eyes were all that Govinda could see. He could not look away from the eyes, or do anything else, but if he continued looking at them, their owner would attack.

More silhouettes appeared with more hostile eyes. There seemed to be an infinity of eyes, somehow fitting onto the ledge outside the cave. The numberless eyes stared at Govinda, overwhelming him with their murderous inhumanity. There came a laugh, and another, and then another, and two at once, and then two thousand, and infinitely more, a deathly chorus of maddening dissonance. Govinda covered his ears, but nothing could shut out the tormenting sound; he wanted to scream to drown it out, but he would become part of the chorus, drawn into it, pulled toward those eyes and open mouths and razor fangs that reached for him... but did not, could not enter the cave.

Suddenly a new part of Govinda's consciousness awoke, separate from the rest.

They dare not enter the cave, the new part thought. *As long as I am in the cave, they cannot reach me... cannot harm me.*

The thoughts were brighter than the numberless eyes, louder than their laughter. For the first time since the laughter erupted, Govinda blinked. For a moment, the blackness stabbed at his soul; he thought he was dead. But it was his imagination; it was not real.

It is not real. It never was real. It cannot be real.

Govinda opened his eyes, and though countless eyes still stared at him, they were less bright, less powerful.

They have no power. They never did have power. They cannot have power.

The laughter stopped. All was silent. Govinda looked into the eyes and saw fear.

Fear? What do they fear?

Govinda blinked again, and the blackness meant nothing. He looked at the eyes again.

They fear me.

He laughed.

The infinite eyes vanished as the silhouettes turned away, suddenly smaller and less deadly than newborn puppies. They scattered and fled, as though Govinda's laughter was the roar of the deadliest predator imaginable. In an instant, they vanished.

Still laughing, Govinda lay back down and closed his eyes, welcoming the comforting blackness. He fell asleep – or perhaps he had always been asleep.

Govinda awoke in the morning with no memory of the haunting encounter of the previous night. Shankar Baba was not in the cave. Hungry, Govinda headed for his own cave. If Devraj had left milk and dried fruit, he would eat that. If not, he would invoke the magic bowl.

To his surprise, Govinda found Shankar Baba in his cave, and the Krishna statue as well. Krishna stood on a low natural ledge at the back of the cave, a pair of ghee lamps burning at his sides. Shankar Baba applied fresh sandal paste to Krishna's forehead and draped silk over his shoulders. Where the cloth and lamps had come from was a mystery, but Govinda didn't ask. If a bowl could produce food upon command, Shankar Baba could produce anything he desired.

"From today, your cave will be Krishna's temple," Shankar Baba informed him. "We shall invite the villagers once a year. You and Devraj will look after Krishna."

"Baba, there is talk of pisachas and spirit possession. Devraj says that when the woodsman's wife went mad, Subahu chained her to the mountain to drive the spirits from her body."

"Wherever they practice jadoo, evil stands at the door."

"But chaining a woman to a post makes no sense."

"Whether pisachas do Subahu's bidding, or he theirs, he knows nothing of denying them their evil desires; indeed, he would not wish to. He claims to be the pisachas' enemy to keep the villagers' favor, but in truth, he is their ally."

"Devraj fears Subahu."

"Love and fear are the only true emotions. Most beings have a balance of the two; higher beings have more love than fear. In lower beings, it is the opposite. Superstitions feed fear the way oil fuels a lamp. A yogi is without fear, pisachas without love."

"Can pisachas harm one who has no fear?"

"What can fear do to the fearless, but fear them? Like attracts like. Demons fear that which is protected by love. They feed on fear the way a villager craves food after a day's work in the field. When a demon feeds on fear, fear increases. Devas, on the other hand, are drawn to love, and the more they love, the more love there is."

"Baba, a goat died in the storm."

"I am aware of all that goes on in these hills. The goat was Kritavat's idea. There is more to it than lightning from the sky."

"Why would they harm an animal?"

"They seek to discredit me. If an animal dies, the villagers may begin to doubt me."

"They would never doubt you."

"The mind is fickle. What a fearful man worships today, he destroys tomorrow. The woodsman loved his wife, but when she failed to give him a son, his anger, born of his fear, led him to curse her. He was unaware that his fear led to her madness."

"I know little about fear."

"You conquered it long ago. Your mind is steady, your meditations deep."

The brunt of their fury spent, the tempests came less often as the moon turned. The sun shone, burning away the chill and spawning fresh growth on the mountain; grass the Champa women would dry on their rooftops for winter fodder.

After his morning meditation, Govinda raced down the mountain to help Devraj with his chores. He found his friend tending the herd in a meadow above Champa.

"The woodsman found more dead animals in the forest," said Devraj excitedly.

"When?"

"Last night. He found a langur and a musk deer in the forest. The woodsman says the leopard killed the animals."

"Shakti isn't the killer. She would not kill more than she needs to feed herself and her cub. If two animals have died, then some other creature is responsible for at least one of them."

"I told you how a leopard chased away the villagers when they brought their sick to Baba's cave. The men say Shankar Baba turned himself into a leopard to scare off the villagers."

"It wasn't Shankar Baba… It was Shakti who frightened the villagers."

"How do you know that?" questioned Devraj.

"She told me."

His mind stretched beyond its limit, Devraj made an excuse and went home.

With the arrival of autumn, the nights grew colder. Govinda went about wrapped in Bhumi Mata's shawl. Their chores completed, Govinda and Devraj headed into the forest in search of adventure, although Devraj avoided known pisacha haunts.

The boys harvested pine nuts and berries, encountered the black bear and her cub, bantered with the langurs, and spread seeds for the cuckoo bird. They climbed the cedar tree and helped the woodsman haul logs back to the village. Govinda was careful not to cross the man, wanting no place in his thoughts. On warm days, the boys dallied by the river near the temple.

The hill people harvested their wheat and millet, relieved to find the yield more abundant than other years. There would be no need to ration grain to survive the winter.

Venturing into the forest one afternoon, the boys observed the langurs chattering from the limbs overhead.

"They're noisier than usual. I wonder what they're saying," said Devraj, looking up at the black-faced langurs.

"They're upset about something."

Govinda got the attention of the largest langur.

Langur, why such a clamor today? he thought, trying to focus the thought so that it was clear which langur he was addressing.

The leopardess has lost her cub.

The thought came many times at once, each with individual distinctions; it seemed all the langurs had replied at the same time.

"The langurs say Shakti's cub is missing. I'm going to speak with the tree."

"You're going to talk to a tree?" asked Devraj incredulously. "I need to check on the cows."

How could anyone speak with a tree, wondered Devraj as he watched his friend head off in the direction of the old deodar.

Sitting against the gnarled trunk of the massive cedar, Govinda felt gentle currents in his spine.

Ancient One, what has happened to Shakti's cub?

He was unsure if the methods by which he communicated with animals also applied to the plant kingdom, but he could think of nothing else.

Something came to him in return, but it was not a thought, or at least not what he would call a thought. It was more foreign to him than the thoughts of animals, which at least functioned in ways somewhat similar to those of humans. This message, if it was a message, came not from the tree's mind, or heart, for the tree did not seem to have such things, but from the tree's essence; it's being. It came timelessly, neither instantly, nor gradually. Once it came, it was Govinda's to keep; it would remain with him for as long as it took him to understand it... forever, if necessary. It was not sent to him; it was planted in him, like a seed, and it rooted in him, somewhere where he was not consciously aware of it, but where it was a part of him. From there, it sprouted into his conscious mind, and he considered and contemplated it, trying to decipher it.

Baba can communicate with this tree, Govinda reminded himself. *I can too.*

And as soon as he believed he could, he found that he had done it.

Evil casts a long shadow over the forest, the tree informed him. *We are patient beings who do not anger easily, but the sorcerer angers us.*

What has he done to upset you? Govinda thought to the tree.

We will not tell you this, but nature will unleash her fury if man does not mend his ways. She appeals to you for help, for it is your race that causes the problem.

But how can I help if I don't know what the sorcerer is up to?

Man has wrought this evil and man must correct it. If we intervene, then man will not learn his lesson.

Because I am a man, I must figure it out?

You are like a seedling to the forest. You must right this wrong, for if it persists, then the mountain will bury the men who live on it.

It must be serious! Again, his mind did not structure the thought with words.

It is. The tree's response came quicker than the others had.

But what am I dealing with? Govinda thought to the tree, resorting again to words, for he still did not know how to intentionally communicate without them. *A few village animals have died, but that hardly seems to warrant burying Champa!*

These sorcerers have planted seeds that do not belong here, the tree told him. *They have upset even us, who are rarely upset.*

Can you tell me anything more?

We do not need to.

The tree's message awakened Govinda's memory of the goat. The villagers believed that lightning had struck the animal, but that did not explain why its neck was cut open or its entrails consumed. Surely a bolt of lightning would not have disemboweled it in such a way.

Are you saying that Kritavat had a hand in the goat's death?

Subahu had already admitted to having had a part in it. Govinda's mind flashed to the frightened animals in the chaan; were they so afraid of the storms which they had endured in the past without harm, or had something else frightened them?

Observe the village priest in the night, the tree advised.

Govinda knew that no one from Champa other than Subahu ventured into the forest after sunset; the villagers convinced themselves that evil moved about the forest at night. Govinda was beginning to believe them.

I will not allow harm to come to innocent creatures, but should I follow Subahu into the forest tonight despite my guru's instruction?

It is necessary! The forest will protect you!

Govinda watched the sun recede behind the western peaks. When he judged that he should wait no longer, he descended the trail to Champa. Venturing to the edge of the forest, he found a hidden

The Tale of the Himalayan Yogis

place from where he observed Subahu closing the temple doors before heading into the woods, passing within a few steps of Govinda.

When the priest was a fair distance up the trail, Govinda followed him. The shaman took the path leading to the forbidden valley where the village lay buried beneath the landslide.

No one dared to enter the valley, by day or by night. In fact, it had been Subahu who had started the superstition that kept the villagers away. He had created for himself an ideal hideout.

Daylight faded, but the moon shone brightly enough that torches were not needed. Judging by the swiftness of Subahu's gait, the priest made the journey often. Despite the many forks in the trail, the shaman knew the way.

Upon ascending the ridge, Govinda watched from the crest. A faint light flickered in the crease of the valley. Subahu descended toward the light.

Kritavat's camp, decided Govinda.

Not wanting to risk being seen on the trail, he descended into the valley through the forest, a ploy made difficult by the dense overhang of trees that blotted out all but a few threads of moonlight.

Govinda's heart quickened as he reached the edge of the forest. On the valley floor before him stood a decrepit chaan, the only building spared by the slide. Govinda knelt behind a boulder as Subahu disappeared into the chaan.

Recalling the words of the conifer, Govinda was determined to discover the sorcerers' plot. He moved closer to the hideout, staying out of sight until he reached the rear of the crumbling edifice.

Govinda pressed his cheek to a crack in the wall and peered inside. Two robed figures were engaged in conversation; one of them was Subahu. He had never seen the other man before. An animal slept near the sorcerer's feet. The unfamiliar sorcerer sat on a wooden bench near the lamp, his spidery fingers tapping absentmindedly on his seat. To Govinda's surprise, the sorcerer possessed the eyes of an adept. He strained to hear their conversation, but the pair spoke in muffled voices.

For no apparent reason, the tantric stood and moved in Govinda's direction. Staring at a section of wall directly in front of Govinda, a wicked smile formed on the tantric's face, sending chills through Govinda. He hastily retreated to the forest, knowing that if he lingered a moment longer, they would discover him.

Climbing part way up the ridge that separated Champa from the forbidden valley, Govinda felt satisfied that he had made a start. He would return in the morning and find out what the shamans had been plotting in the night. The forest slowed his ascent, and he tired before he reached the crest. Shrouded in darkness, Govinda sat on a rock beneath a conifer. The forest was still; not a hint of wind disturbed the trees.

Govinda was about to start for the ridge when he heard snapping sounds in the forest behind him. Whatever was moving through the trees was too small to be a predator, and therefore caused him little concern. As the noise grew closer, Govinda realized that the creature was approaching at an alarming speed. Alerted by the rapidly escalating din, his heart quickened.

A pair of murderous eyes sped toward him. He heard the beast's hot panting as the eyes rose into the air. The attacker passed through a shaft of moonlight, exposing a leopard-like head with lethal fangs.

As Govinda turned to face the creature, his foot slipped on a root, causing him to crumple to the ground. As his body flattened on a soft bed of undergrowth, a collision occurred above and behind him. A sudden gust of wind swung a limb into the brute's path, causing the beast to crash headlong into the branch and collapse to the ground alongside Govinda, landing on the upturned tip of a splintered stick.

The attacker's fall caused a branch to swing low to the ground near Govinda, who used it to pull himself up. He was on his feet in an instant, ready to defend himself, and wisely so, for the collision with the limb only momentarily slowed the animal.

The beast came on the attack again, and this time it found its mark. The animal leaped at Govinda, striking a blow to his head and toppling him over. The attacker's short, muscular torso was a cross between that of a feral dog and a hyena; its forelegs longer than its hind legs.

The foul creature's jaws locked around Govinda's neck. He would have cried out, but his breath could not escape his constricted throat.

The Tale of the Himalayan Yogis

Struggling to breathe under the vice-grip that strangled him, Govinda attempted to club the animal with his forearm, but the beast countered by pinning his arm to his chest.

Govinda attempted to free himself by crawling backward beneath the animal. As the creature maneuvered to stay on top of him, one of its back feet caught beneath an exposed root, and in its attempt to keep its balance, the attacker released Govinda's arms.

The brute fought to stay on top of him, but its back foot was still wedged under the root, slowing it long enough for Govinda to get to his feet. Kicking at the darkness, Govinda struck flesh, then followed with a thrust of his fist that landed squarely on the assailant's muzzle. The attacker yanked its back foot upward, stripping the root out of the hard-packed earth, and then retreated toward the open trail, dodging the low-hanging boughs of the tightly packed trees.

Govinda breathed hard and fast, fully expecting another assault. Had the animal gripped his neck a moment longer, the beast would have crushed Govinda's throat. Reeling, Govinda scrambled to the summit of the ridge. Descending past the bugiyal where the goat had died, he was satisfied that the beast that had attacked him had also killed the goat. Remembering the goat's lacerated neck, he rubbed his throat, which was scraped and bruised.

Exhausted by the time he reached his cave, Govinda slipped under his blanket, relieved to feel the warmth of the fire at his side.

I thought the forest had agreed to protect me, mused Govinda as sleep overcame him.

Govinda slept through the hour of Brahma, drifting in and out of dreams of Bhairav and his dogs.

"Yogis don't sleep through the best hours for meditation."

Shankar Baba's familiar voice filled the cave. Govinda was glad to see someone he loved.

"Am I really a yogi?" asked Govinda sleepily.

"Truthfully, no, but while you're with me, you are," laughed his guru. "I see that you had an adventure in the forest last night."

"I should have listened to you."

"I am not the only voice of wisdom in these hills. The Elder of the Forest advised you well."

"Then you know about my mission?"

"Of course, and I approve, but proceed cautiously; Kritavat is more deadly than poison."

"Then maybe I shouldn't be prying around his hideout in the night."

"Evil does its best work in the dark."

"I thought my time in the Himalaya was for meditation."

Govinda stepped onto the ledge outside his cave.

"There is ample time to meditate if you don't spend all your time under your blanket."

"Something attacked me last night," said Govinda, rubbing his neck. "The tree said the forest would protect me, but when that beast attacked, I was on my own."

"If that were true, you would be dead. The creature that attacked you has never failed to kill."

Realizing that the forest had indeed helped him throughout the assault, he said, "then I am grateful to the forest," speaking more to the trees than to Shankar Baba, though the yogi was beside him and the trees were out of earshot.

"The trees are your allies in this affair," said Shankar Baba. "I shall not be a direct part of it."

"I understand. It's my responsibility to look after the creatures in the forest."

"Think of it as part of your training. If you look after the animals of the forest, they will look after you."

"Did the beast that attacked me also kill the goat?"

"And other animals! Kritavat is cunning. He manipulates nature to serve his twisted ambition."

"Is that why the Elder of the Forest is upset?"

"Kritavat and Subahu plot to spoil the animal kingdom. You love animals, and love is needed to stop these miscreants."

"But what exactly are they doing?"

"I cannot say, but a long time ago before Kritavat strayed from the path… he and I shared the same guru."

"Then I shall need help."

"If you need help, it will be provided, but you are more than able to solve the mystery. In fact, you delight in such intrigues."

"Tonight, I will solve the mystery of Kritavat as well as that of the creature that attacked me."

"Come, have your bath. The stench of that unfortunate creature lingers on your skin."

The rush of snowmelt washed away the residue of Govinda's brush with death. A row of irregular marks on his neck was all that remained of the ordeal.

Govinda spent the day planning how he would deal with the sorcerers. The revelation that Kritavat shared much of the same training as Shankar Baba worried him, but he was determined to complete his mission.

Villagers crowded into the temple to attend evening aarti as Govinda slipped past the sanctum, a borrowed dagger hidden in the folds of his lungi. Reaching the ridge between Champa and the forbidden valley, he waited for Subahu, fingering the dagger's grip as well as its sharpened edges. At all cost, he wanted to avoid another encounter with the beast.

Govinda looked down at Champa. In the moonlight, he saw Devraj running toward the temple. Typically, his friend attended evening aarti, but tonight he arrived late.

Devraj came out of the temple followed by the villagers. The group gathered in the courtyard. Usually, the villagers returned to their homes after the evening ritual, but tonight the men were engaged in an animated discussion. There was no sign of Subahu, and so Govinda returned to Champa to find out why the villagers had gathered.

As he entered the village, one of the men shouted,

"Maybe Shankar Baba's chela can explain what happened."

As he approached the men, Govinda spotted Subahu standing next to Devraj, a look of satisfaction on his face. Devraj was weeping. The boy's father had his arm around him.

"What's going on here?" asked Govinda.

"That's for you to explain," replied a village elder. "We spotted you on the ridge just now. What were doing on the mountain after dark?"

"Why is Devraj weeping?" asked Govinda, ignoring the villager's question.

"Tulsi's dead," moaned Devraj.

"Tulsi dead?"

"Same as my goat," the herdsman interjected. "Something ripped the cow's neck apart and ate the entrails."

"When did it happen?" asked Govinda.

"Just now," Devraj said. "I had gone to the house after milking her. When I returned, I found Tulsi behind the shed."

"Explain why you were on the ridge trail," said Subahu accusingly.

"I was on my way to pay a visit to your guru. It's you who are up to mischief. Just last night a beast attacked me in the forest. See the marks on my neck," he said, pointing to the jagged marks. "The brute that killed Tulsi and the goat also tried to kill me."

"Did you see the attacker?" asked Devraj's father, holding his torch up to examine Govinda's neck.

"I got a glimpse… the animal appeared to be a cross between a hyena and a feral dog. Its fangs are lethal."

The herdsman took a keener interest in the beast's description than the others.

"How did you escape?" asked the herdsman.

"Blind luck!" said Govinda, not trusting the villagers to believe that the forest had intervened.

Turning to Subahu, Govinda continued.

"I saw you and your guru enter the chaan in the forbidden valley. An unreasonable place to meet, isn't it, with all of its demons and ancestral ghosts? Unless, of course, you required utter privacy. What were you doing that required such secrecy? Why should a village priest do anything that merits such confidentiality? Unfortunately for you, I followed you there. I believe your guru became aware of my presence. Almost immediately the beast attacked me."

"Kritavat is my guru, that is no secret," admitted Subahu. "Is a chela not entitled to sit with his guru?"

"Unless the two of you are the cause of these deaths," countered Govinda.

"A serious accusation," said Devraj's father.

"Baba agrees with me." Govinda knew it would be foolhardy to mention that a tree had identified Kritavat as the guilty party.

"It is time the village stopped placing blind trust in Shankar Baba and his chela," declared Subahu, playing on the villagers' doubts and their fear of opposing their priest, without whose protection, they believed, they would be at the mercy of supernatural threats — a belief the priest instigated himself.

"Ever since the yogi installed Krishna in the temple our animals have been dying," claimed Subahu. "Kali is not happy; that I can assure you."

"Nonsense," Govinda countered. "These attacks have nothing to do with Krishna or Kali. You and the tantric are scheming, and I intend to find out what you're up to."

Govinda put his hand on Devraj's shoulder, but his friend was beyond consolation.

Led by Devraj's father, the villagers headed off to see for themselves how the cow had died. As they dispersed, the herdsman approached Govinda.

"I never mentioned this," said the herdsman, "but on the day of the storm, I saw a strange creature on the meadow... moments later my goat was dead."

"What did the animal look like?"

"I can't say exactly. Don't know for sure if it was a dog. It looked more like a hyena. I think yours is the best description... a cross between a feral dog and a hyena. I only saw the animal briefly when the lightning flashed."

Devraj, who had been listening to the conversation, slipped off to show Tulsi to the other men.

Govinda delayed his plan to observe Kritavat. After a few days had passed, while helping Devraj tend the cows, he mentioned that he intended to return to the forbidden valley. To his surprise, Devraj insisted on joining him.

"But what about pisachas?" asked Govinda.

"I don't care if I get eaten. I want to find Tulsi's killer."

"Meet me by the river after evening aarti. Bring a dagger if you have one. The creature is deadly."

His dagger concealed in his dhoti, Govinda attended aarti for the first time since Krishna had disappeared from the temple. Standing near the back, he watched Subahu perform the nightly ritual. After making their offerings, the villagers retired to their homes.

Devraj was waiting for Govinda by the river. The moon provided ample light for their journey to the forbidden valley.

"Are you afraid?" Govinda asked his friend.

"Yes! Are you?"

"A little, but only because that creature is vicious."

"I'm ready," said Devraj, raising his dagger.

"If it attacks, thrust the blade into its chest."

"Whatever killed Tulsi will never kill again," vowed Devraj.

Govinda kept an eye out for Subahu. At the ridge's summit, Devraj paused before starting down the far side. He had never ventured into the forbidden valley. Halfway down the mountain, he exhaled deeply, his courage buoyed by Govinda's reassuring presence. Devraj was intent on finding Tulsi's killer, even if it meant searching a valley inhabited by demons.

The boys reached the chaan where Govinda had spied on the sorcerers, but the stone shed was empty. Scanning the area, they decided to search higher up the mountain.

The boys climbed over boulders and scree; remnants of the landslide that had buried a hundred villagers in their sleep. Though the terrain was rough, the boys navigated by moonlight until they came to a point where the mountain had been rent apart by the slide. An opening loomed directly before them.

Govinda held the Idol's Eye, hoping for an intuition of what lay inside the mountain. Staring into the opening, he signaled to his friend. Somewhere deep inside the mountain, Kritavat carried out the mischief about which the Elder of the Forest had warned him.

"We have to go in without a torch," Govinda said. "Are you willing to do it?"

"As long as you're with me," Devraj declared, a tremor in his voice.

"Stay close. My vision is good, even in the darkness."

Govinda led the way into the opening. Engulfed in darkness, Devraj clutched his father's knife as he placed a tentative foot in front of the other. Only the grating of displaced rocks underfoot disturbed the eerie silence within the mountain.

A high-pitched squeal, followed by the frantic beating of wings, startled the boys. They ducked as a swarm of bats exited the cave.

After stumbling about the pitch-black void, Govinda cupped the Idol's Eye in his hands, hoping for encouragement, but there was only silence.

"We need to keep going."

"Are you sure?" Devraj whispered back.

"I'm not sure..." Govinda's voice trailed off. He was listening with his heart the way Shankar Baba had taught him. Either he heard the faint rumble of a chant, or spirits were conversing in the tunnel. He assumed the voice was Kritavat's.

"Can you hear it?"

"I hear it," confirmed Devraj.

The boys moved deeper into the darkness. The fissure narrowed until Govinda's shoulders brushed both walls of the passage. A few more steps and they had reached the end of the fault, but still, the murmur of chanting continued.

Govinda touched the rock walls around him, searching for clues. Overhead, a faint thread of light streamed down a vertical shaft. He felt the flow of air from the passage and smelled smoke. They needed to climb the rock wall, a dangerous task with torch and rope; without them, it might be impossible.

Groping about the walls of the passage, Govinda discovered what felt like a foothold carved into the rock. He found a second step above the first, and a third, all cut at equal intervals.

It would be a risky ascent. Without hesitating, Govinda began the slow, perilous climb toward the source of the sliver of light above. Devraj followed. The boys climbed, blindly placing one foot after another on the steps. Partway up, the shaft arched at an angle that reduced the danger of falling.

Govinda reached the top of the passage where he waited for Devraj before climbing onto a platform of rock. Resting on his knees, Govinda stared in the direction of the light. Devraj slipped noiselessly onto the platform beside Govinda, relieved to finish the climb.

Govinda got to his feet. Together, he and Devraj stepped toward the light, careful not to alert whoever was chanting. Crouching, the boys peered into a cavern the size of Champa's temple. The scene before them was incomprehensible. Devraj grabbed Govinda's arm, clutching his knife tightly in his other hand.

Attired in a black robe and donning a glossy ebony mask with high cheekbones, narrow eye slits, and yellow fangs carved at the corners of a broad and gaping mouth, a tantric was dancing in front of a waist-high altar. Tied to a post to the left of the altar, a black-backed animal slept. On the opposite side, a leopard cub, tethered to a braided leash, paced restlessly. Govinda was sure the cub was Shakti's son, Durga.

"It's the sorcerer," Govinda whispered.

"But what is he doing?" Pointing his dagger at the sleeping creature tied to the post, Devraj asked, "Do you suppose that's what killed Tulsi?"

"I don't think so."

The boys watched as the sorcerer waved a fist full of incense, painting broad strokes in the air. An opaque cloud hovered below the cavern's arched ceiling, which was charred black. The tantric raised a bleached skull, poured some of its contents onto the altar, and then sipped from the remainder. The sorcerer's chants were forceful, his gestures frenzied. His trancelike dance covered the entire floor of the cavern. As if intoxicated, the sorcerer spun wildly about, his arms flailing from time to time.

As the pulsing energy in the cavern reached a fevered pitch, the tantric stepped to the altar where he made more offerings before picking up a dagger and moving toward Durga. Instinctively, Govinda rose to his feet as the sorcerer lowered the blade to Durga's shoulder. Clutching the rope to prevent the cub from pulling away, the masked figure cut a patch of fur from the leopard's shoulder before releasing the rope. He then approached the creature lying on the opposite side of the altar. Another sweep of his knife loosed a second tuft of fur. The tantric mingled the hair and poured dark liquid over the tangled mass before placing it on the altar.

The boys crept closer, ready to pounce if the tantric tried to

The Tale of the Himalayan Yogis

harm either animal. The sorcerer performed another series of offerings followed by more strident chanting. Govinda found it difficult to breathe, partially due to the smoke, but partly, he sensed, from invisible forces present within the cavern. Durga grew agitated; the other animal slept fitfully.

Raising his hands above his hideous guise, the sorcerer shrieked. Again and again, he cried out, his shrill screams sending chills through the boys' limbs. Durga sprang away from the altar, but the rope throttled his neck. The black-furred hyena-dog sat up and bawled a series of revolting howls before lying down again.

At the center of the altar, amidst the haze of smoke, a form slowly took shape. Govinda and Devraj looked on in wide-eyed horror as a four-legged beast appeared where smoke had filled the air moments earlier. The animal was ghostly, transparent, and dreamlike, but as the sorcerer chanted, the form grew increasingly corporeal until it was as solid as the other animals in the cavern.

The freakish beast was neither cat nor hyena. It had the head of a leopard, but the body of a feral dog. Its coat was an odd assortment of sickly spots on a pale, yellowish body. Seeing the beast, Durga and the hyena-dog withdrew to the limits of their tethers.

"*That* is what attacked me..." Govinda whispered, pointing at the newly materialized beast. "... or another like it. That's what killed Tulsi."

Devraj's hand tightened around the hilt of his dagger.

The strange creature stretched and looked about, scrutinizing Durga and the hyena-dog without approaching either of them. Then it scanned the cavern.

Govinda signaled a retreat out of the animal's sight. Devraj drew a steadying breath as he backed up, but the beast sensed the intruders. Spotting the boys at the rear of the cavern, the animal bore fangs and snarled. Govinda and Devraj shrunk into the shadows, but it was too late.

The brute leaped from the altar with unnatural strength, charging the length of the cave, accelerating with incredible power. Crouching in mid-stride, the animal launched itself at Devraj; its fiendish eyes fixed on its prey. Devraj let out a wail and retreated, clutching his knife with both hands.

Govinda stepped between the advancing animal and Devraj. Switching his dagger to his left hand, he thrust at the animal's chest. The animal's momentum carried it onto the knife. The blade plunged into the brute, barely missing its heart.

The dagger lodged itself in the beast's chest. The brute struck back, pushing Govinda to the side with its foreleg. The creature chose to focus on the smaller prey. Govinda tried to intervene, but the beast was already upon Devraj, clawing viciously at its victim.

Devraj fell onto his back; his head struck the cavern floor. The beast stood on his victim's chest, biting and ripping. Pinning the boy's arms, the creature dug for its victim's heart.

Govinda kicked the beast's forelegs, helping Devraj to free his left arm. Devraj thrust his dagger at the animal's chest the way Govinda had instructed him, but the creature pinned his arm again. Devraj's knife fell onto the rocks.

Govinda kicked the creature, trying to break its durable bones. The beast struck Govinda with a foreleg, pushing him against the cavern wall behind him.

Summoning his strength, Devraj freed his right hand, pulled Govinda's dagger from the beast's chest, and plunged the knife into the brute's heart. The animal bawled twice before collapsing onto his prey.

From his place by the altar, the sorcerer watched. Seeing his ghoulish creation collapse, the tantric rushed forward, gesturing wildly with his hands.

"Stop where you are, Kritavat!" shouted Govinda, kneeling at his friend's side.

The force of Govinda's voice brought the sorcerer to a halt. After pushing the dead creature off of Devraj, he cradled his friend's head in his hands. Devraj's eyes were half open.

"The beast is dead," said Govinda.

"Tulsi's killer is dead?" he whispered, his breath ragged and weak.

"It's dead."

The Tale of the Himalayan Yogis

Sighing, Devraj closed his eyes and died. Govinda pressed his cheek against his friend's chest and then turned to the masked sorcerer.

"What madness possesses you?"

"More will come," the sorcerer retorted. "You can't stop them, for I possess a power greater than the gods. In time, I'll create an army of them. No one can stop me."

"*I* shall stop you!"

Glaring at the masked sorcerer, Govinda pulled his dagger from the beast's chest. Oddly, the blade was bloodless, as were the creature's wounds.

"The chela always turns out like his guru," snickered Kritavat.

"Not in your case, it seems," Govinda shot back. "Why have you disgraced your guru?"

"I am a master. I honor no guru. Who but I can create a living being from smoke and mantras?"

"The gods create life from less. Honor them, if no one else. Why flatter yourself falsely?"

Govinda turned to Devraj. "You have killed my friend. What do you say to that?"

"He had no business coming here."

Govinda approached the masked tantric. Lunging, he ripped the hideous mask from Kritavat's face.

"Pathetic," he scoffed. "I should have left the mask where it was."

Ignoring the abuse, Kritavat replied, "You are even more like Shankar Baba than I imagined."

"I'm going for the village men. They will deal with you."

"But I cannot allow you to do that," replied Kritavat, his lips forming a wicked grin.

As the sorcerer reached for the dagger with which he had cut fur from the animals, Govinda ran toward Durga. With a sweeping arc of his blade, he severed the rope tethering the young leopard. Sensing his freedom, Durga leaped at his captor, toppling Kritavat onto the rocks.

Govinda jumped onto the altar, his feet slipping in a pool of offered blood. With the second swipe of his dagger, he severed the hyena-dog's rope, freeing the animal. The creature, fully alert for the first time since Govinda entered the cavern, vanished through a narrow fissure to the left of the altar.

Seeing the opening for the first time, Govinda followed the hyena-dog, realizing that he might miss his best chance of escape if he lost the animal's trail. He was sure that the animal had not been brought into the cave the way that he and Devraj had entered.

The opening widened, and fifty paces down the corridor Govinda found himself standing in the moonlight. Inhaling the fresh night air as he watched the creature disappear into the forest, Govinda contemplated his next move.

Able to breathe again, Govinda calmed his mind as best he could. Should he return for Devraj, or go for help? He was certain that his friend was dead. To return to kill the sorcerer seemed pointless; surely Durga would finish him off.

Govinda ran down the mountain, his legs carrying him at a reckless pace. He moved with such abandon that he scarcely noticed Subahu, who was climbing to the entrance of the fissure. Realizing that he had passed his foe, Govinda shouted at the village priest.

"Your guru is pathetic!"

Subahu disappeared into the mouth of the mountain. Govinda stumbled down the slope toward the village, racing past Champa's stone cottages. The village men would be of little use, and so he headed for Shankar Baba's cave. Exhausted by the time he reached Baba's shelter, Govinda paused to catch his breath. As he was about to enter, Shankar Baba stepped into the moonlight.

"More heroics," smiled the implacable yogi.

"Devraj performed the heroic deed tonight, and it cost him his life."

Shankar Baba took Govinda in his arms.

"Where is the boy?"

"I left him in the cavern with Kritavat and Shakti's cub."

"Durga will give him a scare, although Kritavat is far too clever to be slain by the cub."

"But Durga was mauling him."

"It matters little. It is not Kritavat's time to die."

"You speak as if this were a game."

"Is that not also what Rukmini said when you were fighting the Moguls?"

"Devraj is dead!" sobbed Govinda.

"Let us see what we can do about that."

The yogi ran a gentle hand over Govinda's forehead. With Shankar Baba involved, he was confident that everything would be all right.

"Take me to the cave," instructed the yogi.

Although it was Govinda who was leading the way to the cave, Shankar Baba outpaced him as always, ascending the ridge and entering the forbidden valley like a giant striding from peak to peak. Not waiting for his chela, Shankar Baba started for the opening in the mountain. Reaching the main chamber, he found the yogi standing before Kritavat and Subahu; claw marks etched on Kritavat's neck and arms. Subahu was tending to his guru. Durga was gone.

"Put your mask on," Shankar Baba ordered Kritavat. "I don't want to see your face."

"What I do is my business," bristled Kritavat. "You are not welcome here."

"It is you who are not welcome here. Go, before the villagers chain you to the mountain."

"Neither you nor the villagers frighten me."

"And what of your creations? If they find you chained to the mountain, they may turn on their master the way that you turned on yours."

"You don't know what you speak of."

"Maybe not, but no mask can hide the fear in your heart. None of Guruji's true disciples know fear."

"Leave us," snarled Subahu. "You have no authority in this valley."

"That is true," Shankar Baba admitted. "I shall leave this hell to devils like you and Kritavat. But be forewarned: if your evil reaches my valley again, I will not be so generous."

"We will meet another day," snapped Kritavat. "I am keen to test the yogic powers the villagers admire so much."

"Your lust for power will be your undoing," Shankar Baba cautioned.

"That is not for you to judge."

"It would be better if you ceased to exist than to continue on this path. If you think you will not have to repay this debt, then you have made a grave miscalculation. Karma pursues a man relentlessly, and it never fails to catch him."

"Your words bore me."

"What do you hope to gain by perfecting evil?" asked Shankar Baba.

"I share my secrets with no one."

"Your plan to bring Tadaka to these hills is a violation of all things sacred. I will not allow it."

Subahu gave his guru a questioning look, but Kritavat ignored him.

"I will take the boy's body and leave," Shankar Baba informed the sorcerers, "but know that the boy's death is recorded in your name."

Kritavat winced as Subahu cleaned the claw marks on his arm. Shankar Baba examined the strange animal's carcass. Not a drop of blood had flowed from its wounds, even the one to its heart. The yogi looked at Kritavat in disgust.

"What purpose is served by inviting demons into our world?"

"I have my reasons."

"But do you know what you do, or why?" questioned the yogi. "Your illusion grows dark. I do not wish to be the one to inform Yogiraj of how far you have descended."

"Descended?" scoffed Kritavat. "I have reached the summit! Show me another man who can conceive life as I have."

"At what price do you play at being a god?"

"That is not for you to decide."

"Unfortunately for you, you are right. Those that judge your actions will do so more harshly than I ever would."

"I do not believe in judgment," bridled Kritavat.

"Know then that what you sew you shall also harvest."

"Then I shall reap the bounty of my brilliance."

"You had more ability than the others, yet you wasted it. I shall leave you to your senseless dream, but let me also leave you with some advice: when the one who has granted you these powers comes for your soul, do not disappoint her, for unlike Yogiraj, Tadaka does not suffer disobedience. I have seen the hells over which she presides. You will not find them to your liking."

"Your advice is of no interest to me."

"My words are harmless, but Tadaka's rage is not. I will go now. I do not expect to see you, or your creations, in these hills again."

Shankar Baba scooped up Devraj's body and carried it out of the cave, Govinda close on his heels. Stepping into the morning light, the yogi adjusted his grip on the body.

"How long has the boy been unconscious?" asked Shankar Baba.

"Little more than an hour. But is Devraj not dead?"

"The state of the body matters little. It can be easily repaired. The state of the soul is more important than the body, and Devraj's soul has not left his body."

"Baba, what was that creature? It had the head of a leopard and the body of a creature that seemed to be a cross between a hyena and a dog."

"Some would call it a *preta*, but whatever it was, the beast was Kritavat's creation, as was the hyena-dog, which he created in an earlier experiment."

"Do these pretas come from another realm?"

"Their bodies are newly formed, but their spirits come from Tadaka's realm. One day I will show you that place. It is not a pleasant realm, but you will find it instructive and hopefully learn a lesson that Kritavat never did."

"Everything about that cave makes me shudder," said Govinda, following Shankar Baba through the forest.

"By thwarting Kritavat's efforts, you and Devraj have done a great service to these hills. Unfortunately, Kritavat has opened the *tirth*. He plans to invite Tadaka and her minions to join him, if he hasn't already done so."

"But isn't a tirth a place of pilgrimage?"

"Tirth is a place for crossing over, like a shallow place where one fords a river. Kritavat has created a bridge for beings like Tadaka to cross over from the lower realms to the world of men. The sorcerer has won a significant victory with the materialization of these creatures, for they do not belong to the world of men. His feat makes our task more difficult."

"But I have already defeated one of his creations."

"With the help of the forest, you succeeded. But Tadaka is another matter. You see, Kritavat tried this once before. From his former association with Yogiraj, he knows that these hills are sacred and that moving between realms is less complicated here. That is why Yogiraj kept a cave in these parts, only Yogiraj's purpose was to commune with the highest beings in creation, not to invite dregs from the lowest hells. When Kritavat first began experimenting some years back, he caused such discord that the mountain crushed not only his twisted scheme, but also a village nearby."

"Then the landslide that buried the villagers was Kritavat's doing?"

"He alone was responsible. And now he has returned to implement his perverted plan. These strange creatures are not his true purpose. As he dabbles in his rituals, his confidence soars. Kritavat's ultimate aim is to ally himself with Tadaka. Should he succeed in bringing Tadaka and her minions into our world, even Yogiraj and the Mahatmas would find it difficult to banish her."

"What should we do then?"

"I intend to see that Kritavat leaves these mountains."

Stopping to adjust the position of the body on his shoulder, Shankar Baba pointed to Champa. "Gather the villagers. I shall bring the body to the temple courtyard. Everyone should know of Devraj's courage and the wickedness of their priest."

Govinda ran down the mountain, reaching Champa ahead of the yogi. He went to Devraj's house first. Devraj's father alerted the others that an accident had befallen his son. By the time Shankar Baba arrived at the cluster of wood and stone abodes, the entire village was waiting for him. Devraj's mother stood beside her husband, tears wetting her hand-spun shawl.

Govinda had already explained to Devraj's parents that the beast that had killed Tulsi had attacked their son. The fact that Devraj had ventured into the forbidden valley did not surprise his parents, for the boy had vowed to search for Tulsi's killer. When their son did not return after evening aarti, Devraj's father and the other men searched

The Tale of the Himalayan Yogis

the forest, but none possessed the courage to venture beyond the ridge where they suspected Devraj had gone.

As Shankar Baba arrived at the courtyard, a woman placed a blanket at the center of the yard upon which the yogi set the body. Devraj's mother threw herself onto her son.

"What has happened to my boy?" she wailed.

Shankar Baba calmly explained.

"Devraj was attacked by an unnatural creature inside a cave in the forbidden valley. The tantric, Kritavat, and his chela, Subahu, are responsible."

As the yogi spoke, Subahu entered the courtyard. The village men seized hold of the priest, but Shankar Baba waved them away. Subahu checked the body for a pulse and placed his hand over the boy's mouth. Then he opened Devraj's right hand and examined his palm.

"Nothing can be done. His soul has departed," Subahu declared.

"The soul remains with the body," countered Shankar Baba.

"Surely you can save him," pleaded Govinda.

"That depends on Devraj," said the yogi.

"Baba, we cannot live without our son," pleaded Devraj's father, his face taut with emotion.

"Baba, please," begged Govinda, unable to bear the thought that his friend was dead.

"The boy served Shankar Baba, and yet the yogi refuses to help," charged Subahu, seeking a reaction from the villagers.

Shankar Baba cast a withering glance at the priest.

"Baba… please," sobbed the boy's mother.

The villagers formed a circle around the body, imploring the yogi to perform a miracle. Everyone knew that the yogi had the power to revive the boy if he chose to.

"I have already healed the boy once," Shankar Baba reminded them. "His life was destined to be short. I dare not intervene a second time."

"But you must," begged the boy's mother. "My son was in your service. Baba, it is your duty to bring Devraj back!"

"Shankar Baba has brought bad luck," declared Subahu, but the villagers ignored the priest; all eyes were fixed on the yogi.

Govinda knelt over the boy's body.

"Baba, please bring Devraj back," he pleaded, looking up at his guru.

"The boy's death was unnatural, the result of an infringement upon the proper workings of the world. Therefore, it would not be wrong to restore the natural way. I can heal the boy, but those present must decide in return: I can continue to live near Champa, or Subahu can, but not both. Subahu and his guru have polluted your land. This misfortune could not have happened if your jadoo superstitions had not supported their actions."

"He has no authority over me," protested Subahu.

"How have they polluted our land, Baba?" asked Devraj's father.

"Tell them what you saw in the cave," Shankar Baba instructed Govinda.

"Subahu's guru wore a strange mask. He invoked spirits that we couldn't see," began Govinda. "His jadoo is different from other sorcerers. He cut fur from a leopard cub and another creature and then offered it on an altar. Then he drank blood and chanted. Out of the smoke, a strange animal with the head of a leopard and the body of a hyena-dog appeared. When the creature attacked, Devraj hit his head against the rocks, but before he died, he killed the beast. Strangely, the animal never bled."

"Is it true?" Devraj's father asked Subahu.

The shaman fidgeted nervously.

"The boy is delirious."

"Everything I say is true," said Govinda.

"The boy is confused," Subahu insisted. "It didn't happen that way."

"Subahu lies," declared Shankar Baba. "I saw the creature myself. Govinda speaks the truth. Although the dagger pierced the preta's heart, there was no blood."

"The yogi speaks falsely," countered the priest, his face fraught with fear.

"Keep silent," ordered Devraj's father. "How dare you speak that way?"

"You all saw Govinda on the ridge above the forbidden valley,"

The Tale of the Himalayan Yogis

stammered Subahu. "It is Govinda who has been invoking demons, not my guru."

"Another word from you, and you will never speak again," threatened Shankar Baba. "I am willing to heal Devraj if the elders agree to confine Subahu to the forbidden valley. If you agree, I shall stay; for how long, I cannot say. If I heal Devraj, but Subahu is allowed to continue as before, then my chela and I shall go."

"Does the council agree to this?" asked Devraj's father, looking to the others. Unanimously, the elders agreed.

"The elders must agree to go to the forbidden valley on each new moon to check on Subahu," Shankar Baba added.

The men grumbled at the idea, but if it meant keeping Shankar Baba, then they would do as he wished.

"Baba, please bring Devraj back!" pleaded Govinda.

The yogi draped a blanket over Devraj. He then placed his hands beneath the blanket, passing them over Devraj's body three times. His hands then hovered near the crown of the boy's head for a moment."

"Done!" the yogi pronounced. Not a person in Champa doubted the decree. Only Subahu seemed dismayed. "Take the boy to his home. By morning, he will be fine. When he wakes, wet his lips and rub his feet with warm milk. Govinda, stay with your friend until you're satisfied that he is all right."

As Shankar Baba stood, Devraj's mother touched the yogi's cloth. Before leaving the courtyard, Shankar Baba clasped Govinda's shoulder and whispered into his ear.

"I have not healed Devraj. What I have done was a show for the villagers. When the signs appear, you must heal him."

The saint then strode out of the village without looking back, leaving Govinda to ponder his guru's words.

Late in the night, long after Devraj's parents had fallen asleep, Govinda held fast to his silent vigil. Shankar Baba's words echoed over and over inside his head, each time sparking a fresh wave of concern for his friend's well being. Devraj's face was ghostly pale, and when Govinda touched his forehead, the boy's body felt as if it had emerged from the stream where the boys often bathed.

What had his guru meant by signs appearing? Govinda waited and watched, but he saw nothing to indicate that he should do something, though he wished there was something… anything… he could do that would cause Devraj to open his eyes.

Sleep had almost overtaken him when he felt a sensation in his right hand as if a small bolt of lightning had struck his palm. A similar feeling in his left hand followed. Govinda rubbed his palms together to ease the sting; his hands felt strangely warm and alive. He examined his hands. To his astonishment, Bhumi Mata's symbols appeared on his palms exactly as the yogini had drawn them.

On his right hand appeared the wings of a swan. On his left hand was a triangle. As Govinda stared at the symbols, the words 'you have been blessed with the ability to heal; use it wisely like your Shankar Baba,' sounded inside his head as clearly as if Bhumi Mata herself were speaking to him.

Instinctively, Govinda knew what to do. Reaching beneath the blanket, he ran his hands the length of the boy's body the way Shankar Baba had done, stopping to let his hands rest on the fatal wound. Upon completing the ritual, intense fatigue overcame him, and Govinda slumped into a chair where he fell fast asleep.

Bands of golden light poured through the window, but it was the nervous excitement of the villagers who had gathered in the room that roused Govinda from his sleep. Devraj's parents hovered over their son, muttering prayers. Govinda stepped to the opposite side of the body and removed the blanket covering his friend. To everyone's astonishment, the boy's wounds had closed. Placing his hand on Devraj's wrist, Govinda searched for a pulse. The boy's skin, which had been cold just hours earlier, felt warm. A faint pulse rose and fell beneath Govinda's fingers.

"Devraj is alive," he announced. No sooner had he uttered the words than the boy's eyes opened, his pallid lips forming a feeble smile. Devraj's mother pressed her cheek against her son's.

Devraj raised his arm weakly before letting it fall to his side. A pail of milk waited by the fire. Govinda rubbed his friend's feet as the boy's mother poured Ganges water between her son's parched lips.

Devraj drifted off, restlessly turning as if caught in the throes of a dream. Upon waking, he tried to sit up. By now, curious villagers

The Tale of the Himalayan Yogis

packed the house. Others peered through windows, hoping for a glimpse of the miracle they fully expected to happen as Shankar Baba predicted.

"Why is everyone crowded around my bed?" Devraj asked in astonishment as his mother helped him to sit up.

"You had an accident," the boy's father explained. "You were attacked by an animal. Baba healed you."

"I want to go to the temple."

"You should rest now," Devraj's father advised.

"No, Father," replied Devraj, shaking his head. "Govinda and I must go to the temple."

"It can wait."

"No, it can't wait."

"All right, but your body is weak."

Devraj took Govinda's hand, rose from the table, and followed his friend through the crowded room and out the door. Those who waited outside the cottage gaped at the sight of the boy whose body had been cold and lifeless the night before. Relieved that their favorite son was alive, the villagers followed the boys to the entrance of the temple, eager to see what would happen next.

Govinda washed Devraj's feet and then his own before crossing the threshold of the temple. Devraj pulled hard on the bell rope, and the resonant chime of the weighty brass bell echoed through the valley. As they had done a hundred times, the boys approached Kali side by side. The sanctum filled with sweetness, more than Govinda remembered.

The boys took turns touching Kali Maa's feet before placing a flower on them. By now the villagers had pushed into the temple.

"In the night, Baba appeared to me in a dream and instructed me to look after her," explained the boy, pointing to the granite statue. "I am to offer Baba's portion of milk to her each morning. I am to serve as priest in the temple and not work in the fields. Service to Kali is to be my life from now on."

When Devraj had finished, Govinda said, "I must go. Baba instructed me to come as soon as you awoke."

"I'm coming too."

The boys walked hand in hand through the village. Climbing the path to Shankar Baba's cave, they frequently stopped so that Devraj could rest. When they arrived at the yogi's cave, Shankar Baba was expecting them.

"You've done well."

Shankar Baba's words flooded Govinda's heart like a monsoon-swollen stream. He knew his guru was pleased with what he had done, but somehow he also knew that he was not to speak of it. Govinda examined his palms, but the symbols had vanished.

"They have done their work," said the yogi enigmatically.

"Baba, why did you insist that the men go to the forbidden valley during each moon?"

"It is time these superstitions stopped. Otherwise, Kritavat's creations will overrun this valley and all of Champa's animals will die."

"Then that is why the Elder of the Forest was upset."

The yogi nodded.

"Now go inside. I have made chai for you."

The boys found a warm fire crackling inside Shankar Baba's cave. The friends sat together, sipping milk chai as they recounted the story of their night in the bowels of the forbidden valley, a bond of bravery forever forged between them.

The snows collected outside Shankar Baba's cave a moon's cycle before they blanketed the terraced plots lower on the mountain. With the first snowfall, Shankar Baba roused Govinda from his morning meditation and led him outside. The sun wreathed the cathedral peaks in gold.

"Come, let us go to your cave."

Govinda followed Shankar Baba up the trail, his steps sinking into drifted snow that numbed his feet and ankles.

"Yogiraj stayed here for many years," Shankar Baba explained. "You are now the age when Shankara debated the great scholars of India. I have taught you meditation and how to master the elements. Bhumi Mata has blessed you, and your body has grown strong these past seasons.

The Tale of the Himalayan Yogis

"Until the snows pass, you should meditate day and night. When you are tired, rest, but not more than a few hours. Spend your days in silence. Should you desire food, you have Maa's bowl. You have everything you need. Your fire will keep the wild animals away."

Govinda circled the camphor flame in front of his guru and then clasped his master's feet before Shankar Baba offered a final instruction.

"This was once my guru's abode. Permit no one to enter. You are not alone here. Yogiraj is present here always. In time, you will awaken to your God-Self, for the Self is Truth, all there is, or ever has been.

"Come to my cave on the day of the guru so that I can observe your progress. Offer water to the sun as it rises over the Five Chimneys. Surya will sustain your health. Remember, the white on the peaks is Shiva's milk. Drink it in. There is no abode closer to heaven than this place."

Shankar Baba stood for a moment at the entrance to the cave, light framing his form. Then he was gone, leaving Govinda to fathom the silence that was already overtaking him.

Seated on the deerskin, Govinda wrapped himself in his shawl and faced the fire. Instantly, he felt a force pulling him within. As if a ship's anchor were attached to his ankle, Govinda plunged to the bottom of a liquid expanse. Before him, a ball of scintillating light slowly formed, expanding until it partially filled the cave. Within the golden bubble appeared a youthful ascetic robed in white. Coal-black hair framed the face of the yogi; his almond eyes were full of compassion.

"Dear one... I come in peace. I come to offer *diksha*. In time, this wisdom will lead you to me."

"But who are you?"

"When you know who you are, you will know who I am," smiled the yogi.

Conflicting Faiths

Emperor Ghazi and his troops reached the outskirts of Delhi. Throngs of cheering citizens lined the avenues to greet the triumphant Emperor and his army. Though weary from the protracted journey, Ghazi could not help but notice the change that had overcome the capital in his absence. Hindus had never welcomed a Mogul ruler with such enthusiasm, at least not in Ghazi's lifetime. In response to the surprising reception, the Emperor reached into a chest filled with *mohurs* bearing Vijayanagar's mark and showered coins on the masses. Eager spectators fell to their knees, hoping to scoop up a coin.

Under Hashim's guidance, Delhi had enjoyed a calm few had known in their lifetimes. Dungeons had been emptied, and Hindus were no longer wantonly harassed on the streets. With the reforms instituted by Hashim, the collective mood of the capital had brightened. After looking after the empire in Ghazi's absence, Hashim could not deny that he too was born to lead.

Hashim bowed as Emperor Ghazi entered the palace.

"Brother, I am pleased on two counts!" exclaimed the Emperor, clasping Hashim's arms.

"Why is that, Your Highness?"

"First, the rumors of Vijayanagar were untrue; the capital had far greater riches than my spies reported."

"And the other reason for your pleasure?"

"Delhi feels fresh. I sense a renewed spirit. I felt it the moment I crossed the Yamuna."

"I have done my best on behalf of the Emperor."

"Hashim, speak less formally. To you, I wish to be your brother."

"My apologies, Ghazi. Running the Empire has made my mind more official."

"Now I am back. You can return to your poetic musings."

"I never left them. In your absence, I have established schools for art and music and philosophy. Priests and religious scholars meet regularly to debate matters of the spirit. I have emptied the dungeons of all but those who would harm others, and done away with public flogging."

"It seems you have indulged your passions in my absence."

"I indulge in what I believe in."

"I have gifts for you."

"I have no interest in gold and gems," stated Hashim resolutely.

"Dear brother, embrace for a moment what I believe in," petitioned Ghazi. "I will not allow my vizier to be a pauper. There are bribes to be paid and women to shower your affection on."

"I have not enjoyed the company of women or paid a bribe in your absence."

"Where is the fun in your life? Enjoy, dear brother… the world is at our feet."

"I hope you will find my work to your liking."

"I like what I have seen so far. Tell me about the spell you have cast over the city in my absence."

"I know no magic; only that men wish to be treated with dignity."

"A noble sentiment. In time, your generosity may turn the people against me, for I am not so liberal as you. They may decide that you should be the one sitting on the Peacock Throne."

"Please, Ghazi; though you speak in jest, I do not approve of your words."

"Come, let us view the spoils of victory."

The twins descended into a complex system of vaults beneath the palace, the servant Junduk keeping pace behind them.

"I have ordered fresh vaults constructed," the Emperor told Hashim as they walked.

"At what cost?"

"More than half the citizens of Vijayanagar fell along with its entire army."

"A life lost for every gem gained."

"Why such pessimism? Your romantic notions prevent you from appreciating the utility of a treasury. Without gold, how would we maintain our palaces or our army?"

"If we endorsed peace, then we would not need such a vast military."

"Without a proper army, we would be invaded from every side."

"I'm sorry. I should be congratulating you in your hour of triumph."

"Since you have no interest in gold, I have brought you a gift that speaks and breathes."

"Speaks and breathes?"

"A Portuguese padre. Vijayanagar traded with the Europeans who have settlements in Goa."

As Ghazi spoke, Hashim detected something in his brother's eyes that hadn't been there in the past. It was a hint of madness, and it reminded Hashim of their father.

Butchering people will destroy a man's soul, he decided.

"I would like to meet this padre," replied Hashim, who had never met a Christian priest before.

"Junduk will take you to him. If you like, I'll place him in your custody."

"Has he been injured?"

"He came down with malaria, but he's fit again. We lost more soldiers to sickness than to swords."

Ghazi swung open the heavy doors to the vaults. From floor to ceiling, mounds of gold bullion, idols, jewelry, and coins filled the chambers. On the floor in front of the treasure stood a sea of mahogany trunks. Ghazi opened one filled with glittering gems.

"My generals are as rich as kings," Ghazi declared, "and common

The Tale of the Himalayan Yogis

foot soldiers are better off than noblemen in other empires. The royal treasury has never known such prosperity."

Ghazi signaled to Junduk, who held up a golden idol of a Hindu goddess.

"I shall present this to Uncle Lufti," said Ghazi.

"It's stunning," said Hashim, taking the goddess in his hands. "It surpasses anything in his collection. Did it come from a temple?"

"No less than the king's private shrine. They call her Saraswati. I'm told the Raja of Vijayanagar himself commissioned her. I considered melting her…"

"Never! It would bring bad luck."

Junduk winced at Hashim's words.

"The mullahs would have you flogged if they heard such talk," teased Ghazi.

"I'm aware of the mullahs' bigotry."

"Bigotry? The ulema is concerned for the welfare of Islam. They would not be pleased if they knew their vizier was fond of Hindu goddesses."

"I suppose it comes from living with Uncle Lufti."

Despite the cold air, beads of perspiration clung to Junduk's forehead.

"Summon bearers to carry the idols," Ghazi ordered the servant. He waited for Junduk to leave the vault before speaking in a hushed tone.

"Watch your words. Junduk is a fanatic."

"Then why keep him around?" asked Hashim.

"Because he's good at what he does."

"Which is?"

"Spying, of course. My spies tell me that tensions have eased in my absence, which upsets Junduk."

"I have tried to govern fairly."

"Then have your reward. Choose an idol if you like."

Dozens of gold idols lay scattered about the floor of the vault. Hashim selected a statue of Shiva riding on his bull.

"What about the others?" Hashim inquired. "You won't melt them will you?"

"I plan to mint coins commemorating our triumph."

"May I keep them?"

"You seem to have a greater interest in gold than you imagined."

"If it means saving these from destruction."

"Remember what happened to Grandfather. His interest in art led to his banishment, and our mullahs are less tolerant than those of his day."

"The statues are masterpieces. It would be a great offense to destroy them."

Junduk returned with a half dozen men, who were instructed to gather up the idols.

"Show my brother to the European's apartment," the Emperor ordered.

The servant led Hashim to a guest apartment in the palace.

A pair of Somalian guards threw open the apartment's silk curtains, exposing a youthful man seated near an open window, his face framed by fading sunlight. The padre appeared to be but a few years older than Hashim; his hair and beard carefully groomed, his skin bronzed by the South Indian sun. The padre's deep blue eyes focused so intently on the book in his hands that he was unaware of visitors.

"Greetings, friend."

Looking up, the padre replied shyly, "Welcome, Emperor. Please come in."

"I am Hashim, the brother of the Emperor. You've met my brother?"

"He saved me from execution."

"My brother tells me you are a padre."

"I'm sorry," stammered the padre, who lacked the grace of a palace royal. "My name is Santiago de Sousa, the son of a Portuguese schoolmaster."

"What brought you to India?"

"I was sent to look after a chapel in Goa. More recently I was assigned to Vijayanagar."

"Then you witnessed the siege?"

"War is barbaric, but then, my people slaughter innocent Goans.

The Tale of the Himalayan Yogis

Your army came for gold. My people seek to convert villagers. In either case, innocent people suffer."

"Did many Christians die in the fighting?"

"Only a handful escaped. Your brother spared me when he learned of my calling."

"My brother has made a gift of you. I am not like those who brought you here. I am interested in all religions, which is why my brother spared you. Will you help me with my studies?"

"What have you discovered in your studies?" asked Santiago.

"I have discovered that truth is an inner experience, and not found in a book."

"Words also contain truth… but yes, spiritual experience ripens in the heart, not on the page. Just now, I am reading Meister Eckhart. His words have helped me understand the suffering I recently witnessed. Listen, if you will. 'In every work, bad as well as good, the glory of God is equally manifested.'"

"May I borrow the book sometime?"

"Of course. If I am to be your tutor, your first lesson can come from Meister Eckhart. He too was persecuted."

"Are you saying Christians persecuted their mystics?"

"Some of our brightest stars were extinguished."

"I thought ours was the only oppressive religion," said Hashim.

"Islam also has a tradition of mystics, does it not?"

"They're called Sufis."

"Surely your mullahs tolerate them."

"Not always," replied Hashim. "The ulema scholars show open contempt for our mystics, but their loathing for Hindus is far greater. My grandfather is a Sufi; my mother was a poet."

"Then you know something of persecution. Perhaps it is a lapse in judgment, but I feel at ease for the first time since Vijayanagar," admitted Santiago.

Hashim knew that he and the padre could be friends.

"Hashim, you must stop this blatant courtship of Hinduism," demanded Ghazi. "Have it as a mistress, but do so discreetly. The mullahs are outraged. These public discussions with Brahmins and Jesuits must stop. After all, you are the vizier of an Islamic empire."

"I never intended to upset the ulema," maintained Hashim. "Their rage is the result of their narrow-mindedness, not my pursuit of truth."

"Allah is Truth, dear brother."

"Allah should be worshipped out of love, not because the religious law demands it. A tolerant heart is better able to know God."

"That may be true for your Sufi friends, but running an empire is a different matter. Your poets arm themselves with fine words, but our foes carry swords. Do you suggest we greet the enemy armed with rose petals and rhyme?"

"If I'm a threat to the mullahs, then I shall resign."

"I won't allow it. An Emperor can count on but a few."

"Then don't mind my mistresses."

"Meet your mistresses behind closed doors… not in full view of the public."

"The mullahs' spies will find me wherever I meet my teachers, but I have a plan. My Brahmin teacher will debate one of the mullahs. If the Brahmin is defeated, then I shall cease my studies altogether. If the mullahs lose, then they must stop harassing me."

"It's a novel idea. I cannot speak for the mullahs, but a debate would bring some excitement to the palace. The mullahs are a self-righteous bunch. If the clerics agree, we'll have the debate during Ramadan."

The mullahs opposed the plan, but the Emperor appealed to the arrogance of Nazir Hussein and Abdullah Khan, convincing them that a public debate would put Hinduism down once and for all. Mullah Khan would represent the clerics since he despised Hinduism more than most.

Hashim sat with Ramlal in the courtyard of his acharya's south Delhi home.

"Baba, the Emperor has agreed to a debate between Abdullah Khan and a member of the Brahmin community. Will you agree to debate him?"

Ramlal considered the offer for a time before nodding.

A stir of excitement swept through the streets of the capital on the day of the debate. Under a waxing moon whose luster was muted by the dusty haze hovering over the city, Hindu and Muslim alike pushed their way into Durbar Square where a thousand torches lit the perimeter of the courtyard. The emperor sat on a gold throne, Hashim on his right and the generals on his left. Robed in black, the mullahs kept to themselves. A handful of jute-robed Jesuits huddled together, teakwood crosses in hand. Santiago de Sousa sat at the edge of the Christian delegation. Hindus occupied seats to the rear of the court.

Armed with scimitars, a line of soldiers stood shoulder-to-shoulder in front of the main gate. From marble balconies, noblemen sipped Egyptian wine from lapis cups as they speculated on the outcome of the debate. Behind latticed walls, harem *bibis* whispered excitedly, roused from their boredom by the novelty of a Brahmin challenging the erudite Abdullah Khan.

A fire blazed at the center of the courtyard, warming the chill night air. The contestants argued resolutely, each man professing the merits of his faith.

"Friend," Ramlal appealed, "Do I demean Allah by affirming that divinity also resides within the good people gathered here, this fire, and the moon overhead?"

"Infidel," retorted Abdullah Khan, relishing the fight. "Allah sits above and apart from his creation. Man, the planets, and the elements are inferior. Those who do not worship Allah are no better than animals."

Ramlal gazed into the fire as he considered his response.

"God is known by many names. Divinity is both feminine and masculine; it dwells in sun and moon, man and woman, Hindu and Muslim."

"Your people lack discrimination. They deify cow dung and worship stones. The prophet Mohammed punished idolaters."

"We Hindus believe in *ahimsa*... non-violence. Punishing a man punishes God."

"Your ahimsa is hypocrisy," bristled the mullah. "I have witnessed your animal sacrifices."

"Does breaking the cup benefit the wine, my friend? Does destroying the vessel of Allah, serve Allah? Taking the life of another must be avoided at all costs. Ahimsa opposes more than violence; it opposes negativity in all its forms. Hatred poisons the mind the way opium poisons the body."

"Allah is the master and man the slave."

"Allah is to be loved, not feared," replied Ramlal. "Man plays the role of lover. God is the beloved!"

"Even your greeting dishonors God. 'Namaste' means, 'I bow to the divinity in you.' Allah does not tolerate heathen practices. Toss your pagan idols into the Yamuna."

The contestants sparred back and forth before Ramlal fell silent. No one, not even Hashim, anticipated the Brahmin's next move. Perhaps even Ramlal had not foreseen what he was about to do.

"Brother, let us put our faith to the test," suggested Ramlal, his eyes fixed on the fire before him. "Surely you agree that the soul is eternal."

"If one accepts Allah."

"Then you do not fear death?"

"Why should I fear that which brings me to Allah's feet?"

"I am prepared to step into the fire if you are prepared to do the same. Will you join me?"

"You speak figuratively. In that sense, yes, I will join you," replied the mullah hesitantly.

"You misunderstand me. I am inviting you to step into the fire with me," repeated Ramlal. "Fire can no more burn the soul than the soil can cover it or water wet it. These empty vessels are not the soul. Come, let us enter the fire together. Being eternal, the soul cannot burn."

Comprehending what the Brahmin had in mind, Abdullah Khan trembled. He scanned the noblemen, generals, mullahs, European emissaries, and royalty who sat on the edges of their seats, eager to see what would happen next. Veiled queens peered through latticed windows, titillated by the Brahmin's bold proposal. Emperor Ghazi leaned forward on his throne.

Abdullah Khan stammered, "Death is not for us to choose... man cannot usurp God's will... I will not enter the fire... I am not a god deciding my fate... what is not written I cannot do."

"Friend, I am not asking you to enter the fire as a god, but as a lover of God."

"I fear God... and you should too."

"Whether you join me, or not, is up to you. Words are useless as fallen leaves, arguments barren like trees in winter. Let us enter the fire together as proof that our religions may coexist. Holy war brings shame to Allah and Krishna alike."

"I have no desire to live with infidels... or die with them."

"Come, brother; let Muslim and Hindu join hands for the sake of our children. We discard lives like pebbles tossed into the Yamuna."

Ramlal took Abdullah Khan's hand and led him toward the fire. The searing heat stung the men's legs as they stood at the fire's edge. Abdullah Khan's body shuddered, the color bled from his face. Trembling, he lost control, defiling himself in the presence of the throng of stunned onlookers. Representing the Emperor and the council of ulema, the senior mullah stood humiliated.

Ramlal released Abdullah Khan's hand and took a step closer to the inferno. As he prepared to enter the blaze, his dhoti caught fire. Unflinching, the Brahmin watched the flames blister his legs.

Hashim rose from his bench.

"NO!" he cried, rushing across the courtyard.

To the horror of every Muslim present, when their vizier reached the Hindu, he tore the tunic from his torso and snuffed out the flames with it.

Clutching Ramlal's ankles, Hashim pleaded, "Ramlal, I won't allow you to end your life because of my selfishness. If you insist on entering the fire, then I shall join you."

Turning his back on the inferno, the Brahmin disappeared through the courtyard gates.

Frustrated by their inability to chasten Hashim, Zahira and the mullahs plotted against the Emperor himself. *Poust,* a potion made from the milky juice of poppies, was their cloak-and-dagger method. Over time, the drink could strip a man of his senses, reducing him to an invalid. First emaciation set in, followed by a slow, lingering death. With the Emperor's mind destroyed, the mullahs would install a puppet on the Peacock Throne. All agreed that Yaman would be that puppet.

Zahira and the mullahs hadn't counted on Ghazi's resilience. His father's opium addiction had resulted in a natural resistance in the young Emperor. It would take time, possibly years, to dissipate his strength, and Zahira and the ulema grew impatient with their failed plans.

Enlisting the support of the generals, they turned to pressuring the Emperor to oust his brother. Ghazi grew increasingly paranoid amidst the dual assault of addiction and political pressure.

"Zahira and the mullahs have demanded your resignation," said Ghazi.

"And the generals? Haven't their newfound riches secured their support?"

"You fail to understand your people. Gold is of little consequence when it comes to matters of faith. The debate has turned even the generals against us. Without their support, I am finished."

"I have no desire to serve those who despise me."

"I have a plan. You shall resign as vizier and move out of the palace. After the storm passes, I will reinstate you."

"Then I'm to have a holiday," said Hashim approvingly.

"I'll send a team of trusted guards to look after you. You can stay with Lufti, or Grandfather if you like."

"I would prefer to stay with the Brahmins."

"Better not!" replied Ghazi, shaking his head. "The mullahs have demanded the execution of your Brahmin friend for the blasphemies uttered in the debate."

Hashim was furious with himself for suggesting the debate. He had been naïve not to recognize the risk.

"I want Ramlal released immediately."

"I can't do that," Ghazi protested.

"Then stop the execution."

"Brother, they wanted to execute you. To save you, I agreed to the Brahmin's execution. Your Brahmin friend humiliated a senior mullah; he must pay the price for his foolishness. Besides, Ramlal was prepared to die on the night of the debate."

The Tale of the Himalayan Yogis

"I intend to free Ramlal," said Hashim as he left the room.

"Act prudently, brother. Your life depends on it."

Hours before the Brahmin's execution, Ghazi freed his brother's teacher. Unknown to the mullahs, a convicted murderer was executed in the Brahmin's place.

The debate's lethal backlash rent the city. Soldiers looted temples and burned Hindu neighborhoods. A thousand Hindus were roped one to another like mules in a caravan and marched barefoot out of the city without food or water. One by one the men collapsed by the roadside, a banquet for the buzzards.

When Hashim heard the news, he rushed to the palace to confront Ghazi, but finding his brother addled by opium; he returned to the Brahmin enclave.

The debate had played into the hands of the Emperor's enemies. In response, Ghazi buried himself in the arms of his women, numbing his mind with intoxicants. After Zahira doubled his dose of poust, palace spies informed the mullahs that Ghazi's health was deteriorating rapidly. It was a matter of time before the opposition would crown their pawn, whether Ghazi lived, or not.

Under a Shiva moon, Hashim lay on a rooftop in the Brahmin enclave. He wished he could visit his brother, but feared it would make problems for Ghazi, and so he stayed with the Brahmins, who treated him as one of their own.

Beneath the night sky, Hashim thought of Govinda. Perhaps his friend was gazing at the same moon from his Himalayan sanctuary. Hashim never doubted that a higher purpose lay behind the events that had turned both he, and his Rajput friend, into fugitives.

On the eve of the Kusum Mela, a favorite flower festival, Hashim set out for the palace. As he left the Brahmin enclave, a lone rider approached in the distance. Intercepted by a horde of turbaned assailants, the rider was beaten and thrown over his horse.

Attributing the attack to another act of Hindu persecution, Hashim continued on his way. Eager to see his brother, he entered the Moti Mahal.

Bandu greeted Hashim at the harem entrance.

"I'll inform the Emperor that you've come," the eunuch said.

Moments later, Bandu returned. "The Emperor invites you to join him."

Hashim followed the eunuch into a smoky den where an assortment of alluring women lay strewn about in various stages of undress. Some of the women were awake; others slept. Ghazi relaxed at the center of the tangle of bodies. A lissome beauty rubbed the Emperor's feet while another massaged his neck and head. The Emperor scarcely recognized his twin.

"Does my mind play tricks on me, or have I become two?" tittered Ghazi. "Join us, brother. I'm relieved that you've come. Remain with me until the afternoon, at least."

At the edge of the mélange of reclining concubines, the nimble fingers of an old man prepared the hookah before handing the hose to a ravishing maiden, who inserted the birch bark tip into the Emperor's mouth. Observing the ritual, Hashim wondered how long his brother could survive such madness.

"Why should I not leave the harem until afternoon?" questioned Hashim.

Ghazi seemed to hear the words, but lapsing into euphoria, he permitted his twin's question to pass unheeded.

Hashim noticed a half-empty pitcher. The color of the liquid told him that it was something other than wine. Hashim was no stranger to intoxication; he had witnessed his father's nightly revelry after his mother's death. The curious liquid worried him. Sniffing the contents suspiciously, he instructed Bandu to pour a cupful.

"Sir, special preparation for Emperor," said Bandu.

Hashim swallowed a mouthful, identifying the taste of poppy milk. He had heard stories of emperors consuming poust and knew they eventually succumbed to madness, or worse.

"Who sent this?" Hashim demanded, clenching the pitcher in his fist.

"Begum Zahira, sir," Bandu revealed. "She prepares it herself and has me serve it late in the night. Begum says it gives the Emperor vigor."

"You serve it nightly?"

"Yes, but only the Emperor drinks it."

The Tale of the Himalayan Yogis

Propping himself against a mound of pillows, Hashim watched Bandu leave the room. The smoke-filled chamber made Hashim drowsy, but he needed to talk to Ghazi, and so he lay on the cushions waiting for the others to awaken from their collective coma.

Hashim rose before his brother. One by one, stupefied minds emerged from smoky dreams, awakening to the monotony of another day in the harem. The Emperor's consorts were not allowed outside the Moti Mahal without an escort, and then only for strolls in the palace gardens. Consorts were permitted to bear a child if the Emperor approved, a thread of hope in an otherwise barren existence.

Ghazi was the last to rise.

"I saw myself hovering over me last night," he mumbled sleepily.

"You haven't looked in a mirror lately," replied Hashim cynically. "Otherwise, you would not have mistaken me for you. Brother, you don't look well. Stay away from this place."

"Nonsense! My women are many, and they all wish to be with me. Tonight you shall play my role while I sleep. Then you will appreciate my exhaustion."

"Let us get away. Why not a trip to the mountains or a visit to the sea?"

"As you can see, I am a prisoner in the palace. If I leave, who will be sitting on the throne when I return?"

As his mind cleared, Ghazi remembered his brother's exile.

"I have not seen you in a moon."

"I needed to be away from the palace," Hashim reminded his brother.

"Your performance at the debate was good entertainment, but it seems I was the only one enjoying the show. The mullahs wanted you flayed."

"Brother, you're being poisoned."

"Nonsense!"

"Poust," said Hashim, holding up the pitcher.

"What of a little more opium? I'm drugged day and night as it is."

"But the poppy water is meant to harm you."

"Harm me? Who is trying to harm me?"

"Have you forgotten that Zahira poisoned Maji?"

"If you think it unwise, I shall not touch the potion."

"Have Bandu continue to bring the concoction, but do not drink it. Zahira must not know."

"Bandu will do as I order," said Ghazi.

An insolent smile formed on the Emperor's face.

"You think I've lost my mind."

"How much opium can a man take?" asked Hashim.

"Life in the palace has been bleak without you," the dispirited Emperor grumbled. "You're the one person I trust."

"Promise me that you'll rest. Visit the harem only every other night."

"But I draw my best moments from a pipe the way you draw yours from poetry and meditation."

"Your best moments aren't real," replied Hashim.

"Who's to say what is real? In my opium den, I become Hafez. The ecstasy of a hundred caressing hands inspires my soul."

"You pay a high price for your philosophy," replied Hashim.

"Every Hindu in Delhi pays a high price for yours, Brother. My addictions surround me with soft music and golden light. Isn't that how Rumi described the mystic moment?"

"Opium is a bottomless well. Soon you'll be unable to climb out."

"Hashim, you and I are both drunkards... only our intoxicants differ. You have your spiritual elixir, and I my women and wine. Addiction has always been the curse of royalty. I dislike sober thoughts."

"What has become of Abdullah Khan?" asked Hashim.

"I'm told he took passage on a ship for Mecca."

"He didn't hold up well in the debate."

"The irony of existence! In the eyes of the mullahs, you're the infidel... and you actually want to know God."

"Am I also an infidel in your eyes?"

"I don't take it seriously," replied Ghazi. "We're all hypocrites here in the palace."

"Thank you for freeing Ramlal. He's with his family in the Brahmin enclave."

Ghazi pulled hard on Hashim's sleeve.

The Tale of the Himalayan Yogis

"Did you not receive my message?"

"What message?"

"Forgive me," groaned Ghazi.

"What need is there to forgive you?"

"You shall find out soon enough."

"Tell me now?" insisted Hashim.

"The Afghan Uzbek Khan and his mercenaries have been hired…"

"To do what?"

Ghazi reached for his wine, but Hashim took the cup from his brother's hands.

"Why have the Afghans been hired?"

"To attack the Brahmin enclave," Ghazi whispered.

"Who hired them?"

"My spies say the mullahs planned it… apparently, Begum Zahira financed it. I sent a messenger as soon as I knew. I thought you'd gotten the message and that's why you came."

Hashim recalled Afghans assaulting a rider the previous night.

"It's by coincidence that I came."

"I tried to dissuade them," Ghazi mumbled, "but they insisted on attacking during the festival."

"The Kusum Mela?"

Ghazi nodded. Gulping wine from a flask, the Emperor spilled some and choked on the rest.

"But the festival is this morning!" realized Hashim, his chest heaving.

"That's why I was relieved when you showed up."

Hashim ran to the stables. The Brahmin enclave was halfway across the city. By the time he approached the neighborhood, large plumes of smoke had darkened the sky. Digging his heels into his horse, Hashim galloped toward the fires. As he neared the Brahmin enclave, a gang of wild-eyed Afghans rode past him.

Hashim scrutinized the bearded mercenaries. One of the men pointed to the smoke.

"We got the heathens," he gloated.

Hashim rode on, his heart pounding harder than the hooves of his horse.

Seeing the smoldering buildings, Hashim despaired. Climbing down from his mount, he combed the smoking ruins. The half-charred remains of flowers and coconuts lay strewn about the grounds outside the temple. But where were Ramlal and the others?

Hashim entered the Yoga Maya temple. Propping himself up against a wall in the inner sanctum, he imagined the fate of his friends. The attack had been in retaliation for the debate.

Overcome by anguish, Hashim was wandering about the narrow lanes when a hooded figure approached.

"The Mullahs have set the Black Seal against you," said the stranger in a hushed tone.

"The what?"

"The assassin who delivers your head on a platter will receive his weight in gold."

Hashim inhaled a long, fitful breath.

"Come, I shall take you to a safe place."

Revelations and Confrontations

Winter wrapped the peaks above Champa in a thick, white shawl.

"How fortunate you are to be exploring the depths of your soul," said Shankar Baba.

"I have you to thank," replied Govinda as he followed the yogi up the mountain.

"None can teach what the soul discovers on its journeys to the realms of spirit. To know the timeless truths, you need only go within, and listen."

They had not gone far when Shankar Baba stopped to watch a flock of black-necked cranes. The graceful birds soared high above the valley, their long, slender necks of a darker hue than their bodies.

"The cranes are flying south again. There must be thousands in the flock," said Govinda, having observed their migration to wintering grounds in the past.

"Even the young ones make the journey, but some won't survive."

"Why is that?"

"The headwinds are fierce, the air bitter cold. Turbulence often forces the entire flock to turn back, only to begin the journey again."

"It seems unfair that such gentle creatures must suffer to survive," lamented Govinda.

"For the Buddhist, the crane is a symbol of wisdom and herald of good fortune. The crane may live for a hundred years, often forming a long-lasting bond with its mate. Over the course of its life, it learns both resolve and self-sacrifice."

Govinda winced as a pair of golden eagles approached the flock. The predators were expecting the cranes.

"The eagles will single out a weak one," observed Shankar Baba.

Winging near the flock, the eagles searched for a young bird, or perhaps an old one. Spotting a fledgling, they attacked. The young crane, already fatigued from its struggle with the headwinds, found itself in a more immediate battle for survival. Diving beneath its pursuer, the untested crane inadvertently separated itself from the flock.

The second eagle struck swiftly. Locking onto the young crane's back with its talons, predator and prey descended in a spiral, the eagle struggling to control its quarry. Seeing her fledgling, the mother crane dove at the attacker, but the other eagle cut her off. There was little the mother could do, but still, she fought fiercely.

"It's painful to watch," Govinda said, looking away.

"Why is death painful?"

"It's unjust."

"Can one know what is unjust without knowing the history of the soul?" asked Shankar Baba.

"Isn't it enough that the cranes must battle wind and cold?"

"Observe what happens next."

Govinda had given up on the young crane when the eagle inexplicably lost its stranglehold on the bird. Exhausted, but uninjured, the crane rejoined the flock. The second eagle, seeing its meal escaping, veered away from the mother bird in pursuit of its prey. As the eagle approached the young one, the mother struck with its sharp, serrated bill, forcing the eagle off course long enough to save her infant.

"Now you see why men live with fear" explained Shankar Baba. "Before getting a human body, the soul emerges from lower incarnations where death may strike at any moment. It's not easy to overcome fear, but it is essential if one is to attain liberation.

"But it hurts to see an innocent creature die."

"Nothing exists in excess. Everything is weighed and measured

The Tale of the Himalayan Yogis

according to our soul's development. Only when the lessons are learned does one have the opportunity for a higher birth. No action is wholly meritorious, or wicked. In all acts, there is some of each. The vulture must have its meal. Do not lament death, for with death comes progress.

"Each man has mountains of karma, but we only carry a small bag of it with us. Karma may appear to be a cruel teacher, but such is not the case. Karma is no more malicious than a summer breeze. Karma is self-made; only the doer must one day face his creation. A Mahatma has faced his karma and overcome it.

"But saints fall ill," observed Govinda.

"The Mahatma's flesh is not what I speak of. I speak of the God-Self that *is* the saint, not the house he inhabits. Identify with your essence. What we see with our eyes may deceive us, but the inner eye sees clearly. Through the spiritual eye, one can know anything. Do you recall Zaim and his men attacking me in the cave?"

"I was sure they would kill you."

"That was their intention, but my inner sight revealed Zaim's karma, and with it, the course of action."

Reaching Govinda's cave, the yogis stepped inside.

"Add a log to the fire," Shankar Baba instructed.

Govinda knew that his guru intended to impart wisdom and placed a pair of logs on the fire.

"Describe your emotions these past days," requested Shankar Baba.

"Turbulent!"

"Why is that?"

"I longed to see Pitaji."

"And this made you sad."

"Sad... also angry!"

"Anger is a thief that steals one's strength."

"I was angry with the Moguls for taking Pitaji and forcing our people to leave their homes."

Govinda felt the heaviness in his heart as he spoke.

"I will reveal something, but you must fortify your heart; otherwise, it could defeat you."

"I want to know everything, Baba. Please don't keep anything from me."

"I shall tell you about your past. Through the fire, you too will view your past," said Shankar Baba. "I see a Rajput king. You are that king and Krishnagarh is your kingdom. You have a son, who you love very much. He is a few years younger than your present age. Though you have an heir, you are unhappy."

"Why is that?"

"Your queen is dead."

Staring at the fire, Govinda's heart hurt at Shankar Baba's words.

"Not long after your queen died, you left Krishnagarh," Shankar Baba continued. "After wandering about, you came upon a yogi whose blessing you sought to renounce the world."

"Was renunciation not the noble thing to do?"

"The pain you felt became the pain of all the good people of your kingdom," explained Shankar Baba.

"But the scriptures sanction renunciation when one's spouse dies."

"True, but that does not free a man from dharma. One's duty in life, especially that of a king, is not to be undertaken lightly. Let us look ahead to see the consequences of your action."

"Have I caused others great pain?" asked Govinda.

"You did what you believed was right. If you hadn't, we would not be sitting here together. See how the drama ends."

Govinda focused intently on the fire.

"I see only flames."

Shankar Baba waved his hand over the fire.

"Now what do you see?"

"I see armies preparing for battle. My son has grown tall, though he is quite young. He's leading the cavalry, but his troops are badly outnumbered. Krishnagarh's army is being slaughtered. The sultan has captured my son. The sultan's scimitar is over my son's head..." Govinda's voice trailed off.

"Detach yourself from your past," Shankar Baba counseled. "There is more."

Govinda gazed into the fire again. "The women, children, and elders in the fort are entering the johar fire!" he observed.

"Now have a look at your life of solitude."

"I see a hermit in a mountain cave."

"Does the cave look familiar?" asked Shankar Baba.

"The cave is my cave. I'm living in that same cave now!"

"Using the same blanket and wearing the same beads."

"But the hermit looks peaceful in his solitary life," noted Govinda.

"And that peace is with you now. You made progress in your life as a recluse. Nonetheless, your people suffered in your absence."

"Baba, who is the man bringing food to the hermit?"

"Do you not recognize him?"

"I do not know him."

"Are you sure?" questioned Shankar Baba.

Govinda examined the figure more closely.

"Devraj?"

"It is he. He too has found his way back to this mountain."

"Baba, why did you accept me as your chela if I failed in my duties as king?"

"One day I will ask you to leave this place to repay your debt. But only after you return to your ancestral land will you learn how the story ends."

"Do you know how it ends?"

"Even the sages find it difficult to foresee the future because the future is not fixed. Free will plays a potent role for souls like you. A man may alter the destiny of his life, but to do that requires perseverance. Your time here in the Himalaya will give you the resolve needed to face the challenges awaiting you."

"What if I fail?"

"We will not let you fail."

"We?"

"In time you will understand. You are roasting the seeds of your past. As I have said, burnt seeds cannot sprout. Come to my cave after seven days."

Govinda touched Shankar Baba's feet, and then the yogi was gone.

The unsettling scenes from Govinda's past haunted him. He tried to think his mantra, but the agonizing vision of his son's beheading and his people entering the johar fire tormented him day and night.

Whenever he closed his eyes, his heart shrunk in sorrow. Grief-stricken, his mind churned in confusion, futilely searching for a way to resolve the guilt that plagued him. Govinda wished he could go to Shankar Baba, but he had been instructed to remain in his cave; disobeying his guru was unthinkable.

Govinda's cave, though warm and comfortable, had become a battleground. His mind wrestled with his heart. He longed to escape to the forest where he could talk to the animals, but his mind wouldn't allow it. Agonizing days and tortured nights passed.

As a child, on those rare days when Govinda felt troubled, he had ridden Kalki into the Aravali Hills or helped Ananta with his temple duties. When those diversions failed to brighten his mood, Mataji took him into her lap and stroked his head until the sadness lifted.

By the fifth day, Govinda had stopped eating, leaving the milk and fruit outside his cave. When Devraj came with fresh milk, Govinda waved it away. Watching his friend descend the mountain, Govinda viewed with skepticism the idea that Devraj was the man who had brought him food in his former life. What if the visions weren't real? What if he hadn't been a king? Govinda knew of no account of a Krishnagarh king abandoning his throne to become a wandering sanyasi. Confusion swirled about him, disrupting sleep and meditation.

When the seventh day arrived, Govinda careened down the mountain, neglecting to put a fresh log on his fire.

"You should have come sooner," said Shankar Baba, stroking his disciple's head.

"You instructed me to come after seven days. I did not want to go against your wish."

"That was your mind speaking. The guru's greatest concern is for his chela's heart."

"I have never been so miserable," moaned Govinda. "I wanted to escape into the forest and not come back."

"The pain would have followed you," Shankar Baba replied sympathetically. "For a tender heart like yours, sorrow is unbearable. Escape was how you responded to the loss of your wife. You were wise not to run to the forest."

"But the pain was almost more than I could bear."

"You must be hungry. Devraj tells me you haven't eaten in days." Shankar Baba handed Govinda a container of warm milk seasoned with saffron. "Come, let us sit outside. The morning sun heals."

Govinda sat facing the wall of sawtooth peaks. Without uttering a word, Shankar Baba took his chela's head in his fingers, holding Govinda's temples like a fragile egg. The clouds shrouding Govinda's heart lifted, replaced by soothing currents that filled him with inexpressible joy. Satisfied, the yogi removed his hands.

"The disciple's devotion causes the guru's blessings to flow."

"By leaving Krishnagarh in my past life, I caused the death of my people and destruction of my kingdom."

"If a king abandons his throne, society inevitably collapses. Though you did not know it at the time, you persuaded the people to escape to Bundi rather than enter the fires because of what happened in your past.

"It is easy to give way to unhappy emotions, but repeated shocks to the heart are like an earthquake shaking a building. Eventually, the foundation cracks."

"Nothing bothered the lamas. When Jinpa died, I was the only one who was upset."

"When anger or disappointment or sorrow floods the heart, those feelings are stamped on the flesh of the physical body, which may one day result in disease."

"Then I am destined to be an invalid," laughed Govinda.

Shankar Baba shook his head. "You will always have perfect health. I will take your imperfections."

"But Baba, I don't want you to suffer due to my foolishness."

"The guru helps in unseen ways. Already, you have been spared death."

"But I have been meditating all these years, and still I became angry, and also sad."

"The yogi gains mastery over the mind through deep meditation and by holding a mirror up to his mind. Every thought and emotion has its opposite. Anger is the antithesis of calm, sorrow the opposite of joy. The qualities of one's mind need to be closely observed. Where you find impatience, you will also find equanimity. Some things you will approve of… others you may shun. The mind contains all these things. Subtle discernment is needed to overcome the pairs of opposites which keep men bound to the wheel of karma."

"The lamas understood the secrets of the mind. I should have paid closer attention to their scriptures."

"A yogi has little use for scriptures. He follows his inner voice. One day, you will hear that voice. Then my work will be done."

"Will there be more pain?"

"A yogi is a warrior. In battle, pain is inevitable. Perseverance is the key to climbing a mountain."

"But I feel like I'm falling down the mountain."

"If you should fall down the mountain, you will end up at my door. In the future, come to me.

"Let's go inside," said Shankar Baba. "It's time you saw something of the worlds beyond this valley." Handing Govinda a piece of cloth, the yogi said, "Put this over your head."

"Our bodies will be safe here by the fire," said Shankar Baba, placing his thumb between his chela's eyebrows.

Removing his thumb from Govinda's forehead, yogi and chela rose above their bodies, traveling through realms unknown to Govinda. In the distance, a murky island appeared. As the travelers flew closer, Govinda saw a swarm of snakes slithering on the ground; peculiar-looking serpents with five or even seven heads. The snakes' diamond markings shone like crystals in the sun. Luminous jewels sparkled on the throats and hoods of the larger snakes. Spitting angrily, the hooded serpents flared as the visitors approached. At the center of the horde of hissing vipers, a king cobra with sapphire eyes and alabaster scales wound itself around a cats-eye throne.

"I am honored, King of Yogis," the serpent king hissed at Shankar Baba. "What brings you to Bhogavati?"

"Sheshraj, your subjects protected us. For that, we are most grateful. One day we shall repay your kindness."

"We must serve Shiva's ambassadors on earth. Who is the fine-looking one at your side?"

Sheshraj surveyed Govinda, his scaly neck extending to give him a closer look.

"Prince Govinda," Shankar Baba replied. "I am taking him to the lower worlds so that he can see firsthand where the evil-minded go when they depart the earth."

"You are fortunate to have one such as Shankar Baba as your guide," hissed the albino serpent.

"I shall require your support again one day," Shankar Baba informed the serpent king.

"We shall swarm the earth in your defense."

As suddenly as the serpents' murky world appeared, it faded. A great eagle appeared in the sky, taking Shankar Baba and Govinda onto his back.

"I am Garuda, servant of Sri Vishnu, who has sent me to guide you through the worlds that exist beneath his feet," the eagle explained.

With Shankar Baba and Govinda on his back, Garuda descended into a dark, misty place where the air smelled like decaying flesh. What little light there was cast a sickly green hue. Govinda sensed fear everywhere.

"Observe the *narakas* where the wicked are imprisoned by their evil tendencies," Garuda communicated to Govinda as he tipped his wings and dove into a seething mass of commotion. Below the travelers, a vile scene came into view. Fierce dogs with razor fangs dragged men here and there. The men screamed in agony, but the dogs ignored their pleas, biting relentlessly at their victims. Packs of ravenous beasts vied for the flesh. Some of the men escaped the ravaging hounds, but their retreat only enhanced the dogs' vicious game. They pounced again and again, impervious to the cries of their victims.

"What have they done to deserve this?" Govinda asked.

"Premeditated killing," Garuda telepathically replied as he winged away to another region.

"Look," said Shankar Baba. "The hell called Kaururu. Those in this region tortured others, among the most heinous acts a man can commit."

Beneath Garuda, men rushed at one another with butcher knives, carving each other to pieces and drinking the blood of the fallen. No one seemed to die as the bizarre spectacle repeated itself again and again. Ax-wielding men, their unshaven faces contorted with loathing, danced and shouted like crazed demons. Madness caused their blood-red eyes to bulge; the smell of death hung over them.

Fanged creatures chased captives while sinister guards looked on with delight. Terrified men ran through jungles, pursued by ravenous beasts. The serrated leaves of poisonous plants cut the men, causing them to bleed profusely. Inmates were felled by arrows, but the men never died from their wounds, although Govinda was sure they wished they could.

"Why do they repeat the same acts over and over?" Govinda asked.

"Perverse desires grip their minds," Shankar Baba explained. "Great Garuda, circle more slowly this time. The scenes are disturbing to my chela. Therefore, I shall offer these tormented souls freedom from their sufferings."

Again Garuda soared over the narakas. Shankar Baba waved his right hand, showering a calming blue light on the souls below.

"The light will cool their agitated minds."

One by one, the men stopped their senseless acts and looked up at the majestic eagle and his riders.

"Garuda, fly lower so that I may speak to them."

Garuda descended into the smoky realm as Shankar Baba continued spreading light everywhere.

"Tormented souls!" Shankar Baba called out. "There is a tunnel of light above you. If you choose, rise into the light and free yourselves from this hideous place." As the yogi spoke, a tube of light formed overhead. Seeing the light, the men shielded their eyes, cowering like frightened animals.

"Go away!" screamed one of the men. "Light is not welcome here."

"But the light can help you!" replied Govinda.

One among the horde seemed to understand. Gazing into the light with but the faintest glimmer of hope in his eyes, the man was instantly pulled from a seething cauldron. His soul flew into the tunnel of light, and he was freed from his tortured existence.

The Tale of the Himalayan Yogis

"You can all free yourselves!" yelled Govinda.

"Be gone! We don't want your help," an angry man snarled, hurling an ax at Garuda, who flew out of range.

"Let us continue our journey," Shankar Baba advised. "Fear prevents them from knowing that their sanskaras imprison them."

Nothing could be more heartrending than the naraka worlds, thought Govinda as he clung to Garuda's back.

Vishnu's eagle dove further into the stifling gloom until Govinda found it difficult to breathe. Choking on hot, caustic smoke that burned his lungs and stung his eyes, he wished Garuda would turn back, but the eagle flew further into the sulfurous atmosphere, which reeked of death and despair.

"Our destination is the pisacha realm of the lower worlds," Shankar Baba said. "There is no other place quite like it. You recall the rites Kritavat performed in the forbidden valley."

"How could I forget?"

"He invoked beings from these very worlds, but his creations were harmless compared to the one who rules this realm. Keep the cloth over your head," advised Shankar Baba, looking over his shoulder.

Govinda clutched Garuda's neck as the eagle winged its way through a nauseating mist. A cacophony of anguished cries stabbed at his ears from every direction. Below them, a putrid pool stretched out until a dense fog obscured it.

An ominous grey mound surrounded by a sickening yellow-green mote appeared through the fog. Garuda circled above it. Pointing to the hill, Shankar Baba cautioned, "Don't look into her eyes."

"Whose eyes?"

Scanning the massive mound, Govinda didn't see any eyes. Wart-like bumps covering the rounded peak leaked noxious vapor like a volcano about to erupt. Garuda kept at a safe distance as he circled.

From the top of the hill, a horde of flying demons poured out of an opening. The hideous creatures had the skinless, eyeless skulls of monkeys, the horns of goats, and the fangs of vicious dogs. Bony legs, bat-like wings, and rat-like tails were attached to hideously formed bodies. Their webbed wings were the color of burnt coal; their serpentine tails whipped from side to side as they flew. The flying demons dove close to Garuda before veering off at the last moment. The tips of the demons' tails were three-pronged and had spiked tufts. Sparks flared from the tufts as the tails coiled and uncoiled. Govinda held tight to Garuda as the demons dove at him.

"They're coming out of that cave," Govinda said, pointing to an opening near the top of the peak.

"That's not a cave," said Shankar Baba. "That's her mouth."

As Garuda passed closer to the peak, Govinda noticed the mouth-like opening ringed with rotting teeth the size of boulders. Above the mouth, a pair of serpentine, reddish slits opened. The malevolent eyes followed the intruders, staring unblinking at them. Heeding Shankar Baba's warning, Govinda looked away while pulling the shawl close to his chin.

The gaping maw exhaled a choking stench and a second horde of screeching demons. The demons dove at Garuda in pairs, bearing fangs before soaring away. One of the monkey devils flew closer than the others, its horns aimed at Govinda. The demon's tail whipped around, throwing a spark that singed Govinda's arm, but the creature had ventured too close. Twisting his regal neck, Garuda ripped the creature in two with his powerful beak.

Govinda looked back at the mountain, which was now on two legs, reaching out to grab him with pockmarked arms. Staring into the depraved eyes of the demoness, he lost his grip and toppled off of Garuda's back. As he fell, Shankar Baba grabbed him by the shoulder, saving him from the cesspool below.

"Hold on!" Shankar Baba cautioned. "Nothing can harm you as long as you're on Garuda's back."

"Who is that?" gasped Govinda, struggling to right himself as his cloth fell into the cesspool and burst into flames.

"Tadaka, sovereign of the seven hells. Speaking her name is enough to attract her. Neither god nor yogi has the courage to face Tadaka. Death at her hands is worse than any other death, for when Tadaka consumes a soul, it ceases to be."

"Forever?"

Shankar Baba nodded. "If the soul is ensnared by her shroud."

Govinda glanced furtively at the demoness; the pain of looking at her hideous face was more excruciating than anything he had ever felt. As Garuda sped away, Tadaka's flying demons chased the eagle until it had flown far above the naraka.

"There must be a way to escape the shroud," insisted Govinda.

"A yogi-warrior might save a man from Tadaka, but it's difficult," Shankar Baba admitted. "Even a yogi's soul can be devoured."

"I'd rather face Zaim any day."

"Agreed! Zaim in his prime was less dangerous than even one of Tadaka's flying demons, and now Zaim is less threatening than a common soldier."

Their journey to the underworlds complete, Garuda soared into the heavens where the air was sweet, the sky cloudless and blue. Govinda was relieved to be far removed from the loathsome regions and the sickening smell of smoldering flesh.

Govinda found himself in Shankar Baba's cave. The yogi sat by the fire, a broad smile on his face.

"Baba, did we visit a dream world, or was it real?"

"A little of each," replied Shankar Baba. "You witnessed the narakas of the lower worlds; illusory planes created by the darkness in men's hearts. But understand that the suffering is real, as is Tadaka! The seven hells are not God's creation. The evil in men has created these realms. All actions, good and evil, bring an equal reaction. That is the way of things."

"But if men could see what we have seen, surely they would think before acting."

"Agreed, but men act impulsively due to their accumulated sanskaras."

"Is Zaim destined to go to one of the narakas?"

"Violence is deeply rooted in Zaim's mind. He took pleasure in it. But now his body is broken. He experiences pain much of the time. The pain he inflicted on others torments him. He will learn from his suffering, and as a result, he will be less inclined to harm others in the future.

"The curse I placed on him will help him to repay his debt. Zaim was headed for unspeakable suffering, which he had earned from a lifetime of cruelty. His leprosy is nothing compared to the pain that awaited him. Only Zaim can save himself, but by bringing on his leprosy, I gave him time to reflect on his actions before it's too late. There is hope for him."

"Pundit Ananta read stories of the seven hells from the scriptures."

"Souls languish there without hope for eons. God himself sheds tears for those in the hands of demons like Tadaka."

"What determines which naraka a wicked soul goes to?"

"Souls are not wicked. Only a man's misguided actions can be called evil, but even they are part of the grander scheme, the play of light and darkness. Kali Yuga is the time when souls learn difficult lessons. Some souls progress slowly, their deeds condemning them to lower realms again and again.

"As you have seen, confusion reigns in these realms. Those who murder, or torture for pleasure, go to the void called Black Poison. In that place, souls consumed by anger and resentment suffer due to their own tormented emotions. Some of these souls become angry with God himself. Dwelling in an abyss of despair, they blame anyone but themselves for their pain. Selfishness reigns in these places."

"Do these tortured souls remain there forever?"

"There is no such thing as eternal damnation. Souls stay for varying lengths. Bhagawan does not punish. A man's actions bring about his fall."

"What about the higher realms where virtuous souls go?"

"Some have learned their lessons better than others. Most souls go to the realm of their chosen religion. Christians live in their heaven and Buddhists in theirs. All is harmonious."

"Are these realms intensely spiritual?"

"In the regions where most souls go, life is hardly different from the way it is on earth. People garden, study, paint, enjoy music… the difference is that no one lacks anything."

"What about a yogi? Where does he go?"

"The celestial hierarchy is infinite. Most souls go to the lesser astral worlds, but those who spend their lives in meditation and service to humanity go to realms where divinity is strongest because that quality is strongest in them. One could say, heaven is as you are. I had you cover your head so that Tadaka would not see your face."

"Why is that?"

"If Kritavat succeeds in bringing Tadaka to the world of men, she will seek out those she knows."

"But the cloth fell off my head," mentioned Govinda, a hint of trepidation in his voice.

"Come, let's wash off the residue of Tadaka and her minions."

After plunging into the river and climbing to his cave, the unsettling memories of his journey through the narakas faded from Govinda's mind, replaced by a contentment that deepened with each repetition of his mantra. Having observed the realms where one's soul might go in the afterlife, Govinda resolved to be more vigilant in his spiritual practice. He had no wish to be chased by fanged dogs or harassed by Tadaka's flying devils.

Crystalline snows fluttered about like benevolent angels, blanketing the mountain. The legendary Himalayan storms would soon isolate Govinda from the world outside.

The ledge outside his cave lay buried, making it impossible for even Devraj to reach the cave. As he journeyed inward with his mantra, Govinda remembered how Lama Norbu and the others prepared themselves for their time between births. The Land of Pure Bliss was their goal, and it seemed they were well prepared.

Although Govinda looked forward to his weekly visit to Shankar Baba's cave, he was content spending solitary days and nights meditating in his cave, his fire his only companion — though perhaps Shankar Baba kept a watchful eye on him from within it.

Another year passed, and another, but Govinda scarcely noticed. Since his exile, he seemed to be existing outside of time altogether. A bearded Govinda emerged from his cave one morning, his limbs longer and thicker than when he first arrived in Champa.

With spring came a steady flow of villagers trudging up the trail to Shankar Baba's cave. The sick and infirm were carried on bamboo palanquins or tethered atop surefooted mules. As Shankar Baba had anticipated, news of Devraj's healing had spread from village to village. Shankar Baba was happy to relieve the suffering of the young ones, but one afternoon a Nepalese Sherpa arrived with his wife's aged father. On a bamboo bier, the dying man was carried by his grandsons.

"Please, Baba," pleaded the sobbing woman. "Save my father!"

After examining the old man, Shankar Baba said evenly, "It is his time. Would you deny an old man his wish?"

The woman and her family listened, but their attachment to the old man was great.

"Please! Help him!" the distraught woman repeated.

"As you wish," replied Shankar Baba. The yogi held the old man's head in his hands the way a mother cradled her infant, tenderly passing his hands over the dying man's forehead and chest. The family waited expectantly for the old man to awaken from his coma, but to their distress, his body convulsed twice and stopped breathing.

"What have you done to my father?" wailed the woman.

"You asked me to help him," replied Shankar Baba calmly.

"But we came for healing," protested the husband.

"What I did was for your father, not for you," said Shankar Baba bluntly. "It was his time. He was afraid of the unknown, so I showed him that there was nothing to fear, and he departed. He will travel faster if you don't hold him back."

The woman grew hysterical.

"But we don't want him to go."

"We have carried him all the way from Kathmandu Valley," the husband added. "Now you have killed him."

"Son, a yogi neither takes life, nor grants it. Karma decides all. Know that your father is content. I will arrange for the body if that will help."

But the disconsolate woman would not be pacified. Weeping bitterly, she took her husband by the arm and left the mountain. The bearers hoisted the bier atop their shoulders, following close on the heels of their parents.

Govinda, who had been helping Devraj bathe the temple goddess, passed the distressed family on the trail. Arriving at Shankar Baba's cave, he knew what had happened, for the scene had become so commonplace that a Champa elder had opened a shop to cater to the needs of the travelers.

"So many need healing," Govinda observed.

"The soul may be ready to move on, but it is reluctant to depart due to the sadness it will cause its loved ones," Shankar Baba said unconcernedly. "It is time we departed this place."

"Many have come since the snows melted."

"This is why I wanted the villagers to believe that it was I who healed Devraj. You were not meant to be a healer."

Govinda ran down the mountain in search of Devraj. He hoped that Shankar Baba would change his mind, but when he and Devraj returned to the yogi's cave, the entrance had been sealed by a massive boulder that a dozen villagers couldn't have moved. The boys climbed to Govinda's cave. Again, the cave was sealed by an enormous rock.

"That same rock appeared when Baba left after the plague," fretted Devraj.

Seeing Shankar Baba climbing down from a ledge above the cave, Govinda said, "Baba, the caves are sealed."

"Indeed."

"But why?"

"These caves are entry points to higher realms. We cannot leave them unattended, or the likes of Subahu and Kritavat will misuse them. Remember your journey to the narakas. Your cave is ideally suited for such travel."

"Baba, who will protect us from Subahu?" worried Devraj. "After you're gone, he will take revenge on us."

"Try he may, but he will not harm your people."

"But I have taken Subahu's position in the temple."

"Do not be bothered by Subahu. His end is nearly upon him."

"If you leave, my people will be sad," pleaded Devraj, searching for a reason that would make Shankar Baba stay.

"You shall make them happy," replied the yogi.

"Baba, speak with the village elders before you leave."

"You will speak for me," said Shankar Baba, placing his hand on the boy's head. "Govinda and I shall go now."

Without another word, Shankar Baba set out on the trail. Govinda took his friend's hands in his.

"We will return. I'm sure of it."

Govinda had no sooner spoken than he regretted his words.

"I think not," moaned Devraj. "This is the last time I shall see you."

Govinda started down the trail, but Devraj overtook him, blocking the narrow path.

"You must promise to return."

"Devraj, you know that I go where Baba goes."

Devraj let his friend pass. Catching up with Shankar Baba, Govinda walked beside him in silence.

"Breathe deeply and keep your mantra going," Shankar Baba instructed. "The mantra is a yogi's only true companion."

"I'll miss Devraj."

"If you are to be a yogi, your mind must not dwell on the past."

"But he's my best friend. We lived here for almost six years, and yet we leave without explanation?"

"You can ill afford to leave your heart in Champa. You will need it in the coming days."

"But how will Devraj manage when Subahu returns?"

Shankar Baba turned and looked back at Govinda's friend.

"You healed Devraj's body after the attack, but I also healed him that night."

"I don't understand."

"The superstitions of the boy's ancestors resided deep in his soul. His fear was hiding in a little-known chakra in the back of his head, preventing Devraj from experiencing freedom. I removed the fear the night you healed his body. He now has the courage to overcome his ancestors' false beliefs."

Govinda walked without speaking for a time before breaking the silence.

"Where does Yogiraj live?"

"He moves from place to place. Truthfully, he is everywhere on this earth, but no one finds him unless he allows them to."

"Is Yogiraj older than you?"

"Older *and* younger. Yogiraj never ages."

"Will I meet him one day?"

"The time is near."

The Tale of the Himalayan Yogis

Shankar Baba stopped at the base of a tree.

"We will rest under this oak tonight," he said. "He feels friendly toward us."

Spreading his blanket on the ground, the yogi settled into meditation, his spine far straighter than the trunk of the old tree. Govinda did the same.

A crisp morning greeted the yogis, the valley shimmering gold in the sunlight. Tossing his blanket over his shoulder, Shankar Baba announced, "It's a long journey to Jageshwar."

"Jageshwar?"

"An ancient Shiva temple that was spared Mogul desecration."

Jageshwar was seven days journey from the forest. Govinda made good use of Bhumi Mata's bowl while Shankar Baba ate a few wild berries along the trail and drank from the streams.

Govinda and Shankar Baba reached the hidden valley leading to Jageshwar. The trail followed a river through a forest of deodar.

"The forest is as old as the temples," said Shankar Baba, admiring the broad trunked conifers. "The Moguls have spared few temples, but Jageshwar is well hidden. For centuries, our sadhu festival gathered in Varanasi, but now we meet in Jageshwar. Thirty-thousand sadhus will encamp near the river. You'll see things of which you never dreamed."

The trail ended at the edge of a cluster of stone temples. At the perimeter of the temple complex, bearded mendicants sat cross-legged by their fires, their matted locks falling to their feet. Clad in loincloths, the sadhus stared at glowing embers, sipped chai, and prepared simple meals.

Shankar Baba walked into the temple courtyard with Govinda at his side. Together, they surveyed the stone shrines. In total, there were one hundred and eight temples, each home to a different god. The larger shrines tapered gracefully like the conifers overhead; others stood low and squat. Only a handful of the temples accommodated more than a few worshippers.

At the center stood the Shiva temple. The throng of sadhus congregating near the temple opened a path for Shankar Baba as he led his chela inside. Recognizing Shankar Baba, a pujari dispatched a boy outside. Moments later, a white-haired priest appeared.

"Pranam, Baba," greeted the senior pundit, his belly shaking with delight at the sight of his old friend. "Come, sit for chai."

The affable Brahmin led Shankar Baba to a camp near the temple.

"Though we haven't seen you in many moons, tales of your greatness reach us," said the priest as he poured chai for the yogi and his chela. "We heard you bruised some Mogul egos in Varanasi, but then disappeared. Rumors circulated that they arrested you, but no one believed it. More recently, we heard that you brought a boy back to life."

"I can neither deny nor confirm the rumors."

"Who is the young chela with you?" asked the pundit.

"I brought Govinda to see the mela."

"The legendary Prince Govinda?"

"… of Krishnagarh," added Shankar Baba.

"The stories of Govinda's courage exceed even his guru's. It is true, then? You killed the Emperor without a weapon?"

"What I have done is of little consequence," Govinda replied indifferently. "Stories grow with time. It has been years since the Moguls sacked my father's fort."

"You shall be our honored guests for the festival."

"Make no special arrangement," requested Shankar Baba.

"Baba, please do not deny us our heroes," pleaded the Brahmin. "The Moguls have nearly destroyed our will."

"Ram and Hanuman are our heroes."

"But your heroics are nearly as great as Hanuman's, and you stand before us. Baba, I request that you preside over the *mahayagya*. That will ensure its success."

"But I am not a Brahmin, nor am I a priest."

Shankar Baba's voice trailed off as his eyes fell on a pair of sadhus making their way through the gathering as a group of pundits approached the camp, obstructing his view. The Jageshwar priest stood to greet the new arrivals.

"Namaste, Punditji," boomed a voice familiar to Govinda.

"Namaste, Mishraji," the Jageshwar priest replied. "Have you just arrived from Varanasi?"

The rotund priest wagged his head from side to side.

The Tale of the Himalayan Yogis

The priest's son spread mats for the newcomers. Shankar Baba waited for the new arrivals before speaking.

"Pranam, Mishraji," said Shankar Baba warmly.

In the gloaming, Mishra had failed to recognize the yogi and his chela.

"Shankar Baba?" Mishra peered questioningly at the yogi.

"I have brought your friend, Govinda."

"Impossible!" roared Mishra. "The sapling has become a tree! The last I saw of you the lamas had shaved your head and wrapped you in robes. By Shiva's grace alone you escaped the Moguls."

"Namaste, Mishraji," said Govinda, happy to see his friend. "As Shastriji predicted, I found my guru."

Mishra sighed, his mood turning melancholy. "I performed the rites for Shastriji this summer past. It was Shastriji who advised us to shift the festival to Jageshwar. Tell us what happened after you left Varanasi with the lamas?"

"The disguise was successful. Twice the Moguls failed to recognize me."

"If you remember, the costume was my idea," chirped the Brahmin, seeming quite pleased with himself.

"I owe you my life, Mishraji."

"And we owe you our dignity. You've been in the Himalaya all these years, but your fame has spread to every village in India. My grandson proudly tells his friends how Grandfather helped Prince Govinda escape."

"It's late," said Shankar Baba, rising to his feet. "We will find a place to sleep."

"You must stay in my tent," insisted Mishra.

"Your tent is at the heart of the camp. We yogis prefer solitude."

"Solitude is the one thing you won't find here," laughed the Jageshwar priest. "The valley is blanketed with sadhu camps."

By the following day, news had swept through the encampment that Govinda and Shankar Baba were attending the festival. Mendicants huddled around fires, exchanging stories of their heroes.

By the third day, an army of ochre-robed figures had invaded the narrow valley. The shallow river beneath the cedars was transformed into a floating garden – crimson, white, and peach petals buoyed about the water after morning oblations. The scent of sandalwood and camphor filled the air.

At water's edge, bearded swamis fingered rudraksha beads concealed inside cloth bags. One mendicant sat submerged in the river, the chill current swirling past his chin.

"Why do they hide their beads?" asked Govinda as he warmed milk over a fire.

"They believe that if another man sees the beads, the benefit of the japa will be lost," Shankar Baba explained.

"Is the belief correct?" asked Govinda skeptically.

"In the market, one should be cautious, but here there is little concern. Bhagawan knows one's heart, and that is what matters most."

A baba walked past Govinda, his body pierced in a hundred places. Silver and brass rings dangled from his ears, chest, abdomen, legs, and arms.

"Why would a renunciate wear so much jewelry?"

"Such customs are peculiar," Shankar Baba said. "Piercing the flesh is a subtle science. Improperly done, it can disrupt the currents of life energy, but if done properly, it enhances the flow. Fortunately, the sadhu understands the *nadis*."

Govinda pointed to a baba with a grotesque patchwork of veins disfiguring his legs.

"That man's legs are badly swollen."

"He has taken a vow never to sit, or lie down," Shankar Baba explained. "By leaning against supports, he sleeps while standing."

"What is the need for such things?"

"It is done to win the favor of the gods, but such practices were not intended for Kali Yuga. Bhakti wins the favor of the gods in this age."

"Is that why Shiva granted boons to Ravana?"

"Shiva is the easiest of the gods to please. Ravana won Shiva's favor through intense penance."

"But surely Shiva knew that the demon had evil intentions."

"Mahadev is all-knowing."

"And yet he helped Ravana," said Govinda.

"Shiva knew what Ravana planned to do, but he also knew that

Ram would defeat Ravana and his army, and so he granted Ravana his boon. The boon enabled Ram to rid the world of the entire race of demons."

Shankar Baba pointed to a small pot. "Take that milk to Mishraji and see that not a drop spills."

Gripping the pot with both hands, Govinda raised it carefully off the ground. The task proved difficult, but he reached Mishra without spilling any milk. When he returned, he found Shankar Baba staring intently into the fire.

"You've seen many curious customs today," Shankar Baba said without taking his eyes off the flames. "What did you see while carrying the pot?"

"I saw nothing at all."

"Good! Maintain that focus while you're here. When you bring water from the river, pay no attention to anything other than the pale of water. Do you understand?"

"I understand," replied Govinda, perplexed by his guru's instruction.

"There should not be a time when you are not thinking your mantra."

Whether he went to the river to bathe, or into the forest to gather wood, Govinda fixed his gaze on the ground as he had been instructed to do.

Not all the sadhus attending the festival donned the saffron cloth of renunciation. Wild-eyed *nagababas* wore loincloths, their lean bodies smeared with ash. Black-robed *aghoras* camped near the cremation ghat, eating rice from skull bowls fashioned from five metals. Red-robed tantrics kept to themselves. Dozens of sects responded to the call for peace, and though they mingled little, they treated one another respectfully.

A pair of tantrics sat in the shadows, agitated by the rumor that Shankar Baba had been invited to preside over the proceedings.

"Why Shankar Baba?" groused one of the tantrics.

"Ignorant Hindus," muttered the other. "I have a plan. My allies in the spirit world will inform me when the time is right. Shankar Baba will be lucky if he lives. Indeed, his destruction may be upon him."

Nodding in agreement, the other man tossed a stick into the fire, rousing a flurry of angry sparks.

Despite the unsettling roar of a tiger in the neighboring hills, the Vedic invocation began an hour after sunrise the following morning at the auspicious moment chosen by a Varanasi astrologer.

Broad stripes painted on their foreheads, a throng of pundits seated themselves in concentric circles around an ancient Shiva stone in the courtyard outside Jageshwar's main temple. With Govinda at his side, Shankar Baba sat at the axis of the multitude. The Vedic ritual would continue for forty days.

Before beginning, Shankar Baba offered a short prayer.

"*Loka samastah sukino bhavantu. Shanti shanti shanti.* May this rite be propitious. May peace spread far and wide. May harmony be restored to the world. Shiva has provided us the means, but we must be of one mind and one heart."

Shankar Baba paused; a look of dissatisfaction furrowed his forehead.

"So long as there is discord, we cannot begin."

Shankar Baba stared at a pair tantrics standing at the perimeter of the courtyard.

"Shiva will not grace our assembly until you leave," said Shankar Baba, pointing to the pair.

"These fools worship you as a god," snapped the tantric. "I cannot allow your fame to spread uncontested. I challenge you to prove your worthiness… if indeed you have any."

The assembly of pundits looked pensively at Shankar Baba.

"Kritavat, you forget that a yogi does not make a public display of his abilities."

"You hide your impotence behind words. Prove that you are worthy to lead this rite, or allow a true Brahmin to make the offerings."

"Why are you disrupting our pious assembly?" Mishra demanded of Kritavat.

"The assembly is presided over by a counterfeit."

"It is ill-advised to place personal ambition above the welfare of our people," warned Shankar Baba. "Leave now, and take Subahu with you."

The Tale of the Himalayan Yogis

Govinda could feel the heat from Shankar Baba's inner fire.

"It is you who must go," Kritavat countered. "I shall expose your folly. Prove to us your worthiness, or let a Brahmin lead the invocation."

Shankar Baba's eyes narrowed as they shifted from Kritavat to the Shiva stone.

"Go to the river and fill this bucket," Shankar Baba whispered to Govinda.

Govinda filled the bucket and returned.

"Pour the water over Shiva," instructed Shankar Baba.

Govinda tipped the bucket, spilling its contents over the oval stone. The gently sloshing water had been visible to the assembly, but to everyone's bewilderment, a stream of milk flowed over the lingam.

"Your trick may impress some, but not those who know the tantric way," scoffed Kritavat, though his eyes did not wholly agree with his words. "You'll need to do more than turn water into milk to satisfy me."

"Fill the bucket again."

Again Govinda went to the river and returned with a pale of water. Again the yogi poured its contents over Shiva's stone. This time, honey flowed from the container. A chorus of cheers echoed through the valley at the sight of the miracle.

"Childish prank!" Kritavat's eyes flashed with malice. "You have shown us nothing! These sadhus are like children cheering the antics of a clown!"

"Kritavat, you haven't learned that a yogi uses his powers judiciously," said Shankar Baba.

"Only weak minds concern themselves with such trivial matters. Step down from your seat, Shankar Baba. You disgrace this gathering."

"Fill the bucket again," instructed Shankar Baba. "I wish to complete my offerings."

Govinda returned with the bucket and poured its contents over the lingam. This time, curd ran over the sides of the polished stone. Again the assembly voiced its approval.

"I challenge you to prove your abilities, and you give us this?" chided Kritavat. "In Varanasi, they hail you, King of Cobras. Show us something worthy of your title, if that is possible! Or is your reputation based on sleight of hand?"

"As you wish. If my offerings are trickery, then surely you will find this trick amusing." Shankar Baba picked up the empty bucket and pressed it against his head. "Kritavat, you have earned your ruin. You have displeased Shiva, the Great Destroyer. Prepare for your death."

Kritavat snickered at Shankar Baba's words.

"Fill the bucket again."

Again Govinda ran to the river and returned with a bucketful of water.

"Death is not so painful as you think, Kritavat."

"You bore me," muttered the sorcerer, his eyes fixed on the bucket.

Govinda was about to pour the water over the lingam when Shankar Baba held up his hand.

"I will make the final offering."

Turning to the sorcerers, the yogi emptied the bucket in their direction. To the horror of those seated nearby, a trio of hissing cobras slithered from the container, their hoods flared. The snakes paused briefly to assess the gathering before rushing forward faster than seemed possible for a snake. In an instant, the cobras reached the tantrics, their flickering tongues tasting the air of their victims.

"It's your turn to perform some magic," laughed Shankar Baba as he walked impassively toward the tantric. "Act fast — I claim no great patience on my part, but Shiva's cobras have even less. The pain you have inflicted on others is about to come full circle."

Kritavat sat as rigid as the wall behind him. Rivulets of sweat formed on his forehead, his fingernails dug into the palms of his hands. Facing the snakes, he stammered incoherently. Frantically trying to conjure up a counter-charm, Kritavat mumbled first one incantation and then another, but his fear-stricken mind could not grasp the intricacies of the spells even though he had cast them countless times.

"For one who had so much to say, you seem strangely tongue-tied," bantered Shankar Baba. "Speak, before Shiva's snakes free you from your wretched existence."

Kritavat drew in a measured breath and then babbled more incantations, but nothing worked.

The Tale of the Himalayan Yogis

"Your magic fails you, Kritavat, but there is a way out. Surrender your pride, and the cobras will not harm you."

"Do something," pleaded Subahu, trembling uncontrollably.

"Coward," Kritavat murmured, though he showed no greater sign of courage.

"Subahu, you did not heed my warning," Shankar Baba chided, standing over the cowering priest. "I gave you ample chances, but still you harbor hatred. What am I to do?"

"Save me, Maharaj," pleaded Subahu.

"So that you can cause more mischief? I leave it to your guru to save you. He knows what must be done."

Shankar Baba turned and walked away, disappearing inside the temple sanctum.

Again Kritavat muttered a charm, and again it did not effect the cobras. Subahu panted, scarcely able to breathe. The cold stare of the hissing serpents was more than he could withstand. Searching for an escape route, he found none. In his panic, he jumped to his feet and ran for the river. The cobras rushed after him, blurring to dark streaks. In a single swift motion, their lethal fangs struck Subahu's legs, and he collapsed, writhing in the dust, his torment short-lived. The venom soon overwhelmed his body, and he lay paralyzed on the ground until he breathed no more.

Seeing his chance, Kritavat pushed madly through the crowd. Again the cobras pursued their prey. Shoving bystanders out of the way, Kritavat raced toward the courtyard gate, but before he could reach the opening the cobras struck from behind, and he fell to the ground. Their task completed, the snakes slithered into the temple where Shankar Baba had vanished moments earlier.

A group of sadhus hovered over Kritavat, convinced that Shiva himself had claimed the miscreant's life. A sadhu jabbed the body with his trident, but the tantric did not move.

The sadhus stood bewildered and transfixed. No one dared to enter the temple, though all eyes were riveted on the entrance. Govinda waited for what seemed an eternity. Picking up the bucket, he went to the river. Returning to the courtyard, he offered a final oblation, bathing the oval stone in cool Himalayan water. As the offering washed over the lingam, Shankar Baba emerged from the temple, water dripping from his lean body. Wrapped about the yogi's neck and shoulders was a trio of cobras.

Govinda fell to the feet of his guru. Shankar Baba touched his shoulder and smiled.

"My work is done here."

In unison, the assembly chanted, "Hara Hara Mahadev – Glory to Lord Shiva."

An arthritic sadhu bent down to touch Shankar Baba's feet. Another did the same. Soon every sadhu in the courtyard had lined up to prostrate at the feet of Shankar Baba, who stood like a deity in the morning light, his eyes blazing like twin suns.

Though the auspicious hour had passed, Punditji announced that the yagya would commence the following morning. For the remainder of the day, sadhus huddled around their fires, sipping chai and recounting the bizarre events that led to the death of the sorcerers.

Mishra, along with a few senior pundits, sat with Govinda.

"Submerge the bodies in the river," advised Shankar Baba, appearing out of nowhere.

"I will organize," said Mishra.

"Wait for my return before beginning the yagya," instructed the yogi.

"Where are you going?" asked Govinda.

"To the forest. The plot to disrupt our ceremony is no trifle. Kritavat controlled many spirits, and they may seek to avenge him. In that case, they will follow me wherever I go. I do not wish to endanger others by remaining in the camp. I shall return after ten days. Until that time, let no one enter the forest on the far side of the river."

"Maharaj, your presence is required here," said Mishra. "The sadhus wish to honor you."

"Honor Shiva. I have little choice in this matter."

"Where will you stay?" Mishra asked the yogi.

The yogi shrugged, and then turned and strode toward the woods.

"Baba, I want to come with you," Govinda pleaded.

"It won't be safe in the forest."

"But I've been with you in the forest countless times."

"Not with soul-devouring demons roaming about."

"But Kritavat is dead!"

"Do not think that body and soul are the same. Kritavat is very much alive!"

Shankar Baba paused near the yagya site. "Dig there. You will find Kritavat's handiwork in the form of a goat's carcass and two crows. Burn the carcasses and prepare a fresh place near the river. And remember... keep your eyes to the ground."

"I shall," promised Govinda.

Shankar Baba had prevented Govinda from following him by telling him the necessary instructions to be carried out in the camp only after everyone else was out of earshot. Govinda had no choice but to remain behind. He watched from the trail as Shankar Baba waded across the river and disappeared among the trees.

Indeed, a goat and two crows were found near the yagya site.

The following morning, the priests gathered to submerge the shamans' bodies. Subahu's body lay wrapped in white cloth, but Kritavat had vanished.

"No great loss," shrugged Mishra. "Animals must have dragged him off."

The sadhus grew restless as the days passed. Disturbed by the attempts to disrupt the yagya, some departed. An astrologer from a nearby village proclaimed that the disappearance of the tantric's body boded evil.

Each night, Govinda carried his pot to the river and made offerings to Shiva. After completing his chores, he stared across the water into the shadow of the trees beyond, hoping that Shankar Baba would return.

As Govinda made his way from the river back to the courtyard on the tenth and final night, a shrouded figure stepped onto the trail in front of him. Govinda felt the figure's breath mingle with his own; a chill passed the length of his spine.

"Allow me to pass," Govinda said, his eyes fixed on the bucket.

"It is you I have come for," the hooded figure whispered raggedly. "Shankar Baba is not here to protect you. Look at me."

"You're dead!" Govinda replied, refusing to look up.

"Your guru may command a few snakes, but I command an army of demons. Look at me."

"I will not. Guruji instructed me not to spill this water."

"Does Shankar Baba believe a pail of water will protect you? He's not here to fill it with snakes. Before the night is over, my demons will devour him."

"Your demons cannot harm Baba."

"You speak of what neither you nor he understands. I swear by the sovereign of the seven hells that there are demons who can devour Shankar Baba," said the wraithlike figure. "Now, give me the diamond."

"What diamond?"

The figure pointed a spidery finger at the pouch around Govinda's neck.

"Give me the pouch. I have the power to end life as well as create it! Now I shall end yours."

The figure waved his hand, causing Govinda's chest to convulse. The bucket slipped from his hands, spilling water over his feet. His head spun violently as he collapsed to the ground.

Barely conscious, Govinda heard a series of sharp cracks in the forest. A leopard sprang onto the trail between Govinda and the shrouded figure. Panicking, the hooded figure disappeared into the forest as suddenly as he had emerged from it.

"Shakti, is it you?" Govinda whispered, too dizzy to stand. But the leopard had also vanished.

Govinda heard a sudden wind in the trees. But was it wind? It sounded more like breath moving through the woods or many breaths... but what was breathing? It was coming closer, though not directly at Govinda. Like a chorus of whispers, Govinda sensed that the voices were inhuman, otherworldly whisperings of a demonic tongue.

Govinda wanted to run, but he lay on the trail staring into the forest in the direction from where the sound came. An enveloping gloom swallowed the trees. As the shadow approached him, he spotted a sooty cloud moving through the air like black smoke riding the wind. The whispers were emerging from the unnatural darkness.

The Tale of the Himalayan Yogis

Govinda stared into that darkness. He thought he saw shapes in it; nightmarish figures with bat-like wings.

Govinda expected the darkness to descend upon him, but it passed over him, following the trail of the leopard. The darkness soared into the woods, haunting sounds fading in its wake.

Govinda stood and stared as the darkness departed. He waited, watching the night; for how long, he did not know.

Govinda was about to return to the safety of the temple courtyard when a great flash lit the forest, glowing orange through the distant trees. The light flickered, dimming and re-igniting in other places. Spine-chilling shrieks issued from the woods. There was something otherworldly about the screams; Govinda felt them more than he heard them.

Govinda feared for Shankar Baba, but there was little he could do without disobeying his guru's instructions, and so he headed back to his camp where he lay awake before drifting into a troubled slumber.

Dawn broke. It was the tenth day, and as he had promised, Shankar Baba walked into the camp as the sun crested the trees, his weary gait giving the appearance of a battered soldier returning from battle. Govinda was the first to spot the yogi, and he ran to greet him. Punditji and Mishra followed. Moments later, a throng of sadhus had gathered around the venerated yogi.

"Baba, you have been away so long."

"Have I have not returned as promised?" asked Shankar Baba, a tired smile lighting his face. "Though I admit I almost didn't make it back."

"Strange things happened while you were away," related Govinda. "Kritavat's body disappeared."

"We think a tiger dragged it off," suggested Mishra.

"I wish that were true," Shankar Baba replied. "Kritavat has eluded the noose."

"But he's dead," protested Mishra. "Everyone saw the cobras attack him."

"The line between life and death mystifies all. Tantric masters have many secrets."

"Are you saying Kritavat brought himself back to life?" asked Mishra.

"He never quite died. The cobras spent their venom on Subahu. What Kritavat achieved was less miraculous, if you would call it so, than what he attempted to do in the forest last night."

"But Kritavat fled when the cobras attacked. I saw him shaking. He couldn't save himself; otherwise, why would he have been afraid?" questioned Govinda.

"Do not underestimate him. He was helpless because I prevented him from using his charms. Also, he fears animals. Fortunately for you, Kritivat could not persuade you to look up from your bucket. Had you done so, I would have been powerless to prevent him from killing you. His deadliest powers require eye contact. Through eye contact, he can lock one's soul in his gaze and separate it from its body, then feed it to Tadaka, or one of her underlings."

"Then you know about the incident on the trail?"

"I was there, my son."

"Then why didn't you help? I suppose you didn't need to; you must have known that Shakti would save me."

"It wasn't Shakti who saved you."

Govinda's confusion gave way to one of comprehension.

"Yogic powers are useful from time to time," grinned Shankar Baba. "It is as easy for a yogi to change forms as it is for a villager to change clothes. Few things frighten Kritavat, but animals with the power to kill, terrify him."

"How do you know so much about this tantric?" wondered Mishra.

"He and I were disciples of Yogiraj."

"The Ageless One?" asked Mishra.

Shankar Baba nodded.

"Kritavat was a brilliantly gifted chela when he was Govinda's present age. That is why the Ageless One accepted him. I had already been with Master for many years when Kritavat arrived. Master had great hopes for him, but in the end, Kritavat fell unripe from the tree."

"What caused his fall?" questioned Mishra.

"Ego is a hollow reed unable to draw nourishment from the soil it grows in. Everyone has the seeds of both liberation and bondage within them. Kritavat wanted to be Master's favorite, but he failed to understand that Master had no favorites. To win Master's favor, Kritavat explored beyond yogic practices, learning forbidden spells and curses. Over time, he became obsessed with them. He mastered many things, but he never mastered his ego or his jealousy. That is the danger of tantric powers, and that is why the yogi avoids them.

"Kritavat became swollen with pride, and so Master sent him away for a while. He instructed me to accompany him. Master agreed that Kritavat could return after six moons. It was my duty to help him overcome his arrogance. While wandering about we were to maintain our vows."

"What type of vows?" asked Mishra.

"The usual mendicant vows. We were to beg for food, speak truthfully, and maintain celibacy, among other things. Master arranged some trials for Kritavat. As I've said before, the more advanced the yogi, the more severe the test. Kritavat needed to change his ways or leave the Mahatmas.

"Kritavat and I went begging from door to door in Kathmandu Valley. Kritavat happened by a young widow's home; she agreed to feed him on the condition that he debate her. The alluring woman was well versed in tantra and the conjugal arts, and she challenged Kritavat to a debate on the merit of the monk's path versus that of a householder. The loser agreed to adopt the other's lifestyle. Kritavat's pride relished the challenge, but he was no match for the bewitching woman, who skillfully defeated him.

"Having lost the debate, Kritavat faced a dilemma. If he adopted the householder life, he would violate the Mahatmas. If he didn't, he would break his vow of honesty. Kritavat came up with a plan; he would share the woman's bed without succumbing to passion."

"Sounds risky," said Mishra.

"Kritavat stayed with the woman for three moons. During that time, I rarely saw him. When I informed him that it was time to return to the Mahatmas, he told me to come back after another moon's turn.

"After a moon's turn, I told him that I was returning to the

Mahatmas and that he should decide. When he didn't come, I left Nepal.

"A year later, Kritavat returned to Master's ashram. His manner was careless and disrespectful, but Master allowed him to stay since Kritavat insisted that he had not violated his vows. Master devised a test to determine the truth. We were asked to assemble in the meditation hall. Master instructed everyone to levitate, a requirement for being accepted into the Mahatmas. As we had done countless times, the group rose above the ground as one. Only Kritavat remained on his mat. But Master permitted him to stay with the Mahatmas, saying, 'Kritavat himself will determine his fate.'

"Kritavat's conceit led him to berate a member of the Mahatmas. Although everyone felt the sting of his ill-tempered tirade, we viewed Kritavat as a means of measuring our compassion. Finding no one to spar with, Kritavat grew increasingly irritable. One day while I was tending the cows, he approached me, walking staff in hand. 'Tell Master I am leaving,' he said. 'Speak with Master before you leave,' I replied. Kritavat accused me of betraying him. After some years, news came that Kritavat was studying with the Nepalese woman who had defeated him in the debate."

"Before the cobras attacked, I offered Kritavat a final chance in the courtyard. He was not in any danger," revealed Shankar Baba. "In fact, the sight of Shiva's snakes brings immense bliss to a yogi. Kritavat fled because his mind is rooted in fear. Had he remained calm, no harm could have come to him."

"Did you expect him to flee?" asked Mishra.

"I expected him to do what he was taught to do, but he has forgotten his training. I devised a plan to save Kritavat, but he's lost his way. Long had I suspected it, but I had hoped otherwise."

"Where is he now?"

"I can't say, but we have not seen the last of him or his trickery."

"Baba, how did you materialize the cobras?" asked Govinda.

"I asked Lord Shiva to protect the sadhus. He chose the means. Kritavat did not come here by accident. And it was no accident that I came either. Where there is light, darkness tries to interfere."

"A new altar has been made by the river," said Punditji. "The astrologers informed me that we could begin tomorrow, but we do not have a lingam."

Shankar Baba headed for the river; Govinda, Punditji, and Mishra followed. Many sadhus followed the group, maintaining a respectful distance. At the river, Shankar Baba sat on the bank with Govinda at his side.

"Shape some mud into a lingam," Shankar Baba instructed his disciple.

Govinda scooped the soft, wet earth into a mound, fashioning a lingam the size of a melon. The lingam properly formed, Shankar Baba leaned forward and blew on it, and then sprinkled sacred ash over it. He then chanted *Om Namah Shivaya* three times. With a crowd of sadhus looking on, the mud underwent a transformation, causing Govinda to blink twice in disbelief. The clay had inexplicably turned into flawless crystal.

"Himalayan *spatak*," proclaimed Shankar Baba. "Its purity cannot be defiled. Now let us begin."

Seated at the center of the Vedic pundits, Shankar Baba instructed Govinda to pour offerings over the crystal lingam. Chants and incantations filled the valley from dawn until noon. The ritual complete, Mishra approached Shankar Baba.

"Baba, will you speak this evening?"

"Have the sadhus gather after their meal."

A sea of bowed heads welcomed Shankar Baba. Few in the assembly had ever seen a saint in action. Attendants erected a marigold-laden dais, but Shankar Baba sat on the ground along with the others. Punditji slipped a garland over the yogi's head and touched his feet.

Shankar Baba spoke in simple terms.

"We are all souls in search of God. Ours has always been the path of truth. The time has come to free Mother India from the shroud of a foreign power.

"Ours is a spiritual army, but we have become small-minded, thinking my god is better than my brother's. Like blind men touching an elephant, one man catches hold of its leg and describes a tree. Another man touches its side and describes a fortress wall. A third man rubs the elephant's ear and calls it a fan. Some of you worship

Shiva… others Vishnu. Shiva is the Paramatma and Shakti his power; Ganesh is his head and Surya his eyes. The parts make the whole, and the whole the parts. Let us not be divided.

"We walk diverse paths seeking a common destination. Pride, the willful son of ego, keeps us from the goal. Spiritual pride is the thief that steals our *punya*. Arrogance caused the tantrics' death. He who commits an act is accountable for it. Fools cling to petty powers. Fix your mind on God even while sleeping. Those without an Ishta-Deva are like orphans. When it is time to depart this world, hold God in your heart. Failing to do this, we have failed to achieve anything.

"The world is a shadowy dream. Awaken from that dream! A life dependent on material possessions is a miserable life. Pity that man! Men live in bondage like parrots in a cage. A well-meaning man goes to the market and purchases a parrot, intent on freeing the bird. He opens the cage, but the parrot refuses to fly away. The bird stays in the only dwelling it knows. Knowing nothing but the confines of the human body, the soul spurns freedom. Human birth is the open door freeing us from the prison we call ignorance.

"Foolish men worry incessantly. Fear is more terrible than a funeral pyre. The pyre burns the dead while fear burns the living. In poor light, a man mistakes a rope for a snake. Fear grips the man until a lamp appears. Then the man never sees the rope as a snake again.

"Seek refuge in the Self. Seek wisdom from those of good character. One day, you will leave this place. At the time of your death, you will review your actions, good and otherwise. If vice outweighs merit, suffering results.

"A yogi's powers must not be used for recognition or personal gain. The perfected *Siddha* acts out of compassion for the welfare of the world. Those who make much of miracles are destined to fall.

"Approach the Supreme with a full heart, not with open hands like a beggar. In that way, we will win the affection of the omnipotent One.

"When one can fill his hands with diamonds, why carry coal? Time consumes beggar and king alike. When we leave this world, our merit accompanies us, nothing else.

"Some sadhus meditate on the formless Being, but what can

The Tale of the Himalayan Yogis

Bhagawan do for us until he assumes a form? Fruit will not grow until we plant the seed. Therefore, choose a form to worship.

"Through meditation, love for one's chosen deity increases, and when the love increases enough, the chosen one enters your heart. Bhagawan is the treasure house of happiness. Take his name with faith and devotion.

"Maintain four dispositions — happiness toward the wise, friendliness toward your peers, compassion for the weak and suffering, and indifference to those who hate you."

"Whether it happens tomorrow, or in a hundred births, we shall reap the fruit of our actions. He who dwells within us keeps a record of all that we do. Solitude is a straight road to the ever-blissful, omnipotent Paramatma."

Shankar Baba fell silent. Rising to his feet, he disappeared through the temple doors behind him.

The peace offering continued for forty days. On the final day, Shankar Baba and Govinda sat by the fire with their Brahmin friends.

"We will leave now," Shankar Baba announced. "Govinda, your training is nearly complete. Until then, you remain mine."

"Baba, stay with us for a few days," Punditji pleaded. "The yagya has been a great success. Let us enjoy the fruits of our offerings."

"Until our people are free, I see no cause to celebrate."

"Where will you go?" inquired Mishra, distressed by the prospect of the saint's departure.

"We shall walk," Shankar Baba stated vaguely. "The Ageless One is expecting us."

"No one has seen the Ageless One in years," replied Mishra.

"Who can predict what Master will do, or where he will appear?"

"A sadhu from the Malabar Coast claimed the Ageless One taught Shankara, Gautama Buddha, Jesus, and Kabir. Is it true?" asked Mishra.

"I cannot say. Master works in secret."

"How will we find him?" Govinda asked.

"He will find us. Many search for Master, but none find him unless he wishes it."

"How did you meet the Ageless One?" asked Punditji.

433

"At the Himalayan shrine called Badrinath, a youthful ascetic approached me as I came out of the temple. He took me to a mountain in Nepal where we spent some years together. Everything I am is due to that great sage who appeared to be no older than Govinda."

"I have heard he moves about with a small group of yogis," Mishra said.

"One cannot predict what Master will do. His life is a mystery to all, including his disciples."

"Does he keep an ashram?" Mishra asked.

"Mostly he stays in far off places. He never appears in public. His words are not written down. Despite his modest ways, Yogiraj is a thousand times more powerful than any of the Mahatmas."

"It's difficult to imagine," said Mishra.

"Stay the night," offered Punditji. "The fire is warm. It is comfortable here."

"A yogi lives for the benefit of the world, not for food and comfort," Shankar Baba reminded his host. "Much good has come from our time here, but more good will come from our departure than from our staying."

Shankar Baba rose to his feet; Govinda scrambled to do the same.

Punditji and Mishra pressed their hands together, but Shankar Baba was already walking away. Like a leopard prowling the night, he moved noiselessly through the forested valley.

"Where will we go?" asked Govinda.

"We shall roam these hills until Master calls."

"How long will that be?"

"I think soon."

IMMORTAL YOGIS

Govinda and Shankar Baba journeyed north for many days, arriving at a ridge overlooking a terraced valley bordering Tibet. Rice fields and potato plots blanketed the valley floor. A rampart of sawtooth peaks towered overhead.

Seeking refuge under an outcropping above the valley, the wanderers relaxed by their fire. Flaxen light swathed the fields below as the sun slipped from sight. Snow peaks blushed magenta in the distance.

"Master loves Nepal," revealed Shankar Baba. "This valley is a favorite of his."

"You once said your master is older than you are. How does one live so long?"

"Immortality was never meant to be the secret it has become, but those who knew the secrets had little choice but to conceal their methods."

"Why is that?"

"Evil kings... warlords... even demons... wanted this knowledge, and those who withheld it were tortured and killed.

"The body possesses the ability to regenerate itself, but it wears out from the friction within. Youth may be preserved indefinitely by those resolute enough to turn their back on discord."

"How does a yogi regenerate his body?"

"The body is composed of air, fire, water, space, and earth. By refining the elements, the yogi lives as long as he likes, but few choose to live indefinitely. Most depart when their work is finished."

"Why?"

The first stars were appearing overhead.

"This life is a brief stop on a long journey through time and space. Once the yogi masters mortality, he travels where he likes."

"While the rest of us, like parrots, are reluctant to step out of our cages."

"In ages past, humans lived much longer, giving them the opportunity to see the consequences of their actions. However, when karma from one life doesn't return until a future incarnation, men fail to connect cause and effect. Consequently, the wheel of karma doesn't serve as the learning tool it was meant to be."

"Obviously, Kritavat doesn't believe in karma, but what possible benefit can come from hurting someone?" asked Govinda.

"Kritavat has chosen to serve himself rather than serve others. In his arrogance, he invokes beings from the lower worlds where he has joined those who would harm others."

"Can love overcome such loathing?" wondered Govinda.

"Without love, there would be no harmony, and without harmony, the universe would self-destruct. The stars and planets exist in harmony. They are alive like you and me."

"Then love is the secret."

"Love is the highest expression of life. There exists more love on earth than the air we breathe, but who would believe it."

A milky radiance flooded the valley as the moon rose above the peaks.

"The moon is full tonight… let us meditate," suggested Shankar Baba.

Govinda closed his eyes and was soon lost to the world. The moon had moved across the night sky when Govinda heard Shankar Baba's voice as if from a distant peak.

"The mountain summons us," said Shankar Baba, pointing to the snowfields overhead.

"We're going up there?" asked Govinda.

Reluctantly, he got up and followed Shankar Baba over a rugged section of terrain. As they climbed, the pale silhouettes of jagged peaks came into view. Pockets of ice and snow stung their feet. The trail was unreliable, but Shankar Baba seemed to know exactly where to place his feet.

Above the trees, the yogis reached a broad, open space where the sun had burned away the snow and ice. Nine timid, triangular-leafed, tawny plants lay before them, miraculously surviving at an altitude that even the heartiest scrub avoided. Having found soil, the plants soaked up the moon's rays. Some of the leaves were smaller and newer than others. Shankar Baba bent down to examine one of the plants.

"There is no plant on earth like these," Shankar Baba declared, caressing the leaves of one of the plants.

"What kind of plant are they?" he asked, wondering if their midnight march up the mountain had been in search of these plants.

"Soma plants. Yogis drink an elixir made from the juice of the soma plant. In ages past, Indra and the gods warred with an army of demons over a pot of soma juice. Had the demons succeeded, they would have been unassailable."

"Do the immortals drink soma juice?"

"Some do. The full moon imbibes the leaves with a special vibration."

"Will you make an elixir from the leaves?"

"These leaves are not for us. We shall pick the new leaves of each of these nine plants, but only after I chant the necessary mantra to win their favor."

"Baba, who are the leaves for, if not us?"

"You need not ask such questions."

Kneeling before one of the plants, Shankar Baba chanted mantras that Govinda had not heard before. Tenderly, he removed three new leaves from the plant before moving to another plant. Shankar Baba repeated the ritual until he had removed the smallest leaves from all nine plants. Placing the leaves in a cloth bag, Shankar Baba faced the moon, his face as bright as the orb itself.

"Master calls."

The yogi led Govinda across the face of the mountain. Although it was closer to dawn than dusk, Govinda felt great exhilaration as he followed Shankar Baba. In the moonlight, they crossed glacial fields and climbed precipices. Deadly crevasses lurked everywhere. High on the mountain, they arrived at an opening cleanly cut from the rock.

"Follow me," he said, marching into the blackness. The blackness was all-enveloping, but Govinda felt secure with his guru leading the way. They tread on for a time, entering deep into the mountain.

"Where are we going?" asked Govinda.

"To your initiation."

"My initiation?"

"Your training is complete. I told you about the Mahatmas. Tonight, you will join them… if you succeed."

"What must I do?"

"That is for Master to decide."

"Kritavat failed. What if I do too?"

"With suitable resolve, you will succeed. Stop here… tell me what you feel."

Govinda searched his heart. "I remember the times when Mataji led me to the Krishna temple. I feel now as I did then."

"There is little difference between Master and your beloved Krishna," said Shankar Baba. "I won't be going any further."

"You won't?"

"My work is done."

Shankar Baba's words pierced Govinda's chest like a Mogul dagger.

"I don't understand," he protested. Uncertainty flooded his mind; the darkness was no longer welcome.

"You must go alone. There is no turning back."

"But you can't leave!"

"I am always with you. Call me, and I will answer."

"But I'll be lost in here without you."

"Take this," said Shankar Baba, placing an object in Govinda's hand. It was the bag containing the soma leaves.

"Your heart will guide you from here," Shankar Baba said gently.

"I'm unsure," stammered Govinda.

"You need not be."

Govinda felt as though the weight of the mountain had collapsed on him. An unbearable heaviness pressured his chest; he found it

The Tale of the Himalayan Yogis

difficult to breathe. Sadness that he hadn't felt since leaving his family now invaded him.

"But why must you go?"

"The bond between guru and chela is unbreakable, but from here you must proceed alone. Doubt not, lest you fall like Kritavat."

"Please, Baba, I want to look into your eyes one more time."

Immediately, a soft, golden light flooded the corridor. Shankar Baba was holding a long, narrow, glowing rock. Govinda gazed lovingly into his guru's eyes. Never had they seemed more powerful, or more affectionate.

"Baba, I am in the habit of following you. When you start down the trail, I try to keep up. Who will I follow now?"

"You will follow your God-Self," Shankar Baba declared. "as will others. It is time for you to lead."

"But am I ready?"

"He is waiting for you," said Shankar Baba, pointing down the corridor.

Govinda stood in place, reluctant to take a step. Wrapping his arms around Shankar Baba, Govinda whispered, "Baba, I love you."

"And ever shall I love you, my son," the yogi whispered back. "The bond between us is greater than you know. I will always be as close to you as your hand. Now I shall go."

Shankar Baba handed the glowing rock to Govinda. Almost instantly, the yogi vanished, leaving only Govinda's brooding thoughts to accompany him as he stepped into emptiness.

How can it be? Govinda thought. *Inside this mountain, there is no sun or moon, yet light comes from the tip of this rock.*

Govinda continued to puzzle over the light as he moved along the narrow corridor that led deeper into the mountain. Although he had not gone far, it seemed like he had been walking for hours. Without Shankar Baba, his legs grew heavy; exhaustion clung to his mind. Fear seized him, sapping his strength and weakening his will.

There is no turning back, but where does this passage lead?

He arrived at a place where two passages, equal in every way, stood before him.

What am I to do now? How can I choose the way when I don't know where I'm going?

Disheartened, he leaned against the wall of the tunnel and examined the passages. One of them appealed to him more than the other, and so he continued walking until the tunnel came to an abrupt end. There was no opening, no possibility of going further. Assuming he had chosen the wrong passage, Govinda sat on the tunnel floor, bewildered by the strange turn of events. Clueless as to what to do, he began to doubt.

This doesn't make sense. First Shankar Baba leaves me, and now the passage ends. Maybe this is the end for me. Even if I find my way back to the entrance, I have nowhere to go. Have these seven years brought me to this?

Fear stalked Govinda's heart. He tried to fend off the feeling, but his apprehension grew, and as it did, the light of the rock faded until he could scarcely see the wall that obstructed his way.

I have walked and walked inside this mountain. If the light fails, what will I do?

Despair cast a shadow on his heart, and as his dejection grew, the light was extinguished completely.

I will stay where I am, Govinda resolved. Placing his hand on the pouch hanging from his neck, he whispered to himself, "Only Krishna can save me now."

No sooner had he uttered Krishna's name than a soft blue light illumined the corridor.

I shall sing to Krishna. Baba may not be at my side, but Krishna is with me.

He sang, softly at first. As his gloom lifted, he sang louder and with greater devotion.

Krishna will help me now, he thought. *He always has in the past. Krishna, you lifted a mountain with one finger. Move this mountain for me now, if you will.*

Govinda felt the mountain tremble against his back. The tremor shook the walls of the tunnel; choking dust enveloped him. He was sure the ceiling would collapse, and so he covered his head with his arms.

The Tale of the Himalayan Yogis

When the dust settled, an iron handle appeared at the end of the tunnel where solid rock had been moments earlier. As Govinda reached for the handle, a door swung open, and he stepped through the opening into a large, well-lit cavern. A low fire burned in the center of the chamber. Around the fire sat some figures.

"Come in, my friend," called a seemingly good-natured yogi who was sitting on the far side of the fire. The yogi seemed barely older than Govinda. Long, raven hair framed his youthful face. His almond eyes were deep pools of understanding.

Govinda had seen the yogi before, but it seemed a veil had been drawn over his memory. Fixing his eyes on the yogi, he took little notice of the others sitting around the fire.

"Join us," said the yogi, gesturing to a grass mat at his side.

Govinda seated himself.

"Where's Shankar Baba?" asked the strangely familiar yogi, who was now laughing.

"Gone," replied Govinda sadly. "He was leading me through the tunnel… and then he vanished."

"Same old Shankar," chuckled the yogi. "He was never the sociable type."

The lighthearted comment drew smiles from the others.

"Baba insisted we climb this mountain… then he led me into a tunnel… said his work was finished… and vanished."

"Don't be discouraged."

"Will I ever see him again?"

"Govinda, you are a son to Shankar. You will see your guru again," the yogi assured him. "Allow me to introduce myself and my brothers. I am Yogiraj."

"Baba's guru?" asked Govinda incredulously. "But… you're too young!"

"Shankar likes to call me Guruji, but he could just as easily be my guru. I wish he hadn't disappeared so suddenly, but that's Shankar."

"It's just that we were together for six years… and now he's gone."

"You'll see him again soon enough. Here there are no gurus and no disciples… all are masters. You could not have come as Shankar's chela."

"But why did he disappear?"

"As your guru, it would have been awkward for Shankar to be present. We are all equals here... cosmic clowns, so to speak."

Yogiraj glanced at his cohorts. His description drew more smiles from the others.

"But Baba says you are his guru!" Govinda protested.

"Shankar is my spiritual brother," stated Yogiraj simply. "He has no more need for a guru than anyone present. Nonetheless, he desired one, and so I played the part. But this ashram is not a place for training. We are here to serve. Meet your humble servants."

Since entering the cavern, Govinda had been so engaged by Yogiraj that he hadn't looked around. The cave, which rose almost six times his height to a conical ceiling, was once again as broad as it was high. Footholds carved into the far wall of the cave led to an opening in the ceiling.

A robust fire burned, but no wood fueled the flame. Oddly, the fire issued no smoke. The fire did not seem to serve as the cavern's sole source of light, but there was no other discernible source from where the light was coming. Even more perplexing was the fact that no shadows appeared within the cavern.

"We call this the Cosmic Flame," explained Yogiraj. "The fire is uncommon in many ways."

"There are no logs," noted Govinda.

"Tonight, the fire burns violet. It welcomes you. Let me introduce my friends."

Yogiraj pointed to a tall, broad-shouldered Indian on Govinda's left who wore a white turban and had an oiled mustache. Govinda was sure the man was a Rajput, and, no doubt, an expert horseman. He could easily envision the man leading a cavalry to battle.

"Meet Chananda," Yogiraj said. "His clan comes from the Great Thar. Chananda is our newest member. He joined us three hundred years ago. Like you, Maharaj Chananda is Rajput royalty."

"Which fortress?" Govinda asked.

"The golden city," replied Chananda.

"Maharaj speaks nine languages," said Yogiraj, "and has traveled

The Tale of the Himalayan Yogis

the world. Oddly, he prefers the ascetic's life to the pleasures of his palaces, although he slips away now and then."

Yogiraj gestured toward a round-faced Tibetan seated beside Chananda. The Tibetan wore a long woolen robe that covered all but his weathered feet. "Meet Lama Dorchen. Dorchen was raised in western Tibet. His master was Marpa, who brought the ancient Buddhist texts from India to Tibet. Dorchen prefers living under the stars to living in the bowels of the earth. He spends most of his time on the high plateaus and only comes here for occasions such as this."

Yogiraj pointed across the fire to a lean, bare-chested yogi with a black beard and solemn eyes. The yogi wore a strand of rudraksha beads the size of walnuts.

"Meet Swamiji. In a different form, and under a different name, Swamiji journeyed to the Middle East to witness that holy birth."

Swamiji was leaning against the shoulder of an aristocratic-seeming Egyptian wearing a silk tunic and matching pants.

"The fashionable one is Akori."

The Egyptian smiled.

"Akori was a pharaoh who mastered the elements," Yogiraj continued. "His appearance hasn't changed in a thousand years! Akori knows the secrets of the pyramids."

Yogiraj pointed to a diminutive, youthful Chinese man.

"This is Deydas Chi. It is not his Chinese name, but it is the one by which you may know him."

Deydas Chi inclined his head respectfully.

"Don't be fooled by the boyish appearance. Master Deydas is the oldest member of our group. I am indebted to Deydas, who taught me the secrets of youthfulness. He prefers living in two places at once. In China, his identical self looks after his clan, which dates back to the Xia Dynasty. His wife is nearly as old as he is."

Yogiraj pointed beyond the inner circle to a fair-haired European who was preparing a drink of some sort.

"Our French brother is Father Girard," Yogiraj said. "We snatched him from a monastery near Chardonnay. Girard still pines for his beloved French cuisine, though he hasn't set foot in Gaul for four hundred years. Girard knows alchemy and fashions gold from granite. He's preparing something special for you."

Govinda suddenly remembered the pouch of soma leaves.

"I have something for you," he said, handing the pouch to Yogiraj.

Yogiraj passed the bag to Girard.

"Soma leaves are nature's finest," Yogiraj explained. "Nowhere in the entire universe is there a more potent medicine. Selfless beings brought this plant to our earth from a distant place."

Father Girard opened the pouch, placed the leaves into a bowl, and began grinding them with a stone.

"Baba told amazing stories about you," Govinda blurted out. "I was expecting a wise old white-haired sage, but you're… so young."

"Appearances never tell the whole story, do they."

Yogiraj slapped Chananda's knee; Akori doubled over with laughter. Even Swamiji shook with mirth at their guest's remark.

"How old are you, Govinda?"

"Almost twenty-two. How old are you?"

Yogiraj's eyes darted mischievously about the chamber. "That's hard to say, isn't it, Chananda?"

An infectious smile dimpled Yogiraj's cheeks.

"Let's just say I stopped counting before Chananda was born."

Again, Yogiraj's friends burst into fits of delight. There didn't seem to be a serious member of the group except for Swamiji, and even he wore a broad smile on his face.

"I guess I don't understand," Govinda confessed.

"You will," Yogiraj assured him. "Before you leave us, you will witness things that will change you forever."

"I already have. I never imagined that a cave could go so deep into a mountain."

"These caves were created before the seas rose a long, long time ago. Like the great temples of Egypt, yogic powers brought them into being. Isn't that right, Akori?"

"Historians believe we Egyptians employed workers to build our pyramids," Akori explained, "but that was not the case for the earliest ones. Those living stones were raised by the power of the mind… not by the exertion of men's bodies.

"A vast network of passages connects secret ashrams and temples throughout the Himalaya. The power of the fully developed mind is without limit, but the entrances to our ashrams are well hidden," Yogiraj explained.

"I understand," Govinda said. "If invaders discovered these caves, they would destroy them."

"They would try, but remember how your cave was suddenly sealed after you had stayed there for many years?"

"Baba sealed the caves."

"Those are not ordinary caves, nor are these," Yogiraj revealed. "As you have seen, we can conceal them and make them known as we see fit. We disguise our entrances in the same way. No one knows the locations of our hidden ashrams, and if a villager happens onto one, the entrance can be sealed at will.

"Only advanced yogis and lamas come here for regeneration. A few like Girard and Akori traveled from distant lands. Ancient secrets are preserved here that will be revealed after the world passes through the great solar initiation, which is to commence in approximately four centuries. Until that time, the caves are known to but a few."

"I am honored to be invited inside."

"You have earned the right to be here. This ashram is your home as much as it is ours. We welcome you and are here to serve our newest member."

"But am I not too young…"

"We're all young, or old, depending on your point of view. Did you think we'd choose to live for a thousand years as white-haired old men?"

"But you are old in truth. I mean… your bodies may be whatever you wish them to be, but your minds and souls are ancient and experienced and wise. I really am the age I appear to be. How can I be one of you?"

"Your soul is ancient too, Govinda. Your mind and soul are experienced and wise and knowledgeable. Age is not a requirement… our requirements are more important ones… different for each… and you meet all of yours."

"What are these requirements that I meet?"

"Once a trial is passed, it matters little what it was. Better to focus on the present."

"If I am to be one of you... what is it that you do?"

Everyone convulsed with laughter. Even Swamiji's dispassionate eyes twinkled at Govinda's innocence.

"Nothing much," Yogiraj managed to say through his laughter. "For us, doing isn't so interesting as being."

"Baba said as much."

"That's because Shankar's been with us for a very long time."

"He has?"

"Of course. How else would Shankar know where to find us?"

"Why such secrecy?" wondered Govinda.

"In time you'll understand everything."

"I feel like I know you."

"You should; you stayed in my cave for five years."

The memory of Govinda's first night in the cave above Champa suddenly flashed across his mind.

"That first night when Baba sent me to live in the cave – your cave – it was you who appeared."

"You saw the yogi, did you not?"

"I was meditating when a golden ball appeared and the form of a yogi – you, I think – materialized. It was the most awesome thing I've ever seen. But I don't remember much after that. It felt like a dream."

"Everything is a dream, Govinda. Our first encounter was no more, or less, real than anything else. I lived in that cave centuries ago. Part of me still stays there. You have done well. That is why you're with us now, for it is time."

"Time?"

"Shankar must have told you about your future."

"Yes... well... he told me, but I never took him seriously."

"Innocence is a virtue."

"But how will it happen? I have no army. I don't even have a horse."

"You have us... and Shankar... and Bhumi Mata. We are here to serve you. No army has ever defeated us. You have other allies as well... the Rajputs will help you as will others. And you have the

The Tale of the Himalayan Yogis

animal kingdom. It is time to liberate our brothers and sisters. Are you ready?"

"But what can the animal kingdom do against the imperial army?"

"Do not underestimate our four-legged friends. But let us not think of the future. Girard has prepared something to refresh you."

The Frenchman handed Yogiraj a silver chalice filled with green liquid. Yogiraj held the cup for a moment before passing it to Govinda.

"Drink this and never grow old."

Govinda sipped the liquid, which tasted like herbal honey. Immediately, the crown of his head began to quiver, and he was overcome with dizziness. Yogiraj placed his hands on Govinda's temples, and a dazzling ball of light entered his head. For an instant, Govinda was sure that his head would explode. A cool breeze swept the length of his body. He felt weightless and transparent. There seemed to be little, if any, substance to his body.

"Within this light, you can know anything," explained Yogiraj. "Ask and the answer will come. Try it."

"Where is Shankar Baba?"

"What do you see?"

Govinda saw the earth suspended in darkness with a broad river winding across the land. At the river's edge stood an ancient city. Somehow, he could see through roofs, floors, walls, and earth. Govinda saw Shankar Baba meditating in his snake-filled grotto.

"I see the Ganges... and Varanasi beside it."

"And?"

"I see Baba in the cave with the cobras."

"Are you surprised?"

"Just moments ago he was with me here inside the mountain."

"Shankar's work was done here, and so he returned to Varanasi."

"But how?"

"By now, nothing we do should surprise you. Ours is a subtle reality, one guided by intention. To the villager, this sort of thing would appear to be a miracle, but to those who fathom the oneness of life, this is ordinary, even commonplace — as it should be."

"Could I do what Baba did?" questioned Govinda.

"Why not!"

"Then I could transport myself to Varanasi?"

"You miss your guru, don't you?"

"Baba means everything to me."

"Time and space are a yogi's allies. In time, I'll take you to Varanasi."

Yogiraj got up and led the others to the footholds carved into the wall. Yogiraj climbed nimbly followed by Govinda. They ascended through a narrow, vertical passage that opened into a small, faintly lit chamber above the main cave. On a raised platform lay a yogi who appeared to be sleeping. His white hair and beard gave him the appearance of an ancient sage about to merge with the cosmos. White silk covered his body; a small rectangular piece of the same cloth covered his mouth.

The yogi's breath is too faint to disturb the cloth, noted Govinda.

"This is the restoration chamber," Yogiraj informed Govinda. "Shankar brought you to us so that you could witness something extraordinary. It has been centuries since one of us underwent regeneration."

"Is he asleep?" Govinda asked.

"Mahesh has been in a unique state of samadhi for forty days. He is about to undergo the regeneration ritual; after which he will never age again. The soma leaves are about to be put to good use."

Silently, the others formed a circle around the platform. They intoned a soft, steady chant. The chamber reverberated with the resonance of potent mantras. Govinda recognized the invocations as hymns to the Mother Goddess.

From a lapis jar, Yogiraj applied scented oil to Mahesh's head, hands, and feet. Then he waited until the cloth covering Mahesh's mouth rippled slightly. The yogi had not been breathing softly; he had not been breathing at all.

Satisfied that Mahesh's breath had been restored, Yogiraj held his left hand above the yogi's chest while his right hand hovered over his forehead. Standing opposite Yogiraj was Deydas Chi, who whispered something that only Yogiraj could hear.

As the monks chanted, the energies within the chamber intensified, causing a bead of sweat to form on Govinda's brow. The cloth covering

The Tale of the Himalayan Yogis

Mahesh's mouth fluttered into the air and fell to the floor. He was awake.

With the help of Deydas Chi and Akori, Mahesh sat up. Unhurriedly, he bent his fragile legs into lotus posture. His bony hands formed mudras as they rested on his creaky knees. Mahesh's spine straightened as he breathed rhythmically in and out. With each breath, he drew strength. A hidden force within the chamber caused Govinda's body to sway as he watched.

Yogiraj signaled to Girard, who placed a silver chalice in Yogiraj's hand. Putting his left hand under Mahesh's chin, Yogiraj carefully poured the cup's contents into his mouth. Mahesh's eyes now shimmered like sapphires.

Yogiraj's hands, which had been moving around Mahesh, now hovered above his head. Forming his hands into a cup, Yogiraj appeared to pour an ethereal substance over Mahesh, whose body was barely visible from within a cocoon of white light. In the space between the cave's roof and Mahesh's head, a radiant pink oval formed. Within the light, Govinda saw the faint outline of a figure. The others in the room looked on attentively. Light flowed from the etheric being into the crown of Mahesh's head, causing his body to stiffen. After his body had absorbed the liquid light, the being poured a similar substance into each of the attendants, including Govinda, before fading from sight.

Yogiraj signaled to Deydas Chi and Akori, who eased Mahesh back onto the platform. Yogiraj took oil from a second jar and rubbed it on Mahesh's head, hands, and feet. Then he nodded to the others. Govinda sensed that the rite was a success.

Yogiraj led Govinda down the carved footholds to a pair of mats near the Cosmic Flame, leaving the others to tend to Mahesh.

"What did you think of the ritual?"

"I can't say," replied Govinda. "The light was so intense that I couldn't see much."

"Did you feel her presence?"

"I'm not sure. Do all the Mahatmas go through this ritual?"

"There is more than one way to regenerate the body. Deydas Chi has never gone through the process, and he's the oldest among us. And Shankar has no interest in it."

"Is that why he looks older than the others?"

Yogiraj nodded.

"Baba says life and death amount to little more than the rise and fall of a wave on the sea. Baba says that if God wanted men to be immortal, he would have made it so that they never died."

"Few in this age do not need to be reborn," explained Yogiraj. "For most, reincarnation is a vital part of the soul's training. Embodiment is an opportunity to balance the mistakes from the past. The Mahatmas remain on earth for the benefit of others since our soul development is complete."

"It's a peculiar fire," observed Govinda. "When I arrived, the flame was purple… now it's white."

"Potent rays from the central sun enter this ashram through the Cosmic Flame. The white flame restores youthfulness, which is helping Mahesh receive his ageless body. For Mahesh, the door to the change called death has been closed.

"In ages past, the Mahatmas possessed master powers, but as humanity fell, our powers diminished."

Rising from his mat near the fire, the yogi said, "Come, there is more to see."

Yogiraj guided Govinda along a corridor leading deeper into the mountain. Other tunnels were connected to the central passageway. At the end of the tunnel, they came to an iron door. Without breaking stride, Yogiraj raised his hand and the door swung open, allowing them to enter a hall roughly half the size of the main cavern.

At the center of the chamber, a five-sided crystal obelisk rose above its amethyst base. The magnificent pillar stood nearly twice Govinda's height. Etched into the pillar's pyramidal crown was the all-seeing eye present on many Tibetan stupas. The cosmic eye symbolized the one who is ever watching over creation and from whom nothing is hidden. Something within the crystal pillar was aware of his presence; Govinda was sure of it.

Around the crystal, a group of yogis sat on grass mats, pearl-colored

The Tale of the Himalayan Yogis

robes draped over their shoulders. Govinda recognized one of the yogis. He had seen the man in Varanasi.

Awestruck, Govinda stared at the arched ceiling overhead. Countless faintly glowing stalactites protruded from the ceiling. Like luminous needles, they emitted a soft, blue light that produced a soothing effect on the body while maintaining a temperature well-suited for meditation.

"These brothers have been in samadhi for almost a moon's turn," whispered Yogiraj after stepping outside the chamber.

As Govinda followed Yogiraj past tunnels leading to unknown destinations, he looked inquiringly at his host.

"Some passages lead to private quarters, others to our temples."

"May I enter the temples?"

"In time."

They returned to the cavern with the Cosmic Flame.

"I see that you have a question," began Yogiraj.

"Why are the Mahatmas always meditating?"

"We meditate for the benefit of the world. The crystal pillar serves as a conduit attracting potent energies that dissolve discord and spread an aura of peace. From this remote ashram, the world is purified. Whatever is required can be radiated from here. No matter how the patient suffers, we offer a cure.

"Men are bound by the fetters of their forging. At present, noxious vapors spread over the earth, inducing a soul-sleep that resists our strongest efforts. When humanity looks away from love, they choose discord and disease, but they cannot survive indefinitely in this condition."

"I don't understand how a crystal can create peace from such a remote place," said Govinda.

"Do not underestimate the power of our assembly of yogis. Unity governs creation. That unity is infinite, becoming many as it transforms into diverse expressions of itself. Its most fundamental expressions are wisdom and love. As the human race evolves, humanity will become wise and loving. As you have seen firsthand, many souls have not yet attained such a state."

"I fought with a few of them," laughed Govinda.

"I'm sure you have. The world is passing through a time when many souls have yet to learn that service to others is superior to service to self; that service to others is service to God. We may be asked to sit on a throne, command an army, serve as a guru, or sit in silence."

"I understand how the role of a king or commander of an army benefits humanity," said Govinda, "but how does a yogi in samadhi benefit humanity?"

"There has been a group meditating here for the past five hundred years. Our monks have the power to silence a storm or prevent a war."

"But how?"

"Universal energies flow into this ashram from dimensions far beyond our time and space. The spiritual bodies of our brothers are well developed. Like magnets, their bodies have two fully enlivened channels, one ascending the spine and the other descending from the crown of the head."

"Kundalini?"

Yogiraj nodded.

"When his subtle energies are perfectly balanced, the yogi enters a state called *nirvikalpa samadhi*. In this state, infinite peace and rapturous bliss result. The yogi becomes as expansive as the universe itself. He sees the stars and planets within the vastness of his own heart. The power of all the sorcerers in Nepal is but a shadow of the power of one who has attained this state."

"When the kundalini rises to the crown of the head, it awakens the yogi's God-Self. From here, the yogi enjoys exalted spiritual states — merging with his beloved Ishta-Deva — a union that radiates wisdom and love to the earth and her inhabitants. The yogi may direct the energies however he wishes so long as it serves others."

"But there is so much suffering and violence and hatred," replied Govinda.

"We are not the only players in the game. I believe Shankar took you on a journey to the seven narakas."

"Are beings like Tadaka also players in the game?" asked Govinda.

"Mankind has been given the gift of free will, but free will becomes a curse on those who deprive others of it. Those who invoke lower beings, use their rituals to spread hatred and fear."

"Your description reminds me of the sorcerer, Kritavat."

Yogiraj sighed. "That one is dear to me."

"But he tried to kill Baba."

"I am aware of everything my chelas do."

"Then you still consider him to be one of you?"

"Kritavat has left us, but he has not left my heart. It is a profound truth that one must have loved greatly to have hated so intensely."

"But I have seen his evil creations. One of them killed my friend."

"But you restored your friend," smiled Yogiraj. "Kritavat would disrupt our mission to prove that darkness is more powerful than light. One day he will awaken from his illusion, and I will be there to serve him."

"But how do you know these things?"

Yogiraj's large, almond eyes flashed. "God's play begins and ends in mystery."

"Baba says you are a thousand times more powerful than any of the other Mahatmas. Is it true?"

"Shankar's devotion makes it difficult for him to be impartial."

"I have a lot to learn."

"Less than you imagine," replied Yogiraj. "To the extent that you are completely in the present moment you are enlightened. If one could be fully in the present, at that moment, he would have full liberation. No thinking about future or past, or what more I can do. To the extent that you can be here, the best future will come, and if you're not fully in the present moment, you'll have a different future. It is to your advantage to be fully in the present for your best future."

"It seems the Mahatmas live in the present."

"A holy atmosphere with one's focus on spirituality, deep meditation, and divine grace, which comes as the result of devotion, are necessary. Divine grace is the final stroke of enlightenment.

"When the period of preparation is complete, mastery dawns. However, a catalyst is required. The last stroke comes from the grace of God, the grace of the master, or the unfolding of your inner consciousness blossoming out into infinity. It can even come in a dream, but one would need to be sleeping in a holy place," smiled Yogiraj.

"Guard your spirituality like the most precious gem. Never allow anything, or anyone, to persuade you to give it up. Don't give in regardless how much pressure is put on you. Moksha won't come if your life contains impurity. In that case, neither God nor guru can do anything for you. It does not mean that you have to be perfect, but it does mean that you try to your best ability to preserve your consciousness and keep your body as pure as you can.

"Liberation means the end of ignorance. We want you in the full power of consciousness, raising you until you realize that you are infinite. We want you to realize that you're the same as we are. We want to remove that which prevents you from perceiving the infinite. That's how we intend to help you.

"Most souls identify with being a man or woman. All that has to go off. Shankar could grant you moksha at any time, but without the experience of growing into enlightenment, it wouldn't be the same. You needed both experience and wisdom… you needed the Moguls and Kritavat and the lamas."

"I have no doubt that Baba has the power to grant moksha, but how does one's Ishta-Deva bestow it?" asked Govinda.

"The avatars and great gurus have taken birth to provide an example, and to teach humanity how to realize their Ishta-Deva. The purpose of a personal god is to give the formless Absolute a form that is perfect. The formless Absolute can't be evolved because there is no difference between the point of no evolution and infinite evolution since the formless Absolute is utterly devoid of everything. On the other hand, Divinity can have relations with every aspect of itself. So, wouldn't it be a better idea to explore Divinity?

"Although being fully attuned to the formless Absolute is ideal as one lives life, the formless Absolute is what you are before beginning your soul cycle. The origin of a soul starts with undifferentiated life energy that emerges from the formless Absolute. The soul forms into a unit that in some way perceives itself as separate from the unbounded Absolute. The soul has individuality and self-awareness. Thus begins the journey.

"With wisdom and experience, your consciousness becomes omniscient while at the same time remaining who you are rather

The Tale of the Himalayan Yogis

than ceasing to exist by merging back into the formless Absolute. Full enlightenment means maintaining your individuality while being omniscient and omnipresent; remaining who you are independent of the formless Absolute. So the ideal would be to move in the direction of becoming Divinity rather than becoming the formless Absolute. Do you understand?"

"I think so," replied Govinda. "You bathe in the stream without becoming water."

"Shankar has taught you well. Be in the water, merge with the formless Absolute in your meditation, but don't revert to being Absolute. Instead, merge with your Ishta-Deva. In your case… Krishna. That is the principle difference between Buddhism and Hinduism. That is why Shankar came for you at Kailash rather than letting you go with the lamas."

"The guru sacrifices a lot for his chela," said Govinda.

"It is nearly impossible to cross the ocean of Maya without the protection of the guru. Now take some rest. Tomorrow, you will receive initiation."

Govinda followed Yogiraj into a chamber with a raised marble platform at its center. On the platform lay a pair of buttery Kashmiri blankets. Sleep arrived the instant he slipped between them.

Soft chants filled Govinda's chamber, causing him to sit up. He searched for the source of the incantation, but he was alone. Sitting on the platform, he noticed a large vessel of water and folded robes which had not been there when he entered the room.

After his bath, Govinda put on the garments, which fit him perfectly. Stepping into the passage outside his chamber, he met Akori, who led him to a room he had not seen before. Inside, Yogiraj sat on a grass mat facing a low altar.

"You slept well?"

Govinda nodded as he entered the room.

"Do you have questions?" asked Yogiraj, gesturing for Govinda to sit beside him.

"I think I understand."

"Then we can begin."

On the altar before them stood a solid gold statue of Krishna.

"Place the Idol's Eye at Krishna's feet."

Govinda removed the gem from its pouch and placed it on the altar.

"Make offerings," instructed Yogiraj, holding up a basket filled with rose petals.

"Now I shall instruct you how to become one with your Ishta-Deva. The process of merging is simple. Let us close our eyes and settle into meditation. Rest your awareness in your heart. Go into your depth and unify your chakras. Breathe into your heart through your chest. Feel yourself becoming one with Krishna. Breathe and merge with him until all limitations lift from within you, and you feel bathed in Krishna's love. It is as simple as a baby feeling its mother's love while being held in her lap. We have all had the experience of merging as infants.

"Allow Krishna's breath to flow into your chakras as if he were playing his flute. There is no limit as to how wide your heart can open. You and Krishna are ONE!"

Govinda's spine straightened as a gentle current coursed the length of his spine.

"Sit with Krishna… merge with him… enjoy his Lila."

Yogiraj rose from his seat and left the room.

At the center of Govinda's inner eye stood a smiling Krishna.

Krishnaji, will you play for me?

Nodding, the divine cowherd held a golden flute to his lips. As Krishna's soft breath flowed through the instrument, Govinda's body thrilled with bliss. With the rise and fall of the melody, rapturous sensations stirred his soul.

A firmament of planets and stars revolved around Krishna. The cowherd's adoring gopis danced about him while a host of beings looked on. The playful Krishna assumed many identical forms and simultaneously danced with each of his gopis. At the center of the Lila, Krishna and his beloved Radha danced hand in hand. When the dance ended, the cowherd's flute fell to his side. Krishna inhaled, drawing the celestial spheres, divine beings, and gopis into his heart. As Krishna inhaled, Govinda's breath stopped, and he was inexplicably drawn into Krishna as well.

The Tale of the Himalayan Yogis

Krishna exhaled a soft, radiant light that spread in all directions. As the light expanded, Govinda became faintly aware of himself again. His form was that of a small, but rapidly expanding ice lingam. The lingam grew and grew, becoming Mount Kailash, perfectly still against the vast Tibetan sky. From Shiva's abode, the maha-mantra, AUM, reverberated silently. Govinda was poised, fully awake within himself, at perfect peace in the infinite expanse.

A hand settled on Govinda's shoulder. His eyes opened to the Krishna murti on the altar.

"How long have I been with Krishna?"

"Since morning," replied Yogiraj.

Govinda pressed his forehead against Krishna's feet and turned to Yogiraj, who was sitting beside him.

"Rare is the yogi who experiences both Krishna and Krishna's breath. Which do you prefer?"

"Krishna," replied Govinda without hesitation.

"Of course, every fiber of your being is woven with the thread of devotion. Did the formless Absolute not appeal to you?"

"I can't say. To be all and nothing… After Krishna exhaled, I saw myself as a lingam. The lingam became Mount Kailash… then everything dissolved into a formless reality."

"Be with Krishna in the coming days. If you should become hungry, think of Akori, and a cup of juice will appear outside the door."

"I have Bhumi Mata's bowl," suggested Govinda.

A knowing smile spread across Yogiraj's face. "Should you require rest, return to your room, but sleep is not needed here. I will send Akori when it is time."

Akori led Govinda into the hall where Yogiraj and a few others sat around the fire.

"Do you know what day it is?" asked Yogiraj.

Having spoken to no one, Govinda shrugged his shoulders.

"Tonight is the anniversary of your meeting Shankar Baba on Kailash."

"Guru Purnima? Then I have been here with Krishna for a full cycle of the moon?"

"In truth, you have been with Krishna forever. But yes, you have been with him since the previous moon."

"I wish Baba were here," said Govinda.

"Every moment with Shankar Baba has been like a bead on your mala. Tonight, I have a surprise for you."

"The flame has changed color again," observed Govinda.

The fire burned yellow-gold with a hint of green.

"The Cosmic Flame anticipates all that we think and do. Tonight, we shall enjoy the wisdom of the guru embodied in the yellow sapphire."

Govinda was admiring the flame when a ball of light attracted his attention. Floating across the room, it hovered near the fire. The form of a yogi coalesced from within the sphere, and a moment later, Shankar Baba stood opposite him.

At the sight of Shankar Baba, Govinda fell at his guru's feet.

"Baba, I couldn't celebrate Guru Purnima without you!"

"I also wanted to be with my guru tonight," said Shankar Baba, bowing to Yogiraj.

"You were in Varanasi. How is it possible that you're here?"

"I've done quite a lot of traveling of late," laughed Shankar Baba. "Have you enjoyed your time with the Mahatmas?"

Govinda nodded enthusiastically. "I shall enjoy it even more now that my guru has joined us."

"I see that you have been with Krishna."

Govinda nodded.

"I asked him to play for me."

"Excellent, but it is always best to be a giver," replied Shankar Baba. "In the future, rather than asking Krishna for something, ask what you can do for him."

"Shankarji is right," interjected Yogiraj.

"Because like me, he also has a great guru," smiled Govinda.

"You do not need a guru now," said Yogiraj.

"Master wishes to talk about the merit of a good and just king," noted Shankar Baba.

"Thank you Shankarji. This wisdom is divinely inspired for the benefit of kings," began Yogiraj. "I shall communicate the words as they appear in the Cosmic Flame."

"Am I destined to be a king?" mused Govinda. "I would rather stay here with the Mahatmas."

"We have plans for you," replied Yogiraj. "Being a raja is the least of what I have in mind for you, but since you are to be a raja, listen carefully.

"Like the lion who rules the animal kingdom, a king must protect his people. A noble ruler must be courageous, majestic, and considerate to the weak."

"My father was all of those things."

"Your father was a just king, and you will be too. A king's worldly duty is to rule well, and that is not an easy task. A king's highest duty is to the gods. His next highest duty is to truth, for the entire world rests on truth. Humility, righteousness, and self-restraint are fundamental to his success.

"A king must care for his people without concern for himself. He must not place too much confidence in anyone. He must conceal his innermost thoughts.

"The people should live in freedom and happiness just as they do in their father's house. The very essence of the king's role is to protect the people. Diverse methods must be employed to do this. Know how and when to use the powers of punishment, and do not hesitate to use them."

"But you said a king must not be too strict."

"I see that you are weighing my words carefully. When a child reaches for the wrong end of a knife, the mother punishes out of love… but punishment should be the last resort. People should be persuaded to act correctly because they understand the benefits of doing so, not because they fear the consequences of not doing so."

"I understand."

"Never fully trust the guardians of the palace. Do things in secret from your enemies. An adversary naturally respects the king who is honored by his subjects. The king cannot be too careful. Wicked people may appear honest, and honest people may appear dishonest.

Even an honest man may become dishonest, for no one is always of the same mind."

Yogiraj fell silent.

"I see the far-reaching influence of your life. And although it will not come overnight, I see the sun rising to dispel the clouds of conflict. I have witnessed the great passages of time. Kali Yuga shall pass… of that I assure you."

"What if I don't succeed?"

"Have the astrologer's words faded from your memory?"

"I haven't forgotten, but conflict grows in my heart," admitted Govinda.

"Conflict is unworthy of you. What is its cause?"

Govinda fixed his eyes on Shankar Baba. "There's no room in my heart for anyone else."

"Your love for your guru is natural, but who was it that taught you to speak, walk, and feed yourself?" asked Yogiraj.

"Mataji."

"Was she not your first guru? And who taught you to handle a sword and ride Kalki?"

"Pitaji."

"Was he not also your guru?"

"But learning to walk and ride are not spiritual lessons. Shankar Baba is my true guru."

"Wandering the Himalaya and meditating in a cave does not define a spiritual life. Had Mataji not taught you to speak truthfully, what chance would there be for spiritual progress?"

"I see."

"Shankar held up a mirror so that you could see your reflection. Through him, you have come to know who you are. The guru teaches through friend and foe alike."

"What can an enemy teach me?"

"An enemy probes one's weaknesses, forcing change from within."

"Then Zaim also served as a guru?"

"What did you learn from him?" asked Yogiraj.

"I learned not to be harbor ill will."

The Tale of the Himalayan Yogis

"Because of Zaim, you befriended Prince Hashim. One day that friendship will prove vital to our cause."

"Must I marry?"

"It is your choice whether you marry or not, but know that Leela's words will also be those of the guru's. When husband and wife live in harmony, that harmony is felt throughout creation.

"There was once a man who yearned for Nirvana above all else. He went without sleep or proper food, believing that austerity would bring him closer to God. His wife grieved to see her husband emaciated, but she did whatever he instructed her to do.

"One day the man left his family in search of a guru. He traveled to many holy places. The man heard about a master who lived in a hut by the Bay of Bengal. He went to the saint and begged him to accept him as a disciple. The wise saint, who was all-seeing, could see that the seeker was sincere.

"The saint said, 'I am not your guru. Your guru resides in the south.' 'Please tell me where' pleaded the man. 'Your guru lives in Nagercoil district.' 'But that is my district,' replied the man. 'That's right,' said the yogi. 'Your guru resides in Ambala village.' 'But that is my village.' 'So it is,' said the saint. "Your guru lives in the house behind the Shiva temple.' 'But that is my house.' 'That is correct,' confirmed the master. 'Please sir, tell me who that person is,' asked the man. 'Your guru is your wife. Return home without delay, for she is waiting to guide you to the divine.'"

"What do you see in the fire?" asked Yogiraj.

Govinda appeared puzzled by what he saw.

"Leela and I have entered a fire, but the flames are not burning us."

"Remember what you have seen tonight. Now, take some rest."

After a night's rest, Govinda was greeted by Chananda, who ushered him into the chamber of the Cosmic Flame where the others assembled around the fire.

"Where is Yogiraj… and Shankar Baba?" asked Govinda.

"Yogiraj will come soon. Shankar Baba has returned to Varanasi. Would you like some juice?"

He had just finished his refreshment when Yogiraj entered the hall, walking hand in hand with a beatific swami about Govinda's age. Govinda had not seen the man before.

Yogiraj spoke with great satisfaction. "Mahesh thanks his brothers for their patience, and for the care they provided during his transformation."

Govinda stared in disbelief at the youthful figure.

Mahesh?

Then the youth spoke. "I am ever grateful. As I lay suspended in the great void, neither alive nor dead, your love restored my body."

Everyone in the chamber marveled at Mahesh's brilliance.

Yogiraj gestured to Chananda, who left the hall.

"We are twice blessed," Yogiraj began. "For Mahesh, who has entered his ageless body, and for Prince Govinda, who is ready to join, or should I say, return to the Mahatmas."

"How is it that I am returning?" asked Govinda, looking at Yogiraj doubtfully.

"In time, you shall remember."

"But I remember my past."

"Our purpose is kept secret until the time is right. Before we reveal the secrets to you, I must ask if you are prepared to continue regardless of what lies ahead."

"You are better able to answer that," replied Govinda.

"Since the fall of the one called Kritavat, I have asked all who would join us if they are ready, for if one fails the result can be dire."

"Then there is a chance that I could fail?"

"Free will is life's greatest gift. The choices we make will determine whether we succeed, or not, just as Kritavat's have. Kritavat is the only Mahatma to have fallen. I hope it will never happen again. We will guide you whenever possible, but ultimately you will determine your fate. Take some time before deciding."

"I require none. I wish to join. If I fail, then I shall face my annihilation."

Chananda returned to the hall carrying a garment similar to those worn by the yogis in the meditation chamber. He handed the robe to Yogiraj and retreated to the side of Deydas Chi.

Unfolding the robes, Yogiraj stepped behind Govinda and placed them over his shoulders. Immediately, Govinda felt a pleasant breeze pass through his body.

"When worn for meditation, this robe has special properties," Yogiraj revealed. "The wearer never grows tired, nor does he suffer from hunger or thirst. But the robe may only be worn within our ashrams."

"But none of you are wearing robes," Govinda observed.

"To put you at ease. But did you not notice our brothers in the meditation chamber?"

"They were all wearing this robe."

"Let us join them."

The group dispersed, reappearing a moment later, having donned robes identical to Govinda's.

Yogiraj led the others to the room with the crystal pillar where eleven mats had been positioned around a twelfth. Yogiraj indicated that Govinda should sit in the centermost spot.

Scanning the room, Govinda observed the yogis who were already deep in meditation. Those who had arrived with Yogiraj joined the others. Govinda was the last to close his eyes, but the pull of his soul was strong. After a few repetitions of his mantra, his mind dissolved into the vast consciousness permeating the chamber.

The passage of time was scarcely recognizable, leaving but the faintest residue in Govinda's mind. During the exalted interlude, his body felt lighter than the robes he wore. When he opened his eyes, the light from the crystals overhead had shifted from blue to gold.

Yogiraj left the hall followed by the others in his inner circle, including Govinda. Returning to the Cosmic Flame, Yogiraj gestured for Govinda to sit beside him.

"The majority of the Mahatmas have been in silence since you and Shankar arrived in Jageshwar," Yogiraj explained.

"Why is that?"

"As you know, there was an attempt to disrupt the gathering. We wanted to ensure that the rite was successful."

"But Kritavat is nothing," protested Govinda. "Baba exposed his plot for everyone to see."

"Kritavat has allied himself with potent forces. His allies nearly match the power that you experienced near the crystal pillar."

"How can that be?"

"Of course his powers are not so great as the forces that work to uplift humanity, but still, do not take his sorcery lightly. As you know, Kritavat was once one of us. He possesses our knowledge and chooses to use it for an immoral purpose."

"I see nothing special in the man."

"Being fearless as you are, I would not expect you to perceive Kritavat as a threat. However, you are unaware of the trouble he caused Shankarji. Had we not intervened, Shankarji would not have returned from the forest."

"Baba had little to say about the forest."

"Shankarji is a true renunciate. Whether immersed in bliss, or on the verge of extinction, he is ever the same."

"Baba possesses greater power than an army of demons."

"Shankarji is rare even among yogis, but you, my son, once possessed powers equal to what you felt near the obelisk."

"But the power near the obelisk is immense," protested Govinda. "There were moments when my body felt light as a leaf."

"Can you say more about it?"

"I paid little attention to it."

"Unknown to you, but not to those in your midst, your body rose from its place, hovering this high above the floor." Yogiraj held his hand out, palm down, at eye level where he sat.

"You mean I floated?" asked Govinda in disbelief.

Yogiraj looked at Akori and Girard for confirmation. The two men nodded.

"I'm sure it was due to the crystal."

Yogiraj smiled as he shook his head.

"Permit me to tell a story," said Yogiraj. "It will help you understand how it is that you are one of us.

"In an age when kings possessed powers equal to the gods, there lived a young king named Raja Aditya, who was dearly loved by his people. Raja Aditya possessed such extraordinary powers that he saw no need for an army, preferring to apply his treasury for the good of

The Tale of the Himalayan Yogis

his people and to honor the sun god, who he worshipped at sunrise each day.

"Hearing that there was a land of vast riches with no army to protect it, a commander from the west invaded Raja Aditya's peaceful kingdom. Arriving at the edge of the capital, the commander sent a messenger to the king's palace and waited for a response. But to his surprise, rather than being received by the king, a boy rode out to meet the commander."

"'Has your king not received my message?' demanded the commander. 'I wish to establish the terms of battle before we attack your city.' The young emissary replied, 'Indeed, the king has received your summons. He wonders if you are aware of his powers, which are of a nature that requires no army to protect his people.' 'So we have heard,' snickered the commander, 'but we do not believe such rumors. Go and inform your king that we shall attack at sunrise. Tell him that Commander Urnadu is insulted that he sends a boy on his behalf.' 'Know that I am not pleased, Commander Urnadu,' answered the handsome youth, 'for you have suffered my people great injury since setting foot in my kingdom.' 'The annoyance of a boy means nothing to me,' replied the commander dismissively. 'Now go and inform your king.'"

"'You fail to understand,' answered the youth, who sat tall on his horse. 'I am the king you wish to inform, and from our conversation, I am satisfied that you and your army are evil-minded. Therefore, leave my country now, or meet your death.' The commander laughed heartily at the youth's bold words, although he was not so dull-witted that he failed to notice an uncanny brilliance in the boy's eyes. 'You are too naive to be a king," scoffed the commander, 'but if by fate you be the king, then gather your soldiers, for we shall attack your city presently.'

"'As I have said, I will not allow you to invade my capital. Tell me who among you have murdered my people and plundered their land.' 'All my men have done this,' replied the commander, waving his sword at his soldiers. 'And enjoyed your women too.' 'A primitive people you are,' replied Aditya. 'For your thoughtlessness, your soldiers shall be punished.' Amused by the audacity of the youth, the commander replied, 'It is you who shall be punished for your insolence. Archers, prepare to execute the boy!'

"A line of archers raised their bows, their arrows trained on Raja Aditya. Anticipating the barrage, Aditya raised his right hand as if it were a shield. Upon command, the marksmen fired, but their arrows failed to reach their target.

"'Have you men lost your skill? Stand closer and fire again,' ordered the commander. In unison, the archers marched forward until they stood but ten paces from the boy. They fired a second round, but once again their arrows fell harmlessly to the ground.

"'Take up your swords, and attack,' ordered the frustrated commander.

"'I think not,' replied the unflappable youth, climbing down from his horse.

"Wave upon wave of soldiers charged at Raja Aditya. Once again the young king held up his hand as if it were a shield. To the astonishment of the commander, as his soldiers rushed to impale the boy, they froze in their steps, their bodies becoming granite statues. Stunned at the sight of his dead soldiers, the commander knew not what to do.

"'My displeasure is great,' said Aditya, 'for your soldiers revel in killing innocent people, mine as well as those of other kingdoms which you have pillaged.'

"Anger born of fear seized Commander Urnadu. Uncertain whether to attack or retreat, the commander's mind betrayed him. Signaling to his infantry, he ordered the army to march on the city.

"As the soldiers moved toward the capital, Raja Aditya uttered a series of mantras. No sooner had he completed his incantation than a sphere of crimson light formed in his hand. Hurtling the ball at the army, it grew in size as it floated in the direction of the soldiers. The massive sphere enveloped the entire army, turning every soldier, horse, and weapon to burnished mahogany. Those on horseback fell from their saddles like puppets severed from their strings.

"Seeing his army destroyed, Commander Urnadu trembled, 'Will you not allow us to leave your kingdom? We have innocent women in our midst.' 'Innocent?' scoffed Aditya. 'I believe not.' 'These women are slaves, which we have captured during our conquests. They have not harmed your people,' replied the commander. 'You speak falsely, Commander. The women are your concubines. They find death amusing and adorn themselves with rubies and pearls stained by brutality. They are hardly innocent.'

"Commander Urnadu knew not what to do. Not only did the young king not need an army; he knew the thoughts and deeds of everyone in his midst. 'What will you do with us?' questioned the commander. 'You and your people shall leave my kingdom and wander barren lands until the last days of your lives,' decreed Aditya. 'But who will enforce this decree?' inquired the commander. 'You are a greater fool than I imagined,' mused Aditya. 'Do you think my powers are limited to the borders of my kingdom? I can know your intentions as easily at a distance as when you stand before me.' 'I don't believe you,' countered the commander.

"'In case you doubt the extent of my power,' replied Aditya, 'I shall engulf the bodies of your dead soldiers in flames, and their remains swept across the land.'

"No sooner had Raja Aditya uttered the edict then a great inferno engulfed the army, reducing the wooden corpses to ashes. A wind arose from the west, scattering the remains across the land.

"'My eyes betray me,' protested the commander. 'Surely this is a trick… a kind of black magic.' 'Call it what you will. Ask your women if they wish to join your soldiers.' 'That is not necessary,' replied the commander. 'We shall abide by your edict.' 'Because of the suffering you have caused, should you attempt to return to your native land, your women will turn to ash as surely as your men have.'

"Hearing the young king's pronouncement, the commander's consort cried out. 'What use have I for this?' she wailed, tossing a gem-studded necklace to the ground. 'Better had you weighed your deeds sooner,' said Aditya. 'Those trinkets are stained by murder. I am but a mirror reflecting your actions back to you.' 'Good king,' feigned the woman, 'can we not atone our sins and return to our homes? What payment demand you for the lives of your people?' 'The seeds of evil bear bitter fruit,' replied Aditya. 'Surely there is something we can do,' pleaded the consort. 'The sentence has been assigned. Know you not your good fortune to escape with your lives? With a wave of my hand, you would all be dust.'

"'Merciful king, we have witnessed your wrath,' pleaded the commander's woman. Thinking the youth desired her, the courtesan employed her charm. 'Have me as your consort, if it pleases you.' 'It does not please me,' retorted Aditya. 'Your offer is poison to my soul. Your self-pity tries my patience.' 'A curse upon your people,' proclaimed the spurned woman. 'I see that you have learned little," replied the king. 'By cursing my people, you curse your own.'

Addressing the commander, Raja Aditya said, 'Have your women place the jewelry they wear on a blanket before me.' The order being more than the commander's women could bear, they hissed like vipers. 'We shall tolerate no more of this,' snarled a consort from her palanquin. 'Until you exorcise your hatred, you have little choice,' advised Aditya. 'Keep your ornaments. However, to purge the cruelty from your hearts, from this moment on, your gems shall be a burden to you.' Before anyone could utter another word against the king, the jewelry adorning the women transformed itself. Shimmering rubies turned to common stone, diamond clusters became lumps of coal, and filigree gold turned to iron so heavy that the women were forced to lower their heads beneath the weight.

"'Until your hearts become chaste, you shall wear your jewels as a prisoner wears iron shackles. Now go, before still darker clouds gather over your future.' Satisfied that the invaders understood their fate, Raja Aditya climbed onto his horse and returned to his palace."

Having listened to the extraordinary account, Govinda asked, "Who was this young king?"

"You don't recall?" asked Yogiraj playfully.

"Recall?"

"You, Govinda, were Raja Aditya, and you ruled the land of five rivers ten thousand years ago."

"If true, there must be a way that I can know that for myself."

"I shall awaken your memory."

Yogiraj pressed his thumb against Govinda's forehead, causing a stream of events to unfold before him as Yogiraj had narrated them.

"Do you not recognize Commander Urnadu?" Yogiraj asked.

"I have no idea who that wicked man was."

"Did he not seem familiar to you? Could he have been Commander Zaim?"

"Impossible!" protested Govinda.

"Is it?" questioned Yogiraj. "Out of ignorance, men repeat their mistakes again and again."

"If indeed I was that king, then I wish to reclaim my powers."

"In time, dear one. Our earth has entered a cycle when such powers are not easily commanded."

"But Baba performs miracles."

"Few yogis possess power greater than your Shankar," Yogiraj agreed. The others in the room nodded. "In the future, great yogis will again walk the earth."

"If indeed I possess the powers you describe, then I shall reduce the entire imperial army to dust this instant."

"I admire your spirit, however, what Raja Aditya did ten thousand years ago is not possible today."

"You have shown me the past, but I want to know the future."

"Doesn't every man? It is easier to look into the past than the future, for the future is not fixed. To an extent, the future can be known from the past, for the inexorable law of attraction brings souls together lifetime after lifetime."

"That's a sobering thought. Then Zaim and I fought because of our pasts."

"It benefits no one to dwell on the past, whether in this life or any other, for the past is a lesser state of the soul."

"Will my karma with Zaim continue?"

"It is finished! Shankarji severed the cord that once bound the two of you. Others are being drawn to your future."

"Like Kritavat."

"Kritavat, yes... but also Leela and Hashim. They too are the result of actions from your past."

"And the Mahatmas?"

"Yes... we too."

"Tell me more about the future, if that is possible."

"Looking deeply into the future may alter it, however four

centuries from now, our world will undergo changes that will render it unrecognizable."

"Must we live with tyranny until then?"

"A few hundred years is not so long, is it Chananda?"

"Hardly more than a good meditation," replied Chananda.

"Some rule by force, but why should the wrong thinking of a few affect the many? Everything in creation influences every other thing. Conditions on earth effect life beyond our planet. Restoring harmony will take time."

"I cannot wait," Govinda replied impatiently.

"Great winds will sweep what remains of the Moguls away long before that time. The time approaches when the world will be restored. The earth will tremble. Mountains will erupt, pouring forth liquid fire and great clouds of smoke. For a time, the sun's light will fail. The seas will rise; tidal waves will wash over the shores. Ash will rain down, and the air will become difficult to breathe. People will despair, thinking the end has come. Demons roaming the earth will be expelled, but they will torment humanity a final time before they depart.

"Mankind will undergo a spiritual quickening as a result of the sun's radiation. When the upheaval passes, peace will prevail. Winds of joy will fill every heart. None will be left out. This I promise you, but to help secure the Golden Age, we have a mission for you."

"So I'm told," smiled Govinda. "I want to know more about this Golden Age."

As Govinda spoke the words Golden Age, the Cosmic Flame doubled in size, becoming a deep violet color.

"The flame approves of your request. No subject gives it greater satisfaction," declared Yogiraj. "Those with violence in their hearts shall perish, victims of their negativity, for evil ultimately destroys itself."

"The way the Emperor died?"

"Like that. Men's actions, good and bad, inevitably return. Those who live harmoniously will feel mysterious winds tickling their hearts. It will happen all over the world, and not just to humans. Animals and plants will feel it too. Great tides of hope, love, and freedom will envelop all of nature. Men will cease making mistakes; they will live agreeably with one another. Animals will have less fear; there will be less fear for everyone."

"It sounds like Sat Yuga."

"Something like that, only greater. The coming time will bring change even to the stars in the night sky. The transformation will be magnificent to behold. The sun and moon will celebrate the moment."

"Will everyone feel it?"

"Everyone! It is the reason why we are here, the reason why I have remained on earth these many centuries. People everywhere will feel the greatest moment of inspiration of their lives… all at once… freedom pouring out the top of their heads… universal love filling their hearts. Everyone will feel it; some more than others depending on their preparation, but all will be uplifted. Every being will feel it. Every grain of sand, every pebble, every tree, and mountain… the sea and its creatures too! Every heart will awaken to the way to live from that moment on."

"It sounds fantastic!"

"The earth will sing. All of nature will hear her sweet note as she awakens from her slumber. Humanity will rise together. A thick veil of ignorance will be removed from the planet."

"As you speak I feel it coming."

"It is destined. The Mahatmas have been assigned the task of ushering in the Golden Age."

Govinda sighed contentedly. He could think of no place where he would rather be than in the company of these yogis.

"Feel the fire in front of you… feel it deeply," instructed Yogiraj. "Fire is the wellspring of a warrior's courage."

"Baba says the fire is a yogi's best friend."

"Have the blessings of the fire before you rest. Place your palms in the flames."

Without hesitating, Govinda reached forward and placed his hands into the center of the fire.

"What do you feel?"

"I feel the immense power of life."

Exile's End

Govinda rose refreshed from his sleep. Wrapped in his blanket, he sat up, unsure whether it was day or night.

Yogiraj was waiting for him near the fire, and he wasted no time in leading Govinda up the carved steps to the restoration chamber.

"Your stay has come to an end," Yogiraj informed his young guest as he ushered Govinda into a room opposite the chamber.

"But I want to stay."

"One day you shall return, but you are needed elsewhere. We shall travel to Varanasi together," Yogiraj continued. "You need only hold the intention to be in Varanasi in your mind, and it shall be. It is best to close your eyes, for the light will be strong."

Closing his eyes, Govinda heard a whirring sound, and his body felt weightless. After what could have been no more than an instant, he heard Yogiraj's voice.

"What better sight than the Ganges?"

Govinda surveyed the cobalt waters cutting a broad swath across the plains. Standing beside him were Shankar Baba and Yogiraj. A yawning banyan tree shaded them from the sun.

"Mind travel is faster than walking," winked Shankar Baba.

"Faster even than Kalki," laughed Govinda.

"Can you feel it?" asked Yogiraj. "Can you feel the oneness of our three hearts?"

The Tale of the Himalayan Yogis

Govinda didn't answer. To be in Siva's city with Yogiraj and Shankar Baba seemed inconceivable.

"We three have been together by the sea, on the banks of holy rivers, by the fire in remote caves, and among the Himalayan forests."

As Yogiraj spoke, Govinda saw three ageless yogis moving along the corridors of time, assuming various roles… Yogiraj always the guide.

"Let us enjoy a dip in Ma Ganga," Shankar Baba suggested.

A suffocating heat bore down on Govinda, slowing his descent to the river's edge. Long-forgotten images of Varanasi flooded his mind as he stood on the banks of the river — Shastriji's ominous predictions, the Moguls pursuing him, Shankar Baba in the cave of cobras, and Leela dancing on the palace roof.

Leela had won his heart, but would he ever see her again, and if he did, would she even recognize him? Govinda stared at his reflection in the water. He had paid little attention to his body over the years. His matted hair and unruly beard reminded him of the unkempt sadhus outside Varanasi's temples. Leela would never recognize him, nor would Mataji, or Ananta, or the people of Krishnagarh. He and Shankar Baba had existed in isolation, beings from another age.

Observing pilgrims making their way to and from the river, Govinda felt strangely self-conscious. He thought of the squat lama who had shaved his head seven years ago; the last time a blade had touched his hair or beard.

Govinda eased his limbs into the dappled current. His body, having grown accustomed to glacial streams, was caressed by the Ganges' tepid waters.

Yogiraj stood beside Govinda, his eyes full of mischief. Disappearing into the river, the yogi surfaced where the current was swift and the channel deep. Circling him, a pod of dolphins darted this way and that.

Standing in the current, Shankar Baba completed his oblation to the sun.

"Yogiraj is like a child. I've watched him play with the dolphins since I was your age. He loves nothing more than to swim with his friends. They always find him."

"Baba, who were the men with Yogiraj?"

"Members of the Mahatmas, but Guruji must have told you that."

"But who exactly are the Mahatmas? Yogiraj said the men are old and from lands unknown to me, but they appear young, and Yogiraj the youngest of all."

"Love ages no man. Out of devotion, the Mahatmas have guided humanity for thousands of years."

Yogiraj emerged from the water.

"Dolphins are like children! They're not burdened by their mind the way thoughts tether men like boats to the shore. Come, let us visit Rohini," he suggested.

Yogiraj nodded as he glided up the monolithic steps leading to the bluffs overhead.

The yogi led Govinda and Shankar Baba past the crumbled foundation of a temple that once overlooked the river.

"Mogul handiwork," said Shankar Baba, pointing to the ruins.

Stopping to purchase mangoes, Yogiraj selected the ripest fruits, but when he offered payment, the vendor waived away the rupees.

"For your sister?" asked the vendor.

Yogiraj nodded and left a mohur on the merchant's makeshift altar. It seemed Yogiraj had plucked the coin from the air.

Yogiraj led the way through the gates of yet another broken shrine.

More Mogul handiwork, mused Govinda.

Signaling for the others to wait, Yogiraj stepped into a secluded garden overlooking the river.

"Baba, have you met Rohini?" asked Govinda.

"A long time ago, Yogiraj decided it was time to return to where he came from, and so he sought his sister's blessing. She asked her brother if it mattered whether he stayed, or departed, to which Yogiraj replied, 'It matters not.' 'Then stay,' advised his sister."

"Is she youthful like Yogiraj?"

Shankar Baba nodded. "The loveliest bloom in the garden."

Yogiraj emerged from the garden.

"My sister has guests with her."

Yogiraj glanced at Govinda, a hint of mischief in his eyes.

The Tale of the Himalayan Yogis

"You may like to have this," he told Govinda, handing him a finely crafted bansari. It was the flute Leela had given him.

"Where did you find this?" he asked, fingering the instrument.

"In the snow."

Yogiraj led his companions past collapsed lintels and crushed icons. Sunlight filtered through a pair of granite columns, lighting a pavilion spared destruction. The yogis entered a garden scented by rose and jasmine bushes.

Three enchanting women sat on a marble bench beneath a shade tree surrounded by flowering bushes. Govinda recognized Rohini immediately. Her youthful radiance rivaled that of her brother. Rohini's calm, lustrous eyes poured forth kindness. Not a wrinkle betrayed her incomprehensible age. Her almond skin was soft and smooth, her posture unassuming. Like Yogiraj, she wore white robes. Her companions dressed in Varanasi's most beautiful silk; one wore a royal blue sari stitched with silver thread, and the other a violet robe embroidered with gold.

At the sight of her brother, Rohini rose to her feet. Taking one another's hands, brother and sister exchanged greetings.

"Bhaiya, who have you brought with you?" Rohini asked in a melodic voice.

"Two Mahatmas."

"Join us. We've been singing."

Rohini spread a blanket on the ground for the newcomers and then handed her brother a bamboo flute.

"And who are your companions?" Yogiraj asked his sister.

"Rajput princesses."

Govinda, whose attention had been on Rohini, shifted to the other women. As Govinda gazed at the winsome princess wearing a blue sari, he noticed the lapis peacock at the end of her necklace. It was the gift he had given Leela before departing for Tibet.

At the sight of the trinket, a Himalayan storm invaded Govinda's chest. He was sure that the young princess with flashing brown eyes and raven hair was Leela. Remembering his bearded reflection, Govinda shrunk back, his heart wilting.

Leela is so beautiful while I am as disheveled as a temple beggar. Maybe she won't recognize me.

Leela glanced at Govinda, but he averted her gaze, fixing his eyes on a boat ferrying pilgrims in the distance. He hoped she wouldn't recognize him. Having lived an ascetic's life, he would need time to grow accustomed to the idea of marrying the spirited girl who had danced away with his heart, for he had long since banished from his mind Shastriji's prediction of marriage.

"Bhaiya, won't you play for us?" asked Rohini.

Yogiraj conjured up a gentle tune. His sister joined him, tapping a clay *mridanga* as she sang. Govinda had never heard a voice so humble, or so sweet as Rohini's. Like a pair of celestial minstrels, brother and sister filled the air with an intoxicating melody.

Yogiraj invited Govinda to play. Raising the flute to his lips, he waited for Yogiraj to resume his melody before joining in.

Leela played *tingsha* bells, glancing from time to time at the yogis. The stately Shankar Baba sat impassively; his eyes closed, his heart wide open. Although distracted by Leela's presence, Govinda played skillfully, the sound of his flute rising above the others.

As the group sang into the evening, a change overcame Govinda. His detachment, the yogi's natural way of life, slowly lifted. At first, he fought the sensation, but as night descended, Govinda stole frequent glances at Leela. Secretly, he played to her, his mendicant's garb unable to veil his feelings.

Leela felt it too. Confused by the yogi's beard, matted locks, and broad shoulders, she failed to recognize the prince she loved. Leela listened to the yogi's flute, probing the notes, which seemed strangely familiar. Whose song was it, and why was it having such a hypnotic effect on her? It went against her nature to sit with music in the air. She would have whirled about the garden had it not been for the yogis in her midst.

Leela's tingsha bells fell silent. Could the young ascetic who played so easily be the Rajput prince who had won her heart? If so, Leela wanted more than anything to run to him, to dance with delight at their reunion, but it was not the place for such celebration.

As the mendicants left the garden, Leela's heart followed them.

"Didi, who is the one who plays so sweetly? My heart knows him."

"Beti," said Rohini tenderly. "Did you not recognize the prince from Krishnagarh?"

"But how can it be? In seven years, I never heard from him… no letter… no news. Word of his capture came; that he was awaiting execution."

"Govinda has been with his guru these many years. Like Ram, your prince has been in exile, but soon he will take the throne. And you shall sit beside him!"

"But he's chosen a renunciate's life."

"Govinda has not chosen a renunciate's life. He went to the mountains to ensure his safety and train as a yogi."

"But Father and I leave for Jodhpur tomorrow."

"Patience, sweet one. We shall arrange everything. That is the gift I offer you today. Leave everything to Yogiraj."

Govinda sat beside Shankar Baba in full view of the burning ghats, watching the Ganges slide past. Yogiraj had inexplicably vanished. The monolithic steps, worn smooth from centuries of coming and going, disappeared into the water. Govinda's lungs labored with the sultry air. After spending seven years where the air was light and fresh, Varanasi was far too smoke-filled and congested. The incessant shuffling of forms to and from the river now haunted him. Distracted by the commotion in the ghats, Govinda wondered if the chaos would ever appear normal again. Years of meditation had refined his senses, and he noticed every passing pilgrim and wisp of smoke rising from the burning bodies.

"In time, you will adjust," offered Shankar Baba. "Varanasi also overwhelmed you when you arrived seven years ago."

"It was such a sweet exile. I expected it to be something to be endured, but it was something to be cherished."

"You have done well."

"I have done little."

"Are you ready?" asked Shankar Baba.

"Ready?"

"To be a king."

"I can't say," replied Govinda.

"Yogiraj described the duties of a king."

"But must I marry?"

Marriage scarcely seemed possible to Govinda after his hermit's life.

"It is time!" Shankar Baba declared.

"But Krishnagarh is no more. I'll be a king without a kingdom. Leela is the pride of Jodhpur. She must have many suitors."

"She is promised to you; she has no interest in suitors. Have you forgotten Shastri's prediction?"

"I haven't forgotten. Seven years in exile…"

"And then…"

"Marriage."

"The time has come."

"Do I have no say in the matter? Have I somehow forfeited my free will?"

"Both destiny and free have roles to play in the drama of one's life. Destiny is the road on which you travel. Free will is the roadside shops you choose to enter along the way. You may stop for chai, buy a mango, or take some rest, but momentary diversions do not alter the course of your life."

"Then destiny is the more powerful of the two?"

Shankar Baba nodded.

"But I want to be with you."

"Yogiraj has promised it. That too is your destiny."

"Yogiraj has vanished. Will you also vanish?" asked Govinda.

"I shall."

"Then who will arrange the marriage? I have no father."

"After leaving you in the tunnel outside the Mahatmas' ashram, I spoke to Raja Rao. He agreed to the marriage seven years ago. He has been informed of your return and intends to honor his agreement."

"And Leela? How did she react?"

"My son, your heart and hers are one. At present, Leela knows that better than you. In previous lives, Leela progressed rapidly on the path; further than you have, in fact. You two have been together

The Tale of the Himalayan Yogis

forever. Did you not feel her devotion in the garden? Was it not as you remembered from the night when she danced on the palace roof?"

"It felt as if we had never been apart."

"Then from where does this doubt arise?"

"It's just that I've been following you all these years. The thought of palace life seems inconceivable after the life we've lived."

"Do not allow your mind to wander from its course. Though the Ganges bends north and south, it moves steadily toward the sea. The river of life twists and turns, but stagnant waters never reach the sea. Your forefathers were royalty."

"My destiny is the same."

"The father arranges everything for the son. Is it not so?"

"That is our tradition."

"In the absence of Raja Chandra, I have arranged your marriage."

"When will the ceremony take place?"

"Raja Rao leaves tomorrow for Jodhpur. Tomorrow, you will ride to Vrindavan to meet Mataji."

"You have arranged all of this?"

"A father's duty… That is why I left you with Yogiraj; someone needed to meet Raja Rao before he departed for Jodhpur."

"Will you attend the wedding?"

"A yogi has no place at a wedding."

"Nor has he a place in arranging a marriage, but a father has a place in both, and you took that place in the arrangements; will you not take the same place at the wedding?"

"I took your father's place in arranging the marriage out of necessity. I shall return to the Himalaya soon."

"Then I shall return too," decided Govinda. "The yogi's life is superior to that of a householder."

"Such talk is not worthy of you. Hear the story of Shukadeva. Under the guidance of his sage father, Shukadeva attained a high spiritual state as a young boy. As a result, he chose the renunciate path and went about without worldly possessions other than his begging bowl and staff. One day, Shukadeva's father sent his son to visit the great philosopher, King Janaka, who lived in a grand marble palace. Upon arriving, the king showed Shukadeva around the palace. Seeing the lavish possessions of the king, who had numerous wives and a treasury of gold, the boy expressed disdain for King Janaka's way of life.

"Janaka, himself a liberated soul, chastised Shukadeva. 'My son, you are more attached to your begging bowl than I am to my wives, palace, and gold.'

"To teach the young ascetic, Janaka instructed the boy to circumambulate the city carrying a bowl filled to the brim with milk. A pair of guards with raised swords accompanied Shukadeva, and if he spilled even a drop, the guards were to cut off his head.

"Shukadeva carried the bowl with great care. After returning to the palace, King Janaka asked him if he had enjoyed the sights of the city. Shukadeva replied, 'I have seen nothing of the city, for the swords of death hung over me.'

"'Excellent,' replied King Janaka. 'This is how one attains Nirvana — through true detachment — the natural state of an enlightened king.'

"So you see, it matters little whether you sleep in a palace, or on the floor of a cave. What matters is the state of your mind."

"But how will I see you if you return to the Himalaya?"

"The guru's true form is light, not flesh."

"But still, I like being at your side."

"One day, we will never part."

Before leading Govinda into the Kala Bhairav temple, Shankar Baba stopped to greet the nagababas inhabiting the cave. The nagas were unimpressive compared to Shankar Baba, who cut an imposing figure with his broad shoulders and tapered waist.

"We shall need your help," Shankar Baba told the ash-covered leader of the nagas.

"We are ready to serve."

"How many nagababas in Varanasi?"

"Nine thousand, but not all have weapons."

"Those without weapons will not be expected to fight. They can serve those with weapons."

The nagababa nodded.

The Tale of the Himalayan Yogis

"I spoke with the nagababas before your return to Varanasi," Shankar Baba explained.

Shankar Baba then led Govinda into the cave of cobras. To Govinda's relief, the cave was empty.

Sunrise came early. As always, Govinda awakened to find Shankar Baba rooted in meditation. When Govinda emerged from the caves, the nagas were bathing in the river. Shankar Baba caught the eye of a young man about Govinda's age with better cared-for hair and beard than most of his kind. The naga was practicing combative techniques with a knife whose edge flashed in the morning light. Shankar Baba summoned the naga.

"Bhaiya, your knife is sharp?" Shankar Baba asked.

The naga nodded, a hint of madness in his smile.

"Cut my chela's hair and beard… but make it nice. Govinda has a wedding to attend."

The naga cut away seven years of growth, leaving Govinda's hair slightly longer than shoulder-length. When the task was complete, Govinda viewed his reflection in the water. It had been years since he had seen his shaven face. He now looked more like how he remembered his father than how he remembered himself. Indeed, he had grown into the very likeness of Raja Chandra.

"This is the second time my hair was cut in Varanasi."

"It was necessary; otherwise, who would recognize you?"

"I'm not sure Leela recognized me in the garden."

"She could not have failed to recognize the music of her flute. Here, put these on." Shankar Baba handed him silk garments. "They were provided by Raja Rao. Your horse is waiting."

After dressing, Shankar Baba led Govinda to the Shiva temple where Mishra was receiving a family of pilgrims. Mishra recognized Govinda immediately.

"Namaste, Govinda!" Pundit Mishra boomed. "The last time you were in Varanasi, the lamas shaved you like a goat. Now you look like the handsome prince that you are."

The bustle in the temple ceased at the word 'Govinda.' A sea of expectant faces vied for a glimpse of the face associated with the name.

Embarrassed, Govinda touched his forehead to the Shiva stone before turning to go. As he slipped out of the temple, Mishra hung a garland on him.

"Your horse is outside," said Shankar Baba.

It was all happening too fast. Govinda's destiny, which he had waited seven years to fulfill, was now upon him.

As Govinda approached the magnificent roan, temple priests lining the path showered him with rose petals.

Govinda dropped to the ground, touching Shankar Baba's feet.

"I am ready, Baba."

"The stallion is a gift from the people of Jodhpur. Raja Rao also wanted you to have this."

Shankar Baba handed Govinda a purse filled with gold.

"The planets have advanced. You have gone from mendicant to monarch in the twinkling of a star."

"I'm humbled," Govinda replied, placing the purse in a saddlebag.

"When you arrive in Vrindavan, purchase saris for Mataji. Her time of austerity is over. Now go with Shiva's blessings!"

"Guruji!" said Govinda, fighting back the tears.

"Ever have I been, ever shall I be," said Shankar Baba, holding Govinda in his arms. "Now go, my son. Your victory is my victory."

Govinda climbed into the saddle and turned the horse. The regal stallion was Kalki's equal in size and strength.

As he rode away, the temple priests called out, "Jai Raja Govinda! Jai Raja Govinda! Jai Raja Govinda!"

Govinda looked over his shoulder for a final glimpse of his guru, but Shankar Baba was already gone.

Kashmir

Emperor Ghazi's health had taken a turn for the worse. Although he refused to acknowledge his declining condition, Ghazi's debilitation troubled Hashim, who suspected that Begum Zahira was once again slipping poison into his brother's cup.

"Ghazi, soon the heat will be insufferable. Let us go to Kashmir. Why not spend the summer on Dal Lake? Mountain air is what you need. Your *hakims* recommend that you get away."

"It's true," Ghazi admitted. "I haven't been well these past moons. I'll meet with the generals and arrange for them to look after things in my absence."

"Kashmir was our last holiday with Maji," recalled Hashim.

"If the generals agree, then we'll depart in ten days. But I don't want a battalion marching with me into the Himalaya. I'll invite my favorites from the harem; you arrange for the cooks and servants. A handful of guards should be sufficient."

"We can enlist Kashmiri soldiers, if necessary."

Hashim hoped that Ghazi would leave his women behind. As long as his bibis were with him, it would be difficult to keep him from his opium. But still, the prospect of being away from Delhi was encouraging.

With the arrival of Summer, the capital had become an inferno. Sleep, the population's sole escape from the oppressive heat, came fitfully.

When the mullahs issued the Black Seal calling for Hashim murder, friends of his grandfather took the prince to a canyon retreat outside Delhi where he lived with a small group of Sufis. After two years, the Black Seal was withdrawn, and Hashim moved into Uncle Lufti's haveli.

"Ghazi needs to get away from Delhi almost as much as you do," Lufti said.

"Won't you join us?" offered Hashim.

"Someone needs to keep an eye on the throne in your absence."

"But it's insanely hot," complained Hashim.

"I am fond of sleeping under the amlaki tree in the courtyard. This summer will be no different."

The young son of Lufti's head servant appeared suddenly on the veranda.

"Sir, *videshi*," the boy informed his employer.

"But I'm not expecting a foreigner," replied Lufti.

Hashim opened the door to find Santiago standing at the entrance.

"Santiago, it is good to see you. Come in; you must be hot and tired."

Hashim led his friend to the veranda. Shaded by bamboo awnings, Hashim and Santiago reclined on cushions.

"In a few days, Ghazi and I will go to Kashmir. My brother's health is failing. The mountains will be good for him. Won't you come along?"

"Thank you for the offer, but I am here on a mission of sorts. When the viceroy learned that I had connections with the Emperor, he asked me to establish trade relations with Delhi. I thought you might be able to help."

"What does the viceroy have in mind?"

"We Portuguese trade the finest horses in Asia. The viceroy thought the Emperor might like some."

"What breed of horses?"

"Arabians," replied Santiago.

"I'm certain the generals will purchase as many Arabians as the viceroy can provide. Consider your mission accomplished. Now, will you join us in Kashmir?"

"I'd like that."

"Then it is set... a holiday in the Himalaya with friends."

Though exhausting, the journey to Kashmir brought Ghazi relief from the relentless pressures of the throne. Upon arriving at the exquisitely carved Lotus Palace, Ghazi retreated to his apartments with his favorites from the harem.

The Lotus Palace stood on the shores of Dal Lake at the heart of a *chinar* forest. Two thousand soldiers camped nearby, a concession Ghazi made to his generals before departing Delhi. The prospect of filling their stables with Arabian horses had put the generals in an agreeable mood.

Hashim was powerless to interest Ghazi in the sights around Srinagar, the historic capital of the region. Consequently, Hashim and Santiago spent their days visiting the many shrines, gardens, and mosques lining the lake. As Hashim and Santiago walked the narrow cobblestone streets, an elfin, spectacled old man followed at a distance. The fellow wore a brown vest and grey salwar kameez; a green *fez* perched precariously atop his head.

"I am Professor Kamur," the man chirped. "Before my retirement, I taught history at the *madrasa*."

"This is Prince Hashim," replied Santiago before Hashim could stop him —Hashim's identity was a dangerously high-profile one— "and I am Santiago, a Jesuit priest."

Santiago extended his hand to the elderly professor.

"Friends, allow me to show you a place of interest to Europeans — especially a priest."

"And what place would that be?" Hashim asked, thinking he knew every place of interest in the old capital.

"The tomb of the man called Yusef," replied the professor.

"Yusef?" questioned Hashim.

"Your friend knows the story of Yusef. He is known to Europeans as Jesus of Nazareth."

"But Jesus's tomb is in Jerusalem," replied Santiago skeptically.

"Maybe. Our ancestors claim that Jesus of Nazareth lived in Kashmir and Tibet. I will show you. The tomb is not far from here."

Hashim looked questioningly at Santiago, allowing the padre to decide whether they would follow the professor.

"Let us see," Santiago decided, not wanting to hurt the kindly man's feelings.

The professor led Hashim and Santiago through a labyrinth of alleys before they reached a solitary tomb in a district called, Rozabal. The vault consisted of an inscribed slab of stone shaded by a weather-beaten roof.

"Tell us why this tomb is special," requested Hashim.

"Our ancestors claim that a prophet of fair complexion healed our sick and taught of God."

"The tomb must be that of another man," decided Santiago.

"Our legends say that Yusef married and raised a family in this valley."

"But that's an insane idea," countered Hashim.

"What proof can you offer?" asked Santiago.

"The tomb is aligned east and west."

"What is so remarkable about that?" asked Hashim.

"Muslim tombs face north and south."

"But any number of foreigners could have been buried here," Hashim pointed out.

"I don't think so," countered the professor.

"Many Kashmiris are of fair complexion. Some even have blue eyes. Surely a yogi could have come down from the hills and healed the sick," argued Hashim.

"If you like, I will take you to meet a yogi who knows a good deal about Yusef."

"Where is this man?" Santiago asked.

"He lives there." Professor Kamur pointed to the hills above the city.

"Can we meet this yogi in the morning?" asked Hashim, who was more interested in the enchanting views than the yogi.

Professor Kamur nodded. "I'll meet you at the flower bazaar near the dock."

"We shall be there."

The Tale of the Himalayan Yogis

Professor Kamur nodded respectfully and headed off to a nearby chai shop.

"What do you think?" asked Hashim.

"I am skeptical," said Santiago. "It is true that almost half of Jesus's life remains a mystery, but I don't think this yogi will come to much. However, having never met one, I am curious."

"The views are superb. It will not be a wasted trip."

The following morning, Hashim and Santiago met the professor at the market near the dock. Having procured horses, they made their way to the yogi's abode on the mountain.

"I have met the yogi a few times," Professor Kamur acknowledged. "He keeps to himself, but if we are lucky, he will invite us inside."

Arriving at a tiny stone hut at the base of a rock outcropping, the men climbed down from their horses. The yogi must have heard the horses because he was standing at the entrance to his dwelling as Professor Kamur approached. The greying recluse appeared to be both gentle and sprightly.

"Namaste!" the yogi greeted his visitors.

"Namaskar, Swamiji!" Professor Kamur replied. "I have brought two travelers."

"You wish to know about Issa, the one called Jesus," said the yogi, directing his words to Santiago.

"That's right," confirmed the professor. "Santiago is a Christian priest. His friend, Hashim, is a prince from Delhi."

"Professor Kamur claims that Jesus lived in Kashmir and Tibet," began Santiago.

"Come inside. We must not discuss profound matters here by the horses."

The yogi led his guests into his hut, which could scarcely accommodate four men. Professor Kamur sat on the threshold of the cramped abode. The yogi's trident, a symbol of renunciation, rested against the wall near the entrance to the hut.

The yogi spread a threadbare blanket for his guests.

"The professor is correct," confirmed the yogi. "The sage known as Jesus came to India as a youth and lived in these mountains where he was known as Issa. Issa was the disciple of an ageless yogi, who initiated him into our ancient practices. Later, Issa lived in a cave on the banks of the Ganges where he perfected his mind through long meditation."

"I find this difficult," replied Santiago.

"That is understandable," the yogi said. "Your priests taught you otherwise, but our sacred book records the account of Issa's life. You will find similar accounts in a Tibetan monastery where lamas also recorded the life of your beloved master."

"But the life of Christ is no mystery," Santiago countered. "Matthew... Mark... Luke... John... all recorded his life's story; and rather well, I might add."

"Do they not agree that Christ left his home as a youth, and that no one knew where he lived, or what he did during the missing years?" the yogi asked.

"Everyone agrees there is a gap in time," conceded Santiago.

"That gap includes much of Issa's life."

"But how could Jesus be buried here when he died on the cross?"

The yogi was silent for a moment.

"Your Jesus did not die on the cross."

"That's outrageous," objected Santiago, shaking his head.

"Crucifixion was a common practice of the time. The image of a crucified savior is in no way inspiring, or spiritual. Fortunately, your savior survived his crucifixion."

"But Jesus died for our sins."

"Then you must examine your beliefs."

Seeing Santiago's anguished face, Professor Kamur spoke. "The Tibetan manuscripts speak of a Dalai Lama from the west named Issa who lived in India and Tibet. The manuscripts say that Issa healed the sick, but fell out of favor with the Brahmins because he taught low caste Hindus."

"The Buddhist records are correct," the yogi stated matter-of-factly.

"I must pray about this," replied Santiago.

The yogi stared intently into Santiago's eyes. "My friend, the conflict you feel is unjustified."

"Of course it's justified," interjected Hashim. "You have cast a shadow over a devout man's faith."

The Tale of the Himalayan Yogis

"I speak not of things said today. The deed was necessary. You will find peace in Tibet. That is all I have to say."

"We should go now," said the professor, stepping away from the entrance.

The unexpected assault occurred with such swiftness that there was little time to react. As Hashim and Santiago turned to go, the yogi lurched toward the door, jostling his guests in the process. Raising his trident, the yogi jabbed Hashim in the chest. The weapon tore through Hashim's tunic and skin, drawing blood. Then, the yogi jabbed him a second time.

Taken by surprise, Hashim reacted after the second thrust. Flinging himself out the door, he lost his balance, and would have fallen had he not collided with his horse. The horse whinnied nervously and shied away, dropping Hashim to the ground. Hashim was back on his feet immediately, struggling to breathe, his eyes sweeping the surroundings for additional threats, his reflexes stringing themselves tightly as cinched rope, ready to mount his horse and gallop away, or fight to save Santiago, if necessary. Then he noticed the impish look on the yogi's face – the yogi, who had made no move to continue his attack – the yogi, who sat down and calmly wiped the drops of blood from the tines of his iron trident.

Examining his wounds, Hashim saw that they were minor. His breathing calmed.

"What have you done?" demanded Professor Kamur indignantly.

"I have spared him the fate of his father," the yogi stated blandly. "I stabbed him a second time for his brother's sake."

"But you've hurt him," protested the professor, wrestling the trident away from the yogi.

"Would it be better that he should die?"

Unwilling to turn their backs on the volatile yogi, Hashim and Santiago stepped backward to their horses. The professor followed. From the entrance to his hut, the yogi watched the men climb onto their horses and descend the path through the forest.

"My sincere apologies," stammered Professor Kamur as they rode off. "These yogis are a strange lot. One moment they're friendly, and the next moment they're stabbing innocent people."

"He meant no harm," Hashim heard himself say, unsure of the truth of his words.

"But you're bleeding."

"I wonder why he called you 'crown prince,' and why he assumed I was going to Tibet," pondered Santiago, ignoring the professor's protests.

"There's a reason why these yogis live alone," sputtered the professor, ignoring Santiago in turn. "They lack social grace."

Professor Kamur regretted having brought the visitors to the yogi.

"Professor, where exactly is this Tibetan document of which you spoke?" asked Santiago.

"Nechung Gompa in western Tibet."

"Is it far from here?"

"If one does not meet with an untimely death at the hands of bandits, or encounter crazed yogis, the journey takes twelve days. Caravans travel to and from Tibet regularly. They stop at Nechung Gompa on their way to Lhasa."

"Where can I meet these people?"

"Make inquiries at Darwaza Bazaar."

Hashim had already forgotten about his wound.

"How was that for an unlikely lesson in Christian history?" he jested.

"It all sounds far-fetched, but the Tibetan manuscript intrigues me. I have always wondered about the missing years," replied Santiago.

"You think the yogi's words had merit?" asked Hashim.

"I can't say."

"Are you thinking of visiting this monastery?"

"I wonder what worn-out beliefs might die if I do," mused Santiago.

"More than your beliefs might die," chuckled the affable professor.

"Let's stop for dried fruit and *bakirkhanis* for Ghazi," Hashim suggested. "Day by day, he grows stronger, though I wish he would join us."

They reached the crowded market. After returning the horses, Hashim slipped a coin into the professor's hand before following the scent of freshly baked bread.

The Tale of the Himalayan Yogis

The friends strolled along quaint cobblestone lanes, inhaling pungent spices, frankincense, and cedar smoke. Vendors vied for their attention, but the pair continued past a row of stone and timber houses until they reached a bazaar piled high with burnished copper, ivory handled samovars, enameled hookahs, and aromatic tobacco blended with molasses. Images of the Buddha stood near symbols of Islam everywhere in Srinagar.

After purchasing fruit, Hashim suggested, "I know a shopkeeper who makes the best chai. His shop is just ahead."

"Prince Hashim Shah!" bellowed the chai walla from beneath a striped fez that seemed better suited for the boy at his side. "Your father great emperor! I have heartache from the news."

"Thank you," said Hashim, grimacing as the chai walla announced his presence. "It happened a long time ago."

"The Emperor's handsome face still makes fresh memory," said the chai walla, gesturing for Hashim and Santiago to sit at his table. "You come for special chai? Emperor's favorite I make for you. And who is your friend?"

"Santiago is from Portugal," replied Hashim.

"You like our heavenly valley?" the chai walla inquired.

"The peaks are more magnificent than anything I have ever seen. Kashmiri sunsets are even more beautiful than those of the Mediterranean."

"Kashmir is my heaven," the chai walla sighed. "This is where I wish to die."

"But you are a young man," teased Santiago.

"Not so young. Whole life I live in Srinagar. I make chai since I am boy."

"Do you know of the tomb in Rozabal and the story of Issa?" Hashim asked the chai walla.

"Everyone knows this place... and this tale."

"Do you believe Christ is buried there?" Hashim inquired.

"I not believe," the chai walla declared adamantly.

"Why is that?" Santiago asked.

"I believe Yusef of Bethlehem live here. My people tell many stories," the chai walla said, "but this not Yusef tomb."

"Then who is buried there?" Santiago questioned.

"I cannot say."

"Which shop has the best bakirkhanis?" inquired Hashim, who had heard enough talk of the tomb.

"Fahid," the chai walla replied. "Fat man with small fez. Next row of shops. Fahid make best bread in Srinagar. He ask high price, but he sell for less. I hear your brother is with you."

"How did you know?" Hashim asked anxiously.

"I am chai walla. I hear everything. Men talking last night about Emperor of Delhi."

"Describe the men," said Hashim.

"Afghan soldier."

"Are you certain?"

"Everyone know Afghan soldier... big swagger... long sword... drink chaang... talk loud."

"No one is supposed to know that Ghazi is here."

"What are you thinking?"

"Do you recall the yogi's words after he poked me with his trident?"

"He said he poked you a second time for your brother."

"I'm not sure the yogi was crazy."

"I agree," said Santiago. "He knew something about me that only one man knows."

"What is that?"

The yogi's words had occupied Santiago's mind since the visit.

"I betrayed him."

"Betrayed who?" asked Hashim.

"Jesus!"

"But you would never betray your Jesus!"

"I committed the greatest sin," said Santiago, his head slumping. "What I did cannot be forgiven."

Hashim looked questioningly at his friend. "What could you have done that was so terrible?"

"Father Valente knows. You will be the second."

"I shall tell no one," promised Hashim.

"We Portuguese have been as ruthless as Uzbek Khan."

"In what way?"

"The executions... I fled Goa because of them."

"What executions?"

"The Goan Inquisition. I murdered the Grand Inquisitor in God's house."

"Speak plainly, Santiago."

"The man responsible for the execution of Goan villagers is called the Grand Inquisitor. His name was Diego Rodriguez. One evening, I was hearing confessions when a Portuguese soldier entered the stall. He asked forgiveness for burning a fishing village. Despite the fact that he was ordered to do it, guilt tormented the man. Diego Rodriguez had issued the orders."

"Why was he ordered to burn the village?"

"Apparently, the villagers refused to convert."

"That's all?"

"When I heard the soldier's confession, I was furious. The soldier claimed that three children had died. As time passed, the story repeated itself. Other soldiers came. I saw the terror on the faces of the Goans. I realized that I too was responsible for the deaths of the villagers, for Rodriguez and his men were acting on behalf of the church."

"What did you do?"

"After comforting a village woman who had survived the slaughter of her family, I came up with a plan. In my religion, there is a sacrament called Holy Communion."

"I have read about it; priests serve the people wine."

"On Easter Sunday, I murdered the Grand Inquisitor."

"How?"

"I poisoned the wine in his communion cup."

"A bold thing to do."

"A cowardly act," admitted Santiago. "Had I the courage, I could have taken the Grand Inquisitor's life any number of times, but I waited for a time when no one would suspect me."

"What is wrong in that?"

"As you can see, I am confused."

"Confusion ill befits a pure soul like you."

"I am no better than the Grand Inquisitor."

"But you are, my friend."

"Listen to the whole story and then decide. After receiving communion wine, Rodriguez was sitting beside the altar when he began to convulse. He tried to stand, fell to the floor, and pulled the altar cloth onto himself. Everything fell from the altar... the Bible... communion plates... Eucharist cups... The candles spilled on him, and his clothes caught fire. He screamed, but I made no effort to help him. Instead, I retrieved the Bible. Rodriguez reached for my robe. I knelt and crossed him, but made no effort to douse the flames. By then, others had reached the altar. But it was too late. Rodriguez was dead."

"Did anyone suspect what had happened?"

"Rodriguez knew what I had done. Everyone else assumed that he had suffered a heart attack."

"You said Father Valente also knows."

"Father Valente is the Cardinal of the Church of Goa. He listened to my confession, which is a private matter between priest and parishioner. He absolved me of my sin. When the opportunity arose, he transferred me to Vijayanagar."

"Considering Rodriguez' cruelty, why do you feel your sin is unpardonable?"

"Holy Communion is our most sacred ritual. During the sacrament, the priest is the servant of the Lord himself."

"Are you so sure you have not acted on behalf of the Lord?"

Santiago paused to consider his friend's interpretation of the story.

"We are taught that the Lord forgives regardless of the sin."

"Then that applies to you as well. I too have witnessed the cruelty of men like Rodriguez. I blamed my religion for their behavior, but now I see that it is the man that errs, not the religion."

"Both share in the responsibility; I am sure of it."

"Santiago, you are too severe. If you show no compassion toward yourself, can it be there for others?"

"I no longer know what to believe."

"I asked myself the same question about Islam. Perhaps you will find answers in Tibet. The Buddhists are a compassionate people. Come, we must not miss sunset on the lake."

Ornately carved *shikaras* lined the lakefront, waiting to ferry locals to and from the bazaar. Hashim chose a boat manned by a pair of sinewy boatmen who easily propelled the craft across the lake's turquoise surface. A soft radiance pervaded the water as the ferry glided past white lotuses seated like queens on emerald thrones. As daylight waned, the lake morphed from turquoise to magenta, and with the fading light, a mystical calm descended over the valley.

Hashim's anxiety vanished as twilight touched his soul. Sunset was the time when fakirs meditated at lakeside shrines, and ascetics turned inward on the mountains above Dal Lake.

A snake worshipper sprinkled flower petals on a floating lamp, offerings meant to propitiate the serpent deity believed by some to rule Dal Lake. From a mosque at water's edge, a muezzin's sonorous call spread across the placid lake. Everything about Kashmir beckoned its residents to a place of inner peace.

"I never thought any place could be more beautiful than the Algarve coast," said Santiago, gazing wistfully at the violet peaks overhead. "The air here has a sanctity about it. The peaks are cathedrals, the lake a suitable place for baptism. One could ask little more of heaven."

"Tomorrow we'll visit the Mogul gardens and stop at my mother's favorite shrine. I hope Ghazi will join us," said Hashim, the tranquil surroundings having driven the threat of Afghans from his mind.

"A peace pervades this valley that I thought only existed by the sea."

"My mother loved Kashmir, not only for its beauty but because the people honor one another's religion. Kashmiris call it *trikasastra* — a blend of Islam, Hinduism, and Buddhism."

At the palace mooring, a canopied shikara lined with Kashmiri carpets and silk pillows awaited Ghazi's women. A second boat pulled up alongside; the smaller shikara would ferry Ghazi and his friends. One by one, Ghazi's consorts stepped onto their boat. Wrapped in *shatush* shawls and embroidered silks, the women seated themselves according to rank.

Side by side, the ferries plied the tranquil waters, gliding noiselessly over Dal Lake's glassy surface in the direction of the Mogul gardens.

Ghazi's concubines would picnic in the gardens while Ghazi, Hashim, and Santiago visited a Kashmiri saint's shrine.

A passing shikara disrupted the dreamy reflections of the peaks, but when the water settled, the masterpieces of light and color reappeared.

"Hashim, why haven't you taken me on the lake until now? I feel better this morning than I have in a long time."

"I tried, brother," Hashim said truthfully, "but when you're with your women, you can't be bothered with fresh air."

"This paradise beggars my women. I no longer care to look at them, having set my eyes on the magnificence about us."

"I'll remind you of your newfound conviction tonight," teased Hashim.

"Are you rogues taking me to an opium den?" joked Ghazi.

"First stop is Lal Ded's shrine, then on to Hazratbal."

"Religion again," complained Ghazi. "I'll get down at the gardens with my harem."

"You can't," taunted Hashim. "You've been kidnapped. We'll stop for *khawa* and *kulcha* after we visit the shrines."

"Have you tasted khawa chai?" Ghazi asked Santiago, acquiescing to his brother's plans.

"Not yet."

"A suitable drink for this paradise."

The concubines' shikara moored at the gardens while Ghazi's boat continued toward the bazaar. Santiago watched the bevy of lithesome women climb down from the ferry, accompanied by a team of hulking eunuchs.

"The Buddhist ruler, Ashok, built Srinagar," said Ghazi, ignoring his harem in favor of recounting his history lessons. "When the Sufis fled Persia, many ended up in Kashmir. Buddhist culture influenced the early Sufis."

"It is obvious why they were attracted to this place," said Santiago. "Dal Lake itself is a mystical experience."

"The valley inspires reverence," agreed Hashim as their shikara moored. "Come; we get down here."

Throughout Srinagar, cone-shaped fez topped the heads of men and boys, their brown *kaftans* covering all but their feet. The maze of constricted passages grew still more congested as the Emperor and his friends approached the shrine of the saint Kashmiris had adopted as their collective mother. The murmur of prayer wafted about a flower-strewn crypt beneath a forest green canopy.

"Ghazi has found his faith," Hashim joked as the twins exited the historic shrine. "He wants to visit all the Sufi shrines."

"Maybe this man will take you," Santiago suggested, pointing to an amiable-looking guide.

"I am honored," replied the rotund fellow with a cropped beard and kindly eyes.

"Take us to all the Sufi shrines," Ghazi ordered.

"That will require the remainder of the day."

"Then let us begin," said Hashim.

"I shall seek out the Tibetans and meet you at the palace," said Santiago.

"Don't start back too late," advised Hashim. "The lake is at its best at sunset."

Santiago headed off in search of a Tibetan caravan.

Pastel shades of light danced on the lake. Santiago stared absentmindedly at the play of contour and color, his mind preoccupied with thoughts of Tibet as his ferry glided across the water. The jarring sound of an explosion disrupted Santiago's peaceful reverie. Anguished cries filled the air, shattering the twilight calm.

The boatman pointed his oar at a ball of fire in the distance.

"What is it?" asked Santiago, uprooted from his trance.

"Boat on fire," said the boatman from the prow. Four shikaras were clustered together; two were in flames.

"Faster."

"Harem shikara," said the boatman as he increased the pace.

"Are you sure?" asked Santiago apprehensively.

"Harem shikara biggest on lake."

Grabbing a long-handled oar that lay at the boatman's feet, Santiago rowed feverishly. As his ferry approached the harem's boat, heads bobbed, and arms flailed in the churning water. From two smaller shikaras, assailants released arrows at the struggling bodies. One by one, the flailing stopped. More anguished cries followed another volley.

A whistling projectile struck Santiago's boatman in the neck. Staggered by the wound, the man dropped his oar. The boatman was about to topple into the water when Santiago grabbed his arm. A second arrow whizzed past, and then another, and another.

Santiago laid the boatman on the deck. The man gasped for air, choking on the blood filling his throat. Crouching beside him, Santiago guided the boat with the oar while assessing the scene of the attack. He recognized the second burning shikara as the Emperor's, but where were Hashim and Ghazi? He was now close enough to see the faces of the men who were releasing arrows as rapidly as they could position them. The words 'Afghan soldiers' stung his mind.

The Afghans' boats moved away from Santiago's, circling to the other side of the harem's ferry to ensure that there were no survivors. The attackers had stopped firing at Santiago.

The cries of drowning victims ceased; the barrage of arrows stopped.

Santiago maneuvered his boat alongside the Emperor's shikara. Climbing aboard, he stepped over burning rugs as he searched for his friends. Santiago spotted the body of a eunuch floating face down alongside the boat.

Their mission accomplished, the assassins retreated.

"Hashim! Ghazi!" shouted Santiago.

There was no reply.

Having searched the Emperor's shikara, Santiago climbed back into his boat and paddled toward the far side of the burning ferry. There, he spotted a familiar figure in the water. Confident the body was that of either Hashim or Ghazi; the padre plunged headlong into the water.

"Hashim?" yelled Santiago, swallowing water.

There was no reply.

Santiago pulled the body into the shikara. The body bore a ghastly wound to the stomach. Scrutinizing the wet clothing, he hoped to identify the body, but the twins had been wearing similar tunics. As he rowed toward the palace, he searched for signs of life, but the body lay lifeless on the boat's deck. Santiago arrived at the palace, not knowing who he had pulled from the water, or whether he was alive.

The Wedding

What is your name, fine horse? Govinda asked.

Sinha of Jodhpur, the horse replied, his thoughts effortlessly communicated.

Sinha of Jodhpur, what heroic deeds have you done?

My daring depends on my master. With you as my master, I am fearless.

Then the name 'Sinha of Jodhpur' shall be known in all the land, for great conquests lie ahead. But first, we cross the river and head south.

As he journeyed to Vrindavan, Govinda's heart ebbed and flowed, swelling at the thought of seeing his mother and despairing that he might not see his guru again.

On the fifth day, he arrived in Vrindavan, the city of Krishna's childhood. After bathing in the Yamuna, Govinda purchased pashmina shawls and silk saris before beginning his search for Mataji. At temple after temple, he inquired into the whereabouts of his mother. After discharging a mouthful of pan masala, a red-lipped pujari directed him to Krishna's garden near the river. Monkeys ruled the grounds, assessing trespassers entrance fees from the limbs of a *bakul* tree near the gated entry.

Govinda spotted a solitary figure clad in white cotton sitting in an open-air shrine amidst the pruned tulsi bushes that spread like a jade blanket over the grounds. Dismounting, he moved silently toward the figure. Sensing someone, the woman turned as Govinda reached the top step of the shrine. It was indeed Rukmini. Standing, she looked at Govinda with familiarity, but not full recognition.

She's looking at me the way she looked at Pitaji, Govinda realized. *It's been seven years; I do look more like Pitaji than my younger self.*

Then the realization hit her. Rukmini's eyes shone brighter than ever before, and she ran to her son, falling into his arms as he quickly set down his gifts and hoisted her into the air. The two spun in a circle, tears wetting their clothes.

"It has been too long," she sobbed. "I had begun to doubt that I would ever see you again."

"I would have come sooner, Maa," Govinda said, holding his mother close to his heart, "but they forbade me."

"Who forbade you?"

"The astrologer... and my guru."

"How you've grown. You look so much like Pitaji on the day we were married."

"I have been searching for you all morning. I should have known you would be in Krishna's garden."

"I asked Krishna to keep you safe."

"He has, Maa. Again and again, Krishna saved me."

"I made him promise."

"He kept his promise."

"Ananta brought news of your exile, but I have heard nothing since. Where have you been all these years? You must tell me everything."

He didn't quite tell her everything – he excluded, or understated, the more dangerous events of the past seven years of his life so as not to unnecessarily worry her – but the morning had become afternoon by the time he neared the end of his story. Rarely did he get more than a sentence out before Rukmini interrupted him with a question or a comment. He showed her Bhumi Mata's bowl and demonstrated its powers. It was late afternoon, and they were both hungry, so he materialized a meal for them.

After eating, Govinda continued with the telling of his tale. He tried to conceal his dejection at being separated from Shankar Baba but failed.

"You miss him, don't you," sensed Rukmini, running her hand across Govinda's cheek.

"Almost as much as I missed you."

"More, I think."

"Baba told me that even though he and I would be apart, his wisdom would come to me through others."

"Has that been the case?"

"It has only been a few days, but yes, I think it's true. Baba said that you and Pitaji were my first gurus."

"According to the *shastras*, that is true."

Govinda continued his account until he reached the subject of his impending marriage.

"You don't seem happy with the idea," Rukmini observed.

"I'm not."

"Krishna married."

"I want to be with my guru… and Yogiraj… and the Mahatmas. If you met them, you'd understand."

"When you left me, you were just a boy. But you've grown to be a great yogi. I can see the change in your eyes."

"But I'm not a yogi. Shankar Baba and Yogiraj are yogis. They neither sleep nor eat. They can seemingly do anything they wish."

"And you can't?" asked Rukmini

"Guruji instructed me to take you to Bundi to prepare for the wedding. These are for you."

He held up the stack of garments he had purchased in the bazaar.

"I'll need some fresh things if I'm to be the mother of a king," agreed Rukmini.

"Our days of solitude are over, Maa."

"I never felt alone. Krishna was always with me. I never stopped thinking of you."

"Tomorrow we shall depart for Bundi."

"It will be good to see Father."

"And Ananta and Ravi and Kamala," added Govinda.

"And all of our friends from Krishnagarh."

The unexpected arrival of Govinda and Rani Rukmini sparked a renewed spirit in the former residents of Krishnagarh. The news of

Govinda's marriage was cause for celebration. Although the wedding would take place on Mount Abu, a distant mountain named after the serpent, Arbuda, the entire community joined in preparations for the grand event.

Rana Yogesh hired masters to train Govinda in swordsmanship, archery, and how to handle a knife. He had been trained in all of these, especially swordsmanship and archery from the earliest possible age, but years without practice had eroded his skills. Ravi, on the other hand, had become obsessed with weapons since the siege of Krishnagarh. In Govinda's absence, Ravi had become far more skilled in the art of war than his cousin. Now they honed their skills together, although Govinda knew that no amount of training would be sufficient to overcome the insurmountable odds he would face in the not too distant future.

News of Govinda's return spread as far as the mud fortresses of Jaisalmer and Pushkar to the west, bringing ambivalent reactions from the Rajput kings. The Krishnagarh prince's disappearance had resulted in seven years of relative peace, and more than a few rajas believed that Govinda's return would rekindle Mogul aggression. Govinda couldn't help believing the same.

A messenger from Jodhpur arrived one afternoon with the wedding announcement. Rajput monarchs from the Great Thar to the Aravali Hills were invited. A thousand laborers prepared the mountain for the royal wedding, which would take place at the Maharaja of Bikaner's summer palace, a compound graced by tropical gardens, sal forests, and fragrant citrus groves. The Maharaja of Bikaner was the elder statesman of Rajputana. Leela's father had assigned a hundred elephants for the royal procession, and twenty-thousand guests were expected.

Govinda and Ravi were sparring with blunted blades when Ananta arrived from Pushkar where he had been performing Vedic rites. Ananta touched Govinda's feet and sighed.

"I had given up hope."

"It's been too long," Govinda agreed, placing a hand on his friend's shoulder.

Rising to embrace Govinda, Ananta said, "You must tell me everything that has happened since you left Varanasi."

"I shall. Perhaps you can help me to understand some things."

"What have I to add to the wisdom you've gained? The Himalayas are the very wellspring of knowledge. When I heard of your return, I came immediately. The wedding is the talk of Pushkar. Every traveler carries the news back to his village."

"People still remember?"

"The legend of a Rajput boy slaying the all-powerful Emperor is told all over Rajputana. You've become a *Puranic* hero of sorts."

"Better they tell Puranic tales than wild stories."

"The Maharaja of Pushkar is troubled," said Ananta.

"Why is that?"

"He fears the Moguls will come when they learn that you've returned."

"If we were united, the Moguls might stay away, but the rajas can't seem to agree on anything."

"Have you heard the news? A new emperor sits on the Peacock Throne."

"I have heard."

"There are rumors that Uzbek Khan assassinated Emperor Ghazi Kashmir, but the official story is that he drowned."

"Why hasn't Hashim assumed the Peacock Throne?"

"Apparently, Hashim also drowned in the accident, but some suspect foul play."

"Hashim… dead?" Govinda tightened his fist on the hilt of his sword. "From whom did you hear this?"

"From the head of a camel caravan. The new emperor is Yaman, Emperor Shah's son by Begum Zahira."

"I look forward to meeting the new emperor, even if he is emperor in name only."

"Perhaps it will be soon," said Ananta.

"If we meet on the battlefield, his rule will be brief," Govinda declared, running his finger along the blade of his sword.

"Then you should practice," bantered Ravi, impatient to resume training.

"I see the hermit's life has done little to extinguish your fire," smiled Ananta.

"The fire of dharma consumes me."

In the days leading up to the wedding, Govinda felt swept about like desert sands in a windstorm. Wherever he went, greetings and gifts awaited him, but the changes occurring within him sorely tested his resolve.

One afternoon, in search of solitude, he rode Sinha to a lake at the northern end of the Aravali hills. Spotting a Marwari herd grazing near the lake, Govinda doubted that he would ever be as free as the horses, whose lean, muscular bodies glistened in the sun. Climbing down, he approached the herd.

"This is the life I long for," Govinda told himself. "To have freedom is to know peace."

But you are destined to free many.

Govinda spun around. "Was that you, Sinha?"

It is I, the white stallion.

"White stallion?" Govinda repeated aloud, scanning his surroundings. "I don't see a white stallion."

I am at the far end of the herd.

Govinda's eyes fell on an old, but proud, stallion, and he ran toward it.

"Kalki?"

It is I.

I never expected to see you again, Govinda thought, shifting to telepathic communication.

Nor I you.

I see you've found your kin.

Many from this herd escaped after the great battle. We live in peace here on the plains.

I'm envious.

I am old now. It is my time to live in peace. But you are coming into your prime; it is your time to ride to battle. You have your father's spirit. You would not be content to graze forever. You are a Rajput. War is in your blood.

Even Marwari warhorses seem to know my future.

Steve Briggs

I know what I know.

An elephant caparisoned in royal blue and five hundred turbaned cavalrymen, their *talwars* shining, waited outside Bundi Palace to escort Govinda to a distant corner of Rajputana. It was a proud day for the residents of Bundi Fort. Their prince had returned a hero, renowned across the length and breadth of India, and his well-wishers gathered inside the fortress gates to give Govinda a triumphant send-off.

The dusty journey crossed a land of few trees and fewer waterways. The supply wagons were nearly empty by the time the royal caravan began its labored ascent to the top of Mount Abu.

As they made their way to the palace, Govinda joked with his cousin.

"Ravi, when the Rajput general was unable to attend his wedding, what did he do?"

"I don't know."

"He sent his sword in his place."

"But you aren't skilled with a sword," teased Ravi.

"I had little use for one."

"Then continue your training," interjected Raja Yogesh.

"If I am to defeat the Moguls, it won't be with a talwar."

"Just how do you plan to defeat them?" Ravi wondered out loud.

"I have no idea."

"During the Great War, Krishna offered the opposing armies a choice," Rukmini said. "The commanders could choose Krishna or his army, but not both. Arjuna chose Krishna, and the Kauravas chose Krishna's army. Arjuna defeated the mighty Kauravas."

"I know you have little taste for adulation, but we are approaching the palace. You had better climb onto your elephant," advised Raja Yogesh. "The groom must make a royal entrance."

Climbing onto the elephant, Govinda was happy to be among the overhanging limbs of the forest. As his elephant lumbered onto the lavish grounds of the maharaja's summer retreat, trumpets sounded, and swords brandished in his honor. Crimson rose petals blanketed

The Tale of the Himalayan Yogis

the tree-lined lane leading to the palace. Uniformed soldiers stood at attention; their mustaches curled at the tips. A priest sprinkled scented water over the elephant's trunk after placing the auspicious mark on the bull's forehead.

On manicured lawns, musicians and dancers entertained guests who had gathered from the far corners of Rajputana. It seemed the entire Rajput nation had crowded onto the palace grounds.

Govinda's exile was the subject of much speculation. Some claimed that he had been tortured by the Moguls only to escape with the help of the Emperor's brother. Others insisted that Govinda had taken refuge in a Tibetan monastery and converted to Buddhism. Nearly everyone dismissed the notion that he had lived in a cave with a yogi who flew from peak to peak, raised men from the dead, and kept cobras as pets. As Govinda climbed down from his mount, onlookers jockeyed for a glimpse of the hero the Rajput clans so desperately needed.

Govinda's host, the Maharaja of Bikaner, greeted the groom's party in his private apartments.

"Welcome, friends. Your presence honors us. Bikaner Palace is your home, my family and staff are your humble servants. Govinda, as you approached the palace, I had to look again to be sure that Raja Chandra himself wasn't climbing the steps. Your father and I were friends and allies. As you entered the palace, I thought to myself, 'If anyone can bring our clans together, it will be Chandra's son.'"

"We are privileged to be your guests, Maharaj-Ji," Govinda replied, "and we thank you for hosting our wedding. I will do all in my power to bring the people of Rajputana together, be that their desire."

"You are wise, Govinda; already you have noticed that not everyone in Rajputana desires agreement among the clans."

"I am more practical than wise."

"There is wisdom in the practical," agreed the maharaja. "Come, let me show you to your accommodations."

Leela and her wedding party arrived at Jodhpur Place at the eastern end of the mountain. Leela whirled into her mother's parlor; her flashing eyes appeared too childlike to be those of a bride.

"*Beti*, a massage will take away the fatigue of the journey," suggested Leela's mother.

"I don't want a massage. I feel like dancing."

"It is time you directed your attention toward your future husband. In three days' time you'll be married, and then your life will change forever. You won't have a moment to think of yourself."

"But I'll never stop dancing."

"There are certain things a married woman must not do, and dancing is one them."

"But Pitaji says I was born to dance," frowned Leela.

"Pitaji dotes on you. As you mature, you'll see the wisdom in my words."

"But I am mature… I'm twenty!"

"Which is old enough to understand why a married woman shouldn't dance. I've tried to teach you, but it's not been easy to get your attention."

"Maa, I can repeat every word you've ever used to describe a proper wife: faithful, reserved, self-sacrificing, generous, kind, sympathetic, modest…"

"Leela, you're a precocious young woman with a generous heart, but there are some things you should know that will make you a better wife. In time, I'm sure you will be a perfect wife, but right now you don't know the first thing about a husband."

"Govinda is not just any husband."

"All the more reason why you should listen to your mother," interjected Deepa, the queen's maidservant.

"Prince Govinda is accustomed to being looked after," the queen continued.

"No, Maa. I saw Govinda in Varanasi, and I'm sure no one massages his neck or washes his feet."

"Still, you should know how to pamper him," the queen maintained. "Isn't that right, Deepa?"

"Listen to Raniji," the maidservant advised the princess. "Men have tender egos… their feet require rubbing daily."

"Deepa is right," the queen agreed.

"Govinda isn't like that."

"The important thing to remember is that a proper wife doesn't draw attention to herself," explained the queen. "She stays in the background. You've grown up onstage. I'm afraid it may not be so easy for you to understand this custom."

"Maa, I don't care about the stage," Leela replied. "I care about *dancing*."

Music, dance, and lavish feasts filled the days and nights leading up to the grand occasion. Camel traders from the Great Thar, cavalry from Chittorgarh, goldsmiths from Kota, Marwari merchants, Pushkar Brahmins, and Ajmer artisans camped side by side at the edge of Nakki Lake. Some came out of curiosity; others from a sense of duty, but no matter the motive, the tented city atop Mount Abu had become the nexus of the Rajput world.

Though no stranger to costumes and makeup, Leela struggled to breathe as her attendants pressed close on every side. A peacock quill applied *mehindi* to her hands and a second quill sketched indigo brows above her striking eyes. Draped from her hair, a gold pendant attached to a string of pearls, rested on Leela's forehead. Filigree chains adorned her plait and ears; attendants painstakingly affixed a pearl *nath* ring with matching rubies to her nose. Servants slipped gold bangles, anklets, and jeweled rings into position, succeeding despite Leela's growing impatience. With the placement of a matching *dupatta* cloth that cascaded from the crown of her head to her ankles, the stunning ensemble was complete, and not a moment too soon.

"Deepa, has there ever been a lovelier bride in all of Rajputana?" the queen gushed as her daughter entered the parlor. The queen's maidservant had been coordinating the assembly of finery and jewels since dawn.

"Maa, I'm so excited that I can hardly breathe!"

"Take deep breaths," the queen advised. "It will calm you."

"I don't care about being calm. I feel calm and excited at the same time."

"Come," the queen instructed; "it is time we started for the palace. We must not be late for the *mahurta*."

In the groom's apartment, Govinda sat, eyes closed, his right hand forming a fist around the Idol's Eye.

Ravi nervously guarded the entrance to the groom's apartment, keeping tailors and servants at bay while Govinda completed his morning meditation. The instant he stirred, Ravi signaled to a troop of servants who filed into the room carrying great mounds of silk. Govinda was not inclined to leave his cushion, but he stood contentedly as the bearers began assembling his costume.

A servant held a plated mirror for the groom. Govinda scarcely recognized the image. It had been less than a moon's turn since he had traded his walking stick for a diamond-studded sword, his matted locks for a satin turban. Gone was his simple waist-cloth, replaced by a silk *sherwani* that stretched beyond his knees. Staring into the mirror, Govinda viewed his impending marriage as a scene from a dream; one that his guru assured him would bring great happiness.

The auspicious hour had arrived, and the wedding parties converged on the palace lawn where a spacious *pandal* dominated the grounds. Red and white garlands cascaded the length of the tent's canopied walls and ghee lamps shone brilliantly outside the tent. The palace gates were thrown open, allowing peasants and noblemen alike to flood the grounds. Everyone wanted a glimpse of the royal couple.

Seated on a crimson mantle atop a silver stallion, Govinda led the *Bharat* as the groom's men followed, dancing to the beat of bass drums and clashing cymbals.

Govinda dismounted, received a gold platter piled high with offerings, and followed a pundit to his place at the center of the pandal. He faced east, the symbolic source of wisdom. On the forehead of his satin turban, the ruby *sarpech* worn by his ancestors refracted light from the still rising sun.

Conches heralded the arrival of the bridal procession. A team of chestnut Mewars drew Leela's carriage. Stepping down from her conveyance, a retinue of handmaids followed in the wake of her breezy gait. Onlookers showered petals on the bride as she made her way to the wedding tent.

An aura of grace swept the bride along, Leela's slippers never seeming to touch the carpeted earth. The bride faced north, forbidden to look at the groom until the ceremony commenced. Priests filed into the tent, ushering in the sacred flame. From a long-handled spoon, a pundit offered ghee into the fire, causing it to hiss and crackle. Raja Rao poured water over the groom's feet and anointed him with offerings. It was time to invoke the gods.

"Please sit." Leela gestured to Govinda, venturing a timid glance at him.

Govinda accepted the gilded chair; Leela took her place at his right hand. The princess removed her dupatta, exposing raven tresses ornamented with pearl and gold.

Govinda turned to her. Speaking words she had rehearsed well, Leela said, "May the nights be honey-sweet for us; may the mornings be honey-sweet for us; may the earth be honey-sweet for us; and may the heavens be honey-sweet for us."

The bride then sprinkled water on the groom's face and limbs, and eleven Brahmins performed the sacred ritual, tossing grain and ladling ghee into the fire at measured intervals. The offerings were meant to bless the couple with health, prosperity, and male progeny.

It was time for the couple to take their vows.

"Be pleased to accept the hand of my daughter, a pure descendant of the Vasishtha gotra," spoke Raja Rao, offering his daughter to the groom.

"I do accept," Govinda said, placing a satin scarf into Leela's hands.

The couple spoke as one, "May our hearts beat as one. May we love each other like the very breath of our lives. As Vishnu sustains the universe, so may we sustain each other. As a guru loves his disciple, so may we love each other steadfastly and faithfully."

Gazing into Leela's eyes, Govinda continued, "Distant though we were, one from the other, we stand now united. May thy eyes radiate benevolence. Be thou my shield. May thou ever have a cheerful heart and a smiling face. May thou be a true devotee of God and mother of heroes. May thou have at heart the welfare of all living beings."

"I pray that I may follow your path," Leela responded. "May I ever enjoy your companionship."

"With all my strength I clasp thy hand," Govinda said. "Together may we follow the path of virtue. Krishna has given you to me. I must protect thee. May we be devoted to each other and make loving parents."

A priest bent low and knotted their garments, a custom believed to bind the couple's soul for seven lifetimes. Smiling, Govinda and Leela took turns leading the other by the hand around the sacred fire. Seven times they circled the fire as conches sounded and rose petals rained down on them.

The sacraments completed, the royal couple gazed into one another's eyes, lost in the moment of their union.

Retiring to their palatial suite after a sumptuous feast, rousing music, and lively dance, Leela broke into a broad smile as she guided Govinda to a gilded mirror.

"Look at you. I would never have recognized you in Varanasi if not for the music you played, and now I scarcely recognize you either."

"Then let me remove this costume so that you 'll know your husband."

"I'll change too."

The couple, having donned loose-fitting cotton, ventured onto the balcony overlooking the palace's scented gardens. A jeweled sky greeted them. Free of his turban, Govinda's hair touched his broad shoulders. Leela wrapped a lock of his hair about her finger.

"Do you remember the morning you came to Jodhpur Palace disguised as a lama?"

"Disguised as a shorn sheep," laughed Govinda.

Leela reached inside her lavender kameez and removed the silver necklace from around her neck. She opened her hand, revealing the delicate jade and lapis peacock.

"I slept with it in my hand every night."

"At first I tried to forget my past. I wanted to be a yogi like Baba, but he explained that I was not destined to be like him. I didn't like hearing those words, but visions of my little Krishna dancing under the moon kept entering my dreams."

"Do you remember our last night on the balcony?"

"The night we fell in love," replied Govinda.

"Will you play for me tonight?"

The Tale of the Himalayan Yogis

Govinda smiled. "If you'd like, I'll play for you every night."

Leela kissed Govinda before retreating inside, returning to the balcony with a finely crafted bansari. He touched the flute to his forehead before pressing the instrument to his lips. Govinda's simple tune filled the night like the scent of orange blossoms. Dismissing her mother's admonition that a married a woman shouldn't dance, Leela spun about, her ebony tresses swirling about her like a breeze in a summer storm.

Under the diamond-studded sky, Leela danced as Govinda played on. Impassioned emotions, which the young bride had held within her during Govinda's exile, now animated Leela's limbs as she circled him. With each pass, Leela's arc narrowed until she joined hands with Govinda, spinning him round and round.

Leading her lover to their satin bed, Leela pulled Govinda onto the soft linen where they fell into a tender, lyrical embrace. Their impassioned souls merged as one, surpassing the most radiant of stars in the night sky. Into the firmament, their spirits soared. From their souls' lofty perch, a song of love spread across the sky.

In the early hours of the morning, Leela reached out to caress her lover, but Govinda was not at her side. The room was dark, but by the faint light seeping through the window, Leela glimpsed his silhouette. Govinda was sitting in yogic posture on the bed.

How little I know of Govinda's past, she thought.

She was keen to know of Govinda's life as a yogi as she lay there watching him, fingering the silver toe rings on her feet. A symbol of marriage, the rings were never to be removed.

Govinda whispered, "Meditate with me. I want to take you somewhere."

Leela easily folded her legs into lotus posture.

"Where are we going?"

"It's a surprise. Just close your eyes and follow my instructions. Let your mind rest in your heart… now feel your soul rise out the top of your head."

Following his instructions, Leela found herself hovering above the bed. Below her, two figures sat side by side on the bed. Govinda took her by the hand as they rose through the palace ceiling into the night sky. Higher and higher they flew until they reached a magnificent swing covered with soft pillows. The swing was suspended from gold-braided ropes seemingly attached to a pair of stars above them.

"A wedding present from our gurus."

"A wedding present?" Leela repeated. "*Our* gurus?"

Sitting side by side, the swing began making long, graceful arcs across the sky. With each pass through the firmament, rapturous bliss coursed through Leela's soul. She sat in awe of the expanse that enveloped her.

"Where did they go? They were here just moments ago," wondered Govinda out loud.

"Who?" Leela asked, peering about. Nothing but stars lit the firmament.

"Our gurus. I suppose they wanted us to be alone on our wedding night."

Leela lay her head against Govinda's shoulder as they swung across the night sky.

"Where are we?"

"Baba calls it the Sphere of the Celestials. The awakened ones come here during yogic sleep."

"What's yogic sleep?"

"Yogis don't actually sleep much. They float into the sky during their nightly meditations, leaving their bodies in mountain caves and other secret abodes."

"Is that what you were doing while you were meditating on the bed?"

Govinda nodded.

"I was just here with Shankar Baba and the others. You'll meet them later."

"I remember Shankar Baba in the garden in Varanasi. He looked intimidating. Pitaji told us about Shankar Baba after he came to the palace to arrange for our wedding."

Leela and Govinda slipped into a tender embrace as a sublime melody reverberated across the sky.

"Krishna and Radha sported on a swing like this," she said dreamily.

"I know."

"I could stay here forever."

"Sometimes the ascended ones swing through the night while keeping watch over the earth. We can come here again if you like."

"I'd like to come often," said Leela, pressing close.

Flower petals rained down onto the newlyweds. In the distance, the melody of a wood flute wafted through the ether, its song echoing off the stars. Leela recognized the tune as one that Govinda had played for her in Varanasi. The etheric melody flowed through their bodies in rhythm with the swing, which arced slowly to and fro, lulling Leela and Govinda into a sweet reverie.

"Do you remember this song?" asked Leela, falling into his arms.

"You danced to it on the roof the night we met in Varanasi."

"It's my favorite."

"That's why they picked it."

"I don't hear the song so much as I feel it caressing my soul."

"That's the way it is here. Music flows like liquid through the spheres."

"Have you been awake long?" Leela asked, leaning against a satin bolster, her fingers playing with Govinda's hair.

"I can't say."

"What were you dreaming about?"

"It wasn't a dream, you know."

"What was it?"

"We were in the higher realms," replied Govinda.

"Then it was real?" asked Leela hopefully.

"As real as this palace. When souls travel, it's not a dream. We were in a realm few can see. The physical world is but a tiny part of our reality."

"It was the most enchanting place I've ever seen. I was hoping you'd say it was real."

"Nothing on earth compares with divine reality. Yogiraj said one day the entire world will be like that."

"I want to return to the swing."

"We shall," Govinda assured her. "It's near the temple where we meet our guides."

"Will you teach me to meditate so that I can get to know divine reality?"

"There's not much for you to learn. We've both meditated a lot in the past."

"I haven't unless you consider my dance routines to be a type of meditation."

"You just don't remember."

Leela looked skeptically at Govinda.

"Do you think your soul could travel so easily otherwise?" asked Govinda.

"I suppose not."

"I'll teach you to meditate, but I'll be reminding you of what you already know. When would you like to start?"

"Right now!" she said emphatically.

Leela's reply reminded Govinda of her confidence as a dancer, and it brought a smile to his face. His fear that married life would somehow impede his spiritual practice was rapidly dissolving.

"Why are you smiling?"

"I remember that precocious girl on the rooftop. She was quite self-assured."

"When you do something you love there's never any fear. I trust my feelings when I'm dancing, just as I trust my feelings when I'm with you."

"Which was all you needed to fly through the firmament last night."

"Why would that frighten anyone?"

"I can't say. No one should ever be frightened by something so close to one's soul."

"I love flying. I was spinning in bliss. Will you teach me to meditate now?"

Holding the Idol's Eye, Govinda closed his eyes.

"You're to meditate on Lord Krishna in your heart."

"How?"

Following Govinda's instructions, she sat motionless on the center of the bed.

"Why the tears?"

"He's so beautiful!" she whispered.

"You learn quickly."

Leela was quiet for a moment.

"Will they come for the Idol's Eye?" she asked.

"They want the diamond at least as much as they want me."

"Then war is inevitable."

"I'm afraid so."

"But it doesn't worry you."

"I worry that it will cause trouble for your family."

"Pitaji has the best cavalry in Rajputana. No army has ever sacked Jodhpur Fort."

"Jodhpur Fort can't withstand the Moguls. Almost nothing can. The Imperial army is stronger than all the Rajput armies combined."

The newlyweds spent languid afternoons exploring the mountain on horseback, picnicking in the forest, and enjoying the hospitality of the Maharaja of Bikaner.

"Maharaj has invited us to picnic in the royal forest. I'm told tigers roam there. If we're lucky, we'll meet one," said Govinda.

"If we're *lucky?*"

Atop Sinha, Govinda and Leela set out for the royal forest.

Mount Abu was an anomaly; a verdant oasis surrounded the Great Thar. The mountain's undulating terrain was strewn with oversized, odd-shaped boulders and shaded with neem and banyan groves.

"Peculiar rocks," observed Leela, pointing at the boulders.

"Like playthings left behind by a giant."

Sinha trotted past the boulders into a sandalwood grove that scented the air with fragrant perfume.

"A perfect spot for a picnic," decided Govinda.

Govinda dismounted and helped Leela down.

"Pitaji says the rajas are hunting today," said Leela, searching the grove for a suitable place to spread the blankets.

"The Maharaja of Pushkar invited me. He strikes me as a man with whom I could easily disagree. He cast a disdainful look when I declined his invitation in favor of our picnic."

"Everyone finds Raja Balveer difficult. It is common knowledge that he sent his daughter to the Emperor's harem in exchange for the Emperor sparing his territories."

"I could never hunt for sport. To me, all creatures are equal; it would be like hunting humans."

"But hunting is all the rajas talk about."

"Then I may not be the one to unite them," decided Govinda. "I love animals. They make the most loyal friends."

"That's not true. Wives make the most loyal friends."

"After wives, animals make the most loyal friends."

The cooks had prepared sufficient food for all the creatures in the forest. After finishing their meal, Leela pulled Govinda into her lap.

"Everyone talks about the yogis you met. Did you learn magic from them?"

"I wouldn't call it magic, but Baba taught me a mantra to protect the Idol's Eye."

"Did it work?"

"The mantra turned the gem into coal."

"What else did you learn?"

Govinda paused; his Himalayan past seemed like another life.

"Let's walk in the forest," he suggested.

The couple strolled among the fragrant trees, eavesdropping on the chatter of birds and monkeys. They had not gone far when Govinda noticed animated chatter among the animals. At first, he assumed they were alerting one another of their presence, but he soon realized that the monkeys were warning of a greater danger.

"The animals are afraid."

"Why?" Leela asked.

"I thought we had frightened them, but the monkeys say a tigress and her cubs are nearby. The crows, on the other hand, are complaining about humans atop elephants."

"Maharaja's hunting party," guessed Leela.

"We should find the tigress before the rajas do. The Maharaja of Pushkar has been tracking a tiger for several days."

"But isn't that what rajas do when they hunt?"

Govinda and Leela moved silently through the forest.

"If we startle her, she may attack to protect her little ones," cautioned Govinda.

"But you have a boon that no animal will harm you," she whispered.

"I do, but you don't. I'm not taking any chances."

They had not gone far when they reached a cluster of boulders standing twice Govinda's height. The tigress appeared on top of one, her orange and black coat shining in the sunlight. Govinda stepped between Leela and the tigress, who growled menacingly.

"I have come to warn you," Govinda told the tiger.

I've been avoiding hunters all morning; my cubs don't understand the danger.

The tigress' thoughts were barely decipherable due to her anxiety; it had been years since Govinda had experienced such difficulty in understanding a foreign consciousness. Communicating with a human was far from the tigress' highest priority.

Govinda heard a series of snaps in the forest. The tigress crouched and snarled. The hunting party was nearby, and closing fast.

Three elephants emerged from the forest, flattening everything in their path. Atop their elephants sat Raja Balveer and two other rajas, arrows poised. Attendants jogged alongside the rajas, bearing spears to stave off any attack on the elephants. More snapping sounds came from the forest; the remainder of the hunting party was not far behind.

Raja Balveer aimed at the tigress, who crouched at eye level with the huntsmen. The tigress stood her ground, roaring at her pursuers, but the rajas, seated on the backs of elephants at a safe distance, had little to fear. Raja Balveer's mahout maneuvered his elephant into position while the maharaja aimed. Govinda shouted, but the raja ignored the warning and fired.

The tigress sprang from the boulder. The arrow passed over the cat's head, shattering against the rocks. The tigress, darting one way before bounding off in another direction, sought to draw the hunters away from her cubs.

A second team of spearmen emerged from the underbrush, closing the circle around the tigress. The tigress paused, searching for an opening between the spearheads. Protected by buffalo hide shields, the spearmen cautiously closed in on the tigress.

Trapped, the tigress ran at the spearmen, but she could not find a way past their weapons. Govinda stood outside the circle, trying in vain to dissuade the spearmen from their task. One spearman found that his taste for valor, in the presence of his master, overwhelmed his judgment. Lunging forward, he broke the circle and thrust at the tigress. Batting his spear out of the way, she sprang toward him.

Govinda followed the spearman through the breach in the circle and slammed into him, knocking him out of the tigress' path. The man was sent sprawling on the ground but spared from being gored. Govinda had put himself in the path of the tigress, and she knocked him to the ground.

Dazed, Govinda looked into the tigress' eyes. Hovering over him, she was fully capable of killing him, but something gave her pause. In that instant, Raja Balveer released another arrow, striking the tigress in the shoulder.

The wounded tigress slumped onto her forepaws. The spear ring quickly reformed around her. A second hunter readied himself for the kill, but before he could shoot, Govinda stepped into the line of fire.

"Stop," he commanded. "The tigress has cubs."

"Stand out of the way!" shouted the raja.

Ignoring the hunters, Govinda pulled the arrow from the tigress' shoulder. The tigress wailed in pain, but the projectile came out cleanly. The wounded tigress crouched on the ground, her injured foreleg trembling.

"You're mad," shouted Raja Balveer. "There's nothing more dangerous than a wounded tiger."

"She has young cubs I tell you!" Govinda repeated. "They're hiding among the rocks!"

"All the more reason to finish her off," one of the rajas replied. "Stand aside; Maharaj wishes to make the kill."

"Then you'll have to kill me first," declared Govinda, tossing the bloodied arrow at the feet of Raja Balveer's elephant.

Leela, who had slipped between the rocks, emerged carrying a cub by the scruff of its neck. The other cub trotted along behind her.

"You'll be killing the little ones' mother," she shouted.

At that moment, the other members of the hunting party arrived. Seeing Govinda surrounded by armed footmen, Raja Rao was outraged.

"Why are you pointing weapons at Prince Govinda?"

"He refuses to get out of the way!" bellowed Raja Balveer.

"Pitaji, she has young ones, but still they insist on killing her."

"Stand aside," ordered Raja Balveer. "The tiger is about to attack."

"What have you to fear?" scoffed Govinda. "You sit atop elephants surrounded by spearmen. The risk is mine."

"The tiger may calm down if we leave," suggested Raja Rao.

Raja Rao instructed his mahout to retreat into the forest. Reluctantly, the other rajas and their footmen followed him.

"I'm not pleased," snapped Raja Balveer as he turned his elephant. The spearmen cautiously followed their masters into the forest.

Ignoring the raja, Govinda bent over the tigress, who was now too weak to stand.

"She's dying."

"What can we do?" asked Leela.

Seeing the cubs looking on anxiously, Govinda had an idea.

"I've done this once before, but I'll need your help."

Leela knelt beside Govinda, a trickle of blood seeped from the cat's wound.

"Fill your hand with her blood," instructed Govinda.

"What?"

"I'll explain later."

Leela cupped her hand near the wound until it was partially full.

"With the blood, draw a triangle on my left hand."

Leela followed Govinda's instructions without questioning him.

"Now draw a pair of swan's wings on my left hand."

Again Leela dipped her finger into the blood and drew a figure.

Satisfied with the symbols, Govinda placed his hands over the wound and prayed to Bhumi Mata. The tigress sighed, her body relaxing for the first time since the attack.

"Is there hope?"

"There's always hope. Devraj was dead, but Bhumi Mata brought him back."

One of the cubs pressed its nose against its mother's side, but the tigress was unconscious.

"For the cubs' sake, I hope she lives," whispered Leela. "How do the symbols heal?"

"I can't say. If the tigress reacts the way Devraj did, she'll sleep through the day. The cubs will need milk whether their mother survives, or not."

Satisfied that he had done what he could for the tigress, they rode Sinha back to the palace.

"After what happened today, I'm sure Raja Balveer will oppose whatever I suggest to the council."

"Raja Balveer is at odds with everyone!" replied Leela. "The others are reasonable men."

In the days that followed, the tigress' wound healed while tensions escalated between Raja Balveer and Govinda.

"Balveer and his friends refuse to attend the council meeting. They're leaving in the morning," announced Raja Rao at dinner.

"I'm too blame for that," lamented Govinda.

"I commend you for protecting the tigress and her cubs," said their host, the Maharaja of Bikaner.

"Once again, we Rajputs stand divided."

ABDUCTION

Jodhpur Palace was unlike any palace Govinda had ever seen. Raja Rao's kingdom enjoyed riches unheard of in Govinda's native Aravali Hills. When he compared his present surroundings to his mendicant's life in the Himalaya, Govinda could only marvel at the opulence he encountered at every turn. Jodhpur's walled-in populace greeted the newlyweds warmly upon their return. Everywhere Govinda went, children rushed to touch him.

In the moons that followed the wedding, Govinda and Leela went everywhere together, and it was not long before the people of Jodhpur had adopted the prince as one of their own.

"Govinda, I want a cat," cooed Leela, snuggling close to him.

"You're missing the cubs, aren't you? I'm glad you love animals."

"I've learned from you."

"I think you've always had it in you. Of course, you can have a cat, but wouldn't two be better? Every creature needs a mate."

"Is that your conclusion, having lived alone for all those years?"

"That's my conclusion having lived with you!"

"Then you're enjoying palace life?" she asked.

"I'm enjoying life with you."

"Then your doubts about marriage are gone?"

"I'll never forget Shankar Baba."

"You miss him."

"More than I miss my father," he replied.

"Today, my students are giving a recital."

"Your children are the best dancers in all of Rajputana."

"I'm only teaching the girls what I love."

"That's all any guru does. Shankar Baba never really taught me anything; he just lived, and I followed as best I could."

"The Osiyan Festival is coming. I want to take the girls."

"You should."

"But Maa insists the Great Thar is no place for children."

"I think it's a great idea. I'll speak to Raniji about it."

"I have my heart set on Persian kittens like the ones my cousin is raising."

After completing cavalry exercises, Govinda walked into the palace, his boots landing hard on the marble floor. A pair of beige and black balls disappeared under the bed as he strode into the room. He removed his boots, which had frightened the kittens. Leela coaxed her young pets from their hiding place.

"Meet Bindu and Loka," she said, emerging from under the bed holding a kitten in each arm. "They're such tiny creatures."

"Fortunately, they'll never be as big as the tiger cubs. By now, the cubs would be as large as a leopard."

"I informed the children about the dance festival."

"But I haven't spoken to your mother yet."

"I told her," said Leela.

"Then Raniji agreed?"

"Maa said, 'If Govinda thinks it's a good idea, then I won't try to stop you.'"

"I think it's a fine idea."

"Maa worries about our safety."

"Your father will send a cavalry escort, but to be safe, it will be best if no one knows you're going along."

"Do you think that's necessary?"

"We can't take chances. Just recently a spy was caught in the market."

"You never mentioned it."

"I didn't want to worry you."

The Tale of the Himalayan Yogis

"Maa's the one who would worry. Come to Osiyan with us; then we'll be safe!"

"The Bikaner and Jaisalmer cavalries are training with our army, and they've placed me in charge."

"You didn't tell me Shankar Baba trained you to command an army."

"He didn't. Just ask cousin Ravi about my skills as a soldier; he thinks I'm useless."

"He's jealous."

"War is something we Rajputs are supposed to know from birth."

"You Rajput *men*, you mean. I'm a Rajput, and I'd be useless in war, but no one has ever criticized me for it."

"We Rajput men, then," agreed Govinda. "Pitaji trained me from the time I could ride, but I still don't like the idea of leading soldiers into battle."

Seven petite dancers swayed atop pillowed howdahs in an elephant caravan led by Raja Rao's cavalry. Leela peered through silk curtains, losing herself in the sandy expanse that was the Great Thar. Her trip to Osiyan as a young girl had inspired her as a dancer; she hoped it would do the same for her students.

Although the desert hadn't changed, its graceful profile had been endlessly shaped and reshaped since her first trip to Osiyan… the major adventure of Leela's life. She had not roamed the Himalaya or lived in the caves of yogis, faced menacing demons or raced atop Kalki across the plains in the moonlight. Govinda had done all of this and more. Leela loved listening to him narrate the stories of his life.

As her howdah swayed, Leela tried to fathom the silence within her husband, a depth from which great currents of courage emerged. With time, Leela hoped to discover the wellspring of wisdom behind Govinda's eyes. She wondered if her father, or any other king, would have faced death to protect a tigress and her cubs. It would take time to fathom Govinda's heart.

Her mother had counseled Leela that love was a slow brewing broth, requiring time and seasoning as it matured. Although she was prepared to wait for love to grow, she was quite sure that their love had not begun as a spark, but as a full flame. The threat of imperial invasion did not worry her. In marrying Govinda, she had allied herself with something larger than Rajput tradition, and she readily accepted her destiny.

Leela closed her eyes to the monotony of the journey, lulled into daydream by the gentle rocking of the elephant. The desert sun bore down on the caravan, and the children grew impatient for the trip to come to an end.

Leela's dream turned tumultuous. Awakening with a start, she peered through the curtains, hoping the enemy troops that had invaded her dream were not real. To her dismay, a horde of armed riders loomed on the waking horizon. She had not yet fully comprehended what she was seeing when the officer in charge of her escort rode alongside her elephant.

"Raj Kumari, horsemen bearing a green flag are headed this way," the officer reported. "I fear they are Moguls."

"What do you suggest?" asked Leela, feigning calm.

"With your permission, I shall order my men to surround the coaches. The intruders are still a good distance away; there is time if we act quickly."

"Instruct the mahouts, and then ride out to meet the Moguls. Do not disclose whom you are escorting. Their presence may be a mere coincidence."

Leela did not believe her words. She feared for the little ones, who peered innocently at the approaching army. Her mother's words now haunted her.

The Great Thar is no place for children.

As she watched the officer ride off, Leela wished that she had never brought up the idea of the dance competition.

"Raj Kumari, they have come for you," the officer stated. "They are led by Commander Jari himself. He claims his cavalry numbers three thousand, and that he will take the girls prisoner unless we turn you over to him. When I told him there were no royals in the caravan, he scoffed at me."

"How does he know so much?" Leela wondered aloud.

"They have their spies."

"What is the size of our escort?"

"Five hundred. We are outnumbered, but our men are superior. Their men are not impressive."

"If the Moguls defeat us, they will surely take the girls. No, we shall not fight. Let them take me, but not the children."

"Raj Kumari, these Moguls have no honor. They may take you and abduct the children too."

"We'll have to take that risk. I'm sure the commander would rather avoid a battle with our cavalry regardless of their advantage. If he demands the children, then we fight to the death. Do you have a weapon for me?"

The officer handed Leela a knife.

"Let us confront the Moguls," the officer pleaded. "Raja Rao entrusted you to me. I can't let them take you without a fight."

"If not for the children, I would allow you to fight, but I won't risk the young ones. Prepare a horse for me."

Leela did not want the children to know what was happening, and so she climbed onto the horse without a word.

"After they have taken me, send a rider to Jodhpur to inform Rajaji and Govinda of what has happened. Send a second rider to Osiyan to inform the people that we have turned back. Return to Jodhpur with the girls without delay," she ordered the officer as they rode toward the Moguls.

The Mogul cavalry was now close enough for Leela to see clearly, and she did not like what she saw. The soldiers seemed to be of one face. They met Leela's gaze with hungry stares, causing her heart to harden as she approached.

Commander Jari spoke first.

"Inform your king that I am taking his daughter to Delhi," he told the Rajput officer, "and that she will be held hostage until Prince Govinda turns himself in. We have not come to make war. Prince Govinda of Krishnagarh is charged with the murder of the Emperor."

"My husband will not come," Leela claimed, though she feared he would. "I could never exchange his life for my freedom."

"Raj Kumari, it matters little what you want. The Emperor will try Govinda for the death of Emperor Shah. I assure you, he will have a fair trial."

Leela knew all too well that a trial would mean certain death for Govinda. For the first time in her life, she trembled. Her fear was not for her welfare, but for her husband. Her capture would mean his execution, and her lapse in judgment would be the cause.

"Fair trial?" she snapped with a mocking disdain. "You intend to execute my husband. Dogs rule by the size of their pack."

"Raj Kumari, do not offend me," Jari replied, loosening his knife from its sheath. "I have orders; otherwise this dagger would have removed your tongue. If Prince Govinda has not come to Delhi within ten days, then you will be executed."

Leela opened her mouth to mock Jari again, but her officer stopped her.

"Raj Kumari, do not anger him. Muslim officers are not accustomed to hearing such words from their women."

"I am not one of their women," she snapped.

"Not yet," Jari said threateningly. "Although I cannot remove your tongue, we do have other means of silencing you. As you can see from the look of my pack of dogs, they have been away from their women."

Ignoring the comment, Leela covered her lips with her hand as she whispered into her officer's ear.

"Tell my husband he shouldn't come to Delhi. Tell him that I'll be all right. See the children safely back to Jodhpur."

When her officer rode off, Leela's dread turned to despair as Commander Jari placed her in the custody of a pair of brutish soldiers, who wanted blood, and, she feared, her.

Raja Rao was the first to receive the news. Led by Commander Kuldeep, his generals gathered at the palace where Raja Rao paced impatiently, waiting for Govinda's arrival.

"The Moguls have kidnapped Leela," Raja Rao informed Govinda as he entered the court. "It was a mistake not to have sent a larger escort, but it's pointless to dwell on that now."

Govinda knew deep in his soul that causes linking him with the Moguls had yet to be resolved.

Speaking to his generals, Raja Rao said, "The Moguls demand Govinda in exchange for Leela. We have ten days. Of course, any trial would be a mockery. If Govinda surrenders, they will surely execute him for the Emperor's death."

"What guarantee do we have that they'll release Leela even then?" Commander Kuldeep questioned. "The only option I see is to free Leela by force. Rajaji, the army is ready to move at your command."

"I appreciate your support, but there must be a better way."

"There is," Govinda declared. "Let us devise a plan to free Leela in exchange for me. Once the Moguls have me, our armies and the nagababas should be ready to attack."

"Wouldn't it be better if you led the attack rather than allowing yourself to be taken captive?" questioned Raja Rao.

"That would be too risky for Leela," Govinda insisted. "I'd rather be the one held captive. The main thing is to free Leela."

"Govinda, we need to be practical," cautioned Raja Rao. "Many lives, including yours, are at stake."

"The Moguls will only free Leela once they have me."

"Before I agree to your plan, I need to know how you intend to go about it."

"I can't say," replied Govinda.

"I can't send my cavalry to Delhi without a sound strategy."

"It may be better if the cavalry remained in Jodhpur."

"What chance would you and some naked sadhus have against an army of three hundred thousand?" protested Commander Kuldeep.

"I shall go in exchange for Leela. I only ask that an escort accompany me to see her safely back to Jodhpur."

"We have time," decided Raja Rao. "Delhi is but a five-day journey. Let us not make hasty decisions."

Before the following dawn, Govinda rode Sinha through Jodhpur's gates, having left behind his royal garb in favor of a commoner's cloth. When Commander Kuldeep delivered the news to Raja Rao, the king was crestfallen.

"Have I learned nothing in all my years?" he asked his commander.

"You have ruled wisely," replied the general. "Should I prepare the cavalry?"

"What choice do we have? I cannot allow Govinda to ride into Delhi alone, and yet we need time to organize our allies."

"But can we ask the rajas to join us? It would mean almost certain death."

"You are right. This is not their affair. Only our troops should go. But I promised the yogi, that in the event of war, I would inform the nagababas. Dispatch riders to Varanasi immediately. I fear the loss of life will be enormous."

"We are Rajputs, after all. Not one of my men fears death," the general reassured his king.

"Judge not a man's fear of death before he faces it. Inform the troops. We depart tomorrow."

"Will you be joining us?" asked Kuldeep.

"I will lead the troops myself."

Sensing the urgency of their mission, Sinha galloped tirelessly across the length of Rajputana. A peasant's turban held Govinda's hair off his forehead as they streaked across the open plains. He had disguised his stallion's nobility beneath a layer of smeared mud and dirt; the stately roan's mane and tail were tangled and knotted. Sinha still looked like a horse of rare quality, but not exceptional enough to arouse suspicion, or so Govinda hoped. As for Govinda himself, despite his fame, there were almost none in the Moguls' lands who knew his face. Dressed as he was, he appeared as little more than a villager. He had concealed his gilded sword along with a bag of mohurs.

Vast stretches of uninhabitable land typified the rugged terrain. Only the heartiest peasants were seen huddling beneath thatched roofs and scrawny trees. Govinda rode on, futilely trying to avoid the scorching sun. His sole comfort was Bhumi Mata's bowl, which fed him daily.

At the northern tip of Rajputana, the road to Delhi appeared. A caravan leader cautioned him that Koli bandits accosted travelers, looting and killing even by day. Knowing the swiftness of his steed, Govinda ignored the warning. It was the Mogul army guarding the river crossings that worried him, for if he was detained, or forced to double back, it could cost Leela her life.

The Tale of the Himalayan Yogis

Govinda reached the banks of the Yamuna River. To his dismay, soldiers guarded the shallow crossings. He had little option but to ride west, which would leave but three days before Leela's execution.

So, what will we do now? Govinda soundlessly asked Sinha as the horse sipped water in the shade of some sparse trees. *We have allies in Delhi; or at least, we used to. Hashim may be dead, but his former friends are probably our friends. Where did he tell me that I could find them? There were two people in two places; Gaziapur was the second place, and Mumtaz Aalim was the person... I'm counting on you to carry Leela back to Jodhpur.*

I will, the stallion replied.

It was night when Govinda arrived at the outskirts of the capital. On the following day, he reached Gaziapur where he found a clear-eyed, white-haired recluse sitting on a rug in the shade of a yawning mulberry tree. The old man was singing to his donkey. He had found Mumtaz Aalim.

"*As-Salamu Alaikum!*" Govinda greeted the old man after climbing down from Sinha.

"Namaste! Slayer of evil emperors," Mumtaz Aalim replied, a wry smile forming as he leaned his head against the trunk of the tree. "I've been expecting you."

"But no one knows I'm here."

"I would not say 'no one.' It is good that you have come. Join me! I too am an outcast... of sorts."

Mumtaz Aalim shifted position on his rug to make room for Govinda.

"Have you any news from Hashim?" asked Govinda, seating himself on the rug.

A shadow crossed the old man's face.

"No one knows the fate of my grandsons. Rumors circulate that Hashim and Ghazi drowned in Dal Lake, but I do not believe that to be true."

"I also don't believe that Hashim is dead."

"Make no mistake, something terrible has happened. And now they've taken your princess. You'll need help in defeating the Moguls. I want to hear your plan for toppling the Empire."

"I've come to demand Leela's release in exchange for me."

"Allow me to offer some advice. Don't count on anyone living up to his promise; at least, not in the palace."

"Are you saying they might execute Leela even if I turn myself in?"

A forlorn look came over Govinda.

"Patience, my son."

"But there is not much time," he protested. "The Moguls plan to execute her within a few days."

"Friends are coming who are familiar with the harem."

"What does the harem have to do with Leela?"

"Your Leela is a prisoner there. Empress Zahira is taking no chances."

"Then Zahira is behind this?" asked Govinda, recalling Rukmini's account of the Empress.

"There is time to save your princess."

Govinda fingered the pouch containing the Idol's Eye for the first time since leaving Jodhpur.

"I understand," said Mumtaz Aalim. "Lord Ram was distraught when Ravan abducted Sita."

"Then you know our Hindu legends?"

"I also know Mogul history, and the Peacock Throne is fraught with conspiracy. Fratricide has been a pillar of succession for decades."

"But why such betrayal?"

"You and Hashim are much the same. At times, I wonder how your virtue will allow you to overcome what lies ahead. Controlling the Peacock Throne means controlling the riches of plunder and taxation. Soon you will see for yourself the fortresses that have been built to house the Emperor's gold and the palace for his elephants. Ten thousand sentries guard the treasury by day and by night. The Emperor's army is nearly three hundred thousand strong."

"The Rajput armies combined are but a fraction... What chance do we have against such odds?"

"You Rajputs are willing to die. That is not always the case with the Mogul," observed Aalim.

"But still, we are overwhelmingly outnumbered. It would be a massacre, would it not?"

"Keep one thing in mind: we Moguls are not a principled lot. A Mogul's loyalty lies with himself, whether heir to the throne or common infantryman. In the throes of battle, our soldiers may desert at the earliest sign of defeat. You will not need to defeat the entire imperial army. Turn back the first line of attack and the rest may not put up much resistance."

"Then we have a chance."

"You are about to enter a world of deception. Behind every pillar lurks a dagger. You will need cunning if you hope to succeed."

"What do you propose?"

"It will be impossible for you to enter the harem. The Moti Mahal is guarded more jealously than the Emperor's gold. The threads of Emperor Shah's intrigue are woven through the warp and woof of the city. My former son-in-law's heirs, his army, his citizens, his harem, and his death have all conspired to bring you to Delhi. They want you because you defeated the most powerful man in all of Hindustan, and they wish to know what kind of man could conquer their emperor and walk away without claiming his riches. Should they capture you… well, let's hope they never do. To agree to the exchange would be senseless. There is a better way."

"Even if we manage to free Leela, won't the Mogul army attack Jodhpur?"

"You have little choice but to defeat them now."

"But I'm not even sure who I'm trying to defeat."

"Empress Zahira is behind much of what is evil in the palace."

"Who exactly is this woman?"

"Zahira was Emperor Shah's favorite before my daughter joined the harem. Still, even after Kameela bore the Emperor twins, Junaid Shah favored Zahira enough to allow her to have a son, and that led to the death of my daughter."

"And to the removal of Ghazi?"

"Ghazi stood in the way of Zahira's plan to put her son on the Peacock Throne. Yaman is a mere puppet, but do not underestimate Zahira. She has decided that it is time to step out of the shadows and rule India herself."

"I've heard stories of her ruthlessness."

"You've met Akori," asked Aalim?

"The Egyptian?"

"Akori is head of our Chisti Order."

"But isn't Akori with Yogiraj?" asked Govinda, removing the Idol's Eye from its pouch and closing his fingers around it.

"Surely you know there is no limit to what our guides can do."

"If the Mahatmas are involved, then what need have we for armies?"

"They choose not to intervene directly. It is up to us to execute the plans," explained Aalim.

"But I'm not even sure what the plan is."

"In time it will become clear."

"I have little time to spare," grumbled Govinda.

"You need only be clear about your actions and help will come."

"If Leela is Zahira's prisoner, she may have already been harmed."

"If that were the case, I would have heard something."

Govinda fingered the diamond, hoping for a clue as to what he should do.

"I can see that you possess powers, but still, patience is required."

"It seems I'm powerless to help Leela."

"Remember one thing, kindness is the conquering power," said Aalim. "Forgive me, but I can offer you nothing but day-old *briyani* and a dusty rug to sleep on."

"By helping me, you put yourself at risk. The least I can do is share my food with you."

"I don't see any supplies," Mumtaz observed, glancing at Sinha.

"A yogini gave me this," said Govinda, holding up Bhumi Mata's bowl. "It fills instantly with whatever food I request."

"A most convenient bowl!" smiled Mumtaz Aalim.

Govinda agonized over Leela's capture. Patience had never been a Rajput's ally, and despite having spent seven years in the Himalaya, Govinda was sure that he possessed far less of the virtue than the average villager.

"I can't wait any longer," he informed Mumtaz Aalim.

"Help is coming."

"What if they execute her while we sit under this tree?"

"They won't harm her until they hear from you; otherwise, how would they ever capture you?"

"There are others they could abduct as well. I can't help Leela by remaining here. I intend to let the Emperor know that I've come for her."

The impulse to take action was as natural to a Rajput as it was for a horse to gallop. Throwing caution to the wind, Govinda saddled Sinha, who was grazing to the rear of the shrine.

"If you must go then allow me to write a letter on your behalf. With the Emperor's seal, at least you will be assured some cordiality, though it will mean little in the end."

"I trust you as much as I trust Hashim. Please keep this for me." Govinda handed the old Sufi the pouch containing the Idol's Eye in exchange for the letter.

"I can see that you place great faith in the gem."

"My faith lies with Krishna; whose power I believe dwells within the diamond."

"You have made a wise choice," Mumtaz Aalim said, closing his fingers around the pouch.

"The Idol's Eye chose for me."

"Then so be it. The gem has guided you to go in search of Leela."

Govinda climbed atop Sinha and headed for the heart of Delhi, a solitary rider entering the enemy camp with nothing but his sword and a letter tucked inside his tunic.

Delhi dwarfed any city that Govinda had ever seen. Ornate mosques, marble palaces, and shops displaying Persian silk and porcelain from China fronted tree-lined avenues. Govinda guided Sinha past gilded chariots pulled by white oxen with horns sheathed in silver. Impoverished Hindus trod barefoot, dodging left and right to avoid the sting of a whip from a nobleman's carriage.

Elephants carried stately women sheltered beneath canopied howdahs. Soldiers rode groomed Mongolian mounts past palanquins bearing Persian aristocrats. Attentive servants jogged along carrying silver spittoons to catch the streams of betel juice discarded by their coddled masters. Lackeys fanned noblemen with horsetail switches.

Court nobles, who had reason to gain the public's favor, tossed silver coins to beggars who grappled over alms in the dust.

Gurgling fountains and lapis-domed mosques graced the capital, diverting the eye from the dust and neglect of unsightly hovels. From the balconies of onion-shaped minarets, muezzins summoned the faithful.

An army cantonment separated affluent neighborhoods from slums housing families living on broken rice and potato scraps. Battlements overlooked lavish mansions staffed by servants assigned to fan guests on sultry evenings.

Govinda headed for the Emperor's palace along the Yamuna River. The palace lay hidden behind a sandstone fortress that obscured the horizon. The complex housed the Moti Mahal, horse and elephant stables, and the palace treasury in addition to the Emperor's palace with its gilded domes and many viewing balconies.

Nearly half of Delhi's citizenry were soldiers. Military encampments stood in plain sight from any avenue in the city, their presence dominating the vicinity near the royal palace. Discouraged by what he saw, Govinda couldn't imagine overturning an empire endowed with such vast riches and consummate military might. The prospect of battling the Emperor's army left him discouraged; the Mogul army would crush him as capriciously as a servant swatted a fly alighting on his master's boot.

At his mother's orders, Emperor Yaman wasted no time in censoring public morals, a move that won the approval of both the mullahs and the generals. Gambling, blasphemy, and beards longer than the length of one's hand were banned, and those who refused to comply faced an angry whip.

On the boulevard leading to the fortress, a Persian juggler performed alongside a snake charmer whose cobra hovered menacingly above its wicker basket. A palmist rendered prophecies beside a fakir who lay on a platform of iron spikes, chatting amiably with a nearby merchant. Nimble dancers, sinewy acrobats, and fruit vendors vied for the attention of those with purses filled with coins bearing the seal of the newly crowned emperor. A dancing bear caught Govinda's eye, and he climbed down from his mount to purchase an apple for the amiable Himalayan beast.

Taut iron chains suspended a wood-planked drawbridge spanning a murky green moat leading to the gates of the royal fortress. Sinha's hooves clopped rhythmically on the courtyard squares as they entered the impregnable walls where Leela was held captive.

Govinda trained his eyes on the balcony overhead. Perched on a throne of rubies and gold sat Mohammed Babur Ali Faez Shah Yaman, his posture every bit as pretentious as his title. Oiled eunuchs fanned the oafish, bulbous-skulled monarch. The young ruler seemed hopelessly bored with the ritual he presided over, but such was the requirement of the Emperor, for if a day passed without his appearing in public, anarchy could result. Such was the insecurity of the Peacock Throne, and such was the expectation of treachery that the citizens of Delhi had come to trust only the sight of the Emperor himself.

A silk string dangled from the Emperor's viewing balcony. At its bottom, supplicants fastened gifts for their ruler. A servant raised the offerings while petitioners prostrated on the ground below.

Govinda guided Sinha toward the string. He was the only man on horseback in the crowded courtyard, and when the palace guards saw him approaching, they quickly surrounded him.

"Dismount!" a guard ordered. "Bow to the Emperor or lose your head."

Swords rose on every side.

"Stand away," Govinda commanded. "I have a message for the Emperor."

Govinda's show of disrespect angered the guards, and a soldier grabbed Sinha's reigns. In a flash of gleaming steel, Govinda drew his sword from its place of concealment. He was about to sever the guard's hand when a voice froze his weapon in the air.

"How dare you raise your sword against the Emperor's guards!" bellowed Yaman from overhead.

"If the guards allow me, I have a letter for the Emperor," Govinda replied, sheathing his sword. "Read it carefully; it bears your father's seal."

Govinda fastened Mumtaz Aalim's letter to the string. An attendant raised the string and handed the message to Yaman.

"Bring it to me," a coarse voice commanded from behind the balcony. Yaman's attendant untied the letter and disappeared through a door before it reached Yaman's hand. Moments later the servant reappeared, letter in hand. The servant whispered something to Yaman, who leaned over the railing to have a closer look at the mysterious rider.

"First I shall read the letter," replied Yaman in response to whatever the servant had whispered.

"Close the gates now!" a woman's raspy voice ordered.

Rather than give the order to raise the drawbridge, Yaman pondered the letter. Upon reading it, he smiled wickedly.

"So *you* are Prince Govinda, and you've come to free your princess," he snickered. "True to your reputation, you Rajputs place chivalry before judgment. FOOL! How dare you ride into my courtyard and not bow down! Get on your knees and beg me not to feed you to my lions. Guards, close the gates and shackle the Rajput!"

The guards closed the circle around Govinda. He had no way out.

Leela suddenly appeared on the balcony, having eluded a eunuch with a dancer's agility.

"The gate is closing!" she cried, avoiding the hulking eunuch who was trying to contain her.

"Are you all right?" replied Govinda.

"It's a trick! They won't free me. Go now, my love, before the gate closes!"

The eunuch tackled Leela, and they fell out of Govinda's sight.

A guard grabbed Govinda's boot, and another seized his reigns. The stallion reared, kicking free of the guard who was holding the reigns. Unable to get out of the way, the guard suffered a violent blow to his head, falling unconscious to the ground.

With the butt of his sword, Govinda bludgeoned the hand that gripped his stirrup. The third guard still clutched his boot. Jerking his foot free, Govinda kicked the guard in the chest, toppling him over.

Free of the guards, Sinha galloped headlong through the startled throng, which fled the horse's path. Streaking across the courtyard,

The Tale of the Himalayan Yogis

Govinda watched the drawbridge rise from the ground. A line of soldiers blocked his path, but he had no intention of slowing down. He only hoped that Sinha reached the span before it was too late.

The bridge rose as Sinha bolted toward it. Soldiers leaped out of the way to avoid being trampled by the charging steed. As Sinha galloped up the sloping span, a sentry swung his mace into Govinda's ribs, tearing his kurta and knocking him off balance as Sinha was about to leap. Gold coins fell like raindrops into the moat. Govinda struggled to right himself as Sinha soared over the water, but the crushing blow plunged him headlong into the moat.

Govinda blinked the water from his eyes and looked around. Sinha had landed safely on the road and was eyeing his master anxiously. Broad rings spread from the spot where Govinda had entered the water. Guards were already lowering the span above him. The instant the drawbridge touched the ground soldiers would pour across. Every commoner in sight who could swim dove into the canal in an attempt to claim the lost mohurs. Amidst the crush of bodies, the Moguls were unable to identify their foe.

Pulling himself onto the far shore, Govinda scrambled toward Sinha clutching his throbbing ribs. With difficulty, he mounted Sinha and headed in the direction of the river, his soaking body leaving a trail of water. He noticed that he still had two mohurs in his kurta pocket.

Guiding Sinha past a troop of soldiers who were unaware of the rider's daring escape, the soldiers peered at him curiously. His torn kurta clung to his drenched torso, but they did not attempt to impede him.

At river's edge, a ferry was pushing off. Sinha galloped down the riverbank and onto the craft, a dozen startled passengers scrambling out of the way.

Scanning the far shore, Govinda spotted a squad of Moguls guarding the ferry's docking point. Gingerly, he dismounted.

Seeing a young, peasant woman and her son at the rear of the boat, Govinda spoke trustingly to the woman.

"*Didi*, I need your help," he whispered. "The Moguls are after me. If your son will sit on my horse and you will walk by my side, the soldiers will think nothing of me."

Before the woman could reply, he slipped two mohurs into her hand, bringing a smile to her face.

"FOOL! I ordered you to close the bridge," raged Zahira, standing nose to nose with her son, her fierce eyes ringed with charcoal. Seething, Zahira loosed a tirade of abuse on her son.

"What does it matter?" he replied, reeling from his mother's rant. "We still have the prize. The Rajput has no choice but to return."

Although she knew it was true, Leela bristled at Yaman's words. Sitting against the wall in a corner, she rubbed her bruised knuckles and toes, the result of her struggle with Itibar Khan. The massive eunuch hovered over her like an executioner. Leela scanned the hall in search of an escape route, a ritual she had performed countless times since being taken captive, but there was no escaping the hulking eunuchs and Sherpa guards who blocked every entrance.

"I warned you not to become too fond of her," Zahira reminded her son. "Your mind is muddled by infatuation. If you had obeyed my order, we would be executing Govinda, and then you would have his princess to yourself. Advise Commander Jari to seal the city. The Rajput can't go far. I'm taking the girl to the harem. She'll be staying with me until they capture the Rajput."

Empress Zahira stormed out of the room, Leela limping after her followed by a pair of burly female guards. Yaman was left cursing his mother's back. The Emperor's face reddened as he grabbed the nearest object, a narcissus in an ornamental pot inlaid with diamonds, rubies, and blue sapphires. Hoisting the bowl above his head, Yaman hurled it from the royal balcony, shattering it in the courtyard below where a crowd had assembled moments earlier. Seeing the wrecked pot, the supplicants scrambled to collect the gems, which rolled like marbles across the stone squares. Hindus and Muslims alike grappled for the jewels. A pair of guards approached the crowd from behind, swords poised.

From his balcony, Yaman watched a Hindu hold his glittering prize up to the sun while a second man donning a fez pocketed a blood-red ruby. The second man was clumsy; he had won the gem through luck. A cunning smile dimpled Yaman's round cheeks as he gestured to a guard with a sweep of his hand. Wielding his sword with the brutal precision of a guillotine, the guard lopped off the hand that held the diamond, catching the gem before it struck the ground. The man screamed, but the others paid no attention as the mad scramble continued.

At the sight of the violent blow, a woman shrieked from behind the Empress' latticed viewing window at the edge of the balcony. Yaman's cheers muffled the woman's cries.

Spotting the severed hand, the Muslim who had pocketed the ruby realized that a similar fate awaited him and dashed madly for the drawbridge. But the swifter guard overtook the clumsy man, and with a sweep of the guard's sword, the hapless fellow's head fell to the ground, his fez cap still affixed to it.

By now the contestants had figured out the morbid game, and those who had collected gems emptied their pockets in front of the guards before seeking safety outside the fortress walls.

Yaman turned to a eunuch who cradled a hookah in his giant hands.

"Did you see it?" the emperor panted excitedly, his formerly blank eyes alive. "Where in all the world can a king command such sport?"

Yaman drew heavily on the hookah, allowing the blue smoke to fill his lungs as he admired the splendor of his city. After a second cup of wine, the emperor's rage subsided, and he became a calm sea awaiting yet another storm. Yaman required an antidote to his mother's venom, and he found two: opium and his nightly visits to the cells beneath the palace. Even his mother had no idea of the delight Yaman took in the suffering of others. In search of the limits of his pleasures, he had yet to find it.

Yaman staggered into the harem. Grabbing a handful of morsels from a silver bowl, he tossed the scraps into a pool of gold and white koi. The fish fought over the food as Yaman turned to face an Oriental mirror. Repulsed by what he saw, Yaman's eyes trailed a pair of concubines as they wandered about a sea of Persian rugs. Slouching onto a silk divan, the Emperor summoned a flurry of nautch dancers with a flick of his royal wrist. A second gesture brought bearers, who approached with fruit and wine; a final gesture brought a eunuch to his side with Leela in tow.

"*Piyaara*," Yaman purred, placing a fleshy hand on Leela's arm. "I understand why your Govinda risks everything for you. Your beauty exceeds anything in the Moti Mahal."

Shifting away from Yaman, Leela replied coldly, "I am a prisoner here, not one of your bibis."

"Be sweet, *meri jaan*," Yaman cooed, his eyes closing as he stuffed a plump fig into his mouth.

Zahira marched into the apartment.

"Idiot! You idle your time away with the wife of the one who will be your ruin. The enemy runs free, and you ogle nautch girls."

"Then Govinda has escaped!" Leela burst out. "The entire imperial army will never catch my Govinda."

"You, my dear, are as insolent as Yaman is dull-witted," barked Zahira. "It's only a matter of time before we capture your prince. And when he is, I'll bring his head to you on a platter!"

"My Govinda can't be conquered," Leela shot back. "You'll see. He defeated your husband, and he'll defeat this pathetic son of yours too. See, he's off dreaming again."

Yaman had lapsed into a torpor, staring absentmindedly at the nautch dancers whirling flirtatiously past though he continued to listen to the conversation between Zahira and Leela.

"Yaman is less than his father's shadow, but what does it matter? The boy is a mere puppet. It is I who rule the empire. Do not forget that your life depends on me."

"Not for long," Leela replied.

"Hold your tongue. A wave of my hand and the surgeons will alter your face so that even your love-struck prince would mistake you for a *Harijan*."

"You do not frighten me." Leela's fiery eyes shot arrows at Zahira.

"You would be wise to fear me," Zahira blandly replied as she left the hall, a trail of eunuchs following in her wake.

Leela retreated to the garden. She needed to get away from Yaman, who had fallen asleep in front of the gyrating dancers. Wherever Leela went a pair of menacing guards followed. Itibar Khan watched from a distance, his cold stare filling her with dread. Rumors claimed that Itibar and his brother Bandu were purchased at a Tunisian slave market for two bags of gold and a Hindu *kanya* of exceptional beauty.

Leela was not prone to despair, but the melancholy that hung over the harem was as thick as the frankincense smoldering in its silver holsters. Sniffing the white jasmine in the garden, Leela longed for Jodhpur. She yearned to whirl about the palace gardens while Govinda played his flute, to be greeted by her father's smile, and to hold her kittens. Her mother's warning haunted her. If she made it back to the fortress of her birth, she would listen to her mother. Leela gazed at the frail clouds overhead, envious of their freedom.

In the brief time that Leela had spent in the harem, she had heard whispers of Zahira's ruthlessness. It was said that the Empress wore a broad streak of jealousy, that eunuchs and harem residents alike feared her, and that those who opposed her tyranny died strange and painful deaths, often languishing in prison for years. Others simply disappeared.

Some believed that Zahira had a secret consort, a shrouded figure seen entering her chambers in the night. Leela had no idea what happened beneath the harem, but one night she was awakened by screams coming from the cellar.

One among the harem community was different. Leela knew from Bandu's gentle eyes that he was a man without malice, the antithesis of his brother, Itibar Khan. Without Bandu, harem life would have been unbearable. In Bandu, the women had a confidant, someone who could lighten the loneliest heart. Bandu was a calm soul, a saintly man assisting a society of women longing for intimacy without the hope of finding it.

The harem inmates indulged in lavish banquets. The elder women treated themselves to sumptuous dishes, but some nubile consorts resisted, preserving their youthful good looks for as long as possible. Previously, this had been in the hope of winning the Emperor's favor and the privileges that it afforded, but with the crowning of Yaman, even that ambition was abandoned.

With its population of three thousand, sentinels guarded every entry point to the harem. Squads of stern-faced Sherpa women patrolled the harem, assisting eunuchs who operated with impunity under Zahira's authority. Idling away sultry afternoons was a way of life, and senior *begums* retreated to underground chambers to escape the heat.

Loneliness caused some to feign illness for the opportunity to speak with a doctor. Although curtains separated patient and physician, women clutched their physician's outstretched hand, kissing and caressing it while he examined their pulse. The residents of the Moti Mahal were forbidden to marry anyone but the Emperor. Gossamer gowns and jeweled necklaces failed to mask the despair that consumed the harem inmates.

At dinner, Leela met Raya, a former wife of Emperor Shah and the daughter of Raja Balveer. The marriage had caused Raya and Zahira to become bitter enemies. The fact that Raya was both a Hindu and a rival wife made her life miserable in the harem.

Feeling a hand on her shoulder, Leela turned to find a young woman wearing a hooded burqa. The woman possessed enchanting, mahogany eyes.

"Do not be frightened," the woman whispered. "I am a friend."

"Who are you?" Leela asked.

"I am Nada. I watched your Govinda ride into the courtyard. He's a brave one."

"He's the bravest man alive!"

"I don't doubt that."

"Govinda will return, and when he does, he'll put an end to the Empress and her son."

"I pray that Allah fulfills your words," replied Nada.

"You do… but why?"

"The harem has been insufferable since Yaman took the throne."

"But the oaf is a mere puppet; a weakling of little consequence."

"I despise him."

"How can you speak like that?"

"Because Empress Zahira has chosen me to marry him. What I saw in the courtyard today sickens me. To humor Yaman, the palace guards beheaded a man. I would rather drink poison than marry the beast."

"No one in the harem will speak to me," complained Leela. "Why do the others dislike me?"

"They're afraid."

"Of Zahira?"

"And Itibar Khan. I'm just as afraid as the others. I'm taking the risk because… you… we… must escape."

"But how?"

"I have a plan, but we must be cautious. There are spies everywhere."

The Emperor and his consorts entered the royal garden for a game of Pachisi. Yaman's stupor had passed, and although mirth was dispensed in small doses in the harem, the group's mood was lighthearted.

Leela and Nada strolled about the *charbagh,* a pair of eunuchs shadowing them. As they passed the Pachisi board, Yaman squealed, "I've won yet again!"

With difficulty, Nada and Leela slipped past Itibar Khan, who hovered in the arched doorway, his body filling the entrance. The hulking eunuch gazed disdainfully at them as they passed. Leela avoided Itibar Khan's eyes. The idea of escape intrigued her, but she gave it little thought, having observed the sentries posted at every door.

Battle

A solitary rider roamed the parched plains to the east of the Yamuna River. Every jarring step of his horse thrust a dagger into Govinda's side. Climbing down, he stretched out on the ground. The mustard harvest was complete, leaving hard clumps of soil underfoot.

Returning to Mumtaz Aalim's shrine was out of the question, for the letter given to Yaman bore the old man's signature. Until he could devise a plan, Govinda would camp outside the city and wait for a sign.

The following morning, Govinda was awakened by a faint rumble. Shankar Baba had taught him to listen to the land, and he pressed his ear to the earth to hear what it had to say. From the west, he heard elephants and horses. From the opposite direction, an army approached on foot.

Fearing that the Mogul cavalry was heading his way, Govinda mounted Sinha and rode in the direction of Varanasi. He had not gone far when he spotted an army of ash-covered figures marching across the fields, their iron tridents rising and falling to the beat of goatskin drums. A horseman led the horde of primitive warriors. As the army of nagababas approached, Govinda recognized their leader.

"Anantaji, I didn't expect to find you here," Govinda said excitedly, riding alongside his friend.

"Raja Rao has dispatched troops to Agra," Ananta explained. "I was sent to Varanasi to gather the nagababas. Raja Rao is planning an attack from the south while we approach from the east. Commander Kuldeep's camp is near Agra."

"Have you seen Shankar Baba?"

"Shankar Baba has a message for you. He says the ground will rise and fall like the sea." He also said to tell you, "'Yogiraj is pleased.'"

"But I barely escaped with my life and Leela is imprisoned in the palace."

"The nagas want you to lead them."

The sight of the sea of loin-covered mendicants poised to march on the capital overwhelmed Govinda.

"The Mogul camp is near the Yamuna," Govinda said. "The nagas are not bothered by the heat. Therefore, we shall engage the Moguls at the hottest time of the day."

The cloud bank to the southwest informed Govinda that hot desert winds were coming. He welcomed the prospect of being engulfed in a sandstorm. If the armies clashed during the *liu*, the Moguls would suffer far greater hardship since its men were unused to being exposed to the hot winds that periodically swept the northern plains. The nagas, on the other hand, were oblivious to hardship. Austerity was their way of life.

"The nagas are ready!" Ananta reported.

"Good. The imperial army is massive."

"*Hari!* There must be fifty-thousand," gasped Ananta, scanning the western horizon.

"As I had hoped."

"You want to confront that?"

"Summon the leaders."

A dozen nagas, few broader than their lances, gathered to hear Govinda's battle plan. The nagas appeared more like half-starved beggars than military officers about to lead their men to battle against the most fearsome army in Asia.

"Do we have adequate water?" Govinda asked. "Our advantage depends on it."

"We babas are like camels. We need little water, but still, we have plenty in reserve," replied a naga leader.

"We shall wait and see what the elements stir up. I am expecting help shortly."

"If you are referring to Raja Rao's army…" interjected Ananta.

"Let us see what comes."

Howling winds brought a sea of sand from the Great Thar, stirring clouds of dust that reduced visibility to a few feet. By nightfall, the conditions had grown still more severe. Nothing compared with the liu; its intense heat and driving winds whipped sand about, blinding the eyes and stinging the skin.

The full force of the storm arrived the following morning, obscuring the sun and causing Mogul horses to grow testy as the hot sand stung their sensitive eyes. There was little that anyone could do but hope that it passed quickly.

On the third day, Govinda woke to a cloudless sky. The winds had done their job.

"Bring me a conch," he requested.

A twig-like baba with matted locks touching his knees scampered off to find one.

Facing his bony troops, Govinda was not encouraged by what he saw. Having lived on alms for much of their lives, the nagas' arms and legs lacked muscle. But in their deep-set eyes, Govinda recognized a steely resolve that gave him hope. Like his Rajput clansmen, the nagas were not afraid to die. Courage was one of the few advantages his troops possessed against the fearsome Moguls, who marched behind a line of bull elephants. Govinda hoped the sandstorm had done its damage.

The baba returned with a pearl-white conch with the words *Jai Sri Ram* carved on it. His lips pressed to the shell; the conch sputtered as the man's breath failed.

"Let me try," said Govinda, tapping the shell's hollow tip before putting it to his lips.

Inhaling deeply, Govinda produced a rich, clarion call that traveled from one end of his army to the other. Three times he made the call before handing the conch to Ananta.

"Tell the babas that no elephant, or horse, is to be harmed," Govinda instructed his officers.

"But their elephants have pikes and blades attached to their tusks," protested one of the nagas. "They will cut us down like sugarcane."

"The elephants will not harm us," Govinda assured the man. "The sun is nearly overhead. Every man should drink his fill before we march. The sound of my conch was a call to the elephants to let them know they will be safe. When the conch sounds again, direct the attack at the heart of the Mogul command. Commander Jari will be riding an elephant bearing the Mogul flag. I shall deal with him myself. Our troops should attack on all sides of me. The soldiers nearest the Mogul command will be their best trained."

"And if the elephants charge?" questioned the naga.

"Then we shall meet an auspicious death," shrugged Govinda. "Should I be killed; Ananta will assume command. Remember, focus the attack on the heart of their army, but wait for the sound of the conch."

The searing sun reached its zenith. What few bushes survived on the parched and cracking plains wilted beneath its relentless glare. The nagas mixed powdered sandalwood and water, spreading the cooling paste across their foreheads, chests, and arms. Their striped markings would have been comical in any other place, but under the summer sun, it could mean the difference between victory and defeat.

Govinda was relieved that the Moguls seemed content to blockade his advance on Delhi; it provided the opportunity to launch a midday assault his adversary would be ill-equipped to counter.

Mogul horses pawed anxiously at the parched earth, unhappy to be saddled in the heat of the day. The horses were not as hampered by the odious heat as their armor-clad masters, who suffered most. In contrast, the nagas donned cotton lungis, their naked limbs staying cool and fresh.

After offering Sinha water, Govinda climbed atop his horse. Sounding a warning to the opposing army's elephants, he waited for a response. It was the critical moment on which the outcome of the battle depended. If the elephants did not reply, there would be no hope.

An eerie silence hung over the plains.

Govinda sounded the conch again, putting the full force of his lungs behind the call. Again he waited for a reply.

"If the bulls don't respond, they'll massacre us," stated Govinda blandly as he signaled for his army to attack.

The chorus of trumpeting elephants brought a smile to Govinda's face. Running his hand over his stallion's muscular shoulders, he sounded the conch a third time and then pointed his sword in the direction of the enemy. As they began their march, the nagas chanted, *"Jai Sri Ram! Jai Sri Ram! Jai Sri Ram!"*

"Only a madman would choose to fight in this loathsome heat," complained Commander Jari to no one in particular.

Certainly, Jari's men didn't relish the prospect. Typically, both sides avoided skirmishing in the heat, but Jari could only assume that his foes believed the sweltering heat to be to their advantage. His scouts had confirmed that indeed it was Govinda who was leading the charge.

"Prepare for battle," Jari ordered. His mahout lowered the imperial army's most intimidating elephant to its knees.

The Mogul commander climbed into the howdah perched on a jade blanket spread across the back of his elephant. His bull bore serrated lances fastened to its tusks. The grey bull, rising unhurriedly to its feet, stood at attention as its commander surveyed his troops. Only a fraction of his forces was visible, so vast was the Mogul ranks. The right wing was thirty-thousand strong, and Uzbek Khan and his infantry defended the left.

The Mogul war machine lumbered toward its foot-bound foe. Leading the charge were a thousand armor-clad elephants, their chests protected by iron spikes and shields of scarred leather. Serrated blades were attached to their tusks and feet. Behind the elephants, a dozen rows of archers were poised to fire. Commander Jari prodded his mount to move faster, but the heat slowed the recalcitrant beast.

"Why so slow today?" Jari inquired of his mahout.

"Sir, he never behaved like this," Raghul replied, procuring a

The Tale of the Himalayan Yogis

barbed stake from the howdah. The mahout prodded the elephant's flanks with limited effect.

"Loathsome heat," muttered Jari, wiping sweat from his brow. Jari's armor was miserably hot; he considered removing it but thought better of exposing his chest.

The row of elephants on either side of their commander was trained to follow the lead bull, and they stood in place, remaining behind their leader. Despite the elephants' heat-induced lethargy, there seemed to be nothing that could stop the Mogul army as it moved on a collision course with the anemic nagas.

"Look at those bamboo sticks. Their bones will dull our swords," sneered Jari as the opposing army came into view.

"Our soldiers will make short work of them," agreed Raghul.

"It's a good thing. This heat is unbearable."

The approaching nagas were now within range of the archers. Jari raised his scimitar, giving the signal to loose their arrows. A shower of arrows arced across the sky, casting a moving shadow over the earth as the projectiles whistled toward their target. The nagas raised crude shields to block the rain of arrows. A dozen nagas fell to the ground; others pulled arrows from their limbs and continued. A second volley followed, and then a third, and a fourth.

Commander Jari gave the signal for the elephants to attack. Raghul prodded his mount repeatedly, but the bull refused to charge. In a hundred battles, this had never happened.

"Give me that," snarled Jari, snatching the barbed stake from his mahout.

Frustrated, the commander jabbed his elephant's ears as nagas battled the infantrymen assigned to protect the elephants' legs. Standing in his howdah, Jari signaled for the other elephants to charge without him, but they failed to respond.

Stabbing his mount in the neck, a stream of blood issued from the thick-skinned bull. The beast shook its mighty head, letting out a deafening bellow that shook its entire body. The other elephants joined their leader, their calls muting the din of drums and clashing swords.

Miraculously, Commander Jari managed to remain upright in

his howdah despite his elephant's wild gyrations. Unsure what to do next, Jari raised his mace and bludgeoned his mount. If the bull didn't respond soon, Jari's elephant riders would be easy targets for the onrushing nagas.

Thrown into disarray by the disobedience of their elephants, many of which had gone down onto their knees, the Moguls climbed down from their howdahs to battle the nagas. Ill-prepared for hand-to-hand combat, the elephant riders were no match for the swarming nagas, who savagely hacked their way between the elephants, breaching the Mogul ranks.

Adding to the confusion, the elephants now obstructed the Mogul archers, who would otherwise have cut down the onrushing nagas. Seizing his opportunity, Govinda sounded his conch and charged toward Commander Jari. Seeing Govinda riding into the heart of the enemy line, the nagas followed their leader through the opening.

Govinda rode alongside Commander Jari, who stood defiantly atop his elephant, the effect undermined by his tenuous foothold atop his unruly mount.

"Climb down, if you have the courage!" challenged Govinda.

"You're hopelessly outnumbered!" Jari shouted back, brandishing his scimitar and stepping out of the basket.

As Jari stepped onto the elephant's back, the beast thrust its head back violently, hurling Jari into the air. The defiant bull deftly caught him in his trunk, raising the commander above his head. Other than Govinda and the Mogul commander's mahout, no one heard the commander's cries for help.

The elephant tossed Jari to the ground. Shaken but uninjured, the commander jumped to his feet, staring into the honey-red eyes of his mount. With a swiftness that belied his massive size, the bull rushed forward, spearing Jari with the iron lance fastened to his tusk. The lance passed cleanly through the commander's armor and chest, killing him instantly.

His wrath spent, the elephant settled peaceably onto its knees. Peering out from his howdah, Raghul spotted Commander Jari dangling from the elephant's lance, a stream of red streaking his

The Tale of the Himalayan Yogis

armor. Uttering a strangled cry, the mahout leaped from the elephant's back and disappeared into the Mogul ranks.

With the help of a naga, Govinda removed the lance from the elephant's tusk and lifted it into the howdah. Propping the lance up so that the Mogul commander's corpse hung like an executed criminal, Govinda climbed into the howdah. As if by instinct, the elephant rose to its feet, towering above the clashing forces that surrounded him.

"Let us ride the length of the battlefield so that the soldiers can see their fallen leader," Govinda instructed the naga.

Govinda raised his sword triumphantly as the elephant lumbered through the raging battle. Seeing the Rajput standing in their commander's howdah alongside General Jari's impaled corpse, the heat, confusion, and loss of command plunged the Mogul soldiers into chaos. Pursued by wraith-like nagas, the soldiers turned and fled. Some of the nagas climbed onto elephants, which directed their tusks and attached blades against their masters.

The carnage was swift and brutal. The elephants trampled the fleeing soldiers and speared many from behind. Foot-soldiers stumbled out of exhaustion, only to be hacked apart by the swarming nagas. The heart of the imperial army severed from its body, its forces had little recourse but to flee for the Yamuna River, all semblance of order abandoned.

As expected, the oppressive heat had taken its toll. Exhausted soldiers collapsed on the parched fields, their armor burning them alive. Some tore at their helmets; others pulled off their boots only to be cut down where they lay, their blood mingling with their sweat.

His troops still outnumbered, Govinda hoped Mogul reinforcements weren't waiting at their encampment by the river. If the Mogul cavalry regrouped, their numbers and superior mobility posed a threat. Everything depended on their generals. If they failed to act, their infantry would be slaughtered, or driven into the river. But if they had a backup plan, then Govinda was leading his men into a trap.

The fleeing Moguls rushed headlong into the river, driven mad by the fear of an enemy that had turned their elephants against them. Some secured rafts and dugouts, but they were quickly dragged down by the mass of men clutching desperately for anything that would keep them afloat. Wearing heavy armor, none of the soldiers could swim. Flailing limbs disappeared beneath the current. Those who returned to shore were speared unceremoniously and shoved back into the reddened water. The river had swallowed almost the entire Mogul force.

Wide-eyed nagas stood at water's edge, staring in disbelief at the scene. Some danced outlandish jigs while others cleaned their weapons, but most just stood and gaped at the spectacle, spearing the odd soldier as he staggered out of the water.

Govinda stood in the howdah, Commander Jari's body at his feet. Before him, an armada of corpses floated past. In the distance loomed the impregnable fortress interning Leela, its russet turrets stabbing the afternoon sky. Govinda's work had barely begun, but already he was thanking his unseen allies for the cooperation of the elephants that had turned the battle in his favor.

Climbing down from his mount, Govinda penned a letter. He was signing it when he spotted Ananta for the first time since the battle had commenced.

"Anantaji, we shall make the Mogul camp our headquarters. Find a mahout and instruct him to take this noble elephant to the ferry. Give the mahout some mohurs and instruct him to deliver the elephant and its cargo to the Emperor's courtyard, but only after parading the elephant through the capital. Instruct the mahout to tie this message to the Emperor's string when he reaches the courtyard."

As the sun disappeared beyond the palace walls, Yaman lay against a mountain of pillows, alternating sips of wine with probes into the gossamer robe of his favorite concubine. Itibar Khan loomed nearby, ever watchful.

"Sir, there is a message for you," a servant stammered.

"Then read it, if you are able," Yaman guffawed.

"Sir, you must come and see for yourself. It is not a message that I can convey."

"What did I tell you? The man can't read," tittered Yaman to no one in particular.

"Emperor, the message is beyond words," replied the servant nervously.

"What is this message that it interferes with my play?"

"A parchment is tied to the royal string… an elephant stands beside it."

"Fool! You have the nerve to bother me about a parchment and an elephant. Pull the elephant up with the rope and burn the…" The Emperor cast his drunken mind about in search of a suitable adjective, "… insipid parchment."

Yaman was both amused with his choice of words and angered by the impertinence of his servant. The bibis lying near him giggled at his wittiness.

"Yaman!" raged Begum Zahira, entering the room in a huff. "Get off your buttocks. Thanks to you, we have a crisis on our hands."

"What is all this fuss about?" Yaman complained. "First, they tell me an elephant awaits me in the courtyard, and now you barge in and disrupt my fun. Can't you see I'm busy?"

"Commander Jari is dead! There's a letter attached to the string. The attendant won't send it up until he sees your fat face."

"Mother, please. Why must you be so unpleasant?"

Yaman untangled himself from his consorts, tried his best to stand unattended, eventually succeeded, and waited impatiently while a servant straightened his robes.

"Now get to the balcony!" ordered Zahira, her eyes flaring.

"This better be justified," Yaman grumbled. "Itibar, bring the wine. This talk of crisis makes me thirsty."

Yaman leaned over the marble railing while Begum Zahira watched from behind the lattice window. Seeing his commander, a lance piercing his bloodstained uniform, Yaman stammered, "S-S-Send up the m-message."

By the time the parchment reached him, Yaman was shaking so badly that he passed the letter to Itibar Khan, ordering him to, "R-R-Read it!"

Untying the string, Itibar Khan opened the letter and began to read.

"Emperor…"

"Louder!" ordered a voice from behind the lattice window.

"Emperor," Itibar Khan began again, "your commander is dead, and your army floats down the Yamuna like a forest cut asunder. Release Princess Leela by noon tomorrow, or we shall sack the palace. Reply before nightfall. Govinda."

"This must be a hoax," Yaman mused, his head reeling. "Get me my hookah!"

Itibar Khan held out a hose.

"It's not a hoax," Zahira hissed, spraying saliva through her latticed window. "Itibar, drag the fool to the harem. And get the Rajput princess. It is time I took over for this clown of an emperor before we all end up like Commander Jari. Send some guards to the courtyard to dispose of the body before everyone in Delhi hears about it. And get me, General Murad. NOW!!!"

Begum Zahira's satin gown fluttered as she sped into the harem. Moments later, Murad entered.

"General Murad reporting."

"You are no longer a general," said Zahira. "You have been promoted to the rank of commander."

"Commander? I... I thank you, Empress. May I speak with the Emperor? Jari's body was paraded through the streets on the back of an elephant like an executed criminal. The entire city is buzzing about it. And the river is full of dead soldiers. The Rajput and his men now occupy the encampment on the far side of the river."

"How many soldiers does the Rajput have?" queried Zahira.

"Ten thousand, but they're not actual soldiers — they're nagababas — and not all are armed."

"Whatever they are, armed or not, they fought well enough to defeat Jari and his men. How many soldiers do we have?"

"Three hundred thousand!"

"Only three hundred thousand?" parroted Zahira. "Then my officers are bigger fools than that drunken lump of flesh they call their emperor. Where are these three hundred thousand soldiers?"

"I... I have no idea where they are, other than the fact that a portion of the troops was dispatched to fight the nagas and the remainder rode south to confront the Rajputs near Agra. Jari was commanding the division that engaged the nagas. Uzbek Khan and his infantry were with him. The other generals are, or were, divided between Jari's troops, Agra, and the city guard here in Delhi."

"Find out how many are dead and where the others are, and report back within the hour. And Commander... if you don't return within the hour, Itibar Khan will remove a few of your fingers and feed them to the dogs while you watch. Do you understand?"

"Yes."

Shaken, Commander Murad rushed out of the Moti Mahal.

Begum Zahira disappeared into the chambers below the harem, emerging an hour later with a pouch in her hand. Commander Murad waited anxiously for her.

"Well?" she demanded of him.

"Half of the troops have gone to Agra to fight the Rajputs," he informed her.

"And the rest?"

"The entire elephant unit has been lost... twenty-thousand infantrymen dead and another forty-thousand are wandering around the countryside without water. They won't last long in this heat."

"And the cavalry?"

"They've reassembled and are ready to mount an attack on the Rajput's camp."

"Prepare the cavalry to strike in the morning, but first, take this to Govinda," ordered Zahira, handing a pouch to Murad. "If he agrees to the terms, the cavalry is to attack his troops while he's on the river. And I might remind you that you do not want anything to go wrong. I'm sure you have heard the fate of the officers who failed in their duties. Your newly attained rank affords you the privilege of knowing that those tales are true."

The Exchange

Commander Murad delivered the pouch and waited for a reply. The message read:

> *Rajput, at sunrise tomorrow, if you are not on a raft in the middle of the Yamuna to be exchanged for Raj Kumari Leela, more than her toe will be delivered to your tent.*

Govinda reached into the pouch and removed a small clothbound object. He recognized the silk as Leela's. Unwrapping the cloth, he recoiled in horror. It contained Leela's toe, her toe ring attached.

"Hideous!" proclaimed Ananta.

Govinda tried to speak. What he meant to say, or to whom, he did not know, but he choked on his words.

"Ready to make the exchange?" grinned Murad. "If not, then her foot will be next."

The Mogul was pleased with himself for conjuring up the notion that a foot would be delivered next.

"Only a fiend would do such a thing," protested Ananta.

"You don't know the Empress," chuckled Murad. "She's capable of anything."

"We'll make the exchange at sunrise," agreed Govinda, "but on the following conditions. I'll be on a raft with two boatmen. Arrange the same for Leela. The rafts will meet in the middle of the river where we'll make the exchange. My army will have orders to sack the fort and spare no one if there is foul play."

"Agreed!" said Murad, before heading back to the palace.

Govinda walked forlornly along the river, his mind tormented by the thought that Leela was captive to such fiends.

Leela tossed about her bed. Nada had informed her of the exchange and promised to help her escape, assuring her that the proposed swap was a trick. The hours crept by as Leela waited, wondering how she would escape when armed eunuchs patrolled the harem day and night.

The creaking of her door followed a faint knock.

"Are you awake?" Nada whispered.

"Yes," Leela whispered back.

"Quickly, my dear, put this on."

Nada handed her a burqa. Leela had never worn one, but she pulled it over the blue salwar kameez she was already wearing.

"Fasten the face covering," Nada instructed her.

"If someone spots us, what difference will it make?" questioned Leela as she fastened the covering.

"It's not like that. Consorts come and go to the guest chambers all night. Tonight, some concubines are entertaining. The mullahs insist their women arrive in full purdah. No one will suspect us."

"I see."

"Now follow me. I'm taking you to a tunnel beneath the palace. It will take us to the mosque in Chandni Chowk. The tunnel is the Emperor's secret passage."

The women made their way to the stairs leading to the underground chambers where senior consorts entertained special guests. Nada carried an oil lantern as they passed a row of lavishly furnished apartments.

"Once we're in the tunnel we're safe," Nada whispered. "No one uses it except for the Emperor when he goes to the mosque."

They entered a dark passageway. The blackness grudgingly receded, closing in again as the light moved on.

Nada and Leela passed a heavily bolted door. As they did, Leela nearly choked. The stench reminded her of Varanasi's burning ghats, but there was something else, something evil about the odor. She felt threatened, as though something was watching her through the keyhole. Nada noticed it too. As they passed the door, they pressed against the far wall.

"Where does that lead?" Leela asked as they continued down the corridor, the door being reclaimed by the blackness.

"I don't know for certain," Nada whispered back, "but I think the chambers are in there."

"The chambers?"

The tunnel cut a long, straight path that seemed to go on forever. It ended abruptly at a stairwell.

"The stairs lead to the inner sanctum of the mosque," Nada whispered. "Only mullahs and high officials are allowed into the sanctum, but the mosque will be empty."

They climbed the stairs and reached a door. Nada opened it cautiously. Raising the lantern, the women scanned the cavernous chamber, but the light was so weak that they couldn't see beyond what the lamp illuminated. Leela had never been in a mosque before and had little idea of her surroundings beyond the domed ceiling and colonnades of carved pillars illumined by the lamp.

"You're safe now," whispered Nada.

"You said we were safe when we entered the tunnel," Leela whispered back, her voice greatly amplified.

"We were, but we're safer now."

"*Safer?*"

"In a moment, we'll be in Chandni Chowk bazaar where there are countless alleys."

"Why are our voices so loud?" wondered Leela as they crossed the mosque.

"Our mosques are designed to amplify the mullah's voice."

"It's eerie," observed Leela. "Are we entirely safe now?"

"Almost."

Leela couldn't help suspecting that they hadn't been remotely safe at any point during the escape.

The Tale of the Himalayan Yogis

Nada led her to another door. Near the door stood a screen separating the sanctum from a row of crypts. The Tree of Life had been carved at the center of the sandalwood screen.

"Out this door and we're safe," whispered Nada, pushing open the door.

Fresh air rushed in as the door swung open, but standing before them was Itibar Khan, his broad shoulders filling the frame.

"I'm surprised, Nada," Itibar Khan said calmly. "I have been observing you these past days. Surely you know that I monitor everyone. Turn around; we're going back the way you came."

"Please, Itibar," pleaded Nada, her voice strangled by panic. "Let Leela go. She has done nothing."

"Without her, we would have no bait for the Rajput. Zahira will not be pleased when she learns you've helped her. Surely you know what betrayal means!"

The walk back down the long, black corridor proved torturous. Nada and Leela shuffled along in front of Itibar Khan, who followed within arm's reach, carrying the lantern. If they walked too slowly, he stepped with his crushing weight on their heels, and if they walked too quickly, he grabbed their shoulders and jerked them backward.

When the women reached the bolted door, Itibar Khan wrenched them both to a stop and handed a large brass key to Nada.

"Unlock the door," he ordered, speaking as if he were trying not to disturb someone.

Nada's hands trembled as she manipulated the key. Again, Leela noticed the disgusting odor, which seemed to increase slightly when the door was unlocked.

"Open it," Itibar Khan commanded, inhaling deeply. The eunuch held a lamp in one hand and a scrolled parchment in the other.

Leaving the key in its hole, Nada opened the door, beyond which there was only blackness. A sickening stench poured through the door, a fetor of fire and death and worse. Nada, who was the closest to the door, retched; her stomach audibly churning. Leela, who was standing behind her, was only slightly less affected. Itibar Khan appeared accustomed to the smell, though he liked it no more than his captives.

The eunuch shoved the women forward. Clutching one another's hand, they stumbled blindly through the door into the darkness. Despite the smothering reek, the air around them felt as though they were in a cavernous chamber, but it afforded no sense of freedom. Instead, hungry, unseen eyes seemed to be staring at them. Leela felt as though something was consuming her strength, a presence she could only describe as demonic. Trembling in the darkness, Leela reached for Nada's hand, sensing that she was similarly affected.

Itibar Khan stepped through the door behind the women and shoved them forward again. The lantern shone on their backs, casting maddening shadows on the stone floor. Part of Leela was glad of the lantern's light, but another part was irrationally afraid of the flame.

It is warm in here, she noticed, *and dry. The air… shouldn't it be cold and damp in a cellar?*

Itibar Khan raised the lantern above their heads, casting its light onto something their shadows had concealed — a fire pit with a pair of blackened chains suspended above it. Beside the pit stood a rusted cage large enough for at least two humans. Its door was ajar.

"You'll be spending the night in there," said the eunuch.

"But Itibar," pleaded Nada. "I am to marry the Emperor."

"*Were* to marry the Emperor, but that was before you revealed yourself to be a traitor. You never wanted to marry the Emperor. Now that you've been spared that fate, you desire it after all? You should've considered more carefully before helping a prisoner escape. Not only would you have realized that escape from the Moti Mahal is impossible, but also that the Empire, in its rulers' wisdom, assigns the best possible fate to each person. If you flee from your position in the Empire, you will only find yourself in a worse one."

"It's warm…" Leela murmured.

"The pit was used recently. Empress Zahira is clever. To ensure that Govinda agreed to exchange himself for you, he was sent a severed toe with a ring identical to the one you wear. Govinda thinks it was your toe. I'm sure the toe will discourage him from further trickery. Had we used your toe, the Emperor would have been upset. The public needs to see a capable ruler on the royal balcony. Soon, you will see firsthand how we do things down here. Now get inside the cage. I've wasted time talking."

The Tale of the Himalayan Yogis

Leela fully intended to obey Itibar Khan, but her body refused to move nearer to the cage, or the pit. Shuddering, Nada stood in place as well. The eunuch shoved them both into the cage, where they collapsed against each other, sobbing in each other's arms.

Itibar Khan locked the cage before making his way to the chamber's exit. Moving quickly, he closed the door behind him. The eunuch had been in the chamber numerous times, but still, he did not like spending more time there than was necessary. Though he had been told that the powers within the chamber were the Empire's allies, he could not help believing that such powers had no allies, only slaves, and enemies. And if ever the Empire left its position as a slave and became an enemy, Itibar Khan did not want the powers within the chamber to remember him.

The eunuch had already missed much of his night's sleep, and he doubted whether he would get any sleep at all after his exposure to the forces within the chamber. He was glad the traitor had brought a lantern; usually, he worked in darkness.

Leela stared at the departing lantern, knowing that it would soon leave them in blackness. When the door closed behind Itibar Khan, the faintest threads of light remained visible through the keyhole and at the edges of the door. Leela expected the slivers of light to darken quickly, but instead, they suddenly shifted, as though the lantern had been dropped and caught again. The muffled sound of something heavy hitting the floor accompanied the shifting light.

The door opened suddenly, and Itibar Khan stepped back into the chamber holding a scimitar in addition to Nada's lantern.

Where did he get that? Leela wondered.

Itibar Khan approached the cage.

"Come," he said, his voice uncharacteristically gentle, sorrowful, and scared. Setting the lantern on the floor, the eunuch unlocked the cage.

Leela looked at Itibar Khan in confusion.

"This is no place for royalty," offered the eunuch.

"Bandu?" Nada cried. "How did you know to look for us here?"

"Nada, you are an innocent child," answered the eunuch whose voice Leela now recognized as Bandu's... "Like my brother, I too have been watching you. But this time, I could not allow my angels to languish in this hell. There have been many…"

"Then you'll help us escape?" hoped Nada.

"I have already helped as much as I can. From here, you must go alone. If anyone sees me, then I will be hung over the pit."

"We will speak of this to no one."

"Try to forget this evil place," Bandu cautioned.

"I've never felt anything so…" Nada's voice trailed off. "What exactly goes on in here?"

"I will not say, except that a sorcerer invokes a demoness named Tadaka here."

"Who is Tadaka?" Nada asked.

The word 'Tadaka' echoed about the chamber as if it was not an echo, but a whisper repeated by a disembodied voice. Leela remembered the name, Tadaka, from Govinda's account of his journey to the narakas.

"Better not repeat the name," cautioned Leela. "Uttering the demoness' name is enough to summon her."

"Step carefully into the tunnel," Bandu advised.

Nada held the lantern high, revealing the body of Itibar Khan. Nada swallowed hard as she stepped over the dead eunuch. Sobbing, Bandu stepped into the tunnel. Leela pressed her head against the eunuch's massive chest.

After Itibar Khan left the chamber, a searing pain had torn through his chest. The eunuch was dead before his body hit the floor.

"Now go, and take this," he instructed, placing a ruby-handled dagger in Nada's hand.

"Bandu, come with us," Nada pleaded, handing the lantern to Leela as she accepted the dagger. "If they find out you killed Itibar Khan…"

"Zahira would never suspect me. She knows I love my brother. Besides, the harem is my home. What good is a eunuch anywhere else? Go quickly, my children."

Bandu disappeared into the blackness.

Nada tugged at Leela's arm, neither woman wanting to linger near the body. But before following Nada, Leela picked up a scroll that lay

The Tale of the Himalayan Yogis

beside the eunuch. Standing, Leela reeled at the sight of the impaled body. She had never clutched a hand as tightly as Nada's. For the third time, they trod the dark corridor leading to the mosque. Again, Nada opened the secret door and guided Leela across the empty sanctuary. A bat dove from its roost, winging about the sanctum.

As Nada reached for the door leading outside, it opened suddenly.

Pulling Leela with her, the women hid behind the wooden screen separating the sanctum from the crypts. Blowing out her lantern, Leela crouched low to the ground beside Nada.

A lamp entered through the door, exposing a bearded face with close-set eyes. A woman joined the man, but the darkness masked her features.

"It's Nazir Hussein, head of the Ulema," Nada whispered.

"It helps when you join me for prayers afterward," Hussein told the woman.

"Be brief," instructed the woman. "I have matters to tend to."

Leela recognized Zahira's voice.

"All the more reason why you should pray, my love," Nazir Hussein said.

"Yes, yes," replied Zahira impatiently.

Empress Zahira and Mullah Hussein knelt on oval rugs facing Mecca.

"I want to use the dagger right now," Leela whispered, tightening her grip on the knife.

"It would please many... including her son," Nada replied in a hushed tone, slipping the weapon into Leela's hand.

Restless, Zahira got up from her rug and carried the oil lamp to the tunnel entrance, her face revealed for the first time.

"Nazir, why is this door ajar?"

"I am praying."

Raising the lamp, she scanned the sanctuary. Again a bat darted about, its shrill sound frightening Nada. Ignoring the bat, Zahira moved methodically among the colonnades, peering behind every pillar. She approached the wooden screen behind which Nada and Leela were hiding.

The Empress walked along the opposite side of the screen, her lamp shining through the carved partition. Lowering the lamp opposite Nada and Leela, she looked through the screen's holes one by one. Fortunately, Zahira was not searching carefully; Leela suspected that the search was an excuse to avoid praying with the mullah. Zahira passed by the fugitives without noticing them.

Leela loosened her grip on the dagger. She had been crouching for so long that her knees ached. Desperate to move her legs, she shifted positions, causing her bangles to tinkle slightly. Spinning around, Zahira held the lamp overhead. Leela stared into the Empress' odious eyes. Zahira stepped close to the screen, peering once again through the openings. Lowering the lamp to the floor, she spotted the fugitives.

Letting out an earsplitting shriek that echoed off the hall's marble dome, Leela wrenched her arm free of Nada's grip, jumped to her feet, and shoved the partition, toppling it onto Zahira.

The weight of the screen knocked the Empress to the floor, splashing hot oil on Zahira's neck. The glass of her lantern shattered, leaving the sanctuary in darkness. The Empress winced with pain as she struggled to free herself from beneath the screen. Leela considered using the dagger on the Empress, but the screen shielded her. Seeing her chance, Leela grabbed Nada by the hand and ran past Nazir Hussein. Absorbed in his devotions, he didn't react to the commotion.

"Stop them!" shouted Zahira.

The women sprinted out the door, darting first one way and then another as they lost themselves in the bazaar's endless tangle of stalls. It was hours past midnight, and canvas covered each shop's wares. In an alley, they stopped to catch their breath and repair their disheveled appearances, to appear less conspicuous.

"Muslim women don't wander around the city's silver district at night. If someone sees us, we'll arouse suspicion," exhaled Nada, appraising the situation.

"We need to warn Govinda."

"It will be difficult. Docking points are well guarded. By the time we reach the river, Zahira will have issued orders to detain all women without escorts."

"But if I go alone dressed as a Hindu girl, then I could cross," suggested Leela.

"It would be risky. The soldiers will detain anyone who looks suspicious."

"But I have to try. Govinda's life depends on it."

"When the shops open, we'll purchase peasant clothes," decided Nada.

"But we have no rupees."

"That dagger is worth a small fortune. Did you not notice the rubies lining the handle?"

Leela examined the dagger and found the handle lined with gems.

"But won't it draw suspicion?"

"We'll have to take that chance. Most Chandni Chowk shopkeepers deal in illegal things anyway. We'll need to find the right stall. What worries me is that the Mogul guard will comb these alleys shortly. It's not safe here, but I don't know where to hide. It has been years since I ventured outside the Moti Mahal."

"Is there a Hindu temple nearby?"

"The Shiva mandir at the entrance to the bazaar has a courtyard. The Mogul guard won't think to look there."

"If we take off these burqas we should be all right," said Leela.

"I can't," giggled Nada.

"Why?"

"I'm not wearing anything underneath."

The night air hung over Delhi's oldest market; the smell of used cooking oil, incense, and rose blossoms confounded the senses as much as the hodgepodge of passageways leading further into the bazaar. Although Leela was hungry, there were more important matters. She followed close on Nada's heels until they arrived at the Shiva temple.

"If only the exchange were taking place later in the day," mused Leela. "Sunrise will come soon, and still the shops haven't opened."

"What are you wearing under the burqa?" Nada asked.

Leela peeled the robe away, revealing her salwar kameez.

The plaintive call of the Imam disturbed the morning calm. Soon the streets would be crowded with Islamic faithful making their way to the Masjid at the far end of the bazaar.

Govinda's ribs ached, but it was his throbbing head that had kept him awake in the night as he reviewed his plan to free Leela. He had considered every scenario, including those involving treachery on the part of the Moguls.

Rising before the sun, Govinda splashed river water on his face and slid his kurta over his head. He then stuffed a river rock inside a pouch, which he secured around his neck. He then went in search of Ananta.

"If anything goes wrong, send armed men on the barge. Have you seen anyone on the other side of the river?"

"Not yet, but they'll come. You're the prize everyone wants."

"Alert the boatmen. I'm ready the moment they arrive."

An hour after sunrise, figures appeared on the far bank of the Yamuna. Govinda climbed onto his raft, which was little more than a rectangle of wooden planks. Waiting for Leela's vessel to push off, Govinda wedged a knife into his sash and placed a sword at his feet. His boatmen were among his best soldiers; they too had weapons at their feet.

Seeing Leela's raft push off, Govinda's craft maneuvered toward the middle of the river. Looking back to the shore, clouds of dust hovered to the south; the Moguls were on the attack. He feared the battle would not go well with Ananta in charge, but this was his chance to free Leela.

The Mogul craft approached. On its platform, a pair of hulking guards flanked a hooded figure wearing a burqa. Govinda was sure the men on the Mogul raft also carried weapons. As the rafts pulled alongside one another, Govinda sensed something was wrong.

"Leela?"

The hooded figure stood in silence. Brandishing his sword, Govinda ran toward the Mogul raft. His boatmen abandoned their oars and brandished their weapons. The guards on the Mogul raft raised bows that had been hidden at their feet, aiming at Govinda's men, who were hopelessly exposed.

Trying to protect his men, Govinda leaped onto the Mogul raft before the archers opened fire. The nagas followed him. Running headlong into one of the archers, Govinda toppled him into the water.

The Tale of the Himalayan Yogis

The second archer fired at Govinda, but he rolled sideways, and the arrow missed its target. Slowed by his injured ribs, Govinda spun back onto his feet, attacking the archer with his sword.

The Moguls fired on Govinda's men. A flurry of projectiles struck the nagas, who fell lifeless into the water. Turning their weapons on Govinda, they held their fire.

Looking past his captors, Govinda saw a second boatload of Mogul soldiers approaching. Leaping into the river, he forced his adversary to either jump in after him or let go. The soldier released him.

Govinda was a strong swimmer, but his injury slowed him. The confusion caused by the attacking cavalry had delayed the second nagas' raft. Spotting Govinda in the water, the nagas pulled him onto their raft, but the swifter Mogul craft overtook them.

Fierce battles raged in the water and on land. Govinda had no idea how Ananta's men were faring, but his situation was dire. From the corner of his eye, he spotted the ominous shadow of a great flock of birds circling over the Yamuna as it headed for the battlefield where the nagas faced the Mogul army.

Distracted by the wraithlike formation in the sky, a barrage of arrows whizzed past Govinda. Two nagas fell dead, and three more were wounded. The Moguls kept at a safe distance, content to release their arrows. None of the nagas had ranged weapons, nor could they swim.

Realizing that the enemy planned to take him prisoner, Govinda dove into the current and swam for shore, but a Mogul craft quickly overtook him. Pulling him from the water, the Moguls shackled his wrists and ankles. Captive, Govinda watched the raging land battle.

"Prince Govinda in chains," gloated an eerily familiar voice. "It's a shame Shankar Baba isn't here."

Govinda spun around to face the speaker. Standing before him was the robed figure that was supposed to be Leela.

"They would have botched your capture had I not been here. My magic is better than you give me credit."

A soldier pulled the robes over Kritavat's head, exposing the tantric's crimson tunic.

"I was not impressed by your magic before, and I'm not impressed now."

"Still brash, I see. But then, that is how Shankar Baba trains his chelas. 'Trust the gods,' he always said. I ask you, where is Shankar Baba now?"

"If I remember correctly, your magic failed in his presence."

"Not really... How do you think I managed to return from the dead?"

"You were never dead. The cobras spent their venom on Subahu. You feigned death and slipped away in the night. Not a very courageous display."

"Is that what you think?"

"Everyone knows that's how it happened," asserted Govinda, testing the strength of his shackles.

"Then I invite you to my chambers beneath the palace. There you will discover the true power behind the throne."

"You think you possess the power to rule the Empire when you haven't the courage to face a cobra. You're a coward."

"You speak boldly for one in chains. Strip away the Rajput's clothes," Kritavat ordered.

"I have nothing of value."

"We shall see. We must prepare you to meet your adoring public."

Kritavat produced a dagger.

"This won't be too painful," he snickered. "I need to give you the proper look of defeat. See that elephant?"

On the river bank stood a bull elephant.

"You'll be paraded through the streets chained to its back," Kritavat said, examining his dagger. "A little blood will help your Hindu brothers understand that their hero is human after all."

"Your schemes never worked."

"But they have! You don't think that useless slab of flesh is running the Empire. It is I who rule from my subterranean throne."

"Where the rodents are your loyal subjects!"

"Speak respectfully," cautioned Kritavat. "Your life is in my hands."

"Is Leela all right?"

The Tale of the Himalayan Yogis

"That depends on what you mean by 'all right.' If you're worried about her toe, that was my idea. Fortunately for her, the toe came from someone else. Yaman has grown rather fond of your princess and would have flown into a rage if she had been harmed. But you took the bait."

"Where is she?"

"Somewhere in Chandni Chowk, but the guards will find her shortly."

"Then she escaped?"

"We have little use for her now that we've captured the prize. She was never more than bait. And it never mattered whether we had her, or not; what mattered was what you believed. Otherwise, we would have guarded her much more… intimately. Yaman is disappointed, but I enjoy seeing the brat pout.

Kritavat's crafty eyes probed Govinda's neck.

"You have something I want."

"This?" asked Govinda, removing the soaked pouch from around his neck.

"I've been waiting for this day since before you were born. With the Idol's Eye, there will be no one on earth, or in heaven, who can stop me."

Kritavat reached for the pouch, but before he could secure it, Govinda flung it into the river.

"Get it," ordered Kritavat, shoving a pair of soldiers overboard.

Unable to swim, the men flailed about the water. Neither of them paid the slightest attention to the pouch, which was swept away by the current. The current also swept the soldiers away.

Flushing with anger, Kritavat raised his knife.

"I should cut your eyes out for that, but I have a use for them," he fumed, carving diagonal lines across Govinda's chest. "I shall offer them to the demoness. You bleed easily, Rajput. Having lived with Shankar Baba, I expected your skin to be thicker."

"Now that the Idol's Eye is gone forever, what use have you for me?"

"Gone forever? Is that what you think? The Idol's Eye is not gone forever. You have delayed my acquisition of it, nothing more. After I make the necessary preparations, I shall use my powers to summon it from the river. If it resists, I shall dam the Yamuna and retrieve the Idol's Eye by hand. As for what use I have for you; maybe I'll use you as bait to catch Shankar Baba the way I used Leela to catch you. Have you heard the news? Raja Rao's army has been defeated… and look there."

Kritavat pointed to the battle on the far bank of the river.

"Zahira is personally commanding the cavalry. She ordered anyone who abandoned his position, executed on the spot."

The raft arrived at the shore where a cavalry escort met it.

Kritavat addressed the officer. "Faizon, rough the prince up and smear mud over his body before chaining him to the elephant… then parade him through the streets. Behead anyone who interferes. Bring the Rajput to the palace before sundown. Empress Zahira will be waiting for him with news of his army's slaughter."

"But sir, should we not use some other means?" questioned Faizon, shifting uncomfortably in his saddle. "The elephants brought bad luck yesterday."

"I thought only Hindus were superstitious. Bind the Rajput to the front of the howdah so that the citizens of Delhi can have a final look at their fallen prince."

From atop his horse, Kritavat fumed over how agonizingly close he had come to possess the real prize, the Idol's Eye. Realizing that the gem was gone forever, he took pleasure in watching the soldiers batter Govinda with the blunt end of an oar.

Before riding off, the tantric shouted, "Soon your soul will be lost, and not even Shankar Baba will be able to find it."

The Execution

Word of Govinda's capture spread quickly throughout the city. Seeing their battered hero chained to an elephant's back, Hindus cursed their cruel rulers. Blood and filth stained Govinda's body and caked his parched lips. A merciless sun seared the cuts on his chest and arms as he passed the throngs of curious onlookers lining Delhi's broad avenues.

The procession entered Chandni Chowk bazaar. The elephant carrying Govinda was passing the Shiva temple when a sadhu appeared on the road. The humble-seeming man raised his hand, and the elephant stopped.

"Stand aside," General Faizon ordered, as a crowd gathered to witness the unfolding drama.

"The prince would like some water," said the sadhu, bowing to Govinda.

"Stand aside!" snapped Faizon. "I have orders to behead anyone who interferes."

Looking up at the officer, the sadhu calmly replied, "If you do not allow me to wet the boy's lips, then I shall ask God to do it."

"Madman," mumbled Faizon, dismounting.

Ignoring the officer, the sadhu continued to bow. Incensed, Faizon raised his sword, intending to lop off the sadhu's head. As he was about to strike the lethal blow, the elephant laid its trunk on the sadhu's neck. Cursing the elephant, Faizon bludgeoned its forehead with the sword's pommel, causing the elephant to remove its trunk. Raising his weapon a second time, Faizon was about to behead the sadhu when the elephant seized the Mogul in its trunk, tossing him defiantly onto the temple steps.

Excited onlookers now blocked the street. The crowd cheered as Faizon's men rushed to their commander's aid. Fearing a riot, the soldiers drew their horses around the elephant and unsheathed their swords.

"Baba, please go before they harm you," pleaded Govinda.

Standing, the holy man made his way toward the temple. As he reached the top of the stairs, an anvil of threatening clouds appeared in the sky. As the sadhu gazed up at the sky, a deafening clap sounded overhead. The cloud unleashed a torrent, sending the frenzied crowd scrambling for shelter. The sadhu nodded at Govinda, who licked rainwater from his lips. Pressing his hands together, the holy man disappeared inside the temple.

Hiding behind a stone pillar a few steps from where General Faizon lay, Nada and Leela looked on in disbelief. Leela had tried to warn Govinda, but the soldiers had converged on Chandni Chowk, leaving her with little option but to hide in the temple grounds. Starting toward Govinda, Nada prevented her.

"There is nothing you can do."

"But he's suffering," groaned Leela.

A pair of soldiers helped their commanding officer to his feet; the downpour had stopped as inexplicably as it had started.

"I want to follow Govinda," Leela whispered, pulling free of Nada's grip.

"If they capture you, it will only make matters worse for him."

Returning to the temple courtyard, Leela leaned against the trunk of a pipal tree. She hadn't eaten since the previous day or slept since the night before the previous one, and the pain of seeing Govinda in his present condition was more than she could endure.

Resting against the tree trunk, Leela looked up to find the old sadhu standing in front of her.

"Eat this, my child," he said, his gentle voice soothing her heart. "It will ease the sadness you feel for your Govinda."

"But..."

"Govinda is like a son to me," the sadhu replied. "You need do nothing. I am watching over him."

"But the Moguls plan to execute him," she moaned.

"Trust, tender heart. Now take this."

The sadhu handed Leela some dried fruits.

"They will give you strength. I have arranged lodging in the temple. You will be safe here, but sit for a while beneath this tree."

The holy man bowed to the tree, muttering some mantras as he did so. The old man was about to go when he noticed the parchment lying on the ground. "Take care not to lose that," he cautioned before vanishing down an alley.

Leela reached for the parchment. Examining the seal on the scroll, she handed it to Nada.

"Do you recognize the seal?" The wax impression appeared to be that of a seamstress.

"It's Zahira's."

"But why would she choose something so ordinary?" wondered Leela.

"It's a long story."

"Let us see what the letter says," suggested Leela, breaking the seal. She tried to read it, but being unfamiliar with Urdu, she handed the parchment to Nada.

Nada began reading silently. "This is most interesting."

"Read it aloud," said Leela impatiently.

"It is addressed to Zahira, which is odd since the parchment bears her seal. The letter reads, 'Preparations are complete. The curse will be activated on the full moon. The twins shall die within the fortnight. Then the Peacock Throne will be ours.

"'I am counting on you to control the mullahs. You know how much they despise me. Although they have given their support to the plan, I trust none of them, and shall direct my powers against them should they conspire against me. Upon the Rajput's execution, I shall depart. K'"

"Who is K?" wondered Leela.

"Whoever it is, they must never know that we have this letter."

The procession continued into the late afternoon. After making its way along Silver Street, the most affluent avenue in all of Asia, the cavalry led Govinda past the lapis-domed monument to Emperor Junaid Shah before heading in the direction of the capital's principle military fortress.

The Red Fort dominated the heart of the city. Recessed mansions with scented gardens lined the parade route as it followed the river. The towering trees lining the road provided little relief from the withering sun, so broad was the boulevard. The elephant bearing Govinda clomped heavily on a bridge as it crossed one of the many canals linking the western suburbs with the river.

Rag-clad children suspended their games, sequined dancers paused, almond vendors waved away customers, and fortune tellers cut short their tales to gape at the beleaguered Rajput as the elephant lumbered through a market neighboring the sandstone fort. Only the pickpockets ignored the passing drama, which abetted their handiwork. When a human juggernaut strangled the street, whip-bearing soldiers offered no warning to those obstructing the way.

Everywhere, Hindus sought fleeting glimpses of their fallen hero. From rooftops, women sprinkled rose water and showered flower petals on Govinda. Brahmins followed behind the procession, chanting and waving incense. To Govinda's relief, there was no violence. Although he had been given nothing to drink or eat, after encountering the sadhu, Govinda's strength was miraculously restored. From time to time, he pressed his fettered hands together to acknowledge the adoring crowds and even joked with the spindly-legged boys who jogged alongside the procession.

The sun was setting as the procession turned onto the boulevard leading to the Emperor's palace. As Govinda passed through an enclave of noblemen's *havelis*, the cheers and chants that had greeted him in other parts of the city were absent. Curious aristocrats stood in doorways and on marble balconies, keen to have a glimpse of the boy who had slain their emperor.

Kritavat, Zahira, Emperor Yaman, and Commander Murad watched as a pair of soldiers dragged Govinda into the Hall of Audience. By appearing in the hall, Zahira violated Islamic protocol.

The Tale of the Himalayan Yogis

Her presence meant the battle had been over for some time, and that the Moguls had defeated the nagababas. Appearing in a black gown, Zahira stared at Govinda's through the slit in her hood.

A palace attendant threw a dingy shawl over Govinda's shoulders, giving him the appearance of a street beggar. Military officers and court nobles stood behind brass railings at the perimeter of the hall. Ladies of the court and senior members of the harem viewed the proceedings from balconies. A latticed window flanked the Peacock Throne.

The magnificence of the Emperor's throne with its glittering diamonds and flashing rubies stood in contrast to Yaman, who slouched on the fabled throne. The Peacock Throne barely supported the portly Emperor. Above his bulbous head hovered a satin umbrella studded with pearls.

"What do you have to say?" asked Yaman, straightening himself as best he could.

"Regarding what?" Govinda answered coolly.

"Regarding the matter for which you are being tried."

"I have done no wrong, other than perhaps thinking the Emperor looks like a circus clown."

Govinda's comment caused more than one court noble to cover his mouth. He heard hushed giggles from behind the viewing screens. Irritated by the insolent remark, Yaman wrinkled his nose; his eyes made even smaller by the girth of his rumpled face.

"The imperial court accuses you of murdering Emperor Junaid Shah," Yaman declared in his most officious voice.

"Why trifle with these absurd accusations? The truth is Emperor Shah fell from his horse and was impaled."

"Ridiculous," Yaman scoffed, shaking his swollen head so violently that his crown teetered. "My father was the finest horseman in all of India."

"And the finest warrior too?" questioned Govinda.

"There has never been a finer warrior than Emperor Shah. His military record is matchless. He was the mightiest Mogul of all."

"Then tell me how, I, a weaponless boy of fifteen, could have slain the Emperor when he was fully armed and mounted."

"Witnesses say you were inside the temple when the Emperor was murdered," Yaman continued, ignoring Govinda's argument.

"No one was murdered. Emperor Shah was injured and fell from his horse. When the horse reared, the Emperor fell onto an iron spike."

"Enough," declared Yaman, straightening his back. "Hear this judgment! I, Emperor Yaman Shah, sentence Prince Govinda of Krishnagarh to elephant execution in the Imperial stadium at noon tomorrow. Take him away. The whole affair bores me."

Yaman tried to rise, but Begum Zahira pushed him back onto the throne.

"Before they take him, Commander Murad has a gift for the Rajput."

Carrying a domed serving dish, Murad placed it in front of Govinda. The commander lifted the lid, revealing Ananta's severed head.

"Recognize him?" mocked Murad.

Burying his face in his hands, Govinda wept silently.

"Empress Zahira struck the lethal blow herself. She's the only woman I've ever known who can make a sword's steel come to life in her hands."

Zahira stood beside Yaman, reveling in her moment of triumph.

"Denying a Brahmin his place in heaven is a rare pleasure," she gloated. "Tonight, Kritavat's nautch girls will dance on the chests of the... what do you call them?"

"Nagababas," Murad interjected.

"Your nagababas have met with a similar fate. Without their prince, your army of wraiths turned and ran. The whole sickly lot of them were ridden down and slaughtered like jackals."

Govinda turned to Kritavat.

"This is your doing. There is nothing so pitiable as a fallen yogi."

"Remove him from my sight," ordered Kritavat with a wave of his hand. "Tomorrow, we'll see who is to be pitied."

As the guards led Govinda away, a messenger entered the hall.

"Cobras!" the breathless man announced. "... cobras everywhere. The courtyard overrun with hissing vipers... gardens too... they're coming over the walls... Seal the palace before they attack!"

The Tale of the Himalayan Yogis

"What are you saying?" demanded Murad.

"Come to the balcony and see for yourself," urged the messenger.

Yaman, Zahira, Commander Murad, and Kritavat made their way to the Emperor's balcony.

"My wine!" Govinda heard Yaman bawl.

Govinda shuffled along as the guards led him into a subterranean tunnel, his shackles clanging against the stone floor. A guard shoved him into a blackened chamber. As he stumbled inside, Govinda felt nauseous and weak, as if someone, or something, was siphoning his life force from his body. Tormented by the ghastly sight of Ananta's head, the scene was shown to him over and over. A malevolent presence lurked in the chamber.

The guards pushed Govinda into the same cage where Nada and Leela had been. As he shuffled into the cage, his foot struck the charred skull of a goat, its eye sockets staring vacantly up at him. He tried to kick the skull outside the cage, but the guards closed the door, and the skull remained inside. Govinda collapsed on the floor as the guards departed the fetid chamber, taking with them the only source of light.

Nada and Leela were resting in the temple guesthouse when they heard shrieks and ran outside to see what was happening. To their horror, a stream of hissing cobras poured out of the temple entrance. As if guided by a shared mind, the cobras flowed over the steps of the temple in a torrent. The ground itself appeared to rise and fall as the serpents slithered toward the palace.

The old sadhu stood at the center of the swarming serpents. As the cobras rushed past him, he smiled mischievously as though the mayhem pleased him. Leela sensed that somehow the sadhu was the cause of the upheaval.

Every Shiva temple in the city spewed cobras from its sanctum. An army of serpents had invaded Delhi, forcing Hindus and Muslims alike into trees and onto the boundary walls lining the streets. Windows and doors were hastily shuttered to avoid the deluge of deadly reptiles. Strangely, no one was bitten by the wriggling hordes.

Word spread that a massive albino cobra had slithered onto the throne, causing the Emperor to summon palace astrologers to the scene. Soothsayers proclaimed that the end was near; a snake charmer waved his *pungi* at the sky, declaring, "The gods are angry!"

Govinda lay on the floor of the cell, his surroundings devoid of light. A eunuch had come and beaten him, but seeming terrified of the chamber; the flogging had been brief. Govinda's wounds stung, but the pangs he felt in his heart pained him far more than the beatings he had endured before, or after, the procession. He blamed himself for the deaths of Ananta and the nagababas.

Govinda opened his eyes as threads of light shone through the cracks and keyhole of the chamber door. The door opened with a jolt, and Kritavat entered the chamber. The tantric slammed the door, hurried through the room to a second door, raised his lamp, fumbled with a key, and muttered something about snakes. Throwing open the door, he closed it behind him, having taken little notice of Govinda.

Sometime later – Govinda had no idea know how long – the door swung open again. A stooped man with coarse, unruly eyebrows shuffled into the chamber carrying an iron pot. The servant ignored Govinda, seemingly searching for someone else.

"If it's Kritavat you're looking for, he's in there," Govinda said, pointing to the second door.

Noticing the prisoner for the first time, the servant stared warily at him. Limping over to the cage, he held up a pot containing bloated leeches nearly the size of mice.

"Blood offerings," grunted the man.

The stunted servant shuffled over to the second door and opened it, mumbling over his shoulder, "Slithering devils everywhere. Omens of doom, I tell you."

"What about omens?" Govinda asked.

"Wouldn't know, would you. Cobras flooding the courtyard… guards fleeing for their lives… the Emperor fouled his gown," sniggered the man before vanishing.

Pangs of guilt prevented Govinda from sleeping. He lay awake on the floor until the door swung open yet again. Kritavat entered the room holding a torch. The sorcerer had not returned to the chamber through the door by which he had left it; apparently, there was another way around. The tantric approached the cage, his torch exposing a wicked smile.

"I wonder how it feels to be trampled by a bull elephant," he grinned, raising the torch near Govinda's face.

"Since you are so curious, why don't you take my place in the arena?" jested Govinda. "It would satisfy your curiosity, punish the guilty instead of the innocent, and spare me an experience I would rather not have."

"Shankar Baba deceived you," retorted Kritavat.

"Why do you say that?"

"He never taught you about darkness."

"Darkness," laughed Govinda. "You mean he never taught me about fear?"

"Not fear... I mean the darkness without which one cannot know light. Your guru pretends it doesn't exist. I can teach you about the dark side. Until you experience the blackness of night, you will never truly appreciate the dawn. Let me tell you about the demoness..."

Govinda cut off the tantric. "You shall lose everything with your twisted philosophy. Shankar Baba taught me about darkness. He took me to the naraka hells where I looked into Tadaka's sickly eyes and smelled her disgusting breath. I saw her rotting teeth the size of rocks and watched her monkey devils fly about like sightless bats. Shankar Baba showed me all of that... and more."

"And yet you think the light will save you. The light in your starry-eyed world is about to be extinguished."

"Whether or not I live, matters little," replied Govinda calmly. "My world will never end."

"You don't know about soul eaters. Have you not studied our scriptures? The Black Age is upon us. Souls will be snuffed out like candles in a storm."

A chilling draft swept through the chamber, extinguishing Kritavat's torch.

"Feel the darkness," he whispered. "She's coming, and when she arrives, she'll want to be fed."

"Your demoness dwells in a different world," Govinda spoke in what he thought was Kritavat's direction. "She cannot come here."

"But she can."

"Not while I'm here."

"I admire your courage. That fool Subahu could have used some."

"As could you," countered Govinda.

"We shall see who has courage. I have an offer for you."

"Your offer doesn't interest me."

"Even if it means Leela's freedom?"

"Leela *is* free. You told me so yourself. And you've already deceived me once."

"Things are different now. Cobras have overrun the palace… the skies are black… a deluge floods the streets… the river spills over its banks. The Empire is under a curse. Soon Tadaka and her minions shall come to power. Then there will be no more yogis… no Emperor's cavalry… no Rajput princesses. Sorcerers who know the secrets of the dark side will be Tadaka's allies. I have seen her at work. Nothing can stop her."

"You talk like a madman."

Govinda wished the tantric would leave.

"The cataclysm has begun, and Leela is a lone girl hunted by the Empire. Free she may be, but she is doomed if I do not save her. Shankar Baba may be able to conjure up cobras, but he can't save Leela. Only I can do that."

"What do you propose?" asked Govinda, playing along. He was interested in any plan, even an insane one if it meant saving Leela.

"It is time I took an apprentice. Subahu was weak-willed."

"Because of his weakness, he followed your illusion of power, and you led him to his death."

"Subahu is dead because he was weak. In her presence, fear is not tolerated. You, Govinda, have no true fear. That's why you will make a suitable ally, for only the fearless are safe in her presence."

"Why would anyone want to be in Tadaka's presence?"

As Govinda spoke her name, another chilling wind swept through the cell.

"Speak her name only when summoning her," cautioned Kritavat.

Suddenly the sorcerer's torch was burning again.

"Am I to be impressed that you can light a candle with your mind?"

"Great beings pay homage to me. You should too."

"Great beings pay no homage to those who revel in human sacrifice."

"The time is coming when men will kill for the wood that warms their homes. I have seen the future... infants disfigured... plagues ravaging the people... oceans washing over cities. Is my recreation so evil by comparison?"

"You have poisoned yourself with self-importance. You pretend to side with the Moguls, but you care only for yourself."

"I am without fear. That is the value of embracing darkness."

"You were not so brave when the cobras approached. And now they come again."

Kritavat flinched. "What do you know of fear? Had I not conquered it, I would have perished long ago. My path does not tolerate fear. Did your Shankar Baba tell you that I cannot be killed?"

"Pride will be your executioner."

"You talk like Shankar Baba. He prattled on about ego."

"Ego is a hollow reed..." began Govinda.

"... unable to draw nourishment from the soil it lives in," chimed in the sorcerer. "Shankar Baba's favorite saying. You have learned well, but your guru's words do not impress me."

"Shankar Baba's words are not meant to impress; they are meant to enlighten. What did you hope to gain by securing the Idol's Eye?"

"You should not have thrown the gem into the river. Shankar Baba never told you?"

"Told me what?"

"Maybe you weren't supposed to know. Maybe Shankar Baba was afraid the dreaded ego would claim his prized pupil since you had the diamond in your possession."

"What was so special about the Idol's Eye?" asked Govinda, feigning ignorance.

"Power!"

"Power? But that's ridiculous," countered Govinda. "No stone can give that."

"You don't know the power of the gem, or you wouldn't have discarded it. Emperor Shah waged war for the Idol's Eye."

"Little good it did him. He had it in his hand when he died," lied Govinda, hoping Kritavat did not know the gem had been a duplicate, and not the real Idol's Eye.

Thinking about Kritavat and the siege of Krishnagarh caused Govinda's face to flush.

"It was you," he accused the tantric. "You're the sorcerer who came to Krishnagarh. You came to find out if the Idol's Eye was there. You persuaded the Emperor to help you get it. The Moguls would never have known about the diamond if you hadn't told them."

"I went to Krishnagarh," admitted Kritavat. "I went everywhere I was allowed to go, suspecting the Idol's Eye was somewhere I would not be allowed to go. When the sentries prevented me from entering the queen's temple, I knew the Idol's Eye was inside.

"After the second cup of chai, a shop owner told me about the diamond. I returned to Delhi and struck a deal with Zahira. She, in turn, persuaded the Emperor to go after the diamond. After all, the Emperor already had Krishna's Consort. He believed that if he had the Idol's Eye as well, he would be invincible."

"Then all this has been for some imaginary powers rumored to be inside a stone?"

"I have the sister stone in my possession," boasted Kritavat.

Reaching into his robe, Kritavat produced a diamond of similar cut and luster as the Idol's Eye.

Govinda recognized the gem immediately.

"How did you get it?"

"You fetch a high price," Kritavat grinned, fingering the diamond greedily. "Zahira has had it since before Emperor Shah's death, but now it is mine, a suitable reward for your capture and the slaughter of those pathetic nagababas. Wouldn't you agree?"

"What about the nagababas?"

"Surely you saw her minions circle above the Yamuna this morning. Tadaka sent them to ensure that the battle went our way. I wasn't taking any chances that the elephants might revolt again, so I dispatched her monkey devils. When the nagas saw demons diving

The Tale of the Himalayan Yogis

from the sky, they turned and ran. With Krishna's Consort in my hands, the control of the Empire has shifted from Zahira to me."

"You can side with your demon friends, or accept the grace of the gods, but not both."

"Shankar Baba has taught you to think of good and evil, but I see the roles of each, and use them as they suit me. My powers come from the Great Soul Eater, and now I will use this diamond to amass the power I shall need to rule."

"Great Soul Eater?" chuckled Govinda. "They attacked Shankar Baba in the forest, and he defeated them."

"Tomorrow, after your execution, you shall face what Shankar Baba faced in the forest. Like a tiger ripping apart its prey, the Great Soul Eater will tear your soul apart. Had Shankar Baba taught you about soul eaters, you would know what to do, but as it is, you will be helpless."

"Then it was Tadaka's monkey devils that attacked Shankar Baba."

"You learn quickly."

"What has Tadaka promised you in exchange for your loyalty?"

"The supreme boon," boasted Kritavat.

"But you're not immortal," countered Govinda. "Her boon applies to humans. That's why Shankar Baba sent cobras after you in Jageshwar, and again here, and why you ran off when the leopard appeared on the trail."

"Yet I am alive. I have proven myself superior to Shankar Baba."

"And what must you do in exchange for your immortality?"

"Please the one who granted it to me."

"Is that why the servant brought the leeches?"

"She feeds on the fear in blood, as well as the souls of the men and animals I offer her. She moves between the narakas and this world whenever I summon her. To prevent her from coming, I would need to die, but that will never happen, and so she will continue to come."

"She doesn't belong in our world. Sooner or later she'll be banished forever. This sort of confusion can only happen when there is great fear in the people. Otherwise, she couldn't come."

"There is great fear in the world, and I will ensure that it not only endures but increases."

"Why did you leave the Mahatmas? Shankar Baba told me that Yogiraj loved you like a son," said Govinda, trying a different tactic.

"Out of jealousy, they forced me out," replied Kritavat acidly.

"Yogiraj jealous? I find that hard to believe."

"Not Yogiraj… Shankar Baba and the others. Before I left, Yogiraj called me to his side and said, 'A guru never abandons his disciple.'"

"But disciples abandon their gurus. Why haven't you gone back?"

"I told you… to master the dark side."

"But in the process, you've created mountains of fresh karma."

"Only the weak-minded fear karma."

"If you think you can have the light one day and invoke Tadaka the next you are mistaken. No action goes unrecorded."

"I am beyond karma," boasted Kritavat.

"You are confused. One attains immortality only after completing one's karma."

"What do you know of immortality? Only the Great Soul Eater can grant it, and she has granted it to me."

"You deceive yourself. Shankar Baba was right. You are a fallen yogi."

"What does Shankar Baba know about fallen yogis? I am tempted to call off your execution so that you can witness my ascent to power."

"I encourage the calling off of my execution, but of what use is power without grace?"

"You talk as if you've met Yogiraj," said Kritavat, his voice softening.

"I have, but of what interest is he to you?"

"I'm curious to know where he is."

"Shankar Baba took me to Yogiraj, but I have no idea how to find him. His cave was deep in the mountains."

"They call themselves Mahatmas, and yet they hide in caves like frightened animals."

"You are mistaken. You had everything when you were with the Mahatmas. Why did you leave?"

"I was more advanced than the others. Yogiraj taught me things that no one else was ready to learn."

"And still you betrayed him."

"Never! I told you I was forced out by Shankar Baba, who, along with the others, was jealous of me."

"Yogiraj talked about you."

"What did he say?" asked Kritavat, unable to mask his curiosity.

"He said you were the only member of the Mahatmas to have fallen, and that he hoped it would never happen again."

"Those who have not attained perfection need the Mahatmas. Do you think immortality is found only at Yogiraj's feet?"

"I know little of immortality."

"Then I shall teach you, but first you must join me. Together, we will conquer these dull-witted Moguls."

"Zahira must find her son insufferable."

Govinda wanted to know more about those who controlled the throne.

"Zahira and Yaman are but pawns in my game."

"As I would be."

"I tolerate Zahira for her cunning. You, on the other hand, would make a fine sorcerer. After all, we share the same tradition."

"Not any longer," countered Govinda. "You abandoned your guru long ago."

"Join me and there be will be no end to your power."

"Thank you for revealing what it is to be a fallen yogi."

"Call me what you like," said Kritavat. "Why not join Tadaka's army?"

"I intend to slay your demoness, not join forces with her."

"You are naive. As it stands now, you will be crushed by an elephant in a few hours. If Leela is fortunate, they'll execute her too. If not, the Great Soul Eater will have her. Think about it. In case you have a change of heart, I shall send Junduk before they take you to the stadium. But once you are in the arena, I cannot help. Now I must go. The Great Soul Eater does not like to be kept waiting."

Kritavat left Govinda to reflect on his impending execution.

He wondered where Leela was; perhaps she was also in a cell somewhere beneath the palace, or maybe she had not been recaptured. He speculated how many nagas had died in the carnage. Praying to Krishna, he summoned the will to face his execution.

Govinda lay on the floor, wondering if it was all about to end. A pair of guards opened his cage, awakening him.

"You are to wash and eat," a guard ordered. "Wear this. Your food is here."

The second guard placed a bucket of water, a bowl of revolting swill, and a white cloth inside the cage. After securing the cage, the guards left. Govinda shoved the swill aside. He washed and changed into the clothing the guards had brought him. Barefoot, and clad in a white cloth wrapped around his waist and thighs, he wished he had Bhumi Mata's bowl, but he had left it at his camp on the morning of the exchange.

The guards were about to take Govinda to the stadium when Junduk appeared.

"Master wants to know."

"Tell Kritavat not to miss the execution."

This time, rather than being chained to the back of an elephant, Govinda trudged along on his own bare feet, his stride impaired by leg irons. During his imprisonment he had been oblivious to the passage of time; the sun-drenched morning told him he had spent the night underground.

It seemed that a storm had assailed Delhi in the night, for the road to the stadium had become a murky terra cotta stream. Govinda slogged through the water, which splashed about his ankles. Fortunately, or perhaps, unfortunately, the stadium was but a short distance from the Emperor's palace. Curious citizens unable to gain entrance into the packed stadium lined the street.

Ahead of Govinda, Emperor Yaman and Begum Zahira rode in a gilded carriage drawn by Mongolian horses. Drummers marched behind the royal conveyance which was flanked by a cavalry squadron bearing drawn swords. Govinda walked side-by-side with a giant African shackled by a double set of chains.

"What is your crime?" Govinda asked the olive-skinned eunuch as the procession made its way through the flooded streets.

"I am guilty of two offenses," the eunuch replied, his head bowed in humiliation. "I killed a man and helped two women escape from the zenana."

The Tale of the Himalayan Yogis

"Was one of the women named Leela?"

"They planned to torture her. I killed my brother to free her."

"You killed your brother?"

"I have seen Kritavat's cruel methods. Some were like daughters to me. I could no longer allow it, and so I took my sword…"

"I am indebted to you. Princess Leela is my wife."

"I know," nodded the eunuch.

"How will we be executed?"

"The strongest elephant in the Empire will trample you and I will be ripped apart by hungry lionesses."

"I have not heard of Moguls using lionesses."

"I will be the first to be executed in such fashion. The lionesses have not eaten since my arrest. Their last meal was the flesh of a human."

Judging from the African's massive chest and arms, it would take many lions to overpower him.

"How many lionesses are there?"

"Too many."

"May I ask your good name?"

"I am called Bandu."

"I am Govinda."

"I am honored to die with you, Govinda."

"And I with you."

A frenzied Hindu emerged from the crowd of bystanders and jogged alongside the Emperor's carriage, shouting, "The gods are angry! Stop the execution!"

A team of soldiers bound and whipped the man as the procession continued on its way.

The execution would be the spectacle of the decade. Zahira had ordered Hindus given liberal access to the stadium to put an end to the legend of their hero once and for all. The upper sections of the arena were allotted the Hindus while court nobles, military officers, wealthy merchants, and the handful of Europeans who made their livelihood in Delhi, enjoyed the best seats. Emperor Yaman and Zahira would watch from the royal box near ground level, flanked by the generals on one side and the mullahs on the other.

A battle between bull elephants would precede the executions; a rematch between Airavat and Gum Gum. As he trudged past, Govinda heard a bystander say that Zahira had personally selected Airavat, for, when sufficiently enraged, the bull was known to have a streak of malice that caused him to trample his victims with a savagery no other elephant possessed. In the aftermath of the elephants' rebellious behavior on the battlefield, there was disagreement in the palace about the method of execution, but Zahira was determined to crush the Rajput's legend once and for all.

Govinda sensed the excitement in the stadium as he and Bandu shuffled along a tunnel to a cell containing a bench where the condemned men would wait until the guards came for them. Govinda heard cheers sweeping the arena, frenzied voices calling for blood.

Govinda and Bandu sat beside one another on the bench.

"Why did you help Leela escape?" Govinda asked, glancing sideways at Bandu.

"I have served the harem for three decades," Bandu said, his words forming slowly. "I have seen infants grow into begums, and begums become murderers. Some were like daughters to me. I have witnessed much kindness and every kind of evil, but what is happening now is too hideous for even a man like me to accept."

"Was your brother involved?"

"We were orphans sold into slavery in Tunisia. They castrated us before our boat reached India. Together, my brother and I ran the harem. I was the one the women trusted, and Itibar Khan was the one who enforced the rules on behalf of the Empress. He was never close to anyone but me. When Zahira rose to a position of power, jealousy led her to poison innocent women, including a rival."

"But isn't that the way with Mogul royals?"

"The Moguls have a saying, 'throne or tomb.' I have always found it to be an ignorant saying. Throne or not, every one of them will end up in a tomb. But I will not. I will end up in the stomachs of lionesses."

"No, Bandu; you will end up in a heavenly realm."

"After the things I have seen, I fear that hell has conquered heaven."

"Do not fear any such thing. I have seen both heavens and hells, and I assure you the heavens are infinitely superior."

Bandu looked at Govinda for the first time, staring into his eyes, examining them as if searching for truth within Govinda's words. Then he looked away.

"Begum Zahira is no longer in control," said Bandu. "The sorcerer has taken over."

"I know about Kritavat."

"I have seen his sacrifices beneath the full moon. Poison to gain the throne is one thing, but Kritavat is mad. You will not see him today because he will be preparing. The full moon is in two days' time."

"You helped Leela because he planned to sacrifice her?"

"I am grateful to be facing lionesses rather than being sacrificed in the chambers below the palace. My heart is sad that I killed my brother, but I have done what is right. I will accept my fate without a fight. I will not give them the pleasure of seeing me wrestle the lionesses. Here, they live in cages, but in Africa, we respect the lion. I will pay that respect now."

With a deep groan, the door swung open, and four guards led the eunuch away.

"I shall look for you in the heavens," Govinda called after him.

Perhaps all too soon, he thought.

Govinda heard cheers which soon turned to boos.

Bandu has refused to fight.

Then the cheers returned; accompanied by the stamping of feet. As the arena shook, Govinda's stomach tightened.

And now the lionesses are upon him.

The guards came for Govinda. They led him through a tunnel to the edge of the stadium. At the end of the tunnel stood Kritavat, robed in black.

"Bandu told me I would not see you today."

"You didn't think I'd violate your final request. I've completed my preparations for the full moon. I had to hurry more than I like to — you'd best die an entertaining death — or else my inconvenience shall not have been worth it."

"I intend to do my utmost to survive. If I fail, I won't have considered the entertainment value of my death."

Govinda walked past Kritavat to the edge of the stadium where he scanned the crowd, which was still on its feet after witnessing Bandu's savage mauling. A line of soldiers stood poised to cut down anyone foolish enough to run onto the field. Although a few women were in attendance, public executions were decidedly a man's affair. Govinda noticed that the wives of a few court nobles were sitting in the front row, their burqa hoods rendering them indistinguishable one from the other.

Anyone of those women could be Leela.

He noticed that two of the women sitting side by side had buried their heads in their hands.

Why have they reacted differently from the others?

The intimacy of the stadium surprised Govinda. Bandu's remains lay in a pool of red near the center of the arena. Attendants corralled the lionesses into a corner, denying the hungry cats their meal.

Govinda noticed a figure standing near the public entrance to the stadium. It was the kindly old sadhu who had summoned rain the previous day. Govinda scanned the royal box at the opposite end of the arena. Emperor Yaman sat on a gilded throne beneath a silk canopy, Zahira on his left and the ever-present hookah on his right. Yaman panted with excitement, a tube fixed to his lips. To Zahira's left sat Commander Murad.

As the spectators settled into their seats, the mahouts led a pair of elephants onto the field. Govinda recognized one of the men as Commander Jari's former mahout. The larger elephant was Airavat; a menacing, bestial giant. The other was Gum Gum.

The bulls grappled with one another, butting heads to the delight of the onlookers. Wary from his previous encounter, Gum Gum backed up frequently to avoid becoming locked in combat. Airavat wasted no time in working himself into a rage.

The elephants sufficiently roused, Govinda was led into the arena to face his executioners. All eyes were on the Rajput as he strode confidently to the center of the stadium. As Govinda approached the elephants, the crowd fell silent. Half of the spectators heralded him as their hero; the other half had come to see his legend crushed.

A spectator high in the stadium shouted, "Govinda Ki Jai!"

The Tale of the Himalayan Yogis

The Hindus took up the chant, raising their arms and pounding their feet as they shouted. Govinda acknowledged his people before glancing surreptitiously at the two women, one of whom he suspected was Leela. One of the women tried to stand, but the other held her down and placed a finger to her lips.

Govinda turned his attention to Zahira, who stared crossly at the cheering crowd. Turning to Commander Murad, Zahira muttered something behind her hand.

Govinda chanced another glance at the women who might include Leela. This time, he noticed a second pair of hooded spectators a few rows higher up. The second pair caught Govinda's eye because one was a man and the other a woman. They were sitting together, which was not customary in the Muslim section of the stadium. The woman wore an identity-concealing hood, but the man wore one as well, which was peculiar.

Goading Airavat, the mahouts directed the bull's attention to Govinda. Eyeing his prey, Airavat abandoned his tussle with Gum Gum, pausing to consider his new adversary. The mahouts' task completed, they hurried off the field. Gum Gum was only too happy to be free of Airavat and kept his distance from the impending skirmish.

Govinda scanned his surroundings in search of something that might save him.

Expectant faces gaped at him from every angle. His eyes met Airavat's; great murky spheres filled with malice. Govinda examined the bull's deadly tusks before shifting his gaze to his adversary's lethal feet. He had never faced a raging elephant, but there was little time to invent a plan since Airavat was about to charge.

A showman as well as an executioner, Airavat trumpeted at the sky, informing the crowd that he was ready. Snorting madly, the bull charged at his foe. Instinctively, Govinda wanted to flee, but knowing that Airavat would easily overtake him, he remained where he was. He needed to communicate with the bull. Otherwise, it would be but a matter of time before he ran out of options. Probing Airavat's awareness, he tried to contact the bull, but a foreign influence interfered.

As Airavat lowered his tusks to impale his victim, Govinda dove to the side, narrowly avoiding death. The bottom half of the stadium erupted at the near miss while the Hindus collectively gasped.

Snorting saliva, Airavat prepared for another pass. This time, as Airavat charged, Govinda feigned the same move, but at the last moment, he dove the other way, once again escaping certain death. Skidding chest-first through the pool of Bandu's blood, Govinda rose to his feet soaked in the reddish muck. Hindu and Muslim alike were now on their feet. The Hindus beseeched their gods to save their hero while the Muslims clamored for his death.

Govinda had exposed his only avenues of escape. Now it became a guessing game. If predator and prey chose the same direction, Airavat would crush his foe like an insect beneath a boy's boot. It was only a matter of time before luck would run its course.

Pausing to scrutinize his foe, Airavat inclined his massive head, first to one side and then to the other, perhaps noticing that this adversary was craftier than his former victims. Staring into his eyes, Govinda decided that his executioner was truly mad.

Once again, Airavat trumpeted at the crowd before lowering his head. Crouching, Govinda readied himself before scrambling to safety for the third time.

Picking himself up off the ground, Govinda was tiring, his youthful agility negated by injury and lack of food. He was about to face Airavat again when he spotted a bright object arcing through the air. Govinda's eyes followed the object, but its path crossed the sun, forcing him to look away to avoid impairing his vision when it could mean the difference between life and death.

"Govinda!" shouted a distantly familiar voice, the speaker barely making himself heard above the cheering spectators.

The hooded man, who Govinda had noticed earlier, had made his way to the arena's front row. No one seemed to notice the shining object or the hooded man; all eyes focused on the combatants. The man moved awkwardly, as though suffering from an injury. Freeing himself from the tangle of raised arms, the hooded man pointed to a spot on the ground midway between Govinda and Airavat.

Airavat stood fifteen paces from his quarry, pondering his next move. The heat from his agitated mind inflamed the bull's eyes.

The Tale of the Himalayan Yogis

Scanning the ground, Govinda spotted the Idol's Eye glistening in the sunlight.

The sweat-drenched elephant drew deep, measured breaths as he prepared for another charge. Govinda rushed forward to seize the Idol's Eye as Airavat launched another assault.

The crowd roared as the contestants rushed headlong toward one another. The onrushing Airavat was about to impale Govinda when he scooped up the Idol's Eye along with a fistful of dust, and dove out of the bull's path, outmaneuvering his executioner yet again.

Standing in the center of the arena, Govinda clutched the Idol's Eye; his mind flooded with hope. Rubbing the dust from the gem, he resolved that he would not die this day.

Summoning a power from deep within his solar plexus, Govinda invoked the mantra to awaken the Idol's Eye. As Airavat rushed forward, frenzied Moguls exhorted the bull to spear his foe. Responding to the crowd, Airavat lowered his tusks. Undaunted, Govinda continued repeating the mantra.

Seeing Airavat moving in for the kill, Gum Gum came lumbering across the field. Lowering his head, the young bull charged into Airavat's side. Having failed to notice Gum Gum's approach, Govinda flung himself out of Airavat's path, narrowly escaping the feet of both elephants. The crowd roared deliriously.

Infuriated by the rival bull's intrusion, Airavat was about to retaliate when Gum Gum charged at Govinda. Thinking that Gum Gum intended to finish off the Rajput, the Moguls cheered him on. But rather than impaling his prey, Gum Gum hoisted Govinda into the air with his trunk. Govinda struggled to elude the elephant's grasp, but exhaustion and injury slowed him, allowing Gum Gum to lift his victim high overhead. Pounding their feet, the Moguls goaded Gum Gum to inflict the death blow.

The arena turned upside down and then righted itself as Govinda was hoisted higher and higher into the air. Expecting Gum Gum to toss him to the ground and crush him underfoot, Govinda clutched the Idol's Eye, his attention riveted on Krishna. Snorting, Gum Gum raised Govinda still higher, arching his neck in such a way that Govinda's feet touched the bull's shoulders. From here, Gum Gum would recoil, thrust his trunk forward and hurtle Govinda into the ground.

To the astonishment of everyone in the arena, Gum Gum gently set Govinda on his back where the exhausted Rajput found himself straddling the elephant's broad neck. Elated to be alive, he rubbed Gum Gum behind the ears. The upper portion of the stadium broke into a chorus of cheers while the lower half stood in stunned silence.

Gum Gum plodded to the center of the arena as Govinda acknowledged his supporters near the top of the stadium. Whispering into Gum Gum's ear, the bull trumpeted three times before lumbering in the direction of the royal box. Govinda wanted to have a word with the Emperor and his mother.

Yaman pulled nervously on his pipe as Govinda approached. Zahira stood beside her son, rage spewing from her eyes. Searching for a means to put an end to the Rajput, the Empress turned to her commander and issued orders that were drowned out by the din.

Commander Murad signaled to the guards, who opened an enclosure at the stadium's edge. Having been denied their meal, five ravenous lionesses rushed onto the field. As a fresh wave of executioners entered the arena, the mahouts corralled Airavat.

Smelling Bandu's blood on Govinda's body, the lionesses formed a circle around Gum Gum, biting and swiping at his forelegs. Gum Gum charged first at one lioness, and then another, but the lionesses attacked from every angle.

The head of the pack was clawing her way onto Gum Gum's back when Govinda slammed his foot into her nose, causing her to fall to the ground. The lionesses leaped again and again, clawing their way up Gum Gum's flanks, bloodying the elephant's sides.

Badly overmatched, the young bull was tiring. Sensing that it was only a matter of time before the elephant succumbed to exhaustion, the lionesses intensified their attack. Eager for the kill, they sank their teeth into Gum Gum's legs, but a well-timed blow from his foot crushed an attacker's skull. Awestruck, the spectators were on their feet again, clamoring for more.

Out of the corner of his eye, Govinda noticed a commotion at the edge of the stadium. The hooded man who had thrown the Idol's Eye

The Tale of the Himalayan Yogis

onto the field was attempting to enter the arena. Though the man had removed his hood, he was too far away to identify. Oddly, the soldiers allowed him to pass, seemingly afraid of the man.

The man approached the mahouts, who also appeared to be frightened. A mahout handed the man a barbed prod and wooden spear.

The man approached Airavat, gesturing to him with the prod. Airavat promptly kneeled, and the man climbed onto the bull's back. Spear in hand, he guided Airavat toward Gum Gum. As they approached, Govinda recognized the man.

"Hashim!" shouted Govinda.

"Use this!" Hashim shouted, tossing the spear to Govinda.

Despite the repeated assaults of the lionesses, Airavat moved alongside Gum Gum. The elephants now battled a mutual foe.

Govinda gripped the spear's shaft with both hands. Thrusting at the lionesses, he put as much of his body into every motion as his injuries would allow without losing his balance on Gum Gum's back.

"My elephant is tiring!" shouted Govinda.

"Guide him to the edge of the arena," Hashim advised.

As Gum Gum lumbered toward the arena's edge, a panting lioness clawed her way onto his back. Feeling the cat's hot breath on his neck, Govinda spun around. Govinda attempted to fend the lioness off with the spear, but his injured ribs hampered his movements. Undeterred, the lioness swiped at him, her claws ripping through his shoulder. Govinda grimaced as the crowd cheered.

Hashim maneuvered his bull alongside Gum Gum. Airavat swept his trunk across Gum Gum's back, knocking Govinda and the lioness into the air. Twisting about as they fell, the lioness landed on her feet. Govinda held the spear out beneath him, allowing it to strike the ground before he did. The weapon slowed his fall, enabling him to land on his feet. Propping himself up with the spear, Govinda's injured shoulder gave out, and his knees buckled.

Seeing Govinda on the ground, the lionesses moved in for the kill. Their leader was about to pounce when Gum Gum speared her with his tusk, lifting the lioness into the air and tossing her aside. The crowd clamored for more.

The remaining lionesses approached tentatively, giving Govinda time to thrust with the spear, which he now held with his left hand. The spearhead struck a lioness in the shoulder, but the spear's shaft snapped. The lionesses charged their defenseless foe, but not before Gum Gum had deposited Govinda safely on the bull's back.

Hashim directed Airavat to the arena's edge with Gum Gum trailing close behind. A soldier recognized Hashim, or perhaps incorrectly identified him as Ghazi.

"Take these," the soldier offered, tossing Hashim a sword and dagger.

"I need another!" Hashim shouted.

A second soldier tossed his sword to Hashim as well, and a third soldier handed one up to Govinda.

"Spread the word that it is I, Emperor Ghazi," Hashim instructed the soldiers.

"I want to confront Yaman," Hashim informed Govinda. "Are you able?"

"I'm fine," replied Govinda, barely able to sit upright.

With his dagger, Hashim cut the hood away from his robe and tossed the cloth to Govinda, who tied it around his wound.

Riding side-by-side, Govinda and Hashim headed for the royal box. The spectators stood, breathless in anticipation. Chants of "Ghazi, Ghazi!" competed with choruses of "Govinda, Govinda!"

The lionesses gave up the attack. Two of their members were dead, and a third limped awkwardly. The massive bulls had been more than the lionesses had bargained. Noticing Bandu's remains on the field, they gathered there and began eating.

Govinda and Hashim approached Yaman, who sat on the edge of his throne, stupefied by the drama unfolding before him. The Emperor babbled and blurted and rambled incoherently as the elephants approached.

From atop Airavat, Hashim stared down at Yaman.

"Yaman, your assassins are second rate."

"Ghazi? But it can't be… you're dead!" gulped Yaman. "Insallah, Ghazi has risen from the crypt."

The Tale of the Himalayan Yogis

Empress Zahira barked a command into Yaman's ear, causing his face to flush with anger. The intoxicated emperor turned to Zahira.

"Mother, don't tell me what to do. NO ONE tells the emperor what to do!"

Raising his hookah, the petulant ruler hurled it defiantly onto the field.

"Get yourself out of this mess," seethed Zahira, pushing her way past the mullahs and disappearing into a tunnel, leaving her delirious son to fend for himself.

"Yaman, you're not the emperor," chided Govinda. "You stole the Peacock Throne from Ghazi, but it remains his."

"Shackle them!" ordered Yaman, but the generals ignored him. "Shackle these men, I say."

"Defend yourself," challenged Hashim, tossing a sword at Yaman's feet.

Yaman picked up the weapon designed for a single-handed grip. Lacking sufficient strength, he grabbed the hilt with both hands. Having never handled a sword, Yaman waved it about in an absurd attempt at defense, but his antics soon tired him.

Instructing Airavat to kneel, Hashim climbed down.

"Commander, arrest this man," panted Yaman.

"But there is some question as to who the real emperor is," Commander Murad replied, uncertain who stood in front of him.

"You fool! Can't you see that it's Ghazi's ghost come back to haunt me?"

"Emperor, you've had too much opium," chided one of the mullahs.

Incensed, Yaman pushed a pair of mullahs out of his way as he stumbled onto the field.

"I'll finish what the assassins couldn't," snapped Yaman.

Yaman slashed wildly at Hashim, who easily parried the inept attacks. Govinda could see that neither Yaman nor Hashim, was skilled at combat. Hashim's primary advantage was his superior state of mind over that of Yaman.

The crowd strained to watch the duel taking place at the edge of the stadium.

With a slash, Hashim drew a trickle of blood from Yaman's upper arm, reddening his robe. Whimpering, the weak-willed emperor flailed at Hashim but missed repeatedly. Hashim easily avoided Yaman's attacks before delivering a thrust to Yaman's thigh. The blade struck bone.

Clutching his thigh, Yaman collapsed to the ground. Yaman was defenseless, and Hashim could have finished him off, but he chose instead to watch Yaman grovel about on the ground. Struggling to his feet, Yaman searched for an escape route. Confused, he hobbled toward the center of the arena in an attempt to escape the gawking multitude.

Yaman's presence on the field drew the attention of the lionesses. The lionesses spotted the bloodied figure limping about in a daze, and seized their opportunity. In a flash, they overtook Yaman, who collapsed beneath them. Before the soldiers could intervene, the lionesses had ravaged Yaman while the throng of stunned spectators looked on. Hovering over their kill, the lionesses dared anyone to approach.

Climbing onto Airavat, Hashim rode past Yaman's remains to the center of the stadium. Govinda followed atop Gum Gum. Together, Govinda and Hashim acknowledged the cheering crowd. Saluting Hindu and Muslim alike, they hoisted their swords, first to the Mogul nobles, and then to the Hindu masses. Circling the field, the princes waved to their admirers before returning to the center of the arena where they crossed swords in a show of unity never before witnessed during Mogul rule.

The guards assigned to the lionesses chased the pack off the field, but not before one of them was mauled.

Smiling to himself, Hashim shook his head in disbelief at the fortunate turn of events. Govinda waved his sword in triumph. With the lions removed, jubilant Hindus flooded onto the field, forming a circle around the elephants and their riders. The soldiers guarding the arena made no effort to stop the mob as it poured out of the stands.

"I need to meet with the generals!" Hashim informed Govinda. "The future of the Empire depends on their support. Come to my Uncle Lufti's palace tonight. Anyone can give you directions."

Three burqa-clad women made their way through the spirited throng as Hashim rode away. One of the women pulled off her hood, revealing herself as Leela. Seeing her approaching, Govinda tapped Gum Gum on the head, who knelt while Leela climbed onto the elephant's back.

"Are you all right?" he asked, hugging Leela tightly.

"You're hurt," replied Leela, seeing his bandage soaked with blood.

"I'll live, which is more than I expected an hour ago."

"Can they come up too?" Leela asked, pointing at the other two women.

Govinda signaled to Gum Gum, and soon all three women were seated atop Gum Gum.

"This is my friend, Nada. If it weren't for Nada, I'd still be captive," said Leela. "And this is Hashim's friend, Safiya,"

"I am indebted to you both."

"You're lucky, you know," smiled Leela. "First the raging elephant… then the lions… We heard they hadn't been fed in days. Poor Bandu… gentle soul… he helped us escape. If he hadn't… it would have been too horrible."

"I can guess closely enough from what Bandu told me."

"You spoke with Bandu?"

"We were together before he died," explained Govinda.

"But how did they discover what he did?"

"I don't know, but Zahira won't give up easily."

"I fear her more than anyone," admitted Leela.

"She's no match for you," grinned Govinda.

The Empress' Doom

After soaking in a mineral bath in Lufti Aalim's underground spa, a team of masseurs kneaded Govinda's aching muscles while a physician cleaned and dressed his injuries. Leela sat beside him, worrying over his wounds. Govinda stroked Leela's foot affectionately, relieved to find all of her toes intact.

After putting on fresh clothes, the young couple ventured into the dining room.

Admiring Leela's violet salwar kameez, Lufti Aalim said, "My dear, never put on a burqa again."

"Only if I need a disguise."

Lufti Aalim led his guests into the library where Mumtaz Aalim, Safiya, Nada, and Hashim had gathered.

"Our apologies," Lufti began. "We Moguls have been poor hosts."

Lufti spoke with an ease and refinement that Govinda had not heard since dining with Raja Rao and his family.

"I am no stranger to hardship," replied Govinda.

"You've faced your share of it," agreed Mumtaz Aalim.

Distressed by the day's violence, Safiya said, "Seeing Bandu and Yaman ravaged by lions..." Her voice trailed off.

"Bandu's death is tragic," Hashim replied, "but surely Yaman deserved what he got."

"Indeed, there was justice in what happened," Nada agreed. "Even as a child Yaman delighted in his depravity. The harem koi pools

The Tale of the Himalayan Yogis

needed constant replenishing. Yaman ordered the eunuchs to hold the fish in the air while he watched them suffocate. Yaman took pleasure in inflicting pain."

"There was one creature who he loved," acknowledged Safiya. "Yaman doted over a parrot named Akbar. He insisted on looking after the bird himself. In that sense, Yaman had a tender side."

"His was an unfortunate life," observed Lufti. "Growing up in a harem with a tyrannical father and a mother like Zahira... is it any wonder he sought refuge in wine and opium?"

"Yaman needed to be free of his mother," Mumtaz Aalim agreed. "He got what he wanted."

"Unfortunately, the rest of us are not yet free of her," interjected Hashim. "She remains a threat to the throne."

"It seems miracles are in the air," said Mumtaz Aalim. "Delhi has witnessed its share over the centuries, but nothing like what has transpired in recent days. Nagababas defeating the imperial army... a deluge like I have never seen... an elephant saving Prince Govinda... cobras flooding the streets... What will happen next?"

"Hashim, how did the generals respond?" asked Lufti Aalim.

"Upon revealing my true identity, they agreed that I should be the next emperor."

"But Bandu told me Ghazi's alive," interjected Govinda, who had been waiting for an opportunity to break the news. "He told me this morning as we waited to be executed."

"Informants claim to have seen Ghazi's corpse," replied Lufti Aalim.

"Bandu said the sorcerer is keeping him alive."

"But how? And where?" wondered Hashim.

"It may be that Kritavat and Zahira are the only ones who know these things," Govinda replied. "Do any of you know how Kritavat became acquainted with Zahira?"

"I shall explain," said Nada. "When Hashim's mother died, Zahira began plotting to seize control of the palace. She was thinking ahead to the time when Yaman would be old enough to take the throne. To help her succeed, Zahira sent emissaries away with instructions to find the most powerful sorcerer in all of India. The messengers were told to offer the sorcerer anything he wanted on the condition that the sorcerer agree to obey Zahira. After six moons, Kritavat showed up.

"We were surprised to see a Hindu coming and going, but mostly the sorcerer spent his days in the underground apartments that soon became his private chambers. During those years, there was talk among the women of blood sacrifices and curses, but only Zahira, Itibar Khan, and Bandu knew what was going on down there. No one else dared go near the chambers.

"As for Kritavat and Zahira being the only ones who know how and where Ghazi is being kept alive, there may be another person who knows. I heard Junduk talking to Zahira. The servant regularly disappears for days at a time, and when he returns, he reports to Zahira. I overheard him mentioning Ghazi less than a moon's turn ago."

"Junduk despises me," Hashim said, "but he was loyal to Ghazi, and he may continue to harbor that loyalty. Send someone for him. Tell him Uncle Lufti wishes to speak with him."

Later that evening, a servant ushered Junduk into the library.

"These are for you if you will tell us what you know about Ghazi," said Lufti, placing two bags of gold coins on the table.

"Ghazi lives," replied the servant sullenly.

"But we are certain that he's dead."

"Then the deception has been successful. Kritavat keeps him alive. The sorcerer needs his blood."

"Why?" asked Lufti.

"Blood curse," mumbled Junduk.

"Tantric curses are common in Nepal," Govinda interjected. "Kritavat lived with a tantric in Kathmandu."

"But who is the sorcerer cursing?" asked Lufti.

"Ghazi's blood connects him to the curse," Junduk explained.

"You're saying the sorcerer has placed a curse on Ghazi?" asked Lufti.

"That's right."

"Where is Ghazi now?" Lufti asked.

"Mizrabad."

At the mention of the abandoned fortress, Hashim's face paled. Mumtaz Aalim closed his eyes, and Nada gasped.

The Tale of the Himalayan Yogis

"I've heard tales of that hell," Nada told the others. "It's an abandoned fortress atop a barren hill. Children from the Emperor's minor wives are often imprisoned there to prevent them from competing for the throne. Vultures sit atop turrets waiting for the prisoners to waste away."

"We must find Ghazi," Hashim declared.

"Leaving now would risk your claim to the Peacock Throne," Mumtaz Aalim reminded his nephew. "Why not have the coronation first, and then go? Remember, Zahira is still a threat. She has the support of the mullahs, and some generals would stake their future with her in exchange for a bag of gems."

"If Ghazi's alive, then he's still the Emperor," Hashim insisted. "The generals have had their fill of Zahira. She lost their support when she took command of the second battle with the nagas. The generals resent a woman leading their army."

"I'll go with you to Mizrabad," offered Govinda.

"I visited the fortress once," Lufti said. "The fort was inhabited by vultures and wild dogs. Take some of my men with you. I have no idea what you'll encounter."

"Yaman's death has necessitated an emergency session of the court. A hearing is scheduled tomorrow. Junduk, I expect you to attend," instructed Hashim.

"I will come," replied the palace servant as he was left the room.

Junduk was leaving when another knock came at the door. Palace guards presented letters bearing the Emperor's seal. Lufti Aalim read the first letter to his guests.

"'Prince Hashim Shah is under arrest by decree of the Emperor of Delhi for conspiring with the condemned Rajput. By order of the Court of Nobles and Council of Mullahs.'"

Lufti Aalim read the second letter aloud. "'Prince Govinda is to be beheaded tomorrow at sunrise for the murder of Emperor Junaid Shah. Members of Lufti Aalim's family harboring the Rajput will be tried for treason. By order of the Court of Nobles and Council of Mullahs.'"

Lufti Aalim tossed the letters into a receptacle before penning a reply.

"Outrageous," he fumed, writing with impressive speed. "No one in the palace has such authority. I'm a member of the Court of Nobles myself, and they have taken no such decision."

"Sounds like Zahira," said Mumtaz Aalim, his snowy eyebrows rising. "She never hesitated to overstep her authority in the past."

Hashim pondered the letters before speaking.

"These edicts bear the seal of a dead and false emperor and are therefore invalid. Since Ghazi is alive, Uncle Lufti has the authority to act on behalf of the Emperor. The generals and court nobles have agreed to meet at durbar tomorrow to discuss the issue of succession. They'll be in for a surprise when I tell them Ghazi's alive."

Hashim penned a reply of his own.

"We must deal with Zahira, otherwise, whether Ghazi lives, or not, the Peacock Throne will never be secure," Mumtaz Aalim reminded the group.

"Baapu is right," Safiya agreed. "Zahira's obsessed with the throne and will waste no time in finding a replacement for her son. If she succeeds, we'll all be food for the lions."

"Zahira controls the ulema," Nada added. "Leela and I saw her with Mullah Nazir the other night. The head of the ulema has a personal interest in Zahira, which we may be able to use to our advantage."

Leela, who had been sitting beside Govinda, suddenly left the room, returning moments later with a parchment.

"This may be useful," she said, handing Hashim the parchment she had taken from Itibar Khan's body.

Hashim examined the seal, which was unfamiliar to him.

"I don't recognize the seal."

"It's Zahira's," Nada informed the group. "Before she joined the harem, Zahira worked as a seamstress."

Opening the parchment, Hashim read the letter aloud.

"Where did you find this?"

"Next to Itibar Khan's body," said Leela.

"The letter confirms the conspiracy as well as Kritavat's role in it," decided Hashim.

"We must show the letter to the Court of Nobles," added Mumtaz Aalim.

"But what of the curse?" Nada asked. "The letter says the sorcerer will activate the curse on the full moon."

"I, for one, do not put much faith in curses," scoffed Hashim.

"Nor I," agreed Govinda. "But I have seen his black magic firsthand. Kritavat is no common sorcerer."

"Then you think the curse is real?" questioned Lufti.

"We should take it seriously," interjected Mumtaz Aalim. "For Hashim's sake, as well as Ghazi's."

"Fortunately, Islamic Law prohibits women from acceding to the throne," noted Safiya. "But who does Zahira have in mind for her puppet?"

"Ghazi is the rightful emperor," replied Hashim. "But public perception is all that matters. The people believe me to be dead, but after my appearance in the arena, they believe that Ghazi is alive, which would mean the rightful emperor has never been Yaman. It has been Ghazi and still is. Zahira will have to convince the people that I'm alive, and that Ghazi's dead, in which case I'd be the next in line of succession.

"For Zahira, the best solution is to arrange for me to die in public. She's already begun with these letters; she'll probably try me for treason against the Empire and sentence me to execution. That would end the line of succession. Zahira would rightfully appoint the next emperor. As for who she would appoint, one of the generals would be the logical choice."

Lufti stamped the letters with Ghazi's royal seal and took them to the guards, who were waiting outside.

"Deliver these to whoever sent you," Lufti ordered the officer of the guards, handing over the parchments. "I imagine it was Begum Zahira."

"But we've come for the Rajput," the officer stammered.

"You don't seem to understand," Lufti countered. "As vizier of Delhi, I have the authority to decide the fate of Prince Govinda. Yaman's edict is invalid because he's dead. The Rajput will not be executed. Prince Govinda is a free man. Now take these messages to Begum Zahira."

The officer accepted the letters and left with his men.

"Hashim, what did you write in your letter?" Lufti asked.

"In so many words, that Yaman's death invalidates the edicts."

"I wrote the same. Also, I offered Zahira a generous pension to vacate the Moti Mahal."

"Zahira is the cause of all this," agreed Safiya. "It is time she was exposed. I have a plan for the hearing tomorrow. I wish to speak before the court."

"But women aren't allowed to speak at court," Lufti replied.

"Then tomorrow shall be an exception."

"I also wish to speak," said Nada. "I believe that only those who have lived in fear of Zahira can bring about her fall."

"In the morning, we will finalize the plan," Lufti advised. "Now, let us retire."

"I detest court politics," complained Hashim over breakfast the following morning.

"It is not the time to reform the system," replied Lufti. "We have urgent matters to tend to."

Lufti was not his usual easygoing self. Along with Safiya and Nada, he had been up since dawn formulating a plan that would expose Begum Zahira. Lufti's scheme required the cooperation of Hashim, who would need guile if he were to have any chance of winning the generals and mullahs to his side. Although Lufti Aalim carried considerable influence among the court nobles, he knew that if Hashim faltered, it would mean imprisonment, or worse. The servant, Junduk, was critical to their ploy.

Lufti Aalim led Hashim into the pillared hall where the generals, mullahs, and court nobles awaited their arrival. Lufti's eyes met those of the bearded mullahs, including Nazir Hussein.

From balconies overhead, Yaman's former consorts watched, veils covering all but their eyes. The Peacock Throne sat vacant, flanked by a latticed marble window, which Zahira added after Yaman's coronation. Stone-faced guards flanked the entrances to the hall.

The Tale of the Himalayan Yogis

Hashim seated himself in a chair below the Peacock Throne. Standing in front of the throne, Lufti Aalim addressed the court.

"Nobles, officers, and esteemed mullahs, the question of succession is clear enough. Prince Hashim is the son of Emperor Junaid Shah and the brother of Emperor Ghazi Shah, and therefore he is the rightful heir to the Peacock Throne. Can there be any doubt in the matter?"

"By lineage that is correct," Nazir Hussein agreed, "but the council is skeptical of Prince Hashim's loyalty to Islamic Law. If you recall, it was Prince Hashim who staged the heretical debate between Mullah Khan and the Brahmin. That farcical affair tarnished the image of Islam, and will not soon be forgotten. As we have all witnessed in the stadium, once more we have reason to question Prince Hashim's fidelity. Who among us did not feel revulsion at the sight of him raising the Rajput's hand in triumph? Treasonous act! I say death to the enemies of Islam! I have no words for my contempt!"

"The court respects your opinion," conceded Lufti.

"The Ulema rejects the proposal that Prince Hashim becomes Emperor of Delhi," concluded Hussein.

"I wish to speak on my behalf," Hashim said, rising from his chair. "There are those who view me as liberal. I do not deny that I have studied religions and philosophies other than my own, but my liberality will serve me well as ruler of a populace that includes many faiths. We should not forget that we are a minority in Hindustan and that if we persist in persecuting the majority, it will one day lead to our ruin. How long can the tyranny continue before Hindus revolt? I stand for a different ethic than that of my father and brother. I stand for a different ethic than the ulema."

"We intend to execute those who side with Hindus," fumed Hussein.

"How many of you were present at Krishnagarh?" Hashim asked, looking around the hall. "I saw the spike that killed my father. I can assure you that Prince Govinda did not murder Emperor Shah."

"What difference does it make?" said one of the generals. "The Rajput has been poison in our wine. Due to his brazen acts, his people have taken heart."

"The military views a Hindu uprising as imminent should

Steve Briggs

a liberal-minded emperor assume the Peacock Throne," said Commander Murad, who had also been present at Krishnagarh. "A show of conciliation would lead to our expulsion. The thought of liberality sickened your father."

"Surely you supported Emperor Ghazi's rule," Hashim reminded everyone present.

"Emperor Ghazi was responsible for our army's greatest triumph," Commander Murad agreed. "The spoils of Vijayanagar are Emperor Ghazi's legacy. The campaign brought riches to foot soldier and officer alike."

"And what about the mullahs?" Hashim asked. "Did you not find Emperor Ghazi's religious views to your liking?"

"Emperor Ghazi was Allah's warrior," agreed Hussein. "Emperor Ghazi exceeded his own father's example in religious conduct."

"Then why not have Ghazi as your emperor?"

"Have you lost your mind?" bristled Hussein. "We have urgent decisions to make, and you chatter like a parrot."

"Absurd," Commander Murad chided. "Everyone knows that Emperor Ghazi is dead!"

The nobles and mullahs broke into a chorus of dissent.

"Hear me out," Hashim appealed, speaking with an authority that surprised even his supporters. "I have come to know that my brother lives."

"Guards, summon the servant, Junduk," Hashim ordered, signaling to the guards at the door.

The guards disappeared, returning a short time later without the servant.

"Why haven't you brought Junduk?" questioned Lufti.

"Sir, Junduk is dead! We found him in the koi pond with this in his back," said the guard, displaying a pearl-handled dagger.

"It is time the treachery was exposed," said Lufti.

Hashim stepped next to his uncle and removed his tunic, displaying a raised scar on his stomach. Turning around, he revealed a similar wound on his back.

"You have been told that my brother and I drowned in Kashmir, but the truth is, I had a sword run through me on the same day when

The Tale of the Himalayan Yogis

Yaman's assassin, Uzbek Khan, abducted Ghazi. I too assumed my brother was dead, but last night Junduk assured me that Ghazi is alive."

"If that be true, then where is he?" probed Commander Murad.

"Mizrabad," replied Hashim. "The point is; Ghazi is still the Emperor. Yaman was an imposter placed in power by his mother."

"If Emperor Ghazi is alive, then the military stands behind him," affirmed Murad.

The other officers, as well as the mullahs, nodded in agreement.

"Do not forget that I served as Ghazi's vizier," Lufti interjected. "As vizier, I order the guards to arrest Empress Zahira. You'll find her behind the screen."

Lufti pointed to the marble lattice beside the Peacock Throne.

"Zahira is responsible for Junduk's death as well as the assassination attempt on Emperor Ghazi," declared Hashim.

A pair of guards disappeared behind the latticed window, returning with Empress Zahira in their grasp.

"Bring her before the court," ordered Lufti, exhaling a sigh of relief.

Women had never stood before the court, but the guards followed Lufti Aalim's orders.

"Begum Zahira," Lufti Aalim began, "you are responsible for my sister Kameela's death, and you ordered the assassination of Emperor Ghazi, all so that dull-witted son of yours could sit on the throne. Yaman has sullied the imperial crown. What do you have to say?"

"I have committed no crime," Zahira countered. "The mullahs will speak on my behalf."

"Begum Zahira is above these counterfeit charges," protested Nazir Hussein. "She has always upheld Allah's will. I can attest to that."

"Princess Nada, will you step forward?" Lufti Aalim requested.

Nada emerged from behind a screen near the hall's entrance.

"Islamic law forbids women standing before the court," bristled Hussein. "Women are not permitted to speak."

"Begum Zahira has spoken," Lufti Aalim replied coolly. "Princess Nada shall have her turn. Nada, tell us what you know."

"Mullah Hussein visits Begum Zahira regularly in the harem's chambers where consorts provide enjoyment for their guests."

"She's lying," snarled Zahira. "Nada herself is guilty of treason. She helped the Rajput's wife escape."

"With Begum Zahira in the custody of palace guards," Nada continued, "I can assure you there are a dozen women who will confirm my words, and much more. Zahira and Hussein have been visiting one another for as long as I have been in the harem."

A titter arose from the court nobles as well as from the women watching from the balcony. Scornful looks appeared on more than one bearded mullah.

"The girl is confused," Hussein protested in his humblest façade. "My visits to the Moti Mahal are of a religious nature."

"Mullah Hussein, are you claiming that your visitations to the harem are for prayer?" asked Nada.

"That is correct."

"Then I assume you are in the habit of praying naked."

"How dare you!" frothed Zahira, struggling to free herself from the guards. "Accuse me… and I'll feed your tongue to the pariahs."

"Your threats no longer frighten me," replied Nada calmly. Removing her burqa hood, Nada's stunning beauty commanded the attention of everyone in the hall.

Holding up the parchment, Nada continued. "I have proof that Ghazi lives because Begum Zahira once again conspires to assassinate Emperor Ghazi and Prince Hashim. This parchment is proof that Emperor Ghazi lives."

Nada unrolled the parchment and read it for all to hear.

> *All preparations have been made. The curse will be activated on the full moon. The twins shall die within the fortnight. Then the Peacock Throne will be ours.*
>
> *I count on you to control the mullahs. You know how much they despise me. Although they have given their support to the plan, I trust none of them, and shall direct*

my powers against them should they conspire against me. Upon the Rajput's execution, I shall depart. K

"Who is this 'K'?" questioned a member of the Court of Nobles.

"A tantric named Kritavat has been visiting the zenana these past moons," clarified Lufti. "Begum Safiya, would you stand before the court?"

Safiya stepped to the center of the hall, carefully adjusting the sleeve of her burqa before addressing the court.

"Mullah Hussein began visiting Begum Zahira seven years ago, but it does not surprise me that the mullahs feign revulsion at Nada's testimony. The hypocrisy is not Hussein's alone. I have seen many of the mullahs entering the harem late at night. Zahira invites them, but always at a price."

"Whore," hissed Zahira.

"Duplicity among the mullahs never raised any suspicion around the harem," Safiya continued, ignoring Zahira. "It made good conversation, but Zahira's crimes are far more contemptible than offering favors to our esteemed clergy. She planned the assassination of Emperor Ghazi, and now she has murdered Junduk."

"I won't stand for this," snarled Zahira, frantically twisting as she tried to free herself.

Drawing a dagger from within her sleeve, Zahira slashed the hand of the guard who held her and tore herself free of the other guard. Brandishing her weapon, Zahira lurched forward, stabbing at Safiya. But before Zahira's dagger could find its mark, Safiya raised a dagger of her own concealed in her sleeve. In her rage, Zahira rushed headlong onto Safiya's weapon, which lodged itself in the Empress' chest, cutting close to her heart.

The hall fell silent as the Empress shrieked.

"That was for my dear Kameela," Safiya said plainly, her words echoing throughout the hall. "... and for Bandu."

Zahira's dagger fell from her hand as she tore at her robes. Wrenching the knife from her chest, Zahira stabbed feverishly at the air. Safiya eluded Zahira's flailing thrusts until the Empress' strength waned and she collapsed to the floor.

Hashim stepped forward to protect Safiya, but she was in no danger. Safiya's knife fell from Zahira's hand. As Zahira groped for the dagger, Hashim kicked it aside, streaking the marble floor with the Empress' blood.

Drawing fitful breaths, Zahira grew pale.

"Victory is mine," mumbled Zahira through a mouthful of blood. "The demoness' curse… is upon… the sons… of Junaid Shah."

The Empress stared coldly at Safiya, her serpentine eyes ringed with death. Zahira's hand searched in vain for her dagger before a final convulsion shook her body. The Empress lay before the Peacock Throne; her eyes fixed on an invisible foe.

Safiya held up Zahira's dagger.

"After Kameela's death, Emperor Shah presented Zahira with twin daggers to protect her from rival wives. Let us see if this dagger matches the one that killed Junduk."

The head guard held up the murder weapon.

"They're identical!" confirmed Commander Murad.

"Begum Zahira died in the manner in which she lived," stated Lufti Aalim. "I think our business here today is concluded. I shall go to Mizrabad to retrieve Ghazi. Until I return, I recommend the court postpone all decisions regarding the Peacock Throne."

The court nobles and generals unanimously agreed to wait for news of Ghazi's status.

The hearing adjourned, Lufti gathered Nada and Safiya close to Hashim, who was buttoning his tunic.

"Finally, Allah smiles on us," whispered Lufti.

The Demoness' Curse

Nada squeezed Hashim's hand as their carriage pulled up to the entrance of Lufti's mansion.

"The monster of Moti Mahal is dead. There will be much celebrating in the harem tonight."

Hashim placed his free hand on Nada's.

"Without your support, I would not have had the courage," he said softly as the carriage stopped beneath the tiled portico outside his uncle's home.

Hashim was the last to climb down. As he approached the entrance, intense pain pierced his chest and upper back, causing him to double over. It was the same pain that had plagued him since the assassination attempt in Kashmir, but now the pain was far more severe. Releasing Nada's hand, he clutched his chest with one hand while twisting his other arm around to his upper back. Searing bolts stabbed at him, causing him to shiver despite the heat.

"What's the matter?" Nada asked, taking Hashim's hands in hers. "You look as if you've seen a *djinn*."

"... not feeling well," Hashim answered faintly.

"The trauma of it all is taking its toll," Lufti Aalim said. "We are all feeling it. A good meal and some rest, and Hashim will be fine."

Hashim tugged at his collar as he walked toward the entrance.

"I'm having trouble... breathing."

As if a serpent had coiled about his neck, Hashim gasped for air before collapsing to the ground.

At the sight of Hashim's ashen face, Nada cried out.

"Zahira and the court didn't cause," decided Safiya, bending down to examine Hashim.

"Go and fetch the *hakims*," Lufti ordered his driver.

Mumtaz Aalim, who had come to the entrance to greet his family, instantly knew what was wrong.

"I'm afraid the curse is real."

"But how do you know?" asked Nada, a look of dread etched on her face.

"The signs are clear. Something is stealing Hashim's life force," decided Aalim.

"Kritavat?" Lufti asked.

"I'm afraid so," Mumtaz Aalim replied.

"Then doctors won't help," said Lufti.

"Probably not, but have them come anyway."

"Will he die?" asked Nada, her eyes riveted on Hashim.

"If we don't find Kritavat soon, I'm afraid there's little hope for Hashim, and probably the same for Ghazi," replied Aalim.

"But Kritavat could be anywhere," Lufti said.

"I know where he is," said Govinda, who had come outside with Leela to greet their friends. "I spoke with him in the dungeon on the night before the execution. He was preparing some blood ritual. I'm certain Kritavat will perform the ritual at Mizrabad, and that the curse originates there."

"Your master has trained you well," Mumtaz Aalim said by way of agreement.

"I'll leave immediately," decided Govinda.

"I'm coming with you," said Leela, clutching his hand.

"I'm going too," Lufti said. "We'll take a hundred of my men."

A pair of servants carried Hashim into the house. Though his breath was shallow and uneven, he was alive.

"Nada and I will look after Hashim," decided Mumtaz Aalim. "Go now; otherwise, it may be too late to save the twins."

The Tale of the Himalayan Yogis

Govinda, Lufti, and Leela rode at the head of Lufti's hired cavalry, pushing on into the night until their horses could go no further.

After finishing their meal, one of Lufti's men approached.

"I wish to speak with you, if I may," the man said.

"What about?" Lufti asked.

"The man called Kritavat was at Vijayanagar."

"Tell us what you know."

"It was the first time any of us had seen the sorcerer. We didn't know him by name, but I'm sure he's the same man. The night following the siege, Emperor Ghazi and the sorcerer argued. The Emperor had called for a few of his harem favorites, but the women were not in their tents because the sorcerer had taken them onto the battlefield."

"Why?" Govinda asked.

"Some sorcerer's rite… Kritavat forced the women to dance over the corpses of the slain soldiers. When the Emperor found out, he confronted Kritavat, but the sorcerer was in a trance and spoke abusively."

"I'm surprised Ghazi didn't execute him on the spot," replied Lufti.

"The Emperor rode back to camp and sent us to get his women," the soldier continued. "When we arrived, the women were weeping. They had watched Kritavat cut the heart out of a dead soldier. The Emperor ordered Kritavat shackled and beaten, and left him to die in the desert. I have no idea how he survived."

"That explains why he's kept Ghazi alive all this time. Kritavat's obsessed with revenge," said Govinda.

The following afternoon, a thinly veiled fortress appeared through the haze.

"Mizrabad!" said Lufti, pointing to the fort.

Rising from a hillock of barren rock, the bleak the edifice inspired despair. Evenly spaced turrets crowned the fortress walls. White-backed vultures perched atop the fortress walls, their puny heads slumping to their chests. The birds appeared well fed, and judging by their numbers; there was plenty to sustain them inside the fortress.

Leela shuddered at the sight of the vultures. A rocky trail led up the hill to the entrance. The plains surrounding the fort lacked sufficient water to sustain anything other than a few thorny bushes bleached by the withering sun.

"Something sinister veils the fort," decided Govinda.

Ascending the trail, the group passed through a series of arched gates, their heavy wooden doors scarred from siege and splintered with age. Forming a single column, Lufti's men passed one by one through the gates. Overhead, vultures inspected the new arrivals.

The group stopped at the main gate, which was secured by massive iron chains. Near the entrance stood a dilapidated hut. A pair of unshaven, dull-witted men emerged. Lufti produced a letter of introduction bearing the seal of the Vizier of Delhi. The sentries scrutinized the parchment before casually waving the riders inside.

"Who's in charge here?" asked Lufti.

"Farokh Amru," one of the sentries replied.

"Sounds like the man is Parsi," noted Govinda.

Inside the edifice, massive stone walls formed an enormous oven, magnifying the sun's intensity beyond reason. Upon entering the courtyard, the arrivals felt their strength wane. Lufti led Leela and Govinda to a shaded space. Droppings and petrified excrement littered the courtyard. At the far side of the yard, a tethered goat dozed at the base of a post. Mizrabad was indeed a hellish place.

"No one of sound mind would accept an assignment here," observed Lufti, squinting at the battlements.

"The goat is here because Kritavat's here," decided Govinda. "It will be sacrificed in his ritual."

"And the vultures are here to claim what's left over," guessed Leela.

"Let's find Amru and see where they're keeping Ghazi," suggested Govinda. "Maybe we won't have to spend the night here."

"I'm in favor of that," she said. "This place makes my skin crawl."

Spotting a splintered signboard with something illegible scratched on it, Lufti and Govinda dismounted, sullying their boots on the filthy terrain. They stepped through a door into an office lit by sunlight filtering through a cracked window. Several of Lufti's men followed them into the office. A broken chair and a string cot were the only pieces of furniture in the room. Lying on the sunken bed, a man wheezed sonorously. The sleeping man wore a dirty lungi, hadn't shaved in days, and reeked of alcohol. Lufti shook the man. Slowly, the dazed fellow opened his bloodshot eyes.

"Are you Farokh Amru?" asked Lufti.

Sitting up, the man nodded. Lufti handed him the letter of introduction.

"Can't read."

"The letter bears the seal of the Vizier of Delhi," explained Lufti. "We've come for Emperor Ghazi Shah."

"Who?" asked Amru, stepping to the door, letter in hand. Squinting in the sunlight, Amru examined the seal as if he doubted its authenticity.

"Emperor Ghazi Shah… he's an inmate here," repeated Lufti.

"No emperor here," Amru replied indifferently.

"He's here I say," insisted Lufti.

Amru held up four fingers. "Only four… two are women."

"Where are the men? Take us to their cells," demanded Lufti.

"Better if she stays behind," said Amru, pointing a grimy finger at Leela.

"I'm coming," Leela said, clutching Govinda's hand.

"As you like," said Amru, not bothering to put on his shirt.

Amru led the group across the courtyard to a military barrack haphazardly partitioned into four rooms. The first three rooms were vacant and reeked of bat guano. The fourth, though it had a cot in the corner with a man lying on it, was no cleaner than the others. The sleeping man was gaunt and nearly hairless — he had no fingers. A stained cloth partially covered his waist. A broken pot lay on the floor. Though the room was the last of the rooms in the former barrack, a half-open door led to what appeared to be a closet.

"Wait here," Govinda whispered into Leela's ear.

Lufti and Govinda followed Amru over to the bed. A foul odor hovered above the body. Govinda tried not to inhale.

"Who is it?" Lufti asked.

"Prince named Kamran," Amru replied. "…been here since before Junaid Shah was Emperor."

"Poor man," replied Lufti.

"Guess they forgot him," added Amru.

"What happened to his hands?" Govinda asked.

"Can't say… punishment, I suppose."

"Where's the other man?" asked Govinda.

"There." Amru pointed through the half-open door.

Lufti stepped over the broken pot and pushed open the door. A barred window allowed a few dust-flecked bands of light into the quarters, but he could see virtually nothing. Lufti stepped tentatively into the darkness.

"I need a lantern," he said, stepping back into the larger room.

"You'll have to make do," Amru said. "We don't get proper supplies."

Lufti stepped into the closet again. Govinda followed him with Leela close behind, waiting while their eyes adjusted to the light. A limp figure lay on a cot facing the far wall. The man was covered by a waist cloth and slept on a stained sheet. On the floor beside the cot was a dented copper cup.

Lufti leaned across the man's body in an attempt to identify him.

"We'll need to wake him," he said. "I can't see his face."

Govinda leaned around Lufti to have a look. Festered welts covered the man's pockmarked arms, legs, and torso. His skin was frighteningly pale and loose. A tarnished medallion rested on the man's chest.

Govinda pointed to the medallion. Lufti bent low to examine it, but the poor light prevented him from identifying it. Removing the pendant from the sleeping man, he retreated. Stepping into the courtyard, Lufti turned the pendant in his hand.

"It's crusted with grime," he said, spitting on the pendant before cleaning the surface with the sleeve of his tunic. After several cleanings, a faint image appeared.

Lufti held the pendant up to the light.

"A pink lotus set in silver," said Leela.

"I think we've found Ghazi," replied Lufti excitedly. "The pink lotus was Kameela's favorite flower. She gave the twins matching pendants when they were young."

Returning to the closet, Lufti shook his nephew's bony shoulder, but there was no response. Lufti shook him again, this time more forcefully, but still, he lay unconscious.

Lufti picked up the half-filled cup and sniffed its contents.

"I doubt we'll be able to wake him until the opium wears off."

Turning his nephew onto his back, he weighed almost nothing. Recoiling, Lufti collided with Govinda, who was peering over his shoulder.

"Hideous," he shuddered.

Lufti pressed close to the wall so that Govinda could have a look. The ghostlike face was indeed Ghazi's, but the man's eyes had been sewn shut. The stitching appeared to have been there for some time.

"*Hari*," recoiled Govinda.

Horrified, both men backed out of the room.

"It's him!" Lufti confirmed. "But why…"

"… the stitching?" said Govinda, completing Lufti's question.

Leela was about to step inside the closet when Govinda raised his arm to prevent her.

"What's the matter?"

"It's too awful," said Govinda.

"What is?"

"Ghazi's eyes have been sewn shut."

"*What?*"

"They're sealed!"

"What kind of hell is this?" wondered Leela.

"Have the cooks prepare soup," Lufti instructed one of his men. "We need a physician, but there won't be one here. I'm going to organize camp outside the fort."

Lufti left the room. A third of his men accompanied him; the others remained with Govinda and Leela, who went in search of Farokh Amru.

"You said Ghazi Shah wasn't here," said Govinda accusingly.

"Man's name is Hashim Shah," countered the Parsi.

"That's what you've been told, but why are his eyes stitched shut?"

"Can't say," replied Amru. "… that way when I got here."

"Same as Prince Kamran's fingers… happened before you arrived," parroted Govinda sarcastically.

"No one's ever posted here for long. I've been here little over a year."

"Why haven't these men been properly fed?" demanded Leela.

"I do what they tell me to do," replied Amru. "Keep them alive… nothing more."

"There are welts all over the Emperor's body," said Govinda.

"Why do you keep calling that sack of flesh, Emperor?"

"Because he's the Emperor of Delhi! Now tell me what's causing the welts on his chest and legs."

"Leeches," replied Amru, his grin exposing a row of rotting teeth.

The Parsi stepped into the courtyard. As Amru left the room, one of Lufti's men entered with a lantern.

"Do you need this?"

"Yes," said Govinda.

Returning to the closet, Govinda held up the light so that he could examine Ghazi more closely. In the lamplight, Ghazi's sunken face looked still more ghostly. His head was little more than a ball of skin pulled loosely over his skull, his hair was tangled and full of lice.

"Must be water shortages," surmised Lufti, returning from the camp. "No one bathes here. When Ghazi wakes up, we'll bathe and feed him. In this condition, he won't be able to travel anytime soon."

"Amru feeds Ghazi enough to keep him alive, but nothing more," said Govinda.

"What about the welts?"

"Leeches," said Govinda.

"Leeches?"

"They're being used to drain Ghazi's blood."

"That has to be the sorcerer."

"The night I spent in the dungeon, Junduk passed through the room with a bowl of bloated leeches."

Leela cringed.

"He's using Ghazi's blood in his rituals," Govinda explained. "In certain rites, the blood of an animal, or even a human, is offered to propitiate wrathful beings."

"Somehow it's linked to the curse on Hashim," Lufti said.

The Tale of the Himalayan Yogis

"Of course," agreed Leela. "Ghazi and Hashim are twins. The blood curse is meant to harm the twins."

"Where's Amru?" asked Lufti.

"He went outside," Govinda replied. "If Kritavat doesn't already know we're here; he will shortly."

Lufti, Govinda, and Leela went in search of Amru.

As they stepped into the blinding intensity of the courtyard, the vultures atop the walls continued to watch Leela. Not finding the Parsi outside, Lufti assigned a pair of his men to guard Ghazi's room. Moments later the guards returned from the barracks.

"He's gone."

Govinda noticed that the goat had also vanished and that the vultures had doubled in number.

"When will the moon be full?" Govinda asked.

"Tonight," Leela replied.

"Then tonight Kritavat will sacrifice the goat, and probably Ghazi as well. The goat's vanished, and the vultures have increased... not a good omen," surmised Govinda.

"I'll post sentries at every entry point to the fort," said Lufti.

"I'm afraid that won't be good enough," Govinda said. "I was raised in a fort. There are underground passages everywhere. If Kritavat's taken Ghazi to some subterranean chamber, then we may not find him in time, if we find him at all."

"Unless Amru knows where he is," suggested Leela.

"But we don't know where the Parsi is," mused Govinda. "We need to find him. Otherwise, Ghazi may not live through the night."

"And if Ghazi dies, Hashim will die too," decided Lufti.

"Every fort has a temple. I'm going to find it," Govinda announced.

"I'll have my men search the fort," Lufti said. "Maybe we'll find an entrance to a tunnel."

Govinda found it nearly impossible to meditate in the cobwebbed shrine, his mind returning again and again to Ghazi's gaunt face. Holding the Idol's Eye against his chest, the specter of impending doom gripped him.

Govinda was about to rejoin the search party when Mizrabad appeared before him as seen from a distance. A misty shroud hovered over the fort like a shawl draped over the crest of a hill. A pair of hideous eyes watched him.

The sun was low when he reached Lufti and Leela in the courtyard.

"We didn't find anything," Leela said.

"I've figured it out," Govinda said breathlessly. "We need to find the place where they dispose the carcasses… probably outside the west wall."

"But there's not much daylight left," Lufti said.

"We should be able to locate the spot from the turrets," Govinda said. "If each of us climbs a wall, we're bound to see it. Look for the vultures; they'll be waiting for their meal."

Lufti and his guards climbed a turret on the west rampart while Govinda and Leela scrambled up the south wall where the most of birds roosted.

"Over there," Leela said, pointing to a rocky area outside the fort.

Govinda followed Leela's finger to a flock of birds packed so tightly together that birds blanketed an entire section of the hill. In addition to the vultures, crows and coyotes had assembled. The area appeared as if a mass burial ground had been unearthed. The bleached bones of water buffalo, goats, cows, and birds were picked clean.

"Let's take the horses," suggested Govinda. "Once it's dark, we'll never find the entrance."

"Do you think we'll find an entrance out there?" asked Leela doubtfully, repulsed by the thought of venturing near the vultures.

"The vultures were keeping an eye on the goat. They've shifted to the hill for a reason. There has to be an entrance out there."

"This is like a nightmare," complained Leela.

"Kritavat is a living nightmare."

Govinda signaled to Lufti that they had found the birds.

"There's one more thing you should know," Govinda explained as they mounted their horses. "The fortress is inhabited by a demoness."

"That explains the revolting feeling," cringed Leela.

"Like the vultures, she wouldn't be here if they didn't feed her."

"How do we fight a demoness?" wondered Lufti.

"I don't know," shrugged Govinda.

Taking one of Lufti's officers with them, Govinda led the group to the spot where the puny-headed vultures had congregated. An acrid stench pervaded the area. Leela hoped the horses would scare off the unsightly birds, but the vultures weren't the least bit startled as they rode up. Sensing that the humans had not brought food, the vultures ignored them. Leela was relieved to find that the vultures took little interest in the search party.

Climbing down from her horse a safe distance from the flock, Leela reeled at the sight of the headless skeletons littering the rocks.

Shrieking, she pointed to a small mound of human skeletons.

"There should be a path leading to the entrance," Govinda said, scanning the rocks. "The entrance will be higher up. No one would drag a buffalo carcass up this hill."

They hadn't gone more than a few steps when Govinda discovered a large, rectangular iron flap among the rocks.

"This is it."

The entrance was similar to the one he had used to escape from Krishnagarh. The covering groaned as it opened. The sound of the creaking cover drew the attention of the vultures, causing part of the flock to alight on nearby rocks. Beneath the cover, a ladder descended into darkness. Assessing the distance to the center of the fort, Govinda was sure that Kritavat's secret chamber lay somewhere beneath the courtyard.

"We'll need lanterns and soldiers," Lufti advised.

"Send a man back to the camp," Govinda replied. "Have him bring buckets of water and more men. We don't have much time. I'm going in."

"I'm not staying here with them," decided Leela, noticing that the vultures were watching her.

"I can't see a thing," said Lufti, peering into the blackness.

"Our eyes will adjust," replied Govinda.

"But what about weapons?" Lufti asked.

"This will be a battle of wills. Weapons are useless against these foes."

"All right, but we may be walking into a trap."

As Lufti's man rode off, the group descended the ladder to the floor of a narrow, low passage that had been cut unevenly into the mountain. The passage smelled of decay. Govinda had rarely navigated such a confining tunnel. They had taken a few steps when Lufti's tunic snagged against a jagged rock protruding from the wall of the passage. Govinda wondered how they dragged a cow's carcass through the tunnel.

"I hope we find him in time," Leela said.

Govinda stepped cautiously at first, but as his eyes grew accustomed to the blackness, he increased his pace. Estimating that they were now under the fort, he paused. Then, as if possessing perfect night vision, he walked up to a door and stopped without banging into it.

Searching for a way to open the door, Govinda ran his hands over the surface of the barrier. Drawing his dagger, he slipped it into the gap between the door and its frame. When the knife touched iron, he lifted the blade, releasing the latch. His weapon poised, Govinda pushed the door open.

Govinda and the others stepped through the door. Through the smoky haze, he peered into a small chamber lit by a single lantern. The chamber was otherwise empty. Govinda spotted another door on the far side of the room. Smoke seeped through the gaps around that door. The sorcerer's ritual was already in progress. He hoped they weren't too late.

Approaching the second door, Govinda heard the faint sound of incantations. The second door was unlocked, and he pushed it open soundlessly. Stinging smoke accosted them, causing Leela to cough.

Peering through the door leading to Kritavat's lair, a robed figure chanted at the far end of the cavern. Kritavat stood before a statue with many hands, each one holding a weapon. Govinda suspected that the idol was a crude depiction of Tadaka. A garland of monkey skulls hung across her breasts, the bones of goats' legs formed a gruesome skirt.

The icon's bulging eyes gazed hungrily at a fire pit into which Kritavat dripped liquid from a long-handled ladle. To the side of the altar stood a stone pillar. A headless carcass lay in the middle of the room, its blood dripping into a bowl. Someone had driven the blade of an ax into a chopping block.

Govinda waited to see if they had been discovered, but Kritavat

The Tale of the Himalayan Yogis

continued chanting, and so he entered his foe's lair. Scanning the cavern, he searched for Ghazi. Not finding him, he trained his eyes on Kritavat.

Govinda stepped to the center of the cavern. Taking no notice, Kritavat continued chanting. A smaller room came into view to Govinda's right. A body lay stretched out on the floor of the antechamber. The faint rise and fall of the man's chest told him that Ghazi was alive.

Govinda signaled to Lufti, who followed him into the smaller space. Together, they were about to lift Ghazi when they noticed a swarm of disturbingly large leeches.

Govinda and Lufti had little difficulty lifting Ghazi, who weighed no more than a couple of sacks of grain. Silently, they retraced their steps through the central cavern and into the adjoining chamber leading to the tunnel. A few more steps and they would be safe. Leela was already breathing easier. Carrying the lantern from the chamber, she led the way.

Govinda was about to step into the tunnel when Leela shrieked. Struggling to free herself from an attacker, she swung the lantern at the man. Catching her wrist, the tribal man wrenched it sharply, causing the lamp to drop to the floor, where it shattered. The tribal dragged Leela into the central cavern.

Lowering Ghazi to the floor, Govinda leaped over the burning oil, but as he entered the central cavern, a second man grabbed his wrist and wrenched it in a way that caused his grip to fail. His dagger fell to the floor. The wild-eyed tribals wore goatskins, their faces and chests were streaked with ash.

"Shouldn't be taking that body just now," said Farokh Amru, emerging from a hiding place.

The Parsi pressed a dagger against Leela's back.

"Amru, I represent the Emperor of Delhi," explained Lufti. "The letter I showed you indicates that this man is to be released."

"Told you I can't read," replied Amru callously.

Amru led Leela and the others into Kritavat's cavern.

"Shackle them," ordered Kritavat, continuing to pour a liquid offering over the fire without turning to face the intruders.

The tribal men shackled the captives to a stone column at the side of the altar. Lufti and Govinda tested the strength of the iron shackles, but the tribals ignored them, confident the chains were secure. The tribals carried Ghazi back into the smaller cave where Govinda had found him. Despite the commotion, Ghazi continued to sleep.

"Bring the leeches," Amru ordered.

The leeches had gone nowhere since being left on the floor. The tribals collected them on a platter, which they placed on the chopping block after Amru had removed the ax.

"For the sacrifice," grinned Amru as he squeezed a leech, causing the liquid from its bloated body to empty into the pot.

"Superstition," scoffed Lufti, continuing to test the strength of his shackles.

"Part of the curse…" replied Amru.

Again and again, Kritavat invoked the demoness as he poured liquid into the fire. Raising the pot containing Ghazi's blood, he poured it into a buffalo's skull and held it in front of the idol. Chanting fiercely, Kritavat poured the contents over the statue's head.

"Leela, are you all right?" Govinda asked.

"I'm fine. What are the offerings for?" she asked.

"Kritavat propitiates Tadaka, but it's not the blood she feeds on; it's the fear in the blood. Fear is her food. Whatever happens, we must not succumb to fear."

Sweat dripped from the sorcerer's brow as the ritual reached a feverish pitch. Liquid sizzled in the fire as Tadaka came alive on the altar. Her eyes ablaze, Govinda looked away, for looming above the idol was something so sinister that even he feared it.

With a wave of his hand, Kritavat summoned Farokh Amru to his side. After receiving instructions, Amru retreated to the smaller cave where Ghazi slept. Amru shook Ghazi, trying to wake him from his torpor. Unable to rouse him, Amru pulled an ember from the fire and dropped it on Ghazi's stomach. Govinda cringed as a pitifully weak cry issued from the cave. Leela buried her face against Govinda's shoulder.

His chin resting on his chest, the tribals dragged Ghazi into the

The Tale of the Himalayan Yogis

central cavern. Govinda had never seen a man in a more wretched condition.

Ghazi offered no resistance as the tribals lay his head on the chopping block. Amru grinned maliciously, demonstrating with the ax what he was about to do. Govinda redoubled his efforts to free himself.

If there was one consolation in Ghazi's execution, it was the fact that his blindness prevented him from seeing what was about to take place. Running the ax blade across Ghazi's neck, Amru informed his victim of what he was about to do.

Ghazi needs to be afraid. If he's not afraid, there'll be nothing to offer, decided Govinda.

When Ghazi didn't respond, Amru ran the blade across his neck again, this time producing a trickle of blood.

"My ax is going to remove your head," howled Amru.

Something within Ghazi stirred at the Parsi's words and his body quaked. Lufti and Leela covered their eyes as Amru wielded the weapon carelessly about Ghazi's head.

Where are Lufti's soldiers? wondered Govinda. *Have the tribals bolted the door leading to the cavern?*

Kritavat continued chanting, occasionally glancing at the Parsi, who danced around the chopping block, waving his ax. Amru's insane tirade sent chills through the captives.

The rite reached its climax, the drizzle of liquid now flowed in a stream into the fire. His chant completed, Kritavat turned to face his victims. Govinda strained to see the sorcerer through the smoke. His eyes ringed with coal dust, the sorcerer looked like death itself.

Kritavat had taken on the appearance of Tadaka. Cackling in otherworldly amusement, Kritavat stepped toward Ghazi. Sneering, he grabbed the ax from Amru and positioned the blade near Govinda's throat.

"Why bother with that drug-addled sack of bones when Tadaka can feast on the fear of a Rajput princess?" Kritavat asked mockingly.

"Sooner or later, Tadaka will turn on you," replied Govinda, keeping his fear at bay.

"When I offer your wife to Tadaka, your yogic trance will become a nightmare."

Tadaka's rage now possessed the sorcerer, and he rushed at Leela with the ax.

"Get that sack of grain out of the way!" Kritavat shouted in a voice strangely unlike his own. "Put *her* neck on the block. Tadaka wants her soul!" shrieked the tantric, pointing the ax blade at Leela.

Lunacy now possessed the sorcerer. The ax hovered near Lufti, and he grabbed for it. Seeing the outstretched limb, Kritavat swung wildly as Lufti dropped his arm, narrowly avoiding having his limb lopped off.

Farokh Amru signaled to the tribals, who moved Ghazi out of the way while the Parsi removed Leela's shackles. Govinda struggled to free himself.

"Kritavat, it's me Tadaka wants!" shouted Govinda, hoping to draw Kritavat's attention away from Leela.

"First her head," cackled Kritavat. "Then you'll know something of the darkness your guru refused to acknowledge... then you will make a worthy offering for Tadaka. After that, I'll offer Ghazi. His twin will die with him. The blood curse is unbreakable!"

The tribals pressed Leela's head onto the block, her cheek resting where Ghazi's had been moments earlier.

"You have forgotten everything," said Govinda. "What you're doing will come back to you. One day, your neck will be on the block."

Kritavat was far too intoxicated to listen.

Then a voice inside Govinda's head whispered, *Help the soldiers find the entrance.*

Wondering what the cryptic message meant, he realized that Lufti's men couldn't find the entrance to the tunnel. He pictured the iron door in his mind, hoping it would somehow aid them. If the soldiers didn't come soon, it wouldn't matter if they ever found the entrance. Time had run out as Kritavat hoisted the ax above Leela's head.

"Get her hair out of the way," Kritavat ordered, "...and put the pot underneath. Tadaka wants every drop."

Leela remained calm despite Kritavat's histrionics.

The Tale of the Himalayan Yogis

Annoyed by her calm, Kritavat screamed, "See the face of death!"

The sorcerer grabbed the goat's head and dangled it in front of Leela, but she looked away. Kritavat produced a bloodcurdling scream as he raised his ax, but as the blade fell, Lufti's men stormed into the cavern. The blow meant for Leela swept horizontally instead, ripping through the chest of the first man.

The soldiers cut down the tribals while Farokh Amru looked on in bewilderment. Kritavat raised his ax a second time, but before the ax fell, a soldier's sword impaled the tantric, the blade passing cleanly through his chest. Withdrawing the ax, the soldier waited for Kritavat to fall, but instead of crumpling to the ground, Kritavat wielded his ax with the fury of an enraged giant, splitting the skull of his attacker before planting the blade in a third soldier's shoulder.

Before the soldiers could capture him, Kritavat vanished into the smoky haze. The soldiers searched the cavern, but the sorcerer was gone.

"Did you bring the buckets?" Govinda asked, waiting impatiently while Lufti's men hacked off his shackles.

"There," said the officer, pointing to the pails of water.

"Pour the water over the fire. It will spoil the ritual and diminish Tadaka's presence in the fort."

After dousing the fire, the men hacked off Lufti's irons. Catching his officer by the arm, Lufti spoke sternly.

"What took you so long? You knew exactly where the entrance was."

"Sir, when I returned with the others, the entrance wasn't there," the officer claimed.

"What do you mean it wasn't there?"

"I returned to the same spot, but the door wasn't there."

"Then how did you find the tunnel?" asked Lufti.

"We searched everywhere. We had given up when one of the men found it exactly where it had been in the first place."

"Sorcerer's trick," Govinda explained. "Kritavat has plenty of them."

"Did he use the same trick to vanish?" Leela asked.

"I don't know," replied Govinda, "but we all saw the sword impale him."

"How is it possible?" wondered Lufti.

"Few understand black magic," Govinda replied. "Shankar Baba never talked much about it."

Govinda turned to the officer. "Have your men search the fort, but leave four here with Ghazi. Put leg irons on Amru and take him back to camp."

"There must be a passage to the courtyard," Lufti insisted. "Somehow Kritavat used his magic to escape through a hidden door."

"He didn't need a door to escape," Govinda claimed. "But we've got to find him! We need to break the curse. Otherwise, we might not be able to save the twins."

In the adjoining room, the soldiers found another door.

"Kritavat didn't use this door," decided Govinda, "but it should lead us to the courtyard. Have the men search for him there."

Before leaving the cavern, Govinda approached the altar. With his boot, he shoved Tadaka onto her back. With the ax-blade, he landed a blow to her chest, shattering the statue. Leading the soldiers up a stairway and into the courtyard, Govinda stepped into the night. The moon was rising above the eastern wall.

"Search everywhere," Lufti ordered.

"Kritavat's mad," Leela whispered, pressing her cheek against Govinda's shoulder.

Govinda rubbed her still tensed neck.

"I pretended not to be afraid, but I was terrified…"

The soldiers climbed parapets and searched inside turrets, but Kritavat had vanished. They had combed the fort, but Kritavat had eluded everyone. Lufti was about to summon his men back to the courtyard when a soldier shouted.

"There!" pointed the soldier.

Kritavat stood on the eastern wall, a full moon framing his robed silhouette. Not far from him, a flock of vultures perched on a turret. The soldiers climbed ladders at both ends of the wall, leaving Kritavat without an escape route. His black silhouette provided an easy target for Lufti's archers.

"Prepare to fire," Lufti ordered.

The soldiers raised their bows.

"It's no use," Govinda said. "You saw what happened when your man ran a sword through him."

As the soldiers closed in on the sorcerer, haunting laughter echoed off the fortress walls. Govinda pulled Leela close.

"It is Kritavat, isn't it?" she whispered.

"It's him," Lufti said. "I think he knows it's over."

Lufti signaled for his men to fire. The first salvo missed to the left, but an arrow from the second round struck its target, causing Kritavat to double over. Plucking the arrow from his stomach, Kritavat tossed it defiantly onto the courtyard below.

"It's not over," said Govinda.

"But the soldiers are almost on him," Lufti protested.

"Govinda!" screeched the tantric, howling like a madman. "Didn't I tell you?"

"Tell me what?" barked Govinda, stepping toward the wall from which Kritavat leered down at him.

"That I can't be killed."

"You told me."

"But YOU can be!"

With a wave of his robed arm, Kritavat spewed a curse at Govinda, causing the vultures to dive. Govinda looked up, but what he saw was infinitely more hideous than a flock of vultures descending. The flying monkey demons that he had seen in Tadaka's hell shot toward him, their wings flapping furiously. The demons bore blade-like fangs as they descended. Their bony legs dangled behind them as they swooped down, circling the courtyard. Govinda tried to shield himself, but he had no means to escape the shroud that fell over him as the devils dove a second time. The Voidweave Shroud struck Govinda, and he found himself under a choking grey mantle, a venomous, putrid gas filling his lungs.

Govinda fell to the ground under the shroud's weight, but there was no ground, nor was there a shroud. Govinda could neither see nor hear. Trapped in an empty void, he gasped for air, but there was none; the void was devoid of even that. Suffocating, Govinda knew that he would die if he didn't free himself immediately.

Govinda's mind reeled as he drew on all the will that he possessed, groping about in the void, desperately trying and failing to touch something – anything – but there was no escape. Govinda was sealed inside death itself, and it invisibly faced him from every direction. His lungs emptied with a horrifying speed, his head throbbed and spun.

Then, as Govinda's lungs heaved for air that didn't exist, he saw her. Hovering above him – if there was an "above" in the void – was Tadaka, her mouth opening to devour his soul, her stinking death-breath choking him as he involuntarily inhaled it in great gasps, for there was nothing else to breathe. A dark, evil force came over Govinda. He felt his life slipping away. He now knew what 'Soul Eater' truly meant. As she drew closer, Tadaka grinned wickedly. As she did, Govinda's alertness waned, his will weakened. Not only was he dying, but Tadaka was pulling his soul toward her gaping maw. Govinda tried to think his mantra, and he managed a few feeble repetitions, but the demoness' power overwhelmed him.

Instinctively, Govinda reached for the Idol's Eye. Clutching it, he cried out for Shankar Baba as the fortress walls spun about him.

Govinda choked and fell onto the courtyard stone. The attack had happened so fast that by the time Leela reached him, the vultures had done their master's bidding and retreated. Alighting on the turrets overhead, they stared down at their victim, their hungry, haunting eyes eager for the feast that awaited them.

Leela tried to revive Govinda, but her efforts were futile. Govinda lay unconscious in the moonlit courtyard.

"What have you done?" she shouted, staring in abject fear at the sorcerer on the wall above her.

"FOOL!" howled Kritavat. "Shankar Baba's chela thought he was a match for ME!

"Capture him!" Lufti ordered his men, who were closing in on the sorcerer from both sides.

Leela held Govinda's head in her lap. Govinda's face was ashen, his body corpselike. Leela had heard Govinda call for Shankar Baba as he fell to the ground, and she began calling for him. Again and again, she summoned the yogi, first softly, then with all the power she possessed. Amidst a torrent of tears, Leela caressed Govinda's head.

Numbed with shock, she covered Govinda's mouth with her hand, but there was no sign of life.

"You've killed him! You've killed Govinda!"

"Fire again," Lufti ordered.

"Why waste good arrows?" Kritavat cackled, leering and raising his arms triumphantly.

With a wave of Kritavat's hand, the vultures descended on the courtyard, landing in a circle around Govinda. Leela sprang to her feet, screaming as she chased the vultures off. The flock retreated to a safe distance before converging again on Govinda's body. Leela hovered over him, protecting his body from the hungry birds. Kritavat danced on the wall, taunting his pursuers.

Govinda felt a horrific sensation as if he was being sucked out of himself. He abruptly lost all his physical senses, though somehow he was still aware of Tadaka sucking him toward her, and of his own body floating in the void behind him, connected to him by a silver cord.

Tadaka's eyes flashed with the sharpness of a blade, severing the silver cord. The pain of the cord being severed nearly obliterated Govinda's being. His awareness flickered at the edge of its end. All that remained was Tadaka and the fact that he was being sucked toward her far faster now; he was almost inside her mouth...

Suddenly, there was an explosion of light, as if a new sun had been born that was all but touching Govinda and Tadaka. Tadaka recoiled, hissing venomously at the light and looming up to become a solid, terrible shadow the size of the universe. The light matched her in size, but it couldn't surpass her. Govinda couldn't tell whether the shadow and the light were both still growing at equal speeds, racing each other to infinity, or whether they were maintaining their present sizes, or even whether size existed anymore.

The shadow that was Tadaka opened its mouth impossibly wide as if to swallow the light whole, capturing it in a shroud of doom. The light seemed to shrink, and for a horrid moment Govinda thought that the shadow would succeed in swallowing it, but the light was concentrating itself, gathering itself to strike. The light thrust forth a blazing spear into the shadow's mouth, and the shadow screamed a scream that all but drowned out Govinda's existence.

The shadow roiled, becoming a boiling black storm cloud of fear and hatred and insanity and suffering and terrifying power. It bit down on the spear of the light, and the light was caught and dragged ever further into the shadow's mouth, though it seemed the shadow was being burned excruciatingly. Great waves of light and shadow emanated from the cosmic conflict, washing over Govinda, alternately reviving him and slamming him back to the brink of extinction.

When each wave of light reached Govinda, he enjoyed a brief moment of clarity, and in those moments, he realized that the light was trapped. It was being swallowed by the shadow, and it couldn't escape, though the shadow might be destroyed along with it, leaving the universe as an empty void.

The darkest wave of shadow yet smashed into Govinda, and for an infinitesimal instant he ceased to exist, but the light, in a final effort, caught his memory before time forgot it and recreated him anew from it.

Govinda found himself briefly in possession of the fullest awareness that he had ever had. He had a body again, and he was in it, the silver cord that connected him to it spun anew and restrung. The light was spent; the shadow was now swallowing it even faster, though the shadow was at its weakest as well. Govinda knew that he had but a moment before the next wave of shadow would forever wash him from the world.

Govinda invoked the mantra to activate the power of the Idol's Eye. The Idol's Eye became a great diamond sword, and Govinda took that sword and slashed out with it, sundering the shadow. The black storm cloud parted, and the captured light shone through.

The light split in two, and for a horrifying moment Govinda thought that he had cut through the light as well as the shadow, but then he realized that the light had split itself of its own accord. In doing so, it had freed the majority of itself from the biting shadow, and the severed limb of light that remained inside the shadow's mouth coalesced into a sphere that shrank until it was invisibly small and then exploded with unimaginable raw, sheer energy.

The greater body of the light seized Govinda in a firm, mighty, warm grip and bore him away from the shadow with great speed, shaping its front into a razor-sharp, screw-like point that stabbed through the fabric of the void and back out into life.

Govinda twisted around for a parting glimpse of the shadow, and through the fading explosion of energy, he saw Tadaka's stunned face, blinking and shaking itself, her charred tongue hanging out and flopping back and forth. The stroke of Govinda's sword had disfigured her face, her mouth scarred by what was now the Idol's Eye again.

The light pulled Govinda through the hole in the void…

Leela held Govinda in her lap, tenderly stroking his forehead. She could see that he was not breathing. She wished she could pour her breath into him, but how? In desperation, Leela scanned the courtyard in search of something… anything. Finding nothing of use, she reached under Govinda's tunic and removed his dagger from its sheath. Pointing the weapon at her hand, she pierced her thumb, causing a trickle of blood to drip onto the ground. Touching her index finger to the oozing liquid, Leela drew a figure on her left hand and then a second one on her right hand. Then, pressing Govinda's head against her chest, she closed her eyes and prayed to Bhumi Mata. With tears streaming down her cheeks, she prayed, first silently, and then aloud. As she prayed, Leela placed her hands on Govinda's chest, and then his forehead. Her tears mingled with the bloodstained symbols, smearing crimson on Govinda's forehead.

Then she waited…

All eyes were fixed on the motionless form in Leela's arms at the center of the courtyard. Kritavat… the vultures… Lufti's soldiers… even the moon seemed to be watching.

"Wake up, my love, wake up!" pleaded Leela. "Wake up, my love, wake up!"

But there was no response, and so Leela closed her eyes to stem the flow of tears cascading from her cheeks onto his. Govinda was not coming back.

The specter of her ancestors possessed her, and she formed an iron fist around the jeweled dagger. This time Leela would not use the weapon to pierce her finger. Instead, she pointed its tip at her heart. If Govinda were dead, she would join him the way the Rajput queens of old had done. As she raised the blade to her chest, a faint voice invaded her mind. Leela hesitated, praying that false hope had not conjured up the voice. Hearing nothing, she readied the weapon.

As she was about to plunge the dagger into her chest, a cold but familiar hand grabbed her wrist, preventing Leela from impaling herself. Leela's eyes flashed on the hand. Recognizing the hand as Govinda's, she dropped the dagger and collapsed on the ground beside him.

Releasing her wrist, Govinda trembled. Gasping for air, he drew in long, fitful breaths. Leela stroked his pallid cheek, elated to feel Govinda's breath against her face.

Confident that he was all right, Leela stood between Govinda and the sorcerer, shielding her lover from harm like a lioness protecting her young. Glaring defiantly at Kritavat, the fire of righteousness raged within Leela's soul. Her eyes swelled, her face reddened. Pointing an accusing finger at the spectral figure on the rampart, Leela shouted,

"Despicable one that curses blameless men. See if you can withstand my curse. May a viper's venom paralyze your heart!"

"But I told you," cackled Kritavat. "I cannot die!"

The soldiers on the wall were almost upon him when Kritavat let out a shriek that caused the fortress walls to tremble. Raising his arms in triumph, the sorcerer turned his back on the courtyard. As the soldiers converged on their foe, Kritavat shrieked again and then dove at the moon, disappearing beyond the fortress wall. As if in response to a command, the vultures took flight.

Mesmerized by what they had witnessed in the full light of the moon, the befuddled soldiers stared in stunned silence.

With Leela's help, Govinda sat up.

"Where's Kritavat?"

"He dove off the wall," Leela replied, caressing Govinda's head.

Govinda tried to stand, but he was too weak.

"Go and retrieve the body," Lufti instructed his men, who had come down from the wall.

"I'm afraid you won't find one," Govinda said, leaning against Leela's shoulder and drawing deep, measured breaths.

"But he jumped to his death! The soldiers will return with his body shortly."

The Tale of the Himalayan Yogis

"I wish it were true, but they won't find a body out there."

"Why do you say that?" asked Lufti.

"It's just a feeling. Somehow I know Kritavat's still alive."

"What happened?" asked Lufti. "You were standing next to me, then suddenly you were on the ground."

"I was… I saw… the… I… don't know… some sort of… I'm not sure I can describe it."

"I didn't know what to do so I painted Bhumi Mata's symbols on my hands the way you had me do it when the tigress was wounded," said Leela.

Govinda said feebly, "I saw… everything… I… I… somehow I knew… the… last thing I remember was… a force came over me… I felt my life… but there was… I would have died, and worse … my soul… No, I can't describe it."

"Let's get out of here," shuddered Leela.

Lufti and Leela helped Govinda to his feet, and they headed back to the camp.

Sitting by a comforting fire, Lufti struggled to come to grips with the bizarre events he had witnessed in Mizrabad's courtyard.

"The men should be returning soon," he said. "If they don't find a body, I'll believe anything."

"There won't be a body," Govinda repeated, sipping a cup of chai. Tomorrow we'll collect the other inmates and start back to Delhi. No matter how weak Ghazi is, he will be better off in the back of a wagon than in that hell."

"The vultures went away hungry," smiled Leela.

"So did Tadaka!" grinned Govinda.

"But won't she return?"

"If they invoke her, but this isn't her world. I don't think she can stay here unless someone feeds her."

"I'm still scared."

"We need to talk to the Parsi. With Kritavat gone, Amru may tell us what's been going on here. It appears that sacrifices have been going on for some time."

"If Kritavat had sacrificed Ghazi, do you think Hashim would have died?" asked Leela.

"That was the plan. Kritavat was using Ghazi's blood to amplify the curse he had placed on Hashim."

"But if Kritavat's still alive, won't he try again?" wondered Lufti.

"Possibly," said Govinda, "but with Zahira dead, he no longer has ties to the palace."

Lufti's senior officer rode into camp with his men.

"Sir, we searched the area," the officer reported. "There wasn't a body on the ground."

"Did you destroy the shrine?" questioned Govinda.

"As instructed. My men scattered the pieces outside the fort."

"Have a dozen men guard the camp," Lufti ordered. "We don't need any more surprises."

Massaging Govinda's back, Leela stared into the fire.

Before retiring, they watched Lufti feed Ghazi watery lentils, which he mechanically swallowed, often nodding off between bites.

"My surgeon will remove the stitches," Lufti said, "but he may never regain his sight. Before we depart in the morning, I'll have my men search the entire fort. There may be others."

Govinda took Leela's hand and together they disappeared into their tent.

"Are you all right?" Govinda asked as they lay beside each other.

"I'm a little shaken. I thought I'd lost you."

"I'm fine, but a part of me is missing."

"What do you mean?" asked Leela, stroking Govinda's forehead.

"It's not easy to describe. The demoness was swallowing me…I mean my soul; I mean… but someone saved me… I think it was Shankar Baba… or maybe Yogiraj. When they pulled me out of her mouth, a part of me didn't make it out."

"Which part?" asked Leela.

"I can't say, but I don't feel like I'm all here."

"You'll be better in the morning."

Although Farokh Amru insisted there were no other prisoners in the fort, Lufti's men found seven children huddled together in a crumbling building at the far end of the fortress. Like the other Mizrabad inmates, Amru had sorely neglected the children. Leela

The Tale of the Himalayan Yogis

cleaned and fed the smallest of the children herself before the group set out for Delhi.

Govinda placed the Idol's Eye on Ghazi's chest, but the gesture caused him to shake violently. Though unfit for travel, the sooner Ghazi came under a physician's care, the better. It wasn't until Govinda saw Hashim that it dawned on him just how near Ghazi had come to death. No one would have imagined that Hashim and Ghazi were brothers; Ghazi looked more like Hashim's invalid uncle than his twin. The morning after they broke the blood curse, Hashim had made a miraculous recovery.

As the days passed, Ghazi's health slowly improved. Lufti's surgeon cut away the stitching, replacing it with bandages that were removed for a few minutes each day while he regained his sight. Gradually, Ghazi became accustomed to seeing again, first in a candle-lit room, and then in the garden in the evening when the light was soft. Ghazi's physician administered small doses of poust to prevent him from suffering the effects of opium withdrawal.

During Hashim's illness, Nada had nursed him back to health. With each passing day, Hashim grew stronger, and as he did, his heart opened to Nada.

One evening, Hashim and Nada were together in the garden.

"I despaired at the notion of marrying Yaman," Nada sighed, "but now I shall place my hope in a just emperor."

"Of whom do you speak?"

"You, of course," smiled Nada. "Your time has come."

"But I have no interest in the throne."

"That is why you will make a fine emperor. Your father and brother were emperors for the sake of being emperors, not for the sake of leading the people. But you will lead the people well. You have already done so during the time your brother was away, and there is no reason why you cannot do so again. You will make a noble emperor; one the people will love and admire."

"If, as you say, I am to be an emperor, then I would like a noble wife at my side, someone who will restore the position of Padshah Begum. Will you be that empress?"

"With all of my heart."

Hashim and Nada spent their days with Ghazi. His fragile body lay on a soft bed. His vision was partially restored, he stared blankly at the silk canopy overhead. His empty gaze was interrupted by fits of coughing followed by painful spasms. Ghazi's pallor was acute; his skin looked like a sheet of parchment that had been crumpled and stretched out again. Despite the efforts of his physicians, Ghazi's mind languished in a perpetual stupor, the result of prolonged malnutrition, opium poisoning, and the curse Kritavat had placed on him. His sallow cheeks and emaciated limbs gave him the look of a man at death's door.

One morning, Hashim and Nada were at Ghazi's side when Mumtaz Aalim entered the apartment.

"How is he?"

"The same," Hashim replied quietly. "His body is stronger, but his mind is elsewhere. When I speak to him, I think he hears me, but his eyes never change."

"It is time you considered the Peacock Throne. Your loyalty to Ghazi is commendable, but his physicians say that his faculties may never recover."

"A physician renowned for curing mental illness is coming today. Let us see what he can do; then we will decide."

"What do you know of this man?"

"I'm told he can know a man's soul by looking into his eyes," said Hashim.

"I'm afraid there may not be much to see. Ghazi's soul has been nearly forced out of its body."

"I don't understand."

"Kritavat placed a powerful spirit inside your brother. The demon usurped Ghazi's mind, stealing his life force little by little until almost nothing of Ghazi's soul inhabits his body. Let us see what the physician has to say. I fear Ghazi's soul is but a fraction of its former status."

Late in the day, after the sun had fallen, a Brahmin appeared at the door wearing a dhoti hitched up between his legs and a cotton shawl draped over his shoulders.

The Kerala vaidya, along with Govinda, was ushered into Ghazi's apartment.

The Tale of the Himalayan Yogis

"I want to be alone with the patient," the vaidya requested, an expression of gravity on his face.

As Govinda was leaving the room, the physician said, "You may remain in the room."

Lufti, Mumtaz, and Hashim were walking in the gardens when they heard a series of groans followed by a spine-chilling scream that shattered the evening calm. Hashim instinctively moved toward his brother's room, but Mumtaz caught him by the arm.

"You must not go inside!" Mumtaz cautioned. "The physician is expelling something unwanted."

"But Ghazi's suffering," protested Hashim.

"When demons are driven out, it can be painful."

Another round of howling followed by the sound of retching, jarred Ghazi's family. At the height of his brother's anguish, Hashim's legs felt unsteady. Seeing Hashim reeling, his uncle eased him onto a bench. Searing pain shot through Hashim's solar plexus and his limbs trembled uncontrollably. Then, as suddenly as Hashim's symptoms had come on, they vanished.

Moments later, the vaidya stepped into the garden; his face strained from exertion. The physician's upper cloth had been removed, and etched across his chest was an ugly row of scratches.

"It's done," the physician announced. "I could not have done it without Govinda. He carries the blessing of a singular yogini."

"We are indebted to you both," said Mumtaz Aalim.

"Follow these instructions carefully," said the physician. "Keep a ghee lamp lit by his bed continuously… and burn incense."

"Will my brother be normal again?" Hashim asked.

"The spirit has been expelled… the curse is broken."

"Will he recognize us?"

"In time, but his liver is damaged, and his lungs are diseased. Had it not been for the bond between the two of you, he would have died long ago."

"Will Ghazi be fit enough to be emperor?" Hashim asked.

"It would kill him," replied the physician with a finality that left little doubt in anyone's mind. "His body is a lamp without sufficient oil to keep it lit. Do not attempt to wean him away from his opium.

His body depends on it; only don't give him much. I will look in on him after seven days."

The physician gathered his supplies and departed.

"He was always the strong one," said Hashim.

"I disagree," said Govinda.

Govinda stuffed his hands into the folds of his shawl, conscious of the symbols that had mysteriously appeared on his palms during the exorcism.

After escorting the Brahmin out, Mumtaz Aalim returned.

"Now we must act. There are those who would seize the Peacock Throne. Nazir Hussein's influence fell along with Zahira, and the ulema has not yet rallied behind one man, but Commander Murad will make his bid for the throne if no one else does. Tonight we should discuss the future of the Empire."

"Whatever you think is best, Grandfather," replied Hashim.

Hashim's family and friends were gathered in the garden when a servant stepped onto the veranda and spoke privately to Lufti. The servant reappeared, followed by a soldier.

"What is it?" Lufti asked the man.

"Sir, I am very sorry to bother you," said the man nervously. "Shall I return tomorrow?"

"My servant tells me you have some information."

"Indeed sir, but would it not be better discussed in private?" asked the man.

"Everyone here can be trusted. Tell us what you know."

"It is just that what I have to say is… unusual. I have not spoken because I doubted whether what I saw was real."

"Tell us what you saw," said Lufti.

"I had the sorcerer in my grasp when he jumped, but when you ordered us to look for a body, I knew there would not be one."

"How did you know?"

"I watched Kritavat fall, but before he reached the ground, something strange happened, which has caused me to doubt my sanity."

"No one here will question what you saw," Govinda reassured him. "We have all seen firsthand what Kritavat is capable of."

The Tale of the Himalayan Yogis

"Kritavat was diving headfirst to the rocks when a mist engulfed him. For an instant, I couldn't see him. Then, out of the mist, a flying creature appeared. It was twice the size of the vultures, but with similar markings. The bird-creature flew off, and the vultures followed it."

"Considering we didn't find a body, your story is as plausible as any," Lufti said. "But why did you wait so long to tell me?"

"I don't believe in black magic," the man replied. "But since returning to Delhi, I have been haunted by recurring visions of that strange bird-creature. I thought if I told someone, it might help me."

"You are not losing your mind," Govinda assured the man. "It is good that you told us."

"Shall I go now?" asked the man tentatively.

"Before you go, can you tell us in what direction the creature flew?" asked Govinda.

"Sir, it flew in the direction of the moon."

The man excused himself, leaving the group to ponder the significance of his claims.

"What do you make of it?" Hashim asked.

"Kritavat mastered many yogic powers before he left his master's ashram," Govinda explained, "and he's obtained more powers since… dark powers. I have little doubt that he could perform such a feat."

"Then we are up against someone more sinister than I realized," acknowledged Lufti.

"He allies himself with malevolent beings," said Govinda. "But no one can harm others and forever avoid the consequences. When Kritavat falls, it will be swift and final. Of that I am certain."

"The notion of Soul Eaters bothers me," Lufti confessed.

"I assure you it is real," replied Govinda, reflecting on his experience with Tadaka in the courtyard.

"It is time we discussed who shall be the next emperor," Mumtaz said, shifting the topic. "I propose that we make a plan to crown Hashim."

"Hashim, what are your thoughts?" Lufti asked.

"It seems inevitable," replied Hashim, a look of resignation on his face. "But if I am to assume the Peacock Throne, I must ask all of you

Steve Briggs

for your help. As you know, ruling the Empire has never interested me. I possess neither the guile nor the ambition to govern. The mullahs will surely catch me in their web, and the generals have witnessed firsthand my faint-heartedness in battle. I'm afraid that I am destined to make a poor emperor."

"You will make a fine emperor," insisted Nada. "The Empire needs a ruler like you, someone who is both wise and understanding."

"Nada is right," Mumtaz said. "May I offer some suggestions?"

"I look to you, Grandfather."

"Lufti has been a fine vizier. He can handle the court nobles and is respected by all. Your uncle has your best interests at heart."

"Uncle, would you accept such a position?" Hashim asked hopefully.

"I'm honored," Lufti replied.

"Then there is the matter of the mullahs," Mumtaz continued. "Nazir Hussein's disgrace has diminished the Ulema's authority, but still, the mullahs have acquired too much power, and if we don't move swiftly, they'll undermine Hashim's rule. I recommend that we replace all but one or two of the mullahs. They have proven themselves to be unworthy."

"I wish to abolish the ulema altogether," Hashim said. "Nada and I invite all of you to join us in forming a new spiritual council; a council that would replace the ulema. If I am to be Emperor, liberality will be my way," Hashim asserted. "There are many such reforms that I wish to make."

"Reforms of a religious nature requires patience," Lufti replied. "And the military?"

"I will invite at least two Rajputs to be among my generals," Hashim said, "but most of all, I would like to form a military alliance with Govinda."

"But I have neither an army nor a kingdom," laughed Govinda, feeling totally at ease with Hashim's family.

"Soon you will," said Hashim. "I intend to help you."

"I can see that you've given this some thought," smiled Mumtaz.

"The Empire has reached a crossroads. If reforms are not forthcoming, the Hindu majority will rise up... and well they

The Tale of the Himalayan Yogis

should… their persecution has been senseless and brutal. After I am crowned, my first order of business will be the reconstruction of the Krishna temple by the Yamuna. I want to assure our Hindu brothers that they can worship openly."

"What else have you considered?" asked Lufti.

"The harem needs reforms," Hashim said. "Nada has helped me formulate a plan for the women. Most of the zenana inmates are unhappy because they have no hope of marriage. I propose that the women be free to marry, and only those who choose to should remain in the harem. Whether they stay, or not, all will receive generous pensions. For those who desire to stay, Nada will look after their affairs, ensuring that they have the opportunity to study and travel if they like."

"You have your mother's heart," observed Safiya. "Your plan would have pleased Kameela."

"Her memory inspires me to make these changes," said Hashim, who then turned to Govinda and Leela. "Friends, you will be leaving soon. But before you depart, I have gifts for you."

Hashim whispered instructions to a servant, who left the room. The servant returned carrying a cushion with Krishna's diadem perched on it. Hashim handed the diadem to Govinda.

"This belongs to you," Hashim said, presenting the jeweled crown to Govinda.

"Where did you find it?"

"After the siege, Zaim's belongings were searched. I wanted to return it to you, but until now I have lacked the authority to do so. The other gift that I wish to share with you tonight is our plan to rebuild Krishnagarh."

Govinda was dumbstruck.

"My father's army laid waste to Krishnagarh," Hashim continued. "You more than anyone have earned the right to rule a kingdom."

"Hashim speaks for all of us," interjected Mumtaz Aalim. "No one here tonight would be safe had you not faced our common enemy against the greatest odds. For that, we are grateful. As future allies, we wish to see your ancestral home restored to its former glory. I heartily support Hashim's proposal."

Steve Briggs

"Leela and I humbly accept your offer," said Govinda. "We will visit Krishnagarh on our return to Rajputana."

Hashim continued. "I have drafted a letter bearing the imperial seal. The letter states that should aggressors lay siege to Krishnagarh, or harm Raja Govinda or his family, the imperial army will assist in repelling the aggressor."

Govinda had never seen Hashim so animated as he was now. It was as if a tidal wave of passion welled within him; as if he suddenly realized that, as Emperor, he had the authority to do great things.

"As Emperor, I will have the means to heal India in ways I never imagined," said Hashim. "And my first wish is to repay you for your friendship. If invaders should attack your kingdom, my army will come to your defense. If your lands are without rain, my treasury will feed your people. No matter how great the need, as long as I am Emperor of Delhi, my resources will be yours."

As Hashim described his plan, Nada fingered a pendant Hashim had given her while the others were away.

"Nada, may I have a look at your pendant?" asked Govinda.

"Of course," said Nada, handing it to him.

"It's lovely… a gift from Hashim?" asked Govinda, admiring the exquisite pink lotus set in silver.

"Yes."

"Does the pendant mean something?" questioned Hashim.

"Ghazi was wearing a similar pendant in Mizrabad," explained Lufti. "The pendant confirmed your brother's identity."

"The pink lotus symbolized all that was sacred to Maji. She gave us matching pendants on our twelfth birthday."

"I remember the day well," recalled Mumtaz Aalim. "We celebrated with fireworks over the Yamuna. Our dear Kameela has helped us find Ghazi."

Govinda handed the pendant back to Nada.

"There is one last thing," said Hashim, gazing affectionately into Nada's eyes. "With Grandfather's blessings, Nada and I wish to marry."

"You have our blessing, my children."

From the Ashes

"We're going home," Leela excitedly said as Govinda helped her into the open carriage that would carry them through the gates of the capital.

"Lufti has provided horses. Shall we ride ahead of the caravan once we reach the countryside?"

As their carriage approached the imposing sandstone gate known as Bara Darwaza, the gaunt, leprous specter of a man stumbled onto the road. Bent from disease, the man looked timidly at Govinda, his begging bowl cradled in his forearms, his face marred by scars.

Observing the scar over the man's brow, Govinda recognized the man as none other than Zaim.

"Commander Zaim?" questioned Govinda, his eyes meeting those of the beggar.

"It has been a long time since anyone has called me 'Commander,'" the man replied meekly, "but yes, I am Amin Zaim. Who are you?"

"An old acquaintance," replied Govinda.

As Govinda tossed a bag to the beggar's feet, Zaim looked up at Govinda hesitantly before dropping to his knees. Having but a portion of his fingers, the former commander of the imperial army scooped up the bag with his forearms. Fumbling clumsily with the drawstring, Zaim employed his teeth to open the pouch. Seeing the bag filled with gold mohurs, Zaim stared in disbelief at his benefactor.

Govinda looked in silent wonderment at his former foe before he and Leela continued on their way.

"But I thought Zaim was your enemy," said Leela.

"He was."

The journey to Krishnagarh took five days. As Govinda approached his clan's kingdom, his senses sharpened. Scanning the landscape, he searched for the familiar haunts of his youth. Crossing the grasslands of northern Rajputana awakened slumbering memories that lifted his mind beyond the monotony of the road … abandoned fortifications atop rocky hillocks and the emerald contours of the Aravali hills, the smell of silver-blue sage and the sight of amber sunsets.

In the distance, Krishnagarh came into view. The winding ascent to the old fortress, one that Govinda had made countless times atop Kalki, proved bittersweet. Large sections of the fort's walls were charred black, and the main gates lay in splintered ruins. Govinda and Leela entered the fortress well ahead of their escort.

Stepping into Krishna's temple, Govinda took Leela by the hand. Scant daylight filtered through the ruined pillars flanking the entrance. Inside, looters had pillaged the sanctuary mercilessly.

"It all began there," said Govinda, pointing to the tall iron spike circled by an ominous stain. Leela flinched at the thought of being impaled on the spike.

The temple was littered with broken stones, rubble, and a wrecked lintel.

"Until the temple is restored, I won't bring Mataji here.

"Is Krishna still in the pond?" Leela wondered aloud.

"Let's go and see."

"Is it difficult?" Leela asked, putting her arm around Govinda.

"Difficult?"

"Seeing the destruction."

"It's an eerie feeling finding the fort empty. I can still see the puppets hanging outside Vaish's shop and Davan staring into the distance and Pitaji riding Kalki through the gates."

Govinda and Leela were walking toward the pond when he spun around suddenly, almost toppling Leela in the process.

"What is it?"

The Tale of the Himalayan Yogis

"I almost forgot about the parchment," Govinda said excitedly. "We need to find the manuscript."

Govinda ran back into the temple, pulling Leela along with him. Scanning the altar, Govinda looked disheartened.

"What's wrong?"

"Nothing but rubble. The Moguls knew that our temples contained hidden treasures and they destroyed the altar searching for it. We'll never know what was in the parchment."

Frustrated, Govinda tossed a few pieces of altar stone to the side.

"Do you think they found the parchment?"

"Had they found it, they would have taken it to Delhi to have it translated."

Govinda sat on the foundation of the altar, upset with himself for having left Krishnagarh without the parchment. Leela tried to console him, but the loss of the parchment caused him great regret, for it was his last remaining link to his ancestors.

The day was approaching its end. Lighting a lamp and raising it, Leela stepped over the broken stones in search of nothing in particular. She stared at the rubble scattered about the sanctum.

"At least this will never happen again," she said.

Lost in thought, Govinda did not reply.

Leela stepped over a fallen pillar and approached the fire pit. Seeing some crumpled materials inside the pit, she bent down to examine them. Discarding a few scraps, she pulled a pair of crumbling, brittle goatskin hides from the pit. Although their seals were broken and their edges charred, the scrolls were still intact.

Holding the parchments up to the light, Leela unrolled one and examined the Sanskrit text that had faded with time.

"I think we've found the parchments," she said excitedly.

Govinda bounded over a fallen pillar and examined the scrolls.

"That's father's seal!"

Leela handed the scrolls to Govinda.

"But the seals are broken," noted Leela. "How can we be sure the Moguls haven't read them?"

"If they had, they wouldn't have discarded them," Govinda

replied. "Some soldier must have found them, and not being able to read Sanskrit, tossed them into the fire pit."

"Aren't you going to read them?"

"Ananta insisted that only the king and head priest should know their contents."

"All right," Leela replied, unable to hide her disappointment.

Seeing the unhappy look on her face, Govinda paused.

"For centuries the Raja of Krishnagarh and his priest have preserved the secret of the Idol's Eye. But now Krishnagarh no longer has a king, or a priest, for that matter. I wouldn't be comfortable being the only one who knew the secrets. Ananta is no more, and I have yet to be crowned. Despite our tradition of male priests, I shall make you head priestess of the queen's temple."

"I like that," Leela grinned. "I've never cared for the old ways."

"I know."

"So how do I become the head priestess?"

"As the future Raja of Krishnagarh, I pronounce Raj Kumari Leela head priestess of the queen's temple."

"Open the scrolls and let's read them," she said eagerly.

"Let's read them in front of Krishna."

"But isn't Krishna at the bottom of the pond?"

"Come!" he said, taking her by the hand.

Govinda had no desire to enter the queen's palace, and so they entered the garden from the outside. The disheveled grounds had an abandoned look. Weeds and creepers had overtaken everything. The pond at the center of the garden, however, looked the way it had the day Govinda had ridden Kalki out the front gates.

"Krishna's in there?" she asked.

"As far as I know. I think we can lift him together."

Leela set the lamp down, and they waded into the water to the spot where Govinda remembered placing the statue. Reaching into the water, Govinda searched the bottom until his hand found the smooth, hard surface of Krishna's shoulder.

"Here he is," he said, running his hands along the contours of the statue until he came to Krishna's head. "You take his head, and I'll carry his feet."

The Tale of the Himalayan Yogis

Govinda guided Leela's hands to the head of the statue. Together, they lifted Krishna out of the pond and carried him to the pavilion where the columns were overgrown with flowering creepers.

Scanning the pavilion, Leela eyed a swing hanging from the ceiling of the garden house and the marble bench opposite the swing.

"Let's put him on the bench," she suggested.

After setting Krishna down, Leela retrieved the lamp and pulled Govinda into the swing.

"Now can we read the parchments?"

"Yes."

Govinda frowned as he examined the parchment.

"What's the matter?"

"I was never much of a student."

"I can read Sanskrit. See, already I'm performing my duties as a priestess."

Govinda handed the scrolls to Leela and held up the lamp.

Leela read slowly, "The History of the Idol's Eye, as chronicled by Raja Chandra Prakash Singh, the eighty-ninth Raja of Krishnagarh."

"Raja Singh lived six hundred-fifty years ago. My father was named after him."

Leela continued: "In the land of Vraj, a prince named Krishna was born five thousand years ago. The young Krishna grew up a simple cowherd, a handsome boy whose playfulness and kindness attracted many friends. His friends followed him through the forests of Vraj, listening to him play his wood flute.

"Later, Krishna led his cousin's army against the evil-minded kings who plotted to plunder the world. After defeating the wicked kings in the Great War, Krishna himself became a king, and his people built a jeweled kingdom called Dwarka for him by the sea. Krishna ruled over a time of peace and prosperity, but the very day Krishna chose to leave this earth, the oceans engulfed his fabled city, for on that day the Dark Age called Kali Yuga descended on Earth.

"Before returning to his heavenly throne, Krishna instructed his grandson to carve a statue in his likeness. The *murti* was crowned with a stunning tiara, and a magnificent blue diamond which Krishna had worn was placed on the forehead of the statue, a symbol of the mystical eye of knowledge.

"The blue diamond possessed great powers, which Krishna himself had imbibed in it. Although the temple housing the Krishna statue crumbled with the passage of time, his devotees built new temples in which to honor him.

"A hunter's arrow ended Krishna's life, but before departing, Krishna informed his relatives that he would appear from time to time as an Ageless Yogi to ensure that his devotees were blessed with perfect masters who could guide them safely across the ocean of Maya. He then instructed his devotees to meditate on him in their hearts, saying, 'whisper my name in your heart and I will come.'

"Kali Yuga grew darker, and Krishna's descendants came under the tyranny of foreign rulers. Although Krishna's people suffered, they never lost hope. When an evil-minded king learned of the blue diamond, he marched on the fabled city of Krishna's childhood. When the king of Vrindavan learned of the imminent attack, he ordered the Krishna statue removed to a safe place.

"Knowing that his Rajput allies were courageous warriors whom the invading ruler feared, the king instructed his priest to take the statue to Krishnagarh in a wagon. The priest went on his way, but the thought of having the jewel for himself played on the priest's mind. The priest decided that since he had risked his life to deliver the statue, he should have the pleasure of holding the diamond and wearing Krishna's tiara, if only for a few hours. And so he stopped his wagon before reaching Krishnagarh and enjoyed the sacred ornaments until the following morning.

"Having held the diamond, the priest decided that he couldn't part with it, and so he turned his wagon and was heading away from the fort when my father, Raja Govinda Singh, the eighty-eighth Raja of Krishnagarh, captured him. A messenger from Vrindavan had forewarned the Rajputs that the priest was traveling with the statue. In case the priest did not arrive, the Rajputs were to find him, for the temptation of stealing the magical diamond would be strong.

"Raja Govinda overtook the priest on the road, and a quarrel ensued. The priest admitted having the statue and tiara in his possession but claimed he knew nothing of the diamond. Knowing that the priest was not telling the truth, Raja Govinda searched the priest and found the jewel hidden in the folds of his robes. Angered, the arrogant priest claimed that only a Brahmin was worthy of caring for the statue and its mystical gem, and therefore, he should be the head priest of Krishna's temple. When Raja Govinda rejected the idea, the priest vowed his revenge.

"The noble Raja Govinda understood the priest's resentment and sent him on his way unpunished. But the priest never forgot the slight he had received at the hands of the Rajput king and planned one day to return for the diamond, which was called the Idol's Eye.

"Time passed, but the priest never forgot the night spent holding the Idol's Eye, nor did he forget the fact that Raja Govinda had disgraced him. And so, years later, the priest returned to Krishnagarh disguised as a mendicant. Intending to steal the diamond, the priest slipped into the temple before dawn. The temple priest, having come to perform oblations for the queen, discovered the thief at the altar. Seeing the diamond missing, the two men scuffled, and the queen was knocked to the ground where she struck her head against the fire pit. The thief escaped, but not before the priest had wrestled the Idol's Eye from him.

"The queen never recovered, and her priest, feeling responsible for the queen's death, renounced the world. Grief-stricken by the loss of his wife, Raja Govinda decreed that no man other than the king, his family, and the head priest would ever enter the queen's temple again. And to ensure that no one would steal the Idol's Eye in the future, Raja Govinda commissioned a duplicate gem cut from blue zircon and had a secret vault made beneath the altar to safeguard the Idol's Eye.

"After the death of his wife, Raja Govinda was never the same. As time passed, he became increasingly withdrawn. Neglecting family and duty, he decided that I was old enough to rule the kingdom and that he would become a wandering mendicant. Govinda left Krishnagarh despite the appeals of his people, who loved him dearly.

"While wandering along the banks of a holy river, Govinda encountered a yogi deep in meditation. Sensing that someone was watching him, the yogi opened his eyes. The yogi prostrated before

Govinda. 'Why does one so wise as you touch the feet of one like me?' asked Govinda. 'Because, great king, I too have renounced the world. And like you, I also felt the pangs of sorrow when I performed the last rites for the queen.' Govinda recognized the yogi, who had adopted the name, Shankar."

'I have been wandering by this holy river for days, but I have not found solace,' said Govinda. 'I am determined to reach the Himalayas. Will you not accept me as your disciple?' 'Our bond is deep,' replied Shankar, 'but I cannot. In a future birth, I will guide you to the goal.' 'Then there is hope, even if this life offers none,' replied Govinda. 'Your people are disheartened,' cautioned Shankar. 'Your son is too young to rule. Return to Krishnagarh where the love of your people will heal your heart.' 'I have taken vows of renunciation; I cannot return,' replied Govinda. 'You shall return to Krishnagarh; if not in this life, then in a future life, for you were born to be a king. Go to the mountains and spend your remaining days in meditation. Now, if you please, I shall return to my sadhana.'

"My father resumed his wandering, but before he found his mountain cave, he sent a letter describing his fateful encounter with the yogi named Shankar. In honor of my father, Raja Govinda Singh, the eighty-eighth king of Krishnagarh, I have faithfully chronicled the legend of the Idol's Eye to the best of my ability."

In service to our beloved Krishna,
Chandra Prakash Singh

Leela lowered the parchment and took Govinda's hands in hers.

"You weren't meant to find the parchment until now because you needed someone with you when you read it," Leela said tenderly.

"Why is that?"

"Because I was the wife of the eighty-eighth Raja of Krishnagarh."

"How do you know that?"

"I had a dream the night when I danced on the rooftop. It was more vision than a dream. I saw myself in a temple. Two men were fighting. One of the men held a brilliant gem in one hand and a brass lamp in the other. As the man was about to strike the other man with the lamp, I stepped between them and fell to the ground. That's all I remember, except that before I lost consciousness, I looked up and Krishna was welcoming me into his arms."

A sea of memories flooded Govinda's mind as he contemplated Leela's words. Could it have happened that way?

Leela skimmed the rest of the first parchment.

"That's the end of the chronicle," she said. "The remainder mentions Rajput traditions, various yogic techniques, and bits and pieces of other topics; not the sort of thing intended to be read from beginning to end."

"Let's see what the second parchment has to say."

"It's much shorter than the first. It says, 'Where the queen's heart dwells… out of that from which our clan was born… remove the sacred dust and see what remains… Krishna's prasad lies beneath… but first, offer water to the yogi.'"

Govinda rose from the swing and held up the lamp.

"Read it again," he said excitedly.

Leela read the parchment a second time.

"What do you think it means?" he asked.

"I think someone wanted to provide a clue that only a Rajput would understand," Leela said, sharing in Govinda's excitement. "And I think it worked."

"A clue about what?"

"I don't know," replied Leela.

"Over the centuries, my ancestors offered their most cherished possessions to Krishna: gold, jewels, silks… the gifts were considered prasad."

"I think the message is saying that the gifts offered to Krishna are hidden somewhere," she suggested.

"But where?"

"Where does the queen's heart lie? Wouldn't that be in her palace?" she asked.

"Mataji's heart was in her temple. I'm sure that's what it means, but what does 'from that which our clan was born' mean?"

"Our scriptures say that we Rajputs were born of a fire sacrifice,"

Leela reminded him. "Do you think the message has something to do with the fire pit in the queen's temple?"

"Let's have a look. But what's that about dust?"

The parchment says, "remove the sacred dust..."

Stirred by Leela's insight, Govinda took her hand and headed for the temple.

The temple was dark. Holding up the lantern, they stared into the fire pit, wondering if they had interpreted the clues correctly.

"Shouldn't we wait until morning?" she asked. "Maybe we'll wake up with some answers."

"Let's search now," Govinda insisted, hovering over the fire pit.

"Remove the sacred dust and see what remains..." Leela repeated as she stared into the pit. "We need to remove the ash."

"But there's enough ash in the pit to fill an oxcart."

Govinda ran out of the temple, returning with a shovel. Wasting no time, he shoveled the ash from the pit until a waist-high mound stood beside it. After removing the ash, he examined the bottom of the pit, running his hands over the charred stone squares.

With the edge of the shovel, Govinda loosened square after square until the flooring in the pit was removed. With the stones out of the way, Govinda examined the soil beneath the pit. Shoveling it away, he unearthed a rectangular iron hatch with a handle.

Govinda pulled hard on the handle, but time and disuse had sealed the covering. Wedging the shovel between the hatch and its frame, he pried the hatch open. The heavy iron grudgingly yielded access to a wooden ladder that descended into a vault.

Lowering the lamp, Govinda peered into a chamber equal to the size of the temple sanctum.

"We're going down there," Govinda said breathlessly. "I'll go first. You hold the lamp."

Leela climbed into the fire pit and held the lamp while Govinda descended into the vault, testing each rung before putting his weight on them. After he had reached the floor, Leela followed. Inside the vault, Leela held up the lamp, but the chamber was empty.

Scanning the vault, Leela tugged anxiously at Govinda's tunic.

The Tale of the Himalayan Yogis

"Let's get out of here," she pleaded, her eyes riveted on a skeleton propped up against the far wall.

"Why such haste?"

"That!" she moaned, drawing Govinda's attention to the bones wrapped in the faded remains of an ochre cloth.

"Judging by the cloth, he must have been a yogi," said Govinda.

A begging bowl sat on the floor in front of the eerie figure. Seeing the copper bowl, Leela started for the ladder.

"We can't give up now."

"I'm not giving up," replied Leela, disappearing through the opening in the ceiling. She returned cradling a porcelain pot in her arms.

"What's the pot for?"

"You'll see." Leela knelt before the skeleton, her heart pounding as she filled the begging bowl with water. Govinda watched over her shoulder as the water filled the bowl. Leela waited, her eyes trained on the bowl. She was not about to look at the ghastly form in front of her.

"Whoever it was, he was meditating when he died. See how the right leg is folded over the left ankle," observed Govinda. "It's the preferred posture for meditation."

"It's hideous. How can you look at it?" scolded Leela, glancing over her shoulder at Govinda. Continuing to avoid the skeleton, she kept her eyes on the begging bowl.

"The yogi decided to leave his body."

"He chose to die down here?" frowned Leela.

"Yes."

"It's working," she shrieked.

"What's working?"

Leela raised the bowl, which was leaking water. She slowly ran her index finger along a faint depression in the floor that the water had exposed.

"But how did you know?" asked Govinda incredulously.

"The final instruction said to offer water to the yogi."

Govinda knelt beside Leela. Removing his dagger from its sheath, he ran the blade along the groove in the floor, exposing an iron covering of similar size and shape to the one they had uncovered in the fire pit. Wedging the dull edge of his dagger under the cover, Govinda raised it from its position. Removing the cover, he peered into the musty void.

"I'm going down there."

"But there's no ladder."

Leela reached for his arm, but Govinda had vanished, leaving Leela holding the yogi's begging bowl. A loud thump echoed from the chamber below, followed by silence.

"Are you all right?" asked Leela, lowering the lantern into the darkness.

"I'm taking the lantern."

Lantern in hand, Govinda scanned the chamber.

"We've found it."

"Found what?" asked Leela.

"Krishna's prasad!"

Eager to be away from the yogi's bones, Leela dropped into Govinda's arms, causing them to tumble onto the floor. Laughing, Govinda pulled Leela to her feet with one hand and raised the lantern with the other.

Surrounding them on every side were teak and mahogany trunks stacked one atop the other. Govinda examined the nearest trunk. Dust obscured the carved mahogany lid. With the sleeve of his tunic, Govinda wiped away centuries of soot.

"I had no idea," he gasped.

Holding the lantern close, Leela read the carved inscription. "'Offerings on Krishna Janmashtami.'" In smaller script was engraved the name 'Rana Samar Singh.'

"Rana Samar Singh ruled over nine centuries ago. It was our clan's tradition that each king offers Krishna a chest of gold and gems during his reign."

"Let's open one," Leela suggested.

The heavy mahogany lid creaked as Govinda raised it. Leela lowered the lamp into the trunk. Scores of scintillating rubies, diamonds, sapphires, and emeralds peered up at them.

"There must be fifty trunks down here," proclaimed Leela.

"My clan is one of the oldest in Rajputana."

The Tale of the Himalayan Yogis

"Let's open some more," she suggested.

Govinda dusted the lid of another trunk. Once again, the inscription indicated that the trunk's contents had been offered on Krishna's birthday in the month of Shravana. Again, they discovered a store of priceless treasures.

Govinda opened several more. Some chests contained exquisite jewelry; others bullion, gold coins, and silver.

"It's all Krishna's," smiled Govinda. "Our ancestors offered everything to him."

"Maybe we can use some of it to rebuild his temple."

"Of course we can. I'm certain Krishna would want you to have a beautiful palace with lotus tanks and flowering gardens on every side."

"Do you think so?" Leela asked, her eyes dancing.

"I'm sure of it."

Leela wrapped Govinda in her arms, and together they spun in a circle.

"Are you happy that we came to Krishnagarh?" Govinda asked Leela back in the garden.

"Oh yes," she replied, pulling Govinda onto the swing.

Wrapping him in her arms, Leela pressed her lips to his. Everything but the kiss dissolved, and when the kiss ended, they kissed again. Entwined as one, they slipped into a deep and blissful slumber as the moon rose over Krishnagarh.

Epilogue

Leela and Govinda found themselves soaring above the earth. Higher and higher they flew until they arrived at the gates of a magnificent temple fashioned from pastel shades of light. Other buildings of comparable beauty surrounded it.

From the top of the temple stairs, Yogiraj greeted them.

"Welcome to the Celestial City. The gateway to this heavenly place is through the crown of the head, which few can pass through."

Yogiraj led them into a cavernous hall of polished stone. The hall rose to a vaulted ceiling and was flanked by gardens with fountains and flowering bushes. Sunlight poured into the hall through sections of the roof that opened to a cloudless sky. Mysteriously, half of the sky was a starry night and the other half radiantly sunlit.

At the center of the hall stood an octagonal altar. Atop it blazed a flame of violet, gold, and white. Though the flame burned brightly, there was no apparent source of fuel.

Ushering his charges toward the flame, Yogiraj explained, "The divine flame burns without end. Enter it without fear, for if a trace of fear remains the flame will burn."

Govinda and Leela looked at each other. Leela held out her hand, and Govinda clasped it in his own.

"It reminds me of the fire in the Mahatmas' cave," he said.

"I feel only love," whispered Leela.

"We're ready," said Govinda.

Yogiraj turned to the fire. Pressing his hands together, he gazed intently at them.

"Become One with the eternal presence of God's heart, become One with the love of life that owns all, gives all, sustains all, protects all, illumines all, and frees all. Become One with the life stream of Creation, which will enable you to calm the hearts of men, walk on the waters, and gaze down the corridors of time until perfection returns you to your royal home forever."

Turning to the fire, he continued. "I offer these sweet souls who have attained purity of heart. Receive your children and convey them to the Hall of Coronation where the Ageless Ones have gathered."

Yogiraj then gestured for them to enter the fire. Hand in hand, Govinda and Leela stepped into the enveloping flame.

Wave after wave of fire engulfed them as their souls were transmuted into light's pure essence. Sublime currents of violet fire whirled about them, entering the bottoms of their feet and traveling the length of their bodies before pouring out the tops of their heads. The divine flame shifted from violet to white, circulating throughout their bodies, lifting them higher and higher with each cycle.

Rising above the divine flame, they found themselves in a pillared chamber at the foot of a gold and bronze-veined staircase leading to a pair of gilded thrones. Standing before Govinda and Leela were twelve blue-robed, seemingly benevolent, genderless beings. Taller than humans, they were exceedingly magnificent. Their fathomless eyes radiated warmth; their hands held staffs fashioned from primordial light. One of the beings, the apparent leader of the group, held a golden scepter crowned with a lapis sphere.

The leader gestured for Govinda and Leela to ascend the staircase where Yogiraj and Rohini stood attired in floor-length robes. Behind them stood several Mahatmas who Govinda had met in their Himalayan abode.

"Please be seated," said Yogiraj.

Rohini motioned for Leela to sit on the left and Yogiraj gestured for Govinda to sit on the right. A crown bearer stepped forward and handed a jeweled crown to Yogiraj, who placed it on Leela's head. A second bearer placed another crown in Yogiraj's hands, which he put on Govinda's head.

"These are not the crowns of royalty," explained Yogiraj, "but the crowns of illumination, which shall grace your souls from this day forward."

From the essence of his being, a blue light emanated from Yogiraj's chest. As it expanded, the oval light formed a faceted, gem-like sphere. The light grew in size until it obscured Yogiraj. From within the light, a being of indescribable beauty appeared. In Yogiraj's place stood Krishna, who placed his hands over the couple's hearts.

"My children... you stand at the very altar of life. You are mine, and I claim you."

As mysteriously as he had appeared, Krishna dissolved back into the gem of light, which contracted until it disappeared altogether. In its place stood Yogiraj, a knowing twinkle in his eyes.

The light illumining the chamber faded, and Govinda and Leela fell into a sweet slumber. When they awoke, they found themselves arm in arm on the garden swing, the Idol's Eye glistening in the moonlight. The palace pond's indigo surface shimmered, reflecting the moon and cascade of stars overhead.

"Have we been asleep all this time?" asked Leela dreamily, gazing in wonder at Krishna.

"I don't think so."

A gentle breeze passed through the garden. Mysteriously, the wind brought with it the playful melody of a wood flute. An intoxicating tune filled the air, the scent of sandalwood permeated the night. Leela searched for the source of the music, but she found none within the walled garden.

Coaxed from the swing by the playful melody, Leela whirled gracefully about the garden, circling Krishna, and then Govinda.

Pulling Govinda from the swing, they danced arm in arm into the night.

Glossary

A

Aacha— good, fine
Aarti— ceremony of light
Acharya— teacher
Aghora— type of sadhu (holy man) that lives in or near cremation grounds
Agni— god of fire
Ahimsa— non-violence
Aloo—potato
Aloo Paratha—flat bread with potato cooked into it
Amlak— sour fruit used in Ayur Veda
Amrit— nectar of immortality
Ap Kaisa Hai— 'Greetings, how are you?'
Apsarasa— celestial dancer in Indra's court
Arjuna— a hero of the Great War
Ashram— a Hindu hermitage where mendicants live
Atma— soul
Avatar— an incarnation of God

B

Bakirkhanis— a type of cake
Bandar— monkey
Bansari— wood flute

Baapu— endearing term for father
Bara Darwaza— big gates to a city
Bardo Thodol— Tibetan Book of the Dead
Bawarchi— chef
Begum— term of respect for Muslim women; a queen
Beta— endearing term for son
Beti— endearing term for daughter
Bhagawan— God
Bhaiya— brother
Bhajan— a devotional song
Bhakta— a devotee of God
Bharal— Himalayan blue sheep
Bharat— India
Bhava— spiritual mood, transcendent love for the Divine
Bhuta— ghost
Bibi— south Asian girl friend
Bidi— hand rolled cigarette
Bijak of Kabir— famous works of the poet Kabir
Bilva Leaves— leaves sacred to Shiva. The trifoliate leaves are believed to represent various trinities – creation, preservation and destruction.
Bodhisattva— one who has attained enlightenment
Bolo— listen, 'hear what I have to say'
Bon Po— ancient spiritual tradition of Tibetans
Brahma Mahurt— the auspicious hour before dawn
Brahman— the totality of all
Briyani— rice mixed with vegetables, spices, and raisins
Bugiyal— high altitude Himalayan meadow or grassland
Bum Bum Bole— salutation to the auspicious one, Lord Shiva
Burfi— milk sweet cut into squares
Burqa— Muslim woman's gown

C

Chaan— shepherds shelter in the mountains
Chaang—home brewed liquor

Chador— veil
Chai— tea
Chai Walla— tea vendor
Chapati— flatbread
Chappal— sandals
Charbagh— Muslim garden divided into four sectors
Charkoni— starting and ending place in a Pachisi game
Chela— disciple of a guru
Chinar— type of tree in Kashmir
Choli— tight fitting blouse worn under a sari
Chuba— waterproof Tibetan coat made of skins

D

Dacoit—bandits
Dakshina— gift to the gods
Damaru— small two-sided drum shaped like an hourglass
Darshan— to have a glimpse of the Divine
Dasha— period of time in Vedic astrology
Deodar— Himalayan cedar, a conifer sacred to Hindus
Deva— Hindu god
Devanagari— alphabet/script used in Hindi and Sanskrit
Devi— goddess
Devi Annapurna— goddess of food
Devic— pertaining to the gods
Dharma— one's allotted duty in life
Dhoop— incense
Dhoti— loosely wrapped cloth Hindu men wear at the waist
Dhuni—sacred fire
Didi— elder sister
Diksha— initiation or blessing conferred by a gury
Diya/Divya— light, a small leaf boat carrying an oil lamp
Diwali— festival of lights
Djinn— fiery Muslim spirit
Dolu— a type of yellow dye
Dosha— imbalance or impurity in the body

Dupatta— veil
Durbar— public meeting of the Emperor
Durga— Hindu goddess that defeated the great demon
Dussehra— Hindu celebration known as Victory Day

F

Fakir— mendicant
Fez— hat

G

Ganesha— elephant god of Hindu religion
Ghazal— form of rhymed poetry popular in Persia
Gompa— Tibetan monastery
Gopi— female devotee of Lord Krishna
Graha— one of the nine planets
Gufa— cave

H

Hakim— physician
Hanuman— monkey god
Hara Hara Mahadev— appellation meaning 'Hail Lord Shiva'
Hari— Lord Vishnu
Harijan— untouchable in the traditional Indian caste system
Hatha Yoga— yoga system involving physical exercises and breathing techniques
Hati— elephant
Hati Darwa— elephant's entrance or door
Hati Mahal— elephant palace
Havan— sacred fire
Haveli— large home or palace
Hiranyagarba— Hindu concept of creation being a great, cosmic egg
Hookah—water pipe
Hoopoe— a colorful bird, notable for its distinctive "crown" of feathers

Hsun Ok— a ceremonial vessel used to make offerings to Buddha

I

Indra— Hindu god ruling heaven
Insallah— Muslim phrase meaning 'God's willing'
Ishta-Deva— personal aspect of God

J

Jadoo— type of black magic
Jaggery— raw sugar
Jai— victory
Janmasthami—birthday
Japa— method of meditation using prayer beads
Jeldi— go quickly
Jhootha— liar
Jihad— religious crusade
Jiva— individual soul
Jivan Mukti— a realized soul
Jizya— infidel's tax imposed on non-Muslims
Jodhpur— billowy pants popular in Jodhpur
Johar— Rajput ritual of self immolation by fire
Jyotishi— a Vedic astrologer

K

Kafta— tasty balls made from flour, ghee, and spices
Kaftan— a silk or cotton coat reaching the ground
Kakad— barking deer
Kakaji— uncle
Kala Bhairav— Hindu god of annihilation
Kala Chandra— seven-year cycle of the moon also referred to as black moon
Kali Yuga—great cycle of time when humanity falls into ignorance
Kanya— young girl, virgin

Karma— universal law of action and reaction
Karpura— camphor
Katora—bowl
Kaururu— one of many hells mentioned in Hindu scriptures
Khawa— green tea
Khus— a flavoring added to drinks; believed to be cooling and calming
Kofta— savory sphere made from chickpea flour and spices
Krishna— popular Hindu god
Krishna Janmastami— Krishna's birthday
Kulcha— type of bread
Kumari— young girl
Kum Kum— red dot placed on the forehead
Kundalini— spiritual energy of a yogi
Kurta— loose-fitting shirt worn by Hindus
Kusa Grass— grass woven into floor mats
Kusum— flower

L

Lak— numerical indicator for 100,000
Lila— divine play
Liu— desert windstorm in north India
Loka— realm of heaven
Lords of Karma— celestial beings that review the actions of humans
Lord Vishnu— Hindu god of preservation
Lungi—a peasant's waist wrap

M

Mahabharat War— the great war
Mahadev— name for Shiva
Maharishi— great sage
Maha Shanti Yagya— great peace ritual
Mahatma— great soul
Maha Yagya— a very large Vedic ritual

Mahout— one who rides, trains, and looks after elephants
Mahurt— auspicious time to undertake an action
Maji— informal term for mother
Mala— holy beads worn by yogis
Mandala— geometric pattern representing the cosmos
Mandir— temple
Mangal— the red planet
Mantra— holy sound or word used in meditation
Mataji— mother
Maya— illusion of Creation
Mehindi— brown dye used to draw on hands of a bride
Mela— holy festival
Meri Jaan— beloved
Mewar— horse from a region of Rajputana
Mohur— gold coin
Moksha— state of enlightenment
Momo— Tibetan dumpling filled with vegetables
Monal— peasant
Moti Mahal— pearl palace
Mridanga— percussion instrument
Mrityunjaya— death averting Vedic ritual
Mudra— auspicious sign or gesture
Muezzin— Muslim chosen to lead the call to worship at a mosque
Mullah— Muslim cleric
Murti— image or idol expressing the Divine
Musth— periodic condition in bull elephants characterized by glandular secretion and aggressive behavior during mating season.

N

Nadis— subtle vessels or channels of the body through which energy flows
Naga— serpent or snake
Nagababas— mendicants
Nama— name
Namaskar— Hindu greeting

Namaz— Islamic obligatory prayers
Narakas— 7 hellish realms
Nath— Nose ring
Nautch— temple dance
Navagraha— nine planets
Navratri— autumnal festival celebrating the nine nights of the goddess
Neem— a tree in mahogany family whose leaves are used in Ayur Veda
Nirvana— enlightenment
Nirvikalpa Samadhi— total absorption of consciousness, transcending

O

Ojas— lustrous appearance of the skin

P

Pachisi— ancient board game of India
Padshah Begum— Mogul Empress
Pallu— loose end of a sari that hangs across front of the torso
Pan—bits of areca nut with powdered betel leaf and lime
Panchang— Hindu calendar
Panchdhatu— five metals
Pandal— large tent
Paramatma— Supreme Soul
Paratha— Indian flatbread made from wheat
Pisacha— flesh eating demons
Pitaji— respectful term for father
Pitris— ancestors
Piyaara— darling
Poust— drink made from poppy plant
Prabhu— master or prince in Sanskrit, can also be a term for God
Prana— subtle breath, means, "I want to live."
Pranam— respectful gesture, bowing down
Pranayama— yogic breathing technique
Prasad— items offered to Hindu gods

Prema— Divine Love
Preta—a demon in the form of a four legged creature
Puja— ceremony honoring the Vedic gods
Pujari— Hindu priest
Pungi— musical instrument made from a guard
Punya— merit from a past life
Puranic— very old, ancient
Purdah— Islamic practice of preventing men from seeing a woman
Purnima— full (full moon)

R

Raja— king
Raj Kumari— princess
Rajput— warrior clans from Rajputana
Rajputana— region of India that is Rajasthan today
Rakshasa—demon
Ramadan— holy month when Muslims fast
Ramayana— a favorite Indian scripture chronicling the life of Ram
Rangoli— colorful geometric painting often found at the front door of an Indian home
Rani— queen
Rasgulla— syrupy desert made from fresh cheese formed into balls
Ratna— term for size of a gemstone
Ravana— great demon from the Ramayana
Rig Veda— one of the four principle Hindu scriptures
Rinpoche— highly respected Tibetan lama
Rishi— sage
Roti— flat bread
Rudraksh Mala— dried seeds from a tree strung as a necklace

S

Sadhana— spiritual practice
Sadhu— Indian holy man
Safarchi— attendant

Salwar Kameez— loose fitting blouse and pants
Sama Ritual— Sufi dance involving whirling about
Samosa— triangular shaped deep fried snack
Samsara— cycle of birth and death. "wheel of suffering"
Samvartaka— the fire that destroys creation
Sani Abishek— ritual performed to propitiate the planet Saturn
Sankalp— intention, wish, resolve
Sanskara— deep impressions of the mind
Sanyasi— wandering ascetic
Saraswati— Hindu goddess of wisdom and fine arts
Sarpech— a gem worn on the turban
Sat Chit Ananda— pure bliss consciousness
Sat Yuga— great cycle of time when goodness prevails on earth
Seva— service to guru
Shakti— energy within
Shaktipat— a guru bestowing spiritual power to another person
Shakun— an omen
Shani Abishek— ritual honoring the planet Saturn
Shanti— peace
Shastra— knowledge, often a scripture
Shastri— seer or astrologer
Shatush— shawl woven from chin hairs of a goat
Sherwani— long coat like garment usually made from heavy material
Shikhara— the peak or tower of a Hindu temple
Shikara— Kashmiri boat used on Dal Lake
Shiva— Mahadev, Hindu god of destruction
Shunyata— empty state of mind
Sidha— one who has mastered supernormal powers
Siddhi— supernormal powers like levitation
Sitaphal— sugar apple
Snanam— holy bath
Solja— salty butter tea
Soma— name for the moon, plant with divine powers, spiritual elixir
Spatak— Himalayan crystal
Subji— vegetables
Sufi— Muslim who seeks inner or mystical experience

Sufism— sect of Islam emphasizing the mystical
Surya Siddhanta— astronomical treatise
Sutra— scriptural verse
Swastik— health

T

Tali— plate of food
Talwar— a type of sword similar to a sabre
Tamasic— foods that are decaying, foul or promoting laziness or ignorance
Tandoori— a cylindrical clay oven using charcoals or wood for heat
Tantric— a practitioner of one of the esoteric traditions common in Asia
Tapasya— austerity
Tara— Buddhist goddess
Taslim— gesture of respect when greeting the Emperor
Teek Hain— common expression meaning 'OK' or fine
Tekke— dervish monastery
Tilak— spot placed on forehead after entering a Hindu temple
Tingsha Bells— small cymbals used for accompanying spiritual songs
Tirth— an auspicious or holy spot linking man's world with the higher realms or heavens
Topi— hat
Trikasastra— practice of blending three religions (Buddhism, Hinduism, Islam) unique to Kashmir
Trishul— trident
Tsampa— a staple in the Tibetan diet usually made from ground roasted barley
Tulku— a Tibetan Buddhist that chooses to be reborn to continue his work
Tulsi— plant sacred to Lord Vishnu that bears seeds used for making a mala (necklace)

U

Ulema – council of mullahs

V

Vaidya— Ayur Vedic physician
Vastram— holy cloth
Vayu Gaman Sidhi— power for levitation
Vibhuti— sacred ash
Videshi— foreigner
Vizier— prime minister

W

Wajad— Sufi phrase for spiritual ecstasy
Walla— a man or vendor

Y

Yak— slow moving beast of burden common to Tibet
Yama—Hindu god of death
Yagya— Vedic ritual involving chanting and offerings
Yogini— female mendicant
Yoni— place of passage, womb

Z

Zenana— Muslim harem

ABOUT THE AUTHOR

As a teenager, Steve Briggs met his guru at a meditation retreat in the Swiss Alps. After studying English Literature at the University of Arizona on an athletic scholarship, the author received a Ph.D. in Vedic Studies and traveled internationally instructing thousands in the art of meditation.

Sent to India by his guru, the author embarked on a seven-year odyssey taking him from Cape Comorin in the south to the high Tibetan plateau. Along the way, he initiated India's government and corporate leaders into meditation, encountered saints and sadhus, and astrologers and artists. He sipped yak butter tea with lamas at windswept Tibetan monasteries and hiked the paths of Vedic India's time-honored pilgrimages. As the guest of a Maharaja, he shared the fervor of thirty-million pilgrims at the Maha Kumbha Mela, the world's largest religious festival.

The author's first book, *India: Mirror of Truth, A Seven Year Pilgrimage*, was a popular memoir about his time in India.

Steve is now working on the second book of *The Nirvana Chronicles*. You can contact the author at sbriggs108@yahoo.com